P9-ECJ-589

WITHDRAWN
UTSA LIBRARIES

A CONSTANT REMINDER

A
CONSTANT
REMINDER

**Based on
Historical
Facts**

A NOVEL

Isaac Charchat

Shengold Publishers, Inc.
New York

ISBN 0-88400-109-1
Library of Congress Catalog Card Number: 84-51586
Copyright © 1984 by Isaac Charchat

All rights reserved

Published by Shengold Publishers, Inc.
New York, N.Y.

Printed in the United States of America

LIBRARY
The University of Texas
At San Antonio

Prologue

There are many who claim that the Holocaust began when Adolf Hitler became Chancellor of Germany on January 30th 1933. Even Hitler described that day the beginning of 'the greatest Germanic racial revolution in world history,' and declared that 'We are the last who will be making history in Germany.' His ego thrived on the romantic self-destruction of German myth and legend; Hitler truly believed that the German people would either emerge triumphant, or perish. But even defeat could be glorious if there were no victor, no vanquished—only complete and utter destruction.

This fatalism expressed itself in many ways, but none more telling than Hitler's adoption of the swastika armband. Armbands were traditionally worn by those in mourning, and who would mourn the Reich if it perished? It was as though Hitler subconsciously mourned the final end of the German people, even as he celebrated his greatest political triumphs.

If we must choose a day and say 'This is the day the Holocaust began,' it would have to be in December of 1924. The 20th to be exact; the day Adolf Hitler walked out of Landsberg Prison after serving just one year of a five year sentence. At that time, Germany lay in ruins, her pride shattered, her economy bankrupt. Crushed by the Treaty of Versailles, her borders were inundated by millions of refugees from the East, most of whom were Jewish. Although the Nazis lacked unity and credibility after the abortive Munich putsch, Hitler made the transition from convict to Chancellor just in nine short years. Brilliantly, he manipulated the dark frustration of the German people; their hatred and despair were the raw materials he forged into an awesome weapon of destruction.

Though Hitler's satanic genius still overshadows a host of accomplices, no historical cataclysm occurs overnight or as the result of one man's efforts. So it was with the Holocaust; there are many men who must bear equal responsibility for the parts they played. One of those men was an American named Henry Ford.

Obsessed by the belief that international Jewry was conspiring to dominate the earth, Ford used his vast wealth and influence to spread that conviction throughout the world; Adolf Hitler was his most fervent pupil and admirer. In fact, Hitler's year of comfortable confinement at Landsberg was just long enough for him to compile Henry Ford's racial theories into a book of his own—*Mein Kampf*. Henry Ford defined 'The Problem;' Adolf Hitler provided 'The Final Solution.'

Thousands of Eastern Jews recognized the impending danger and yearned to escape from Germany during the twenties and early thirties, but America closed her doors and Great Britain cut off emigration to Palestine; there was no escape. Like the people in this story, most Jews had to be smuggled into Palestine. Ironically, their only ally was Egypt; the Camp David Accords were not the first time Jews and Egyptians pledged to work together towards a common goal.

What you will read in the following pages is based on a true story, the story of a young Swedish Jew and his coming of age in a gathering storm.

To my thirteen grandchildren
Ruvan
Avrom
Debby
Maxy
Leon
Steve
Judy
Sammy
Charlie
Levi
Jeffrey
Reuben
Michelle
their parents, their children
and their grandmother Cecilia.

ONE

London, England
July 22, 1912

Gerald Bass brushed the trailing edge of his mustache back from his upper lip with a gnarled forefinger and cleared his throat decisively. It was an unconscious habit and one that the staff of the London Savoy often mimicked with relief. It usually indicated that the old man had found nothing to criticize.

As manager of the most elegant hotel in London, Bass did not have to stand behind the polished mahogany registration desk like a clerk, but he relied on his own eyes and ears to insure that the Savoy maintained its reputation for perfection.

Having completed his rounds for the day, Gerald Bass pulled out his oversized gold watch and snapped open the cover. It was just past three. The lobby was practically deserted—most of the hotel guests were enjoying high tea in their rooms or the sumptuous lounge. Thus far, the day had gone smoothly and Bass was looking forward to taking tea in his office. He had a definite weakness for the fresh scones and homemade marmalade that would be nestled alongside a pot of steaming tea on his antique side table. Afternoon tea was the only time Gerald Bass allowed himself to truly relax.

Satisfied that everything was in order at the front desk, Bass gave his assistant manager a cursory nod. "It looks quiet enough, Johnson," he said. "I shall be in my office."

"Yessir," Johnson replied, relieved to be rid of his superior. The assistant manager respected Bass and admired his abilities, but could never muster the depth of passion for the hotel that Bass seemed to expect. For Johnson, the Savoy was his job; for Bass, the hotel was his life.

As Bass stepped out from behind the registration desk, the glass doors of the lobby burst open. The manager froze with displeasure as one of the junior porters ran towards him, arms waving.

"Mr. Bass! Mr. Bass!" the porter shouted excitedly. "It's the Jewish lad—he's had the tar licked out of him at Windsor Castle. He's—"

"Lower your voice." Bass interrupted, his voice filled with menace. To his embarrassment, a half-dozen guests looked up from their newspapers to see what the commotion was all about. Bass made a mental note to discharge the porter for his lack of discretion, then he started to ask which "Jewish lad" when the lobby doors opened again. The uniformed doorman came in escorting a middleaged woman Bass vaguely recalled as a maid or governess. There was a young boy with her.

"Good Lord," Bass muttered under his mustache. "It's the Isaacson, the Swedish lad." The woman looked close to panic. The boy was a mess.

One eye was purple and discolored like an overripe piece of fruit and his nostrils were encrusted with dried blood. His left ear was cut and was badly swollen. Streaks and dots of dark red stained his torn shirt and his school tie was pulled off to one side. The pearl gray jacket looked as though it had been through a rugby match.

The woman tried to hold the boy close to her, but he kept pulling away. He looked sullen and defiant. Bass noticed he was limping.

The hotel manager quickly diverted them away from the elevators and ushered them into his office. Suspecting that Benjamin Isaacson looked worse than he really was, Bass's first thought was to minimize the damages before he sent for the boy's mother. He dispatched the doorman for warm water, towels, and some antiseptic. When they arrived, the woman started to wash the boy's cuts and bruises. To his immense relief, Bass saw that the damage was not serious. The boy wasn't even lame—he had just lost a shoe. Bass tried to find out what had happened, but the boy would say nothing and the woman just kept repeating that an English boy had beaten up 'her Benjamin.'

Gerald Bass was shocked and dismayed. It was bad enough that the son of a guest had been physically abused at Windsor Castle, the King's home. Even worse, it had been Bass who had recommended the excursion to the boy's parents. The manager couldn't understand it. Isaacson seemed like a quiet boy, not at all the type to pick a fistfight. Besides, he was barely nine years old. What could have happened? Gerald Bass rubbed his forehead and sighed. There would no doubt be the devil to pay when Anschel Isaacson discovered what had happened to his son.

They were almost done cleaning up the boy when Riva Isaacson swept into the room. Anger and worry creased her face. She rushed to her son, certain that he was seriously injured, but Benjamin insisted he was fine. 'At least the lad's not a whiner,' Bass thought.

It took a few minutes to convince Riva that Benjamin had sustained no permanent damage. Then she turned to Bass in a cold fury.

''Why was I not informed immediately that something had happened to my son?'' she demanded. ''Everyone in the hotel knew that a Jewish boy had been beaten up in Windsor Castle but me. I see I guessed correctly that my son was the victim.''

Bass flushed, inwardly cursing the hotel grapevine. Despite his best efforts to quash the staff's obsession with gossip and rumor, the grapevine continued to flourish.

''My apologies, Madame,'' Bass bowed. ''There simply wasn't time. I was anxious to ascertain whether or not we needed a doctor, so that one could be sent for. I know how upset you must be.''

''No, I don't think you do,'' Riva snapped. She knew she was over-reacting, but it was mostly because she was so relieved that Ben wasn't seriously hurt. She hadn't known what to expect when she first heard the news.

''Would you like me to send someone for Mr. Isaacson?'' Bass asked diplomatically.

''No, thank you,'' Riva said. ''We'll manage until he returns.'' With that, she shepherded her son and his governess out the door.

Bass sat down heavily and stared at the silver tea tray on the side table with its wicker basket of scones. He had completely lost his appetite. He scowled and jammed his forefingers into his vest pockets—a gesture that indicated furious displeasure. Thanks to the bumbling porter shouting across the lobby, any chance of keeping a lid on the incident was long gone. But what worried Bass the most was the banquet scheduled for that evening.

By eight o'clock, half the peerage in England would be gathered in the Savoy's main ballroom for a grande fête. If there was one thing Gerald Bass had learned in all his years managing the hotel, it was that London's society matrons loved nothing better than a ripe bit of scandal to bandy across the dinner table. What had happened to the Isaacson boy would provide more than enough grist for their mill. Then another thought dawned on the hotel manager. If the disaster at Windsor Castle became a topic of conversation at the banquet, it was almost certain to be picked up by the newspapers. Bass shuddered at the thought and felt his stomach turn over.

It was going to be a long evening.

•   •   •

For Benjamin Isaacson, July 22nd had promised to be an ordinary day, much like the previous three—dull and boring. Benjamin's brother, Herb, and his sisters, Ida and Frieda, were bedridden with the flu. Benjamin's mother, not about to take any chances with her oldest son, had thought it best that he remain confined to their suite at the Savoy. It was luxurious enough, but nine-year-old boys are seldom impressed with opulence. Benjamin was bursting with energy and curiosity—all of London was waiting to be explored. He might just as well be in prison, he thought morosely.

There was one consolation that had brought a smile to Benjamin's face that morning. Since his mother always skipped breakfast and his brother and sisters were served in bed, Benjamin had his father all to himself. Breakfast alone with his father was something he looked forward to.

"Good morning, Benjamin," his father boomed. "I have some good news for you." With a crisp snap, Anschel Isaacson unfurled his napkin and spread it across his lap. "Sit down."

Benjamin hurried to his chair, trying to imagine what kind of surprise his father had in store for him.

"You seem to be healthy enough, so your mother had decided to take Mr. Bass's suggestion and send you to Windsor Castle today." Anschel grinned broadly at the way his son's face lit up. "If the truth be known, I suspect you've been underfoot these past few days. Even your mother's patience has its limits."

Benjamin could hardly contain his sense of excitement. He was about to escape from the Savoy—and without Herb and Ida to tag along and ruin things. "When are we going?"

"Right after you finish breakfast. Greta will take you because your mother doesn't want to leave the other children." Concealing an amused smile behind the palm of his left hand, Anschel watched his son wolf down breakfast. Benjamin made a half-hearted swipe at the crumbs on his chin and was already out of his chair by the time Anschel laid a restraining hand on his shoulder. Benjamin looked up happily.

"Son, I want you to find out everything you can about Windsor Castle, so you can report to Herb and Ida. It will cheer them up, even if they learn that real castles are built on stone foundations, not on clouds."

Benjamin nodded solemnly. It was not often that his father made a special request.

"I'll have Williams bring the Ford to the front of the hotel." Anschel deliberately kept the tone of his voice casual. The Model T was his pride and joy. He was certain Benjamin would be thrilled by the prospect of having it all to himself.

Anschel had gone to great lengths to acquire the car when the Isaacson family first arrived in England for their summer vacation and never seemed to tire of praising its virtues. Though Henry Ford's production line masterpiece had taken America by storm, there weren't many Model Ts in Europe, and virtually none in the Isaacson's native Sweden. Even in England they were rare, and the sight of a Model T always drew a crowd. Benjamin's father waited expectantly for a reaction from his son, but none was forthcoming.

"Don't you have anything to say?" Anschel asked hopefully.

"May I be excused?"

Anschel sighed and waved his hand. "Go along, and have a good time." Who could understand the workings of a child's mind?

Benjamin raced through the hotel suite to his room, where his mother had already laid out his clothes for the day: a Prince of Wales suit, complete with gray woolen knickers, a gray jacket with black piping, a starched white shirt and Eton tie, and a pair of patent leather shoes. A grimace of distaste crossed his youthful features.

"I'll help you dress, Benjamin." His mother startled him, entering the room as she spoke. A sense of vitality radiated from her small frame, still attractive and slim-waisted, even after four children. Her eyes were blue-gray, set above fine cheekbones that scalloped down to a firm, determined jaw line. Her jet black hair, fine as silk, was pulled straight back from her forehead, perfectly complimenting her creamy complexion and accentuating the graceful curve of her neck. There was nothing cold about Riva Isaacson's beauty and no trace of the petty vanity that often marred women with similar good looks. She smiled at her son. "I laid out your clothes myself, Benjamin."

"Do I have to wear those funny things?"

"You do."

She helped her reluctant son to dress, then carefully knotted the school tie around his neck. Riva Isaacson believed in honoring traditions.

Once she discovered that Windsor was the home of the prestigious Eton School, as well as Windsor Castle, she was determined to see that Benjamin was properly attired.

Her handiwork complete, Riva stepped back for a moment to examine him. Except for the exasperated look on his face, Benjamin looked exactly like any one of a thousand English schoolboys. "You look fine," his mother reassured him. His clear blue eyes mirrored his dissatisfaction and a rebellious lock of corn silk insisted on poking out from beneath the short-brimmed gray cap. Riva pushed it back in place and pronounced him ready to leave.

"Don't forget your Swedish-English dictionary either," she called after him, as he dashed out of the room. "We're here to learn, as well as to enjoy ourselves."

He said hurried goodbyes to everyone, then grabbed Greta by the hand and forcibly led her down to the hotel lobby. She tried to slow him down. "Benjamin, please, I'm a governess, not a piece of luggage."

"But we're late," Benjamin protested. "Williams is already waiting with the Ford." They spoke in Yiddish, the language Greta was most comfortable with.

Williams had parked the Ford outside the entrance to the Savoy Hotel, in between two horse-drawn carriages. It looked strange and out of place, like an ungainly intruder into an age of elegance and grace. The automobile was all rectangles and sharp corners, lacking the graceful curves of a turn-of-the-century carriage. As always, the car was surrounded by curious people, too polite to ask Williams any questions, but not too polite to stare; most had never seen a Model T up close.

When Ben and Greta appeared at the Savoy's entrance, Williams gracefully opened the car door and bowed slightly. The chauffeur looked aloof and disinterested, but Ben knew from experience that Williams was coiled like a spring, ready to pounce on anyone who might mar the shiny black finish of 'his car' with an oily fingerprint. Williams shared Anschel Isaacson's love of automobiles.

Benjamin clambered into the Ford, enjoying the crowd's attention as Williams walked to the front of the Model T and cranked the engine to life. The engine caught with a backfire that frightened every horse within earshot and a number of pedestrians as well. It belched and rattled and threatened to stall, but Williams managed to get to the driver's seat fast enough and throw the car into first gear with a grinding jerk. They bounced over the cobblestone streets of London, with Williams swerving constantly to avoid foot traffic and horse-drawn cabs. Benjamin clenched his teeth to avoid having his jaw snapped shut.

If the truth were known, Benjamin much preferred Elka, the old mare who drew the family carriage back in Stockholm. The Ford was noisy and uncomfortable; it seemed tinny and ramshackle when compared to the rich finish and plush upholstery of their Sunday carriage back home. Benjamin did not understand his father's fascination with the car, but Anschel seemed so enthusiastic that Benjamin never dared express his true feelings. Once he did muster the courage and ventured an opinion to Greta. 'I don't like it either,' she had replied in a conspiratorial whisper. 'But your father never does anything unless he has a good reason. He's got something in mind, you mark my words.' As usual, Greta was right.

Several days after Benjamin's conversation with his Governess, his father had remarked that it was an interesting coincidence that Benjamin and the Ford Motor Company were born in the same year—1903. ''But there is an important difference,'' Anschel had laughed. ''I did a better job with you than Ford did with his Model T jalopy. When I start building cars, I'll build them like you—sturdy as a rock.'' Benjamin was not overly impressed, but he didn't want to disappoint his father, so he feigned interest whenever Anschel praised the virtues of the automobile or tried to teach him something about mechanics. He always nodded sagely when his father declared that Sweden had to 'keep up' with America and England, a sentiment that Anschel expressed on a daily basis.

Despite the discomforts of the journey, Benjamin did bask in the inquisitive stares of the local people when they arrived at Windsor. To judge by their reaction he could have been a member of the Royal Family.

They were just in time for the eleven o'clock tour and hurried to the main entrance, where twenty or twenty-five people were already assembled. Greta Kaminsky had hoped for an easy day, but it was not to be. Benjamin had interpreted his father's request for a full report literally and set a grueling pace.

She made it through the first half of the tour, but after lunch, when Benjamin insisted on arriving at the Round Tower of the castle ahead of the rest of the group, Greta thought her feet would never stop aching. As soon as they stepped into the cool interior of the tower, he began bombarding her with questions.

''Benjamin, please. I can only answer one question at a time. If you—''

''Greta, you know I'm supposed to learn everything there is to know about Windsor Castle.'' Benjamin interrupted her for the third consecutive time. His cheeks were flushed and there was a note of desperation in his voice. "Please, Greta, just tell me what a 'moat' is. I can't find it in the dictionary."

"I think it's what they call the water that surrounds a castle," she sighed. Normally, she would have rebuked him for his rudeness, but she saw the earnest expression on his face as he studied his Swedish-English dictionary and let it pass. Greta Kaminsky rubbed the small of her back, wishing there was somewhere to sit. A hundred rooms in Windsor Castle, she groused to herself, but not a single chair that wasn't roped off with gold braid. What was the use of a chair if you couldn't sit in it? The English were a strange people, she decided.

Even though it was unbearably hot and humid, Greta Kaminsky did not really mind touring old castles with her young ward. She was actually more of a companion than a governess anyway; a plain woman in her thirties with a poor complexion and an ever-increasing waistline. She had been employed by Benjamin's mother, who felt more comfortable with someone from her native Estonia, and Greta appreciated the opportunity that had been given to her. Though the language was next to impossible to learn, she much preferred life in Sweden to the grinding poverty she had known in Estonia. Her outlook on life was practical and somewhat mercenary, but she did have a natural affinity for children. She understood Benjamin's present sense of self-importance. Despite her aching feet, the expression in his clear blue eyes was so intense, she could not resist a smile.

"I know you want to please your father, but don't you think it would be better if you spent more time looking at the castle and less time with your nose buried in the dictionary?" Greta did not wholly approve of too much time spent with books; she was convinced it was unhealthy. Benjamin simply ignored her. Unconsciously, he tugged at his collar in a vain effort to loosen his tie—the starch irritated his neck. He looked up as the lead members of the group strolled into the Tower, then turned back to his dictionary like a race horse entering a starting gate. He wanted to take advantage of the extra few minutes to search for several unfamiliar words.

The tour guide waited patiently for the stragglers to catch up. After they were all reassembled, he cleared his throat ostentatiously and began a monotonous monologue memorized intact from a 1905 Encyclopaedia Brittanica article.

"The Round Tower was constructed during the reign of Henry II in the latter part of the twelfth century and occupies the former site of a stockade built by William the Conqueror, who constructed the mound on which the castle stands. Henry II added walls to the south, east and north. The Albert Memorial Chapel occupies the site of what was originally a royal chapel, built by Henry the III. The chapel was declared the center of the Order of the Garter in 1348 by King Edward the Third."

As the guide droned on in a poorly concealed Midlands accent, Benjamin frantically thumbed his dictionary. There were so many words to know. Though he spoke excellent Swedish and German and thanks to his grandmother, passable Yiddish, he found English difficult and confusing. Without raising his eyes from the minuscule print, he pelted Greta with questions. Before she could complete the answer to one, Benjamin interrupted with another. "Greta, what is a mound? A chapel, Greta, what is a chapel? How do you spell 'garter'?"

Greta threw up her hands in despair. Despite the English classes she had attended in Stockholm, her understanding of the language was not much better than Benjamin's and she was exhausted by his incessant demands for translations. Her patience was wearing thin and she was just about to suggest they leave the tour and find a place to rest when a young English boy appeared behind Benjamin and tapped him on the shoulder. To Greta's relief, his appearance put an abrupt end to Benjamin's ceaseless chapter.

Greta had been hoping Benjamin might make some new friends. Though he never complained, she suspected that he was a bit homesick for Sweden and his friends in Stockholm. Besides, a new friend would occupy Benjamin's attention and give her a much needed respite.

The English boy had a very pale complexion and high cheek bones set under a shock of fine, brown hair. He was a couple of years older than Benjamin, who turned and smiled a greeting. Greta wasn't the least bit worried about the language gap; young boys never had any trouble communicating.

"My name is Geoffrey Armstrong. What's yours?"

"Benjamin."

"You're a bit of an odd lot," the English boy observed. He seemed friendly enough.

"My English not so good," Benjamin grinned.

"So I gather. Go to Eton, do you?" Armstrong eyed Benjamin's tie.

"Eating? I eating later."

Armstrong smiled thinly. "Moron. Eton is a public school."

"School I know!" Benjamin exclaimed happily. He didn't notice the shock registered on Greta's face. She wasn't fluent, but she knew what the word 'moron' meant. She reached for Benjamin's hand, but he slipped away. He was not about to desert his new friend and turned back to Armstrong with a friendly grin.

"What language were you speaking?" Armstrong asked. "You understand 'language'?"

"Yiddish," Benjamin replied hesitantly.

Armstrong sneered. "Well, well . . . another Jew trying to push his way in where he doesn't belong." Armstrong suddenly jabbed a forefinger into Benjamin's chest. "You've no right to wear Eton colors. Take off that tie and jacket now or I'll send for the police."

The smile faded from Benjamin's face. He didn't understand the words, but there was no mistaking the tone. He turned to Greta for a translation but stopped when he saw the horrified expression on her face.

Armstrong grabbed him by the shoulder and spun him around. "The least you can do is remove the tie," he snapped. "Take it off!" Confused, Benjamin tried to step back, but the older boy was stronger and kept a firm grip on Benjamin's jacket. Instinctively Benjamin's fist came up and struck the other boy's hand away. Armstrong's features reddened with anger but Greta dragged her charge out of harm's way before anything else could happen.

"Please . . . please . . . is all misunderstanding," Greta stammered. The focus of the crowd began to shift away from the tour guide. "His mother just want him to be like English boy." Greta's hands were shaking.

"Well, he's not an English boy," Armstrong snarled at Greta. "He's a fraud. I wear a Harrow tie because I'm a pupil there. I have a right to wear it. Your Jew-boy hasn't earned the right to wear an Eton tie and I want him to take it off now. We don't need you and your kind in England." Greta was speechless. Benjamin stared at her with a confused expression on his face.

"I said, take it off you bloody Jew!" Armstrong shouted at Benjamin. Before Greta could stop him, Armstrong lunged forward and yanked Benjamin's tie. Benjamin stumbled, clutching Armstrong's sleeve to break his fall. It separated from the jacket with a loud tear and Benjamin tumbled to the floor.

"You bloody little twit!" Armstrong screamed. He kicked Benjamin in the stomach and aimed a second blow at his face, but Greta pushed him off balance and the kick just grazed Benjamin's head. Armstrong fell to the stone floor with an indignant yell. As he scrambled to his feet, Benjamin threw himself at the older boy, arms flailing. His onslaught caught Armstrong by surprise and Benjamin landed three good punches before Armstrong's superior weight and size shifted the balance. He threw Benjamin to the ground and straddled the smaller boy, pounding his face with blow after blow.

Greta was practically hysterical, but no one in the crowd made an attempt to intervene. The tour guide finally pulled Armstrong away, but not before he landed a final punch that glanced off Benjamin's ear. Armstrong's school ring left a deep gash in the lobe. Benjamin staggered to his feet, blood streaming from his nose and mouth. With a wild look in his eyes, he bolted for the main doors. Greta ran after him. She managed to catch up with him in the gardens and grab him by the arm.

"Benjamin, are you all right?" she gasped.

"Just leave me alone," he yelled, shaking off her hand. He used the end of his tie to staunch the flow of blood from his nostrils. "Just leave me alone."

Greta was stricken by the sight of his bruised and bleeding face. "Benjamin, I'm so sorry."

"What was wrong with my clothes?" Tears of rage filled his eyes.

Greta tried to console him but Benjamin just looked away, his fists clenched. Sensibly, she hurried him to the car and ordered Williams to drive them home. The chauffeur asked no questions.

The ride home was made in stony silence, with Benjamin staring listlessly at the passing countryside. Greta's mind was in turmoil. She remembered the intense hatred on Armstrong's face when he had said that England did not want 'her and her kind.' She had also felt the animosity of the crowd; they had agreed with Armstrong. Greta had been spoiled by living in Sweden, where one's faith was a minor matter. She had assumed that England would be the same.

Nervously, she fingered the tiny gold crucifix around her neck, a keepsake from her aunt. Greta's father was a Polish Catholic and her mother was Jewish. Her father had not practiced his faith and her mother had concealed hers, for the sake of practicality, so Greta had been raised without much religion. She had never felt the loss. Since coming to work for Riva, she had simply fallen into the patterns of the Isaacson household. From Riva's mother, she had learned Yiddish and how to observe the rituals of Judaism, but she never considered herself 'a Jew,' or a Catholic for that matter.

Greta Kaminsky's age and temperament had made marriage unlikely, so she had decided that if her lot was not to be exciting, it would at least be comfortable. Her whole life centered around the Isaacsons and her sunny third floor room in the Stockholm house. It wasn't a great deal, but it was enough for Greta Kaminsky. All she wanted was to be left alone to live her own life in peace; any talk of religion and politics only served to give her indigestion. She had often tried to puzzle out why other people would care so deeply about someone else's religion, but the answer always escaped her.

Riding back to the Savoy, Greta came to the realization that she had arrived at a turning point in her life. Geoffrey Armstrong had intruded into her private universe. His words were a harsh reminder that as far as the rest of the world was concerned, she would be judged as a Jew, whether or not she wore a crucifix. She shivered involuntarily.

Not until they arrived at the Savoy and Mr. Bass took them to his office did Greta Kaminsky feel safe for herself or for Benjamin. In a kind of delayed reaction, the full emotional impact of what had happened did not strike Greta until Riva Isaacson appeared. Only then did Greta begin to sob uncontrollably.

●   ●   ●

After leaving Bass's office, Riva set herself to calming Greta. That accomplished, she sat Greta and Benjamin down in the suite's formal parlor and began asking questions. Anschel arrived half-way through the story angry and excited. He had heard enough rumors from the hotel staff to set his blood boiling. He made Greta begin all over again, but never once interrupted until she had finished. Then he sent her to the kitchen to start dinner, knowing that the best thing she could do was occupy her hands. Gratefully, Greta disappeared from the parlor, leaving Benjamin alone with his parents.

"Are you sure you feel all right, son?" Anschel asked.

Benjamin nodded yes. "Papa, that boy said I was a dirty Jew. Why would he say that? Doesn't he realize that we are God's chosen people? I think we should tell King George about what happened. If he knew, he'd take care of it."

"I don't think the King of England would be interested, Benjamin," his father said gently.

"But if we were back in Sweden, King Gustav would want to know. We'd go and see him—just like the time . . .''

"Son, England is not Sweden."

Benjamin stared in surprise. "You mean he wouldn't be interested in something that happened in his own house?"

Anschel sighed. He and Riva had always known that an incident was bound to occur. Sooner or later their children would have to learn that not everyone considered the Jews God's chosen people. Like most parents faced with explaining an unpleasant truth to a child, they had discussed a dozen ways to handle it, but had never arrived at a satisfactory solution. Anschel felt a tightness in his chest as his son looked at Riva.

"Why did you dress me the wrong way, Mama?"

"It wasn't your clothes, Benjamin," Riva replied evenly. "What angered the other boy was the fact you are a Jew, just like your father and me.''

''And that's something you should be proud of,'' Anschel added forcefully. Riva shot her husband a warning glance, then resumed by explaining what her son already knew—that Jews have customs and beliefs that differed from other faiths.

''Like keeping Kosher?'' Benjamin interrupted.

''Exactly,'' his mother smiled. ''It's not unusual for people to dislike or fear the unfamiliar and Jews are not the only people who experience prejudice. It's just a part of life we learn to adjust to.''

''Forgive me, Riva, but you are wrong,'' Anschel burst out. ''Sugar-coating the truth does not make it more palatable.'' He paced the living room, building up a full head of steam. Benjamin had never seen his father so agitated. Normally, Anschel dealt with problems in a cool, unruffled manner.

''Anschel,'' Benjamin's mother interrupted, ''please sit down and relax.'' Her husband slowed for a moment as though considering her request, then quickened his pace again.

''I think better when I walk,'' he grunted, as though she were unfamiliar with his habits, even after ten years of marriage. Riva Isaacson sighed and motioned to Benjamin to sit next to her on the horsehair sofa. She hoped her husband would exercise some restraint. Anschel took up a position by the living room fireplace and hooked a thumb in his vest pocket.

''Benjamin, your mother is trying to describe something called 'anti-Semitism' in the gentlest way possible. We've all experienced it and it is not easy to understand, but I want you to pay close attention and do your best. All right?'' He did not wait for a reply, but plunged directly into a blunt, straightforward description of what it meant to be a Jew in a Christian world.

Benjamin was stunned by what he heard. ''But Papa, the English boy was the only one who ever said anything about—''

''What people say in public and the feelings they express at home in front of their children are two different things. Armstrong's parents might smile and nod to you in the lobby of the Savoy Hotel, but their son was probably more honest about expressing their true feelings. He was just repeating what he had learned at home.''

''But why would people hate other people without even knowing them?''

''It's a combination of fear and ignorance,'' Anschel's eyes flashed. ''During the past few years, son, more than a quarter of a million Jewish refugees from eastern Europe have come to England. They're not at all like the English or even the English Jews. They're different. They cling to the ways of the old country and cluster together in the same neighborhoods. They speak English poorly or not at all, so they seem strange and alien. Most of them are simple tailors, or cobblers, or furniture makers who were forced to flee for their lives by the Russians or the Poles.

"Right now, there are a lot of people in England who have no work because times have been hard. They blame the refugees, saying that the Jews have taken jobs away from Englishmen. Even though this is untrue, when times are hard people look for a scapegoat. You understand, Benjamin? Someone they can take their frustrations out on. An easy target for their anger. People who won't fight back."

Benjamin was overwhelmed by the bitterness in his father's voice and the anger seething beneath the surface like molten lava. The words became meaningless sounds, static that crackled around the white hot core of his father's anger.

Anschel pointed a finger at his son. "Understand this, Benjamin, the boy you fought with probably doesn't know why he hates Jews. He's just parroting what he's heard. Most people who are anti-Semitic are no different."

Benjamin could not meet his gaze. Like most children, Benjamin relied on emotions, not words, to guide him. His father's intensity left him bewildered and spinning like a compass brought too close to a magnet. Benjamin's mother sensed his turmoil and reached out, taking his hands into her own. "You must not expect to understand everything at once, but as you grow older, you will. And with understanding will come acceptance. It's better to avoid a confrontation. Better to just walk away, not fight . . ."

"No, Riva!" her husband thundered. His bushy eyebrows knotted together, and his beard bristled with indignation. "I'll not have my son believing that. The boy was right to fight back." Anschel's pale blue eyes were ice cold.

"Anschel, please!"

"If you let people abuse you once, they'll do it again."

Confused, Benjamin looked to his father. Never before had he heard his parents disagree or even raise their voices to each other. Silently, he listened while they argued.

Suddenly, Anschel whirled on his son. "One day, we will have a homeland of our own, but not by accepting the world as it is. If we seek the false comfort of acceptance, we will never have the strength to do what we must. When your grandfather, Nissen, was a boy in Russia, a group of . . .''

''Anschel, I'll not have you frightening the boy with stories like that. You're not at a Zionist meeting.'' Riva's blue-gray eyes glittered like polished steel.

Anschel's lips compressed and he glared at his wife, but he respected her wishes. He drew a deep breath and turned to his son. ''You've heard me use the word 'Zionism,' haven't you.'' It was a statement, not a question. Benjamin nodded. He knew his father was involved in something called 'Zionism,' but it was just a word. Now, as Anschel explained what it meant, Benjamin listened intently, aware he was receiving knowledge of special value. Anschel kept his explanation simple, wanting his son to understand the major concept of Zionism: that the Jewish people would never be truly safe or free until they possessed a homeland of their own. And that homeland could only be one place—the land that God gave to Moses and Abraham, the Land of Palestine.

Benjamin thought for a moment, trying to sort through the welter of emotion. ''Does that mean that we're going to live in Palestine?''

''That is my dream.''

''When are we leaving?''

''That's something you'll have to ask your mother.'' His father laughed unexpectedly, signaling a sudden change in mood.

''Mama?''

''Benjamin, I don't want to upset you, but this is a subject that your father and I disagree on.'' Riva Isaacson was a pragmatic woman with a keen intellect and ideas of her own, not about to have her son confused or filled with romantic ideals. She preferred known dangers to unknown ones, and though she loved Anschel deeply, she would never leave Europe. Unlike her husband, who considered himself a Jew above all else, Riva thought of herself as a European. Europe was her home, not some barren land that had ceased to be a nation more than two thousand years before. The whole concept of a Jewish homeland was alien to her.

Riva realized how impressionable Benjamin was, so she chose her words with special care. She wanted her son to understand that Jews could pray to God regardless of where they were; when the Messiah was ready for his people to return to Palestine, he would let them know.

When she finished speaking, Riva studied her son thoughtfully. The uncertainty on his face was unmistakable and she sensed it was in part due to the discord between herself and her husband. Wisely, she digressed to explain that people could disagree on certain matters and still love each other very much. Benjamin listened closely, but his mother could see that he was exhausted.

"Benjamin, I think you've had more than enough to think about for one day," she smiled, concealing her dismay at the way his eye was swelling. "Why don't you wash up and change your clothes. I'll have Greta get some ice to put on that eye."

She kissed him gently, then he stood up and walked towards the hallway. No sooner had he turned the corner than he heard his mother begin to speak in a low, angry voice.

"Anschel, I can't understand why you insist on badgering the boy. And the last thing he needs to hear is a gruesome story about how his grandfather..."

"Riva, I've tried to make you understand..."

The sound of his parents' voices faded as Benjamin closed the bedroom door and began to undress. He tried to assimilate what he had heard, but his head ached and he felt physically ill. It had never occurred to him that he might be 'different' from anybody else, or that anyone might dislike him just because he was Jewish. Worse than that, his parents were arguing because of him; he had become a source of discord. For the first time in his young life, he felt very much alone.

● ● ●

The Isaacsons left England during the last week of August and Benjamin was not sad to see the white cliffs of Dover fade astern as the ship headed northeast towards the Baltic Sea. A damp wind blew off the Channel, driving most of the passengers to the warmth below. Benjamin was grateful his mother had insisted he wear a woolen jacket. He stood alone at the railing and watched the oily gray swells rolling in from the North Sea. He was glad to be away from the noise and mayhem generated by his brother and sisters below deck. Little Freida was already seasick and screaming at the top of her lungs.

"Benjamin?" Anschel Isaacson appeared beside his son. "What are you doing up here alone?" Benjamin shrugged his shoulders.

"Nice and quiet up here, isn't it, son?" Anschel leaned against the railing and stared out at the waves. Benjamin always felt comforted by the strength of his father's presence and treasured the time they were able to spend alone, away from the rest of the family. Content to remain silent, father and son stood together sharing the quiet moment.

After a while, Anschel rested an elbow on the pitted mahogany railing and turned to face his son. "Your mother and I are a bit worried about you.'' Ever since the incident at Windsor Castle, Benjamin's attitude had fluctuated between quiet withdrawal and outright belligerence. Twice, he had made a nasty scene in public. Riva was in favor of a direct confrontation followed by some strong discipline, but Anschel prevailed on her to be patient. ''Give the boy some time,'' he had urged. ''He's got a lot to digest.'' Reluctantly, she had agreed not to press the issue. Now, as Anschel stood beside his son, he sensed the boy was ready to talk.

''Son?''

Benjamin hesitated, until curiosity overcame reluctance. ''Father, if they don't like Jews in England, why did we go there?'' It was the first time he'd mentioned the incident voluntarily. ''Why didn't we go someplace where people like us?''

''Don't make the mistake of thinking that England is an exception. Anti-Semitism is quite common throughout Europe, especially in the East.'' Anschel was careful to keep his tone conversational; there was nothing to be gained by lecturing.

Benjamin thought for a moment. ''Then why don't we stay in Stockholm, where people at least don't bother us?''

''There's more to the world than Stockholm,'' Anschel laughed. ''Son, I love Sweden, but I'd be a fool to trust her. You see, people don't bother us in Stockholm because the Jewish population of Sweden is minuscule, not because our countrymen are fond of Jews. If as many Jews emigrated to Sweden as to England, believe me, there would be plenty of trouble.'' Then he told Benjamin the real reason why the Isaacson family settled in Sweden.

''Your grandfather had six daughters and was terrified they would marry outside of their religion. He chose Sweden because there were strict laws prohibiting intermarriage between Jews and Gentiles.''

Benjamin stared at his father in surprise. He had never imagined that such a thing could be true. He looked down, compulsively twirling one of the horn buttons on his coat.

''What happened to Grandfather when he was a boy? What were you going to tell me that day that made Mama so cross?''

Anschel hooked a finger under Benjamin's chin and drew his son's face up until their eyes met. ''Your mother wasn't angry, she was just trying to protect you. But I think you're old enough to handle the truth.'' Grandfather Nissen's story was not an unusual one. One day, a platoon of drunken Cossacks returning from a boring patrol stopped in Nissen's village. When they left, the village was a smoldering ruin; nine Jews were dead. Though Anschel's voice was neutral and his words plain, Benjamin's face mirrored his fear and horror; few things are as graphic as a child's imagination.

Anschel knew that Riva would be furious with him for telling Benjamin, but it was time. They could no longer protect their son from the realities of the world, to do so would be to saddle him with a dangerous handicap. Now, Benjamin would have to come to his own understanding. Anschel had always hoped to spare his children the indignities he had experienced, but seeing the unhappiness on his son's face, he realized what a vain hope it had been. He had once planned to free himself from the oppression and bigotry of Europe by emigrating to Palestine and starting a new life, but that was before he had met Riva Nadelson.

She was beautiful and witty and alive, and when he had asked her to marry him, she had replied "Yes, yes, and forever, yes." Then he spoke of building a life together in the free air of Palestine and her reaction shocked him; she would have no part of Palestine. Even the thought of living in Sweden dismayed her, and she tried to convince him to remain in Estonia, close to her family, but Anschel would not hear of it. His family was originally from Estonia, and he was all too familiar with the anti-Semitism that characterized the Baltic States. He would not raise his children in such a place. It was the first disagreement they had ever had. Anschel spent many long evenings, vainly trying to persuade Riva, but she would not change her mind. She would never accept a future that included Palestine.

Anschel was first and foremost a pragmatist, a man willing to sacrifice to obtain what he wanted, and what he wanted more than anything else in the world was Riva Nadelson as his wife. For her, he would abandon his plans to emigrate, but he would never live in Estonia. Riva understood and she too compromised; they would live in Sweden. She also agreed to travel every summer, once the children were old enough. Anschel loved Sweden, Denmark, and Norway, but he knew they were just "border states." Their language and culture extended only as far as their geographical borders and Anschel did not want his children limited by a provincial upbringing. In exchange, Riva extracted a small concession. When it was time for the children to be born, she wanted to return to her family in Estonia. It will make me feel more secure, she had told him. He had agreed without hesitation.

He smiled, remembering Benjamin's birth. Riva had misjudged the timing of her first baby and Benjamin had been born at sea. They hadn't even passed through Swedish territorial waters when the doctor had ushered Anschel into the ship's miniature hospital ward for a glimpse of his new son.

"Are we going to England again next year?" Benjamin's question cut across Anschel's reverie, bringing him back to the present. He suppressed a grin when he saw the dismay on his son's face.

"No," laughed Anschel. "Next year we go to France. After that, who knows? But right now, young man, you're going below decks. Your mother will think that we've both fallen overboard." Benjamin laughed happily and followed his father down the companionway.

•   •   •

Anschel Isaacson was true to his word and every succeeding summer the family planned to travel to a different country. Before leaving, the children would always spend extra time learning about the country they were about to visit, and the long hours of study served to heighten their anticipation. The end of each school year was marked by frantic preparations for the trip abroad, and the entire household came alive with excitement. Even Greta, who regarded travel as punishment for the sins she had once hoped to commit, begrudgingly confessed her enthusiasm. Paris and Rome served in turn as the family's base for the summer of 1913.

In every city, the routine was identical. Once everyone settled into their accommodations, Riva Isaacson set to work. She was not a woman who believed in unproductive time; just because the children were on vacation was no reason to be idle. With the meticulous planning that characterized everything she did, Benjamin's mother scheduled a daily round of cultural excursions to museums, churches, and historical sites.

These "educational" forays were interspersed with side trips to the surrounding countryside, picnics, and visits to local homes of Jews and Gentiles, chosen to show the children how people in other countries lived and worked. And touring was no excuse for laxity in observance of the Sabbath; the Isaacsons worshipped in local synagogues wherever they found themselves. Greta never ceased to be amazed by Riva's inexhaustible vitality. Her own enthusiasm tended to flag by lunch time.

For Ben, June, July, and August were the best time of the year because Anschel did his best to devote the summer months to his family. As always, there was business to conduct, but only on a very limited basis. Anschel took advantage of his presence in different European countries to strengthen his overseas connections and make new business contacts, but usually spent no more than two or three hours a day on business—the rest of his time was reserved for the family.

• • •

June of 1914 found the Isaacson family in St. Petersburg. Of all the cities Benjamin had visited, St. Petersburg impressed him the most. Built from scratch on the marshes of the great Neva River, Peter the Great's "window on the western world" was intended to demonstrate that Russia had come of age. Its spacious boulevards were lined with imposing palaces and magnificent private homes, designed by the best French and Italian architects in the world. The overall effect was a classical harmony unmatched in Europe. Culturally, St. Petersburg was a monument to literature, ballet, music, and theater. Commercially, the city was Russia's largest seaport and most important manufacturing center, combining both roles with style and grace.

Despite the political unrest that lay beneath the glittering surface of *salon* society, St. Petersburg was still considered a stable place for investment and a splendid city in which to enjoy oneself. The Isaacson children were nothing less than overwhelmed by the magnificence of Czarist Russia.

One particular morning, late in June, Ben and his brother Herb dressed quickly and rushed downstairs before Greta called them. It was to be a special day—Anschel had promised to take them boating on the Neva. That meant an entire day, free of Ida and Freida. No little sisters to tag along and slow things down.

When the boys galloped into the dining room, Anschel was already seated at the table, and he surprised them by failing to criticize their unceremonious entry. Instead, he waited until the entire family was assembled, then rose and began to pace. It did not bode well for the day's plans.

"I must return to Sweden," he announced. Cries of protest and disappointment rose from the table. Anschel held up his hands for silence.

"This is not an ordinary business problem," he explained. "A situation has arisen that I wish to share with you. I want all of you to forget your disappointment for a moment and listen carefully." Anschel withdrew a letter from the breast pocket of his jacket and held it up for everyone to see. Riva toyed with her teacup.

"I usually don't discuss the details of my business with my family, but this is something that affects all of us."

The world was in the midst of a great transformation, he told them. New inventions and manufacturing techniques were revolutionizing the way things were done, but none would have so great an effect as the automobile. The Ford Model T parked in the Isaacson's carriage house in

Stockholm would soon replace the horse and buggy forever. The children glanced at each other surreptitiously. Once their father started talking about automobiles, there was no stopping him.

"Millions of people will no longer be separated by time and distance," Anschel declared, his eyes filled with the excitement of his vision. "A journey that used to require a full day in a horse and carriage now takes only a couple of hours in an automobile, and we're fast approaching the point where mass produced automobiles will cost little to own."

Herb burped aloud, earning a sharp reprimand from his mother. Ignoring the interruption, Anschel explained how he and his brother, Samuel, had organized a small group of influential friends and petitioned Henry Ford for a license to manufacture Model T automobiles, first in Sweden and Germany, then in other strategic European countries.

The children came alive at the mention of Henry Ford's name. Everyone knew about Henry Ford and how he started with nothing to become one of the richest, most admired men in the world. He was an inspiration to every ambitious schoolboy in Europe.

"Are you and Mr. Ford going to be in business together?" There was awe in Ben's voice. Anschel cast a sidelong glance at his son and in that split second, Benjamin saw the cold fury in his eyes. The abrupt shift in his father's mood startled him.

"I received Mr. Ford's reply yesterday afternoon." Anschel ripped the letter from its envelope and read aloud in a tense, bitter voice. The letter consisted of two short sentences: Henry Ford was not interested in discussing a licensing agreement with Anschel Isaacson; Henry Ford did not do business with Anschel Isaacson's "kind of people." The children stared at their plates, feeling ashamed without knowing why. Only Benjamin flushed angrily; he was old enough to realize exactly what the letter meant.

"I want you all to remember this," Anschel shook the letter furiously, and his fist came down on the polished surface of the table, rattling the china. "There are many people in this world who will judge you simply because you are a Jew. It doesn't matter what kind of person you are—the fact that you are a Jew is enough. You must remember this, and be strong. We have endured as a people because we have not dared to forget who we are. One day we will reclaim our sovereignty as a nation. You must all be strong for that day."

What Anschel did not tell his family was that he had already made substantial commitments, based on his confidence that Ford would grant a manufacturing license. Financing had been arranged, factory space had been leased, and tooling equipment had been ordered—even some of the management staff had been signed to contracts. In his enthusiasm, Anschel had overlooked one of his cardinal rules: if you are a Jew, never forget it.

That the world's largest manufacturer of automobiles had placed him in a difficult position did nothing to alter his belief that the automobile was the wave of the future, and Anschel Isaacson intended to be a part of that future. Once his group in Stockholm was reorganized, he planned to form a consortium with a French or English company to manufacture a European automobile; there was much to be done. He saw no point in cutting the children's summer vacation short, so he and Riva decided the family would remain in St. Petersburg until the end of August, then rejoin him in Stockholm.

The next morning, the entire family accompanied Anschel to the steamship depot on the Neva River, where a ferry waited to take him to Kotlin Island and a steamship to Stockholm. After saying farewell, the family stood clustered on the pier and watched until the ferry was out of sight.

June 28th was a beautiful summer day, warm and pleasant, without a hint of rain. Sunlight played over the Neva, creating sparkling diamonds of light on the sapphire waves, and pleasure boats cut graceful swathes through the water. But Anschel's departure had cast a pall on the day, and the children were quiet and withdrawn.

"What we all need is a large helping of *morozino*," Riva declared as she led everyone off the dock. A generous serving of Russian-style ice cream always seemed to brighten the children's spirits and chase away the downcast expressions. She piled the family into a horse drawn carriage and directed the driver to a sidewalk café known for its *morozino*. But before they reached the restaurant, the course of their lives was irrevocably changed.

A thousand miles away, in a country that would one day be known as Yugoslavia, a nineteen-year-old unknown Serbian political agitator named Gavrilo Princip assassinated Francis Ferdinand, heir to the Austro-Hungarian empire, and his wife. Europe's Golden Age was over.

It would be nearly two long years before Anschel Isaacson saw his family again.

•   •   •

The world was shocked by the events in Sarajevo and when Anschel Isaacson first learned of the assassination, he sent a letter to reassure Riva that any rumors of war were groundless. There had been talk of war in 1908 when Bosnia and Hercegovina were annexed by Austria, but in spite of the rhetoric, war was avoided. Likewise, the Balkan Wars of 1912-1913 had amounted to no more than a local crisis. There was no indication that the tragedy in Sarajevo would be any different. The monarchs of Europe were closely related, and the specter of war was so terrible to contemplate that most Europeans were convinced that the era of widespread conflicts was over. It was a tragic illusion. In mid-July, Austria delivered a harsh ultimatum to Serbia. The Serbs accepted some conditions, but a promise of support from the Czar led them to reject the majority of demands. Tension rose to a fever pitch, culminating in a declaration of war by the Austro-Hungarian Empire on July 28. Within four days, Western civilization was at war.

The atmosphere in St. Petersburg remained deceptively gay. Kaiser Wilhelm was thought of as a buffoon and the ruling House of Hapsburg was perceived as a rotting edifice, ready to collapse of its own weight. Czar Nicholas II had not been surprised when his cousin, the Kaiser, declared war. On his orders, the Russian army had been quietly mobilizing for several weeks.

The first week of August saw military units in full battle regalia marching through the streets of St. Petersburg to the sound of brass bands. Russian flags adorned most homes and the sound of boot heels on cobblestones reverberated through the city. Army units in field gray and olive drab paraded in endless columns to staging areas outside St. Petersburg, and the colorful blue and white uniforms of sailors from the Kronstadt Naval Base became a common sight.

Filled with excitement, the Isaacson children watched the spectacle from the balcony of their second-floor apartment. Nothing they had ever seen compared to the sight of Imperial Russia readying for war. The citizens of St. Petersburg lined the streets and filled the air with enthusiastic cheers, decorating the troops with garlands of flowers. During those first few days, everyone was a patriot, carried away by the martial music and chauvinistic slogans.

While her children participated in the festivities from the balcony, Riva sat at the kitchen table, her tea untouched and growing cold. There was a queasy knot in her stomach. She had been nervous after the assassination of the Archduke, but Anschel's letter had given her a sense of security. She had debated leaving the city when the Russian mobilization began, but everyone seemed to consider it an exercise in saber rattling—nothing to worry about. Even when war was declared, no one believed it would last long or affect their lives to any great degree. Though

St. Petersburg was far removed from any possible danger, Riva Isaacson did not relish the prospect of remaining in a country at war any longer than was absolutely necessary.

That afternoon, she decided to book return passage to Sweden. As she prepared to leave for the ticket agency, Benjamin ran to her side and insisted on going with her. With Anschel gone, he had become very serious about his "responsibilities" as "the man of the house." She regarded her son with affection, noting the grave expression in his eyes. He's growing up, she thought to herself. Against her better judgment, she allowed him to go with her, leaving the other children with Greta.

Riva and Benjamin tried to make their way through the crowds, but gave up a block from the apartment. The streets were a solid mass of humanity; it was impossible to move. Riva was terrified she and Benjamin would be separated in the confusion, and she clung to his hand all the way back to the apartment. It took them nearly a half an hour to retrace their steps.

"Trouble always comes in threes," Greta predicted dourly when she heard the story.

The next day, Riva tried again, leaving after a bitter argument with Benjamin, who was fiercely disappointed at being forced to remain behind with Greta and the other children. It distressed Riva to see his wounded pride, but she was not about to take any unnecessary risks; Benjamin would stay in the apartment. She took a horse-drawn hansom to the steamship agency, only to discover that it was impossible to book passage from St. Petersburg to Stockholm or anywhere else. "Perhaps tomorrow, Madame," the clerks told her. The Russian mobilization had placed tremendous demands on the country's transportation systems and military needs received top priority. Civilians hoping to make travel arrangements mobbed the steamship offices and railroad ticket agencies, but during that first week of August there were no ships available for civilian passengers. Confusion was rampant as the country moved to a war footing. Riva's friends tried to reassure her that the war was nothing to be concerned about, but Riva remained unconvinced. Beneath the pageantry and flowers, she sensed an undercurrent of repressed fury that terrified her. Day after day, she racked her mind for a way to escape from the city, but she could think of nothing.

The children were enjoying themselves immensely, and Riva was grateful they were in no immediate danger; the Isaacsons were neutral Swedes and had nothing to fear. But emotions ran high in St. Petersburg, and Riva took the precaution of warning her children not to speak German or Yiddish in public. A carefully orchestrated propaganda program against Germany had already commenced, and Riva didn't want her family to be caught in the cross fire.

Every day, Riva fought the crowds and battled her way to the steamship offices, and every day she stood in a long line only to be told the same thing: there were no passenger ships available. The Russian naval base on the Neva created security problems and monopolized St. Petersburg's shipping. For all practical purposes, it was impossible to leave by sea.

After being turned away for the third consecutive day, it occurred to Riva to try an alternative route—overland, to her family in Estonia. Her chances of booking a passage from Estonia to Stockholm were bound to be greater than her chances of booking passage from St. Petersburg. By enlisting the aid of a business associate of her husband, she managed to obtain reservations for herself, Greta, and the children for the following Thursday.

Since any train could be requisitioned by the miliary without notice, Riva had no way of knowing whether or not they would actually be leaving until the train was out of the station. She debated sending Anschel a cable, but even if it got through, she reasoned, they might still be trapped in St. Petersburg if the train was requisitioned. Not wanting to misinform her husband or cause him needless worry, she decided to wait. She would communicate with Anschel once they reached Estonia.

When Thursday came, Riva paid an extra deposit on the apartment so they would have a place to return if the train failed to materialize, and led her family to the station. Standing on the platform was an agony of uncertainty, but Riva's prayers were answered and the conductors finally gave the boarding signal.

The journey proved uneventful and they arrived in Dorpat hot, tired, and unannounced. Years before, when Riva's father had died, Anschel had bought her mother a spacious home in an elegant residential section of the city. It was the house in which all her children, with the exception of Benjamin, had been born.

As the taxi lurched to a halt in front of her mother's house, Riva felt tears sting the corners of her eyes. A wrought iron fence separated the front yard from the street and the entire property was framed in green by mountain ashes and well-tended evergreen shrubs. The house had been recently painted—she recalled having sent the money, and from the street it looked warm and inviting and, above all, safe. For Riva, Dorpat represented the security of home. She had been born and raised in Dorpat;

her family had been a part of the Jewish community there for centuries. There was a continuity to life in Dorpat that she found missing from her life in Sweden, a sense of belonging that Anschel never understood.

She watched the children run up the front walk and heaved a sigh of relief. She was home. Now she would have a haven, a safe place in which to think and to plan.

TWO

Dorpat, Estonia
August, 1914

It was nearly ten o'clock at night and Riva was bone weary, but for the first time in weeks, she felt truly relaxed. The house was peaceful, and St. Petersburg seemed like a dream now that the children were safely tucked in bed upstairs. She and her mother, Beile, sat in the kitchen, resting their arms on a scarred wooden table that Riva remembered from the time she was a young girl. The formal parlor was more comfortable, but there was an intimacy and warmth about the kitchen that both women preferred. They talked quietly, content to be in each other's company.

Beile studied the lines of fatigue on her daughter's face with a sadness all parents feel as they watch their children grow older, and she let the conversation meander, allowing Riva time to regain her equilibrium. They spoke of relatives and friends, how Dorpat had changed, and a dozen trivial things that served to reconnect the parted strands of their lives. By unspoken agreement, they avoided the subject of the war and stayed in the past; unlike the present or the future, the past was a safe common ground full of warm memories and pleasant moments.

It was midnight before Riva brought up the war and why Anschel had left the family in St. Petersburg. Beile listened without interrupting as the weeks of pent-up fear and anxiety poured from her daughter's heart. Finally, there was nothing left but nervous exhaustion, and Beile reached across the table to take Riva's hand.

"These are sad times," she sighed. "Thank God you and the

children were able to get out of St. Petersburg before things got worse.''

Riva squeezed her mother's hand, too drained to express her feelings. Though Beile Nadelson was in her early sixties, she carried her age with a youthful vigor that belied her years. Beile never seemed to change; she was always a source of strength and love.

''It will be nice to have my grandchildren around me,'' Beile smiled tiredly. ''We haven't had a good long visit in many years.''

''I wasn't planning on a long visit, Mama,'' Riva yawned. ''As soon as I can book passage, the children and I are returning to Stockholm.''

Beile looked at her hands and began rotating her wedding band back and forth. It was an old habit that always signaled bad news.

''Mama?''

''Riva, the Germans have already mined the Gulf of Riga. Unless the war ends quickly, you and the childrenm may be here indefinitely.''

Riva braced herself against the edge of the table as a black wave of nausea threatened to overcome her. Her mouth felt dry and, for a moment, she was afraid she might actually lose consciousness. She drew a deep breath to clear her senses, then looked up at her mother. ''From what I hear, Mama, they expect peace talks to begin soon. Once they do, the war should end fairly quickly.''

''You're probably right,'' Beile agreed. She smiled encouragingly, but her voice lacked conviction.

•   •   •

Hopes for an early end to the war faded as the fighting escalated and peace talks failed to materialize. It became quickly apparent that the length of the conflict would be measured in terms of years, not weeks or months.

The first two weeks in Dorpat were the most difficult, marked by tension and a vague, lethargic depression. Beile, Riva, and Greta did their best to keep everyone's spirits up, but it was a constant struggle. It gnawed at Riva's heart to see how much the children missed Anschel. She also had to contend with several unpleasant confrontations between Greta and Beile over the children. While Greta was determined to continue their training and education just as though they were back in Sweden, Beile came of a different culture and generation; she felt they should be brought up according to the old traditions. Again and again, Riva found herself mediating between the two women as the discord expanded to encompass an endless range of issues. The skirmishes continued until Riva finally exploded one night and laid down her own rules. Neither Beile nor Greta was pleased with the end result, but Riva's intervention restored a measure of harmony to the household. There were other minor problems, but life inevitably settled into a stable pattern.

The highlight of any day was a message from Anschel. Sometimes there would be no word for weeks at a time—then six letters would arrive in a single day. Every one contained the same promise: "Ill join you as soon as I can. All my love, your husband and father." Riva read each one aloud to the assembled family and they always talked afterwards but she began to notice a drift in the children's attitude. Every letter placed a little more distance between Anschel and his children. Benjamin, being the oldest, tended to idealize his memory of Anschel and tried to pattern himself after what he thought Anschel would want him to be. At times, Riva could detect a vein of resentment in Benjamin as though he blamed Anschel for deserting them, but she could never coax him to talk about it. It was some consolation that Herb, Ida, and Freida came to accept Anschel's absence, and with the exception of a few nightmares and tearful tantrums, they finally adjusted to their new surroundings.

To the children's delight, Beile spent a great deal of time baking and devoted herself to spoiling them as much as her daughter would permit. Greta was convinced that Beile was engaged in a competition for the children's affection but that was untrue. Beile Nadelson loved having her grandchildren around and treasured their time together, storing the memories like carefully mounted photographs against the empty days of the future.

Although she was genuinely fond of Anschel and appreciated his generosity, Beile had always distrusted his politics and resented his refusal to live in Dorpat. She had been lonely since her husband's death and longed to have her daughter and grandchildren nearby. Like Riva, she felt that one should remain close to one's family and that Zionism was a dangerous illusion. Occasionally, she had to suppress a twinge of guilt that her enjoyment of the children came at the expense of a separation from their father.

Every day, the house filled with cousins, aunts, uncles, and old friends. Riva welcomed the constant activity; it took her mind off Anschel and the war. She also usurped the responsibility of running the house and it helped to make the long days pass. Only at night, when the house was still and she climbed into an empty bed, did she allow herself the bitter luxury of missing her husband. Before falling asleep, like tens of thousands of wives and mothers all over Europe, Riva would murmur a brief prayer for the war to end and her family to be reunited.

The children were enrolled in school in mid-autumn. Herb and Ida funneled their energies into study and new friends. Freida was still too young for school and spent most of her time with Beile. It was Benjamin who concerned his mother the most. He was withdrawn and often moody; of her four children, Benjamin had the greatest difficulty adjusting to Dorpat.

The other children were younger and took the change in stride, but Benjamin was old enough to realize that Stockholm and Dorpat were separated by more than the Baltic Sea. Dorpat's culture reflected its German heritage and a clear prejudice separated Gentile from Jew, permeating every aspect of life. Like his father, Benjamin found the atmosphere oppressive and threatening; there was an undercurrent of malice that surfaced in subtle ways. Sometimes it came as a disdainful glance or a snide remark, barely audible. On other occasions it could be seen in the reluctant nod of a neighbor passed on the street, or heard in the patronizing tone of a local shopkeeper. Herb, Ida, and Freida were all too young to notice, but Benjamin felt the coldness and rejection, a feeling that was fully justified the day school began.

At the close of the first school day, Benjamin left the building and began a six-block walk to *cheder*, a Hebrew school, where he would study Judaism and the Hebrew language for two hours every afternoon. Most of the Jewish boys attended the *cheder*. As he left the school grounds, he reached into his pocket and withdrew a black embroidered yarmulke that he set firmly on the back of his head.

"I wouldn't do that if I were you." A slight, curly haired boy stood a few paces behind Benjamin. Like Benjamin, he was on his way to the Hebrew school.

Benjamin stared at the boy for a moment. "When you go to *cheder*, you're supposed to wear a yarmulke as a gesture of respect."

"Not here," the boy shook his head. "But you probably wouldn't know that. I can tell by the way you talk that you're not Estonian."

"I'm Swedish."

"It doesn't matter what you are. If you wear that yarmulke, you'll be asking for trouble."

"I wore it to *cheder* in Sweden, and I'll wear it here," Benjamin replied coldly. The boy studied him, then shrugged and walked away.

Halfway to the Hebrew school, Benjamin caught up with three classmates on their way to *cheder*, but they ignored him, so he walked three or four paces behind them, lost in his own thoughts. Suddenly, he was shoved from behind and found himself face down in the dirt, momentarily stunned. He rolled to a sitting position and looked up. A muscular blond teenager towered over him, a faint smile on his lips. Benjamin's three classmates cowered against a building while a half dozen Christian boys taunted them for attending a ''Jew school.''

''Did you trip?'' the blond jeered. An adolescent cruelty marred his youthful features. ''You Jews always seem to be so clumsy.''

Benjamin bit back a reply; sometimes it was better to let things pass. As he scrambled to his feet, the blond's arm flashed out and swiped the yarmulke off his head. That was more than Benjamin was willing to tolerate. He lunged forward with a yell and a scuffle ensued. It ended quickly when Benjamin found himself on the sidewalk again, nursing a bloody nose.

''Try that again and I'll break your legs,'' his opponent spat. He held up Benjamin's yarmulke for everyone to see and slowly ripped it in half. Then he threw the two pieces on the ground. ''These Jew hats are not made very well,'' he smiled maliciously. ''You should get yourself a decent cap.'' The blond signalled his friends and they disappeared down an alley.

By the time Benjamin pulled himself together, the other Jewish boys had disappeared. He wiped the blood from his face with a coat sleeve, then made his way to *cheder*.

Herr Jakelsky, the prinicpal, stood at the gate like a toll collector, counting heads and urging the boys to hurry. Though attendance was always taken in the classroom, Herr Jakelsky felt his visible presence on the street was an important reminder to those boys who might be considering skipping Hebrew school. If they did, they would have to answer to him and that was never a pleasant prospect. Herr Jakelsky was an old-fashioned man with a humorless expression that mirrored his belief in strict discipline. He tolerated no foolishness.

When he saw Benjamin walking up the street with a swollen nose and blood on his shirt, he shook his head. ''You are Benjamin Isaacson, the new boy?'' he snapped as Benjamin reached the gate. ''The boys told me what happened. Go to my office immediately.'' Summarily dismissed, Benjamin did as he was told.

When Herr Jakelsky appeared at the office door, Benjamin was totally unprepared for the vehement reprimand he received. The principal was furious at Benjamin for wearing a yarmulke on the street.

''You're in Estonia, not Sweden. In Estonia, we do not look for trouble by flaunting our religion. Rudy Kurtz gave you what you deserved.''

''But . . .''

Herr Jakelsky was not interested in hearing Benjamin's explanation. "Just don't make a spectacle of yourself in public again. Now get to class. You are late."

Benjamin's face burned red and he spent the entire two hours of class with arms crossed and teeth clenched, not hearing a word the teacher said. He did learn that "Rudy Kurtz" was the ringleader of a Christian gang that often plagued the Jewish boys on their way to *cheder*.

Benjamin tried to slip into the house unnoticed, but Greta spotted him. "What on earth happened?" she exclaimed.

"I tripped and fell." Benjamin had never lied to Greta and salved his conscience with the thought that he was telling at least part of the truth. He didn't like deceiving her, but he intended to deal with Rudy Kurtz himself; he was old enough to settle his own problems. As Greta took his shirt to clean it, her lips pursed together in a frown, letting him know she did not entirely believe him, but she did not question him further.

Before leaving for school the next day, he took another yarmulke and stuffed it into his back pocket. Rudy Kurtz already knows who I am, he reasoned, so it doesn't really matter whether I wear it or not. On his way to *cheder*, he jammed the yarmulke on the back of his head. Herr Jakelsky was irritated but helpless on this one issue. No Jew could forbid another to wear a yarmulke.

There was an ugly confrontation almost every afternoon, making the six-block walk to the *cheder* a daily agony. Usually, the abuse was verbal; sometimes it was worse. Benjamin and the other boys altered their route to avoid the gang, but more often than not, the Christian toughs would be waiting to make their lives miserable. It was during the second week that Kurtz singled Benjamin out for special treatment, roughing him up and pushing him headlong into a thorn bush.

Herr Jakelsky said nothing when Benjamin limped up to the *cheder* trying to pull the torn edges of his shirt together and smooth his disheveled hair. Benjamin's face and hands were covered with bloody scratches from the thorns, and his jacket sleeve was ripped from elbow to wrist. He shuffled past the principal and took his seat in the classroom, setting his mind on a list of irregular Hebrew verbs written on the board.

Just before class ended, Herr Jakelsky strode into the room. He asked Benjamin to stand and delivered a scathing lecture in front of the entire class. He felt that Benjamin was attempting to undermine his authority and accused him of being responsible for the trouble all the boys were having. Not once did the principal mention Rudy Kurtz and his gang. Benjamin shook with fury at the rebuke.

"Mr. Isaacson wears his yarmulke out of stubborn willfulness, and he gets what he deserves,'' Jakelsky concluded after what seemed like an eternity. "It's too bad the rest of you must suffer as well." He glared at Benjamin and stomped out of the room. No one waited for the teacher to officially dismiss the class.

Benjamin bolted out of the room and was halfway down the front steps of the *cheder* when a voice called out after him. He whirled, and found himself face to face with Meilach Gorsky. Gorsky was six months older than Benjamin and at least a head taller. He had a reputation for being a practical joker and good with his fists. Benjamin considered ignoring him or brushing him off, but he was uncomfortably aware of Gorsky's superior size. He had the additional disadvantage of standing on a lower step, forcing him to look up at the older boy.

"What do you want?" Benjamin snapped. He had endured enough abuse for one day and was not about to be intimidated.

"By the look of you, you could probably use a friend." Gorsky grinned innocently, revealing a set of comically spaced white teeth. His complexion was dark and his bushy eyebrows grew together in a straight line beneath a bristly crop of jet black hair. Benjamin detected no malice in Gorsky's warm brown eyes.

"I can take care of myself," Benjamin growled. "I don't need any friends." He turned and started down the steps again.

Gorsky hesitated for a moment. Like the other boys at the *cheder*, he had regarded Benjamin's arrival with suspicion. The Jews of Dorpat were a clannish lot and their children were no different—strangers were strangers. Benjamin was Swedish, and therefore not just an outsider but a foreigner as well. His attitudes seemed strange, almost arrogant, and he unconsciously reinforced that perception by standing aloof from the rest of the boys; they misread his self-imposed isolation as conceit. Even Benjamin's knowledge of Hebrew did not register to his credit; Hebrew was a language the other boys regarded with studied indifference.

Meilach Gorsky stood at the head of the stairs and laughed out loud at the determined set of Benjamin's shoulders. Despite Benjamin's unfriendly attitude, there was something about him that attracted Gorsky. It was easy for him to overtake Benjamin's short-legged strides.

"Are you always this stubborn?"

Benjamin stopped. "Are you always such a nuisance?" Meilach gaped at Benjamin, then broke out laughing.

"What are you laughing at?" Benjamin asked hotly. At that, Meilach began to laugh all the harder. Disgusted, Benjamin turned and started to walk away, but Meilach's hand shot out and caught him by the shoulder.

"No wait, wait," Meilach gasped, wiping tears of laughter from his cheeks. "You just got beaten up by the *goyim* and chewed out by the principal. You're a foreigner with a funny accent. You're conceited and arrogant, yet you still have the *chutzpah* to tell me you don't need any friends. You're unbelievable." Benjamin was about to protest, but Meilach raised his head and cut him off. "And the way you speak Hebrew is enough to make anyone dislike you."

Benjamin stared at Meilach, trying to decipher his intentions. "Then why waste your time talking to me?"

"I want us to be friends," Meilach replied with a finality that precluded any argument.

Benjamin's mouth dropped open in surprise. "I thought you just said . . ."

"I did," Meilach grinned. "But you've got style and I like that. You can help me with my Hebrew verbs, and I'll help you with your . . . other problems. Fair enough?"

He accepted Ben's lack of response as a yes and put an arm across Benjamin's shoulders. "So, tell me, who do you think will win the war?" They both broke out laughing.

The next afternoon, Meilach and four of his friends walked to the *cheder* with Benjamin. All wore yarmulkes. Rudy Kurtz and his friends evidently disliked even odds because none of the Jewish boys were bothered that day.

Benjamin and Meilach became fast friends and were soon nicknamed "the twins" by the rest of the school. They made an odd contrast. Benjamin was small for his age, very fair and reserved. Meilach was tall, darkly handsome and gregarious. Somehow their differences complemented the relationship, cementing the bond between them.

It was not long before Rudy Kurtz struck again. This time the victim was Willi Seigel, the curly haired boy who tried to warn Benjamin against wearing a yarmulke the first day of school. Like most of the other boys, Willi had taken to wearing a yarmulke to Hebrew school. He was well liked at the *cheder* and when he appeared at Herr Jakelsky's gate with his shirt ripped to shreds and his jacket missing, it disrupted the entire class. Rudy Kurtz had outdone himself, sending Willi off with a mutilated yarmulke and an ultimatum: any Jew caught wearing a yarmulke was in for "Real Trouble."

That day, on the way home from school, Benjamin and Meilach could talk of nothing else. Benjamin wanted desperately to gather a group of Jewish boys and combat the threat head-on, but Meilach vetoed the idea.

"Nobody around here wants to fight back, Ben. It's too dangerous," Meilach frowned. "If a gang of Christians beats up a Jew—that's just a little high-spirited fun. But if we were to beat up some Christian boys, we'd be dirty Jews ganging up on helpless Christians. And most of our parents would probably give us a licking as well."

"We can't just keep on taking it," Benjamin sputtered. "We have to fight back. We have to do something."

"For a runt, you always seem to want to slug it out," Meilach grinned. "Trust me. I'll think of something."

Benjamin did not have to wait long. The next morning, Meilach confided that he did have a plan, and promised to explain it after *cheder*. Benjamin spent the entire school day squirming in his seat, trying to imagine what Meilach had dreamed up. Twice he was reprimanded for not paying attention in class. All the way home that afternoon, Meilach maintained an infuriating silence until they reached the Isaacson house.

"Just get me a large cork, a laundry bag, and about twenty feet of string," Meilach instructed him. "I'll meet you out back."

Mystified, Ben did as he was asked and met Meilach behind the house. They walked to an old hemlock tree growing near the Isaacson's back fence. Meilach pointed to one of the lower branches. Hanging from it was a large gray hornets' nest Ben had never noticed.

"What are you going to do with that?"

"You'll find out soon enough," Meilach promised as he knotted the string around the large end of the cork and stuffed the laundry bag into his jacket. He climbed to the hornets' nest and deftly shoved the cork into the open hole of the paper cone. Then he rocked the nest until it broke free of the branch, placed it in the laundry sack, and pulled the draw strings closed. The autumn chill made the hornets sluggish and slow to react.

"What are you going to do?" Benjamin repeated.

"Be patient."

Meilach led the way through a maze of alleys that brought them opposite a darkened warehouse whose hulking presence dominated the empty street. Like sightless eyes, small opaque windows pierced the red brick walls. A peeling sign hung over the front doors. It read "Property of the University of Dorpat."

Benjamin suddenly wished he were elsewhere, certain that anyone who saw them near the deserted building with an oversized laundry sack would assume they were thieves and summon the police. A shiver ran up his spine and he stifled an impulse to suggest they leave.

Two minutes later, they stood at a barred gate on the side of the building. It was not locked. Meilach checked to see if anyone had noticed them, then pushed the gate open and slipped down a flight of damp cement stairs to a basement entrance. A heavy steel fire door obstructed their way. Gently, Meilach set down the laundry bag and started to rummage between the foundation stones. After an interval that felt like an eternity to Benjamin, Meilach extracted a large iron key and inserted it into the lock. The bolt snapped open with an audible crack that made Benjamin jump. He was certain the entire neighborhood knew they were burglarizing the building.

"What . . ." Benjamin began, Meilach raised a finger to his lips and disappeared into the basement. There was nothing but darkness within. Once inside, Meilach closed the fire door and fumbled with a match. As it flared to life, he used it to light a kerosene lantern that hung from a peg near the threshold.

The lantern created a puddle of yellow light, casting twisted shadows across an unearthly landscape. For a moment, Benjamin was completely disoriented by the sight of a Roman villa, complete with olive groves and a view of the Mediterranean. Then he realized it was a theatrical set. As his eyes grew accustomed to the faint light, he saw dozens of different sets and props.

"Great place, isn't it?" Meilach whispered. "The University of Dorpat Theater stores all its stuff down here."

They followed a convoluted path between the sets to a narrow door. Meilach opened it cautiously and held the lantern up. Beyond lay a windowless room with a table, chairs, and an old couch. A rotting side board leaned against one blackened wall.

"It stinks in here," Benjamin grimaced.

Meilach rubbed his hands together. "Rudy Kurtz's father is the head custodian of the university. He lets Rudy and his friends use this room as a clubhouse." It was surprisingly warm in the warehouse basement and the two boys were already sweating heavily. Benjamin was certain he could hear the angry hornets beginning to stir.

"What now?" Benjamin whispered. Tension formed an iron band around his chest. Without another word, Meilach opened the laundry sack and gingerly removed the hornets' nest. He was careful not to dislodge the cork.

He carried the nest at arm's length and braced it in a corner behind a moth-eaten chair. Then he rubbed his fingers in the coal dust on the floor and blackened the length of the string to make it less conspicuous. Fascinated. Ben watched as his friend led the free end of the string back to the door. Crouching on one knee, Meilach looped the string around a protruding nail on the outside of the door and tied it securely.

"Let's get out of here," he whispered. The two boys retraced their path, stopping at street level to be sure no one saw them. They sped across the cobblestones and hid behind a discarded carriage that partially blocked the mouth of an alley.

"Now we wait." Meilach squatted on his ankles, watching the building. Ben envied his friend's composure—his own heart pounded furiously.

Not much later, Rudy Kurtz and a half dozen of his cronies walked up the street. They were laughing and indulging in a bit of high spirited horseplay. Relaxed and unsuspecting, they disappeared down the steps to the basement. Later Ben would swear that he held his breath until they reemerged, yelling and screaming and swatting their faces and clothing. The "twins" doubled up with laughter.

"That will give . . . the kids at *cheder* . . . something to buzz about," Meilach gasped. Benjamin groaned at the pun and playfully jabbed his friend in the ribs.

Rudy Kurtz showed up for school the next day, his face swollen with red welts. Three of his freinds had to spend the day in bed with ice packs. Though neither Ben nor Meilach would claim any credit, rumors flew through the *cheder* that "the twins" had struck. Unwilling to admit they had been ambushed, the Christian boys described their misfortune as an "accident," but the message had been received. From that time on, Rudy Kurtz and his gang limited their harassment to insults shouted across the street and none of the boys wearing yarmulkes were assaulted. Benjamin remained suspicious of the uneasy truce, but when he confided his doubts to Meilach, his friend shrugged them off. "They're just bullies," Meilach replied. "I think we've heard the last of them."

Mainly due to his friendship with Meilach, Benjamin's attitude improved steadily, and he became himself again. His moody spells all but disappeared and he regained much of the cheerfulness lost when he first arrived in Dorpat. The school year passed more quickly than Benjamin imagined, and the two boys spent most of the following summer in each other's company. Life seemed very quiet until September, when school began. Meilach appeared on the Isaacson's front doorstep one afternoon, looking pale and serious.

"You'll have to find someone else to visit," Greta teased him. "All the cookies are gone." Meilach was famous for his voracious appetite. To Greta's surprise, he did not banter with her.

"Is Benjamin here?" he asked.

Greta studied him suspiciously. Meilach usually appeared on Friday afternoons to help Benjamin with his "deliveries" of food to needy families. Helping one's less fortunate neighbors was a Jewish tradition on holy days, but many Jews, like Benjamin's mother, didn't wait for a special occasion. Every *erev Shabbat*, the Sabbath eve, they sent pots of steaming chicken soup, gefilte fish spiced with saffron, and a honeyed pastry called *teigelach* to the poor, the old, and the sick. It didn't matter whether the recipients were Jewish or Gentile—only that they were in need of a good hot meal. Riva's specialty was chicken soup that contained an entire boiled chicken.

Friday afternoons, before sundown, Benjamin, Ida, and Meilach delivered the plates and pots of food to a half dozen families. Meilach's presence had aroused Greta's suspicions because he had mentioned he would not be helping Benjamin for Rosh Hashanah; he had prior family commitments. Now he stood at the door acting strangely.

"Of course Benjamin is here," she frowned. "He's polishing his shoes for services at the synagogue. Have you forgotten this is Rosh Hashanah eve?"

"Everyone knows that it's the beginning of the Jewish New Year," Meilach replied absently. "Could I just see Benjamin? Please?"

"He's in the basement." Greta watched Meilach disappear through the cellar door. Thoughtfully, she tugged at the fold of skin beneath her chin. "They're up to something," she muttered and shook her head in disapproval. Then she returned to the kitchen to supervise Ida, who was ironing Benjamin's suit.

Benjamin looked up and smiled as Meilach thundered down the stairs. "What are you doing here? I thought you were supposed to be with your family."

"If you lived in the Jewish quarter instead of this fancy neighborhood, you'd already know why I'm here. You were right about Rudy Kurtz. He and his friends are up to their tricks again. I saw them hanging around in front of Glickmann's bakery, complaining about Rosh Hashanah. They say they're tired of having the city stinking of 'Jew food' and watching Jews parade around the streets like they owned the city. Ben, there's trouble brewing."

"A lot of people are going to be out on the streets tonight," Benjamin put down his polishing rag. "Nothing would deter them from going to the synagogue on Rosh Hashanah. What do you think Kurtz and his friends are up to?"

"I'm not really sure," Meilach replied. "I don't think they have the guts to really hurt anyone, but they'll probably harass a lot of people and make things unpleasant; try to ruin the holiday. I'm sure they'll try to stop the deliveries, just out of pure spite."

"I figured Rudy would never let the hornet's nest pass," Benjamin sighed. "He's been waiting a long time to even the score."

"Maybe it's time we got a bunch of people together and took care of Rudy Kurtz once and for all."

Benjamin laughed. "Now you sound like me. You know better than that. What we need is a strategy, not an army."

"Benjamin? Are you still down there?" Ida's voice echoed down the cellar staris.

"Yes, Ida," he shouted back.

"Mama says the soup is almost ready. We should leave soon."

"I'll be up in a minute." Benjamin turned to Meilach, who looked at him expectantly. "I think what we have to do is make our deliveries just like nothing is going to happen. We can't really do anything about Rudy Kurtz and we can't let him frighten us off the streets with a bunch of wild threats. If we stay in a group and mind our own business, maybe nothing will happen."

"What about Ida?" Meilach asked.

Benjamin thought hard. "I think we'll still take her. If we don't, she'll know something's up and raise havoc with Mama. Besides, Kurtz and his friends might just ignore us if we've got a couple of little girls with us. Why don't you get Sam Lefkowitz and his sister to make the rounds with us? That will give us a good-sized group."

Meilach nodded in agreement. "I'll meet you in fifteen minutes."

Benjamin, Ida, Meilach, and the Lefkowitzes left the Isaacson house a half hour later, laden with cast iron pots and platters of gefilte fish and *teigelach*. Heavy lids covered the pots, but the unmistakable aroma of chicken soup enveloped them like a fog. Benjamin noticed that Sam Lefkowitz's hands were shaking.

Benjamin kept up a stream of banter to mask his own anxieties; if Kurtz was really out to even the score, there was no way to stop him. It galled Benjamin that all the cards seemed to be stacked in Kurtz's favor. He was Christian, he had the advantage of a large gang, and if trouble occurred, the police were bound to look the other way. Who cared if a few Jews got roughed up? It was nothing unusual.

Benjamin knew why Rudy had stationed himself in front of Glickmann's, five blocks away from his customary hangout. Every Friday afternoon, Benjamin passed by the bakery to make his deliveries. Rudy knew it and he was waiting.

Bypassing the bakery was an option that never occurred to Benjamin. He knew that avoiding Kurtz would only delay the inevitable, and when the final confrontation would come, any sign of weakness would make Kurtz all the more bold and aggressive.

Despite Kurtz's advantages, and his posturing and threats, Benjamin felt that his best choice was to face Kurtz head-on. His instincts told him Kurtz was a bully without the stomach for a real face-to-face confrontation. So Benjamin decided to gamble, and followed the same path he took every Friday afternoon past Glickmann's bakery. If he was right, nothing would happen. If he was wrong, and Rudy called his bluff, someone was liable to get hurt—probably he. He gulped hard at the thought. Halfway to the bakery, he wavered for a moment, realizing that he might not be the only one to suffer; if anything happened to Ida, he would never forgive himself. But he was already committed to a course of action and the force of his decision propelled him forward. For Benjamin, once a decision had been thought out and made, there was no going back. It was a trait he had inherited from Anschel.

They could see the front of the bakery from two blocks away, and the sight of Rudy Kurtz and a dozen other Christian boys leaning against Glickmann's building was enough to stop Lefkowitz and the girls dead in their tracks. When Rudy Kurtz caught sight of Benjamin, he grinned like a death's head, and his friends straddled the sidewalk as if they owned it. Rudy was an extraordinarily handsome young man with strong white teeth and a prominent jaw. His close cropped blond hair had bleached out during the summer and looked like white gold in the afternoon light. He had grown taller since Benjamin last saw him. Kurtz uncoiled from a slouch and languidly stepped out to block the sidewalk.

"Well, well, well," he bowed with mock courtesy. "It's my favorite Jew."

"Hello, Rudy," Benjamin replied pleasantly. He fixed his gaze on Kurtz's eyes, not willing to concede an inch. Rudy stared back as his friends encircled Benjamin's group. The gang's motion was casual and unguarded, like a predator that knows it has nothing to fear from its prey; after all, Jews had a reputation for docility.

The Jews of Dorpat had unconsciously encouraged that reputation by refusing to defend themselves; it was too dangerous, too risky, they said. Their reluctance to fight back had made them an easy target. Rudy Kurtz based his confidence on past experience.

"I see you're stinking up the streets like you always do on Friday afternoon." Rudy crossed his arms.

Benjamin was not going to be provoked. "Why don't you step aside and let us pass. Nobody is looking for trouble."

"Trouble?" Rudy looked offended. "We wouldn't dream of it.

We're just out to help the Jews celebrate their New Year properly, right?'' The other boys snickered in agreement. ''You know, Isaacson, until you put on that skullcap the first day of school, I actually thought you were a decent Christian.''

''Appearances can be deceiving. A lot of people who look like decent Christians really aren't.''

The implied insult was not lost on Kurtz, but he chose to ignore it. He gestured to the black iron kettle in Ben's left hand. ''I'm curious to see the kind of poison you're feeding to some of our poor Christian neighbors. I want to see if it looks as bad as it smells.''

Meilach squared his shoulders and stepped forward, balancing two plates and a pot in one hand. ''Why don't you just . . .''

''It's all right, Meilach,'' Benjamin restrained his friend. ''I think Rudy has a point. After all, the aroma is unmistakable.''

''Ben, he's just going to dump it out in the street,'' Meilach protested heatedly. Benjamin just waved him off.

Pale and tense, Ida stood next to Sam Lefkowitz's sister. Sam was behind them and looked ready to faint.

''Be my guest, Rudy,'' Benjamin smiled disarmingly as he removed the cast iron lid from the pot and handed it to Ida. He held the kettle out for Kurtz to look into.

Ben saw the flicker of triumpth in Kurtz's pale blue eyes as he stepped forward. Suddenly, Rudy's arm shot out to knock the pot from Benjamin's grasp, but Ben was too quick, jerking the kettle back out of reach. Ben plunged his free hand into the hot soup, skimming a handful of broth, fat, and chicken skin off the surface, then swung at Kurtz. Ben's hand connected with the side of Rudy's face with a loud smack.

''Oh God, I'm burned! I'm burned!'' Kurtz screamed, clutching at his eyes. ''I can't see!'' Yellow broth and globules of hot fat ran down his cheeks. He staggered, one hand over his eyes, the other groping for support. Meilach whipped the lid off the pot he was carrying and smeared a second boy. He yelped in pain, and clutched his woolen cap to his face. The rest of the gang began to back away, glancing at each other uncertainly.

The sight of Ida and the Lefkowitzes removing the lids off their soup pots was all the incentive the gang needed. They scattered and ran, leaving only Rudy Kurtz, who was still trying to wipe the soup out of his eyes with a shirttail.

''Are you all right, Rudy?'' Ben inquired solicitously. ''That was terribly clumsy of me.''

''You burned me, you dirty Jew.'' Rudy was practically in tears.

"Since you enjoyed the first serving so much, perhaps you'd like seconds." Benjamin swung the pot back as though he intended to empty it over Kurtz's head. Rudy covered his face with his arms and ran as fast as he could, leaving the five young people laughing and jubilant.

"For a minute, I though you were going to do it," Ida giggled.

"This stuff is too valuable to waste," Ben grinned. "Besides, he'll feel like he's been marked for life. Chicken fat is impossible to scrub off."

"That was quite a display," Meilach teased. "Not quite as impressive as watching the walls of Jericho fall, but still pretty impressive."

"Joshua at least had a horn," Ben replied with a straight face. "All we had was my mother's chicken soup. Come on, we've got deliveries to make.

Rudy Kurtz did not bother them again.

THREE

Dorpat
December 1915

In Anschel's absence, the honor of lighting the Hanukkah candles fell to Ben that December. The first night of Hanukkah, he lit the first candle on the gleaming brass menorah and recited the blessings in flawless Hebrew. The lighting of the candles was usually a solemn and joyous occasion, but this night had a melancholy quality about it. Though no one voiced the thought aloud, the ceremony was a keen reminder that 1915 marked the second year the Isaacsons had celebrated Hanukkah without Anschel. The atmosphere in the Dorpat house was somber, and the news of one German victory after another had done nothing to dispel the gloom.

The next morning, Beile decided to take matters into her own hands; she was not about to permit anyone, including her daughter, to squander the joys of the season. She employed her considerable charm and culinary talents to bolster everyone's spirits and coax smiles to reluctant lips. In those instances where food and charm failed, she was not above administering a well-deserved rebuke. By the time Ben lit the second candle that evening, her efforts had returned an unmistakable cheerfulness to the Isaacson household, which lasted through the rest of Hanukkah.

It was towards the beginning of January that Beile began to worry about her daughter. Riva leaned on Beile's strength and tried hard to bury her loneliness for the sake of the children, but the separation from Anschel had created an aching void that nothing seemed to dispel. Beile found it difficult to understand Riva's sense of loss; after all, it wasn't as though

43

Anschel had died. Yet for Riva, separation carried with it an uncertainty that was almost worse. She had lost weight and acted oddly distracted at times. She had also become quarrelsome and overprotective of the children. Beile watched her daughter with increasing concern, but was reluctant to press the matter. Give it enough time, she told herself; it will pass. But despite Beile's optimism, nothing changed. Riva remained withdrawn and uncommunicative, going about her daily routine with a mechanical detachment.

Ironically, Ben's adjustment to life in Dorpat had a negative effect on Riva: it freed her to focus on the war and how much she missed Anschel. Though she loved the city and the warmth of family and old friends, she could never quite escape the feeling that she was a prisoner in her own home. She had trouble sleeping, and Beile often woke in the middle of the night to the sound of her daughter's footsteps descending the stairs to the kitchen.

Anschel's letters remained a source of joy for Riva, and for a few brief hours after receiving one, she would emerge from her shell, gay and talkative, with a healthy flush to her cheeks. But her euphoria would quickly fade and the following days would find her quiet and moody. Again and again, Beile tried to make her talk about her feelings, but Riva refused to discuss the subject. She kept her emotions bottled up and private.

The winter of 1915 was particularly cruel, and the progress of the war was hampered by heavy snows. Despite the temporary lull, both sides remained committed to total victory, making peace a distant dream. Riva's depression deepened with the drifts of snow that banked against the Dorpat house like a smothering veil.

When the family celebrated Passover in April, Riva kept staring at Anschel's empty place at the head of the table, barely touching her food and speaking only when someone addressed a direct question to her. She was not cross with the children, but they sensed her distance and it disturbed them. Unable to reach her daughter, Beile resigned herself to Riva's self-imposed isolation.

Spring of 1916 arrived late in Dorpat. When it did, it came all at once and had a certain unreal quality. The ragged yew hedges turned green almost overnight and the scent of blossoms perfumed the air with new life. The sudden respite from the harsh Baltic winter took everyone by surprise. People busied themselves repairing the damage done by the heavy snows and tried to ignore the sound of German artillery; the front lines were less than thirty miles from Dorpat.

The German threat was a major topic of conversation in Dorpat that spring, but not for Benjamin and Meilach. They spent the month of April consumed by endless discussions on the subject of Meilach's fast-approaching thirteenth birthday. On that day, at his bar mitzvah, Meilach would stand in front of family, friends, and the entire congregation to receive his father's blessing and make the transition to manhood in the eyes of the Jewish community. For any Jewish boy, his bar mitzvah was the most important occasion of his young life.

As the great day drew closer, anticipation gripped the Gorsky household like a fever. Meilach and his father, Yakov, were together constantly, laughing and planning, and the close bond shared by father and son was plain to see. At first, Benjamin had shared Meilach's growing excitement, but excitement slowly faded into envy as he realized that his own transition to manhood would be made without Anschel. Benjamin's thirteenth birthday was only a few months away, but for him, there would be no laughing with his father, no planning, no special sharing. Benjamin tried to hide his feelings behind a facade of casual indifference, but whenever he saw Yakov Gorsky place his arm around Meilach, or heard the pride in his voice, it filled Benjamin with a jealous despair he did not fully understand.

•   •   •

Meilach Gorsky's bar mitzvah proved to be a memorable occasion. Just before Meilach recited the *haftorah*, a section of scripture he was required to memorize and deliver, Yakov Gorsky stood and placed a magnificent silk tallis across his son's shoulders. It was the high point of the ceremony, and the entire congregation rose as one, solemnly welcoming Meilach into their midst. The bar mitzvah was everything Meilach had expected, and more.

Benjamin attended the reception after the service, then slipped away unnoticed, avoiding the evening celebration. He had no desire to dance and feast; the sight of enthusiastic friends and relatives crowding around Meilach and his father with their congratulations practically moved him to tears of frustration. It had taken all his self-control just to stay through the reception.

He returned home from Meilach's bar mitzvah feeling depressed and alone. Shunning dinner and his mother's offer of a game of chess, he went straight to his room, where he stretched out on the bed and stared at the ceiling. He was filled with jealousy and self-pity; he felt empty and betrayed, as though Anschel had deserted him intentionally. All he could think of was his own bar mitzvah, and the more he thought about it, the more angry he became. He sprang out of bed, yanked the straight-back chair away from his desk and sat down. Rummaging through the center drawer, he found some ruled paper and a steel-tipped pen. He was vaguely aware that what he was about to do was wrong, but he pushed the feeling aside and began to vent his anger in hastily scrawled lines across the paper. He wrote furiously, choosing the words that would wound his father the most. He filled the blank pages with loneliness and frustration, wanting to hurt his father as he had been hurt. He blamed the war for separating them, he blamed Henry Ford for Anschel's untimely departure, but most of all, in his bitterness, he accused his father of being selfish, uncaring, and indifferent to his family. "Whenever there was a choice," he wrote, "you chose your business over us. I hope you are satisfied." Benjamin's final salvo was a paragraph about his mother's unhappiness. He fell asleep at his desk just after midnight.

The following morning, he considered throwing the letter away, but in the end, self-pity won out, and he posted it the same afternoon. Later that week, when time had dissipated the force of his anger, he began to regret the letter, realizing how selfish and callous he had been. One night after dinner, guilt and remorse finally drove him to tell his mother about it. His confession startled her out of her preoccupation with her own problems; his feelings were an uncanny reflection of her own unhappiness.

Riva sat her son down at the kitchen table and listened without interrupting as Benjamin purged his emotions. They talked well into the night, and while she refused to sympathize with him, she did understand his motives and refrained from pointing out the obvious: that Anschel was separated from them through no fault of his own. She suggested that Benjamin send a second letter, apologizing for the first and explaining why he had sent it.

"Your father will understand," she promised. When she sent him off to bed, he came around the table and hugged her tightly, and it suddenly occurred to her that she couldn't remember the last time she had hugged Benjamin or any of her other children. As she sat alone in the silent kitchen, she realized that without Anschel, the children needed her more than ever. Somewhere, she would have to find the strength.

That night, Riva wrote Anschel a long letter, reassuring him that she and the children were fine. Though she felt defeated and heartsick herself, she was careful not to burden him with her own loneliness. Anschel was bound to be deeply wounded by Benjamin's letter and she wanted to soften the blow as much as she could.

If Riva had realized just how much Anschel would be affected, she would not have slept at all that night. As it was, she remained awake until well after two, when sheer exhaustion finally overtook her.

● ● ●

Anschel Isaacson sat motionless, staring out a salt-flecked window towards the coast of Sweden. It was an exceptional day, even for early May. The Baltic was a deep shade of midnight blue and brilliant sunlight sparkled off the random whitecaps, forcing him to squint. But Anschel had no interest in scenic views. Impatiently, he pulled a gold watch from his vest pocket and checked the time; it was near three. He still had a good two hours to wait before the ferry docked in Copenhagen.

Unconsciously, his hand sought the slim packet of letters in his breast pocket; they were a cruel reminder that his children were growing up without him. He had recognized Riva's last letter for what it was, and he admired her courage, but Benjamin's letter had cut his heart. He had read them both a dozen times, and in the end, they served as a catalyst for his decision.

Since the beginning of the war, Anschel had tried unsuccessfully to get his family out of Dorpat. Meanwhile, the German army had advanced steadily eastward, driving through Poland, Lithuania, and Latvia like a juggernaut. By the summer of 1916, Germany had extracted a terrible price from the demoralized Russian army, and now stood no more than a good day's journey from Dorpat. Even more disturbing were the spreading rumors that a revolution in Russia was imminent; how much longer Czar Nicholas II could hold on to his tottering throne was a matter of open speculation. If the Czar was overthrown, resistance could collapse, or worse, the Communists might accede to power. In that event, a German occupation might actually be the lesser of two evils.

Having tried every conceivable alternative without success, Anschel was forced to admit that it was impossible for Riva and the children to escape from the continent until the war ended. If there was a way out, Anschel himself would have to find it from the inside. If not, he belonged with his family anyway. The situation in Estonia could degenerate into chaos at any time.

Once his decision was made, Anschel made his preparations quietly, unwilling to become involved in a long, drawn-out confrontation with his family in Stockholm. He knew they would try to dissuade him. He also knew that nothing they said could induce him to alter his decision; two years of separation was enough.

The morning of his departure, Anschel's brother, Samuel, accompanied him to the station where he would board a train for southern Sweden and a ferry connection to Denmark. Just before boarding, Anschel handed his brother a thick stack of envelopes addressed to Riva and the children, warning Samuel not to say anything about his leaving. Anschel knew how Riva would worry if she believed he was in danger; he preferred her to think he was safe in Stockholm. The letters he gave to Samuel would be posted every few days, so Riva would not feel out of contact. Armed with a determination to see his family and a leather money belt filled with Swiss gold, Anschel embraced his brother, then boarded the train. He never looked back.

The route he had chosen formed a great semicircle, slicing through Denmark, Germany, Poland, Lithuania and Latvia, then across the German lines to Dorpat. It was circuitous, but it represented his best chance of arriving in Dorpat safely; there were too many risks in a more direct approach. It would be difficult, but it could be done. With luck, he would be in Dorpat in three or four weeks.

The journey through Denmark proved to be quick and uneventful, but it took Anschel nearly ten days to make arrangements to cross the German border. Once in Germany, there were endless delays, and at times, Anschel thought in despair that he could make faster progress on a bicycle. Sometimes, he would spend days pacing an anonymous room in a welter of anxiety, waiting for a train. Then, when it came, he would travel forty miles, only to be delayed again. It was frustrating and he found the inactivity maddening, but Germany was a nation at war and traveling civilians always received the lowest priority. It was mid-June by the time he reached Poland.

Traversing Germany had been difficult, but crossing occupied Poland was even worse. The victorious Germans were suspicious of all civilians; time and time again, Anschel was forced to prove his status as a neutral Swede, or failing that, to draw on his supply of Swiss gold. Once, he was forced to knock a German station guard unconscious. After Anschel had paid him a large bribe, the man had become greedy, deciding he should have it all. Anschel had no choice but to overpower him and disappear. Luck was with him; by the time the guard revived, Anschel was thirty miles away.

Anschel received his worst setback in a tiny Lithuanian hamlet, waiting for a train that never came. His gold had served him well as a passport, but it was no immunity against disease. After spending thirty-six hours trapped in a damp, draft-ridden rail station that was little more than a three-sided shed, Anschel began to shiver uncontrollably. His fever quickly rose to 104 degrees and he became virtually helpless. He might well have died in a nameless Lithuanian village if a kindly local farmer hadn't found him wandering beside the road and taken him in. Ironically, the man was a Gentile, not a Jew.

For three days, Anschel tossed in a feverish delirium punctuated by incoherent images and the blur of a woman's face framed by a dark kerchief. When the fever broke early the third evening, Anschel woke feeling weak and drained. Gently, the strange woman wiped his brow and helped him to sip a thin broth. Panic seized him for a moment when he suddenly realized he had no idea where he was, but the woman soothed him and something in her voice made him trust her. He drifted back into a restful sleep.

As he slowly regained his strength, Anschel came to know and respect Emil Kuzsma and his wife. They were simple people, generous and caring despite the tragedies that had befallen them. Their only child, a son, had been killed early in the war, and their farm had been decimated by German soldiers who confiscated their livestock and crops. Their faces were lined with sadness, but they faced the present and the future with an open honesty and a stoic acceptance that touched Anschel deeply. Many would have taken his money belt and left him for dead; instead, the Kuzsmas shared their food with him and nursed him back to health, asking nothing for themselves.

From the Kuzsmas, Anschel learned that no Jews remained in Lithuania. Over the objections of many Lithuanians, the Czar had ordered the Jews driven deep into Russia; after centuries of pogroms and abuse, he was afraid they would rise up and ally with the Germans, forming a fifth column behind Russian lines. Anschel was shocked, but not surprised; it was typical of the insanity generated by the war. What amazed Anschel the most was the way Emil Kuzsma and his fellow Lithuanians viewed the expulsion as an act of God. Somehow, they believed, God had influenced the Czar to remove the Jews from the path of the advancing German army, thus sparing their lives.

Characteristically, after three weeks in bed, and a week of nervous pacing around the tiny living room of the farmhouse, Anschel decided to leave. His host protested, pointing out that Anschel was far from recovered, but Anschel would not be swayed. Aside from his impatience, Anschel had another reason for leaving as quickly as possible: he realized that his presence was an imposition. The farmer and his wife barely had enough food for themselves, and even gold could not buy food where there was none.

Anschel struck out for Dorpat early one September morning, ignoring the dizziness he still felt from time to time and the racking cough that had never left him. Day after day, he pushed on towards Estonia and his family. The constant rain and freezing dampness took its toll, and his health began to deteriorate. Somehow, he forced himself to continue.

Forty miles from Dorpat, just south of the German lines, his luck ran out. For weeks, he struggled in vain to find a way across the lines, but nothing worked; security was too tight. Anschel became weaker with every passing day and more desperate to get through the lines before his health failed completely. He finally found an undertaker willing to risk smuggling him across the lines in exchange for a small fortune in gold; horse-drawn hearses laden with coffins were permitted to cross the lines during lulls in the fighting.

The undertaker was a pudgy man with greedy eyes and the face of a cheat. His insincerity and duplicity were so plainly visible that Anschel had second thoughts about entrusting his life to the man. But Anschel Isaacson had run out of time; there was no other way. He watched uneasily as the undertaker drilled a dozen tiny airholes through the side of a cheap pine coffin. You'll have plenty to breathe, the undertaker sniveled. Like Christ himself, you'll rise from the dead, only quicker. When the holes had been darkened with stain to make them less conspicuous, Anschel stepped into the coffin, gagging himself with a strip of linen so that his coughing spasms would not betray them. As the lid closed, and the undertaker nailed it shut, Anschel wondered if he would ever see his family again.

●　　●　　●

Unaware of Anschel's desperate struggle to reach Dorpat, the Isaacsons' family life followed its usual routine. As always, the summer ended too quickly and school once again became the day's occupation. Benjamin had resigned himself to a bar mitzvah without Anschel, trying hard but unsuccessfully to convince himself that it really didn't matter.

One afternoon late in September, Ben stood in the synagogue, his tousled head bent in prayer as he recited the *shemoneh esreh*, the Eighteen Benedictions. As the time for his bar mitzvah neared, Benjamin had devoted himself wholeheartedly to his spiritual preparation and had made it a point to attend *shachrit* services in the morning, *mincha* in the afternoon, and *maariv* in the evening. At first, he interspersed his ritual prayers with prayers for a miracle, hoping that Anschel would somehow appear in time for his bar mitzvah. But he had come to understand that such prayers represented a childish, selfish desire on his part that was unworthy of a boy about to become a man, and he abandoned them.

As he faced the altar, reciting the *shemoneh esreh*, the front door of the synagogue swung open violently and Greta hurried towards him, her heavy shoes clomping on the polished wooden floor.

"Benjamin!" she said breathlessly, grabbing his shoulder.

"Greta, please," he whispered out of the side of his mouth. Once begun, the Eighteen Benedictions had to be recited to their conclusion.

"Benjamin, listen to me!" Greta's pale face was flushed from the cold and she was gasping for breath. "Benjamin, your father is here!" she blurted out.

Benjamin stood numbly, barely able to comprehend the news. He felt paralyzed. "Where?"

"At the house. You must come quickly. He's . . ."

Benjamin didn't wait for her to finish. Removing his *tallis*, the Eighteen Benedictions forgotten, he bolted out of the synagogue, leaving Greta to follow as best she could. As his legs pounded on the sidewalk, covering the half-dozen blocks to the Dorpat house, his heart sang; he felt as though he were flying. His prayers had been answered! He could hardly believe it. As he neared the house, he caught sight of Beile standing on the street corner and ran to her side. To his surprise, she looked sad and careworn.

"What's wrong?" he gasped, his breath coming in great ragged gulps.

"Your father is not well, Benjamin. You must prepare yourself." Beile laced her arm through his, forcing him to walk.

"What do you mean, 'not well'?" Benjamin gasped, trying to slow his breathing. "Where is he?"

"Upstairs, in your mother's bedroom, but Benjamin . . ."

He broke away from her and ran through the front door, sprinting up the stairs to his mother's room. Riva stood at the foot of the bed with Doctor Timmerman, the family physician. They both turned as he burst into the room. His mother's eyes were red and swollen. They stared at each other in silence, then Riva whispered his name and held out her hand. Slowly, he walked up and took it. As he did, he had a clear view of the bed.

Though the bedroom was hot and stuffy, the man in the bed was covered with heavy blankets. It was his father, but it was not the Anschel Isaacson Ben remembered. The Anschel Isaacson who had bid farewell to them a lifetime ago on the station platform in St. Petersburg was a robust, vigorous man. The stranger in the bed was an empty shell.

A coldness welled up in Ben's heart; he felt weak, his knees rubbery, as though they might give way at any moment. *My God*, he thought. *My father is dead.* The shadow lying on the pillow looked like a death mask. The eyes were closed and sunken deep into the skull, surrounded by dark brown circles of bruised flesh. The skin stretched loosely over the cheekbones, as if the tissue beneath had somehow been removed; it had a sickly white pallor that made a harsh contrast with Anschel's unshaven face.

Thin strands of hair were plastered to his forehead and there were flecks of spittle on the bloodless lips. His breathing was so shallow that the covers barely moved. Ben knelt by the side of the bed. "Father," he whispered. There was no response. Ben felt as though he'd been dealt a physical blow.

"Riva, would you mind?" Timmerman asked. "I'd like to examine Anschel again." Benjamin didn't move.

Riva placed her hands gently on Benjamin's shoulders. "Come downstairs and we'll talk."

When they entered the kitchen, Beile and Greta stood up from the table. Beile let them alone to talk and climbed the stairs to see if Dr. Timmerman needed anything. Greta excused herself to finish some meaningless household chore. Once they were alone, Riva told Benjamin what she knew of Anschel's odyssey through war-torn northern Europe. He listened in stunned silence.

"Dr. Timmerman said that your father has a good chance of recovering," Riva said calmly. Ben had no way of knowing that it required all of his mother's strength to maintain her composure; what Timmerman had actually said was that Anschel was lucky to be breathing at all. "A relapse of pneumonia is very serious, Benjamin. Your father has pushed himself to the limit."

Benjamin was silent for a moment. "You mean he may . . ."

"I won't lie to you, Benjamin. We don't really know. He will need all our help and our prayers, and God willing, he will survive."

"Why did he come? Why did he take the risk?" Benjamin sprang to his feet and started pacing restlessly. It must be an inherited trait, Riva thought dully.

"Why couldn't he have waited until the war ended?" Benjamin demanded. Suddenly, he stopped pacing. With dawning horror, he remembered the letter he had sent, then his prayers. A black wave of guilt cascaded over him, leaving him weak and filled with shame. It was almost more than he could bear. His prayers had been answered, but in a way so horrible to contemplate that it left him trembling.

"My letter," he whispered. "He came because of my letter. And I prayed . . .'' Riva stared at his stricken face, powerless to speak. The connection had not occurred to her.

"That is sheer and utter nonsense.'' Beile Nadelson stood in the kitchen doorway, her presence filling the room. "Your father came because he loves his family and could no longer bear to be separated. It had nothing to do with your letter or your bar mitzvah or your prayers.''

"It was my letter,'' Ben replied miserably. "I know it was.''

"You give yourself too much credit,'' his grandmother snapped. Her words were edged with anger. "To believe that a man of your father's intelligence would be moved by the self-indulgent moanings of an adolescent boy is absurd. What is required now is strength. Your father needs you to be strong for your mother and the other children, not weak and filled with self-pity.''

Benjamin stared at her in shock. His grandmother had never spoken to him so harshly. It jolted him, which was exactly what she had intended.

"Do you understand me, Benjamin?''

Benjamin nodded slowly. He still believed that his letter was in some way responsible for Anschel's condition, but he knew his grandmother was right. Unconsciously, he squared his shoulders.

"Good.'' Beile turned to her daughter. "Riva, there is much we must do.'' Crisply, she assigned duties to her daughter and her grandson; work, like food, was a weapon to be used against despair. By then, Riva had recovered herself, and as they left the kitchen, Beile saw the resolve in Benjamin's face and noted her daughter's composure. She was quite pleased with her performance. There's fire still in these old bones, she thought with satisfaction.

Anschel was still unconscious the following morning, and Ben wanted to remain home from school, but his mother was adamant. "The doctor said your father may be unconscious for two or three days,'' she told him. "There's no point in your staying home right now. Besides, Anschel would not want you to miss school or your bar mitzvah lessons. Please, Benjamin, do as I ask.'' Reluctantly, Ben complied with her wishes.

The next three days passed with agonizing slowness and filled Ben's imagination with guilt and doubts. Each day he watched the clock until the last hour of class was finished, then endured two more endless hours at the *cheder*, Meilach would walk him home, trying his best to keep Ben's spirits up but Ben hardly heard a word he said. Entering the house, Ben would throw his books on the floor and dash straight upstairs where he would sit by his father's side until it was time for him to go to bed. Anschel remained unconscious.

The afternoon of the third day, Anschel opened his eyes briefly, but by the time Ben returned home, he was asleep again. The doctor seemed pleased by the news and assured everyone that the prognosis was good, and the following day Ansclhel regained full consciousness.

As time passed, Anschel grew stronger, and his cheeks lost their deathly pallor. Every day when Ben returned home from school, he helped his father to the greenhouse, where they would sit together in the late afternoon warmth and talk. Being with his family was the best tonic Anschel could have had, and he made steady progress. Ben would always treasure the hours he and his father shared on those warm afternoons. For Anschel, their talks were a vital part of the healing process; for Ben, they resolved all the loneliness and insecurity caused by the separation.

When Ben finally worked up the courage to ask his father about "the letter," Anschel stared at him blankly and disclaimed any knowledge of it. Relief flooded Ben's face, and Anschel was pleased his son would not have to carry an unnecessary burden of guilt. Then, to his surprise, Ben insisted on telling him.

"I want you to know the truth," Ben explained, his voice full of remorse. Miserably, he told his father about Meilach's bar mitzvah and the letter he had written. Benjamin was so involved with his sense of guilt that he did not see the intense pride on his father's face. Anschel covered his mouth, seized by a spasm of coughing. When he looked up, into his son's troubled eyes, he thought to himself: it has been worth the risk. Everything he had gone through had been worth the cost to see his son become a man. Anschel beckoned Benjamin to his side and embraced his son.

•   •   •

Towards the end of October, after dinner one night, Riva asked everyone to move to the living room; Anschel had an announcement he wanted to make. As they formed a semicircle in front of the roaring fireplace, Riva surveyed her family with a thankful heart. Her mother was as feisty as ever, and the children were thriving. Best of all, Anschel was looking more like himself every day, fortified by Beile's carefully prepared menus and Riva's smorgasbord dishes. Riva Isaacson had much to be grateful for.

Anschel made a great production of settling into his chair and organizing himself, letting the suspense build. Suddenly, he broke into a broad grin. "It is time we started planning for a momentous occasion."

Everyone knew he was referring to Ben's bar mitzvah. A surge of excitement ran through Ben as Anschel and Riva described their plans for the event; everyone was assigned an important job except for Freida, who at six was too young to be given any serious responsibility. Ben sat at the edge of the couch, opposite his father, his face flushed with pride. Anschel regarded his son with affection. "You really didn't think that I'd miss your bar mitzvah, did you, son?"

● ● ●

No effort was spared in anticipation of the occasion; no detail was too small to be overlooked. The furniture was polished to a mirror gloss and the entire house was scented with the fragrance of bee's wax and lemon oil. Every rug was hung on the clothes line and beaten until the nap stood out and the fringes were white and fresh, and the entire house was scrubbed from the basement to the attic. Riva Isaacson would not be satisfied until everything was perfect.

For the entire week preceding the bar mitzvah, friends and relatives streamed in and out of the house, helping to prepare the enormous quantities of food the guests would consume. To everyone's amusement but Beile's, Meilach was a constant presence in the kitchen, testing and sampling the pastries. Her nerves remained steady, but there were times she thought they would never be ready when the day arrived.

Every afternoon Ben closed the door to his room and studied the *haftorah*, a section of scripture he was expected to recite at his bar mitzvah. He began by committing the words to memory, then practiced the melody to which they would be sung. He spent hours singing at the top of his lungs, compensating for his lack of pitch with a large measure of enthusiasm. Herb and Ida were fully occupied, helping Riva put the house in order and finalize plans for the party. No one seemed to have time for anything but the preparations.

Typically, it was Anschel who noticed there was a problem—Freida. She had Riva's dark curly hair, and a perpetual sunny smile that her father had noticed was missing of late. Since she was only six, no one expected her to help, and her efforts to contribute always met with an exasperated "Later, Freida, I'm busy right now." After witnessing one such incident between Freida and Greta, Anschel disappeared unexpectedly. When he returned an hour later, he called for her.

"Could you spare a moment?" he asked. Eagerly, she followed him through the greenhouse. A horse-drawn cart stood outside the greenhouse door, laden with magnificent potted plants and flowers. "I need someone to be responsible for these plants and flowers," Anschel explained. "Such things are essential to a successful bar mitzvah, and I was wondering if you would accept the responsibility."

Freida accepted the commission solemnly, her dark curls bouncing as she ran through the greenhouse and out to the cart. To the driver's amusement, she immediately began giving instructions, fearful that the plants might be damaged as they were carried from the cart to the greenhouse beds.

"She's her mother's daughter," the driver laughed. He knew the Isaacson family well.

Day after day, Freida occupied herself in the greenhouse, pruning, transplanting, and watering. She made elaborate lists in labored print, planning where flowers and plants would be placed and what arrangement might be the most attractive. It exhausted Beile just to watch her. Once Freida had a part in the festivities, her sunny smile returned.

Three days before the bar mitzvah Ben was practicing up in his room when he heard a tremendous commotion outside the house. At first, he thought that the Germans had finally broken at the Allied lines and were swarming through the streets of Dorpat. Then from inside the house, he heard people running, slamming doors and shutters, and shouting instructions. He dashed to the window.

Thirty or forty people were gathered in front of the Isaacson house. Some carried signs that read "Stop the Jewish Blasphemy." All were shouting and yelling. Quickly, Ben removed his *tallis* and tucked his shirt into his pants, then ran downstairs.

Riva blocked the foot of the stairs, screaming at Herb to stay away from the windows. Ben eased around his mother and caught sight of his father, who stood motionless in the dining room, watching the crowd. He hurried to Anschel's side. Everyone else had sought refuge in the kitchen, which was windowless and easily defended. Ben heard Greta trying to maintain some kind of order.

"What's happening?" Ben asked his father breathlessly. Riva forged past him with Herb in tow and disappeared into the kitchen.

"Perhaps our neighbors prefer that you sing on key," Anschel replied dryly. Ben was confused.

"You mean they're out there because of me?"

Before Anschel could answer, Elsa, the Isaacson's Christian maid, bolted across the dining room like a frightened deer. She wrenched the

French doors open and escaped through the greenhouse. Greta appeared at the kitchen door.

"I tried to stop her but she was terrified what might happen if—"

"Thank you, Greta," Anschel cut her off. The less said, the better. "Please go back to the kitchen." Then he instructed Ben to close and bolt the doors. Though they were mostly glass, locking them could do no harm.

Several people outside the house saw Elsa running for the safety of the neighbor's yard and sounded an alarm. Like a predatory animal, the crowd smelled her panic and it exhilarated them. Elsa's terrified exit gave them the scent of blood. As a single mass, the mob surged towards the greenhouse door.

Ben watched the crowd move around the house, darkening successive windows like segments of film, slowed to appear as single frames. Then his gaze shifted to the French doors of the dining room and the greenhouse beyond. The first person he saw was an obese German woman carrying an enormous sign attached to a wooden pole. He recognized her as one of his neighbors.

She swung the pole in a wide arc as she approached the glass greenhouse door, then seemed to freeze as the heavy sign hesitated at the apex of its arc. For a brief moment, she was obscenely framed by the glass and woodwork; then the placard descended like a guillotine, shattering the glass door into a thousand shards of crystal rain.

A dozen people followed her into the greenhouse; there was no room for the rest. Ben's throat constricted as he watched the havoc. The intruders forgot the house temporarily and indulged their passion for destruction on the greenhouse. They overturned benches and tore the plants and flowers from their clay pots, smashing the empty vases against the house or stone floor. Even the wicker furniture was ripped apart.

Ben noticed the obese woman scratch her forearm on a miniature rose bush. Enraged, she lifted the plant and threw it through the glass side wall. He would always remember the expression of immense satisfaction on her face. After demolishing the greenhouse, the mob would have broken into the Isaacson home, but Freida disrupted their plans. In all the excitement, no one noticed her sneak to the side door, where she could see into the greenhouse. When she saw her lovely flowers being destroyed, she started to scream hysterically.

The sight of a distraught six-year-old girl caught the crowd off guard. While an adult would have been assaulted, Freida's hysteria threw the mob into confusion.

Anschel beckoned Riva to care for Freida, then took advantage of the lull to step outside. He found himself face to face with the obese German woman, whose name was Karla Spitz. She glared at him belligerently. Anschel held up his hands and spoke loud enough for everyone to hear.

"Mrs. Spitz, if you have a problem or complaint you wish to discuss, you and several of your friends are welcome to come inside and discuss the matter in a civilized manner." Anschel's voice was calm and steady, and he made no reference to the destruction that had taken place. The crowd was astonished at his audacity; an invitation was the last thing they expected.

Anschel's offer placed the onus of a reply directly on Karla Spitz's ample shoulders. She hesitated, looking to her fellow rioters for support, but no one said anything.

"Why don't you come in?" Anschel smiled disarmingly. "You might cut yourself on the broken glass." She could hardly do anything but accept. Once she and the other ring leaders were inside the house, the situation was defused and the crowd began to disperse. Anschel's gamble had paid off; nothing deflates a riot quicker than boredom.

Fragments of window panes, clay pottery, and discarded placards covered the floor of the greenhouse and littered the lawn outside. Ben heard the crunch of broken glass as the people mounted the stone steps to the dining room doors.

Benjamin's father motioned his unwelcome guests to chairs in the living room. Anschel remained standing; it gave him a slight psychological advantage. Despite his thin frame and sunken cheeks, he was still a figure of some authority.

"You have broken into my house for a reason?" he asked Mrs. Spitz. His tone was almost cordial, as though they sat in a cafe discussing the weather.

Karla Spitz felt like an actress who had forgotten her lines in front of a full house. She had come to do battle, not chat in the Isaacsons' living room. Anschel's politeness unnerved her. She sensed she had been outmaneuvered and struggled for a way to regain the upper hand, but she could think of nothing. Anschel stood motionless, waiting for her reply.

As the silence grew uncomfortably long, her nervousness increased. Her companions stared at the floor like errant school children in a principal's office. She smoothed the wrinkles from her dress and tried to organize her thoughts.

"We can no longer close our ears to the devil's music!" she blurted out when the silence became at last unbearable. "As good Christians, we can no longer afford to be polluted by blasphemy.'' Her chin quivered uncertainly and there was a defensive note in her voice.

''Blasphemy?'' Anschel sounded shocked. ''What blasphemy?''

''Do not be coy with us, Herr Isaacson,'' Karla Spitz replied primly. She had regained some of her lost momentum. ''Only a deaf man could fail to hear your son wailing his heathen chants every afternoon.''

''As a learned woman, Mrs. Spitz, I'm certain you already know that both Christian liturgy and Hebrew liturgy are firmly rooted in the books of the Old Testament. You must forgive me if I find it hard to accept that my son's singing of a passage from the Old Testament can be construed as blasphemy of any kind. To call it such would be to describe your own religious practices as 'blasphemous.' Surely you do not wish to do that.'' The sarcasm of Anschel's response was veiled by a pleasant tone.

Karla Spitz was undeterred. ''Like most Jews, Herr Isaacson, you are clever with words, but that changes nothing.''

While she repeated the entire litany of her complaints, her greatest concern remained Ben's ''heathen chants.'' She insisted the transgression stop immediately, and it was obvious that her companions agreed. ''We were afraid this type of thing might happen when we saw a Jewish family move into this neighborhood,'' she concluded. Though Anschel Isaacson's greenhouse had been destroyed, it was once again Karla Spitz and her friends who were the aggrieved parties.

Anschel pursed his lips for a moment, then looked down at the floor, apparently lost in thought. ''Mrs. Spitz, I can see that we are not about to agree on the subject of liturgy and I will concede that my son's loud singing might be annoying to you and these other good people. But that is cause for complaint, not a reason to wreck my home.'' One of the men sitting on the sofa remarked snidely that a rich Jew shouldn't have any trouble building a hundred new greenhouses.

Anschel turned calmly to the man, and although his tone was level, his eyes flashed with unmistakable anger. He pointed to Freida, who still sobbed in Riva's arms. ''Tell me, Mein Herr, how much will it cost to repair my child's shattered feelings?''

There was no response. Anschel had gained a measure of control; it was time to use it.

''I think we've discussed this matter enough.'' Anschel stood ramrod straight and there was cold steel in his voice. He gestured towards the door. As everyone filed out, Karla Spitz decided to have the last word. It was an urge that had always been her undoing.

''I'm not really concerned about a few tears or some crushed flowers. I am concerned with the blasphemy your son screams at the top of his lungs every day. It is my soul involved, not yours. We are good Christians of sound German stock, and we live in a good Christian town. Though we are not ruled by the Kaiser, we are proud of our German accents and do not wish to be defiled by Jews.''

"I find a German accent most becoming," Anschel smiled in response. "It's the intolerable German arrogance that always accompanies it I cannot abide.''

Two of the men with Mrs. Spitz snickered while she gasped in outrage. Not everyone in the greenhouse appreciated her Teutonic superiority. Gently, Anschel took her arm and guided her out the door.

Ben watched her disappear down the front walk. "What should we do now, Father?''

Anschel smiled. "Just sing a little softer, my son. God will still hear you.''

Anschel found it ironically appropriate that the section of scripture Benjamin had been singing dealt with God's admonition to Abraham to take his people out of a foreign land and lead them to the soil God had chosen for them—the land of Palestine. It was coincidence that passage happened to be the *haftorah* for the week Benjamin was born, but Anschel always regarded it as an auspicious omen. Perhaps his son was destined to fulfill his own dreams.

Three days later, Anschel placed the silk *tallis* across his son's shoulders, and Benjamin received his father's blessing to join the men of the Dorpat congregation as an equal.

•   •   •

March of 1917 witnessed the abdication of Nicholas II as Czar of all the Russias, and by December, Anschel Isaacson's worst fears were realized: Lenin negotiated a separate peace with the Central Powers and removed his bleeding country from the war. To the despair of the Allies, the Kaiser took full advantage of Russia's exit to move his troops from the east to strengthen the western front. But the reprieve proved only temporary.

By the summer of 1918, the Czar and his family were dead, executed by a firing squad of revolutionaries; it seemed to mark the beginning of the end. Within weeks, Germany's allies collapsed in rapid succession. Bulgaria and Turkey capitulated to the Allies first, and the disintegrating Austro-Hungarian empire surrendered in October. The end of the war was in sight.

Though morale was low and her resources were all but depleted, Germany refused to surrender. Its trooops still occupied an enormous area, from France in the west to the Crimea in the east, and she was loathe to admit defeat. Only when revolution broke out within Germany itself did the exhausted nation finally capitulate. Pending a treaty draft, an armistice was signed on November 11th, 1918, in an old French railroad car at Rethondes. The war was over at last. People danced in the streets and embraced perfect strangers. Everyone was filled with the joy of just being alive.

In Dorpat, the Isaacsons celebrated quietly with a special dinner, but there was an empty place at the table. Anschel had never fully recovered his strength and, early in September, he suffered another relapse. He had been bedridden nearly three months when the war ended in November, and the house smelled of disinfectant and overheated rooms.

On those days when Anschel felt strong enough to converse, he and Benjamin had long discussions about politics and Zionism and the future. Anschel could never resist an opportunity to speak about Palestine, and he and Ben had plenty to talk about. During the dark days of 1917, before America's might had turned the tide against Germany, England had been desperate for support. As a result, Great Britain's Foreign Secretary, Lord Balfour, had written to Baron Rothschild, head of the English branch of Europe's premier banking family, promising British support for a Jewish homeland in Palestine. It had been intended as a political gesture to rally Jewish backing for the war, particularly in America. Though the letter, which came to be known as the Balfour Declaration had failed to grant all the concessions the Zionist leadership had hoped for, it was a tremendous step forward. The British government had committed itself in public to the concept of a Jewish homeland in Palestine. For their part, the British had everything to gain. Jewish support for the war was a powerful factor, and after the war, a pro-British political entity would be a stabilizing influence for British interests in the Middle East.

"It's a fragile beginning," Anschel told Benjamin as they sat together in Anschel's bedroom. "But it's the first official step towards making our dream of a Jewish homeland in Palestine a political reality."

Despite the future possibilities created by the Balfour Declaration, Anschel was increasingly concerned by political developments in Europe during the days that followed the armistice. Russia was torn by civil war, the Austro-Hungarian Empire had splintered into a host of unstable nations, and Germany was in chaos. A new historical era had begun.

Whenever Anschel raised the subject of the armistice, Ben's attitude was always the same. "The Germans started the war, and they lost it.

They deserve whatever they get." With a few exceptions, it was an attitude that most people shared.

When the drafts of the Treaty of Versailles were made public, Anschel felt saddened and suddenly very old and tired. The terms imposed upon Germany by the victorious Allies were harsh to the extreme. Germany was to be stripped of its pride, its material possessions, and its status as a sovereign nation. A crushing schedule of reparation payments guaranteed that the shattered German nation would never be restored to its former glory.

Despite his misjudgment of the events in Sarajevo four years earlier, Anschel Isaacson was a shrewd judge of European politics. He saw the Treaty of Versailles as a catastrophe, not a "Final Peace," as it was hailed. "Social and economic stability lead to peace," he lectured his son, "not punitive measures. This treaty will lead to disaster. If history has taught us anything, it is that the ungenerous conqueror will aways face his enemies again."

For Anschel, watching his son grow to manhood from a sickbed was a depressing and disheartening experience. He had always been a strong, vigorous man, and he found it humiliating to be taken care of like a helpless infant. There was so much to impart, so much he wanted Benjamin to know, and for the first time in his life, Anschel did not really feel up to the task. He seemed to be so exhausted, all the time.

Benjamin enjoyed talking about Palestine, but he had noticed a certain change in his father since the relapse. Anschel seemed almost driven, and had begun to lecture more than discuss. Gone was the generous sense of humor that once characterized their talks. In its place was a seriousness of purpose Benjamin did not wholly understand, especially when Anschel seemed to be sympathizing with the defeated Germans. He also noticed a change in his parents' relationship.

A tug of war had developed between Anschel and Riva over their son. Hemmed in by the narrow confines of his sickroom on the second floor, Anschel found a kind of vicarious freedom in planning for Benjamin's future. To him, that meant a break with the past, and a new life in Palestine. Terrified she might lose her husband to pneumonia and her son to an empty dream, Riva lost no opportunity to insist that Ben remain in Dorpat; he belonged with his family. Ben dealt with the conflict good-naturedly, to the occasional irritation of both parents.

One day, Anschel sent for him. "Benjamin, I am not a well man," he began.

"Papa, you'll live forever. In a few . . . ."

Anschel raised a hand to silence his son's protest. "It is the truth. Without becoming maudlin, let me say that I've tried my best to give you the benefit of my mistakes. Listen to me now.

"Europe is a hostile place for Jews to live. Through the centuries we have survived by God's grace and our own good wits. We have always been outsiders in our own countries, occasionally acceding to power, but always thrust away in the end. Our people have been scapegoats and the object of hatred and derision for thousands of years. Whenever there is political instability, it is the Jews who suffer the most."

Anschel began to cough, wiping the yellow phlegm from his lips with a linen handkerchief. He was pale, and beads of perspiration glistened on his forehead.

"Papa, we can talk later."

"No, my son, the future is too important to be postponed," Anschel wheezed. He asked Benjamin to rearrange his pillows. When he spoke again, his eyes remained closed.

"Pick your fights carefully, Benjamin, and never waste yourself on fruitless vengeance. Don't hide in the past. Your future and the future of your unborn children lie in Palestine, not here. With inflation and . . ."

Benjamin's mother called upstairs. "Benjamin! It's time for you to come down for dinner and let your father rest."

"Tell her it's all right," Anschel whispered, exhausted by his efforts.

"I better go, Papa. I'll come back after dinner." Tenderly, Ben pulled the covers over his father's chest.

After his son had left, Anschel's thoughts floated on the surface of his consciousness. He knew he had been rambling, but it was hard to keep things in order when you were so tired all the time. There was something important he had to tell Benjamin, but he couldn't quite remember what it was. So many things to say. If only he had more strength.

By the time Ben returned after dinner, his father was fast asleep. He seemed to be breathing easier, so Ben quietly left.

Six weeks later, Anschel Isaacson was dead.

Everything had seemed to be going so well—Anschel's condition took a turn for the better towards the end of November, and by the first week of December, he was much improved. The Isaacson house returned to normal, and Herb and the two girls were allowed to play as loudly as they pleased. Beile breathed a sigh of relief as she saw a smile return to Riva's face.

It had become apparent to Dr. Timmerman that Anschel Isaacson's health was assuming a cyclical pattern. The second relapse had drained his meager resources, and his subsequent improvement did not guarantee his recovery would be permanent.

As Anschel grew stronger, Dr. Timmerman pronounced the prescription that Anschel had been longing to hear for most of his adult life; he recommended that the family relocate to a warm, dry climate.

"The winters here are too cold and damp," he explained to Riva. "If you remain in Estonia, or return to Sweden, you must forgo any hope of a complete recovery and be willing to risk another relapse."

Anschel's illness had accomplished what all his years of rational argument had not. While he greeted the news with unabashed joy, Riva was stoic. Though she would never willingly emigrate to Palestine, Anschel's health was her first concern. She tried to speak of Italy or southern Spain, but her husband was adamant, and she no longer had the heart to fight with him. Reluctantly, she agreed the family would leave for Palestine as soon as possible.

Resigned to the move, Riva applied herself to the preparations with an intensity that left Greta breathless. though she was still in her thirties, Greta did not relish change of any kind. "I've had enough excitement during the past few years to last a lifetime," she replied when Riva asked her to accompany the family to Palestine. "Dorpat is just fine for me." She managed to hold out for two days, until the children cajoled her into going. "Why not?" she finally relented. "After all, I am Jewish, and what better place is there for a Jew but the Land of Abraham?" Greta had finally decided which part of her heritage would claim her.

Anxious to remove Anschel from any further danger, Riva planned to leave just after New Year's Day. She and Beile talked incessantly about what to take, what to leave, what could be purchased once they arrived. Together, they oversaw the packing of suitcases, trunks, and crates that contained the accumulated possessions of a lifetime. Though she had been told that many of her fine linens and clothes would be inappropriate for Palestine, Riva still insisted on taking them. She was going to carry as much of "home" as she could.

Always, the two women avoided speculating on what would happen when the final day arrived. Beile was too old and too set in her ways to leave Dorpat; she would remain behind, once more alone in the big house, counting the memories of the past. Both women knew that they would probably never see each other again.

For Benjamin, those days in December were the most exciting of his life. He and Meilach let their imaginations run free during endless conversations about the impending move and what life in Palestine might be like.

Meilach vowed he would join Benjamin as quickly as possible; together they would share the adventure of a lifetime.

"You can live with us at first," Benjamin promised breathlessly. "Then we can decide what we're going to do."

"I'll want my own camel," Meilach warned him.

"You get what you deserve. A jackass." Ben ducked to avoid a punch. It was an almost magical time for the two boys.

Two days before the scheduled departure, Riva gathered the children early in the morning and set off on a final round of farewell visits. When they returned shortly before dinner, Dr. Timmerman's horse-drawn sleigh was parked in the circular driveway. Riva rushed into the house and found her cousins Frankel and Ira sitting at the foot of the stairs. There were tears in Frankel's eyes.

"Frankel, what happened? Is it Anschel?"

Numbly, Frankel nodded. "Riva, I thought he was better . . . I had no idea . . ."

Without waiting for an explanation, Riva pushed past Frankel, and ran up the stairs, clutching the long folds of her dress. Benjamin raced after her.

Dr. Timmerman met them at the bedroom door. "I'm afraid it isn't good, Riva."

Anschel lay on the bed, racked by a fit of coughing. He was conscious, but shivering beneath the blankets. Beile sat by the bed, wiping the sweat from his face.

"What could have . . ." Riva stopped in mid-sentence when she saw the galvanized bathtub in the corner of the room. There were puddles of water on the floor and a bar of soap floated on the surface of the water. Her hands clenched together, turning the knuckles white and bloodless.

Timmerman removed his glasses and rubbed his face. "We can talk downstairs," he sighed.

Riva walked around him, and Beile stood as her daughter approached the bed. "Dr. Timmerman, my place is beside my husband. We'll talk here." Dipping a wash cloth in a chipped enamel basin, she sat down and began to wipe Anschel's brow. "Who brought that tub in here?" she asked quietly.

"It was an accident, Riva. No one meant any harm," Beile explained. Riva did not interrupt as her mother told her the story.

Apparently, Frankel and Ira had come to bid Anschel farewell. Beile had an errand to run, and asked them to stay with Anschel until she returned. Once his mother-in-law had departed, Anschel decided to take advantage of her absence and indulge himself with a bath.

"You must help me, Frankel," Anschel had grinned. He was still too weak to walk more than a few feet. "I haven't had a decent bath in three months and I'm not going to Palestine smelling like a sickbed."

Even though Anschel insisted he was well enough to bathe, Frankel and Ira were still dubious. "Aunt Beile never said anything about a bath," Frankel said suspiciously. "I don't want her angry with me."

"Beile is my mother-in-law, not my keeper," Anschel snapped. When he threatened to go downstairs alone and pour his own bath, Frankel finally capitulated. He and Ira carried the galvanized bathtub to Anschel's room and lugged buckets of hot water up from the kitchen.

Aided by Frankel, Anschel slipped into the tub with a sigh of contentment. The two cousins kept the water hot, but Anschel suddenly began to shiver. Panic-stricken, they wrapped him in a blanket and put him back to bed. When Beile returned a couple of hours later, Anschel's temperature was one hundred and four.

"These things just happen, Riva." Timmerman said when Beile finished speaking. His face was creased by sadness.

"How bad is he?"

Timmerman hesitated for a moment. "If we can't get the fever under control during the next few hours . . . Riva, I'm sorry. To be honest, there isn't a great deal I can do."

Riva nodded woodenly. "I understand."

The doctor picked up his hat and coat off the chaise next to the bed. "Send for me immediately if there's any change, or if you need me for anything." Timmerman looked stricken. He had known Riva since she was a little girl, and now, when she needed him most, he was powerless to help her. Beile saw him to the door.

Benjamin and his mother kept a vigil by Anschel's bedside through the night. By dawn he was worse. His breathing was labored and shallow, and Benjamin saw the life ebbing from his eyes. For the next twenty-four hours, he drifted in and out of consciousness. Anschel Isaacson died early the following morning.

While some volunteers from the *chevra kaddisha*, the burial society, made all the necessary arrangement for Anschel's burial, Benjamin sat downstairs in the living room. Clutched in his right hand was a small pin, a gold Star of David that Anschel had given him. Benjamin had seen the pin often in the past; it had been in Anschel's family for three generations, and he had always worn it on special occasions.

During one of his brief periods of consciousness, Anschel had asked Benjamin to hand him a box sitting on the dresser. When Benjamin brought it to him, Anschel took the pin out and gazed at it for a minute.

Though he was weak, and barely able to whisper without coughing uncontrollably, he pressed it on Benjamin, and extracted a promise from his son—the next time the pin was passed on to another, it would be on the soil of Palestine.

"Never forget, Benjamin, *lekh lekha*. The future of our people lies in the land that God gave to Abraham," he had rasped weakly. *Lekh Lekha* were the words God spoke to Abraham. In Hebrew, they literally mean "go forth," and in the context of scripture, they meant "go unto the land I have chosen for you."

Those were the last coherent words Anschel Isaacson uttered. They would be burned in his son's heart forever.

FOUR

Shiva
Dorpat, 1918

The day of Anschel's funeral, Ben avoided the family carriage, and chose to walk instead. Ida walked in silence beside him. She didn't relish the prospect of a three-mile trek back to the house, but she knew Ben would be glad to have her company. Collars upturned against the freezing wind, they followed the carriage ruts out of the cemetery, then turned towards the heart of the city.

Ben was dreading *shiva*, the traditional seven days of mourning. For an entire week, the Dorpat house would be filled with people he barely knew and their muted laments about "fate" and "God's will." It would be like that for the entire week; a mind-numbing ritual. Throughout *shiva*, the Isaacsons would sit on low stools as a reminder that death brings all men low, and greet the mourners who would come to offer their melancholy condolences. At the moment, Ben didn't much feel like talking to anyone. His mind was still trying to grapple with the harsh reality that his father was gone.

When Ben and Ida reached the house, their fingers were stiff and their cheeks were dead white from the cold. Most of the funeral party had already arrived, and as Ben and Ida walked in, a sympathetic crowd enveloped them. Friends, relatives, and many people they had never seen before jammed the rooms and hallways. The press of bodies was claustrophobic and Ben had to stifle an urge to blindly run from the house. Ida read the expression on her brother's face and tactfully drew the guests away, giving him room to breathe.

He wandered into the dining room and sat by himself off to one side, letting the crowd swirl around him until it was time for *minchah*, the afternoon prayer. Three times each day during *shiva*, it would fall upon Ben to lead the special services; *shachrit* in the morning, *minchah* in the afternoon, and *maariv* in the evening.

When the clock struck four, Ben rose and led the congregants in prayer, reading from a worn leather prayer book that had belonged to his grandfather. When the service ended, he resisted the impulse to return to his quiet oasis in the dining room and instead took his place on one of the low stools set aside for the immediate family. He sat for a time, absorbed in his own thoughts until Shlomale Gorsky, Meilach's nine-year-old brother, tugged at his sleeve.

"Benjamin," the boy whispered. "There's a *goy* here."

Ben raised an eyebrow. "Where?"

Solemnly, Shlomale pointed to a nervous young man who looked to be nineteen or twenty. He was obviously uncomfortable and out of place. "When you were leading the *minchah* services," Shlomale said, "he held his book like the others, but he didn't read it. He just kept staring at the book; his eyes never moved."

Ben smiled. "That's Arnold Pilpin. He's a medical student at the university and he's as Jewish as you and I. He just can't read Hebrew." Shlomale scrutinized Ben's face suspiciously.

"Why can't he read Hebrew?"

"He never went to *cheder*."

"Why not?"

"You'll have to ask his parents." Ben pointed to the elder Pilpins, who were sitting across the room.

In a voice loud enough for everyone to hear, that is exactly what Shlomale did. Pilpin blushed with embarrassment and his parents were speechless. Why hadn't Arnold Pilpin gone to *cheder* like everyone else, Shlomale demanded. Madame Pilpin tried to ignore him, but to her dismay Shlomale insisted on an answer. The situation became increasingly awkward and Ben was just about to rescue the Pilpins when to his surprise, Arnold Pilpin turned to his mother with the same question. He had wanted to attend *cheder*, but instead his mother had arranged for him to be tutored in French, German, and Latin; if her son was to be a doctor, he had no need to waste his time learning a useless language and meaningless history. While she squirmed uncomfortably under Arnold's gaze, her husband simply stared at the floor in silence, offering no support. He agreed with his son. Arnold finally sat down when his mother promised to discuss the matter at home, but Shlomale kept after her until Meilach was forced to drag his little brother into the kitchen.

Ben rubbed his eyes wearily and stretched his legs; the height of the stool made his muscles cramp and his back ache. He looked over at his mother who sat ramrod straight, her face sad but composed. If the stool caused her any discomfort, she gave no sign of it. Ben shifted his gaze to the window and the snow-covered street beyond.

His thoughts wandered, finally settling on the last words his father had spoken—*lekh lekha*, and it occurred to him that the last time he had read Chapter Twelve of Genesis was at his bar mitzvah nearly two years before. Maybe it's time to read it again, he thought. Somehow, he felt it might bring him closer to Anschel's memory. Ben walked across the living room to the walnut bookshelves lining the walls on either side of the fireplace and pulled the *chumash*, the Five Books of Moses, from its place. He carried the book to the dining room and settled himself in a corner to read, letting the soaring prose fill his mind and blot out everything else. Hardly five minutes had passed before someone intruded on his solitude.

"I'm sorry about your father."

Benjamin looked up to see a young girl with long brown hair standing in front of him. There was an open, honest intelligence in her deep blue eyes and unlike many of the guests, there was no trace of practiced sympathy in her expression. She was undeniably attractive, with a creamy complexion and full red lips. Her features were delicate but strong, and a slight upturn to the eyes and mouth hinted at a dry sense of humor. She wore a plain dark dress that did nothing to detract from her striking figure. At any other time, Ben would have been delighted to meet her, but not on this day. He thanked her for her sentiment, then abruptly returned to his book. To his surprise, the girl ignored his tacit dismissal and introduced herself as Bluma Feldman.

"It's not good to sit by yourself during *shiva*," she gently chided him. "If you share yourself with others, it helps with the pain."

"How would you know?" Ben grumbled. He was in no mood to hear lectures from a teenage girl he'd never met.

"My father died last year," she replied evenly. There was no reproach in her voice and her gaze never wavered. Ben blushed in embarrassment.

"I'm sorry," he sighed. "Please sit down and accept my apologies." She sat next to him on a chair and pointed to the gold Star of David pinned to his lapel.

"Was that your father's?"

"Yes. He gave it to me the week before he died."

"Then it must mean a great deal to you."

She had a frank and open manner that Ben found enormously appealing; her directness was a refreshing change from the platitudes he'd been hearing all day. As they talked, Ben realized that Bluma Feldman was one of those rare people who wasted no words on idle amenities; conversation for its own sake did not interest her. When she spoke, it was because she had something to say. When she listened, she listened intently; she was not one to miss much. She was from Riga, in Latvia, and had come to Dorpat for her schooling. She lived with an uncle not far from Ben's house. As it turned out, they were distantly related by marriage; she had come to Anschel's *shiva* with her aunt, a second cousin of Anschel's.

She was deeply moved when he told her of his promise to Anschel, and it didn't surprise Ben to find out that she too believed in a Jewish homeland in Palestine. What impressed him most was her astonishing grasp of the issues involved and the strength of her commitment; his own feelings had not yet crystallized to the same extent. As sunset approached, they reluctantly ended their conversation.

"It's almost time for *maariv*," Ben said.

"I know. Afterwards, I must be going." After the final prayer, everyone would be leaving.

"I hope we see each other again."

She smiled and nodded in response. Then she disappeared into the living room.

For the first time that day, Benjamin felt alive. Talking with Bluma had somehow made his burden lighter, and the way they had shared each other's thoughts left Ben feeling he had known her all his life. She was someone he wanted to see again.

The next six days of *shiva* passed much like the first. Bluma came every afternoon to help Beile and Greta with the guests and the food; Riva hardly moved from her low stool in the living room. Ben found himself looking forward to Bluma's arrival every morning; she was the one bright spot in his life. Ben introduced Bluma to Meilach the second day and it seemed only natural that they became instant friends. Though Riva was too preoccupied to notice the growing friendship between her son and Bluma Feldman, it did not escape Beile. Despite the crowds of people that came and went during the day, Beile knew how lonely *shiva* could be and she was pleased that her grandson had found someone to help him pass the empty hours.

When the seven days of mourning were over, the Isaacson family began the hard adjustment to a life without Anschel. The first few days were the worst, exacerbated by the sad process of unpacking. Beile and Greta put the new clothes back on the shelves; they wouldn't be needed in a climate like Dorpat's. There was a brief flare of tempers when Riva tried to unpack Ben's trunk and he insisted on leaving it untouched. I'll be needing it one of these days, he had explained defensively. Too tired to argue, Riva helped him push it to the back of his closet.

The next day, Ben and the other children returned to school. It was time to resume their lives again.

Riva's decision to remain in Dorpat came as a surprise to no one. With Anschel gone, there was no longer any reason to emigrate, and Sweden had always been a foreign country to her. In Estonia, she was surrounded by family and friends and the memories of a lifetime. There she would stay.

Money was not a problem. Anschel had left them well-provided for and his brother, Samuel, managed Riva's share of the family business in trust for Ben and Herb. That gave Riva the freedom to live where and how she pleased. Benjamin was intensely disappointed by Riva's decision to stay in Dorpat, but he took his mother's feelings into consideration and avoided the subject of emigration. He had no desire to add to her burdens.

Anschel's death left a gaping hole in the Isaacson's family life and everyone coped with the loss in a different way. Riva occupied herself with the details of running the house and became active in the local synagogue. Herb and Ida were quiet and withdrawn for the first few weeks and Freida had nightmares she could never remember. Beile kept them as busy as she could, knowing the pain would subside to a dull ache with the passage of time.

Benjamin resolved to make the best of his life in Dorpat; at least he had his dreams of Palestine. Dorpat would have to do until he was old enough to start his own life. But despite his best intentions, trouble began the week after Anschel's *shiva*. With all the activity surrounding *shiva*, Ben never had the right opportunity to tell Riva about his promise to his father. It was best to wait until the confusion subsided, he had thought.

The evening he chose came at the end of a quiet day. His mother had collapsed in a comfortable arm chair and closed her eyes. Anschel's death had aged her; she seemed tired and drawn. The other children had already gone to bed and only the comforting click of Beile's knitting needles broke the quiet. Unconsciously reaching for the pin on his lapel, Ben proudly told his mother about the promise he had made to Anschel. He was so absorbed by the importance of the trust Anschel had placed with him that he failed to notice the astonishing transformation in his mother. She sat bolt upright, every muscle tense, and her eyes narrowed coldly. She listened without commenting until her son finished. He smiled happily, completely unprepared for what his mother was about to say.

"Anschel was not himself at the end." Riva's voice was taut. "Such a promise is meaningless."

"But—"

"There are no 'buts' about it, Benjamin," she snapped coldly. "You are not obligated or bound by a promise made to your father when he was delirious."

Benjamin felt the blood rush to his face. "He wasn't delirious when I . . ."

"I don't want to hear any more, Benjamin, and I want you to forget this lunacy." Riva was quivering with anger. Ben looked down at the floor, his jaw muscles rigid.

Beile sucked in her lower lip and sighed. "Riva, try to understand. Benjamin . . ."

"I understand perfectly," Riva lashed back. "And I'll raise my children the way I see fit." She stood and left the room, setting a pattern that would be repeated again and again in the future.

With Anschel gone, Riva was determined to have Benjamin forget about Palestine. She had lost her husband; she would not tolerate the loss of her eldest son. The future she planned for Benjamin did not include Palestine and she used every means at her disposal to discourage him, never missing an opportunity to voice her criticism. Beile's efforts to soften her daughter's attitude met with stubborn resistance; Riva remained convinced that the only way to confront the issue was head-on.

Oddly enough, had she said nothing, there was an excellent chance that Ben might have spent the rest of his life in Dorpat. Benjamin wanted desperately to please his mother, and if she had been more understanding and less adamant, the significance of a young boy's bedside promise to his father might have faded with time. The cost of keeping that promise and splitting his family apart might well have proven stronger than his need to honor Anschel's request.

Benjamin had been thrilled by his father's vision of the future; it appealed to his sense of adventure. Few teenage boys can resist the lure of travel and excitement combined with an idealistic cause; Ben was no different. But the dream was a safe one, the kind any adolescent would cherish. It was a fantasy without risk. Reality was Dorpat, and while it might be dull, it was safe and secure.

Riva's determination to destroy the dream only strengthened it because it forced her son to make a choice; to deny the dream would be to deny his father's memory. Anschel's belief in a Jewish homeland was an integral part of his character, the two were inseparable. Ben felt an obligation to defend it, a need to keep the dream alive because it was a precious bond that still linked him to Anschel. Unwittingly, Riva's obstinacy pushed her son farther and farther away.

Over time, their arguments grew increasingly bitter. As Riva became more brittle and intractable, Benjamin grew more stubborn. The more his mother denigrated Anschel's dreams of Palestine, the more Ben leaned towards his father's views. It was a constant source of discord in the family and only Ben's deepening relationship with Bluma and Meilach's sense of humor kept him from becoming sullen and morose.

Ben graduated from school in the spring of 1920, and the prospect of spending three years in the narrow confines of a college classroom left him cold. He was nearly eighteen; he yearned to start his own life. And unlike many of his graduating classmates, Benjamin knew exactly what he wanted to do and where he wanted to go. The only question was when.

Every so often, he would open the door to his closet and stare at the brass-bound steamer trunk wedged in the corner. In his mind's eye, he could visualize the morning he and Herb would drag the trunk from its resting place to a waiting taxi. He had imagined the details of that final day so many times that it assumed a feeling of reality, as though he were leaving the following day. There were only two things left to do before that day actually arrived: pick a date and tell Riva. But despite his confidence, Ben shrank from the inevitable confrontation he knew would arise.

Again and again, he made elaborate plans to break the news, but something always seemed to interfere; the timing was never right. Everything conspired against him. The biggest setback came in mid-summer, when Palestine was torn by anti-Semitic riots. Riva pounced on the spreading violence as a perfect example of just how dangerous and unstable Palestine was. But Benjamin saw the riots in a different light. If there were more Jews in Palestine, he reasoned, the Arabs would have to think twice before assaulting them.

As he moved closer to a final decision, Ben broached the subject to Bluma; he wanted a trial run before he spoke to his mother. To his surprise, she was less than sympathetic. "The timing is all wrong," she told him. "Your mother still needs your help with the other children and you're crazy to pass up a university education." Having expected her to be supportive, Ben felt betrayed and resentful. It was the cause of their first real disagreement.

His conversation with Bluma did lead him to realize that postponing a decision would not make it any easier. He was tired of being on the defensive, tired of having his life planned by other people. There were exciting things happening in Palestine and he wanted to be a part of them. Riva's plans for his future meant three boring years at the university followed by a dull career in Dorpat. She had never understood what Zionism was all about and never would. What Ben craved was action; education could wait.

One summer afternoon, sitting at the broad rosewood desk in his father's study, Ben set a date. August, he thought. The first of August would be perfect. He kept rolling the date around in his mind, saying it out loud until it began to feel right. I leave August first, he decided. Once the date was made, Ben felt exhilarated; he could hardly wait to tell everyone. Of course, Riva would have to be the first to know.

Ben chose a time when he felt she would be most relaxed and receptive—just after dinner on a Saturday night. Barely able to contain himself, he waited until they were alone in the living room and broke the news in a firm but reasonable voice. He had known Riva would be upset but the violence of her reaction stunned him. What he had thought would be a difficult but calm and rational discussion quickly degenerated into a shouting match that lasted the better part of a half-hour. Flushed and trembling, Riva finally ended the battle with a pointing finger leveled at Ben's face.

"You're going to the University of Dorpat this fall whether you like it or not!" Riva's voice cracked with the intensity of her emotions. "I am your mother and I know what's best for you. And I don't want to hear another word about Palestine. I'm sick of Palestine. Do you understand me?"

"I understand you, Mama," Ben snapped back. "But I'm still going."

"If your father were alive . . ."

"If my father were alive, we'd be in Palestine."

Riva turned on her heel and left the room. They were trapped in a stalemate.

It was Beile who restored Riva's sense of perspective. Later that evening, after Riva had calmed down, Beile pointed out to her daughter that Benjamin was eighteen and old enough to do as he chose, with or without Riva's consent.

"But I can't let him throw his life away on a pipe dream," Riva protested.

"Have a little faith in your son," Beile replied gently. "There are many good reasons why Benjamin should go to the university, but 'Mama says to' isn't one of them."

Riva stared at her mother, then nodded imperceptibly. Beile was right, her son was no longer a boy.

Riva waited until the children were in bed, then asked her son to rejoin her in the living room. They sat on the edge of their chairs, eyeing each other like two contestants in a sparring ring. Benjamin waited for his mother to start the conversation.

"Earlier this evening, you told me you could learn far more by emigrating to Palestine than sitting in a classroom for the next three years. Is that correct?"

Benjamin was surprised she had heard anything he had said. "That's right. I'd be helping to build a new country. I can't think of anything more important." There was a certain eagerness in his voice. If Riva was willing to listen, perhaps there was a possibility he could persuade her that Palestine was his real future.

"How are you planning to build a new country?" Riva asked. "By farming?"

"There's nothing wrong with farming," Ben shot back. He was not going to let his mother intimidate him.

"I'm not saying there is." Riva saw the youthful determination in his face and phrased her reply carefully. "I'm just saying that you should consider all the alternatives. After all, Benjamin, the decisions made at this point will determine the future course of your life."

Benjamin stared at his mother in astonishment. He had expected an ultimatum, not a discussion. The thought did cross his mind that her sudden willingness to talk was a pretense, a ruse, but he dismissed it. She had never bothered to conceal her true feelings in the past; why should she now? Besides, nothing she could say would change his mind.

"I'm listening, Mama," he said.

Instead of trying to convince her son that the realities of farming were a far cry from the romantic ideal, Riva chose a different tack. She reminded Ben of the emphasis Anschel placed on education and how he had hoped that Ben would choose business as his profession. To Anschel, business was as honorable a profession as law or medicine. Perhaps more so, he had often laughed. When one made the rounds from doctor to doctor, or lawyer to lawyer, one never really knew whether or not he was hearing the truth or being duped. But business was differnt; it was a relationship of equals. You knew when someone was trying to take advantage of you, and he knew whether or not you were treating him fairly. Anschel believed there was a challenge and an excitement to business missing in other professions; an opportunity to build and create, to provide jobs for people and make things happen.

"There is more to business than just making a profit," Riva explained. "There's . . ."

"That's true," Ben interrupted. "But what does that have to do with Palestine?"

"Hear me out, Benjamin," his mother said. She sat quietly, hands folded on her lap. Patiently, she explained that one could not build a modern nation on crops. If Palestine was to grow and prosper, she would need industry, banking, commerce, and manufacturing; she would need resourceful men with skills and capital. Those men were the hardest to find.

"You have the ability and the potential, Benjamin. If you so choose, you can be one of those men, but not without an education. I think your father would agree that the best way you can help to build a Jewish homeland in Palestine is by using your head as well as your hands. Benjamin, we both know that I cannot stop you from going to Palestine; you're old enough to make your own decisions. But before you do, please think about what I've said. There's a great deal a stake."

In spite of himself, Ben found his mother's point of view logical and persuasive. And he knew in his heart that she was right about his father; Anschel would have said exactly the same thing. Even so, he bridled at the thought of abandoning his plans.

To her credit, Riva sensed that she had said enough. She rose from her chair and kissed him gently on the forehead, then went up to her room. Too keyed up to sleep, Ben wandered into the kitchen, looked for something to eat.

He found Beile sitting at the kitchen table. Glad to have her company, he pulled out a chair opposite her and sighed as he collapsed into it. His conversation with Riva had thrown his feelings into turmoil and he needed to sort them out. Unlike his mother, Beile was always a sympathetic listener; Ben never hesitated to share his feelings with her. He often wished that his mother was as easy to talk to.

Beile offered to fix him a snack, but he shook his head. What he really needed to do was talk. The fulfillment of his dream lay practically within his grasp, yet he felt torn between the decision he had made to emigrate and the inescapable logic of his mother's arguments. Slowly at first, then with an increasing force on their own, the words poured out of him. Finally, when there was nothing left to say, he leaned forward and stared at the scarred table top, feeling emotionally drained. Beile reached out and took his hand into her own.

"I can't tell you what is right, Benjamin. You must decide that for yourself. Just bear in mind that your mother wants nothing but the best for you. And if she seems unreasonable at times or ridicules the ideals you believe in remember that she has suffered a terrible loss."

"That was almost two years ago."

"Do you miss Anschel any the less?" When Ben remained silent, Beile surprised him by saying she did not disapprove of his plans for Palestine.

"I never thought I'd hear you say that, Grandmother."

Beile laughed. "I never though I would either. But times change, Benjamin. One thing I learned from your father is that you cannot make someone into something they are not. Each of us must have our own dreams, and follow our own paths."

Ben regarded her with affection. "I wish Mama would understand that."

"In time, she will," Beile promised. "Love and fear can do terrible things to all of us. Your mother just needs time."

Ben rose from the chair and kissed his grandmother on the cheek. "Thank you," he smiled. For the first time in months, he felt at peace.

Beile Nadelson climbed into bed that night feeling every one of her sixty-eight years. As she lay beneath the covers, waiting for sleep to come, she said a prayer of thanksgiving. She knew without asking that Ben would enroll at the university. There would be problems in the future, but for the present, she could ask for no more. "If he still chooses to emigrate in three years, I won't be the one to stand in his way," she promised herself. "And if Riva does, I'll box her ears, like I did when she was a little girl." The old lady laughed out loud at the thought and closed her eyes.

Beile Nadelson died peacefully in her sleep that night.

They buried her next to Anschel in the Jewish cemetery outside Dorpat. Benjamin said *kaddish*, the prayer for the dead, with all the love and affection that filled his heart. In the months that lay ahead, her grave was marked by a score of small white pebbles, one to mark each visit of those who missed her.

• • •

To Riva's relief, Ben enrolled at the University of Dorpat that fall, and while he did not share his mother's enthusiasm at first, his outlook brightened considerably when he discovered that Bluma and Meilach would be attending college with him. The idea of spending three years with his best friend and the girl he found irresistable made the length of time he would be in school seem less daunting.

While Bluma chose political science and Meilach opted for history, Ben decided to study economics. The twinge of regret he felt at abandoning his plans to emigrate was quickly overshadowed by the academic demands of freshman year. The give and take of classroom discussion and the stimulating exchange of ideas held an appeal for him he had not anticipated and he came to relish the daily intellectual challenges. Best of all, Ben's home life became a study in tranquility. He and his mother rarely argued and they both made a sustained effort to preserve their truce on the subject of Palestine.

The second week of classes, Ben, Bluma, and Meilach formed a Zionist study group which quickly grew to more than thirty members. For Ben, the Zionist Society was an ideal outlet for the pent-up energy and idealism inside him, and it soon came to absorb nearly all his free time. Riva viewed Ben's involvement with increasing alarm; Jewish political groups were an easy target for Gentiles in search of a scapegoat. But she struggled to keep her feelings to herself and was not about to endanger the fragile understanding that had developed between her and her son. "At least I can be grateful they're not doing anything but talking," she often reassured herself, and the truce was preserved.

• • •

Ben found the following three years hectic and rewarding, punctuated by summers that seemed unbearably dull by comparison. The combination of his studies, the Zionist Society, and his maturing relationship with Bluma, kept him fully occupied, and as he prepared for final examination towards the end of his senior year, it was with a sense of disbelief that time could pass so quickly.

As graduation approached, Ben expected his mother to begin a campaign intended to keep him in Dorpat, but to his surprise, Riva said nothing about the future. It was not, as he assumed, because her opinions had changed.

During the previous three years, Bluma Feldman had been a constant presence in the Isaacson house, and even though her political views had horrified Ben's mother, her quick wit and ready smile had earned Riva's respect and affection. But what impressed Riva the most was the look on her son's face whenever Bluma walked into the room; the passion they felt for each other was plain to see. To Riva, the obvious implication was marriage, and a marriage between Ben and Bluma represented her best chance of dissuading Ben from emigrating. She knew there was nothing like a wife and children to settle one down to the business of living. The more she thought about it, the more convinced she became that Ben would marry Bluma and settle in Dorpat.

While Riva Isaacson could not have been prouder when her son accepted his diploma in the spring of 1924, she waited in vain to hear the word "marriage." Still, she kept hoping.

Even though there was no question of their love for each other, graduation left Ben and Bluma in a quandary as they tried to reconcile marriage with their plans to emigrate. They couldn't leave for Palestine together unless they were married; Bluma's mother would have died at the thought. But if they did marry, it meant months of preparation followed by months of visiting relatives.

Aside from the delay, there was another consideration: if Bluma became pregnant during that time, it would be almost impossible to leave. That much Ben and Bluma knew from experience; Meilach had been married during his second year at the university, and by the time he graduated, he had one child at home and another on the way. Despite his best intentions, Meilach was now permanently tied to Dorpat; his growing responsibilities and the pressure from his family left him no other choice.

Having seen what happened to Meilach, neither Ben nor Bluma wanted their future dictated by chance, so they ruled out marriage. After talking it over, they decided that Ben would emigrate first and Bluma would follow as soon as she could. Once they were both in Palestine, marriage would be a simple proposition; there would be no need for a massive formal wedding, nor would they run the risk of being ensnared by either of their families. It meant being separated, but it seemed the only logical alternative.

Ben unconsciously encouraged his mother's hopes for an early marriage by saying nothing about Palestine. Instead, he told her he planned to visit his Uncle Samuel in Stockholm in November. The reason he gave was a plausible one: in November, he would turn twenty-one, the age at which he was eligible to claim his inheritance. There were arrangements he needed to make with his Uncle Samuel.

In the back of his mind, Ben saw the trip to Sweden as a stop on his way to Palestine, but decided against mentioning this to his mother since he was loathe to mar his last few months with her with argument and dissension. Meanwhile, Riva managed to convince herself that Ben was just waiting to claim his inheritance before marrying Bluma. Had she known the real reason for his trip to Sweden, the kind of risks Ben was planning to take, she would have done everything in her power to block his inheritance.

It was his intention to arrange the estate Anschel had left him so he would be able to withdraw his capital once he established himself in Palestine. Though he could have emigrated with enough funds to live comfortably and left the remainder of his inheritance safely earning dividends in Sweden, his youthful idealism recoiled at the thought of a partial commitment. He was well aware of a derisive slogan, popular at the time, which said: "Palestine gets people without money and money without people," and the truth of the accusation stung him. Regardless of however small his contribution might be, there would be no reservations, no holding back. He was prepared to commit everything he owned to a future in Palestine.

But November seemed a lifetime away and Ben was looking forward to an idle summer spent with his family and Bluma. Although she had originally intended to return to Riga after graduation, Ben persuaded her to stay in Dorpat until he left for Sweden. It would make the impending separation less painful.

Ben and Bluma passed the lazy days of June just as they had planned—reading, relaxing, and enjoying each other's company. It took them a couple of weeks to adjust to the leisurely pace, but by the end of the month they had established a routine that seemed almost sinful when compared to the grueling demands of the previous three years. It was to be a summer they would always remember.

•　•　•

Meilach Gorsky took the stairs leading from his apartment to the front landing two at a time. Once again, he was late for work and he knew his father would be furious. As the owner's son, Meilach was expected to set an example for the employees, and Yakov Gorsky did not consider tardiness as the best way to do it. Meilach dashed from the building into the bright July sunlight and promptly found his path blocked by a sidewalk argument.

"You liar!" screamed a man wearing a Russian peasant's blouse; there was scattered laughter from the small crowd that had gathered.

Meilach recognized the man instantly; he was an orthodox Russian Jew named Tzibale, an impoverished fruit vendor. The object of his scorn was a blond woman in a light summer dress with her back to Meilach. His curiosity piqued, Meilach lingered to watch the scene unfold. The woman shook her fist at the fruit peddler and yelled an insult that Meilach missed. Tzibale snickered coarsely in response.

"You know what you are?" he sneered. "A whore! A lying WHORE!"

Incensed, the blond woman grabbed a three-foot length of iron rod resting on the open tailgate of Tzibale's pushcart and raised it over her head to strike him. The weight of the rod slowed her swing, giving Meilach just enough time to reach out and seize her wrist.

"No need for violence," he muttered. She stumbled back into him, struggling to break loose, but he held her securely around the waist. He was not about to let go until she dropped the rod.

"You pig!" she screamed. "You're hurting me!"

Meilach heard the excited shouts of the crowd in the background and made an effort to keep his voice calm and reasonable. "Just drop the rod and . . ."

A black blur flashed in front of Meilach's face; suddenly he couldn't breathe. Using a nightstick to pinion Meilach by the throat, a burly policeman yanked him away from the woman and forced him to the ground. When he released Meilach from the choke hold, Meilach tried to rise, but the officer struck him viciously on the side of the head. The last thing Meilach heard before he lost consciousness was the blond woman, hystericaly shouting that he had tried to molest her.

By the time a distraught neighbor pounded on the Isaacsons' front door with the news that Meilach had been arrested, half of Dorpat had already heard the story. Standing on the threshold, Ben and Bluma listened in stunned silence to a recitation of rumors that were flying around the city. One claimed that Meilach had beaten a Christian woman, another said he had tried to rape her. Yet another alleged he had tried to rob her.

"I'd better get to the police station," Ben said tersely. Bluma nodded in agreement, then led the Isaacsons' frantic neighbor into the kitchen to calm her down.

As Ben raced to the station house, he feared for his friend. Nothing incited a mob so quickly as the accusation that some Jew had molested a Christian woman, whether it was true or not. Two blocks from the police station, his worst fears were confirmed. A half-dozen uniformed policemen stood on the front steps, holding an angry horde at bay. From the insults the mob screamed and the placards Ben saw, he had no doubt what the crowd wanted: Meilach Gorsky.

Ben realized he had no chance of reaching Meilach. Even if he was able to force his way through the crush of bodies blocking the street, the police would never let him in. In despair, he ran back towards the house to get Bluma. Somehow, they had to get through to Meilach; together, they would work out a plan.

Meanwhile, word of Meilach's arrest sent shock waves through the Jewish community and, that same afternoon, the Elders formed a committee to deal with the crisis. No one who knew Meilach believed the charges, but unless he was proven innocent, and quickly, the incident would be a perfect pretext for anti-Semitic riots or a pogrom.

There was little for the committee to go on. The Christian woman, a Frau Kimmelman, was nowhere to be found. She had disappeared after giving the arresting officer a statement in which she accused Meilach of trying to drag her into his apartment building and rape her. There were also statements from a dozen bystanders who said Meilach had indeed grappled with her and pulled her towards his building. The fruit vendor, too, corroborated the woman's story. The "investigation" was beginning to look like a dead end.

Through the committee's influence, Ben finally obtained permission from the police to see Meilach. Though a full day had passed since the incident, there was still an ugly crowd outside the police station. As he pushed his way to the front steps, Ben was grateful that his blond hair and blue eyes allowed him to pass for a German; the crowd was looking for trouble and would have been pleased to release their hostility on any Jew who happened by.

Once inside, a turnkey led him to Meilach's cell. His friend lay on a narrow metal cot, his face concealed by an arm.

"You have five minutes," the turnkey grinned. "Take any longer and you can rot in there with him." He relocked the cell door, then returned to the front desk, leaving Ben alone with Meilach.

"Meilach?" Ben said gently. "Meilach, it's me, Ben."

Meilach groaned and lifted his arm to reveal a series of cuts and bruises across his face. One cheek was swollen and discolored, the other was split wide open. Dried blood encrusted Meilach's upper lip and from the crooked angle of his nose, Ben guessed it was broken. The Dorpat jails were not known for their hospitality, particularly if you were a Jew.

Ben suppressed his sense of rage. "Are you all right, Meilach? Do you need a doctor?"

Meilach shook his head and winced involuntarily. "I'll live." It was difficult for him to speak.

"I want to know exactly what happened," Ben said softly. "Tell me everything—don't leave out any details."

Ben left the Dorpat police station more confused than ever. What Meilach had told him was practically worthless; he hadn't even seen the woman's face. The only fact Ben had learned that he didn't already know was that Tzibale had called Kimmelman a whore just before she picked up the iron rod.

After he returned home and filled Bluma in on his conversation with Meilach, they sat together on the back porch. Again and again they went over the incident, looking for a clue to all the unanswered questions. Why were Tzibale and the woman arguing? Why had the woman suddenly disappeared? How did the policeman appear on the scene so quickly? But above all, why would Frau Kimmelman accuse Meilach of trying to molest her? And why would the witnesses back her up when it was obvious that Meilach's intent was to prevent a violent confrontation? He would hardly molest a woman or try to rape her right on the street in front of a crowd.

"None of this makes any sense, Ben." Bluma stood and restlessly paced the length of the porch. "There's something very strange going on here and I have the feeling that the answer lies with Tzibale."

"The fruit vendor?"

Bluma stopped pacing and turned to Ben. "How much do you know about him?"

"Not much," Ben replied. He had seen the short, unkempt peddler many times during the preceding month; Meilach's street was part of his regular route. He always wore a ragged black ankle-length coat and he was so dirty, it was commonly said that if Tzibale bathed in honor of the Sabbath, he did so with a thimble. But he seemed harmless enough, just another Russian refugee struggling to eke out a living as best he could.

"Since Frau Kimmelman has disappeared so conveniently, the only person who really knows what really happened is Tzibale, and for some reason, he isn't telling the truth," Bluma frowned. "I'd say it was time we found out a little more about our friend Tzibale. If you want to know the truth, I don't even think he's Jewish."

She stroked her chin thoughtfully, oblivious to the startled expression on Ben's face.

First thing the following morning, with the full approval of the stymied Committee of Elders, Ben and Bluma organized the Zionist Society into an efficient task force and began asking questions about Tzibale. Where did he live? What were his habits? Who were his friends? As Bluma had predicted, people who were reluctant to speak with the police or the Jewish investigators felt less inhibited about talking to freshly scrubbed university students looking to write an article for the college newspaper.

That night, they all met at the Isaacson house to share what they had learned. As each person made his report, Bluma listed the salient facts on an unlined yellow pad.

1. Tzibale had been in Dorpat nearly a month, yet he had not joined a synagogue, nor made any attempt to become a part of the closely knit Jewish community in Dorpat.
2. Tzibale claimed to have been a farmer, but his hands were soft, not hard and calloused from a lifetime in the fields.
3. Many of the people on Tzibale's route had noticed that he never bothered to count his change. He simply threw it into the cash box. That was out of character for a man who supposedly lived on the verge of starvation.
4. Two local barflys swore they had seen Tzibale drinking in a bar with several Gentiles. That was highly unusual; orthodox Jews did not drink at all, let alone in the company of Christians.

The most important bit of information uncovered was the reason for Tzibale's argument with Frau Kimmelman. An old woman who lived on the floor below Meilach had seen everything, but she had been too terrified to talk to the police.

The old woman said that Frau Kimmelman bought some fruit, and when she went to pay for it, she discovered her purse was gone. She then accused Tzibale of stealing it and he retaliated by calling her a lying whore. It was at that point that Meilach became involved.

"I can understand why Tzibale would not have mentioned Kimmelman's purse to the police," Ben spoke out over the half-dozen arguments that raged; every member of the Zionist Society seemed to have his own theory. "But why didn't Kimmelman point the finger at him for robbing her?"

Bluma laughed softly and everyone looked at her in surprise. "Because it didn't matter whether he stole the purse or not. It was all planned, right from the beginning. Tzibale is not Jewish, he's an agent, a provocateur planted by the Communists to spark a pogrom, and Kimmelman was working with him."

"But why?" someone asked, a puzzled expression on his face.

"Study your history," Bluma retorted, irritated by the astonished disbelief she saw on the faces in the living room. "It certainly wouldn't be the first time that a Communist posed as a Jew in order to start a pogrom or make people think we Jews favor the overthrow of the government." For centuries, the Russians had coveted the Baltic States as a path to the sea and as a buffer against Germany's ambitions. Now that Germany was in ruins, there was a perfect opportunity to seize control from within by fostering violence and political instability. For nearly two years, beginning in the summer of 1922, anti-Semitic incidents in Dorpat had increased in scope and frequency, and while Bluma had always suspected the Communists, there was never any proof.

"Just one problem," Ben pointed out. "If it was all a setup, how did they know exactly when Meilach would appear?"

"Meilach wasn't part of the original plan," Bluma explained. "He was an unexpected bonus. Tzibale was to be the culprit, but when Meilach intervened, Tzibale didn't need to take the risk. The tipoff was the purse. They must have planned for Tzibale to be accused of stealing, then he and the woman would fight. The police officer, who had to be a part of the plan, was waiting around the corner to arrest Tzibale only God knows on what charges. As for the crowd, the policeman could manipulate them any way he wanted. Who's going to argue with a policeman?

"After a while, the charges would be dropped and Tzibale would be released, but the damage would have been done. You'd have every Gentile fanatic in the city running loose in the Jewish Quarter. The Communists would like nothing better." The implications were staggering, and as the inescapable logic of Bluma's words struck home, the expressions of disbelief turned to fear and outrage.

"It's no longer enough to prove that Meilach is innocent," Bluma continued grimly. "There's too much damage already done. The only way out is to prove that Tzibale isn't Jewish. If we can do that, for once the rumor mill will work in our favor. The Communists are the first ones people will blame."

"And just how are we going to *prove* that Tzibale isn't Jewish?" Ben wondered.

"We'll hire a prostitute to see whether or not he's circumcised. No Gentile would undergo such an operation just to play a part."

Ben laughed delightedly at the sheer genius of her ideas, but three or four of the men in the living room actually blushed. Nothing pertaining in any way to sexual matters was ever discussed in front of a female. Bluma noticed their discomfort and grinned at Ben.

"Let's do it," he grinned back.

• • •

The prostitute only confirmed what they already knew: Tzibale was not Jewish.

Rumors ignited the city. The only thing the good burghers of Dorpat feared more than a Jewish conspiracy was a Communist one. A wide-scale investigation was launched, but nothing was to come of it. Predictably, Tzibale disappeared and Russian intrigues became the major topic of conversation.

Meilach was released the following day and the Jewish community heaved a collective sigh of relief. The threat of imminent bloodshed had been defused and life returned to normal.

While everyone in the Jewish quarter preferred to forget the entire incident as quickly as possible, to Ben, Tzibale was a foretaste of things to come, a very small part of a much larger plan. If he had ever had any doubts about emigrating, they disappeared with Tzibale, and just after Meilach's release, Ben decided to go ahead with his plans no matter what happened. After his trip to Stockholm, he would travel on to Palestine, stopping in Berlin for a week or two to visit his cousin Herschel. He had only one time constraint—he wanted to be in Jerusalem on April 1st for the official opening of the Hebrew University, the first wholly Jewish institution to rise on the soil of Palestine in nearly two thousand years. It was an event he did not want to miss.

Ben tried to convince Meilach to emigrate as well, but between his family and his father's business, Meilach was too firmly entrenched in Dorpat. "Maybe in a few years," Meilach had smiled. But the look in his eyes saddened Ben; he knew Meilach would never leave Dorpat.

Telling Riva was the hardest thing Ben had ever done. She was disappointed, hurt, and angry, but there was a kind of resignation in her careworn features as she argued with him. She had pinned all her hopes on a marriage between Bluma and her son, but as the summer months had passed without an engagement, she had begun to suspect that Stockholm would only be a stopover for her son. In her heart, she had known he was bound for Palestine and nothing she could do would hold him, but still, she went through the motions.

When all the words that had to be said were finally said, Riva shook her head wearily. "Go if you must," she whispered. She could fight no longer.

His last few weeks in Dorpat passed all too quickly, especially the precious moments spent with Bluma. He had no way of knowing when he would see his family again, and the thought of being separated from Bluma plagued his heart. Though Riva still refused to give him her blessing, she supervised the packing, checking to see that her son had everything he needed, and she insisted that everyone accompany him to the railroad station where he would take a train for the coast.

When the final day arrived, they bid each other farewell on the station platform in Dorpat and Ben took a seat in his assigned compartment. Surrounded by strangers, he stared out of a dust-streaked window at the people he loved and contemplated his future with a sense of loss and loneliness. The picture of Bluma and his family waving as the train left the station was one that would be forever framed in his memory. For a moment, he felt as though he might never see them again.

• • •

Stockholm had changed very little in all the years Ben had been away. The city was much the same as he remembered it from the spring of 1914—snug, prosperous, and tidy. It was good to see his Uncle Samuel again and renew the old ties with his father's side of the family, but Ben was possessed by an impatience to begin his journey. Not until he was on the boat train for Germany would he really feel that he was on his way to Palestine.

To his dismay, it took him three long weeks to settle the details of his inheritance and make the necessary arrangments with his uncle. It was a dreary and depressing experience, but when the formalities were finally dispensed with, Ben found himself possessed of a substantial estate. He told his uncle of his plans, and Samuel Isaacson thought his intention to invest in Palestine was foolhardy and reckless, but he refrained from criticism once he saw how determined Ben was.

On the day Ben was to leave, Samuel stayed home from the office and drove him to the station. Though he only knew his father's brother from letters, childhood memories, and rare visits, Ben felt very close to the portly man who stood before him.

"I want to thank you for everything, Uncle Samuel," Ben smiled as the conductors gave the signal to board.

"It seems like a thousand years ago that I bid your father good-bye on this very platform. Now, my brother's son is a man. Life passes so quickly." They embraced, then Ben turned to board the train.

"Shalom," Samuel whispered as Ben disappeared from sight. "God be with you."

FIVE

Hanukkah
December 24th 1924

The Sassnitz–Trelleborg boat train clawed its way south towards the German port of Sassnitz, the hull vibrating from the impact of heavy seas. Windblown spray and driving rain made it almost impossible to distinguish between the horizon and the foaming gray crests of the waves. Seated next to a window inside the train, Ben tried to ignore his queasy stomach and hoped the railroad car wouldn't be pitched off its special tracks by the ferry's violent motion. There were three other people sharing his compartment, a curly haired man of thirty and a middle-aged couple, but no one seemed inclined to talk. From the expressions on their faces, Ben saw that he was not the only one concerned with his stomach and his safety.

Ben reached into his breast pocket and withdrew a letter from his mother that Samuel had passed onto him two days before. He felt guilty for not having opened it sooner, but if the truth were known, he was afraid to read it, afraid he might change his mind. So he had put the letter aside, waiting until he was on the boat-train for Germany and irrevocably committed. A wave of homesickness passed over him when he caught sight of his mother's delicate script on the envelope. He unfolded the cream-colored stationery and began to read.

My Dearest Ben,
For years, I have been afraid I would have to write this letter to

89

you. But, like most things we fear, the anxiety is always worse than the object of our fear.

When you left last month for Stockholm to visit your father's relatives and claim your inheritance, I knew that our lives would never be the same again. I wanted to explain to you why I tried to keep you from going, but the right words never seemed to come. I hope I've found them now.

Though your father and I were from two different worlds, I fell in love with him from the first day we met. I had never known anyone like him. He was unafraid, outspoken, a true visionary. My father warned me that Anschel was full of dangerous ideas, but I was prepared to live with the risks that might entail, and I've never regretted a single day.

Unlike your father, I have always beleived it is a Jew's fate to try to live peacefully in a Christian world until the Messiah comes for us. I feared the unknown. I never cared for the world outside my door. It exhilarated Anschel. Your father yearned for Zion. He loved the challenge.

You are very much your father's son, so like him in your need to be challenged, your reluctance to accept things as they are.

Ben—my dearest son—I knew years ago, when Anschel died, that part of him lived within you; a part that would remain restless and dissatisfied. I was fearful that your going to Palestine would mean we would never see each other again. I fought you for so long because I wanted you to stay with me, with the rest of your family, as young men have done here in Dorpat for a dozen generations. But I can fight no longer.

I know now that I cannot reach out and bring you home any more than I could expect Anschel to renounce his dreams of Palestine. I pray that you will find what you seek and satisfy your heart in a way that your father never did. If you do, then perhaps both of you will rest at last. I love you, my son. Wherever you go, part of me goes with you. I pray to God that when you reach Jerusalem, you will find the homeland that you feel is yours.

We all love you and miss you.

Your Mother

The letter moved him deeply, bringing back the anguish he had seen on her face when they said ''good-bye.'' He felt a flood of love for his mother and a pang of guilt for not having opened the letter sooner. His mother still believed he was making a mistake, but she had done the most she could; she had told him that she understood and had given him her blessing. Ben kissed the letter and returned it to his pocket. As he looked up he noticed the couple sitting across from him were staring. Embarrassed, the man looked away, but the woman met Ben's eyes and smiled.

"You are reading a letter from your girlfriend, ja?"

Ben flushed. "No."

"You are bound for Hamburg?"

"Marta," the man scolded, "leave the poor boy alone." Then he turned to Ben and apologized for intruding on his privacy.

"Please don't apologize," Ben laughed. "As a matter of fact, I am bound for Hamburg. I'll be catching the Berlin Express tonight. By the way, my name is Benjamin Isaacson."

The couple introduced themselves as Johann and Marta Krechtser, which inspired the curly haired man to join the conversation. Johann was in the wool trade and his wife Marta was a lively woman with graying red hair. They lived in Altona, a suburb of Hamburg. The other man was from Fulda, a medieval town in central Germany. His name was Michel Zadek and he was a wholesale distributor of children's novelties. Zadek had the sunny disposition and enthusiastic personality that one would expect of someone in his line of work. Conversation helped to take everyone's mind off the storm outside and made the long hours pass more pleasantly. Towards one o'clock in the afternoon a conductor announced that owing to the weather, the ferry would arrive in Sassnitz two hours late. Marta Krechtser turned to Ben and pointed out that he would miss his connection to Berlin because of the delay.

"I'll get a hotel room in Hamburg for the night," Ben shrugged.

Johann Krechtser shook his head negatively. "This is a Christmas Eve, as well as the fifth night of Hanukkah. There won't be a room to be had in all of Hamburg."

Impulsively, Marta invited Ben to stay with them for the night, and after he gratefully accepted, she extended the invitation to include Michel Zadek, who was forced to decline.

"Thank you for your kindness," he said. "But I am orthodox and, as you know, traveling after sundown constitutes a breach of the Sabbath. I'll just have to find someplace to stay in Sassnitz."

●　　　●　　　●

True to the conductor's prediction, the boat train arrived in the German port of Sassnitz just before sundown, making it impossible for Michel Zadek to accompany Ben and the Krechtsers to Altona. It came as a great disappointment to Michel that he and Ben would part company so quickly. They had enjoyed each other's company immensely.

"Perhaps you could visit my wife and me in Fulda?" Zadek asked, as he gathered his bags.

"I'll be in Germany only for a couple of weeks before departing for Palestine," Ben explained. "I'm afraid I won't have the time."

"Oh, you'll love Fulda," Michel beamed, refusing to accept Ben's negative response. "It's the pride of central Germany, a masterpiece of medieval architecture. Hannah and I have plenty of room, and I know you'll love her cooking. There's so much to see—the castles, the churches, the—"

"Michel, I—"

"Benjamin, you couldn't be in such a hurry that a few days more or less would change your plans," Zadek insisted. He looked crestfallen.

"All right, all right," Ben laughed. "I promise to try."

Ben helped Zadek carry his luggage outside and wished him luck in finding a place to stay. It was with genuine regret that he watched the friendly toy vendor disappear into the darkness shrouding the platform.

Instead of reboarding, Ben strolled alongside the train to stretch his legs. After the stale air of a closed compartment, the brisk wind blowing off the Baltic felt refreshing and invigorating. Ben savored the salt tang in the air, watching the trainmen couple an engine to the railroad cars on the ferry. When they finished, a whistle shrieked and a conductor shouted the "all clear." Reluctantly, Ben returned to the stuffy compartment.

He chatted with the Krechtsers for a while, but the warmth of the compartment made him sleepy and he found it difficult to hold up his end of the conversation. Without realizing it, he dozed off in his seat as Marta Krechtser was telling a story about a niece who had once visited Stockholm. The next thing Ben Knew, Johann Krechtser was gently shaking his knee.

"We are in Altona, Benjamin," he smiled. Ben nodded and rubbed the sleep from his eyes, stifling a yawn.

Marta and Johann Krechtser lived in a brick row house on one of the back streets in the Jewish section of Altona. It was an old house, but neat and comfortable and not too far from the station. By seven o'clock, Ben had finished unpacking his bag in the guest room.

"Can I make you a late supper?" Marta called out as Ben descended the stairs. She had become very fond of him in the short time they had known each other. Already, she was assuming the role of surrogate mother.

"No thanks," Ben replied. "I've been sitting for too long. What I'd really like is a walk."

"If you change your mind, just help yourself to the food in the icebox," she said. "If Johann and I retire before you return, we'll leave the door unlocked."

Ben thanked them again for their kindness and let himself out the front door. The Krechtsers were a gracious couple and Ben appreciated their hospitality, but he felt something was missing. As Johann had reminded him, it was a Sabbath eve, the fifth day of Hanukkah. It was also Ben's first holiday away from home, and he missed the traditional warmth of a Friday night family dinner. Stepping off the Krechtsers' stoop, he turned right and walked towards the center of Altona.

The streets were decorated for the holiday season, but the festive buntings did not conceal the shabby appearance of the buildings. Even though it was Christmas, the displays in the stores were meager at best, and most of the people Ben passed wore clothes that were old and threadbare. There was an air of neglect about the city, reflected by the look of the people on the street; it was a harsh contrast to the snug prosperity of Sweden. Anschel had been right when he predicted that the Treaty of Versailles would leave Germany in ruins for years to come.

Ben strolled for blocks, inhaling the crisp, clean air and admiring the Hanukkah decorations in the Jewish quarter. The houses looked festive and inviting, their lights casting pale shadows through frosted panes of glass. Ben tried to imagine the families gathered within, sitting around the polished tables. If the people inside those houses were anything like his own family, every bit of silver, crystal, and china would be gleaming with spotless perfection in honor of the Sabbath. The rooms would be filled with the aroma of holiday delicacies and fragrant with the scent of candle wax and lemon oil. Occasionally, through the fine lace curtains that graced most windows, he glimpsed people celebrating together. Each familiar scene underscored the miles that separated him from his own family. He closed his eyes for a moment, recalling the hearty taste of his mother's *kreplach* soup.

He walked a few more steps, then stopped in front of an imposing brick house that looked particularly inviting. The house was richly decorated for Hanukkah and a large bay window afforded Ben a clear view of the dining room. A dark-suited man with a neat Van Dyke stood at the head of the table. From his solemn expression, Ben guessed he was saying *kiddush*, the traditional Sabbath prayer. The man's wife and children stood in a circle around the dinner table, hands clasped in devotion.

The scene struck a chord deep inside Ben. He felt a strong kinship with the family standing around the table and longed to partake of the warmth of Friday night prayers with them. He wanted to share himself with others, to be a participant, not just a spectator. Leaving Dorpat had marked a turning point in his life, and he needed to reaffirm his identity as a Jew, as though that would somehow preserve his link with the past.

Something within him that Ben did not fully understand compelled him to walk up the front steps. He was certain he'd be invited in; it was after all the Sabbath and Hanukkah as well.

He reached out to ring the doorbell, but to his surprise, the button was missing from the small brass dome that housed it. He looked closer. Inside the dome were the exposed ends of the bell wires, separated by a few millimeters. It wouldn't take much to force them together. After a brief search, Ben found a splinter of wood and inserted it into the empty hole. To his delight, the bell rang. A woman answered the door, wearing an inexpensive lace cap that identified her as the family maid. An expression of open hostility pinched her features.

"What do you want?" she demanded.

Ben started to explain, but to his astonishment, the woman cut him off in mid-sentence. Her voice was filled with indignation.

"How did you ring this bell? Can't you see that it was taken apart on purpose to prevent anyone from ringing during the Sabbath? You'd better leave now before the master gets raging mad." She tried to close the door, but Ben's hand shot out to prevent it from latching.

"I mean no harm and no disrespect. All I want to do is speak to the master of the house."

From behind the maid, a deep male voice bellowed, "Whoever it is, get rid of him!"

"You heard Herr Hessemann!" the maid whispered fiercely. "Get out!"

"If it's another *Ostjude* come for money or a job, tell him to get out of here or I'll call the police. This is a sacrilege! I will not have my Sabbath defiled!" Herr Hessemann sounded outraged.

"Please leave now," the maid begged. The belligerent tone of her voice had vanished and in its place was genuine fear. "If you don't leave, I could lose my job, and I'd have no money to feed my children." The belligerent scowl on her face had vanished, replaced by a pleading expression. Though he seethed inwardly, Ben offered no resistance as she closed the door in his face. Slowly, he turned and retraced his steps to the Krechtsers' house. His mind churned with confusion and anger. He could not imagine a stranger being so rudely treated on a Sabbath eve in any of the homes he was familiar with.

By the time Ben returned to the Krechtsers, he was relieved to discover they had alreayd retired for the night. He went straight to the guest room, careful not to wake them. Ben lay on the bed, fully dressed, and turned the experience over and over again in his mind. Hessemann was obviously a wealthy man, and from all outward appearances, a pious

Jew. Why would he turn someone away from his door without even listening or coming to the door himself? Was he such a religious fanatic that the mere ringing of a bell on the Sabbath was enough to override all other considerations?

What galled Ben the most was that Hessemann had assumed that he was an *Ostjude*—a Jewish refugee from eastern Europe. Millions of Jews had been driven from their homes in Russia and Poland by war and revolution and had fled westward with little more than the clothes on their back. Thousands of these hapless refugees converged on the great port city of Hamburg, hoping to find passage to America and a new life in a new world. They were to be bitterly disappointed. America had closed her doors to Jewish immigration and Great Britain, bowing to Arab pressure, severely restricted the number of people who could emigrate to Palestine. Most of the *Ostjuden* were left stranded in Germany, a country that could barely feed its own population.

Hessemann's attitude infuriated Ben because it was so unreasonable. Refusing a stranger the barest hospitality because of a small infraction of the Sabbath was unconscionable. Hessemann had barely finished praying to God when he rebuked a fellow Jew who was probably homeless, destitute, and hungry.

●   ●   ●

The next morning at breakfast, Ben made no mention of the incident, but he did ask the Krechtsers about the family who lived off Elbchaussee in an elegant brick house. The callousness and cruelty of Hessemann's attitude still rankled Ben, and he had decided to confront the man and somehow hold up a mirror to his hypocrisy.

"That is the home of Jacob Hessemann," Johann Krechtser explained. "Like myself, he trades in woolens, but he's a very important man. He owns big warehouses in Berlin and Cologne. He trades everywhere."

"Why would you be interested in that house?" Marta wondered. When Ben made a feeble reply, she studied his face with a penetrating stare, much as his mother might have. Then she leaped to the wrong conclusion. "He does have a very beautiful daughter named Sarah," she observed slyly.

Ben ignored her innuendo. "Is Herr Hessemann a religious man?"

"Oh, a very religious man," Marta replied sarcastically. "If you doubt it, just ask him. He loves to flaunt his piety almost as much as he loves to flaunt his money."

"Now, now, my love," her husband interrupted with a wave of his hand. "It is not our place to disparage the piety of our neighbors." He stood, then excused himself from the table. "I have some papers to work on upstairs in the study. If you want me, I'll be there. Have a good day, Benjamin." He gave his wife a peck on the cheek and left them sitting at the kitchen table.

Ben made small talk for a while longer, then excused himself on the pretext of going for a walk. To his acute embarrassment, he actually blushed when Marta good-naturedly bantered she had never known anyone quite so fond of walking. Avoiding her eyes, he quickly pulled on his coat and left.

Although it was still early in the morning, Ben was surprised to find the streets completely deserted. Then he remembered it was Christmas Day as well as the Sabbath. He wandered towards Elbchaussee, trying to form a plan of some kind.

There was no sign of activity at the brick house with the bay window, so Ben leaned against a gas lamp and stared at the house, speculating how to approach Hessemann. A few minutes later, his dilemma was resolved when the door opened and the Hessemanns appeared, one by one. As they crossed the threshold, each brought two fingers to their lips, then reverently touched the *mezuzzah* attached to the door frame.

Herr Hessemann led his family down the front steps, and Ben's first thought was that Hessemann's voice was far more impressive than his appearance. He was tall and ungainly and dressed completely in black. A fedora of the same color was perched uncomfortably on his head, its brim nearly covering his eyes. Hessemann's face was long and craggy, with deep seams and furrows along the cheeks, as though someone had plowed but not harrowed. With his narrow shoulders squared and his gaze leveled straight ahead, he was the perfect image of a successful German burgher. Right behind Hessemann came his wife, a rotund, moon-faced woman with the vacuous features that befitted her role as her husband's shadow. The expensive cashmere coat she wore only added to her bulk, making her appear equally tall and wide, and she clutched the handrail as she descended the front steps, clearly terrified she might topple to destruction at any moment. A young girl and two teenage boys followed Frau Hessemann down the steps. Like their parents, the children were dressed in black. The larger of the two boys slammed the front door with tremendous force, announcing to the neighborhood that the Hessemanns were on their way to *shul*. Given their appearance and demeanor, Ben knew they had to be bound for a synagogue.

Choosing a direction away from Ben's post at the gas lamp, Hessemann set a brisk pace that his wife was hard-pressed to match. Ben waited until they were almost out of sight, then followed them. The Hessemanns walked purposefully for several blocks, then turned and disappeared into an unassuming brick building. As Ben walked up to the door, he noticed a small plaque bearing the Hebrew greeing, "God Welcomes You." He waited a few minutes, nodding politely to people arriving for Sabbath services, then entered the synagogue.

The outside might have been plain, but the interior of the synagogue was airy and impressive. Stained glass windows cast colorful patterns across the room and the main sanctuary gleamed with gold. The congregation Herr Hessemann belonged to was a wealthy one.

Ben hung his coat in an alcove and took a seat towards the front with the rest of the men. According to custom, the women sat in a cordoned-off area to one side. Casually, Ben studied the congregation. There were no *Ostjuden*, just well-dressed German Jews, and Ben could feel their curiosity; strangers were always an object of attention.

The rabbi entered from a side door, flashing a practiced smile at the congregation as he took his seat on the *bimah*, an elevated platform that could be seen from anywhere in the hall. Thick reading glasses gave him a professorial cast, an image that he obviously relished and enhanced with a tweedy three-piece suit.

Immediately after the cantor concluded the *shachrit* service and the holy Torah was returned to the Ark, the rabbi stepped forward to deliver his sermon. He chose to discuss Pharaoh's dream of the seven lean cows who ate the seven fat ones, yet remained thin and bony. The rabbi declared in stentorious tones that Joseph's interpretation of the dream as abundance followed by famine was a perfect metaphor for the Jews of Germany. Stroking his neatly trimmed beard and absently readjusting his glasses as he lectured, the rabbi told his congregation they had an obligation as German citizens to help rebuild the shattered German nation, just as Joseph had helped Pharaoh.

"Though these may be difficult years for Jews, we must persevere and honor our duty. The lean years will eventually pass, and prosperity will return again." On that note, the rabbi cleared his throat and stepped down from the pulpit. The theme of the sermon was one that Ben had heard before; it struck the same note of passive acceptance Ben had heard so often in Dorpat.

At the end of the service, the rabbi stood by the door to greet his congregation as everyone filed out. Ben was near the end of the line, just ahead of the Hessemann family, and he could feel Jacob Hessemann's presence behind him. He was sorely tempted to confront the man right in front of the rabbi, imagining himself turning to Hessemann with a tight smile, and saying, "Hello, I'm Benjamin Isaacson, the man you had thrown off your steps for ringing a bell on the Sabbath." In the end, his sense of propriety triumphed over temptation, and he said nothing. Instead, he kept his gaze fixed on the rabbi, who greeted and disposed of his congregants with remarkable speed. When Ben's turn arrived, he reached out and shook the older man's hand firmly; the rabbi's grip was surprisingly strong. There was a pause as he studied Ben carefully.

"You don't look familiar to me. What is your name?"

"Benjamin Isaacson. I am Swedish."

"Well, Mr. Isaacson, I am Rabbi Bromberg," he smiled. "I hope you enjoyed the service."

"I found the sermon . . . interesting." Ben hesitated, then decided to plunge right in. "In all honesty, I feel there might be another way to interpret the story of Joseph and Pharaoh's dream."

"Really? Perhaps you'd like to join us for the Talmud class after prayers this afternoon. We could discuss it then."

"I would," Ben replied. He always relished a good debate. Bromberg told him to come around three in the afternoon, then turned away to greet the Hessemanns. Ben considered waiting for Hessemann outside the synagogue to introduce himself, but he decided to wait. Given Hessemann's extreme piety, it was a sure bet he belonged to the Talmud class. "That's where we'll get to know each other," Ben promised himself.

When Ben returned to the synagogue that afternoon he found a group of men that included Jacob Hessemann already gathered around a polished oak refectory table. Ben noted the old rule held—wherever Jews assembled, one's status was determined by one's proximity to the rabbi. It didn't surprise him to see Herr Hessemann seated close to Rabbi Bromberg. Ben murmured a greeting to the group, then pulled up a chair near Hessemann.

The rabbi opened the class by introducing Ben and repeating the gist of his sermon to refresh everyone's memory. When he finished, he gestured towards Ben.

"Mr. Isaacson would like to commence our discussion this afternoon by expanding on the topic of my sermon." Bromberg sat back and crossed his arms to listen, like a professor about to hear a student dissertation.

"I believe that one could interpret the story of Joseph in a radically different way," Ben began. Bromberg pulled his glasses down and gave Ben a sharp look over the lenses. As Ben returned the stare, he noticed Bromberg's glasses were bifocals. The irreverent thought occurred to him that bifocals were appropriate, providing the good rabbi with one view up towards God and another one down on the congregation.

"You disagree with my interpretation?" Bromberg was less than pleased, having assumed that Ben would merely be adding gloss to his own commentary.

Ben smiled disarmingly. "As you said, Rabbi, for Joseph, Pharaoh's dream was a warning of impending disaster. And I agree that the dream still has relevance today, but not as a mandate for Jews to rebuild Germany. I see it as a call to action, but action of a very different kind." Ben turned to the group. "The message is a simple one: prepare for the future while you can. The pogroms in the east and the outbreaks of anti-Semitism you've all seen are no dream; they're real. As the seven lean cows devoured the seven fat ones, so will we Jews be devoured by those starving around us. Pharaoh could not afford to be complacent. Neither can we. Now is the time to muster our strength and secure a place where we will be safe; a place that God has already set aside for us." Ben paused for dramatic effect. "The land of Palestine."

Several men at the table looked eager to comment, but before they could speak, Rabbi Bromberg quashed the discussion with a gruff "thank you" and an abrupt change of subject. There would be no talk of Zionism in his synagogue. Out of deference to him, no one brought up the subject of Palestine again.

The class ended with evening prayers. Bromberg shook hands with everyone, gave Ben a cursory nod, then left. Some of the men followed him out, but most remained behind, forming a circle around Ben. They asked the usual questions—where was he from, were there many Jews in Sweden, what was it like for Jews in Sweden. Then they turned to the subject of Zionism.

"Despite the good rabbi's views, I have donated quite a bit of money to the Zionist cause," remarked a lawyer addressed as Rechts-Anwalter. "But I don't put much faith in it. Politically and economically, I find the entire concept of a Jewish homeland in Palestine is badly flawed. We Jews must learn to survive wherever we find ourselves. This is what we have always done."

"The future can be different," Ben replied. "God set aside Palestine as. . . ."

"Come now, Mr. Isaacson," Rechts-Anwalter scoffed. "Palestine is a politicial issue, not a religious one. God's instructions to Abraham were meant for Abraham. I really don't see how they can be applied to us, thousands of years later."

"The laws God gave to Moses were not just meant for Moses," Ben riposted.

"I am not one to dispute the Word of God," Rechts-Anwalter said with a self-deprecating smile. "But it seems to me that if God wants us to return to Zion, he'll let us know just when to start packing." A ripple of laughter ran through the group.

"German Jews have been persecuted since the time of Martin Luther," Ben pointed out. "What more of a sign do you need?"

"We've always dealt with hatred," one of the men explained with a shrug. "And Palestine is hardly the land of milk and honey. The Arabs hate us more than the Germans do."

"True," Ben admitted. "But there's a reason why we are treated like outsiders wherever we go; we don't belong. Sweden is not my home, nor is Germany yours, Our destiny as a people lies in Palestine, but we must make it a reality for ourselves, just as Abraham did."

"Very eloquent, but I've heard enough claptrap about Palestine to last me a hundred lifetimes," griped an elderly man with a bushy white beard. "We are German citizens and we like our lives here. We are comfortable. Our futures are here. If the Poles and Litvaks who have no future want to go traipsing off to the wilds of the Levant, let them do it. They have nowhere else to go. We have worked hard to build what we have, so our children could enjoy the fruits of our labors. We have no need of Palestine."

"Do you really believe that the Germans will ever accept you as equals? Or will treat you as being any different from the most illiterate *Ostjude* who's spent less than twenty-four hours on German soil?" There was an edge to Ben's voice.

"We ask only to be left alone," the old man replied stubbornly.

"They'll never leave you alone," Ben snapped back.

"Look, Benjamin," Rechts-Anwalter laughed easily. "You're a convincing speaker and a fine young man, but you have to look at things from our point of view. We have roots here, strong roots. We have to be practical."

"Then be practical!" Ben urged. "The greatest threat facing Jews today . . ."

"I would like to talk further, but I really must be going now," Rechts-Anwalter smiled pleasantly. "Perhaps another time."

The group began to break up, leaving Ben feeling frustrated and deflated. As Ben prepared to leave, Hessemann came up to him. He had stood on the outside of the discussion group, listening but not participating in the debate. Ben had become so involved in the discussion that he'd quite forgotten about Jacob Hessemann.

"You made some very interesting comments about Joseph, Mr.

Isaacson. However, I am not certain about your particular interpretation." Hessemann gave him a patronizing smile and asked where Ben was staying.

"I'm staying with the Krechtsers, but I'm afraid I don't see much of them. They've been very kind, in spite of the fact that they're not very religious," Ben replied with a twist of sarcasm. Hessemann missed the irony of the remark, unaware that Ben was the *Ostjude* he had thrown off his property the previous evening.

"I agree," Hessemann replied self-righteously. "I'm sure that the company of such people could not be very stimulating to someone like yourself." He stopped to think for a minute. "Why don't you come to my home for dinner tomorrow night?" Not on the Sabbath, Ben mused.

"I'd be delighted," Ben answered. He couldn't have planned things any better.

"Good. I'll be looking forward to seeing you at five o'clock. It should be a most interesting evening." More interesting than you might imagine, Ben thought to himself as Hessemann turned to leave.

Although Ben had intended to leave Monday morning, he decided to let events run their course and spend a few extra days in Hamburg. The Krechtsers were delighted to have him stay. It didn't surprise Marta that Ben was having dinner with the Hessemanns.

"I had planned a big dinner for tomorow, but don't worry," she teased him, thinking his interest lay with Hessemann's daughter. "We'll have it on Monday, after your business is attended to."

"It's Herr Hessemann I'm going to see," Ben reddened involuntarily.

"Of course," Marta smiled. "Who else?"

Ben was mortified.

The following day, Ben dressed with great care. Taking his leave of the Krechtsers, he covered the half-mile to Elbchaussee in less than fifteen minutes. As he rang the doorbell, he half-hoped the maid would recognize him and try to throw him out again; it appealed to his sense of drama. But to his disappointment, the maid did not remember him. Blankly, she took his coat and hat as Frau Hessemann welcomed him.

Ben placed a yarmulke on the back of his head and followed her into the salon. As they walked in, Jacob Hessemann rose from the sofa to greet him, then introduced his two sons, Julius and Manfred. The boys shook Ben's hand limply, then took their seats without uttering a single word; Hessemann's wife disappeared into the kitchen.

"Please sit down, Mr. Isaacson." Hessemann motioned Ben to an overstuffed wing chair next to the fireplace and reseated himself on the sofa.

"I'm delighted you could come," Hessemann smiled expansively. "Tea?" As if on cue, the maid served steaming cups of tea with lemon wedges and a crystal pot of raspberry preserves to use as a sweetener.

They talked for a while and Ben explained he planned to spend some time in Berlin visiting his cousin Herschel, a doctor at Berlin University Hospital, then emigrate to Palestine. Ben made several attempts to involve Julius and Manfred in the conversation, but Hessemann's sons limited their responses to monosyllables and kept their gazes riveted to the floor. It was almost as though Ben and Hessemann were in the room alone.

Suddenly, Hessemann placed his cup on a side table and sat back, clasping his hands together. Ben could almost see the wheels turning behind the small black eyes.

"Tell, me, were you bar mitzvahed?" The question was so unexpected that Ben burned his upper lip on the hot tea. It was a question one usually reserved for potential suitors.

"Both my parents were conscientious Jews, and I was given a thorough education," Ben grimaced, rubbing his lip. "That included a bar mitzvah."

"And your family is Swedish on both sides?" There was a hopeful tone in Hessemann's voice and Ben wondered what he was driving at.

"My father was born in Sweden, but my mother is Estonian."

Ben's host paused for a moment, an involuntary expression of distaste flickering across his face. Estonia was part of Russia, and like most German Jews, Herr Hessemann had an instinctive abhorrence of anything from the "barbarian" east.

"But you and your father are actually Swedish?" Ben felt that he was being "qualified." For what, he wasn't sure.

"That's right," Ben replied with a broad grin. He decided to enjoy the interrogation. "But my father's father was Estonian, like my mother."

Without realizing it, Hessemann let out a sign of relief. "But you're really a Swede, not an Estonian," he said heartily. "That's good, very good. More tea?" Ben shook his head negatively. "You seem to be very well off—has your family been successful in business, or are they professional people?"

Ben answered perfunctorily, growing irritated with Hessemann's prying. Several times, he tried to steer the conversation, but Hessemann never gave him the opportunity to do anything but answer questions. Just as Ben was beginning to doubt he would ever get a chance to bring up Friday night's incident without being rude, Frau Hessemann interrupted her husband's interrogation with a question of her own. Ben took advantage of the interlude to use their facilities.

On his way back from the bathroom, Ben heard a peculiar noise behind the closed kitchen door. Quietly, he pushed it open and looked inside.

A young girl of sixteen or seventeen sat on the floor, trying to spoonfeed stewed chicken to a small gray cat. She was attractive, with short, dark hair and delicate hands. She wore a pleated skirt and a white cotton blouse monogrammed with the initials *S.H.* Even though her clothes were square-cut, they did not entirely conceal her lovely figure. Ben suddenly realized why Marta Krechtser had presumed his interest lay in Sarah Hessemann, not her father.

"What's wrong with you?" Sarah scowled with furious impatience, unaware she was no longer alone. The cat licked one of its paws regally, ignoring the food. Tears of frustration ran down the girl's cheeks.

"Why don't you pour a little milk on it?" Ben suggested. "That will moisten it."

She scooped the cat into her arms and scrambled to her feet, startled by his sudden appearance. It took her a minute to find her voice.

"We can't mix milk with meat! The food is kosher!" Sarah was shocked at the impropriety of his advice. She looked down and nervously smoothed the wrinkles out of her skirt. "Don't you know that's a sin?"

"For a cat?"

"Of course. Kosher is kosher." She put the cat down and it scurried into the next room. "This is a strictly kosher household, and my father would never tolerate anything that is not kosher, including Katzele."

Ben smiled. "When Moses explained 'kosher' to our people, I don't remember him mentioning anything about cats having to be kosher."

"My father says that observing the dietary laws of *kashrus* is the most important thing we can do as Jews. Everything in our house must be kosher. We even have kosher candles and shoe polish."

"Kosher candles and shoe polish?" Ben tried not to laugh. "Why do they have to be kosher? You don't eat them, do you?"

"Of course not," Sarah giggled.

"Then what's the difference?"

She thought seriously. "I'm not sure."

"There isn't any difference," Ben whispered secretively.

"But that wouldn't make sense."

"Of course it doesn't make sense. It's all nonsense." They looked at each other and burst out laughing. There was something about Sarah Hessemann that Ben found enormously engaging.

"But father told me," she still looked doubtful. "Are you completely certain?"

"As certain as I am that your initials are *S.H.*"

"How did you know my initials were *S.H.*?" Her dark eyes sparkled. Ben pointed to the monogram and the girl blushed deeply.

"I am so foolish," she said shyly. "Of course you saw my monogram." Ben introduced himself and she confirmed what he'd already guessed—that she was Jacob Hessemann's only daughter, Sarah.

"Are you going to be a rabbi?" she asked.

"No. I'm just travelling through on my way to the International Zionist Federation in Berlin."

"Oh, a Zionist!" She looked ready to pounce on him. "Then you can help me! You must help me! Can you get me into a *hakhsharah*?" A *hakhsharah* was an agricultural training camp for young people on their way to Palestine.

Ben gaped at her, overwhelmed by the sudden transformation. He hardly expected the shy daughter of an orthodox German burgher like Hessemann to even know what *hakhsharah* was, let alone want to join one.

Sara took a deep breath, as though her entire life hung in the balance of what she was about to say. "If I don't leave this house, I'll die. My father is so religious that my life is unbearable. He doesn't just do what God has told the Jews they must do, he makes things up to prove to God that he's more worthy than the next Jew. He makes us recite things and do things that send my friends laughing. I can't go out. I can't have parties or wear makeup or anything. I won't even be able to go to the university."

"Sarah, please. . . ." Ben was embarrassed by her passionate outburst. He tried to say something, but her words kept pouring out in a confused tumble, as though a dam had been breached.

"I've got to get out of here. My mother does everything my father tells her to. She doesn't even have a mind of her own. If he has his way, I'll be married next year to some fat old poop I've never seen before. I'll do anything to keep him from marrying me off to some religious fanatic like himself."

She paused to catch her breath, looking around to make sure no one was listening.

"Please help me to get to a *hakhsharah*," she pleaded. "They have a religious Zionist camp outside of Fulda and if I could just get there, I'd have a chance to live my own life. Please help me, Benjamin. You are a Zionist, a man with a purpose. You understand. Won't you help me? Please?"

"Sarah, we don't even know each other." The intensity of her expression made him feel distinctly uncomfortable.

"Please, Benjamin. There's no one else who can help me."

"I'm a guest in your father's home. It would be improper for me to interfere in a family matter." He winced at the hollow ring of his excuses. She looked so desperately unhappy, he felt guilty for not helping her.

"You're just like everyone else," Sarah blurted out.

"There's nothing I can do," Ben replied stiffly. Her accusation annoyed him. "Besides, the last thing I need is to be saddled with a sixteen-year-old runaway."

"I'm seventeen, not sixteen, and I . . ."

They were interrupted when the door opened and Jacob Hessemann appeared. Sarah looked away sheepishly and excused herself from the room.

"I see that you met my little Sarah," Hessemann said proudly. "She's very skilled and devout, not like most of the young girls one sees today." To Ben's surprise, Hessemann was not at all upset; most orthodox fathers who found their daughters alone with an unmarried man even for a minute would have been furious. Then Ben recalled Hessemann's careful appraisal of his clothes and bearing at the synagogue the previous day. And the questions about his family and background. With a shudder, Ben realized that Herr Hessemann was considering him as a prospective son-in-law.

"Sarah is quite charming, don't you agree?" Hessemann prompted. "She'd make a fine wife for a good man." Ben had to suppress a laugh at the clumsy attempt to manipulate him.

"Yes, Sarah is very charming. We were just discussing Zionism." Ben wondered if Hessemann would be as pleased with his daughter if he knew what she really thought.

"Zionism? With Sarah?" Hessemann raised an eyebrow. "How strange. I am curious about your enthusiasm for the subject. Perhaps we can discuss it at dinner." With a sweeping motion he indicated they should proceed to the dining room. He intended the gesture to be courtly, but the effect was comical—like a head waiter who'd had too much to drink.

Once they were seated around the table, Herr Hessemann dominated the conversation. His sons never spoke and Frau Hessemann limited herself to whispering an endless stream of instructions to the maid. Sarah kept stealing looks at Ben; she was the only member of the Hessemann family with any animation or spontaneity.

"So tell me," Hessemann boomed from his seat at the head of the table. "How did your grandfather come to live in Sweden. That's most uncommon for an *Ost* . . . ah, I mean Russian Jew . . . ah . . . a Jew from Russia. Most unusual. Not that he was Russian, but. . . ." Hessemann stammered, embarrassed by his inadvertent reference to what he viewed as a blemish on Ben's family background.

"I understand what you mean," Ben cut in after he let Hessemann flounder. "Actually, it's rather an interesting story."

"Please tell us!" Sarah exclaimed. Her father turned to her in surprise, then rebuked her with a stilted homily on proper manners; women did not speak at his table, unless it was to the maid. Watching him lecture Sarah, Ben suddenly understood why ringing a bell on the Sabbath was more important to Jacob Hessemann than someone who might be starving to death on his doorstep. Hessemann was concerned about appearances; nothing else had any real meaning. He was incapable of relating his religious beliefs to other people; other people served only as witness to his own piety. It was not difficult to see where Sarah's frustration came from.

"As I told you, my grandfather came from Estonia," Ben repeated when Hessemann finished with Sarah. Ben was pleased to see Hessemann wince slightly when he accented the word 'Estonia.' "My grandfather was not a rich man, but he loved life, especially his wife and six daughters."

"Six daughters!" Sarah was amazed.

"Sarah!" This time her mother spoke, and her father contented himself with a disapproving glare. Sarah's impassioned outburst in the kitchen no longer surprised Ben; it showed she had spunk and a mind of her own. Considering who her parents were, it was a wonder she had any personality at all.

"I apologize for the interruption, Mr. Isaacson," Hessemann glowered. "I hope it won't happen again."

"Anyway," Ben resumed, "my grandfather had everything he desired except a son to carry on the family name. He had resigned himself to being the last of the Isaacsons until one morning when he woke everyone early and announced that he'd had a vision. According to the vision, he would have a son, but only if he left Estonia. Therefore, the family was immigrating to America. He would go first, then send for his wife and daughters. Naturally, they all thought he was demented."

Sarah could not help but giggle, and Ben grinned in response. The

Hessemanns sighed in despair as Ben continued. "He was so sure of himself that he went straightaway to the nearest dock and jumped aboard the first available ship. It happened to be bound for Sweden, but that didn't bother him. He planned on taking a ship from Sweden to America."

"I didn't realize that Jews were allowed to travel so freely in the east, especially in those days," Hessemann said disdainfully. What he actually meant by "Jews" was *Ostjuden*.

"You're quite right," Ben admitted, letting the slur pass without comment. "My grandfather couldn't get proper papers, so he had to outwit the authorities. He cut the imperial eagles off an official government envelope and pasted them together with some printed Russian text on two pieces of hinged cardboard. Most of the police and border guards were completely illiterate, but they knew what those eagles meant, so they permitted him to leave without interference." Hessemann harumphed into his napkin, as though such deception was immoral, and Sarah covered her face to keep from laughing. Julius and Manfred kept eating as though they hadn't heard a word.

Ben finished his story, relating how the boat landed in Stockholm and his grandfather began by fixing gas meters, then became involved in manufacturing them. "He brought his family to Sweden, had two sons within three years, made a fortune, and lived happily ever after."

"But I thought you said he was bound for America," Sarah said. "Why did he stay in Sweden?"

"Sarele, you are impossible," her father shouted. He threw his napkin down. "Benjamin already explained how his grandfather went into business."

"It's all right, Herr Hessemann. Sarah is right. My grandfather did not happen to stay in Sweden because of business." Ben relished the opportunity to deflect Hessemann's anger away from Sarah. "As I mentioned, my grandfather had six daughters. Like any good father, his gratest fear was that one of his daughters might marry a non-Jew. With six to worry about, my grandfather felt particularly vulnerable. While waiting in Stockholm for a ship to America, my grandfather discovered that intermarriage was allowed in the United States but not in Sweden. In Sweden, it was illegal for a Jew to marry a Gentile. Grandfather felt that Swedish law gave his daughters an extra measure of protection, so he stayed, and every one of his daughters married another Jew."

"What a marvelous story!" Sarah clapped her hands with delight. She seemed so alive. Ben marveled how two people like the Hessemanns could produce so exquisite a creature as Sarah.

Hessemann glared at his daughter, ready to start lecturing again.

Unwilling to witness another scene, Ben distracted Sarah's father by plunging into a dissertation on the subject of Zionism. Hessemann vented his annoyance by excusing Sarah and the two boys from the table.

Trapped at the table by Ben, who continued to extoll the advantages of a life in Palestine, Hessemann twisted and squirmed uncomfortably. He made polite sounds of acknowledgment from time to time, but Ben could see that his attention was wandering. Motivated partly out of sympathy for Sarah, and partly by a malicious desire to snap Hessemann out of his disinterested complacency, Ben decided to bring up the subject of Sarah and the *hakhsharah*. She would probably never be allowed to speak long enough to do it herself.

Casually, he suggested that Sarah seemed like an exceptionally pious young woman who might benefit greatly by fulfilling God's divine commandment to settle in the Holy Land. He was careful to phrase his conversation in the orthodox platitudes he knew would appeal to her father. Herr Hessemann stared into space, nodding politely, unaware of what Ben was leading up to. Frau Hessemann beamed and Ben realized she was misreading his intentions. She assumed he meant Sarah would make a fine wife for a man bound for Palestine; a man such as himself. It was time to put an end to that misconception, he decided.

"Have you considered enrolling Sarah in a *hakhsharah*?" Ben asked offhandedly. Hessemann's gaze shifted to Ben's eyes. For a moment, Ben thought that he hadn't been heard, and was about to repeat himself, but Hessemann spoke first.

"Why would you suggest a thing like that?" Hessemann's expression was neutral, so Ben continued.

"I honestly think that a girl like Sarah would benefit greatly from the experience and—"

"How dare you say such a thing!" Hessemann shouted and jumped to his feet. "My daughter is not that kind of girl and I will hear no more about this!"

"Don't you think that's a bit narrowminded? After all, a *hakhsharah* is a place. . . ."

"Of sin and immorality," Hessemann sputtered. "I wasn't born yesterday, young man. I know what those 'agricultural communes' are like—young boys and girls sleeping together and doing God knows what else! It's revolting!" Poor Frau Hessemann became so upset she developed a case of the hiccups.

"Herr Hessemann . . . ," Ben tried again.

"I think we have discussed this matter enough," Hessemann cut him off rudely. His wife hiccupped in the background, trying to conceal her dismay and her breach of decorum behind a napkin. "If you want to know more about the *hakhsharah*, perhaps you should speak to Rabbi Bromberg. I'm sure he'll enlighten you. Good evening." Dinner was obviously over. Ben thanked his distraught hostess and left the table, finding his own way out.

On the way back to the Krechtsers, Ben literally shook with anger; he kicked an empty bottle in disgust. The entire evening had gone haywire. He had become so involved in Sarah's problem that he had lost the opportunity to mention Friday night. "Not that it would have made any impression on Herr Hessemann if I had," Ben muttered aloud.

When he arrived at the Krechtsers, Marta greeted him with a broad grin and told him that someone was waiting for him in the parlor. To his surprise, Sarah sat on the edge of the couch.

"What are you doing here?"

"Mama wanted me to give you this." She held up a small brown paper bag.

"How did you get here before I did?" Ben asked as he opened the bag. The delicious aroma of cinnamon and caramel filled the air—Frau Hessemann had sent pastries.

"I know all the back ways," she smiled. Her cheeks were flushed crimson from the cold. "Mama felt awful that Father got so angry. She made him promise to apologize the next time he sees you." Frau Hessemann evidently considered Ben too good a potential suitor to risk losing, despite his head-on collision with her husband. Ben and Sarah stared at each other in silence.

"I'm sorry I was rude to you in the kitchen," Sarah looked down. "You're not really like the others."

"Thanks."

"Then you're not angry with me?"

"Of course not."

"And you'll help me get to a *hakhsharah*?" Her gaze was steady and unflinching; he had trouble meeting it. "Will you help me?" she asked again.

He sympathized with her, but didn't want to commit himself, so he sidestepped her question. "Where would you go?" he kept his voice low, so Marta would not hear them.

"Fulda—the camp I told you about. I'll walk there if I have to. I'll steal my mother's bread and walk." Ben pointed out that she'd freeze to death halfway there. She tossed her head defiantly.

"If I do, then it's God's will. But I'm going, whether you help me or not."

"What about your parents?"

"Mama doesn't need me and once I've left, Father will never want to see me again," she said with a trace of sadness. Ben found himself being led down a path.

"You're asking me to break the law. You're not even eighteen yet."

"You're a Zionist, aren't you?"

"That has nothing to do with running away from home."

"Zionists break the law all the time. They scheme and plot and deceive the police every day. Otherwise, how could they get Jews past the British blockade? Just think of me as another settler who needs to be smuggled." Her expression was full of mischief. Ben's resistance finally collapsed and he asked her if there was a safe time they could meet.

"I knew it!" she shrieked with delight. "I knew you would help me!"

"For God's sake," Ben whispered fiercely. "Why don't you just shout it in the streets." Sarah covered her mouth with her hands.

They agreed to meet at noon the next day. Sarah's mother and father would be gone, and the maid had the day off. Her brothers would be busy at *cheder*.

"Just remember, I'm not promising anything," Ben warned her.

"Oh, thank you, Ben! Thank you!" Before he could stop her, she threw her arms around him in a bear hug.

"Don't thank me just yet, and don't get so excited," Ben cautioned as he broke away from her. "Nothing may come of it. I just want to think about it." Though he still refused to give a yes or a no, she knew he would help her.

"Whatever you say, Ben," she replied demurely.

After she left, Ben sat in the living room, munching the pastries that her mother had sent. He empathized with her situation, but aiding her would complicate his plans. It would take time, and it was no small responsibility, especially if Hessemann involved the police. In truth, he hardly knew Sarah and already she was clinging to him, looking to him for all the answers. But she was sincere, he reminded himself, and he had decided to spend a few extra days in Germany anyway. Besides, if the camp was near Fulda, he could visit Michel Zadek as well as help Sarah. He made up his mind: he would help Sarah get to a *hakhsharah*. It was the right thing to do, he told himself. Pleased with his decision, he got ready for bed, imagining the delight in Sarah's face when he gave her the news.

As Ben slipped beneath the covers, a disturbing thought occurred to him. The feel of Sarah's body pressed against him had lingered long after she had gone and he remembered the strength of her embrace. He fell asleep reassuring himself that his interest in Sarah amounted to nothing beyond one Zionist helping another.

Having made the decision to help Sarah, Ben was anxious to set his plans in motion. At breakfast the next morning, he told the Krechtsers that he would leave for Berlin that evening. With difficulty, he dissuaded them from accompanying him to the station.

He and Marta spent the morning engaged in small talk and Ben was grateful that she made no mention of Sarah. After an eternity, the hall clock chimed eleven forty-five, and Ben excused himself on the pretext of doing a little last-minute sightseeing.

"The exercise will be good for you," Marta smiled. He felt guilty about not telling her what he was planning, but it was better she stayed in the dark about his intentions. He didn't know her well enough to gamble. Though she disliked Hessemann, she might feel it was her duty to warn him that his daughter was about to run away.

Ben covered the distance to Elbchaussee in record time, arriving breathless. As he reached for the bell, Sarah startled him by jerking the door open. Before she could say a word, he stepped into the vestibule and raised a finger to his lips. Her eyes shone with the glow of a born conspirator.

Step by step, he explained the plan as Sarah listened calmly, stroking Katzele. Unconsciously, Ben kept looking out the window, as though he expected the entire neighborhood to come flying out of their houses in shocked indignation at what he was about to do. When he finished, he made Sarah repeat the instructions back to him.

"I am to be on the platform for the Berlin Express, which departs at exactly 6:35 tonight. I am to wear a good dress and a heavy coat. I should cover my head with a scarf and speak to no one."

"And?"

"I'm not supposed to bring any suitcases or bags with me, nothing that would draw attention."

"Perfect," Ben complimented her. "Most of the clothes you have would probably be inappropriate for the *hakhsharah* anyway. I'll pick up some things for you before we leave, or we'll get them in Berlin."

"But I haven't any money to buy clothes."

"Don't worry about that. Just remember—when you get to the station, ask the station master for the track number. Don't forget: the Hamburg–Berlin Express. And whatever happens, don't leave the area. Any questions?"

"No," she replied quickly. "Katzele and I will be waiting for you."

"Katzele!" Ben exploded.

"I can't leave her here . . ."

"I'm sorry, Sarah, it's out of the question. Absolutely impossible. We've got enough problems as it is."

"But . . . ," Sarah's voice was full of misery.

"If you want my help, the cat stays here," Ben said with finality. "Besides, what would she eat? How would she void herself on the train? What would you do with her at the *hakhsharah*?" Sarah remained silent.

"Then it's all settled," he said, glad to have the issue resolved. He leaned forward and kissed her on the forehead. "Trust me, Katzele will be far better off here in Altona."

"Okay," Sarah whispered. He squeezed her arm, then checked the street and let himself out.

She watched him jog up the street and disappear around a corner. Shivering with the cold and anticipation of the adventure about to begin, she held Katzele close to her and climbed the stairs to her room.

SIX

The Hamburg-Berlin Express
Monday, December 29, 1924
6:15 PM

Ben hurried down the Krechtsers' front steps to the waiting cab and threw his bags onto the forward seat. He waved to Marta and Johann one last time, then climbed into the open carriage and covered his legs with a blanket. The leather seat was stiff from the cold. With a flick of his switch, the driver set the horse in motion.

As the carriage wound through the streets of Altona, it occurred to Ben that he was insane to have involved himself with a seventeen-year-old girl. What had he been thinking of when he agreed to help Sarah Hessemann run away from her parents? He must have lost his mind. One of his bags bounced off the opposite seat.

"Damn it!" he growled, lunging for the case. Angrily he wedged it in a corner and returned to his thoughts. Sarah had probably forgotten the instructions he had given her and ended up at the wrong railroad station. Or her father wrung a confession from her and locked her in a bedroom. Or any one of a hundred other unpleasant possibilities. Ben was suddenly aware of the sweat running down the sides of his rib cage, despite the intense cold.

The ancient carriage swung dangerously as its wooden wheels caught in the icy ruts scoring the streets. Ben's case tumbled out of the corner again, and he had to brace his legs to avoid being pitched forward.

"A thousand cabs in Hamburg and I end up with a one-horse *droske*" he muttered. "*Kutcher!*" he shouted, using the Yiddish word for driver. "What's the matter with you? You're going to kill us both!" As if to emphasize his point, the *droske* bounced onto a smooth stretch of pavement with a bone-jarring leap, then skidded and shuddered as the wheels hit another patch of ice-covered cobblestones.

"*Kutcher!!*"

The driver finally responded by reining the swaybacked mare to a fast walk. She wheezed between the traces like an old bellows.

"Sorry," the driver mumbled in a thick Polish accent. "My mind is on other things."

"So is mine," Ben snapped. If Hessemann discovered their plans, would he call the police?

"They let the maniac out, you know." The driver turned. His face was a bright cherry red, broken by coarse white stubble, and his hooded eyes watered continuously. He ran a sleeve across his nose and sniffled. To Ben's dismay, the old mare was left to pick her own way.

"What maniac?" Ben humored the driver, trying to keep his eyes on the road. He was fearful the horse might bolt or run over a pedestrian.

"I'll tell you what maniac," the driver spat. "Adolf Hitler, that's what maniac." He jabbed the air with his switch for emphasis. For the next five minutes, Ben was subjected to a full-blown biography of the obscure Bavarian politician. The driver kept repeating that Hitler's Nazi Party posed an enormous threat to Jews everywhere.

Swathed in scarves, the driver's face had the appearance of an unformed ball of putty, barely shaped by an artist's hand. Though he had to be the better part of fifty, none of his features was clearly defined, except for the liver-colored lips, which twisted furiously as he spoke. They looked like a scarred gash on his unlined face. He suddenly stopped in mid-sentence when he realized that Ben was watching the road ahead, not listening to him.

"Don't worry about the horse. She knows her way." The driver was anxious to regain Ben's attention. "Did you hear what I said? Do you know who Adolf Hitler is?"

"I've heard of him." Ben had read somewhere about Hitler's attempt to take over the Bavarian government during the previous year and vaguely recalled he had been arrested. It was nothing of consequence; strictly a local matter. Ben had never given it a second thought.

"Do you realize he's free?" the driver's voice was bitter. "Five years they gave him and he's out in one. You can bet you'll be hearing more from Adolf Hitler."

"Do you lecture all your fares? Or just the lucky ones?" Ben was growing annoyed with the driver's obsessive monologue.

The driver took no offense. "Just the Jewish ones."

"What makes you think I'm Jewish?"

"No gentile would stay with a Jewish family like the Krechtsers, even if they're not orthodox. That's the way it is in Germany today."

The driver's comment reminded Ben that the Jewish community in Hamburg was small and closely knit—if the driver knew the Krechtsers, then he probably knew the Hessemanns as well. Ben would have to avoid being seen with Sarah until the driver was gone. Silently, he willed the trip to be over. If something went wrong or she was late, every minute could be important. The driver broke in on his thoughts again.

"You don't seem very concerned."

"What?"

"Every Jew should be concerned," the driver exclaimed, gesturing angrily with his whip. He used it like a conductor would use a baton, each stroke conveying a message. "If that madman has his way, there won't be a Jew left in Europe." They were back to Adol Hitler again.

"I'm sure that it will take more than one man to drive the Jews out of Europe."

"You're right! That's the whole point. How do you think he got out of Landesberg Prison so quick? He has friends everywhere, and not just in Germany." Ben sighed, resigned to his fate as the *kutcher* railed against Hitler in exhausting detail: Hitler claimed the Jews betrayed Germany during the war; Hitler said there was a Jewish conspiracy to keep Germany in ruins; Hitler had sympathetic friends all over Europe.

"You seem well versed for a cab driver," Ben observed sarcastically. He was nearing the end of his patience. "Do you teach politics at the university in your spare time?"

"I wasn't always a *baal-aguleh*," the driver retorted. *Baal-agule* was a Hebrew phrase for a freight porter with a horse and cart. "Four years ago, I had a big fur business in Poland. Lots of friends. Money. A big house. Then Grabski came to power and started with his 'Jewish sanctions.' We all thought it would pass, just like all the other hard times. But it didn't. It got worse and worse. Then the riots started, may Grabski rot in hell." The driver was like a spring, being wound tighter and tighter.

"I lost the business first, then the house. They kept squeezing until we had nothing left but the clothes on our backs. I had two choices. I could use what little money we had left to get out and try to find work, or I could stay and watch my family starve to death in an unheated tenement room.

So now, I drive a *droske* in Hamburg and send money back to Poland so my family can eat.''

"Why didn't they come with you?"

"I waited too long to believe the truth. By then, there wasn't enough money to pay off the right people. I barely got out myself. If I can earn enough, I'll send for them and we'll emigrate someplace we can start over again. Maybe America.''

"America has its share of Grabskis," Ben replied, thinking of Henry Ford. The horse shied at a pedestrian and the driver turned to calm her.

"You don't have to believe me," the driver continued. "Ask around. Find out for yourself. The Nazis will make Grabski and his friends look like saints. If there is a devil, Adolf Hitler has a pact with him." The driver turned away.

Ben was about to argue with him, but he stopped himself. What was the use? The man was lonely and separated from his family; his obsession with Adolf Hitler was probably just a way of keeping his mind occupied. It was best to leave him alone.

A moment later, they rounded the last corner, and Hamburg Station rose in front of them like a gigantic gray stone and glass behemoth. The station was brightly lit and the streets were jammed with traffic. Horse-drawn carts and wagons vied with cars and taxis for curb space. Drivers swore in frustration and pedestrians darted in and out of traffic.

Streams of heavily bundled people made their way to the main doors carrying suitcases, dragging trunks, or clutching parcels wrapped in brown butcher's paper and tied with string. Skillfully, the coachman maneuvered the *droske* towards the front entrance. Ben felt a tremendous sense of excitement. His next stop would be Zionist headquarters in Berlin.

"You mustn't forget what I told you," The driver shouted over his shoulder.

"Of course not," Ben replied absently. His deep blue eyes flashed with impatience as he scanned the crush in front of the station, trying to catch a glimpse of Sarah.

The cab slid to a halt in front of the station's main entrance, and Ben leapt out. He intended to pay the driver and carry his own bags, but the driver was too quick. Before Ben could stop him, he grabbed the suitcases from the *droske*.

"You don't need to see me to the train," Ben protested. "I'd prefer to carry my own bags." All he wanted to do was get rid of the driver and find Sarah.

"I insist," the driver replied stubbornly.

"What about the *droske*?"

"It won't go anywhere. Besides, now we'll have a few more minutes to talk." He was already halfway to the station entrance. Outmaneuvered, Ben resigned himself to the driver's company. All the way to the platform, the driver jabbered about Adolf Hitler and his Nazis. Ben started to worry; if anyone who knew the Hessemanns saw Ben and Sarah together, there was bound to be trouble. He hoped that Sarah would have the wit to disappear if she saw him with the talkative driver. A scene in the station could mean the end of Sarah's freedom, and if the authorities got involved, of Ben's as well.

The Berlin Express platform was mobbed and Sarah was nowhere in sight. Perhaps she'd seen the driver and was waiting for him to leave? Ben tried to reclaim his bags but the driver asserted his right to carry Ben's luggage directly to the compartment. Ben breathed easier when he saw the seats were empty. The driver placed the luggage on the landing by the door and wiped his nose with a gloved hand.

"Thank you for everything," Ben smiled thinly, eager to be rid of him. He paid the driver in Swiss francs and included a generous tip. As he turned away, the cabbie grabbed his arm, the fingers pressing through Ben's thick coat. At first, Ben thought he was going to thank him for paying in foreign currency instead of worthless German marks, but instead, the driver was back to his predictions of doom.

"You think I'm just a foolish old man, but I know what I'm talking about. You listen to me. The black times are coming. For your own sake, remember what I've told you." His eyes burned with an inner torment, as though life had seared away everything inside, reducing his existence to a single purpose. Before Ben could reply, the cabbie turned and was gone.

Ben shuddered, relieved to be free of the depressing *kutcher* and stepped back onto the platform. Crowded at any time, Hamburg Station was a madhouse during the Christmas holidays. Thousands of people jammed the broad concourse. Ben scanned the crowd. The gothic clock suspended from the vaulted ceiling read 6:22, leaving him exactly thirteen minutes before the Berlin Express left the station.

The station's concave ceiling acted like an echo chamber for the clashing sounds rising from the platforms. Engines released jets of steam with earsplitting shrieks, vendors hawked sandwiches, fruit, and cold drinks and uniformed porters tried gamely to make headway through the dense crowd. The babble of a thousand conversations in a score of different languages made it impossible to hear anything. Sarah could be calling for him from ten feet away and he still might not hear her. He spun in a circle, hoping to catch sight of the girl.

A solid mass of humanity engulfed him, broken by islands of piled luggage and the parallel tracks separating the station platforms. The crowd was relatively well mannered and polite but blocked his line of vision. He pushed his way to the base of the platform, hoping she might be there.

Eight minutes to spare.

He searched the main walkway in a frenzy, bobbing and weaving through the mêlée. Twice he thought he had found her, only to mumble a quick apology when a young girl turned to reveal a stranger's face. Again and again, he jumped up on his toes to see over the packed multitude.

"Where is she?" he muttered, glancing at the clock again. Six twenty-nine. Six minutes to find Sarah and board the train.

He dashed from one platform to the next, ignoring the shocked exclamations as he elbowed people out of his way. If Sarah didn't appear within the next few minutes, he would have to leave without her. He felt a momentary twinge of relief; she was not a responsibility he really wanted. If he were free of her through no fault of his own, so much the better. He considered giving up the search and boarding, but the thought of Sarah facing Jacob Hessemann's wrath alone filled him with guilt and dismay. In Hessemann's ignorance, he was capable of anything. Ben pushed through the crowd until he caught sight of a conductor's blue uniform.

"Can you help me?" Ben shouted.

The conductor looked up from his clipboard. "I am busy."

Ben had to yell to make himself heard over the noise. "I'm sorry to disturb you, but I'm trying to find a seventeen-year-old girl who was to meet me here for the Berlin Express. She's about three inches shorter than I am. She has black hair just covering her collar and—"

"*Nein, Mein herr.*" The conductor cut Ben off with an annoyed wave of his hand. "I have seen no one of that description. Consult the station master. Perhaps she left a message with him." Rudely, he turned back to his clipboard.

Ben stifled a nasty remark; he didn't have the time to waste. A faint shout announced the departure of the Berlin Express. Ben spun and saw the train slowly edging away from the platform. Muttering apologies to people he jostled out of the way, Ben dodged through the milling crowd and ran towards his coach.

Reaching the entrance to his car, Ben leapt onto the narrow running board. The train was moving just fast enough to throw him off balance, and it took a moment to regain his equilibrium. He was about to climb in when the door slammed shut in his face.

Through the window, Ben saw no one; the angle of the corridor blocked his view. The train was still moving slow enough for him to jump off, but he was determined not to be left behind. He tightened his grip on the handrail and wedged his feet securely on the short, narrow step-up to the carriage door. He tried forcing the door. It refused to move. He heard people shouting for him to let go.

The train gathered momentum.

"Open the door!" he yelled. Someone had to be within earshot.

No one appeared.

An instant later, the Berlin Express cleared the station and Ben was immersed in freezing blackness. Swaying heavily on the uneven tracks, the train built up to a full head of steam, threatening to toss him from his fragile perch. With a sickening feeling in the pit of his stomach, Ben looked down at the snow-covered ground, reduced to a gray-white blur by the speed of the train. His ears burned from the cold. Helplessly, he clung to the handrail as the train left the suburbs of Hamburg behind; jumping was no longer an option.

As he peered through the glass, a middle-aged couple appeared in the passageway. Ben breathed a sigh of relief.

"Please open the door! *Bitte! Offnen sie die Tur!*" he yelled over the clatter of the carriage wheels. He gestured frantically at the interior handle, "It's stuck!"

They stared at him, then the man grabbed his wife's arm and propelled her through the car. Ben felt a shock wave ripple through his body. What were they doing? Where were they going? "They're going for help," he said out loud. "I must have frightened them and they've gone for help!" There could be no other explanation.

The wind sliced through Ben's woolen suit like a steel-edged razor. He cursed the impulse that made him pack his gloves in the suitcase—his hands were already stiff from the cold, and he was in serious danger of falling off. Unless he could warm his exposed fingers against his body they would freeze. Somehow, he would have to latch himself to the train.

He grasped the railing with one hand and struggled to remove his belt with the other. Panting from fear and exertion, he tried to thread the belt through the railing and around his back. He finally succeeded after a half-dozen frustrating attempts, wincing at the pain in his numbed fingers as he forced them to pull the belt taut and buckle it closed. Strapped to the train like a window washer to the side of a building, he whispered a prayer of thanks to the man who had cut the leather so thick and stout. He shifted his weight to relieve the aching in his legs and lower back; the pressure of his weight against the belt was beginning to reduce circulation to his lower body.

Ben concentrated on the empty passageway, willing someone to appear before he froze or lost his grip. After an eternity passed, the connecting door to the next carriage opened.

Two men and an elderly woman stepped into the car. The woman wore an expensive stole and one of the men sported a monocle. The woman was the first to see him and let out a startled cry, raising a gloved hand to her throat.

"For God's sake," Ben yelled, "open the door!"

All three gaped at him. Rime coated his hair. His face was dead white from the cold; his lips a deep shade of bluish purple. One of the men started forward, then stopped and pivoted, as though someone had called to him from the compartment adjoining Ben's.

"What are you waiting for?" Ben screamed.

Something was wrong.

The man nodded, then led his two companions down the corridor without looking at Ben again. Only the woman gave a brief, horrified glance backward.

"What the hell is the matter with you people?" Ben screamed to the empty corridor. He pounded on the window with his fists. Frantically, he racked his brain. Why wouldn't they help him? Did they think him a madman? An Anarchist? Were they afraid of him for some reason? What was it? Exhausted, he slumped against the rocking car.

It really doesn't matter, he thought grimly. He was on his own, and if he didn't keep his wits about him there was a good chance he would die. He closed his eyes for a moment and tried to regain his composure. If he could not shout his way into the car, he would have to break the glass.

Clenching his teeth to keep them from chattering, he leaned against the belt and reached down to remove one of his boots. As he did, the compartment light played across his hands. They looked shiny and wet. He held his palms up to the light and a wave of nausea passed through him. The flesh was ripped and torn. The cold had numbed his hands, deadening the nerves. He had been unable to feel the skin tearing on the loose screws protruding from the hand rail. Horrified but fascinated, he watched the drops of blood whipped off his hand by the freezing wind.

Seized by anger, Ben pulled off his right boot and slammed the heel against the compartment window again and again, screaming at the top of his lungs. The glass vibrated with the force of his blows, but refused to give way.

Ben continued his frenzied pounding until, at last, a conductor entered the carriage. He was dumbstruck by the sight of Ben outside the window.

"Open the door!" Ben cried, pointing to the inside latch with the heel of his boot. "Hurry!" Nearly thirty minutes had passed since the train left Hamburg Station. He could not hold on much longer. The conductor started towards the door.

Suddenly, a white-haired man appeared at the compartment door opposite Ben's and grabbed the conductor's arm. When the conductor tried to break away, the passenger tightened his grip, speaking rapidly.

The white-haired man was not tall, but he had an air of authority about him, despite the stained celluloid collar and threadbare suit. His face was deeply lined, etched by the force of buried anger. The eyes were a flat blue and very cold, set above protruding cheekbones that tapered down to a receding jaw. He could have been anywhere between forty and sixty.

When he released the conductor, he stared directly into Ben's eyes. Exaggerating his pronunciation so Ben would understand, he mouthed the word *Jude*.

Jew.

The white-haired man pointed to the gold pin Ben wore in his lapel. The Star of David Anschel had given him. To Ben's horror, the conductor smiled wanly and shrugged. Then he turned and walked off. The white-haired man reentered his compartment.

For the first time in his life, Ben realized he was capable of killing another human being without hesitation and without regret. Had he been able to reach through the glass, he would have strangled the white-haired man in a blind rage.

The train lurched, and for a moment, Ben had the sickening sensation that his belt had broken free. Frantically, he clutched at the handrail, tearing his hands again. His breath came in short, painful gasps. He caught a glimpse of himself, reflected in the window glass of the carriage door. What he saw was a ghostly caricature of himself—hair blown to the side, clothes askew, his face milk-white and distorted by the irregularities in the glass. It was like a vision from a nightmare.

But he wasn't dreaming.

Summoning the will, Ben bent down and put his shoe back on. His arms ached from holding his body upright against the train, and his legs felt like lead weights. He tried to flex his muscles to keep them functioning.

A piercing whistle split the air.

Vision blurred from the slipstream, Ben strained to see what lay ahead. Bright pinpoints of light seemed to dance in the clear air in front of the Berlin Express. He rubbed his eyes on the coarse wool of his coat, then turned forward again, squinting against the full force of the wind.

He hadn't imagined anything. There were lights ahead—the running lights of another train. The Berlin Express lost momentum as it slowed to pass a disabled train. Ben felt a surge of adrenaline course through his system as a plan formed in his mind. If the train slowed enough, he might be able to climb onto the roof, make his way back to the caboose, and climb down to safety.

He looked to his left. Faintly silhouetted against the compartment lights was a side ladder leading to the roof. In order to reach it, he would have to lean to the side as far as possible and then jump to reach the ladder. He tried to loosen up his cramped limbs.

Tentatively, Ben stretched towards the ladder, measuring the distance. It was farther then he thought. He turned and looked ahead. The Berlin Express was fast overtaking the other train.

"God damn them," he yelled in frustration. He thought quickly, reviewing his options. If he jumped and fell, he would probably freeze to death or break a leg in the fall. If he remained where he was, he would probably freeze to death unless someone let him in, and that didn't seem too likely. With the jump, there was at least a chance he could make it. He might not get another opportunity.

Not much of a choice.

He would try for the ladder. Tired and clumsy from the cold, he unbuckled the belt. It slipped from his fingers and disappeared. Now there was no going back. Without the belt, he wouldn't last another ten minutes.

He made a final attempt to concentrate. It would have to work the first time; there would be no second chance. His breath came in ragged gasps, the icy air burning his lungs. Painfully, he flexed his fingers and whispered a prayer for good luck.

He waited until the last possible moment, when the two trains were side by side. As the Berlin Express passed her disabled sister and began to pick up speed, Ben tensed for the jump. He took a deep breath, leaned back, and sprang towards the ladder.

His left hand connected with the upright support, sending jolts of agony up his arm as it took the full weight of his body. Twice his forehead struck the side of the carriage before his right hand found a grip. Hanging from a rung, his legs flailed helplessly over the void, pedaling against the side of the train until they connected with the bottom step of the ladder. Straining at every joint, he climbed to the coach roof.

He paused at the top and locked both arms around the ladder brace, trying to slow the wild beating of his heart. He was still alive. Through the cold and the pain, he felt a surge of elation.

"Halfway home," he grunted, conscious of the growing lump on his forehead. He scanned the top of the car, searching out a catwalk or runway of some kind. A flattened walkway ran down the length of the coach, but it was meant to be used while the train was stationary, not pitching from side to side. He would have to chance finding handholds as he went.

A wrenching jolt nearly dislodged him. The Berlin Express had passed the disabled train, and her throttle was wide open again. Looking out over the edge of the coach, Ben saw nothing but frozen bushes lining either side of the tracks. Snow stretched away into the darkness without the slightest sign of life.

He crawled to the catwalk and down the length of the coach roof, clutching at anything that offered the slightest handhold. It took all of his strength to avoid being catapulted off the slippery roof by the car's heaving motion.

Then suddenly, he was violently yanked to the side. He held on.

Another lurch threw him ninety degrees to the side. One leg hung over the side of the train. Nauseating vertigo caused the bile to rise in his throat. He forced himself to concentrate and struggled back to the catwalk.

He faced the wrong way—towards the front of the train. Precariously, he turned on the icy metal and resumed his perilous course to the caboose. Twice he crossed the dangerous gap between cars, always looking for a way down to safety, never finding one. Finally the dome of the caboose loomed ahead. Less than a half dozen yards left to go.

The sleeve of his overcoat caught on the jagged metal edge of a roofing sheet. His left arm wouldn't move.

The car hit a hillock.

Ben was up in the air, no longer physically connected to the Berlin Express.

Half a second later, he hung from the side of the caboose, dangling in the wind. His hands clung to two jagged sheets of tin, curled back from the roof. He prayed the rivets would hold his weight. The sharp edges ripped into his palms, sending fresh sprays of blood through the air.

The car shook wildly over the warped tracks, threatening to dislodge his precarious grip. Branches from saplings lining the railbed whipped at his heels. Methodically, he searched the side of the caboose with his feet, desperate for a foothold. He found one, just above a compartment window, and used it to boost himself back to the roof.

He crawled down the length of the caboose, forcing himself not to hurry. Grasping the ladder, he set one foot on the rop rung and began to climb down. When he reached the landing, he closed his eyes to hold back the tears.

The latch was stiff, but not locked, and Ben dislodged it with an elbow. He fell forward into the caboose. As he rose to his knees, a blast of warm air struck him, numbing his face and causing his hands to ache ferociously.

Ben slammed the door shut and crawled to a bench, grateful to be alive. Leaning against the wooden sidewall with his eyes closed, he waited for his heart to stop pounding. Slowly, the warmth thawed his frozen limbs. His body ached unmercifully, but he welcomed the pain. It cleared his senses. He looked down and tried to flex his fingers. Before he did anything else, he would have to attend to his bleeding palms. Reluctantly, he rose from the bench and began searching the caboose for something to use as a bandage.

He couldn't find a first-aid kit, so he rummaged through the mail sacks and packages strewn around the caboose until he found a parcel wrapped in a white linen sheet. Using his teeth, Ben ripped long strips of cloth from the edge and made a crude dressing for each hand. It was awkward, but it would have to do for the time being. Then he sat down to gather his strength and think.

Jude! The word echoed in Ben's mind, rekindling his anger. He remembered the loathing and hate that twisted the white-haired man's face and wondered if he was one of the Nazis the driver had been raving about. He seemed to qualify. The sight of Anschel's Star of David, proof that Ben was a Jew, was all it took—that was reason enough to leave him hanging off the side of the Berlin Express to freeze or fall to his death. It didn't matter what kind of human being Ben was; only that he was a Jew.

Ben had experienced hatred and he knew how dangerous a mob could be during a pogrom, but no one had ever singled him out of a crowd and tried to kill him because he was a Jew. The more he thought about it, the more outraged he became. what made it worse was that no one had been willing to help him. There would be an accounting, Ben promised himself, but later. First, Ben would have to find out if Sarah was on the train. Then there would be plenty of time to deal with the white-haired man.

Ben looked down at his hands. The white linen wrappings looked almost like gloves, except for the palms, which were already stained crimson. He stood up, grunting from the cramps in his legs. Bracing himself against the swaying motion of the train, he walked out of the caboose.

The adjacent car was a fourth-class carriage, in reality little more than an open freight car. The walls were drab olive in color and lined with hard wooden benches instead of cushioned seats. A small coal stove in the center of the coach barely threw enough heat to keep the frost off the windows.

Ben closed the door behind him and slipped his hands into his coat pockets. There was no need to appear conspicuous. As he looked around the depressing interior of the fourth-class car, he recalled a joke he heard on the ferry from Sweden: "Why are you traveling fourth class?" asked the one traveler. "Because there's no fifth class," replied the other.

Fourth class was uncomfortable, crowded, and carried a certain stigma with it. Before the war, only the poor and the indigent traveled fourth class. But the jobs were scarce in 1924 and the German mark was hardly worth the paper it was printed on, leaving most people little choice. Six years had passed since the end of the war, but the bitter consequences of defeat could still be seen on the faces in fourth class. They were the remnants of Germany's prosperous middle-class—unemployed professors and schoolteachers, intellectuals without journals to write for, chefs without kitchens, entertainers without stages, students without a future. Their unspoken resentment and humiliation was a palpable presence, roiling beneath the surface. They hid behind newspapers or a disinterested glance, afraid of the questions they might be asked. Most of the people would not meet his gaze. Their clothes were not much better than rags.

A few had small baskets of food, but in deference to those who did not, they avoided opening them. Fourth-class passengers were used to traveling on an empty stomach. From time to time, one would smoke a jealously guarded homemade cigarette, but packs of cigarettes were not displayed or offered. Tobacco was too precious a commodity to share. The passengers in fourth class were a study in defeat, and their silent despair was a reflection of the country's shattered pride. While the German economy lay in ruins, the human cost could be measured on their faces.

A man seated near the exit stared at Ben from over the *Berliner Tageblatt*, and Ben returned the stare. Though creased by bitter lines at the corners of the mouth and eyes, the face was still youthful enough to appear boyish, topped by close-cropped sandy hair and broken beneath the nose by a Prussian moustache. A small red scar ran from above one eyebrow back to the hairline. At first glance, it gave him a rakish appearance, but if one looked closer, the real effect was threatening. He was not slouched on the bench, like most of his fellow passengers but sat ramrod straight, his shoulders squared.

The man behind the newspaper wore a once elegant Wehrmacht uniform, bearing the insignia of an *Oberleutnant*—a first lieutenant. Its threadbare condition made it obvious that he had been discharged some time ago, but Ben assumed he wore it out of pride or defiance. Even though an unsympathetic populace heaped jokes and abuse on ex-army officers, many preferred the dignity of the uniform to anonymity of civilian rags.

"You have a cigarette?" the soldier asked quietly. The question surprised Ben. Wehrmacht officers were nearly all aristocrats. They did not make conversation with strangers.

"I don't smoke or drink."

"Then you must be one of those Jews who don't indulge." In a society known for its consumption of beer and partiality to brandy and cigars, Jews were a notable exception. Rarely did they smoke or drink.

"I am a Jew, but I do not smoke or drink out of personal preference. It has nothing to do with my religion." Ben's tone was chilly. Being addressed by a German officer did not seem like much of an honor right at the moment.

The German eyed him carefully. "I meant no offense."

"None taken," Ben replied. The soldier returned to his paper. Ben immediately regretted his curt tone. If he was to find out if Sarah was aboard the train, he needed answers, not a confrontation. Perhaps the solider had seen her.

"Listen," Ben said, leaning forward. "Have you seen a young girl wandering around the train, looking for someone?"

"*Nein*," the officer replied noncommittally. He didn't even bother to look up. Ben wondered if he was telling the truth or simply unwilling to answer. Ben looked around the room for a pretext to resume the conversation casually.

A passenger in the far corner of the coach caught Ben's attention. As Ben watched, he fumbled with a small cardboard box and furtively withdrew a cigarette. Then he slipped the box back into an overcoat pocket as though it were filled with gold. Only after checking his pocket to be certain his trove was secure did he light the cigarette that dangled from the corner of his mouth. The thin blue smoke drifted across the room. The *Oberleutnant* looked up when he smelled the tobacco. A hungry expression came over the officer's face as he watched the man inhale the acrid smoke with obvious satisfaction. That was Ben's cue.

Nonchalantly, Ben removed a handful of silver coins from his pocket and jingled them in his bandaged palm, walking towards the smoker. Everyone stared openly. Silver currency represented real wealth; it was a rarity in postwar Germany. When most people had wheelbarrows full of worthless paper marks, the man who had silver or gold was a man who could have what he wanted. Curiously, Ben felt no fear at the ostentatious display—even in a starving Germany, people were still too self-disciplined to steal.

"How much?" Ben asked casually.

The smoker stared at the money, his own cigarette forgotten. "How many do you want?"

"Ten."

The man paused and pointed to a British half-crown. Ben handed him the money and could not resist adding an extra shilling to emphasize their respective positions to everyone in the carriage. People did not hesitate to answer your questions when they knew you had money.

The man removed the box from his overcoat and counted out ten well-rolled cigarettes. Ben took them and nodded in thanks, a gesture which the man silently returned. As he walked back towards the *Ober-leutnant*, Ben had the undeclared attention of everyone in the car.

"I thought you didn't smoke," the officer observed, lowering his newspaper.

"I don't." Ben held out the cigarettes for him.

The German was puzzled and more than a little suspicious. "Why would you buy cigarettes for me?"

"Why not? Maybe you'd do the same for me if our roles were reversed."

The *Oberleutnant* shrugged and took the cigarettes. He lit one with enormous satisfaction and pocketed the others carefully.

"*Danke*," he said, extending his hand. "My name is Stiffler, Kurt Stiffler." Instinctively, Ben reached out, then backed off as he remembered his damaged hands. Stiffler's eyes narrowed with surprise when he saw the bloodstained palm. He had assumed the wrappings were for warmth.

"What happened to you?"

"You wouldn't believe me if I told you." He had no reason to think that Kurt Stiffler was any different than the callous conductor or the white-haired man, but the ex-Wehrmacht officer insisted on hearing the story.

"We have little else to do and I am genuinely interested. Please."

Stiffler listened without interruption as Ben related the details of his experience; everyone else heard the story as well. In fourth class, privacy was a luxury no one could afford. Besides, nothing broke the monotony like hearing someone else's troubles. When Ben finished, Stiffler's upper lip curled in disgust.

"I've seen that type before," he spat. "He's a Nazi. But you mustn't think all Germans are like that. Germany is still a civilized country. Before the war, scum like him would not have been allowed to walk the streets." The violence of Stiffler's reaction caught Ben off-guard. Whoever the Nazis were, their reputation preceded them. Ben suddenly wished he had paid closer attention to the eccentric *kutcher*.

Stiffler's jaw muscles started working and he suddenly sprang to his feet. The scar above his eyebrow pulsated a livid red and he bristled with indignation, as though he were the offended party.

"What are we going to do about this?" Stiffler demanded.

"I hadn't really thought about it," Ben replied warily.

"We must seek out this man and confront him. Honor demands it."

"You have no interest in this. Why should you want to do anything?"

"Jackals offend me. And the Nazis are no better than jackals. Unless we remind them of who and what they really are, they'll be snapping at all our throats. Where is he?"

"Three cars up. Maybe four." Ben wondered what the soldier had in mind. Stiffler's pale complexion was flushed and he looked like an angry bull. Ben was beginning to regret having spoken to the volatile ex-officer; he'd had enough problems for one day. He started to suggest that Stiffler forget about the whole matter, but Stiffler was already heading for the compartment door. Reluctantly, Ben followed his lead and a crowd of curious passengers formed behind them.

Stiffler came to a halt at the rear of the third car when he saw a conductor staring at them from the opposite end of the carriage. The conductor smiled at first, then paled visibly when he caught sight of Ben. Ben and Stiffler slowly walked the length of the carriage, stopping at Ben's assigned compartment. Half the passengers in fourth class stood behind them. Ben noticed that his bags were still neatly stacked where the *droske kutcher* placed them.

"Are those yours?" Stiffler asked Ben, pointing to the piled bags. He stared at the conductor.

"They're mine."

Stiffler stepped forward, bringing him face to face with the frightened conductor.

"Are you the man who left my friend hanging on the outside of this carriage?" There was a brittle edge to his voice.

Alarmed, the conductor looked at Ben, then stuttered, "Uh . . . I . . . I . . . I'm not sure."

Stiffler turned to Ben. "Never mind this spineless worm. Where's the other man? The Nazi?"

"In the compartment to your left," Ben gestured. Faces peered out of cabins and the aisle was jammed with curious people. Stiffler reached out and slid the compartment door open with a resounding crash, then stepped in and yanked the white-haired man out of his seat.

"Did you see that man hanging outside the train before?" he asked politely, nodding towards Ben.

The white-haired man was speechless.

"Answer me!" Stiffler shouted.

Involuntarily, the man jumped.

"Didn't you hear me?" Stiffler radiated violence, and people began to back away. "Are you deaf? Or dumb? Perhaps deaf and dumb?"

"I heard you," came the sullen response.

"Well then?"

"I had my reasons."

"What reasons?" Stiffler smiled unexpectedly. His tone was friendly and inquisitive, as though he and the white-haired man were two old friends discussing a soccer match. The unexpected smile lulled the white-haired man into a false sense of security.

"If you don't know already, I'd be happy to tell you," snarled the white-haired man. "The man is a Jew. Why concern yourself in this affair? One Jew more or less doesn't make a difference to anyone."

"Ah, but it does," explained Stiffler patiently. He sounded like a schoolmaster lecturing an errant pupil. "This gentleman is more than a Jew, he is also a fellow human being and a guest in our country. Did I mention he is my friend as well? No? Well he is, and I think he is entitled to a little courtesy and a little respect. Don't you agree?" The white-haired man glared at Stiffler, debating how dangerous his antagonist really was.

"I suppose you are one of these Nazis?" Stiffler observed with an air of resignation. Though he seemed outwardly calm, Ben sensed that Stiffler was ready to explode without warning. He was like a loaded revolver, waiting for someone to pull the trigger. The white-haired man hesitated, then squared his shoulders in defiance.

"Yes, I am a National Socialist, and proud of it," he boasted, oblivious to the way Stiffler's eyes narrowed. "Only the Nazis have the courage to speak the truth in Germany today. All patriotic Germans are National Socialists. The stinking Jews have preyed on the Fatherland long enough, robbing our children of their birthright and tainting our race with their polluted blood. Soon, all Germany will awake and crush them." His eyes shone feverishly.

"So you're saying that all Germans who are not Nazis are disloyal?" Stiffler's voice was deceptively neutral.

"I am saying that Jews are communists and traitors who would destroy our way of life. Germany's defeat was their greatest victory. As for you, Herr Oberleutnant, I suppose that you are the last of the Junkers," he sneered. "A lover of the Jews—a traitor and a disgrace to the uniform you wear. Tell me, Herr Oberleutnant, how much did they have to pay you to . . .''

Stiffler's fist lashed out and caught the Nazi on the chin; he reeled backwards and crumpled into a seat. Stiffler hauled him out of the corner and braced him against the compartment wall. Again and again, he pounded the older man in the stomach, face, and ribs.

''You animal! You Nazi pig! You filth!'' Stiffler was on the verge of losing control completely, but no one dared interfere with his fury. Though he felt no compassion for the Nazi, Ben thought that it might have been kinder to strangle the man.

Finally, Stiffler dragged the man over to Ben. ''This is the right man?'' he asked belatedly.

''Yes. Yes, it is.''

''Just wanted to be sure.'' Contemptuously, he released the white-haired man, who sank to the floor. ''You filthy, stupid animal! Just because your pisspot jailbird leader is out on the streets again doesn't mean you run the country. Your kind is a blight on the Fatherland.'' Stiffler grunted disdainfully and kicked him in the head. The crowd was silent, awed by Stiffler's rage.

Then Stiffler placed his boot on the moaning Nazi's chest like a big game hunter who just bagged a trophy. Posing for a moment, he looked at Ben with a crooked grin, ''But where are my manners? Would you like a turn?'' Ben was struck by the contrast between Stiffler's boyish, good-natured invitation and the bloody wreck beneath his boot.

''It looks like you've done for both of us,'' Ben observed. The white-haired man seemed barely conscious.

''Nonsense,'' Stiffler scoffed. ''This Nazi excrement tried to kill you. It's only fair that you express your feelings to him in turn. Besides, we have an obligation to set an example that Germany wants no part of his kind's murderous hatred.'' Stiffler glared at the spectators, challenging them to disagree. No one did.

He grabbed the man by his jacket lapels and leaned him up against the wall next to Ben. Gently, he slapped the man's cheeks to revive him. The Nazi opened his eyes and moaned.

''We're awake!'' Stiffler exclaimed gleefully. ''After you passed out, Herr Nazi, it occurred to me that you were never properly introduced to the man you tried to murder. After all, if you're going to kill a man, you should at least know his name. This is Herr Isaacson. He has some things to say to you.'' He propped the man up and stood back to watch.

The white-haired man opened his eyes. A steady stream of blood ran down from the corner of his mouth. One eye was swelling shut and two of his front teeth were broken. Ben saw the hatred in his eyes, cold and explosive—the kind that pounced on you from behind in dark alleys.

The white-haired man hawked weakly and spat a bloody glob of phlegm at Ben. It hit the floor several inches from Ben's foot. "My day will come, *Jude*," he rasped. Suddenly, Ben relived those terrifying moments on the outside of the Berlin Express. He wanted to smash the white-haired man's arrogant sneer to a bloody pulp, but his hands were too badly injured to form fists. Ben felt the crowd anticipating his response, urging him to take his revenge. He had to do something.

"Our friend seems to feel that Jewish blood is polluted," Ben said grimly. "Perhaps he'd like a sample."

Stripping the improvised dressings off with his teeth, Ben pulled the man's face toward him and rubbed his bloody hands over the white-haired man's cheeks and eyes until he gagged and coughed, blinded by Ben's blood. Red liquid trickled down his face onto his jacket, staining his collar and shirt. He slumped to the ground, unconscious.

The crowd stared as Ben crouched down and wiped his hands clean on the man's coat. Then he carelessly tore broad strips of cloth from the man's shirt and used them to wrap his hands. The terrified conductor turned and walked to the back of the car, where he began to sob.

Stiffler leaned over the Nazi. "Have you fallen asleep again? Ah, well. If you can hear me, hear this: You got off easily this time. If I ever see you again, I'll really give you cause for regret." Then Stiffler walked up to the conductor, who tried to back away. The conductor tripped on a bag and fell heavily against the compartment window.

"I'll bet you thought we forgot all about you," Stiffler grinned maliciously. "But we didn't. Are you a good friend of the Nazis? Is that why you didn't let my Jewish friend onto the train, Herr Schaffner? What's wrong? Are you feeling ill? Or are you also deaf and dumb, like our friend on the floor?"

"*Mein Gott*," the man replied in a shaky whisper. "Please don't hurt me. I don't know. I don't do things like this. It's the Nazis. They make you think crazy. I never did anything like that before. I swear. I don't know why I did it—my family would be ashamed if they knew—please, you mustn't tell anyone."

"We won't have to tell them," Stiffler smirked. "One look at your face, when I get finished with you, and they'll know."

"Kurt, please, there's been enough violence." Ben motioned for Stiffler to leave the conductor alone.

The conductor stumbled towards Ben clutching a clean handkerchief. Tears streamed down his face. "I'm sorry. Please, I'm so sorry. I'll never do it again. I swear it on my mother's grave. You must believe me." Trembling uncontrollably, he bound Ben's hands. "Which compartment are you in? I'll carry your bags there for you. Even better, I'll see you get a first-class compartment, all to yourself."

"My compartment is right here." Ben was sickened by the conductor's whining attempt to appease him.

"I'll find you another one, a better one, a much better one," the conductor promised anxiously, staying as far away from Stiffler as he could. "Please, just follow me. You'll see. You'll like it."

"Not yet," Ben replied, cutting off the frightened man's babbling. "I'm trying to find a young girl who was supposed to meet me at the station. I'm afraid she missed the train, but I want to be sure she's not on board." Ben described Sarah and the conductor recognized her immediately.

"She's in a second-class compartment, sitting in the middle of the floor on her luggage. No one can make her budge. All she does is cry and pet a small cat she has wrapped in a shawl."

"That's Sarah!" Ben exclaimed, forgetting he had told her not to bring the cat. "Take me to her."

"Of course, of course. Anything you want. Anything. I'm here to serve you." The conductor grabbed Ben's bags and led the way, grateful to have escaped Stiffler's wrath. As they walked towards the head of the train, Stiffler asked if Sarah was Ben's sister.

"We're not related. She's a young girl I met in Hamburg. She's running away from home and I agreed to help her."

"How romantic," Stiffler boomed. "Are you in love with her?"

"No, I am not in love with her," Ben replied quickly. For some reason he couldn't identify, Stiffler's suggestion that he and Sarah were lovers annoyed him. "I'm just helping her to get settled in a *hakhsharah*. That's all."

"A what-sara?"

Ben's response was drowned by the noise as they passed from one car to another.

"A *hakhsharah*," Ben repeated. He grinned at the puzzled expression on Stiffler's face. Before Stiffler could reply, the conductor stopped and pointed to a compartment. Inside, Sarah sat on a basket, stroking Katzele. Ben pushed through the door and caught her up in his arms. She buried her face in his shoulder, sobbing with relief. In spite of himself,

Ben felt the tears well in his own eyes. He broke their embrace and held her at arm's length.

"Sarah, Sarah . . . where were you? Why didn't you meet me on the platform? I went crazy trying to find you."

"Oh, Benjamin," she sniffled. "I was so frightened. When I didn't see you on the train, I thought you'd changed your mind, or that my parents had found out and had you arrested. I was so scared." She wiped her eyes with the back of her hand.

"Why weren't you on the platform?" he repeated gently.

"I was about to leave when I saw Katzele staring at me," she sniffled. "I know what you said, but I just couldn't leave her. No one would care about her like I do and I was afraid Father would take out his anger on her. So I decided to take her and just get on the train. Once we were aboard, I knew you wouldn't make me leave her in a strange place. But you never got on the train and. . . ." She burst into tears again and Ben folded her in his arms.

"It's all right now, little one," he whispered.

Stiffler tapped Ben on the shoulder. "Hey, my friend, the conductor is quivering outside. He wants to know if you would like your bags in an empty first-class compartment down the corridor. What should I tell him?"

"Tell him 'yes,' " Ben replied, nodding at him over Sarah's shoulder. "Tell him that would be fine."

As he held Sarah, Ben was suddenly aware that the other passengers in the compartment were all smiling at him. "She's been waiting for so long," said an elderly woman hesitantly. "We felt so bad for her. Will she be all right?"

"She'll be fine," Ben promised.

"Listen," said Stiffler, moving back towards the door to the compartment. It was obvious he felt out of place. "I'm going back to fourth class . . ."

"Absolutely not," Ben cut him off. "I won't hear of it. Get your bags and I'll see you in a minute."

"But. . . ." Stiffler began.

"If you aren't back here in five minutes, I'll be coming after you," Ben warned.

"*Jawohl, Mein Kapitan*," Stiffler replied with a mock salute. He grinned broadly and walked out.

As Ben led Sarah to the compartment, she noticed his hands. "Ben! What happened?" Briefly, he told her.

"It's my fault! It's all my fault! I'm so stupid . . . ,'' she sobbed.

"Stop that. It's all right now." Ben held her, stroking her hair. Without warning, she broke away from him.

"I am so foolish," she said angrily. "Thinking only of myself."

"Sarah . . ." Ben began.

"Just a minute," she sniffed, rummaging through her purse, removing several white linen handkerchiefs.

"Give me your hands . . . ,'' she instructed. "Let me bandage them for you." She was all organization and efficiency. Tenderly, she removed the improvised bandage he had tied around his palms and replaced it with a proper dressing.

"You're very good at that," Ben said. Sarah beamed with pleasure at his compliment and it made him feel good to see her happy.

Ben stood and excused himself to change his clothes. After finding the lavatory at the end of the car, he stripped off his torn jacket and pants, washed, then dooned a fresh shirt, slacks, and a woolen sweater. After combing his hair, he balled up the discarded clothes and stuffed them into a trash receptacle. He walked back to his compartment feeling more like his old self. He had barely settled in when the compartment door opened and Stiffler stuck his head in. "Did the reunion party start yet?"

"No," Ben laughed, "we were just waiting for you." Sarah settled herself against Ben's shoulder. The feel of her weight warmed him.

Stiffler opened one of his packages and dug out a bone China demitasse. Filling it from a battered silver pocket flask, he raised it in a toast.

"Ben, I know you don't drink," he said, "so I will toast for the two of us. *Zum Deutschen Volk!*" He tossed the drink down in a single gulp then smacked his lips with exaggerated satisfaction, and dropped into the seat opposite Ben and Sarah.

"I want you to know that I appreciated your 'help' with our Nazi friend," Ben smiled.

"No problem. I enjoyed it." The expression on Stiffler's face showed that he had. "I daresay you would have done no less had your hands been in better condition."

"I feel as you do about jackals."

"So, Mr. Isaacson," Stiffler raised his eyebrows, "tell me, since Swedes are always neutral, and Jews don't fight at all, how did you get so tough?"

"It must be because I'm a Zionist," Ben laughed.

"Does that have anything to do with this young lady joining a . . . a . . ."

"*Hakhsharah.*" Sarah supplied the missing word.

"Exactly what I was about to say." Stiffler saw Ben yawn. "Perhaps you'd rather rest than talk. You've had quite a day."

"I'm tired, but not sleepy," Ben replied. He felt sluggish and his entire body ached, but he had no desire to sleep. He looked across at Stiffler's open face and felt an unexpected surge of affection. It wasn't because of what Stiffler had done to the white-haired man—if anything, that would have made Ben far less likely to feel any friendship. It was something about Stiffler himself, a winning quality that shone through the bitterness and anger, revealing the basic decency of the man beneath.

"Let's talk for a while," Ben suggested.

"All right, then you can start by telling me what a whatsara is."

"It's an agricultural commune the Zionists established to train young people as farmers to start a new life in Palestine," Ben explained.

"Knowing the Arabs, I would think it better to train men as soldiers, not women as farmers," Stiffler observed.

"We do," Ben responded, feeling a rush of pride at the use of the word "we." "But people have to eat as well as fight."

"Why would Sarah want to be a farmer?"

Sarah blushed and shrugged her shoulders, so Ben answered for her. "What Sarah wants is freedom. A place to start fresh, free of the oppressive customs of our own people as well as the prejudice of others. A place where you aren't pushed off a train because you happen to be a Jew. A place you truly belong to; a homeland. Is that right, Sarah?" She nodded shyly.

"I think a Jewish homeland is a good idea," Stiffler remarked, pouring himself another drink. Something in his voice touched a nerve in Ben. Though Stiffler was not a Nazi, Ben guessed he shared a common German prejudice: Jews did not belong in Germany, whether they'd been in the country for ten days or for ten generations. To Stiffler, Jews were not really Germans. They were a kind of foreigner.

Stiffler was a man of reason and honor, capable of liking someone who was Jewish, but never "Jews." Although Stiffler would have resented the implication, Ben realized that men like him were only one step away from the Nazis; victims of the blindness of their class. They would never freely join the fascists, but their bias made them susceptible. They could be seduced into hatred.

"Germany for the Germans and Palestine for the Jews?" There was a sarcastic note in Ben's voice. He didn't like Stiffler any the less, but couldn't let the thought pass.

''What's wrong with that?'' Stiffler replied defensively. ''Shouldn't people be with their own kind?'' Ben shook his head.

''What do you mean by that?'' Stiffler demanded.

''It's ironic,'' Ben sighed. ''I'm afraid you are more of a Zionist than most Jews are.'' Stiffler looked startled at the thought of himself as a Zionist. Ben explained how most European Jews considered themselves Germans or Estonians or Poles first and Jews second, unlike their Christian neighbors, who considered them Jews, period. Stiffler rubbed his chin thoughtfully.

''I never thought of it quite that way,'' he mused. ''I met a lot of Jews during the war, but they weren't much like you.''

''How do you mean?''

''The Jews I knew were a quiet group. They weren't the outspoken type. Never looked for trouble. Never defended themselves when they were insulted. Not that they couldn't fight,'' Stiffler added quickly. ''They were good soldiers. Took a lot of casualties and I always respected that—won more Iron Crosses for their numbers than anyone else. They fought harder than a lot of Germans.''

''Stiffler,'' Ben said acidly, ''they were Germans. Just like the white-haired man who left me hanging off the train.''

Stiffler repeated his point that the Nazis did not represent the people of Germany. They were an aberration, the freakish offspring of a misbegotten war. They were a minority.

''It's not just the Nazis,'' Ben replied. He tried to describe what it meant to be a Jew in a Gentile society, but Stiffler found it hard to comprehend. He had no frame of reference, no way to relate to a situation where a man's life and fortune hinged on his religion. Stiffler's world had always been rigorously governed by an ironclad set of rules, conventions, and beliefs. There was an order to life. There were prescribed responses to every situation that were not open to question. The individual was never called upon to speculate, only to obey.

Stiffler's character had been formed by a world vanished in the smoke and ruin of war. He was essentially a nineteenth-century man, who saw life in black and white; there were no halftones, no shades of gray. Sitting across from Ben and Sarah in the overheated compartment, he struggled to reconcile his own sense of honor with the realities of postwar Germany.

''Ben, I'm a German, and I love my country. Germany was raped by the Treaty of Versailles and the rest of Europe is taking advantage of her weakness, economically and politically. Between the communists and the fascists, people are confused and afraid. They don't know what to believe. You must try to understand how easy it is to inflame a people who have suffered a terrible defeat, as we have. The Swedes might be saints, but they didn't just lose a war.''

"They didn't just start one either," Ben remarked dryly. Seeing the look of stricken pride on Stiffler's face, he hastened to add: "Kurt, I don't credit anything to the innate goodness of the Swedish people. We're left alone because there are less than five thousand Jews in all of Sweden. I'm sure that Sweden would be no different than the rest of Europe if our numbers increased.''

Stiffler stared silently at his empty cup, then filled it again. He felt as though he had been cast adrift, spinning aimlessly, without direction or purpose. Everything he had believed in was tarnished with doubt. When Ben had asked him why he was going to Berlin, he was almost embarrassed to admit he was gambling on finding a job. It was humiliating to think that he would soon be forced to accept any kind of employment, just to be able to buy food.

"I don't know, Ben," Stiffler sighed. He was slightly tipsy and fast becoming maudlin. "I used to think that honor was all a man needed. That was what my father taught me. Blood, honor, and steel. If he lived to see the end of this war, he wouldn't have understood it either. Machine guns, tanks, planes, refugees, homeless children. No one dreamed it would be such a slaughter. I watched my men writhing on the ground, coughing their lungs out from the mustard gas. Thousands dead to gain a hundred yards of ground. After three years in the trenches, none of it made any sense anymore.''

Stiffler rubbed his face tiredly. "I can understand the hatred of an enemy in battle—that's a clean white-hot hate that keeps a soldier alive and sane. But I have to be honest with you, Ben, I don't really understand the kind of hate that drives our white-haired friend and others like him.''

"I know." Ben reached out and squeezed Stiffler's forearm. His friend looked discouraged and depressed.

"Can you imagine? I'm twenty-seven years old. I have no profession, no home, no money, no prospects. And the worst part of it is that there are thousands of others, just like me.''

"You have your honor, and your name," Ben smiled.

Stiffler looked up, slightly cockeyed. "You're damned right. And, as our Nazi friend discovered, that still counts for something in Germany." With a typical mood swing that often accompanies large quantities of schnapps, Stiffler cheered up considerably. "When I get to

Berlin, I'll find a job and things are bound to get better. From where I sit, they can only improve.'' He looked over at Sarah, who had fallen asleep.

"She's a sweet girl," he observed, pouring himself another schnapps. Stiffler downed the fiery liquid in a single gulp. "You know something? I'm hungry."

"There are sandwiches and fruit in the small case," Ben whispered. Stiffler rummaged through the basket and dug out two chicken sandwiches. Ben was surprised how hungry he suddenly felt.

"I've been meaning to ask you something," Stiffler said between mouthfuls. "You look like a Swede and speak German well enough to pass for one, so how did our Nazi friend know you were Jewish?" Ben pointed to the Gold Star of David in his lapel and told Stiffler how he had come by it.

"Perhaps you shouldn't wear it. These are difficult times for Jews. It doesn't pay to court trouble."

"You sound like a governess; besides, what do you call befriending Jews and beating up Nazis, if not courting trouble?"

"That's different," Stiffler grinned happily. "That's just plain fun."

The sound of their laughter woke Sarah. "Did I miss anything?" She yawned and rubbed the sleep from her eyes.

"Only a chicken sandwich," Stiffler smiled.

Ben dug out three apples and another round of sandwiches and the three of them feasted. When the food was gone, Sarah snuggled up against Ben and quickly fell asleep. Stiffler followed her example, his snores drowning out the sound of her regular breathing. Ben closed his eyes, hoping the gentle motion of the train would lull him to sleep, but sleep would not come.

His conversation with Stiffler reminded him of his mother and family back in Dorpat. They had never seemed so far away; he felt as though they existed in another lifetime. Careful not to disturb Sarah, he reached into his breast pocket and withdrew the letter his mother had sent to him in Sweden. In the dim half-light that illuminated the compartment, he reread the words she had written. Then he folded the letter and replaced it in his breast pocket.

Life is strange, he thought to himself. When he left Dorpat, he thought of himself as part of the greatest undertaking of the Jewish people since the legions of Rome destroyed the Temple and dispersed the children of Abraham to the four corners of the earth. All he had foreseen was April 1st and the opening of Hebrew University. The trip to Berlin was supposed to be just a train ride from one place to another. Now he was sitting with a runaway girl and a German ex-army officer, trying to ignore the ache of his torn palms.

His mother had been right, he smiled to himself. Dorpat was a lot safer than the outside world. But his father had been right too. Where nothing is risked, nothing can be gained. Ben closed his eyes and promptly fell asleep as the Berlin Express sped towards its destination.

SEVEN

First Day in Berlin
Tuesday, December 30, 1924
5:30 AM

Kurt Stiffler drew heavily on a cigarette, savoring the sharp taste. It was unusually good tobacco for postwar Germany. He stared at Benjamin Isaacson's rumpled form, wedged up against the corner of the compartment, injured hands crossed on his lap. His face was peaceful and composed in sleep. The girl was curled up against him, breathing regularly.

Stiffler flexed his legs and arms, stifling a yawn. Although Stiffler had no particular fondness for Jews, Isaacson was different. Scrappy, he thought. And generous. A good man to have behind you in a fight. Stiffler looked down at his own bruised knuckles and smiled. It had been a long time since he'd had the opportunity to resolve his feelings so simply. Outside, the lights of Berlin cut through the early morning darkness. He crushed the cigarette and leaned forward.

"Benjamin . . . wake up—we're almost in Berlin." Still half-asleep, Ben yawned and groped for his watch.

Stiffler saved him the trouble of looking. "It's five-thirty." Though Hamburg and Berlin were only separated by 160 miles of flatland, the tracks and equipment were in such poor condition that it had taken nearly twelve hours to cover the distance between the two cities.

Ben blinked and slid out of his corner without waking Sarah. He stood in the middle of the compartment and stretched his aching muscles with a grimace of discomfort. He dropped into the window seat next to Stiffler and winced as he gingerly fingered the lump on his forehead.

"Still suffering from last night's adventures?" Stiffler grinned.

"Yes," Ben admitted, staring at his bandaged hands.

"They'll be all right. The scars will remind you to tell the story to your grandchildren."

"I don't think I'll need any reminders. It isn't an experience I'm likely to forget."

"Welcome to Berlin, capital of the Reich." Stiffler pointed to the jagged skyline just barely distinguishable against the darker background of the north German plains.

As they entered the outskirts of Berlin, its appearance took Ben by surprise. Berlin was known as a city of beauty and sophistication. It was famous for its glittering cabarets and elegant people, its symphonies and plays, its operas and sidewalk cafés. But the Berlin that lay before Ben that December morning made Hamburg look like a jewel. Even though it was physically untouched by the war, Berlin looked drab, grimy, and unkempt. Everything was dulled by a tarnish produced by years of neglect. Many of the buildings looked abandoned, their unpainted trim and peeling exteriors providing a silent reminder of the disaster that had overtaken the Reich.

The city seemed to sprawl away to the horizon, its streets poorly lit by brass lamps with dirty glass globes. Even at this early hour, groups of ragged men gathered around garbage can fires to warm themselves. It was not what one expected of the capital city of the most populous nation in Europe.

"You should wake the girl," Stiffler broke in on Ben's thoughts. "We're almost in the station."

Fifteen minutes later, the three friends stepped onto the platform at Nordbahnhof, buttoning their coats against the early morning frost. As they walked the length of the train towards the station concourse, Sarah's broad smile froze into a mask of fear. A police detachment stood at the end of the platform, scrutinizing the passengers.

"Just a routine check," Ben assured her.

"Are you sure? My father has lots of connections in Berlin. He knows everybody. Do you think he's alerted the police? Oh, Ben, what if they're looking for us!"

"Don't worry about it, Sarah. There's no way he could have notified the authorities already. It's too soon," Ben smiled.

"I'm scared, Ben. I don't want to be sent back. He'd never let me out of my room again until he found some horrible old man to marry me off to,'' she said faintly. For all her spunk, this was her first experience in the outside world.

"Don't be afraid," Stiffler smiled, squeezing her shoulder. "They'll never stop you as long as you're with us. We won't let them."

"Trust us Sarah," Ben held her hand. "Everything is going to be fine."

In spite of his confidence, Ben's heart raced as they approached the police checkpoint. A bored police inspector asked their names, politely raising a finger to the brim of his hat when he saw Stiffler's Wehrmacht uniform. Satisfied with their replies, the inspector waved them through. Ben and Sarah both gave an audible sigh of relief once they stood outside the station.

"See," Stiffler laughed. "Nothing to it."

"Now what?" Sarah asked brightly, her spirits restored. Ben stared at her. He hadn't thought past their arrival in Berlin. She certainly couldn't stay with him at his cousin Herschel's.

It was Stiffler who solved the problem of what to do with Sarah by suggesting that Ben rent a room along Grenadierstrasse, in the Jewish section of Spandau. Spandau was filled with hundreds of bed and break-fast places, run by Berliners hoping to pick up extra money by renting rooms. Sarah would be safe there, lost among the thousands of *Ostjuden* who inhabited the quarter, until Ben could make arrangements for her to leave for the *hakhsharah*.

It took them fifteen or twenty minutes to walk to Spandau and everything Ben saw confirmed his initial impressions of Berlin; it was dismal and dreary. Spandau was no different. The streets were lined with turn of the century houses badly in need of repair. They stopped at the first sign they encountered but the interior of the house was stale and musty, and the room they were offered reeked of mildew. They hurried back to the street, grateful to be breathing fresh air. Ben rejected two other places before they found a lovely third-floor attic with a private bath and kitchen. Since the building was partially empty, the large parlor was not sub-divided into smaller cubicles, leaving a spacious living area. Sarah would enjoy the privacy of the entire apartment. The landlady was a crusty old woman who did not really believe Ben's story that Sarah was his cousin, but she was used to people who came and went and never gave their real names. Besides, she was hardly in a position to turn away paying tenants. She took the money Ben gave her and stuffed it in her voluminous bosom, then disappeared down the stairs, puffing and wheezing.

Ben dug through his suitcase and came up with a few articles of clothing he had bought for Sarah in Altona, just before the driver came to pick him up. He laid them out on the bed and promised they would shop for the proper clothes the next day. He had made arrangements for the landlady to provide all of Sarah's meals, so there was nothing left to worry about.

"I'll be by later, after I see Herschel," Ben smiled. Sarah stared at him, then burst into tears. He and Stiffler looked at each other in surprise.

"What's wrong?"

"I don't know," she cried. "I feel so foolish and afraid. I just don't want to be abandoned in such a strange place."

"We aren't deserting you," Ben explained. "It is just too risky for us to be seen together. Your father might have given a description to the police, or told them to look for us at Zionist Headquarters. And there are things I must do. You'll be fine with the landlady. Just don't go out, all right?" She nodded miserably, folding Katzele in her arms.

Assuming all was well again, Ben gave her a kiss on the cheek and pulled his coat on. He was about to leave when Stiffler stopped him.

"I think there's something else bothering her," Stiffler said. Ben turned to Sarah.

"Please don't think I'm a ninny," she pleaded, tears running down her cheeks.

"Tell us what's really bothering you, Sarah. It's your parents, isn't it?" Stiffler said gently. She wouldn't meet his gaze. "You know, Sarah, it's only natural for you to miss them, even if you and your father didn't see eye to eye."

Ben stared at his friend, surprised by the depth of his sensitivity. It had never occurred to him that Sarah might miss her parents after the way they treated her.

"I've written them a letter," Sarah sniffed, "but I'm afraid to mail it. I want Ben to read it first." She reached into a pocket in her blouse and handed Ben two neatly folded sheets of paper.

Dearest Mama,

As I write these lines, I am preparing to leave this house forever. I know that it is cruel and sinful to leave without telling you, but I also know that you and Papa would never give me your permission or your blessing to do what I am about to do, so this is the way it must be.

By the time you receive this letter, I will be en route to a *hakhsharah*. After I finish my training there, I will be bound for Palestine. Dearest Mutti, I know you will be asking yourself why I would want to do this, so I'll try to explain.

Do you remember my seventh birthday? We were at Grandpapa's house and it was *Pesach*, the first *seder* night. That evening, while my cousins were helping Grandma Goldy prepare the *seder* meal, I was in the dining room, practicing the *Manishtana*, the Four Questions that I would ask after we were all gathered around the table. Papa was helping me, and he suddenly smiled and asked me what I wanted to be when I grew up. I know you both remember my reply. I said that all I wanted was to be Jewish. I had tears in my eyes because there was nothing else in the world that I wanted as much.

Papa raised me onto Grandpa Arnold's chair. Then he hugged me and kissed me and as he held me tight, he prayed to God to make me strong in mind and body. He prayed that I might serve Him and set a proud example for others to follow.

Mutti, God has answered Papa's prayers. I hope that you and he understand.

I love you both very much, and I pray that my loving brothers, Manfred and Julius, will come to see, as I have, that there can be no higher way to honor God than to pray to Him on the soil of the land He has set aside for us.

I will write as often as I can.

Love and kisses,
Sarele

Ben folded the letter and carefully placed it in his pocket. He looked up and felt a tug at his heart when he saw the anguish on Sarah's face. "Sarah, this is one of the most beautiful letters I have ever read. I hope your parents realize just how beautiful it really is. I'll mail it for you today."

Sarah ran into his arms, somehow still keeping hold of Katzele. After a moment, she pulled away and he wiped the tears from her face.

"I've got to go," he whispered. "Remember, wait for me. If there's a problem, ask the landlady for help." Ben eyed Katzele, who glared back suspiciously.

"Don't you go anywhere, either," Ben jabbed a warning finger in the cat's direction.

Once on the street, Ben drew a deep breath. "Well, Kurt, now that Sarah's taken care of, I think I'll head for Zionist Headquarters on Meineckestrasse. It's a place I've been waiting to see for a very long time, and there's an old friend of my father's that I want to see. What are your plans?"

"I have no plans, but since a person such as yourself needs an escort to keep him out of trouble, I hereby volunteer to show you the way." Stiffler was actually relieved to have something to do, something that would postpone facing the uncertainty of his bleak prospects for the future.

It was a sunny winter morning, cold and dry, and the two friends set off at a brisk pace. They walked east on Spandauer Damm for several miles, then turned north towards the city's center. Crossing the River Spree, which sliced Berlin into northern and southern halves, Ben listened to Stiffler bemoan Berlin's dilapidated condition.

"This used to be one of the most beautiful cities in Europe," Stiffler sighed. "Now it seems as though the city is dying. It reeks of decay and abandon."

"I wouldn't describe that as decayed or abandoned," Ben pointed to the soaring spires of a magnificent Romanesque cathedral. He felt badly for Stiffler.

"Ah, yes, the Gedachtniskirche. All that's left of the German spirit."

"For God's sake," Ben poked his friend in the ribs. "You sound like a mortician. It's a beautiful morning, we're alive and well, and the sun is shining. What more could you want?"

"You're an optimist."

"And your cynicism is less than genuine. I saw the way you talked to Sarah." They both laughed.

Ten minues later, Stiffler pointed to an imposing three-story building that fronted on a small park. "That's what you're looking for, my friend."

Ben left Stiffler standing on the sidewalk and mounted the steps to the heavy doors. A discreet bronze plaque read: *Bürohaus der Zionistischen Vereinigung für Deutschland*—Headquarters of the German Zionist Federation. This was the place Anschel had spoken of so often; the nerve center of the Zionist movement in central and eastern Europe. In this building, men made decisions that would affect the course of Jewish history.

"I'll wait for you out here," Stiffler called out as Ben entered the building. Too absorbed in his own thoughts to reply, Ben waved absently.

Originally a sumptuous personal residence, No. 10 Meineckestrasse still retained certain domestic touches—flowing curtains, well-kept plants, lovely prints and paintings, and a number of baroque pieces that no one would buy to furnish an office building. Ben guessed that the former owner had left a great deal behind.

The atmosphere was anything but homey. It crackled with electricity. Secretaries bustled from office to office; all sorts of people sat waiting for a conference or stood in lines for information; volunteers asked ceaseless questions about travel permits, shelter, or donations. The building echoed with the rasping sounds of Yiddish, German, Polish, Russian, and other languages that Ben did not recognize.

The people at No. 10 Meineckestrasse formed a government unto themselves, modeled after the English system, which they greatly admired. They had a small cabinet, staffed by 'ministers'; an informal parliament, divided into ministries and departments; and a complete bureaucracy. They even arranged to have the same street number as No. 10 Downing Street, referred to themselves as "Ten Meineckestrasse."

Ben walked up to the reception desk and cleared his throat to attract the secretary's attention. She was busy transcribing notes from a large pad and ignored him completely.

"Excuse me," Ben said politely.

"Yes?" she asked without looking up.

"My name is Benjamin Isaacson and—" Ben was cut off in midsentence as the secretary turned to answer the whistle of a speaking tube. She listened with an indifferent expression on her face, jotting several names into a bound notebook. Then she replugged the tube and started talking to the secretary behind her. She was not much interested in Ben or what he had to say. Annoyed at her attitude, Ben decided to bluff his way in. Leaning over again, he tapped her on the shoulder. She turned quickly, with a startled look on her face.

"I have an appointment with Mr. Kaplan," Ben said authoritatively. "It's very urgent, and I'd like to see him immediately. I've wasted enough time already."

Chastened by Ben's tone of voice and his mention of the General Director's name, the secretary mumbled an apology and excused herself. At Ten Meineckestrasse, as at Ten Downing Street, mention of the right name was a key that unlocked any door. A few moments later, she returned and led him to an office on the second floor.

To his astonishment, the door was guarded by a heavyset man in a Wehrmacht-style uniform, including the mandatory black leather boots, polished to a mirror shine. He had a livid scar on one side of his face and had the appearance of a man who relished trouble. His eyes narrowed when he saw the bandages on Ben's hands but he said nothing. Ben gave him a wide berth.

The secretary led him through an outer waiting room and showed him the door to an inner office, instructing him to knock. Before Ben could thank her, she was gone.

"*Komm*," was the weary response to his knock.

Herr Maurice Kaplan, General Director of the Zionist Federation, was a slender, gray-haired man with prominent cheekbones and luminous brown eyes that glared at Ben from behind gold-rimmed glasses. Wisps of hair drifted onto his high forehead like vines looking for a place to root. He was reputed to be brilliant but moody and ruthless; prone to brief conversation and intolerant of those who wasted his time.

Ben had caught Kaplan in the act of sorting through the morning mail, which he continued to do, in spite of Ben's presence. Instinctively, Ben held out his right hand. Kaplan started to take it, then stopped when he saw the bandage. Without commenting, he gestured to a chair.

"I'm afraid I don't remember any appointment with you, Mr. . . . ." He had already forgotten Ben's name.

"Isaacson," Ben replied. "And you didn't have an appointment with me." At that, Kaplan raised his eyebrows. The expression on his face clearly indicated that he was not a man to be trifled with.

"I hope you have a good explanation," Kaplan said sharply. "If you don't, you are going to have a very unpleasant conversation with Hans."

"The one with the shiny leather boots?" Ben grinned.

"I wouldn't make jokes if I were you. Hans doesn't have much of a sense of humor. Neither do I."

Silently, Ben handed Kaplan a yellowed envelope. Kaplan's expression became quizzical when he saw the handwriting on the envelope; he recognized it as his own. He unfolded the sheet and skimmed the contents. Slowly, a smile spread across his face.

"Anschel Isaacson," he said thoughtfully as he handed the yellowed envelope back to Ben. "How could I not remember? You are his son?"

"Yes, sir. Since I was on my way to Palestine, I thought I'd stop and see you."

Kaplan came out from behind his desk and shook Ben's hand again. His grip was clammy, but strong. "Your father was a fine man and a great help to our efforts here. I've often regretted never having actually met him. He died during the war, didn't he?"

"That's right," Ben answered. "The year the war ended."

"His death was a loss to us all," Kaplan replied. "Please accept my belated condolences." Something in Kaplan's voice betrayed the real feeling beneath the expression of sympathy: Anschel Isaacson had been a valued resource in the past, but that was history; it counted for nothing. Ben's father was a well gone dry and Kaplan was not a man to remember the past with any sentiment. He was only interested in the present and the future.

"What brings the son of Anschel Isaacson to Ten Meineckestrasse?" The brusque manner returned. Maurice Kaplan had fulfilled his obligations to Anschel with a kind word to his son. Now it was time to get rid of Ben and get back to work. "If you're interested in the details of emigration, you can talk to any of the people downstairs. They'll see that you get all the information you need. Now you must excuse me."

Ben had not expected much from Maurice Kaplan, but he found the Director General's abruptness offensive. Anschel Isaacson had been a staunch and generous supporter of the German Zionist Federation. That should have some meaning.

When Ben didn't move to leave, Kaplan became impatient. "Was there something else, Herr Isaacson?"

"As a matter of fact, there is."

Ben described Sarah's problem and asked for Kaplan's help to settle her in a *hakhsharah*. Kaplan scribbled a few brief notes and promised to make the appropriate arrangements on Sarah's behalf. He told Ben to check with the receptionist in a couple of days. Then he rose from his desk and extended his hand.

"Nice to have met you, Benjamin."

When Ben did not take the Director General's outstretched hand, an irritated expression creased Kaplan's face.

"Was there something else, Herr Isaacson?" Kaplan sighed.

"There's something I think you should know about."

"Be quick about it. I have a lot to attend to." Kaplan no longer bothered with a pretense of politeness.

As Ben described his experience on the Berlin Express, the Director General became suddenly interested. Kaplan thrived on information; it was his lifeblood.

"Your experience is not an isolated one," Kaplan remarked after Ben had finished. "That type of thing is beginning to happen all over Germany more and more frequently. It's going to get a lot worse." Swiveling his chair back and forth in a half-circle, Kaplan eyed Ben thoughtfully. Then he excused himself from the room, asking Ben to wait.

He reappeared two or three minutes later with a tall, powerfully built man he introduced as Zorach Hanovi. Hanovi had a massive head with thinning reddish brown hair combed straight back from the forehead, and heavy, brooding brows. He walked with a slight forward slump to his shoulders, as if to make his height less conspicuous, and kept his hands jammed into his trouser pockets. Except for the eyes, he could have been anybody's grandfather. They were flat, cold, and hard, the irises matching the midnight black of the pupils. Even when he smiled, revealing even rows of large white teeth, the eyes remained expressionless; like the eyes of a hawk examining the entrails of its prey.

Dispensing with the preliminaries, Hanovi asked Ben to repeat his story. Kaplan stood by the window and listened intently as Hanovi questioned Ben about the white-haired man and Stiffler. Hanovi was intrigued by the fact that Stiffler was a German officer who had been willing to help a Jew.

"Such men are rare," Hanovi muttered, as though he did not believe a word Ben had said. Something about his tone and manner made Ben feel almost guilty, as though he had been lying. Kaplan beckoned Hanovi to join him by the window.

The two men conversed in a low whisper, but loud enough for Ben to hear them without straining. Information on Nazi activities in Berlin was apparently in short supply at Ten Meineckestrasse. Kaplan and Hanovi were discussing the ramifications. They spoke of Ben's experience on the Berlin Express and made it clear that they were impressed by the way he handled the situation.

At first, Ben was embarrassed to hear himself discussed as though he weren't there; then he heard Hanovi lament the fact that Ten Meineckestrasse didn't have someone like Ben to find out more about what the Nazis were planning in Berlin. The incident on the train had given them an idea of some kind.

"That's the kind of set-up we need here," Hanovi expounded. "Nothing could be more ideal than the combination of a Jewish foreign national and a German officer with unquestionable credentials. They'd be free to move around and keep their ears open without raising any suspicion."

"I agree," Kaplan murmured. "That's the kind' of intelligence information we need."

Ben's heart started to pound faster as he listened to Kaplan and Hanovi. Did they have an assignment for him? Would they want his help? He could hardly contain his excitement at the prospect of actually working for the Zionist organization. It would be well worth delaying his trip to Palestine. Tactfully, he tried to find a way to interrupt, but the two men ignored him and continued their conversation.

"I'd like to help," Ben finally blurted out. Kaplan and Hanovi turned to look at him.

"Help with what?" Kaplan asked.

"I'd be happy to find out more about the Nazis for you. Just tell me what you want me to do."

"Ten Meineckestrasse cannot afford to become involved in petty intrigues," Kaplan said. There was nothing in his voice to suggest that he felt otherwise.

"But you just said. . . ."

"If it became known that we were involved in those kinds of activities, the results would be disastrous. It would destroy everything we've been working for. If people want to tell us things, we listen to what they have to say, but that's all. Do I make myself clear?"

Hanovi said nothing. His face remained expressionless, except for the eyes, which bored right through Ben. It was then that Ben realized they had intended him to overhear their conversation. They wanted the information, and they needed his help to get it, but they weren't willing to take any risks—not even to go so far as acknowledging Ben's involvement.

"Of course," Ben smiled as he rose to leave. "I understand completely. If I should hear anything, I'll let you know."

Kaplan shook Ben's hand. "Call us in a day or two about Sarah Hessemann. We'll do what we can."

Ben offered his hand to Hanovi, but Hanovi kept his hands in his pockets. Ben understood it was not meant as an insult; Hanovi was simply reserving his judgment.

"From what you told us, you have a certain talent for getting out of a jam," Hanovi smiled thinly. "It's a useful talent for a man to have. For Jews, it's often the only way they get out of trouble." It was Hanovi's way of warning Ben that he was on his own. If there was trouble, there would be no help forthcoming from Ten Meineckestrasse.

As Ben walked out of Kaplan's office and back down the corridor to the first floor, he felt like he was floating on air. Unlike the armchair Zionists back in Dorpat, Kaplan and Hanovi were serious men; men who made things happen. Even though his association with them was to be unofficial, Ben was still thrilled with the idea of making a real contribution to the cause. Somehow, he would figure out a way to get them the information they needed. And when he did, Hanovi would be pleased to shake his hand. Ben wondered what Hanovi's real name was. He was sure it wasn't Zorach Hanovi—"Hanovi" was the Hebrew word for "the prophet." Perhaps it was a code name.

As he rounded the corner outside Kaplan's office, Ben tripped over an outstretched pair of legs, and the man responsible mumbled an incomprehensible apology. Distracted from his thoughts, Ben suddenly realized the halls of Ten Meineckestrasse were jammed with refugees. He had been so excited by the prospect of meeting Maurice Kaplan, he hadn't noticed the men seated on narrow wooden benches along the walls. They stared at his expensive clothes with more wonder than envy. It made him feel uncomfortable.

They were surprisingly quiet and they reeked of poverty. Their eyes had the hollow look of men without purpose. Ben felt the dull edge of their despair gnawing at him. He could see the questions on their faces: was Ben someone important? Someone who could help them? Should they stop him and ask him to put in a word for their future? A word that might help their wives and their children?

Ben felt their desperation enshrouding him like a thick mist, making it difficult for him to breathe. It gave him the oppressive sensation of being dangerously adrift, as though he too might fall into the morass of hopelessness that had devoured the people staring at him. He quickened his step. By the time he reached the front door, he was almost running. To his relief, Stiffler was standing across the street, reading posters on a kiosk. Ben hurried down the front steps and rejoined his friend, glad to be free of No. 10 Meineckestrasse.

When Stiffler asked about his meeting with Kaplan, Ben did not mention Hanovi and simply relayed the information that Kaplan had offered to help Sarah. There was no need to say any more. Ben gave Stiffler his cousin Herschel's address and together they set off towards the Tiergarten, the city's most elegant residential district. They walked south along Potsdammerstrasse, recrossing the River Spree, and into the park.

"The Tiergarten has one of the most magnificent parks in the world," Stiffler boasted as they passed a small group of people skating on a small lake in the center of the park. "It fronts along the river and forms an oasis of beauty in the heart of the city. If we had more time, I'd show you the zoo and the botanical gardens." Tall trees lined the river bank and stone walking paths led through trimmed hedges and copses of gray birch. Stiffler drew Ben's attention to the stately homes bordering the park. They showed no evidence of decay or neglect. Handsome wrought-iron work graced the entrances and leaded French windows reflected the afternoon sun in diamond shapes.

"These homes once housed the cream of Berlin's aristocracy," Stiffler said. The cynical tone had returned to his voice. "Now they're the preserve of the *nouveau riche*. Family counts for nothing. Money is everything."

"Stiffler, you are impossible," Ben admonished him as they left the park. "Which way is No. 74?"

"One block down, and to the left," Stiffler grinned.

When they found it, Ben hesitated in confusion. No. 74 was a bakery.

"I thought you said your cousin was a doctor at Berlin University Hospital," Stiffler laughed. "Why would he live in a bakery?"

"I don't really know. Maybe I got the address wrong."

"A fortunate error!" Stiffler exclaimed in delight. "Even if it's the wrong address, I'm starving. Let's go in and get some *kuchen*. The aroma is driving me crazy."

Ben pushed the door open and walked up to a small, dark-haired woman who stood behind the counter. She greeted them dully and asked what they wanted.

"I'd like a coffee ring, please," Stiffler beamed.

She looked under the counter. "We don't seem to have any more. Just a moment." She turned towards the back of the store and called out, "Karl! Bring out some more *kranz-kuchen*. We have customers."

A minute later, a burly man with a huge mustache appeared from the back room with a coffee cake. Resentfully, he tossed it on the counter as though he had been grossly inconvenienced. He stared at Ben and Stiffler as the woman wrapped the cake.

Ben smiled when she handed his purchase to him. "Could you help me with a small problem? I was given this street number as the home of a cousin. I was told I could find him at No. 74."

"That's odd," she murmured. "What's his name?"

"Herschel . . ."

Ben heard a terrible yell, twisting in time to see the burly man charge at him from behind the counter. The man grabbed Ben's lapels, his face contorted with rage.

"That dirty Jew! That sex maniac! I'll kill him! I'll break his damned neck! He'll regret the day he was born! Do you hear me?"

Stiffler grabbed the man by the back of his collar. "We hear you, Herr Baker," he said quietly, his voice filled with meance. "For the sake of your own health, I would recommend you try to relax. You'll live longer."

"Please, Karl," the woman begged, pulling his arm. "Please don't do this. Let him be." The man stared at Stiffler's Wehrmacht uniform and reluctantly released Ben. He allowed the woman to lead him through a curtained doorway at the rear of the bakery.

"What was that all about?" Ben wondered as he straightened his jacket.

Stiffler shrugged in response. "Who knows? You can't seem to go anywhere without getting into trouble."

When the woman reappeared, she asked Ben and Stiffler to follow her to the back of the store. They pushed the floor to ceiling curtains aside and stepped through into a small apartment.

The bakery was typical of a small commercial establishment—store out front, apartment in the rear. This particular apartment had four rooms and a small kitchen. Through an open bedroom door, they could see the burly man, sitting on a bed with a melancholic expression on his face. He looked up and glared at them. Wearily, the woman pushed back a long lank of black hair from her forehead and sat down at the kitchen table, asking Ben and Stiffler to join her. She paused for a moment, trying to gather her thoughts.

"Herschel is your cousin?" she asked. Ben nodded. "Odd. You're the second person in as many days to come looking for him. A pretty young girl was in here late yesterday afternoon. I'll tell you the same thing I told her. Herschel was living here with us until a week ago. He and my husband had a violent argument and he left."

Ben looked at her expectantly.

She sighed. "He left here with my daughter, Helen. They didn't tell us where they were staying." She fidgeted with the worn edge of the table cloth.

"This cake looks delicious," Stiffler said hungrily, eyeing a coffee ring on the kitchen table. "Do you mind if I. . . ." The woman shook her head and Stiffler helped himself to a large piece.

Ben felt momentarily stunned by what the woman had said about Herschel and her daughter. He had heard rumors that his cousin was living with a *shikse*, a gentile girl, but he found it hard to believe. Herschel came from a very orthodox background. To an orthodox Jew, no offense was greater than becoming involved with a person who was not a Jew; even non-orthodox Jews were suspect. The woman seemed to read his thoughts.

"My daughter is a nurse at the same hospital where Herschel works. Times are hard, even if you're a doctor. He needed a place to live that he could afford and we needed the extra money, so he boarded with us. I guess he and Helen . . . being together so much. . . ." She gestured helplessly, unable to voice the obvious. "Anyway, when Karl found out that Herschel was Jewish and that he and Helen. . . . It became impossible for Herschel to live here any longer."

"Surely you could have talked . . .," Ben began. The woman cut him off.

"Talk with him? Please. My husband was so angry that he joined the Nazi SA in retaliation."

"That's a bit extreme, isn't it?" Ben tried to conceal his distaste.

"The worst part is that I'm Jewish," she added ruefully.

Momentarily stunned, Ben could think of nothing to say. Seemingly oblivious to the conversation, Stiffler helped himself to another piece of cake.

"You see," she continued, "my husband didn't suspect that my daughter and Herschel . . . were romantically involved. But it had gone on for so long that everyone else in the neighborhood knew. Karl was the last to find out, and when he did, he just exploded. There was no dealing with him." She wrapped her arms around herself as though she were cold.

"So," she smiled faintly, "my husband, Karl, dressed up like a storm trooper while his Jewish wife pins on a swastika armband. Then he kisses me tenderly and goes off to some other part of town to harass Jews." Seeing the expression on Ben's face, she paused. He looked down at the table, embarrassed for her.

"I know he loves me very much," she said lamely, as though that explained everything. "He'll do anything I ask. He just has to play his games once in a while. He's like the rest of them—a little boy at heart."

Ben stared at her in disbelief. How could any Jew live with a gentile who made a hobby of abusing other Jews. Ben's expression betrayed his thoughts.

"Look," the woman said curtly. "They won't talk to me, but I'm sure you can find them at Berlin University Hospital. That's where I sent the girl who was here yesterday. I hope you find him."

They left her sitting at the kitchen table. As they reached the door, she cried out to them. "Please take Herschel and Helen a message for me. Tell them I understand and tell my baby I love her." Ben nooded to her. Tears streamed down her cheeks and she covered her face with her apron.

"You lead a very strange life, Benjamin Isaacson," Stiffler commented as they walked towards the hospital.

At the hospital, the head nurse told them that Herschel was playing in a concert at the Schloss Charlottenburg, Berlin's premier concert hall. He wasn't expected at the hospital until late that evening.

"I'm beginning to feel like I'm on a carousel," Stiffler joked. The concert hall was off Spandauer Damm, back towards Spandau.

As they walked past dozens of small shops, Ben noticed the unusual number of record stores playing American popular songs. When he asked Stiffler about it, his friend described the rising enthusiasm for American records as a sign of the times. Stiffler seemed to think that the blaring music was one of the heaviest burdens imposed on Germany by the victorious Allies.

By contrast, there were none of the street musicians one expected to find during the Christmas holidays. Instead, beggars and panhandlers filled the streets. Many were crippled or maimed during the war, missing arms or legs; others were cruelly disfigured. Silently, they reached out for money, retaining a shred of tattered dignity by refusing to speak. They were the broken remnants of men the nation preferred to forget. Drunks were commonplace, sitting in doorways or directly on the sidewalk. It was a sad and depressing scene to witness.

Ben also noticed a large number of people who were neither drunks nor panhandlers. They were poorly dressed, but appeared respectable enough. They seemed to be wandering aimlessly.

"You know, Kurt," Ben remarked, "I've seen some of these people before, when we were walking in the opposite direction. What are they doing?"

"They're what's left of the German middle class," Stiffler said. "They've no money and no chance at getting a job, so they just walk around to convince themselves they have something to do." Ben heard the bitter note in Stiffler's voice; Stiffler knew that only a thin line separated him from those people wandering the sidewalks. Suddenly, Stiffler stopped and caught Ben's arm. He pointed towards a group of men in formal clothes strolling down Spandauer Damm. "Take a good look, Benjamin," he sneered. "This is what we've come to."

"Who are they?"

"Who knows?" came Stiffler's derisive reply. "They could be English, French, Dutch—anything. They come here to collect reparations, or buy foundering German companies for a fraction of their real value. Above all, they come to gloat. How they love to gloat. Nothing pleases them more than to see Germany in ruins." Stiffler stopped to light a cigarette. He looked sullen and morose.

"There will be a reckoning one day, Ben," he said, exhaling forcefully. "I promise you that."

"That's what I'm afraid of," Ben replied. He watched his friend stare at the foreigners with such loathing that it chilled him. Later, having recovered its strength, Germany would exact a terrible retribution for the humiliations it had suffered. What frightened Ben the most was the certain knowledge that the Jews of Germany would be first to feel the nation's wrath. He was relieved when the baroque façade of the Schloss Charlottenburg finally came into view and put an end to the uncomfortable silence that fell between him and Stiffler.

The two young men heard the strains of an operetta floating through the high arched windows. Ben bought a ticket for himself and offered to buy one for his friend, but Stiffler declined the invitation.

"I never developed an ear for music," he explained moodily. "I'll wait outside and watch the parade."

Ben found his seat, then scanned the orchestra. He had no difficulty recognizing his cousin, who sat with the first violins. Herschel had not changed at all since Ben had last seen him in Dorpat the year before. Herschel was a frequent visitor to Dorpat; his parents still lived there.

Ben enjoyed the music, a lilting piece by Kalman entitled *Czardas Furstina*. The lively melody raised Ben's spirits and helped to wash away the dreary emotions accumulated during the day. For the first time in weeks, he was alone and able to relax. Settling back into his seat, Ben half-closed his eyes and anticipated his favorite passage.

Abruptly, he jolted fully awake.

Three rows down and two seats over was a profile that looked familiar. His heart started to pound. Ben leaned over the seat in front of him to get a better look. His face flushed with excitement and he suddenly felt short of breath.

He had not been mistaken. It was Bluma.

What was she doing in Berlin? Why wasn't she in Riga? A dozen questions raced through his mind, and it took all his self-control to remain seated. What he wanted to do was leap the three rows between them and fold her into his arms. Then another thought chilled him. Had something happened to his family in Dorpat? The concert became unbearable.

When the performance finally ended, Ben vaulted over a row of seats and pushed his way to the aisle. Working against the crowd, he forced his way to her row and stopped in front of the empty seat next to her.

Bluma was busy searching for something in her purse and didn't notice him at first. Ben watched her, feeling as though it had been years since they last saw each other. Her fine brown hair was arranged the way he liked it—parted on one side and swept back; and she was dressed as she always dressed; in plain sensible clothes that in no way detracted from her beauty. Seeing her made him wonder how he ever could have left her behind.

Suddenly she looked up.

"Ben," she breathed. His knees felt weak. He held out his arms and they embraced right in the sixteenth row of the Schloss Charlottenburg.

"What are you doing in Berln? Is everything all right? Did something happen to my family?"

"Your mother asked me to bring you a message," she replied, her face glowing. "She wants you to come home. Your brother and sisters miss you, too."

"Then there is nothing wrong, no trouble?" Ben was incredulous. "You came all the way just to tell me that my family wants me to come home?"

She nodded affirmatively. Holding Bluma closely to his side, Ben led her towards the lobby.

"I don't believe you. My mother wrote to me, giving her blessing. She knows I wouldn't change my mind unless something happened at home. And you know it too."

Bluma nodded solemnly. When Ben saw the expression on her face, he broke out laughing.

"You really came to see me!" Ben was exhilarated. "You've changed your mind and you're going to Palestine with me!"

"I just came to deliver a message."

"Liar."

"Okay. You're half right," she teased. "I'm not going to Palestine right now. I can't. But after you left for Sweden, I got to thinking about how long we might be apart, and I wanted to see you one more time. So I hopped on a train in Riga and here I am." It was typical of her to surprise him like this. Ben took her claim and retrieved her coat. They sat next to each other on a red cushioned sofa in the lobby.

"How were you planning to find me?"

"Your mother told me you would be staying with Herschel."

"Ah. Then you must be the dark-haired girl who asked for Herschel at the bakery."

"That's right. Did you meet Karl? He was something else again." Bluma shuddered in mock horror.

"I met Karl. Where are you staying?"

"At a hostel. I got in late yesterday, and by the time I tracked Herschel down, he had already left for the concert. I figured you'd probably be here." She smiled brightly.

"I love you, Bluma."

"And I you, Benjamin Isaacson," she whispered, running her fingers through his hair to straighten it. Looking down, she saw his bandaged hands. He hadn't changed the dressing since the previous evening and there were dull, rust-colored stains showing through the linen.

"My God! What happened?" Ben repeated the story of the Berlin Express.

"The things we feared are beginning to happen, Ben," Bluma said sadly.

As he described his meeting with Kaplan, Ben suddenly remembered Sarah. He was almost embarrassed to tell Bluma; it all sounded so improbable.

Bluma arched an eyebrow. "A little girl? And you're helping her run away from her parents?"

"She just happens to be running away. All I'm doing is helping to get her settled in a *hakhsharah*.'' Ben winced at the defensive note in his voice.

"How old is this 'little girl'? Twelve? Thirteen?''

Ben blushed and mumbled something.

"I didn't hear you,'' Bluma teased.

"She's seventeen.''

"What!'' Bluma exclaimed. "Old enough to be a wife and mother, and you call her a little girl.''

"Bluma, there's nothing. . . .''

"Oh, I know,'' she laughed delightedly. "But I could never resist playing the deceived lover.''

Just then, a slender man holding a violin case in one hand and a pince-nez in the other came striding through a side door into the vestibule. An attractive young woman with blond hair and deep blue eyes accompanied him.

"Ben!'' Herschel shouted, rushing over to enfold his cousin in an enthusiastic embrace. "We saw you inside the theater with Bluma. You made quite a spectacle of yourselves.''

He turned and hugged Bluma. "What a wonderful surprise!

"Ben. Your hands.'' Herschel's grin faded into furrows of concern. He wanted to examine Ben immediately, but Ben shook his head.

"I'll tell you the whole story later on and you can examine me then.''

"Ben, I really think you should let me look at them now,'' Herschel insisted.

"Later.'' Ben stepped around Herschel and smiled at the young woman who stood behind him. "You must be Helen.''

"I am. Please forgive Herschel.'' She rolled her eyes comically. "It's the overwork. But he is right. You should have those hands taken care of.'' Her smile was warm and friendly and Ben took an immediate liking to her. After the official introductions had been made, Helen asked if Ben and Bluma felt like having coffee.

"That sounds wonderful,'' Bluma shivered. "I think we could all use something hot to drink.''

"There's a fine café next door,'' Herschel said. "Why don't we go there right now?''

"Herschel, I have a good friend waiting for me outside,'' Ben explained. "Do you mind if he joins us?''

"By all means, bring him along.'' Herschel looped his arms around Ben and Bluma. "You'll find that Berlin is the most exciting city in the world. Germany is a fantastic place for a young person to be.''

It startled Ben to hear his cousin describe Germany in such glowing terms, considering that Herschel was a Jew who could hardly afford an apartment, despite his talents as a medical doctor and a concert musician. But he kept his thoughts to himself. There would be plenty of time to talk later on.

Once they were outside the concert hall it took Ben a minute to spot Stiffler's distinctive uniform. Stiffler waved and crossed the street to join them. Ben introduced him as the "Scourge of the Nazis." Bluma greeted Stiffler warmly, but Herschel and Helen were more reserved and more than a little curious. Not many Jews could claim a Wehrmacht officer as a friend.

As they walked towards the café, Ben told Herschel and Helen about Sarah and the *hakhsharah*. Herschel managed to wheedle Ben into an explanation of how he had injured his hands.

"Unbelievable," Herschel shook his head in shock when Ben finished.

"Thanks to Stiffler, it's going to be some time before my white-haired friend tries another stunt like that. Stiffler is a good friend and a great patriot," Ben grinned and slapped Stiffler on the shoulder. "Not only is he the scourge of the Nazis, but he doesn't like Reds either. He thinks that Germany should be rebuilt for Germans, by Germans." Ben jabbed at Herschel for his rose-colored remarks about Germany and young people.

"Well," Herschel smiled and waved airily, "I think that Germany will fully recover only if everyone, Jew and gentile, foreigner and native, work together to rebuild it, regardless of where they come from."

Stiffler eyed him coldly, noticing Herschel's slight Estonian accent. "What you say may be true, Herr Doktor, but only if the Jews and foreigners who come here remember they are Jews and foreigners, not Germans."

"You're not suggesting that there is a difference between German citizens based on where they were born or how long they've been here?" Herschel smiled, ready to good-naturedly contest the point. He seemed oblivious to the tension in Stiffler's voice. Remembering Stiffler's remarks on the train about Jews and familiar with his quick temper, Ben adroitly changed the subject. It defused the situation temporarily, but it was obvious that Stiffler and Herschel were bound to lock horns. Ben knew there would be trouble if they sat down together.

Fortunately, the growing animosity between Stiffler and Herschel had not gone unnoticed by Bluma. She tugged Helen's sleeve.

"You know, Helen, I think it's terrible to leave that poor girl alone in an apartment on Grenadierstrasse. The café can wait, I think."

Ben shot her a grateful look.

"But I'm half-frozen," Herschel protested. "It must be a forty-minute walk to Spandau."

Helen patted him on the arm. "Bluma's right, dear. Let's go see the girl. I'm sure you won't freeze solid in forty minutes."

Stiffler took advantage of the change in plans to excuse himself, claiming exhaustion. He pressed his address on Ben and extracted the promise of a visit. Taking his leave of the ladies, he nodded to Herschel and disappeared into the night. Despite his fondness for the ex-soldier, Ben was glad to see him go. There had been enough excitement in his life during the previous twenty-four hours. He had no desire to witness a confrontation between his friend and his cousin.

They walked together, laughing at Bluma's running monologue on the antiquated train service between Riga and Berlin.

Halfway to Grenadierstrasse, a cardboard sign caught Ben's attention. It was nailed on the door of a seedy restaurant, and read NO JEWS ALLOWED, in crudely lettered Gothic script. He stared at it, unaware that the others had continued walking. They came back to retrieve him.

"What does this mean?" Ben asked.

"Nothing really," Herschel replied. "We'd better keep moving or we'll freeze to death."

Ben was about to argue with his cousin, but Bluma gripped his arm and squeezed it gently. Out of courtesy to her, Ben held his tongue.

They had walked for several blocks when an old truck stopped on the street corner in front of them and disgorged a half-dozen brownshirted SA troopers. Efficiently, they off-loaded bales of pamphlets and began distributing them to passersby.

To Bluma's dismay, Ben broke free of her grasp and walked over to the Nazis. A square-shouldered young man smiled and handed one of the leaflets to Ben. It bore a simple message:

HITLER IS FREE
AND IN FULL COMMAND OF THE NAZI PARTY!

"Is this more of what you call 'nothing?' " Ben handed the circular to Herschel, who crumpled it and dropped it to the pavement.

"If you ignore them, they'll leave," Herschel said. "There are too few of them to cause any real trouble. They're just celebrating Hitler's release from prison. It's been going on for the past few days, but by next week, it will all be forgotten."

A crowd began to gather around the Nazis, encouraging them. People cheered as the brownshirts painted slogans across the windows of nearby stores. *Juden Heraus*—"Jews get out" was plastered on a half-dozen windows along with the warning *Sofort!*—"right now!" One window bore the admonition: "Hitler is free. Germany awake!"

No police appeared to discourage the vandalism.

"They're just bored," Herschel explained.

"They don't look bored to me," Ben commented sarcastically as they reached the busy intersection of Kurfursten Damm.

A full parade was underway.

More than a hundred uniformed Nazis marched in uneven columns, singing the *Horst Wessel Lied*. As the haphazard ranks passed rows of parked taxis, outwalkers planted little Nazi flags on each hood. The cabbies laughed and waved. Ben watched the display with a mixture of anger and fascination.

"Turn around, Ben," Herschel tapped him on the shoulder.

Behind them stood a building with an inner courtyard separated from the street by a pair of wrought-iron gates. Beyond the gates was an exclusive restaurant. There was a large sign on each gate. One read JUDEN, the other read VERBOTEN.

"So?" Ben replied. "It's identical to the first sign we saw—JEWS FORBIDDEN. The only difference I see is price. This place looks more expensive."

"There is another difference," Herschel smiled sardonically, "this restaurant is owned and patronized by Jews."

This time, Bluma could not restrain Ben. He couldn't decide what made him angrier—the sign or Herschel's casual indifference. What Ben saw as an intolerable outrage, Herschel accepted without question. Bluma tried to distract him by reminding him about Sarah but he refused to go anywhere until he'd seen the café for himself.

"How did I know you were going to say that?" Bluma sighed.

As Helen and Herschel preceded them into the café, Ben hung back slightly and whispered to Bluma. "How can Herschel pretend to love a country where this type of thing happens?"

"Herschel is no different than the other German Jews I've met," Bluma whispered back. "They all want to 'belong,' so they ignore what's happening. They tell themselves that it doesn't mean anything—that it's all a game. They really believe it will all simply disappear one day."

"Along with every Jew in Germany," Ben muttered as the maître d' welcomed them. He indicated they would have to wait for a moment before being seated. They stood just inside the gates.

"Why do these places make a pretense of cooperating with anti-Semitism?" Ben started to cross-examine his cousin.

"It's because of the *Ostjuden*. Jews are anxious to disassociate themselves from the *Ostjuden* in the eyes of their fellow Germans.''

''I should have guessed.''

The maître d' returned, and in a thick Bavarian accent, asked them to follow him. As they entered the main dining room, he turned and pointedly asked if Herschel's party objected to sitting next to a group of ''Polish guests.''

''No, we don't,'' Herschel replied quietly. The phrase ''Polish guests'' was apparently a polite euphemism for *Ostjuden*.

The five ''Polish guests'' at the next table conducted their business in loud and very coarse Yiddish. They waved their arms, gesticulating enthusiastically, and spoke directly into each other's faces with heavy accents and a wild abandon that clearly marked them as *Ostjuden*.

A clean-shaven German at a neighboring table began a vulgar imitation of the refugees, pronouncing ''was'' as ''voos'' and aping their mannerisms. His friends roared with laughter, which encouraged him to get louder. People at other tables began to laugh. The five *Ostjuden* fell silent, looking at each other uncertainly.

''I know those men,'' Herschel shook his head. ''Watching that display, you probably wouldn't guess the comedian and his friends are German Jews of Polish descent—*Ostjuden*, one generation removed.''

''They're Jews?'' Ben couldn't believe it.

''That's right. They're so eager to be considered pure-blooded Aryans that they out-German the Germans.''

''Why would you want to stay in this country?'' Ben fumed.

''Don't you understand, Ben? The problems faced by German Jews are generally of their own making. We can make good lives for ourselves here if we stop acting like a bunch of immigrants. If you want to get along in a new country, you have to adopt new customs, new ways of doing things. German culture is one of the richest in the world. We need to become adept at German culture—not victims of it. After all, this is the land of Beethoven and Schiller, Heine and Goethe.''

''It's also the land of Adolf Hitler and his Nazis,'' Ben shot back.

''Really, Herschel. I have to agree with Ben. What you're saying makes no sense at all.'' Bluma's ire was aroused. ''You're suggesting we deny who we are, as though we should be ashamed to be Jews. That's no different from what our friends at the next table are doing, ridiculing the *Ostjuden*. I don't think you can worship God as a Jew on Rosh Hashanah and Yom Kippur, then hide behind a German mask the rest of the year.''

''I'm not hiding behind anything,'' Hershel replied defensively. They fell silent for a moment as the waiter served coffee.

"What's the difference?" Bluma asked after the waiter left. "The German Jews at the next table are trying to appear more German than the Germans by ridiculing their own kind. All you're recommending is that they be more subtle about it."

"All I am saying," Herschel replied with exaggerated patience, "is that we shouldn't look for trouble. Why antagonize people by needlessly flaunting strange customs and traditions? It's offensive to native Germans. We have to be realistic about the way things are."

"And what if one happens to be proud of Jewish culture and traditions? What should one do then?" Ben asked his cousin. The German Jews continued to mock the embarrassed refugees. It was a humiliating spectacle.

"In that case, one should not come to Germany," Herschel answered.

"In that case, where should one go?" Ben replied sarcastically. "I'd like to know, just in case there's another war or communist revolution. Most of these *Ostjuden* didn't have much choice about coming here."

"They could go to Palestine, I suppose." Herschel sipped his coffee and sighed, suddenly changing the subject. "This coffee is excellent. I have always enjoyed this restaurant."

"How could you enjoy it with this kind of thing going on?" Ben gestured, unable to disregard the situation at the adjacent table. The mimic now had the attention of most of the restaurant.

"I ignore them," Herschel said calmly, "just as you should."

"It's all right for you to ignore them," Ben sputtered. "But then, you're not the one on the receiving end."

"Ben!" Bluma warned. She saw the red flush creeping up the back of his neck and knew he was close to losing his temper.

"What should I do?" Herschel asked quietly. "Create a scene every time I see a Nazi or a childish German Jew? Would you have me act as outrageously as they do?"

"Sometimes, that is the only thing some people understand," Ben replied grimly as he rose from his seat.

Bluma reached out to stop him, but he pulled away. His face burned with anger. He felt an overwhelming urge to subject the mimic and his friends to the same kind of humiliation they were inflicting on the forlorn *Ostjuden*.

As he approached their table, a waiter walked by with a loaded tray. With a quick jolt, Ben knocked the waiter off balance, sending the contents of the tray cascading over the German Jews.

The waiter stammered an apology.

Ben surveyed the faces at the table. All but one of the men were splattered with food and wine. Enraged, the mimic turned on the waiter.

"You clumsy, stupid, ignorant . . ."

"It's not his fault, it's mine," Ben interrupted. He turned to the waiter. "Go and get something to clean up this mess."

"*Jawohl, mein Herr,*" the waiter stuttered, grateful to be absolved of responsibility. He ran towards the kitchen. Silence fell over the dining room.

"Look what you've done!" the mimic snapped. He wiped bits of pastry off his lapels.

"From the sound of your voice, *Herr Jude,* I assume that you are the leader of this merry group. How much damage have I done, *Herr Jude*?" The man stared at Ben in shock. No German Jew wished to be identified as one in a public place, especially by a gentile. From Ben's appearance, the mimic assumed that Ben was gentile.

"Please, there's no need to. . . ."

"But I insist." Ben's voice was needle-sharp and dripped with sarcasm. He noticed the mimic's diamond tie pin and matching gold cuff links. Carelessly, he threw a fistful of dollar bills on the table. "Will this cover the damage, *Herr Jude*?"

"It's really not necessary. . . ."

"Ah, but it is. Is that enough money?" Ben pointed to the dollar bills, wilting in the spilled wine and coffee. When the mimic didn't respond, Ben poked his chest.

"I spoke to you," Ben growled. Mortified, the man refused to speak.

"What was that? Have you nothing to say, *Herr Jude*?" Ben asked mercilessly.

"Uh . . . please . . . Please accept my apology for being . . . uh, so clumsy, *Mein Herr.*" The man was desperate to placate Ben and put an end to the embarrassing scene.

"How can you apologize for being clumsy? I was the clumsy one," Ben smiled viciously. "You shouldn't be so quick to accept the blame for something you didn't do. And one other thing, *Herr Jude,* you should be more careful about the things you say in public. What one man finds funny, another might find humiliating. Don't you think so?" The man stared at Ben in astonishment, realizing that Ben was referring to his treatment of the *Ostjuden.*

"Good. Then the matter is settled. Pick up the money, *Herr Jude.*" The man made no move.

"I said, 'Pick it up!' " Ben roared. With a single motion, Ben pried the man's hand open and jammed the money onto his palm. The mimic winced as Ben squeezed his hand into a fist around the soggy bills.

Ben turned and walked back to his table. As soon as he sat down, the mimic and his friends quickly paid their tab and left. Gradually, people began talking again.

"Ben, you're red as a beet. Calm down," said Bluma. "Try to breathe deeply."

"Relax, cousin," Herschel advised dryly. "Perhaps I shouldn't say this while you're so angry, but all you did was humiliate a Jew by calling him one. No one could witness what you just did without feeling that being a Jew is a contemptuous thing. That kind of display just creates a deeper sense of shame. By the way, it doesn't make any converts to Zionism, either." Herschel sighed heavily and held out a plate to Ben. "The waiter brought us some strudel. Try some."

"I can't," Ben replied between clenched teeth.

"Please, Ben," said Helen, "don't judge them too harshly. They're basically decent, hardworking people who want to be accepted by the society they've always lived in. Ironically, the men who just left all consider themselves to be good Jews."

"Then how can they treat other Jews like trash?" Ben retorted angrily. He had grown up with hypocrisy in Dorpat, but he had never seen Jews actually turn on each other in public. To do so was an act of self-destruction. Helen understood his frustration and tried to explain how German Jews maintained a sharp distinction between their religion and their nationality. They were Germans first and Jews second. The *Ostjuden*, were foreigners, aliens. German Jews considered themselves Germans and wanted to be accepted as such. They did not want the scorn and abuse heaped on the *Ostjuden* directed at them.

"It's truly pathetic, Ben," Helen continued quietly. "The Germans won't allow any Jews to join clubs and business organizations, or participate in social functions. It no longer matters whether you're a German Jew or an *Ostjude*. If you're a Jew, you don't belong. So, the German Jews form their own exclusive groups and post signs that say 'JUDEN VERBO-TEN.' do you know what they do then, Ben?"

Ben stared down at his coffee.

"They brag to their friends that they belong to exclusive clubs that don't take Jews. Even though everybody knows it's a charade, they still play the game. It makes them feel like real Germans. It's sad. Whatever pride they have left is paper thin."

The quiet force of Helen's words had a calming effect on Ben. He didn't like what she was saying, but he knew she spoke the truth.

"What you're really saying," Ben said softly, "is that the *Ostjuden* are responsible for German anti-Semitism."

"The *Ostjuden* have changed everything," his cousin replied. "They're like an invasion force, millions strong. Most of them can't even speak German. Look, Ben, I realize it doesn't sound very noble, but if these people moved on to America or Palestine, anti-Semitism in Germany would disappear overnight."

"Do you really believe that, Herschel?" Ben asked. He was amazed at his cousin's callous attitude. "Do you really believe that getting rid of the *Ostjuden* would solve the problem? That you can simply wait for the Messiah right here, camouflaged as a good German? That you will be hated any less, or spared when the pogroms begin again because you speak flawless German and dress like a burgher?" Ben was no longer angry, just bone tired.

"Let's see how Sarah's doing," Helen suggested tactfully. "We've spent enough time in this place."

Since Ben was tired and had yet to check on Sarah, Herschel hailed a *droske* and all four of them piled into the back. Five minutes later, they stood on the threshold of 379 Grenadierstrasse while the landlady gave vent to her maternal instincts and berated them for deserting poor Sarah. While Herschel tried to explain that he didn't even know the girl, Ben managed to escape and took the stairs to the attic three at a time.

"Sarah?" he called out cheerfully as he pushed the door open. Sarah sat in the middle of the floor, cradling Katzele. It reminded him of the first time he had seen her, spoon-feeding the cat in the Hessemann kitchen. Her eyes were red-rimmed and tears trickled down her swollen face.

"You look like you've been crying for hours," Ben said sympathetically. He crouched down beside her. "I have lots of exciting news to tell you."

"How could you leave me like this?" she cried miserably. "It's been a whole day."

"Sarah . . ."

"I was frantic," she sniffed. "I thought you'd been killed—or maybe arrested."

"Well, I'm here now." Ben leaned over and hugged her tenderly. Her childishness would have grated on his nerves a week earlier, but he had come to enjoy having her depend on him. He knew her spirits would rebound after she heard about Kaplan and the *hakhsharah*, so he sat her on the couch and gave her the news. It was just what she needed to hear.

Impulsively, she leaned over and kissed him, then ran to the bathroom to wash her face before they went downstairs to join the others.

Herschel, Helen, and Bluma were sitting in the front parlor. The overprotective landlady had recovered from her bout of indignation and insisted on serving tea and cake. She clucked over Sarah like a mother hen. They spent a half hour in pleasant conversation, then Ben stood and told Sarah they had to be leaving. To his surprise, Bluma wanted to remain behind.

"Please," Helen said. "There's plenty of room for you and Ben at our apartment. Herschel and I are on night duty at the hospital, so you'd have the place to yourselves."

"I'll take you up on your offer tomorrow night, Helen. This is Sarah's first night in a strange place, and she should have some company." Bluma smiled sweetly and placed her arm protectively around the younger woman's shoulder. "Besides, it will give us a chance to get to know each other."

Ben suspected that there was more than maternal instinct motivating Bluma. Though she may not have realized it herself, Sarah was a very attractive young woman, and Bluma was not about to have any competition.

As they said their good-byes, Herschel asked Ben to accompany them to the hospital. "I want to see those hands," he insisted.

•   •   •

"Palestine is the only place Jews will ever be able to be themselves," Ben squirmed while Herschel cleaned his cuts with disinfectant. "Ouch!"

"You're very fortunate," his cousin murmured. "It's a miracle that no permanent damage was done."

"The kind of behavior we saw tonight is indicative of what's happening in Germany today."

"The tendons seem fine." Herschel worked quickly. He tried unsuccessfully to ignore Ben's lecture.

"You and Helen could start fresh in Palestine, far away from your prospective in-laws and their bizarre ideas. I'll even bet you could make a better living there."

"Done!" Herschel exhaled and snipped the last piece of gauze away.

"You do good work, Doctor," Ben smiled.

"Thank you, Ben. Now I can get to work on a paying patient."

"You know, Herschel, they could use men like you in Palestine," Ben said softly. "They need good doctors there."

"Please!" Herschel begged. "No more propaganda!"

"All right," Ben laughed. "I won't say any more. Just promise me that you'll think about it?"

"I will. Now, why don't you go to the apartment and get some rest?"

EIGHT

Second Day in Berlin
Wednesday, December 31st, 1924

Ben slept fitfully and awoke just past seven, unable to sleep any longer. It was cold in Herschel's apartment and outside, it was dark, overcast, and depressing. Ben rolled out of bed and dressed quickly. He left a short note for Herschel, then strolled out to explore the neighborhood around the Tiergarten.

He had not walked far when he decided to stop in a small café and appease his growling stomach with coffee and a cinnamon pastry. No sooner did he sit down than he regretted his choice of cafés. The coffee was bitter, the pastry was stale, and the wind whipped through a dozen cracks in the dilapidated building. Ben drew up the lapels of his coat to ward off the drafts and shivered. If nothing else, he thought to himself, I'll enjoy the climate in Palestine.

He was the only customer in the shop and made small talk with the waiter, who suggested a walk through the city to the Unter den Linden. "You'll see everything worth seeing," the man promised. Ben paid his bill and took the waiter's advice.

He felt better for having eaten something and walked steadily until he reached the Unter den Linden. Lined with magnificent Linden trees, the broad boulevard was Berlin's equivalent of the Champs Elysées. Most of the great department stores fronted on the Unter den Linden's wide sidewalks, and brass plaques displaying the names of famous German companies were attached at eye level to many of the buildings. Elegant cafés and specialty shops nestled between the impressive buildings, and sumptuous residences lined the side streets.

Ben read the names of the department stores: Wertheimer's, Tietz, Goldmann—the most exclusive stores in the city. Ben smiled as he watched groups of beautifully coiffed women walk through the heavy bronze doors. He chuckled to himself: even in the midst of an economic disaster, there were still plenty of people willing to pay the highest mark for the most expensive item. As he turned the corner, the smile faded from his face.

A uniformed Nazi stood on the curb, handing out leaflets to people on the sidewalk. Ben held out his hand for one.

"We must spread the truth," the young Nazi said earnestly as he handed Ben a copy. "See the names on these stores? Wertheimer's, Tietz, Goldmann—all Jews. They get richer while we starve. It's time we Germans did something." Ben glanced down at the leaflet.

It was a single page, printed on cheap rag paper. Across the top, in the inevitable gothic script, it announced:

FOR THE INFORMATION OF TRUE GERMANS

In the center of the page was a crude drawing of a fat, horned devil with the word *Jude* printed beneath. The devil was grinning hideously and displayed uneven rows of decayed teeth. He was peeling potatoes and hoarding them in a large barrel. He threw the peels towards a starving widow and her child. Over their heads was printed the word *Deutschland*. Below the drawing was another line of print:

THE JEW STEALS THE BEST
AND THROWS THE DREGS TO GERMANY

Through the thin white paper, Ben saw the silhouette of another drawing on the opposite side. He flipped the leaflet over. The reverse side showed a trim, uniformed Nazi peeling potatoes into a bubbling pot. The same widow and child stood by the pot, helping themselves to the stew with expressions of gratitude. The other half of the page was taken up by the horned Jew, shown shriveled and emaciated. He was on his knees, face twisted with hatred and disappointment, feeding on the potato peels tossed to him by the disdainful Nazi. There was a caption on this drawing as well:

THE NAZI RESERVES THE BEST FOR GERMANY
AND THROWS THE WASTE TO THE JEW

Ben looked up into the young Nazi's face, searching for a clue to his motivations, a basis for his hatred. There had to be some reason why he so willingly spread lies in the name of truth. But there was nothing but sincerity in the clear blue eyes; no trace of deception, no concealed dishonesty. It horrified Ben that the clean-cut German, so neatly dressed in a shabby, makeshift uniform, actually believed the propaganda he dispensed.

Momentarily off balance, Ben turned and blindly walked away. At the end of the block, he almost bumped into another pair of Nazis, handing out the same leaflet. He suddenly realized that there were Nazis on nearly every street corner, spreading propaganda. Herschel's words about "celebrating Hitler's release" came back to him; his cousin had been wrong. The Nazis and their propaganda were not about to fade away in a week. They were there to stay.

Ben's hands clenched into fists as he realized he was powerless to do anything. Angrily, he shoved them into his pockets. His right hand touched the paper with Stiffler's address. Fifteen minutes later, Ben walked up the two flights of stairs to Stiffler's apartment. The hallway smelled faintly of tobacco and urine. As Ben knocked, several large flecks of peeling brown paint floated to the floor.

The door opened and Stiffler appeared in a patched undershirt and suspenders. His face broke into a warm smile.

"Benjamin!" he growled, practically dragging Ben into the tiny apartment. "How fortunate! I have just been given a bottle of Liebfrau-milch as a gift from some old war buddies. You must have some with me."

The room was drab and depressing, containing no more than the bare essentials: a table, two chairs, a spartan bed, and a rickety chest of drawers. The doorless closet held nothing but Stiffler's well-pressed uniform. The ex-soldier read Ben's expression.

"Not the Tiergarten," he smiled. "But then again, I've enjoyed far less appealing accommodations on the eastern front."

Without consulting Ben, he filled two glasses. "Oh, I forgot. You don't smoke or drink. Ah well." He raised the first glass in a toast and downed the golden liquid, following it with the second.

"So, what brings you here?" he asked, refilling his glass. "Nostalgic for the old times already? Shall we have a talk?" He rubbed his hands together enthusiastically. Ben thought to himself, what a waste. Stiffler was a fine man with enthusiasm and ability, marooned in a rattletrap building with nothing to do and nowhere to go.

"What's the occasion?" Ben pointed to the wine bottle, which was now half empty.

"To celebrate my joining a paramilitary group," Stiffler replied, wiping his mustache. "It's supported by an industrialist who pays less than a living wage, and in return, we keep the communists away from his factories and bash in the heads of any lunatics in need of discipline."

"Like the Nazis?"

He laughed. "You'll never forget that man, will you?"

"No, I won't," Ben replied with a tight smile. "And he's not liable to soon forget us. But he's part of the past now. I'm talking about the Nazis who are alive and kicking. Apparently, they're coming up in the world. Now they're authors."

"Authors? Of what?" Stiffler's eyes narrowed. Ben took the crumpled flyer out of his pocket and proffered it to Stiffler.

"I've seen trash like this before. They just can't seem to develop a sense of taste. You know," he mused, "if the truth were known, the captions on these ought to be reversed."

"My sentiments exactly," Ben agreed. "Get your uniform—I have an idea."

Stiffler burst into laughter. "I love the way you think, Benjamin. Action, always action. You remind me of General von Hutier, always ready to storm the gates of hell."

By asking some of the street people, Ben and Stiffler quickly discovered that the central distribution site for the flyers was located on Potsdammerplatz. For once, Ben knew the way and led Stiffler to a vantage point on the opposite corner.

Across the street, eight or ten Nazis passed out leaflets to everyone who would take one. Behind them, dozens of bound reams of leaflets sat in stacks; twice, mesengers arrived to keep other locations supplied.

"Only a Nazi would use a street corner as an office." Stiffler muttered.

"What about the Reds?" Ben asked facetiously.

"They're more like anarchists," Stiffler grinned. "They prefer basements. What now?"

"Somehow," Ben said thoughtfully, "we have to figure a way to get all those flyers to a printing press."

"No problem at all," Stiffler replied offhandedly. "Just follow me."

Stiffler squared his shoulders and marched over to the corner. Crisply, he saluted the Nazis. They were impressed by his uniform and returned the salute enthusiastically.

"Oberleutnant Warner," he introduced himself. "Headquarters is furious. These miserable pamphlets have a printing error in them. Why have you been distributing them?''

The Nazis all looked to a thin blond man who seemed to be in charge. ''What kind of error, Mein Herr?'' the man stammered.

''You idiot,'' Stiffler said fiercely, pointing to the caricature of the Jew on the pamphlet. ''Are you totally ignorant? Can't you see? Where is the Jew's skullcap?''

''I don't see one,'' the Nazi replied nervously. ''I am not a printer, Mein Herr, just a loyal party member doing as . . .''

''Enough,'' Stiffler cut him off. ''I am sick of hearing excuses. We must have skullcaps on these drawings immediately.'' He turned and hailed a cab. As it pulled to a stop by the curb, he snapped orders at the confused Nazis.

''Rebind those loose pamphlets. Load them into the cab for reprinting. And send the men home until tomorrow. Quickly!'' Frantically scrambling, they obeyed his orders.

The Nazis saluted again as the open cab pulled away. Smiling slightly, Stiffler returned the salute with a casual wave. Then he turned to Ben. ''Now, where the hell are we going?'' He was obviously feeling very pleased with himself.

''Ten Meineckestrasse,'' Ben told the driver.

''I might have known your Zionist friends would be involved in this,'' Stiffler smirked.

''They're not,'' Ben replied blandly. Stiffler gave him a puzzled look. ''At least, not yet.''

When the cab pulled up in front of Zionist Headquarters, Ben left Stiffler in the cab to safeguard the stolen flyers. He dashed into the building, ignoring the protests of the receptionist as he bounded up the stairs to Kaplan's office. Hans guarded the door.

''Mr. Kaplan is busy,'' he said gruffly.

''He'll see me,'' Ben snapped. ''Tell him I'm here.''

Hans hesitated for a moment, then turned and knocked on the door. The General Director stood behind his desk, pointing to a map. Half a dozen well-dressed men flanked him.

''This man said you would want to see him,'' Hans said.

''Did he?'' Hans seemed to wilt at the tone in Kaplan's voice.

''Mr. Kaplan,'' Hans stammered. ''I . . . I thought . . . I mean, he said. . . .''

''I have something I think you'd like to see,'' Ben interrupted, laying a copy of the leaflet on his desk.

Kaplan looked up, his expression neutral, "And?"

"Take a look out the window," Ben said.

Kaplan turned around and parted the curtain. His guests moved to the windows. Stiffler was slouched on the back seat of the open cab, his boots propped up on a stack of literature. He looked up and smiled innocently. Kaplan stared at the back of the open cab, which was completely filled with bundles of leaflets. Then he turned back to Ben.

"Very interesting. You have brought us—I would guess 50,000 copies. Do you agree? 50,000 copies of a Nazi pamphlet. It was very kind of you to take them out of circulation, but what's the point?" Kaplan shrugged. "The Nazis will only print more. Why didn't you just have them burned?"

"I propose to overprint them and turn them into anti-Nazi propaganda. It will make the Nazis look like fools, save us a great deal of money, and provide every Jew in Berlin with a good laugh." Ben was quite proud of his idea.

Kaplan smiled, then broke into laughter. "I take it you have a printing press?"

"No, sir," Ben grinned. "But I'd bet you know where I can find one."

"That's one bet you'd win," Kaplan nodded. He thought for a moment. "Take these to 1223 Spandauer Damm. They'll be expecting you. The men there will help you with your plan. But remember, you're on your own. What you do with those pamphlets is your own business." Kaplan nodded a dismissal to Ben, then turned back to his guests.

The address Kaplan gave them was on the basement door of a rundown apartment building. A heavily bearded *Ostjude* answered their knock and introduced himself as Felix Levin. As Kaplan had promised, they were expected. The printer instructed his two teenage sons to start unloading the taxi and invited Ben and Kurt to see his operation. Ben asked how Kaplan had managed to contact Levin so quickly, but the printer seemed unable to tear his gaze away from Stiffler's uniform.

"What's the matter?" Stiffler asked with a grin. "Haven't you ever seen a Wehrmacht uniform?"

"Not in this part of town," Levin replied. He gave Stiffler a sidelong glance that conveyed his suspicions; German officers inspired little trust in eastern refugees. Anxious to begin, Ben took the printer by the arm and outlined his plan. The *Ostjude* stroked his gigantic beard and roared with laughter. He guaranteed Ben would be pleased with the results.

When the cab had been emptied, Ben left Stiffler to help the printer and went to pick up Sarah and Bluma. Levin would need all the help he could get. On the way back, they stopped to buy food, soap and towels. Typically, Bluma was thoughtful enough to purchase some small gifts for the printer and his sons.

By the time they arrived back at the printer's shop, Stiffler and the bearded *Ostjude* had become fast friends. Levin had found a bottle of slivowitz for Stiffler and the two men were busy castigating the communists as they fed the presses. Ben, Sarah, and Bluma were immediately put to work binding reams of leaflets.

They finished just before sunrise. Stiffler had consumed the entire bottle of slivowitz and lay draped over a chair, snoring softly. Too excited to sleep, Bluma and Sarah had insisted on helping until the last bale of pamphlets was bundled and ready.

''So, this is your answer to the Nazis,'' Levin observed as he wiped the sweat from his forehead with a grimy hand. The two boys loaded the last of the packets into the back of the printer's truck.

''No,'' Ben replied. ''My answer is Palestine.''

''Please, don't start on that,'' the printer threw up his hands. ''I've already been worked over by the best.''

''What's the matter with Palestine?'' Ben asked.

''It's a lot of trouble for nothing. First, you have to fight the British Empire to get in, then you have to fight the Arabs for the privilege of staying. And even if it was easy to get there, who wants to live in a desert? What can you say about a place where the most reliable source of water is your own sweat.''

''But Palestine offers freedom . . .,'' Ben tried again.

''You Zionists never give up,'' the printer laughed. ''My cousin wrote me about life in America and that's where I am going. In America, I can be both free *and* rich. So why should I swat bugs and fight Arabs for the thrill of plowing sand? Besides, if God wanted us to stay in Palestine, we'd still be there. Now, wake up your friend and let's get going. We don't want to disappoint our good Mr. Kaplan.'' Ben nodded. How did one fight freedom and money? Why not America? Ben shrugged the thought off. He was too tired to deal with it.

They spent the morning canvassing Berlin. The printer drove with Sarah and Bluma for company up front, while Ben and Stiffler rode in the back. Every time the truck stopped, Ben would feed Stiffler packets while the ex-soldier was placing flyers for people to take. Though it was new year and most of ths shops were closed, there were enough people on the streets to attract attention. No one dreamed of questioning a man wearing a Wehrmacht uniform. Towards noon, Ben signaled the printer to pull over.

"We've one more stop to make," he grinned, bleary eyed. "Take us to the corner of Potsdammerplatz, if you please."

Stiffler gave Ben a quizzical look, wondering why Ben would want to pay the Nazis on Potsdammerplatz a visit. He was tempted to ask but decided to let events run their course. He always enjoyed a good surprise.

Levin parked the truck diagonally across from the corner of Potsdammerplatz. To Ben's satisfaction, the Nazis were still there, passing out leaflets. By the dozens of bundles behind them, he saw that Kaplan had been right; the loss of 50,000 pamphlets hadn't even slowed the Nazis down for a day. He was relieved that the men on the corner were not stormtroopers, they were just unemployed Germans who either sympathized with the Nazis or were earning a few marks for an easy day's work. They would not interfere with his plans.

Ben jumped out of the truck and instructed Sarah and Bluma to stand on the corner with Katzele and pretend to be lost, knowing that two attractive young women would have no problem gathering a crowd. As they began stopping pedestrians to ask for directions, Ben and Stiffler offloaded the reprinted flyers, piling them on the corner. People who stopped to talk naturally saw the stack of pamphlets and helped themselves to a copy. Many started to laugh, attracting more pedestrians. Soon, a crowd of several dozen people had formed, blocking the sidewalk.

Inevitably, the Nazis across the street became curious and several wandered over. They were aghast to see their own pamphlets, cleverly redesigned and over-printed with a new caption:

THE NAZIS KEEP THE PULP AND THROW YOU THE PEELS

Self-conscious of their armbands and humiliated by the laughter of the crowd, the Nazis quickly disappeared.

"All right," Stiffler grinned. "We've had our fun. Now let's get out of here before they send the goons."

Unobtrusively, they joined the crowd and guided Bluma and Sarah back to Levin's truck. As Ben slammed the door to the cab, he smiled at Bluma.

"I think we'll stick around here. I'll meet you and Sarah back at Grenadierstrasse later on."

"What are you going to do?" Bluma frowned suspiciously.

"Don't worry about us. Just see that Sarah gets home."

Ben signaled Levin, and as the truck pulled away, he saw the disapproval on Bluma's face. She was less than pleased, but he knew she would understand.

Stiffler rubbed his hands together gleefully. "Just what do you have in mind for us, Herr Isaacson?"

"Just lean against the side of the building and look disinterested."

"Then what?"

Quickly, Ben outlined his plan.

NINE

Nazi Headquarters
Berlin

As Stiffler had predicted, the "goons" were not long in arriving. Barely five minutes had passed when a car and a truck screeched to a stop at the corner of Potsdammerplatz and disgorged a dozen angry storm-troopers. A balding man in a leather coat barked a series of orders that sent the Nazis wading into the crowd, pushing and shoving people out of the way. While half the group began ripping leaflets out of people's hands, the rest of the stormtroopers gathered up the bundles stacked by the curb and loaded them into the truck. They dispersed the crowd quickly, ignoring the shouts of indignation.

"You'd think they owned the place," Stiffler sniffed.

"Just play your part."

As the crowd disappeared, the balding Nazi mopped his forehead with a handkerchief. Stiffler's uniform caught his eye. He walked towards them.

"Did you see who was responsible for this?"

There was no suspicion in the Nazi's voice, just irritation and curiosity. As Ben had hoped, with all the confusion, no one had connected them with the truck and the pamphlets. They were just a couple of innocent bystanders.

"Perhaps," Stiffler replied casually. He fenced with the Nazi for a while, not wanting to seem too cooperative. He and Ben had agreed it would be a mistake to appear too eager at first. They let the man persuade them of the importance of his mission, then gave an imprecise description of two men that would have fit half the population of Berlin. The Nazi wrote everything down in an expensive leather-bound notepad.

"You are true Germans," he beamed and snapped the pad shut. "We will catch these Jew-lovers, and I assure you we will see that they are appropriately punished. If you remember anything else, please let me know. My name is Manheim and you can reach me anytime at Nazi Headquarters."

"It's gratifying to know someone is looking after the interests of our Fatherland, Herr Manheim," Stiffler smiled.

"God only knows what the Jews will do next," Ben added. He was careful to keep any hint of sarcasm out of his voice.

The Nazi studied them pensively. "We could use men such as yourselves. Every day, we grow stronger, but the enemy still outnumbers us. We need the help of every loyal German we can get."

Ben and Stiffler looked at each other, as if trying to decide what to do.

Manheim smiled. "You'll be compensated, of course."

"Why not?" Ben shrugged. Manheim motioned them towards the back of the truck, and they climbed aboard.

The stormtroopers welcomed them enthusiastically, shaking their hands and slapping them on the back. Despite their reputation, the stormtroopers surprised Ben. He had expected hardened fanatics, but the men in the back of the truck acted more like university students on an outing. There were a couple of ex-soldiers, privates, who treated Stiffler with great respect, and the rest were not much different than the average man you'd expect to meet on the street.

"You'll have a great time," promised a young man who sat next to Ben. He was a carpenter by trade and had been out of work for more than a year before joining the Nazis. "Once you finish in the classroom, you'll get to ride with us, and that's where the fun is."

"Classroom?" Ben asked.

"It's no big deal. Can you believe it? They actually pay you to read about Jews." The young carpenter laughed. He had a warm, friendly manner and a winning smile. "My name is Werner Sauer. Where are you from?"

"Hamburg," Ben replied, deciding it was best to stick as close to the truth as possible.

"I was born and raised right here in Berlin," Sauer explained proudly.

As Ben talked with Sauer about how hard it was to find a job in Germany, he found himself liking the young Nazi very much. It occurred to Ben that under different circumstances, he and Sauer might have become good friends. The friendly carpenter seemed to view the Nazi Party as a meal ticket, not a way of life, and was describing how he had become a carpenter when the truck began to slow.

"We're there," he smiled.

Nazi Headquarters turned out to be an aging stone structure that occupied the better part of a city block. Heavy iron gates barred the entry to a spacious courtyard paved with cobblestones, and the truck came to a halt while two guards pushed the gates aside and waved them through. Manheim dismissed the stormtroopers, then led Ben and Kurt to a second-floor anteroom where a humorless clerk took their names. Ben gave his name as Benjamin Erhardt and Kurt used the name Kurt Rutman.

"You will each be paid five marks a day," the clerk snapped. "There is a brief introduction you are already late for, and three days of instruction and training. At the end of that time period, you will be informed as to what arrangements will be possible. Fritz Heyl is your instructor. Manheim will show you the way." Manheim turned and Ben started to follow, but Stiffler remained standing in front of the clerk. Ben saw the set of Stiffler's shoulders and prayed there wouldn't be trouble.

"Your manners leave a great deal to be desired." Stiffler's voice was steely. The clerk looked up in surprise; no one had ever questioned his manner before. He was about to administer a sharp rebuke when he saw the expression on Stiffler's face. Without hestitation, the rebuke faded into a mumbled apology. Ben was afraid that Manheim would be offended, but the Nazi was delighted and complimented Stiffler on his bearing.

"We need men like you, Rutman. Men with leadership experience and ability. Too many of our recruits are lacking in discipline and training."

Manheim guided them down a wide hallway to a large open area that had been created by knocking down the walls of half a dozen rooms to create a "classroom." Rows of battered desks filled the room. A dozen young men in ragged street clothes sat facing the instructor and a free-standing blackboard.

"Wait here and I'll have a word with Heyl," Manheim told them.

Stiffler noticed that Ben's attention was focused on a life-sized poster portrait of a man who looked vaguely familiar. The face was gaunt, framed by wisps of fine white hair, and the skin looked fragile, as though parchment had been stretched over the bones. Even in old age, the jaw was square and determined, the eyes keen and unimpaired.

"Do you know who that is?" Stiffler whispered.

Shock coursed through Ben as he recognized the wizened face. "It's Henry Ford," he muttered. Ben found it hard to believe. What were the Nazis doing with a full-length portrait of Henry Ford?

"Gentlemen, take a seat," Manheim waved, interrupting Ben's thoughts. "I leave you in Herr Heyl's capable hands."

Fredrich Heyl was an unemployed public school teacher, nicknamed "the Ferret" by every class he taught. It was a creature that Heyl's appearance conjured up at first glance. His face was narrow and pointed, the chin, mouth, and nose tapering forward, as though funneled directly at the viewer. His glittering eyes darted back and forth, never fixing on any object for more than a second or two. His hands moved continuously from his back pockets to his front pockets as though in search of a place to hide. Just watching him made Ben feel nervous and out of place. Stiffler made himself at home, slouching in a chair and putting his boots up on his desk.

Heyl was cataloguing the effects of the Treaty of Versailles in sharp, bitter language, dwelling on the role played by the Jews in Germany's defeat. He kept repeating the fact that every man in the classroom was unemployed because of the Jews. As the other "students" filed out at the end of the lecture, Heyl handed Ben and Kurt a small packet that contained four books and several printed sheets.

"This four-volume set is your textbook. Don't lose it," Heyl glared at them. "You're being paid to study it. And be prepared to discuss it. You'll be judged on how well you master the lessons we teach you. Learn well and you'll have a future with the Party. Collect your stipend on the way out." Heyl turned on his heel and disappeared down the hall.

Ben and Stiffler found their way back to the clerk, who paid them five marks apiece. To Ben's amusement, the clerk was excessively courteous to Stiffler, prefacing every sentence with "Yes, Herr Oberleutnant," or "No, Herr Oberleutnant."

As they strolled out of headquarters Ben made a mental note that the complex served a wide variety of purposes—there were a number of offices and apartments in addition to the "classroom" facilities. A group of well-dressed businessmen standing around a Mercedes-Benz in the courtyard drew his attention.

"Who do you think those men were?" he asked Stiffler once they were back on the street.

"Money men."

"What does that mean?"

"Who do you think pays for all that? The building, the fancy uniforms, the cars? Where do you think the Nazis get the money to pay you and me five marks a day to listen to rubbish?"

What Stiffler said made sense, and as they walked towards Grenadierstrasse, Ben decided to return to Nazi Headquarters the following day and continue the charade. There was so much more to learn. Now he understood why Kaplan and Hanovi had been so eager to find out more about the Nazis and what they were up to.

"You're playing a dangerous game," Stiffler sighed when Ben told him of his intention to return the next day. "If they find that you're a Jew, you'll end up feeding the fishes in the River Spree." When Ben didn't reply, Stiffler's eyes narrowed suspiciously. He reached out and grabbed Ben's arm.

"It's Kaplan, isn't it? He put you up to this."

"The less you know the better. As you pointed out, it could get dangerous."

"Well, I'm going back with you tomorrow. If you do get into trouble, I'm a good cover. Nobody doubts the word of a Wehrmacht officer."

Ben shook his head and smiled. "I don't understand. You don't really care much about Jews, Kurt, and there's nothing in this for you. Why bother?"

"There is something in this for me—helping a friend. And it won't hurt me to learn about the Nazis. Sooner or later, it will come to a fight. The more I know, the better off I'll be. Besides, I promised Bluma I'd look after you."

Ben nodded in appreciation. He was glad of Stiffler's company and secretly relieved that he would not be stranded alone in Nazi Headquarters. They parted at Grenadierstrasse, agreeing to meet at Herschel's apartment the following day.

Ben was eager to begin studying the materials Heyl had given him, so he stopped at the Grenadierstrasse apartment just long enough to be certain that Bluma and Sarah were safely settled. He didn't tell them what he was doing, only that he was involved with something that might take a couple of days.

Sarah took his explanation at face value; she was still preoccupied with the day's excitement; Bluma knew him better. She suspected what he was up to, but she agreed to stay with Sarah on the condition that Ben checked with them every evening.

"I don't want you taking any unnecessary chances," she worried. "If we don't hear from you, I'll be sending out the troops."

Ben hurried to Herschel's empty apartment, anxious to get to Heyl's "textbook." He took just enough time to brew a pot of tea, and as it steeped, he began to read. The four books were a set collectively entitled *The Eternal Jew*, by Henry Ford. The same Henry Ford who had refused to grant Anschel Isaacson a license to produce Model Ts because the Isaacsons were "the wrong kind of people." *The Eternal Jew* was the German version of a series originally published in English under the title, *The International Jew, The World's Foremost Problem*.

The introduction began with a warning: there was a worldwide Jewish conspiracy to dominate the earth. The purpose of *Eternal Jew* was to reveal that conspiracy to the light of day. Ben turned the pages of volume one with enraged fascination.

Page twenty-three: "The sole winners of the war were Jews."

Page twenty-eight: "As nature encysts the harmful foreign element in the flesh, building a wall around it, so nations have found it expedient to do with the Jew."

Page twenty-nine: "Every commissar in Russia today is a Jew."

The book made accusation after accusation, portraying Jews as diabolical conspirators and cunning parasites. The list of crimes was incredible: the Jews started the American Civil War, the Great War, the Russian Revolution; the Jews were consolidating their control over the world by manipulating the international money supply; the Jews were motivated by an insatiable lust for power and money; the Jews believed they had a divine mandate to conquer the world and form a nation within other nations.

There was a special section reserved for German Jews. German Jews served in the Wehrmacht only to sabotage its offensives and aid the Communists; they controlled the economy, food supply, and the nation's industries. In collaboration with their fellow Jews abroad, they structured the Treaty of Versailles to keep Germany in ruins, leaving them free to exploit the situation. One quote summed it all up: "The Jews of Germany were not German patriots during the war . . . they can never become assimilated with any nation. They are a separate people, always were, and always will be." In short, all Jews were traitors; they were the source and cause of Europe's problems.

The book stopped just short of advocating outright violence as a solution, but the question of what to do with the Jews, now that the conspiracy was unmasked, remained opened and dangling: "Imagine for a moment that there were no Semites in Europe. Would the tragedy be so terrible, now? Hardly! They have stirred up the people in all countries, have incited them to war, revolution, and Communism. They believe in the saying that 'there is good fishing in troubled waters.' '' It didn't take much intelligence to see that the step from quarantine to violence was a small one. Ben began to understand the reason Henry Ford's portrait was hung in Nazi Headquarters.

That night, when Ben put down the final volume, his mind was a welter of confusion. The lies contained in *The Eternal Jew* were so blatant, so preposterous, that it was hard to accept that any rational person would believe them. And yet, the Nazis considered *The Eternal Jew* mandatory reading, a textbook of Nazi philosophy. It was close to four in the morning when Ben finally collapsed into bed.

He slept fitfully that night and awoke bleary-eyed to the sound of Stiffler pounding on the door to Hershel's apartment. He dressed quickly, half listening while Stiffler described his evening with a Norwegian dancer. On the way to Nazi Headquarters, Ben tried to discuss what he had read, but Kurt had spent the evening otherwise occupied. Briefly, Ben outlined the contents of their "homework." To his surprise, Stiffler started laughing.

"Nobody is going to credit that nonsense. These Nazis are crazy. Really, Ben, you do the German people a great injustice if you think they're gullible enough to believe that garbage."

"You're wrong, Kurt. Just watch the faces of the students in our class."

"The ones who are asleep, or the ones who are awake?"

"Just listen and watch."

Herr Heyl was in rare form the next morning and began his lecture by quizzing his students on *The Eternal Jew*. Ironically, Ben was the only student who had read the entire four volumes.

"A man like Mr. Erhardt will go far in the party," Heyl rasped. "The rest of you still have to learn that there is more to the movement than beating up a few Jews and painting slogans on storefronts. To defeat an enemy, you must first understand him. That is why you're all here.

"Now, next to the blackboard, you see a portrait of Henry Ford. It is a copy of the one Adolf Hitler keeps next to his desk at Party Headquarters in Munich. I know you have all heard of Henry Ford because of the Model T automobile, but what you might not know is that he is also one of the most courageous Aryans in the world." Heyl's tribute sounded so melo- dramatic that Ben almost snickered, but as he surveyed the faces in the classroom, only Stiffler seemed to share his amusement; the others listened with rapt attention; even the mention of Henry Ford's name seemed to be enough to invoke awe and respect.

Henry Ford was the epitome of the self-made man, living proof that a man could start with nothing and still have it all. Millions of people all over the world looked up to him and dreamed that one day, they too might emulate his success. He was widely regarded as the man of the century and a potential presidential candidate.

To a nation reeling from defeat and economic disaster, his life story provided an inspiring example. As he demonstrated again and again in *The Eternal Jew*, Ford was particularly fond of the German people and publicly admired their efficiency, their ingenuity, and their superlative racial stock. Germany was a nation in search of heroes, and she found one in Henry Ford. As Ben had discovered, many of the articles in *The Eternal Jew* were warnings directly addressed to the German nation, where the established order had been torn asunder, leaving a political vacuum. A vacuum that Hitler and the Nazis hoped to fill. Ben began to perceive the shadows beneath the surface. Heyl started writing dates on the blackboard.

"Henry Ford ran for political office in the United States back in 1918, but was defeated by a narrow margin. It was then that he became suspicious and first began to investigate Jewish activities. By 1920, he had amassed sufficient evidence to publish his findings in his personal newspaper, *The Dearborn Independent*. They tried to silence him, but nothing could shroud the truth. Your textbook, *The Eternal Jew*, is actually a collection of the articles that have appeared in Mr. Ford's newspaper. Unselfishly, Mr. Ford has used his position and his tremendous wealth to bring the world the truth about the Jew. Through his generous efforts, *The Eternal Jew* has been translated into sixteen languages and can be bought for just a few pfennigs, an amount that even the most destitute can afford." Heyl droned on about the millions of copies in print and how the book would influence the course of world opinion in the coming years.

"Never underestimate the power of the written word. When Henry Ford started, there were five or six organizations in the United States dedicated to protecting society against the Jews. Now there are 120. We can do the same here in Germany. Henry Ford is living proof that the truth will be heard."

By the morning of the third day, any doubts Ben may have had about the appeal Ford's book had for the German people were gone. The book focused the rage and frustration of a faltering nation and identified the elusive, shadowy "they" of a thousand complaints and unfulfilled dreams. Here, at last, was a salve for the lacerated pride of the German nation.

Who really started the war? The Jews.

Why did we lose? Who betrayed us? The Jews.

Who kept Germany in poverty? The Jews.

How can Germany regain her pride and rightful heritage? By getting rid of the Jews. It was a litany all too easy to remember.

Contrary to what Ben had thought, Hitler was not an original; he had a mentor in Henry Ford, one of the most popular and influential men in the world. Henry Ford had provided Adolf Hitler with an ideal scapegoat, and in America, he had already proven that anti-Semitism was far from a political liability—Heyl had boasted that a survey of American college students rated Henry Ford as the third most admired man in history, right after Napoleon and Jesus Christ. One day, Heyl promised, Hitler's name would join the other three.

Heyl had opened his lecture that third day by reading from a newspaper article that appeared in *The Chicago Tribune* in 1923, the year before Hitler's abortive *putsch* earned him a sentence in Landesberg Prison. In that article, Hitler had referred to Ford as "his personal inspiration," and told the reporter, "I wish that I could send some of my shock troops to Chicago and other big American cities to help with the elections. We look to Henry Ford as the leader of the growing Fascist party in America."

As Ben sat in the chilly classroom, the pieces of the puzzle revolved in his mind, one question leading to another. Like a kaleidoscope, the pattern kept changing, but the colors remained the same. Was Adolf Hitler really a has-been politician, his career stained and ended by a jail sentence? Or had he just suffered a temporary setback? Did the well-dressed "money men" in the courtyard of Nazi Headquarters comprise a small group or represent an international cartel of businessmen and industrialists? Was there more than an ideological link between Ford and Hitler? Was Ford one of Hitler's money men?

It made sense. Both men were using anti-Semitism to build a political base. Ford wanted to be President; Hitler wanted to rule Germany. Both men were skilled in manipulating the press. And there was more than a shared hatred of the Jews involved—Ford wanted to build plants in Germany, but was barred by a restrictive clause in the Treaty of Versailles, a treaty Hitler had publicly sworn to abrogate. Did Ford help to spring Hitler from prison? Was he helping to finance the Nazi party?

There were other questions to be answered as well. How united were the Nazis? Contrary to Ben's initial impression, Berlin seemed to operate independently of Nazi Headquarters in Munich. Would Hitler be able to consolidate the Party under his command? There were also rumors of a split at the top that Ben wanted to trace.

Even though the rank and file were clearly jubilant about his release, it was said that more than one party leader was disappointed to see Hitler freed early. Hitler's prestige had suffered a severe blow when the putsch in Munich failed and rumor had it that jealous rivals sought to supplant him. Yet Hitler had maintained a low profile since leaving Landesberg Prison; he seemed almost reluctant to appear in public. Why?

There was only one way to find the answers to those questions. Ben would have to remain in Nazi Headquarters and accept a position when his "training" was finished. He was well liked and trusted, and he knew Heyl would recommend him. It would be risky, but well worth the chance to find out some answers.

At the end of the third day, Heyl asked Ben and Stiffler to report to Manheim's office for assignment. On their way, Stiffler debated ending his part in the charade but realized that if he left at that point, it might cast suspicion on Ben. So he resigned himself to remaining a Nazi recruit and accompanied Ben to Manheim's office. The Nazi leader greeted them effusively and asked them to sit down.

"We are assigning you to Heinz Strohl," Manheim smiled. "He's not a particularly effective man, but I'm hoping that some of Oberleutnant Rutman's leadership qualities will rub off on him. If they don't, I suspect Strohl will be taking orders from one of you before the month is out."

While they waited for Strohl, they talked about the latest news: Hitler had written a book while in Landesberg Prison. Manheim was very excited about the possibilities.

"The book will have a tremendous influence. It will ensure Hitler's international reputation, and practically guarantee that. . . ." Manheim was interrupted by a sharp knock on the door.

"Come in, Strohl."

When Heinz Strohl walked in, Ben felt his stomach knot in fear. Heinz Strohl was the indecisive blond Nazi that Stiffler had ordered to load the pamphlets into the taxi. He recognized Stiffler instantly, staring in shock. Before he could speak, Stiffler vaulted out of his seat and landed a right hook that sent Strohl halfway across the room. He lay on the floor, unconscious. Manheim was appalled.

"Why did you do that?"

Stiffler improvised quickly. "I know this man. He is a piece of slime who insulted my family. I did what honor required."

Manheim crouched on the floor, trying to revive Strohl, who moaned slightly and stirred. Ben's mind raced. If Manheim found out who they really were, both he and Kurt would end up in the River Spree. They had to get out before Strohl came around.

"Perhaps I should take Rutman home," Ben suggested. "We could continue this conversation tomorrow, after the Oberleutnant has had an opportunity to reconsider his rash actions."

"Perhaps that would be best," Manheim agreed. He was irritated and angry, but unsuspecting. "Be in my office at eight sharp."

They left the office, trying to walk as quickly as possible without breaking into a run. Down the stairs, two at a time, into the sunlit courtyard—all they needed was a few more minutes and they'd be clear.

"Stop them!" Manheim screamed from his office window; Strohl had come around. "Shoot them if you have to!"

Werner Sauer was one of the guards at the front gate. He stood not more than a dozen paces from Ben, blocking the other guard's line of fire. For a split second, they stared at each other, and Ben could see the reluctance in Sauer's eyes.

"Move!" screamed the other guard. Sauer stood his ground and hesitated before drawing his weapon, giving Ben and Stiffler just enough time to dart into one of the ground level offices. They ran past a startled secretary into an empty back room. Conscious of the shouts close behind, Ben yanked a window open and waited until Stiffler dropped to the ground below, then jumped after him.

They ran through the maze of alleys behind Nazi Headquarters until the sounds of pursuit faded, then disappeared. Heaving and panting from a combinaton of fear and exertion, they hid behind a small grocery store that backed onto the alley.

"That was too close," Stiffler gasped, struggling to catch his breath.

"The next time you come along to protect me, wear a mask." Ben started to laugh, but ended up coughing.

"We'd better separate," Stiffler decided as he straightened his uniform jacket. "They'll be looking for us. You know where to find me."

"Agreed."

Ben waited for a few minutes after Stiffler opened the back door of the grocery store and cut through to the street, then set off in the opposite direction. He had a lot to tell Kaplan and Hanovi.

• • •

Maurice Kaplan's expression never changed as he listened to Ben recount his experiences of the previous three days. Kaplan asked questions in a flat, disinterested monotone, like a shopkeeper checking his inventory. He barely glanced at the books and articles Ben placed in front of him.

"You've been a very busy man, Mr. Isaacson," Kaplan observed when all the questions had been asked. "First you're in the printing business, then you're a distributor, and now we discover you're a provocateur. I can see why you didn't show up yesterday."

"Yesterday?" Ben was bewildered.

"You were supposed to find out about the arrangements for the *hakhsharah*," Hanovi said.

Ben had been so involved at Nazi Headquarters that he'd forgotten about Fulda. Why would they bring up Fulda? It seemed so irrelevant compared to what he had learned at Nazi Headquarters.

"I thought it was more important to. . . ."

"And so it was," Kaplan cut him off. "Now we must make arrangements to get you out of Berlin immediately. It's too dangerous for you to stay."

Ben started to protest. "But I. . . ."

"You and Miss Feldman and Miss Hessemann are scheduled to leave on the next express for Fulda. It leaves at seven A.M. tomorrow morning. Hanovi will give you the necessary tickets and information. Now you must excuse me." Kaplan stood up. That was it. No word of thanks, no personal congratulations—not one word of appreciation. Ben's face flushed angrily and he strode from the room.

"Downstairs, third door to the right," Hanovi said. Ben heard the other man's footsteps close behind him.

Once the door to Hanovi's office was closed, Ben started to vent his frustration. "What kind of man is Kaplan? And how did he know about Bluma? He's. . . ."

"Worried," Hanovi interjected. "It's much worse than we thought." Patiently, "the prophet" explained that Kaplan was distraught; Ten Meineckestrasse had underestimated the Nazis' strength as well as the depth of their commitment and organization. That error in judgment would be corrected immediately, but even so, the future looked darker than ever. Hanovi looked grim.

"If the questions you raised are answered the way I think they will be, within five years, the Nazis will be a major political force. But that's no longer your concern."

"What does that mean?" Ben asked.

Hanovi handed him an envelope. "As Mr. Kaplan said, it's too dangerous for you to remain in Berlin. In that envelope are your tickets for the Fulda Express. Stay at Grenadierstrasse and take a cab to the station first thing in the morning. Don't worry about your cousin, we'll see that he knows what happened. Just stay in Fulda until you hear from us. The people who meet you at the *hakhsharah* will let us know where you're staying. Any questions?''

''Just one. How did Kaplan know about Bluma?''

Hanovi grinned like a crocodile. ''We have our sources. Oh, I almost forgot. As long as you're in Fulda, Mr. Kaplan would appreciate it if you'd speak to the local congregation. They're isolated and very conservative. They need to know what's happening here in Berlin. And don't worry about Henry Ford. We'll be alerting the Anti-Defamation League in the United States to his activities here.''

''You never miss a bet, do you?''

''We try to do our best.''

As Hanovi walked Ben to the front door, he reached out and shook Ben's hand. It was as close to saying thank you as Hanovi would get.

That night, Ben explained to Bluma and Sarah what he had been doing and told them to start packing. As he watched them, he realized what good friends they had become. He was glad that Sarah now had someone to call a friend.

Just before they turned in for the night, Bluma walked Ben to the street and kissed him gently. ''You were crazy to take a chance like that.''

''I know.''

''I love you, Ben.'' He kissed her deeply.

The next morning dawned clear and windy. At the last minute, Ben decided that a conductor might raise an objection if he saw Sarah's pet, so they placed Katzele in a wicker basket lined with a towel. Sarah carried the basket under her arm, keeping one hand on the lid.

Ben waited until the last possible moment to send for a cab. The last thing he wanted was to be standing around at the station. Though he guessed that Ten Meineckestrasse would have people watching them, he didn't want to take the chance of being recognized by some overzealous Nazi before they boarded the train. Despite Ben's apprehensions, everything went as planned. They all breathed a sigh of relief when the final whistle sounded and the train began to move. They were on their way to Fulda.

TEN

Fulda
January, 1925

As the train sped south, the broad expanse of the north German plain gradually gave way to the sandy woods of Brandenberg. Far removed from the decay infecting Berlin, the snow-covered pines and well-ordered farms of central Germany resembled a completely different country.

Sarah was nervous and distracted for the first part of the trip; her landlady relished a good disaster and had frightened Sarah with a wad of newspaper clippings describing terrorist attacks on the trains running to and from Berlin. Sarah was so convinced some fanatic would try to derail the Fulda Express that she had everyone in the compartment sitting on the edge of their seat by the time they left the outskirts of Berlin. Ben found himself wondering how he ever agreed to get tangled up with her. Sometimes it seemed like more trouble than it was worth.

An hour out of Berlin, they passed through the ancient city of Leipzig, leaving the soft hills of Saxony behind for the dense, gnarled woods of Thuringia. The fairy-tale quality of the mountain forests made a magical contrast with the stark severity of the Prussian plains surrounding the capital.

It was close to noon when the forbidding peaks fell away to reveal a broad valley piercing the mountains. Not far distant, and well below them lay Fulda, nestled in a wide bend of a river sharing the same name. The town was bracketed to the north and south by magnificent hills, capped by a rolling carpet of glistening snow.

Dozens of church steeples dominated the skyline, preserving the town's medieval appearance. Even from a distance, Ben could distinguish the ancient peaked roofs of the houses crowding the narrow streets. Though an occasional factory chimney marred the view, the vast majority of buildings dated back to the Middle Ages. The train slowed gradually and the station rail yard became visible, a stark and grimy intruder into a perfectly preserved past.

As Hanovi had promised, they were expected; Ben never ceased to marvel at Ten Meineckestrasse's organization and efficiency. A young couple named Fritz and Leisl welcomed everyone to Fulda and helped to load the luggage into an ancient vehicle. Ben cranked the engine over for Fritz and the truck roared to life. Skillfully, Fritz coaxed the old gears to respond as he negotiated the twisting cobblestone streets that led out of town.

As the young people talked, the travelers were surprised to discover that Fritz and Leisl were not really Zionists. They were like many Jews who felt an obligation to help, but had no particular desire to emigrate to Palestine or become too deeply involved. The men at Ten Meineckestrasse always found a use for such people. Sometimes they were used for their contacts or asked to perform a small service—in this case, they were tapped to drive Ben, Bluma, and Sarah to the *hakhsharah*.

Ben noticed that Sarah did not participate in the conversation. She was numb with anxiety.

Thirty minutes from Fulda, the road deteriorated to a bumpy track riddled with rocks and frost heaves. Gamely, the old truck pitched and bucked. Ben was just about to suggest walking when Fritz stopped outside a small farmhouse on the outskirts of a forest. Leisl started to laugh. When Ben asked her to share the joke, she pointed to the conveyance that would take them on the last leg of the journey.

To Bluma's delight, a gaily painted cart stood by the side of the house with a bay mare in the traces. She pawed the ground and snorted, eager to be off.

A grizzled old man emerged from the house, swathed in a rank bearskin coat. He mumbled a greeting, then hauled himself up to the driver's seat, groaning and complaining in Yiddish. Without waiting to see whether everyone was aboard or not, he clucked to the mare and the cart started to move. Ben had to leap onto the cart's tailgate to avoid being left behind. He yelled at the driver, but the old man ignored him and promptly dozed off, allowing the horse to follow her lead through the dense woods.

Only the sound of the mare's hoofs breaking the crusted snow disturbed the silence of the forest. Mounded snow covered the sparse patches of open ground and formed a thick coating on dark green pines and hemlocks. Twice, they startled a deer into flight. Though Sarah was still apprehensive, the cart ride seemed to calm her nerves. Ben and Bluma snuggled together and enjoyed the twenty-minute ride like a couple of schoolchildren on an outing.

"Look!" Sarah called out excitedly as an open space appeared at the end of the tunnel of trees. Her cry roused the driver from his slumber and evoked another series of muttered complaints in Yiddish.

Before them lay a broad snow-covered plain, completely enclosed by a simple wire fence. Horses and cows clustered around stacks of winter forage, and a flock of sheep grazed on a windblown patch of field.

In the center of the valley stood a collection of weather-beaten houses, barns, and outbuildings that appeared well-tended but badly in need of painting. Ten or twelve open-sided sheds housed every imaginable type of farm implement: plows, harrows, tractors, balers, spreaders, and several pieces of equipment that none of them recognized. As they approached the *hakhsharah*, the mare whinnied, causing the farm horses to lift their heads and nicker in response.

The driver guided his horse through the gate and tied her to a wooden post. "You're there," he grunted as a horde of coatless teenagers erupted out of the long wooden dormitories and descended on the cart. They stood in a circle, shivering in the cold. They were obviously excited to see newcomers—any visitor was a treat, but Katzele was an instant success.

For the first time since leaving Berlin, Sarah smiled happily, the care gone from her face. The unknown was now known. Jumping down from the cart, she basked in the attention Katzele received and chattered happily with the strangers who would soon be her friends.

Ben and Bluma climbed down from the cart, and a rugged young woman in her late twenties stepped forward. She introduced herself as Trudi Weiss, a member of the Religious Committee For Fulda and explained that new arrivals were her responsibility.

"We were afraid Sarah might be lonely," Bluma explained, "but she seems to be doing fine."

"You have nothing to worry about," the young woman assured them. "We're all family here. We hold the future of Palestine in our hands, so every person entrusted to us is a precious charge." Ben and Bluma saw the pride in her face as she surveyed the excited group of young people.

"Would the two of you like a tour of the camp?"

"I wish we had time," Ben declined regretfully, "but I have a friend in Fulda, Michel Zadek, who is expecting us for dinner. We'd best be going."

Ben walked over to say good-by to Sarah. His heart fell when he saw the stricken look on her face. Her lips began to tremble, and she wrapped her arms tightly around herself. For a moment, she simply stared at him, then she burst into tears. The young people stood around her, silently supportive. Each of them knew exactly how she felt. They had all left behind a familiar way of life, homes and loved ones. They understood what it was like to be lonely. Ben took Sarah into his arms.

"It's all right," he said, caressing her hair.

"I'll never see you again," she wailed.

"Of course you will, Sarah," he promised. "How could I ever let you disappear from my life?"

"Oh Benjamin, I feel so alone."

"I know, I know . . . ," he comforted her. "But we'll write. And before you know it, we'll all be in Palestine."

Sarah's eyes met Bluma's. "You, too, Bluma?"

"Me too, Sarah."

Suddenly, Katzele squirmed out of Sarah's coat and jumped to the ground. Meowing with delight, he rolled in the fluffy snow, wriggling and pawing at imaginary mice.

"He looks so happy," Sarah sniffed.

"I know. And you will be, too."

She took Ben's hands in her own and whispered the words every Jew holds precious, "Next year in Jerusalem!"

"*Leshanah haba'ah b'Yerushalayim*," Ben whispered back. She turned and walked away with the other young people.

"I guarantee she'll be fine," Trudi Weiss smiled.

"By the look of it," Bluma observed, "you know how to take good care of them."

"We do," she answered. "All it takes is a little love and devotion."

• • •

Ben tried to describe Michel Zadek to Bluma on their way into town, but no description could do justice to the original. Zadek sat across from Ben and Bluma in the back of an open *droske*, his black eyes flashing excitedly. His pudgy hands cleaved the air like windmill blades.

"I could hardly believe it when you sent word to meet you back at the station. Such a surprise! Such a wonderful surprise!" Zadek bubbled. "You're both going to have a marvelous time. I can't wait for you to see

Fulda. Fulda has such a rich history, such drama. It's like living in a wonderful novel. Spend a little time here, and I guarantee you'll forget about Palestine. On the way to my house, I'll give you the quick tour. It's still early. You don't mind, do you? Or would you rather go straight to the house?'' The enthusiastic toy vendor hardly drew a breath between sentences.

Bluma burst out laughing. ''We're in your hands.''

Fulda was everything Zadek had promised. Despite its size, the city possessed a tranquil beauty usually seen only in small villages untouched by the twentieth century. They drove through the streets while Michel conducted an uninterruptible monologue about the city and how it grew up around a Benedictine Abbey founded in the middle of the eighth century.

''There are so many churches,'' Bluma remarked.

''From Fulda, Christianity spread throughout central Germany. That's why there are so many cathedrals here. St. Boniface himself is buried in one of the crypts.''

Michel interrupted his historical lecture to point out his own house, a modest two-story affair in a middle-class neighborhood called Judenberg—Jewish Hill. They drove on to the center of town, past the Michaelskirche, a Carolingian-style church over a thousand years old, and the castle of the Prince-Bishops of Fulda, since converted into a museum. Zadek promised to show Ben and Bluma the paintings and frescoed ceilings in the castle the following day.

''They're masterpieces,'' he boasted.

They passed through a quaint park full of twisted old trees whose trunks were stripped of bark. Their odd shapes intrigued Bluma.

''Why are they so deformed?'' she asked.

''They used to quarter cavalry horses here in the old days,'' Zadek explained. ''The beasts would eat the bark and scratch themselves on the trunks, stunting the trees.''

''Is there anything about Fulda that you don't know?'' Bluma laughed. Looking to the north, she noticed a great walled building. From the center of the structure emerged a huge, conical roof, covered with gray slate.

''What is that?'' she asked Zadek.

''That's the Frauenberg. The walls were built to protect the people from massacres during the religious wars.''

''Massacres?''

''Of course,'' Zadek beamed. ''The town's had so many of them, only a scholar could give you a complete tally.''

''I'm not sure I understand what you mean,'' Ben said. The thought of pastoral Fulda being the site of religious massacres struck him as incongruous.

"Fulda is the religious center of Germany," Zadek rattled on. "Saint Boniface and his pupil, Saint Sturmi, built a monastery here in the eighth century. Old Saint Boniface chopped down Donar's Oak, which stood atop Mount Gudenbery and—"

"Donar's Oak?" Bluma interrupted.

"Yes. Donar's Oak was a sacred tree, worshipped by the people who lived here. Unable to gain any converts, Boniface invited everyone in Hesse to the base of the tree for a demonstration. When everyone had gathered around the tree, he cut it down. They were awestruck at his effrontery, certain that he would be struck down by their gods. When nothing happened, they concluded that his god was more powerful than their own, so they converted to Christianity. Ever since that time, Fulda has been a center of religious activity for the entire country. Penitents and pilgrims still come to the local shrines and legend has it that the Messiah will return to earth here. It is a very holy place, even for the Jews."

"Why were there so many massacres?" Bluma wondered.

"Well, it's a bit complicated," Zadek began. "During the Reformation, Catholics and Protestants fought battle after battle, and many of those battles were fought around Fulda. Traditionally, the winning side would massacre the losing side. First, the Catholics would kill the Protestants, then the Protestants would massacre the Catholics." Zadek laughed, then shook his head sadly. "Whenever they tired of killing each other, they'd turn on the Jews."

Ben was aghast. "If what you say is true, why would Jews consider Fulda a religious center? The Reformation was nothing to them."

"That might be true, but a holy place is a holy place, even though every square in town has been drenched with Jewish blood at one time or another."

"But, why did they remain?" Bluma asked, genuinely puzzled. "It doesn't make sense to me."

"Fulda was their home. Where else would they go? Besides, it was God's will."

Ben looked at his friend sharply. Zadek was a very religious man, but his streak of fatalism took Ben by surprise. It seemed out of character.

As they passed through a small square, Michel instructed the driver to stop and described the atrocities that had taken place there during the sixteenth century. A mob of zealous Protestants had sealed the square off and herded a thousand Jews into the confined space, using it like a pen. When the square was filled, the Protestants poured oil on the Jews and set them on fire. The bodies burned for two days. The odor and decay made the area uninhabitable for almost a month.

Ben and Bluma quietly surveyed the square. It was paved with well-worn cobblestones and surrounded by tidy sixteenth-century homes that all had the same clean, freshly scrubbed appearance. Small shops and a coffee house made the square a perfect setting for strolling lovers. It did not look like the kind of place where a thousand people had been burned alive. They drove on in silence, unable to forget the carnage that Zadek had described—the terror, the agony of that day, the screams, the fire, the stench.

No one spoke until Zadek stopped the *droske* near a small house. "During the Middle Ages, a group of Catholics forced a rabbi, his family, and the leaders of the congregation to commit debaucheries in front of this house."

"How horrible," Bluma whispered.

"That wasn't the end of it, either," Zadek continued authoritatively. He seemed dispassionate and immune to the catalogue of horrors, reciting the gruesome facts like a schoolboy anxious to impress the headmaster. "When the Catholics grew tired of the exhibition, they beheaded the Jews and stuck their heads on spikes for the crows to pick at."

The carriage passed the foot of Judenberg, completing the circle back to Zadek's house. Again, Zadek broke the silence.

"This entire area has been burned down more than twenty times. Knights, priests, Catholics, Protestants, soldiers, mercenaries—all had their day. They'd surround the houses with a ring of torches and walk inward, burning as they went. If Jews tried to escape, men with swords or axes would cut off their heads and toss them to dogs." Here, even Zadek began to falter. "It must have been pretty gruesome."

"Why didn't they at least fight back? Or flee?" Ben asked.

"Fight back with what? Flee to where? Let me tell you a story." The carriage came to a halt in front of Michel's house. As they stepped down he pointed to the street.

"In 1806, cavalry units of Napoleon's Grande Armée passed through Fulda on their way back from the Battle of Jena. The streets of the lower town were deserted and the French searched the area looking for people to question about the movements of enemy units. Finally, they came to this road, where my house stands." Zadek paused for effect.

"A platoon of chasseurs saw a group of dirty, bedraggled Jews dancing down the hill. A French sergeant cantered to the side of an old Jew who was kneeling in the street, chanting in Hebrew. The Frenchman dismounted and lifted the old man up. 'Why are you singing?' he asked.

'What happened here?' The old Jew looked at the Frenchman in a daze. He smiled, then kissed the sergeant's hand. 'When the Catholics heard that the Catholic French army would pass through Fulda, they drove out the Protestants,' he said. 'Then they began to massacre the Jews. The next day, the Protestant Prussian army marched through. They forced the Catholics to flee and celebrated their victory by killing more Jews. Now, you have come and driven out the Prussian Protestants. We are celebrating because no one is left to kill us. It is God's will, and we are thankful.' ''

Hannah Zadek stepped out of the front door, shivering from the cold. ''Michel,'' she scolded her husband. ''Why are you keeping our guests out in the cold? Have them come in.'' She was a plain woman, several years older than her husband, with a toothy smile and sharp, angular cheekbones. She wore an inexpensive wig that sat slightly askew; like many ultra-orthodox Jews she wore a *sheitel* to hide her own hair in public. Prudently, Ben introduced Bluma as a friend, a co-worker in the Zionist movement.

After Zadek's grisly tales, dinner turned out to be more cheerful than they expected. Michel's wife prepared a superb kosher dinner, and Michel entertained everyone with anecdotes from the toy trade. Hannah Zadek programmed the evening with brusque efficiency, sending the men to the synagogue and dragging Bluma off to meet with the women of the congregation. Knowing how Bluma resented the orthodox tradition of separating men and women, Ben chuckled at the gracious way she swallowed Hannah's ''invitation.''

Actually, Hannah's efficiency dovetailed perfectly with Ben's plans. He couldn't admit that Ten Meineckestrasse had sent him to speak to the congregation, but he could, as an invited guest, address the group. He planned his speech on the way to the synagogue and sat impatiently, waiting for the service to end. When it did, Zadek introduced him.

Ben began by drawing a parallel between the stubborn reluctance of the ancient Jews to obey God's command, '*lekh lekha*,' and modern Germany. He spoke of Fulda's nightmare history and linked it to current events, concluding with a description of what the Nazis were doing in Berlin. The congregation nodded in solemn agreement.

''God set aside the land of Palestine as a haven for his people in a world filled with hatred. The signs of the times are plain to read. It is incumbent on us to follow God's will and seek our future in Palestine.''

Ben's speech was stiff and not very eloquent, but he felt that he had made an impression. He had expected a burst of enthusiasm but to his surprise, confusion rippled through the congregation. The rabbi stood up.

"Mr. Isaacson," he said firmly. "I enjoyed your talk, and you raise many valid points, but surely you must realize that we cannot return to Palestine. It is not our place. Any such redemption must come at the behest of the Messiah and the Messiah alone, not by the work of any mortal man. It would be blasphemous for us to presume to do His work."

Ben was speechless. They had seemed so receptive.

"Ah," Ben tried to collect his thoughts. "Do you . . . I mean are you trying to say that you feel it is God's will that you remain here in Fulda, until the Messiah descends from heaven and commands you to leave, even if that means harassment or death?"

"What else would you have us do?"

Ben remained silent for the rest of the meeting, listening as the men passionately argued trivial points of Talmudic law. He wanted to stand up and scream at them. They were so preoccupied with details, they had forgotten about survival.

Ben's disappointment was painfully obvious to Zadek. "I would have warned you, if I had known what you were going to talk about," he apologized mournfully. "My congregation is ultra-orthodox."

"Don't worry about it," Ben squeezed his shoulder. As they walked out of the synagogue towards Zadek's house, a young man with a barely discernible beard ran up to them. Ben recognized him from the meeting.

"Ah," Michel grinned, "Benjamin, this is Hermann Kishk, one of our more enthusiastic members."

All the way back to Zadek's house, Hermann plied Ben with an endless stream of questions about Berlin and the Nazis. When they arrived at the front door, Hermann turned to Zadek. "If you don't mind, I'd like to talk to Benjamin alone for a second, all right?"

"Of course," Zadek replied with surprise. He bid Hermann good evening and left the two men standing on the stoop.

Hermann turned to Ben with a serious expression. "I've listened to what you said about the Nazis, and I think you're right. For a long time now, I've felt that every Jew in Germany should leave this place. We're all in terrible danger."

"I thought the Jews of Fulda had been placed here by the hand of God." The humorous edge in Ben's voice was lost on Kishk.

"There's going to be massacre, worse than any of the others. I really think they are planning to kill us all. It's only a matter of time, and once they start, they won't stop until every Jew in Germany is dead. I want to go to Palestine, just like you said." Hermann gestured wildly with his arms as he spoke and there was a feverish cast to his eyes.

"Is this something you just decided?"

"No, but after listening to you, I thought the time was right. Will you tell me what I should do?"

Ben stared at Hermann Kishk, wondering if he was in complete possession of all his faculties. What had Ben said that touched Kishk, but no one else? Kishk struck him as the type to be carried away by the excitement of the moment. Ben was tempted to tell him to think about it overnight; he didn't want to make any complicated arrangements with Ten Meineckestrasse, then suffer the humiliation of having Kishk change his mind the next day.

"It's not a game, Hermann. Maybe you should think about it for a while."

"I am entirely serious," Kishk replied anxiously. "You must help me. There's no one else."

Ben smiled. "All right. I'll do everything in my power to help you get to Palestine. Just sit tight and someone will contact you within the week."

"Good night, and God bless you." Gratefully, Hermann pumped Ben's hand. Ben watched him disappear into the darkness. The thought occurred to him that Kishk was the first person he had ever persuaded to emigrate to Palestine. In a small way it helped to make up for his lack of success at the synagogue.

Later that night, as they talked about Palestine and the congregation in Fulda, Michel suggested that Ben and Bluma stop in Leipzig on their way back to Berlin. "The Jews of Leipzig are far more sophisticated and cosmopolitan. I'm sure they'll be more receptive to your message. When you decide to leave, I'll call a friend of mine, Hans Schonbaum," Zadek promised, eager to assuage Ben's disappointment. "By the time you arrive in Leipzig, everything will be arranged."

"Why not?" Ben smiled. Even though Hanovi had instructed them to remain in Fulda, there was nothing to be accomplished by staying; they might just as well try their luck elsewhere.

● ● ●

As Michel had said, Leipzig and Fulda were worlds apart. Fulda was a pastoral reminder of the Middle Ages; Leipzig was a bustling commercial center, encompassing more than a dozen major industries. Located at the confluence of the Pleisse, the White Elster, and the Parthe, the city had been a natural meeting point for the ancient trade routes serving northern Europe for more than a millennium. Its factories produced steel, chemicals, textiles, and paper; its smoked meats and sausages were world famous; and the skill of its furriers was second to none.

Culturally, Leipzig was best known for its publishing and printing houses, booksellers to Germany and central Europe since the fifteenth century. Even during the economic depression of the twenties, the city remained vital and alive.

Leipzig's Jewish community was prominent, wealthy, and influential. They dominated the fur and printing trades outright and shared in the ownership of the remaining commercial and industrial interests on a roughly fifty-fifty basis with gentiles. The Jews of Leipzig were a force to be reckoned with. They were the mainstream of German Jewry, not a backwater eddy.

Ben called Hans Schonbaum from the station, and Michel Zadek proved to be as good as his word—everything had been prearranged. "Your timing is perfect," Schonbaum announced. "I'm giving a little fund-raising party tonight, so I can guarantee you a full house. We're always delighted to hear news from the capital. Why don't you come around seven o'clock? That will give my guests an opportunity to assemble and relax before your talk."

"We'll be there," Ben promised. It was perfect, he told himself. There would be a big difference between talking to an isolated orthodox congregation, with the rabbi sitting in the front row, and a group of twentieth-century realists. At last Ben felt like he was about to accomplish something. He and Bluma checked into a hotel for a few hours of rest. They were both asleep in minutes.

That evening, they found Schonbaum's house without any trouble. The neighborhood was filled with impressive homes that looked more like miniature palaces. Each seemed to compete with the next, striving to appear more sumptuous and overwhelming than its neighbors. The address they'd been given was a huge house with a white marble façade, bathed by outdoor lights. Dozens of cars and carriages lined the curb.

When the butler opened the front door to admit them, Ben and Bluma saw that a large crowd had already gathered. The guests congregated in small groups and the sound of a string quartet drifted over the conversation. Liveried waiters moved among the guests, bearing trays of delicate canapés and champagne. Everyone wore elegant evening clothes. Unconsciously, Bluma smoothed the wrinkles from her navy blue dress.

"Welcome!" their host boomed, appearing in the foyer. Hans Schonbaum was a stubby man with a fringe of gray outlining his shiny pate. He greeted them warmly and suggested they circulate until it was time for them to speak. "Please, make yourselves comfortable," he urged, then left to greet other new arrivals.

Helping themselves to champagne and canapés, Ben and Bluma studied their surroundings. The salon was at least seventy-five feet long and half as wide, lit with magnificent crystal chandeliers. The walls and intricately carved woodwork formed a perfect background for the Renaissance paintings Schonbaum's wife collected. It was a far cry from the simple functions they had attended in Estonia.

A small bell rang and Vera Schonbaum rose to speak. She was a beautiful woman, magnificently attired in a flowing satin gown. It was impossible to ignore the exquisite diamond and emerald choker she wore or the large ruby on her left hand.

As she spoke, Ben felt as though the walls were closing in on him. It was worse than Fulda. The Jews of Leipzig were opening a school; a German-language school to teach *Ostjuden* how to speak German properly. According to Vera Schonbaum, most *Ostjuden* thought they were speaking German when they spoke Yiddish, and it was causing a great deal of embarrassment and ill-feeling in Leipzig. By learning proper German, and German customs, the *Ostjuden* would be gradually assimilated into the community, and the problem would be solved. The purpose of the soirée was to raise money for the school.

"They should be teaching them Hebrew, not German," Ben sputtered to Bluma. Their hostess finished speaking and her guests applauded politely as she introduced Ben and Bluma.

"These fine young people bring us the latest news from Berlin," she announced.

Ben strode to the informal lectern, sensing the audience's boredom. Dulled by Vera Schonbaum's lecture, they were already chatting among themselves. If Ben wanted their attention, he would have to capture it. He filled his lungs.

"*Lekh lekha!*" he shouted. Startled by his shout and the use of Hebrew, the guests turned in surprise. Hebrew was not a language spoken outside a synagogue.

"You have all heard those words before, so I'm not going to bore you with more Zionist interpretations of Genesis. What I want to talk about tonight is survival. Teaching *Ostjuden* to speak German is the last thing you should be doing. They'll never be a part of Germany, and neither will you. What the *Ostjuden* need is a Jewish homeland, not lessons in German grammar. Please believe me, before this decade is out, every Jew in this room will need that homeland as well." The audience shifted uncomfortably. They had come for a pleasant evening, not a harangue from a twenty-one-year-old Zionist who wasn't even German.

Ben ignored the annoyed expressions and plunged into a detailed description of the situation in Berlin. He warned of the growing threat posed by the Nazis, and the ever-increasing pressure caused by tens of thousands of refugees. He was angry and passionate, and he indulged his sense of frustration. Bluma watched in resignation, knowing his words fell on deaf ears. Twice Vera Schonbaum politely tried to end his speech, but Ben had built up a full head of steam and would not be deterred. When he finished speaking, no one applauded. Bluma wanted to leave, but Ben was in a combative mood and insisted on remaining. For the next two hours, Ben argued with businessmen, factory owners, publishers, and bankers. In the end, it was a complete waste of time.

The Jews of Leipzig were attuned to politics and understood the realities of the world, yet they dismissed the warning signs around them as hysteria and exaggeration. Walking back to the hotel with Bluma, Ben realized that despite their eloquent arguments and well-reasoned objections, Vera Schonbaum's guests were really no different than the isolated congregation in Fulda.

Ben had heard the same arguments a hundred times in Berlin and Fulda—we are German citizens, our lives are here; this is our culture; the *Ostjuden* are the ones responsible for all the trouble. Even worse, there was a new twist; one businessman had dismissed the Nazis by pointing out to Ben that they were no more than hired thugs, nothing to worry about. "Right here in Leipzig," he had laughed, "there are a number of Jewish industrialists and plant managers who use hired Nazis to keep Communists and jobless *Ostjuden* away from their factories."

It was a disheartening evening. Bluma listened quietly as Ben vacillated between rage and frustration.

"Bluma!" Ben exploded in exasperation. "What's wrong with those people? They know we were telling the truth. Why won't they face it? Can you believe some of them have Nazis on their payrolls? And use them against *Ostjuden*, fellow Jews?"

"I had a hard time accepting that one too."

"Bluma, is it me? Am I doing something wrong? Using the wrong words? These aren't uneducated farmers—they're intelligent, powerful people. I just can't accept that they don't see what's happening."

Bluma nodded. "They know what's happening, but they insist on sticking their heads in the sand. They're like the people back home—too afraid of the future to think about it."

They walked for a while, hand in hand. Bluma finally broke the silence.

"Ben, let's go back to Berlin tomorrow. We're just wasting our time here. These people aren't going to listen to anything they don't want to hear."

They were on the first train to Berlin the next morning.

• • •

They spent the balance of their first day in Berlin relating their experiences to Herschel. They roared with laughter at the story of Levin and the reversed cartoons, but the mirth faded from Herschel's face as Ben described his incursion into Nazi Headquarters.

"Those kinds of incidents create a lot of trouble for everyone," he frowned. "They're dangerous and provocative. The people you spoke to in Leipzig had the right idea. Assimilation is the only alternative to emigration."

That was all Ben needed to hear. He and Herschel were on their way to a first-rate conversational brawl when Helen remembered that someone from Ten Meineckestrasse had stopped by with a couple of complimentary tickets for Ben and Bluma.

Bluma was astounded. "How could they know we decided to come back? And then send someone over here before we even arrived?"

"I really don't know," Helen replied.

But Ben knew. It was Zorach Hanovi's way of letting him know that Ten Meineckestrasse was looking out for him. They must have another use for me, Ben thought, wryly. They wouldn't waste the manpower and effort if they didn't.

"Anyway, the tickets are for a local Jewish theater run by Ida Klinger," Helen went on. "She sponsors these plays to help pass the time for *Ostjuden* who have nowhere to go and nothing to do. It reminds them of home."

"They're staged in a giant indoor shelter, and the plays are good enough to attract real theater-goers," Herschel added. "You'll love it."

That night, Ben and Bluma found their way to Madame Klinger's, where hundreds of people jammed the makeshift theater, filling the wooden benches and forcing latecomers to sit on the floor. They looked strange at first, until Ben realized that most people were wearing several layers of clothing. Refugees quickly learned that one carried everything of importance or value—they never knew when they'd be asked to move on without warning.

Madame Klinger herself appeared from behind the curtain to receive a thunderous ovation. Modestly, she inclined her head, then held up her hands for silence and introduced the play.

It was written by Sholom Aleichem, a man who saw into the hearts of his people with rare clarity. Like most of his stories, the play chronicled the hardships of Jewish life in a small Russian town. It was a tale of heartbreak and suffering, alleviated only by the indefatigable humor and deep faith of the characters. Its portrayal of life in Czarist Russia reminded Ben of the childhood stories his grandfather told.

The actors were not professionals, but they understood their roles as few actors could. They were from the small villages of Poland and Russia that Sholom Aleichem depicted. They had lived the lives of the characters they played. There were no heroes in Sholom Aleichem's stories, only people.

As the play unfolded, the audience actually participated, shouting out encouragement when the characters encountered the harsh disappointments of life, and sharing their grief when sadness threatened to overwhelm them.

Many people in the audience wept openly; the essence of the play struck too close to their own lives. Huddled together in wretched refugee shelters, driven from their homes, and left without possessions or hope, they could not help but be touched. The stories contained such power for two reasons: they were rooted in real experience, and they were written in Yiddish, a language the author had singlehandedly established as a literary medium.

It surprised Ben to see tears streak Bluma's cheek. She leaned into him and whispered, "Ben, I don't want to stay any longer." In response, he simply put his arm around her and held her close. As he did so, he noticed that the couple sitting to his left seemed equally moved.

The man was close to fifty, dressed in a shabby jacket and pants. He was barrel-chested, with a thick neck and broad shoulders. His nose canted to one side, having been badly broken and never properly set. He looked like a powerful man, but there was a gentle quality to his face. The woman next to him appeared much older because her face was dark and deeply lined, like a piece of old leather. She wore her hair drawn back into a bun.

The man sat motionless, tears trickling down his face. The woman cried in complete silence, her eyes fixed on the stage. Their emotions were so plain to perceive, so raw and exposed, that Ben felt drawn to them. Instinctively, he wanted to reach out and comfort them. He was so engrossed by their pathos that the applause signaling the end of the play caught him by surprise.

As the curtain fell, the man and the woman sat numbly, not joining in the applause. Ben stared so intensely, that the man finally sensed his gaze and looked up with an embarrassed smile.

"You must excuse us," he said, blowing his nose. "We cry too often when the play is sad."

"Not at all. I see you were deeply moved."

"Yes. Sometimes the play makes us remember too much. I am Heinkel Cohen. This is my wife, Mina." His wife continued to stare at the stage, entranced.

"Would you like to join us for some coffee?" Ben asked impulsively.

"We have no money for such things," Heinkel said sadly.

"Please, be our guests."

Heinkel accepted Ben's invitation with a smile and gently shook his wife until her eyes came into focus. "We are going for coffee, Mina." She nodded, drawing her coat around her.

They walked to the café in silence, not wanting to break the mood created by the play, each person lost in his own thoughts. When they arrived at the coffee house, a waiter showed them to a cozy table in the warmest corner of the café, seating Ben and Bluma across from their guests. The cold air seemed to have revived Mina Cohen somewhat, but her eyes still had a glazed look. They drank their coffee slowly, inhaling the rich aroma.

"Oh," Mina Cohen finally spoke. "This is wonderful. I cannot recall the last time I had real coffee."

Heinkel brushed his fingers through his graying hair. "It is very good coffee, a *mechayeh*. Very good." They spoke in Yiddish.

"Did you enjoy the play?" Bluma asked, seeking to start a conversation. Heinkel looked down into his cup.

The woman smiled wanly. "We were very moved. It was so . . . so very true, so like a bad dream, a terrible nightmare." She shook her head sadly and returned to her coffee. Something about the way she spoke sent chills up Bluma's spine.

"Are you all right, Mrs. Cohen?" Ben asked, concerned about her appearance. "Was it something in the play?"

"It reminded us of something that happened in our village in Lithuania," her husband quietly explained. For some reason, he seemed reluctant to meet Ben's gaze.

"What happened?" Bluma asked.

"The Russian police came to our village one day . . . ," he started. Then he faltered. Ben noticed that Cohen's hands were trembling.

"You don't have to tell us," Bluma put her hands over Cohen's. "Perhaps we should talk about something else."

"No, Heinkel," his wife blazed to life. "Tell them. Everyone should know what animals they are." Cohen looked at his wife in despair. Suddenly, Ben wished he had not been so impulsive. There was a stricken look in Heinkel Cohen's eyes as he began to speak.

"Late one afternoon, four policemen came to our village. They were drunk and bored, looking for excitement. They tied the horses outside the house we used as a synagogue and urinated on the front door. Everyone bolted their shutters and locked the doors, hoping the policemen would tire of their game and leave."

"Everyone but the butcher," Mina interrupted. "He was too proud to hide, too strong to cower. He kept his shop open, so naturally, the policemen went there first. They grabbed his daughter." Ben felt Bluma's hand tighten.

"Mina, please," her husband tried to calm her. Ben noticed her eyes were crystal clear.

"She was a beautiful girl, with long dark braids. She was sixteen years old, always so cheerful, so fragile, so innocent. She was a . . . a. . . ." The woman struggled for the word. "She suffered like the little *Tsarevitch.*"

"She had hemophilia?" Bluma supplied the word.

"That's right," her husband replied. But the woman seemed oblivious to them, reliving the experience in a world of her own.

"They dragged her out of the shop by the hair and stripped her naked. Then they raped her, one at a time. Each one had his turn. After a while, she didn't even moan anymore." Mina Cohen's eyes burned with the intensity of her emotions. "Her mother must have suffered the agonies of the damned. To raise a child, love her with all your heart, to see her grow. . . ." She spoke loud enough for everyone in the café to hear.

"Mina," her husband whispered brokenly.

"When they finished with her, they stood her up against a wall while the blood ran down her legs. . . ."

"Mina! That's enough!" her husband cried. The woman began sobbing hysterically. Bluma ran around the table and took Mina Cohen into her arms.

"Didn't anyone try to stop them?" Ben asked, already knowing the answer. Resistance would have resulted in a massacre. Heinkel Cohen covered his face.

"Her father tried to stop them," Mina choked. "He came running out with his big butcher knife, but they just laughed. They nearly beat him to death."

Bluma stared at Mina Cohen in horror. In the isolated Jewish villages of the east, such an atrocity affected every member of the community with a depth of feeling almost impossible for a non-Jew to understand.

"Mina never got over it," Heinkel whispered. She began to wail and her husband took her into his arms. She covered her mouth with her hand, trying to stifle her terrible grief, unable to control herself. She looked up at the ceiling, crying out to God, "Why? Why did they have to do that? She was so young!" Tears poured out of her like a stream of liquid pain.

"They killed her!" she screamed.

Heinkel Cohen pressed his wife's face into his shoulder while the German patrons of the café stared in shock. Angered by the disruption in his café, the barman walked over with a look of hostility on his face. He was a beefy man with close-cropped hair.

"Get that lousy drunk out of here!" he shouted. "Take your Yiddish crap and get out!"

"She's not drunk," Bluma flared.

"Not drunk?" the bartender laughed. "Jews get drunk on coffee. She's ruining my business. Now get her out before I drag her out by the hair!" As he reached for Mina Cohen, Ben stood up and smiled disarmingly.

"No need for excitement," he assured the bartender. The man hesitated for a moment and Ben lashed out, kicking him in the testicles. The bartender collapsed on the floor, clutching himself and gasping for breath. Bluma helped Heinkel Cohen with his wife, and they left the café at a half run.

Two blocks away, they stopped beneath a street lamp to catch their breath. Mina Cohen slumped against her husband in an exhausted stupor.

"I'm sorry we ruined your evening," Cohen apologized. "I hope you won't get into trouble for what happened in there."

"Don't worry about it. I enjoyed it."

"It is always this way," Cohen sighed with resignation. "Our lives run like the play; someone else wrote the parts. We have no other lines, no other choice . . . nothing but pain."

"Heinkel . . . ," Bluma began.

"Please don't. Thanks for the coffee." He started to turn away.

"You must be hungry," Ben broke in, reluctant to abandon the couple to their private hell, but Cohen held up his hand and shook his head.

"You're very kind, but you see what happens. We tried to run away from it, but we can't. No matter how far we run, it always comes back to haunt us. When she's in pain, all I can do is pray for it to end, and when it finally does end, all I do is fear its return. There is no end to it.'' He turned and walked off into the darkness, supporting his grief-stricken wife.

Bluma turned to Ben and buried her head in his shoulder.

''Ben,'' she cried quietly, ''I feel like . . . like . . .''

''I know,'' Ben replied, holding her tightly. ''I do too.''

ELEVEN

Berlin/Wiesenstrasse
January 1925

Ben and Bluma sat together in Herschel's darkened apartment, deeply affected by the Cohens' tragedy. It was hard for them to accept that people like the Cohens had no future; their lives were a series of days, one lived after another. They had no hopes, no dreams, only nightmares.

"I think we've made the same mistake Vera Schonbaum and her friends have made," Bluma said. When Ben opened his mouth to protest, she shook her head vehemently.

"I mean it, Ben. We've been looking at the *Ostjuden* like they were some kind of nameless, faceless mass. In all honesty, they're as strange and alien to us as they are to Vera Schonbaum and people like her. We don't understand the *Ostjuden* because we don't know who they really are or what it's like for them."

"What are you getting at?"

"I think it's time we found out for ourselves," she murmured pensively. "Old clothes, that's what we need. Old clothes."

"Why would we need old clothes?"

"Because we're going to become *Ostjuden*."

They rose early the next morning and borrowed some of Herschel's and Helen's old work clothes out of a closet trunk. Bluma roughed up the material with a dinner fork and tore some of the edges and seams, creating a ragged appearance. Ben skipped shaving and Bluma carefully smudged her face and hands with blacking from the coal grate.

"Ugh," she grimaced, looking at herself in the bathroom mirror. Ben came up behind her and kissed her on the back of her neck.

"You look radiant."

"Ben, please. You'll ruin my makeup," she deadpanned. They laughed together.

"There is one advantage to our charade," Ben grinned. "At least the Nazis won't recognize me."

After leaving a vague note for Herschel, they tramped north over the River Spree into the sooty nether world bordering the railroad yards of Berlin. Near the tracks, there was a large complex for homeless *Ostjuden* known as the Wiesenstrasse Shelter. It had been established by the Berliner Verein, a private association, and provided housing for *Ostjuden* refugees.

"You'd think we were on our way to prison," Bluma said. Twice they had stopped to ask where Wiesenstrasse was, and each time, they had received a look of pity and sympathy.

As Ben and Bluma neared the railyards, the stench of uncollected garbage became overwhelming. Old factories lined the neglected streets. Derelicts slept in doorways and abandoned buildings. One man wrapped in a tattered army blanket made his home in a wooden packing crate that had been left on the sidewalk. Bluma shuddered involuntarily.

Wiesenstrasse was a filthy, foul-smelling avenue littered with trash. It ran parallel to the main rail lines. Scummy pools of liquid flooded the cobblestones and refused to freeze. Screeching brakes, whistles, and the clattering wheels of passing trains shattered the air. The odor of gas and diesel fumes was overpowering.

Built at the onset of the Industrial Revolution, the shelter had once been a factory, a haphazard collection of buildings, interconnected by tunnels and enclosed walkways. The soot-stained red bricks looked ready to crumble, and Bluma swore that she saw the whole structure tremble when a train passed by.

"I'm already depressed, and all I've seen is the outside," she said. They climbed three short steps to the front office door. Once inside, they were in a different world.

The interior was immaculate. Everything was freshly painted an antiseptic white, with simple wooden furniture and no curtains. The floors were gouged and scarred, but scrubbed to a dull shine. The smell of cleaning fluid permeated the air. It was indifferent, impersonal, and mechanical, but clean as a hospital. Functional, sterile, cold—but safe. They were so preoccupied with the vivid contrast between interior and exterior, they didn't hear the receptionist.

"May I help you?" she repeated impatiently.

"Uh, yes." Ben was careful to mask his fluent German and made his reply in stumbling Yiddish. "We have no . . . "

"No place to stay," she cut him off. Ben nodded miserably.

"See the man over there," she said curtly and pointed to the far end of the room. She turned back to a stack of papers. She's like the building, Ben thought to himself, functional, but sterile and cold. They trudged to the end of the room. Without looking up, a man in wire-rim glasses asked their names.

"Benzl Ben-Anschel."

"Amulba," Bluma murmured, spelling her name backwards. Ben detected the jittery note in her voice, but the clerk ignored it. He was used to dealing with nervous refugees; *Ostjuden* always seemed terrified of officials. The clerk, a German Jew, couldn't understand it. But then again, he had never lived in a small village in Russia.

"Papers, please."

"Lost."

The clerk looked at them with a long-suffering expression. Few of the Jews entering Wiesenstrasse had papers of any kind. Fortunately, passports and papers were not required to gain admittance. If you could speak Yiddish, that proved you were a Jew. If you were a Jew, that was enough.

"Can you sign your names?"

"I think so," Bluma replied timidly. The clerk pushed a registration book and steel pen across the desk.

"Try," he drawled sarcastically.

Bluma took the pen and laboriously spelled out her name: A-M-U-L-B-A, her forehead furrowed in concentration. She checked the spelling twice. Ben had to look away; he was afraid he would start to laugh at her charade.

"That's an odd name," he muttered. "Where are you from?"

"Lithuania."

"It figures," he frowned knowingly. "Show me a bizarre name and I'll show you a Lithuanian. Now you sign," he said to Ben. Quickly, Ben printed out his name: Benzl Ben-Anschel.

"Another one," the clerk sighed. "How did you pronounce that?" Ben repeated the alias.

"Hmmm," the clerk grunted. "That was an improvement over the last time you pronounced it." The clerk handed them each a numbered locker key. Unmarried couples were housed in separate dormitories.

"You can get *morgencafe* and bread at any time. Stay out of trouble."

That was it. Like the receptionist, the clerk turned back to his paperwork. Ben and Bluma looked at each other uncertainly. Nothing was said about the future, nothing about how long they would be staying, nothing about anything. Ersatz coffee, a locker, and a cot; that was it. They agreed to settle in, then meet in the dining area in thirty minutes.

Wiesenstrasse's dormitories formed an endless maze. Uninterrupted rows of surplus cots and warped lockers filled every open space, a plain wooden chair separating every other cot. Shelves propped on crates served as desks; bare bulbs with conical metal shades illuminated the dormitories. There were no frills, nothing of a personal nature. It looked like an army barracks. To save space, toilets had been placed in the corridors, but there were sinks and showers located in special rooms on the top floor. Ben soon learned that the water running from the taps was always tepid, never hot, because the gas heaters never kept pace with the demand. It was uninviting, barren, and uncaring, but it was better than the street.

Ben glanced at his key, then walked over to an unoccupied bed with the same number. He stretched out for a moment and tried to absorb his new surroundings.

"What happened to the guy who was here yesterday?"

A ragged *Ostjude* stood at the foot of Ben's bed looking like a volcano about to explode. His expression was meant to be intimidating, but he was slightly cock-eyed and the net effect was comical instead of threatening.

"I want your locker key," the *Ostjude* shouted.

Ben rolled off the bunk and stood up. He was a full head taller than his antagonist and outweighed him by forty pounds.

"What did you say to me?"

The *Ostjude* who introduced himself as Yitzakh sighed. "Nothing. Everybody is bigger than me." To Ben's amusement, the *Ostjude*'s anger disappeared instantly and he sat on the neighboring bed.

"The man who slept on your cot was my business partner. His locker is the only one in the room that locks securely, so we kept our inventory there. Now, you're here and he's gone, probably with all the merchandise."

Ben handed him the locker key. He snatched it away and rushed to the locker practically ripping the door off its hinges. It was still packed with boxes.

"A miracle!" he exclaimed. "An honest man."

Ben tapped him on the shoulder. "I thought this place was for people without jobs or a place to stay."

"A man has to have something going for him," the *Ostjude* rubbed his hands together gleefully. "Say, Blondie, you speak German?"

"My name is Benzl, not Blondie, and yes, I do."

"You speak it well?"

"Fluently."

"Then I am in a position to offer you employment." He sounded like a factory owner looking to hire a new foreman.

"What are you talking about?"

"How do you expect to get out of here? Where will you go? Where will you stay? How will you eat? You need money, money, money!" The *Ostjude* was a bundle of nervous energy.

"I hadn't thought about it yet."

"You hadn't thought about it yet?" The man started to laugh, amazed at Ben's ignorance.

"What's so funny?"

"What are you?" he asked, wiping the tears of laughter from his eyes. "An idiot? A moron? One doesn't escape from prison on good looks."

"No one here is a prisoner. Anyone is free to leave whenever he pleases." Ben didn't know whether to be annoyed or fascinated by the volatile *Ostjude*.

"You're new here," the *Ostjude* smiled tolerantly. "But you'll learn quick enough. Let's be realistic, my friend—"

"I'm not your friend," Ben interrupted.

"You will be. Listen, from the look of you, I'll bet you've got a girlfriend. Am I right?"

"That's right."

"See!" he exclaimed. "I know everything! Now, she doesn't want to live here for the rest of her life. So if somebody else comes along with money before you, she might take off without you."

"No chance."

"I've heard that before," the *Ostjude* cackled. He began to unload the locker, handing several boxes to Ben. "Take these to the bed," he directed. Exasperated, Ben complied. The *Ostjude* arranged them on the bed and opened them, one by one. Some contained ribbons, thread, and needles. Others held little dolls, scissors, and inexpensive knives. The largest box was filled with framed reproductions of a medieval master-piece by an unknown German artist. They were poorly matted and the quality of the printing was atrocious, but Ben recognized the sallow, hollow-cheeked face of Martin Luther.

"What in God's name are you doing with these?"

"I sell them," the *Ostjude* grinned.

Ben frowned in disgust. Though most people remembered him for the Ninety-five Theses, there was another, darker side to Martin Luther, a side Anschel had told his son about after Madame Spitz and her friends had broken into the Isaacson greenhouse.

In the years following his excommunication from the Roman Catholic Church, Luther opened his arms to the Jews of Germany. He demanded full and equal rights for Jews and battled tirelessly against the corrupt practices of the entrenched clergy. Supported by the nobility, Luther attracted thousands of converts from Catholicism, and began to dream of Germany as a nation bound by a single faith. But that dream was threatened when the Jews remained steadfast to their own religion.

In retaliation, Luther turned on the Jews with a vengeance, issuing an edict in 1543 that advised the German people on how to deal with Jews. It began with " . . . their synagogues or churches should be set on fire, and whatever does not burn up should be covered or spread over with dirt. Their homes should likewise be broken down and destroyed, their prayerbooks and Talmuds removed, their rabbis forbidden to teach, their privileges revoked, and young Jews set to work in fields." It ended with an exhortation to violence: any resistance to the new order was to be countered by driving every living Jew from German soil.

By the time Luther died in 1546, poor communications and his own failing health crippled his new campaign and he failed to overcome twenty years of preaching love with three years of hate. The Edict did not become formally embedded in Lutheran doctrine or take root in distant Sweden or Denmark. Even so, it was not without effect; the Jews of Wittenberg and the area surrounding Luther's home province received the full brunt of his frustration. The rest of the world might not remember the dark side of Martin Luther, but the Jews of his birthplace would never forget.

"Do you know how Luther felt about Jews?" Ben asked. "And what he did?"

"Of course. But so what? I have an obligation to sell my customers what they want."

"How could anyone respect himself as a Jew after selling those portraits of the old Jew-baiter to good Christian *hausfrauen*?"

"I don't sell to Christians," the diminutive peddler laughed. "I sell only to other self-respecting Jews."

"You're not serious!"

"What better way to show your good Christian neighbors your appreciation for one of Germany's greatest heroes? Stick Martin up next to a portrait of the old Kaiser and you're a patriot. All good German Jews are anxious to be thought of as patriots."

"You're unbelievable."

"Listen, neighbor, I'm going out to sell this stuff this afternoon in front of Wertheim's. You come along and I'll give you half. How's that? Help you keep your girl."

"Half seems very generous," Ben observed.

"Name's Yitzakh," the little man said, extending his hand. Ben took the hand and shook it firmly.

"All right, Yitzakh, I'll go, but first I've got to stop at the dining room."

"Not to eat, I hope?"

Half of Wiesenstrasse's first floor was a gigantic dining hall filled with battered plank tables and camp benches. Bluma sat alone at a table with a cup of coffee and piece of bread. A small bite was missing from the bread. The coffee looked untouched.

"Better get used to it," Yitzakh burst out before Ben introduced him. "The coffee is made from pure chicory. *Morgencafe* or morning coffee is the polite name, but good manners forbid my telling you what we really call it. The bread is spongy and barely edible. You'll be eating a lot of it."

"I can hardly wait," Bluma grimaced. All three of them laughed.

•   •   •

"*Iss Frankreich,*" Yitzakh repeated.

"Still not right. *Aus Frankreich. Aus*—'out of' or 'from.' From France." Ben corrected him for the third time.

It was a cold, crisp January day and Ben strode down the Unter den Linden at a brisk pace, carrying two sawhorses and a large box of merchandise. Yitzakh struggled gamely to keep up, but the table top and boxes he carried were too much for his short legs. Breathlessly, he called out for Ben to stop on the corner of Potsdammer Platz.

They made a strange pair. Ben was tall and blond, with broad shoulders and a narrow waist. Yitzakh was almost pear shaped with dark curly hair and a runaway beard. Even with his funny hat, he barely came up to Ben's shoulder.

"Let's try it again," Ben suggested. "*Meine liebe Dame, eine schöne Kravatte, eine . . .*"

"Enough! Enough!" Yitzakh cried.

"I thought you wanted to learn how to speak German correctly. No one will buy anything from you with that atrocious accent. They'll think you're a barbarian."

"You talk to the old biddies," Yitzakh gasped, trying to catch his breath. "That's what I have a front man for. With your blond hair and flawless German, they'll swoon at your feet."

"And if they don't swoon when they see me, I'm sure they'll faint when they get a look at you."

"Just remember that a German *hausfrau* likes all things from France, except the people."

Ben laughed. "Will I be able to retire after today's haul?"

"Only if you bag us a rich widow."

The department stores on Friedrichstrasse lined the sidewalk like baroque palaces. The street was alive with peddlers, anxious to take advantage of the foot traffic generated by the selling giants. Yitzakh directed Ben to assemble the sawhorses just to one side of Wertheim's front entrance. Three other peddlers were already set up for business. As they arranged the inventory, Yitzakh instructed Ben in the art of selling.

"Don't let anyone walk by without buying something. Remember— just because they bought something from the man next to you doesn't mean they won't buy from you as well. And never let them buy one of anything. Always offer four for the price of three." Their margin was such that Yitzakh could have offered five for the price of one and still cleared a small profit.

Yitzakh began grabbing at potential customers, shouting in a grating accent. Most people tried to ignore him. Ben watched quietly, an idea forming in his mind. He tapped Yitzakh on the shoulder.

"Why don't you let me try?" Ben suggested. "After all, did you hire me to act as a front man, or to lug sawhorses?"

"A bit of both," Yitzakh twinkled.

A stout *hausfrau* emerged from Wertheim's and was about to enter her carriage when Ben called out to her in flawless German. "Frau Kirschbaum!" Startled, the woman turned.

"My name is Heindel," she said.

"What a coincidence!" Ben exclaimed. "You look very much like Frau Kirschbaum. I called out because I had promised that good lady I would sell her four of these beautiful French bows for the price of three, when they came in." The woman eyed the ribbons and remarked how lovely they were.

"Please, Frau Heindel, allow me to apologize for the misunderstanding by offering you the same discount.'' Greedily, the woman took advantage of the price reduction. Again and again Ben used the simple ploy with enormous success. Yitzakh was thrilled. Their table was the busiest on Friedrichstrasse. Ben's first problem arose with an overbearing woman in a black cashmere coat.

"I will have three of those," she barked, pointing to a box of lavender ribbons. Her wide shoulders and square face made her look like a character from a Wagnerian opera. Ben had no trouble envisioning her with a horned steel helmet and a spear.

"I'd be delighted to sell you four for the price of three," he smiled.

"Don't give me your sales pitch. I need only three. I want only three. Will you sell them to me or not?" Ben stared at her in confusion. Yitzakh quickly intervened.

"Uf korse, lovly frowlin," he bowed. He handed her three lavender ribbons and took her money. She stomped away.

"What was that all about?" Ben exclaimed.

"How should I know?" Yitzakh shrugged. "Why would anybody insist on buying three when they could have four for the same price? Maybe she's a yeke." He used the Yiddish expression for a humorless blockhead.

Sales were so brisk that two-thirds of their inventory was sold within thirty minutes. Ben commented that selling was easy, once you got them to the table. He noticed that a lot of people seemed in an awful hurry.

"Wertheim's sells the exact same merchandise for three times the price we do. Those people were afraid the clerks would chase us away before they could buy."

"Oops!" he gasped. "Speak of the devil and he'll appear."

Several men wearing vests came out through the bronze doors and motioned for the peddlers to disperse. One by one, they forced each peddler to close down and leave. One of the men walked over to Ben and Yitzakh.

"Move on!" he growled. "You've had your fun, now take this junk over to Tietz's. You'll do much better there."

Ben stepped forward, prepared for a fight. Yitzakh placed a restraining hand on Ben's arm.

"We were just planning to go over there," Yitzakh smiled.

"That's good," the man smirked. Then he turned to Ben. "Trust me. Their prices are much higher than ours. You'll make a killing."

As they dragged their belongings down the street to Tietz's, Ben asked why Yitzakh had restrained him.

"It's a public street," Ben argued heatedly. "We have just as much right here as anyone else."

"You do have a lot to learn." The street-wise peddler appraised his partner. "I don't know how you ended up in Wiesenstrasse, what with your fancy language and soft hands, but I do know this: now that you're here, you're no different from any other *Ostjude,* and if you ever want to get out of here, you'd better do as you're told. Besides," Yitzakh sighed. "We'll get a lot of healthy exercise this way."

Ten minutes later, they were set up in front of Tietz's and sales resumed at the same pace. While Yitzakh was talking to a customer, Ben stole a look at his hands.

Though Yitzakh was only thirty, the peddler's hands were aged, rough, and thickly calloused. All the fingernails were chipped or broken. By contrast, Ben's clean hands and trimmed nails looked like they belonged to a concert pianist, not a refugee. He made a mental note to wear gloves the next day.

The balance of the day passed in much the same way—they'd set up shop, sell like crazy, then be forced to move on. Though Ben was constantly irritated by the attitude of the clerks and the store managers, Yitzakh refused to be anything but cheerful. Ben began to develop a deep respect for his friend's powers of observation and survival. Yitzakh taught him how people learned to live with what they cannot change.

That evening, Ben had to admit that he felt a rush of pride when they divided the day's profit, and he insisted that Yitzakh eat with Bluma and himself to celebrate their success. Like Ben, Bluma was discovering that life at Wiesenstrasse was not at all what they had imagined it to be.

"We need shirtfronts!" Yitzakh exclaimed the second morning. With regular shirts being so expensive, the ingenious vendors devised a kind of dickey with cuffs and a collar, all attached by elastic, but with no sleeves or back. For many Germans who could not afford the price of a shirt, the dickey was a perfect solution. They were always a good seller.

Ben was astonished to discover that the peddlers traded as furiously with each other as they did with the customers. A box of bows would be exchanged for half a dozen dickeys, a cache of sewing needles for a dozen pairs of scissors, a bit of costume jewelry for a tie. Each time, the price rose as the seller made a profit. Sometimes, the profit achieved on the initial trade was lost when the seller was forced by demand to repurchase his goods at a higher price. The fierce bargaining sessions that pitted peddler against peddler were more than a way to make an extra profit; they were a matter of pride and reputation. In an existence lit by small triumphs, outfoxing a shrewd trader was one of life's special pleasures.

Ben adapted quickly to the underground life led by most *Ostjuden* in Berlin, learning more every day. As long as one didn't remember the past or think of the future, life was palatable. The more Ben learned, the more convinced he became that Palestine was the only place for the *Ostjuden*. Their courage, their resilience, and their faith would be wasted anywhere else.

On the sixth day, they set up in front of the candy-cane logo that adorned Tietz's department store. Almost immediatley, a steely-eyed clerk evicted them, and they moved on to Goldmann's where they remained undisturbed until a young girl asked them to leave.

"Listen, I've got a wonderful tip for you!" she blurted out. "Wertheim's is running low on towels. Go there! You'll do much better!"

"Sorry, sweetheart," Ben grinned. "But we like it here. I'm sure we won't ruin you."

"Oh, dear," she groaned. "Please leave, I don't want to see anyone get hurt. My boss is watching, and he can get very angry."

Ben turned around and saw the store manager, chomping a cigar in the front window. Ben smiled broadly and tipped his hat. During the week, he had come to know all the store managers by sight and made it a point to irritate them whenever he could.

Ignoring the girl, he turned back to the table and handed a pair of collars and cuffs to a customer. He thanked the customer and rearranged the towels in a more attractive fashion. When he looked up to serve the next person, a great bull of a man towered on the opposite side of the table. The man gave him a tiny smile, then picked up the edge of the table and threw it at Ben and Yitzakh.

"Now get out of here!" he screamed. *"Schnell!"*

"We were just leaving," Yitzakh yelled back. Contemptuously, the man kicked one of their valises out of his way and returned to the store. They moved to a corner to regroup.

"That clerk looked more like a gorilla than a man," Ben gasped.

"You're learning," Yitzakh laughed.

"Why did they waste their time sending a girl out to lie and make excuses, begging us to move on? Why didn't they just send out the gorilla in the first place?"

Yitzakh explained that it was all part of a game the store managers played with the itinerant peddlers. Nearly all the department stores were owned by Jews, and they knew the *Ostjuden* were going to peddle their wares; there was no way to stop them. Rather than sending security right away, they tried to avoid hurting fellow Jews by warning them first.

"But that doesn't stop them from sending the thugs out, if they have to," Ben said bitterly.

Yitzakh shrugged. "Business, just business. They pretend and we pretend. Let's get set up again." They reassembled the table and started selling again. Suddenly, the expression on Yitzakh's face changed.

A large group of men in bright red shirts ran down the street waving crimson flags. They shouted socialist slogans and tossed rocks and bricks through store windows.

"Communists!" Yitzakh spat. "They're always stirring up trouble."

"Oh, God!" Ben cried out, grabbing their valises.

Yitzakh looked puzzled. "What's the matter with you? They're not after us."

Ben pointed in the opposite direction. Black vans offloaded scores of policemen armed with short heavy clubs. Viciously, they began to restore order by assaulting and arresting everyone in sight. They used the clubs with lethal efficiency, bludgeoning anyone in their path. People fell to their knees bleeding or clutching broken bones.

Ben and Yitzakh gathered their belongings and tried to slip down a side street, but a group of Communists grabbed the table top and sawhorses to use as a barricade. Yitzakh screamed in fury and seized the edge of the table. Ben helped him, but they were too badly outnumbered. Their merchandise spilled into the street.

The police were everywhere, swinging their clubs like scythes. *"Genug ist genug!"* they yelled. "Enough is enough!" Methodically, they carved a swathe through peddlers, Communists, and innocent bystanders. Screams and shouts filled the street.

Desperately, Yitzakh tried to recover their inventory, falling to his hands and knees and stuffing collars, bows, and towels into an open valise. He didn't see the two policemen come up behind him. Ben shouted a warning, and Yitzakh hunched his shoulders in time to deflect a vicious blow.

Frustrated, one of the policemen kicked him in the side. As he did, the toe of his boot caught in Yitzakh's pocket, ripping the flimsy material and sending his store of coins rolling across the pavement. Yitzakh unballed himself and started to crawl after the coins. Ignoring the fleeing Reds, the two policemen started to laugh and make fun of him.

Ben tried to step in, but three more policemen joined the first two, enjoying the sport. "Leave it alone," they warned him, tapping his chest with a club. "It is just a *schmutziger Jude*." A dirty Jew.

Ben's hands clenched into fists, but he forced himself to keep them at his sides. Again and again, they kicked Yitzakh in the stomach and ribs. Furious at his inability to help his friend, Ben realized he had been spared because the police assumed him to be an unemployed German. *Ostjuden* did not have blond hair and blue eyes, or speak perfect German.

The policemen toyed with Yitzakh, first pretending to help him find his coins, then stepping on his hands or poking him, using their clubs like cattle prods. They pushed him back and forth, tripping him, then yanking him up again.

Finally, a black van pulled up. One of the policemen looked down at Yitzakh and spat. "You and your little Red friends are through. show up around here again and I'll kill you." The man raised his club and bashed Yitzakh on the side of the head. Then he stepped into the van and was gone.

Yitzakh was barely conscious and covered with blood. Ben helped him to his feet, praying there was no permanent damage. Yitzakh was surprisingly bulky for such a small man.

As they shuffled past the display window of Goldmann's, avoiding piles of trampled merchandise and broken tables, Ben caught sight of the store manager. He was still standing in the window, chewing his cigar.

Only now he was smiling.

Ben spat at him, hitting the polished glass protecting the man's face.

It was dark by the time Ben and Yitzakh returned to Wiesenstrasse. They limped into the dining room empty-handed; the merchandise had been ruined and even the sawhorses and platform were gone. They had barely enough money to pay for the trolley.

Bluma had been anxiously waiting and when she saw Yitzakh's face, she came rushing over. "Oh my God!" she cried. "What happened?"

"I'm all right, I'm all right," Yitzakh muttered as he collapsed into a chair. "It looks worse than it is."

Bluma ran to the kitchen for hot water and some antiseptic. When she returned she bathed Yitzakh's cuts and bruises, then bandaged the shallow gash on his brow. As she worked, Ben told her what had happened.

"It's unbelievable,"she said tersely.

"You get used to it," Yitzakh shrugged despondently. "Maybe tomorrow we'll do better."

Ben looked at his friend's battered face and felt sick inside. Yitzakh had been beaten, he had lost what few possessions he owned, and he faced a bleak future alone. It made Ben feel ashamed for the comfort and security he had enjoyed all his life.

"Yitzakh," Ben said. "There's something I want you to know." Quietly, Ben told his friend the real reason why he and Bluma had come to Wiesenstrasse.

Yitzakh nodded. "I should have guessed. You two were hardly the typical Jewish refugee couple."

"I hope you can forgive us for deceiving you," Ben apologized. "I want you to know that the way we both feel about you wasn't part of the charade."

"Forget it," Yitzakh grinned. "So I didn't know your real name. Who cares?"

Ben dug into his trouser pocket and extracted a British five-pound note. "Since I couldn't do much to help you this afternoon, I hope you'll allow me to help you now." He handed the five-pound note to Yitzakh. "This will see that you get a fresh start."

Yitzakh's eyes widened when he saw the denomination. "It will do all of that," he whispered. To Yitzakh, five English pounds represented a small fortune. He pocketed the money carefully.

"You didn't have to do that," Yitzakh grinned, "but I'm glad you did." Then the smile faded from his face and his expression became grave. "I know you'll be going back to your way of life, and I'll be going back to mine, but there is something I'd like you to remember. You look like a German, and I can see you've got plenty of money, so maybe being a Jew gets forgotten in some little corner of your mind. But don't be fooled. Sooner or later, while you're at the opera, or eating strudel and drinking coffee on the Friedrichstrasse, someone you may or may not know will walk up to you. He'll look at your nose, or your mouth, or your hair, or the Star of David you wear on your lapel, and you'll see in his eyes that you revolt him. If you're lucky, he'll just spit on you and call you a dirty Jew. If you're not lucky, maybe he'll try to kill you. You don't have to be an *Ostjude* to know what it means to be a Jew."

"I know," Ben whispered. There was nothing else he could say.

"I've had enough for one day, so I'll say good night." Yitzakh rose to his feet with a groan. He looked at Ben and Bluma fondly. "May God keep you both."

Then he walked towards the stairway and out of their lives.

• • •

The six days that Ben and Bluma spent at Wiesenstrasse were an education in hopelessness, guilt, and despair. Like Ben, Bluma had found that the people she befriended formed a nation of the dispossessed. Most of the refugees were men, forced by circumstances and a lack of money to leave their families behind. They dreamed of earning enough to bring their families to Germany, then on to America. But the harsh realities of life in Germany and the American immigration quotas put an end to any hope for the future. For a while, the refugees would send enthusiastic letters and what little money they earned back to their families in the east. But gradually, the letters and money would dwindle as the crushing burden of the present blotted out the future. Lonely men and women formed liaisons, seeking the comfort and consolation of companionship as a buffer against the cruelty of their lives. With no identity to stand between them, they simply faded into another life, left with only bittersweet memories of the past.

Though the vast majority of the people in Wiesenstrasse were adults, occasionally there was an exception to the rule, and a family with children arrived. They were always accorded special treatment, both by the administrators and the residents. Children were especially precious to people who understood how fragile and tenuous life could be.

When Ben and Bluma left the shelter and returned to the apartment, they were exhausted and depressed. Helen and Herschel listened sympathetically while Ben summed up their experience.

"We talked to hundreds of people," he said wearily, "and it was always the same—everywhere we found the same terrible resignation. People desperate to work, to find a home, to escape the crushing despair. People with nowhere to go, nowhere to stay, nowhere to belong. I don't know how I can make you understand what it's like."

He paused for a moment, seeking the right words. "You feel as though the earth had simply disappeared, leaving nothing but an endless void. You fall endlessly, hoping to reach bottom and praying that when you do, you won't be smashed into a thousand pieces by the impact." Emotionally drained, Ben and Bluma slumped on the couch, staring at the floor.

Herschel gave them both something to help them sleep while Helen made up the bed. "Sleep now," she said. "We'll talk about it later."

Ben slept fitfully for nearly twenty-four hours, dreaming of endless gray corridors and tunnels that led nowhere. When he finally awoke, he reached over to discover that Bluma had gone. The smell of brewing coffee roused him to pull on a pair of trousers and pad into the Pullman kitchen.

"Bluma?" he yawned.

To his surprise, Hermann Kishk, from Fulda, smiled at him across the kitchen table. Ben stared, finding it hard to believe that Kishk was really there.

"Good morning!" Hermann said brightly. "There's fresh coffee in the pot. Let me pour you a cup."

Ben sat down heavily and rubbed his eyes while Hermann fixed the coffee. He placed a platter of chocolates and pastries on the table, then took a chair opposite Ben's. As they talked, Ben was astonished to discover it was nearly two in the afternoon.

"Herschel's at work," Hermann explained. "Helen and Bluma got tired of waiting, so they left to visit somebody. I don't remember the name."

"You still haven't told me what you're doing here," Ben said between mouthfuls of pastry.

"I was afraid I might change my mind if I stayed in Fulda, so I left for Berlin the day after you did. I've spent the last few days roaming around, just killing time until you showed up. Isn't Berlin a fantastic place! But that's not important because what's really important is what happened to me after I got here." Hermann had not lost his breathless manner or habit of running sentences together. Ben was about to ask what had happened when Hermann started again. "I never imagined what it would be like, how thrilling it could be."

"What could be?" Ben finally got a word in.

"Love. I'm in love. Madly, passionately, absolutely in love. Oh, Ben, I never believed it would happen to me. I never dreamed I could fall in love at first sight, I mean I knew such things happened, but not to me."

"First sight?"

"I was sitting alone on a park bench and she sat down next to me and when I saw her face, I knew she was the one for me." Hermann described the relationship's rapid progress.

"But you haven't even been in Berlin for a full week!"

"I know, I know."

"I think you had best tell me the whole story. It couldn't take too long," Ben added wryly. "And please, start with her name."

"Gisèle," Hermann burst out. "Gisèle is her name, and she works as a swimming instructor in a gymnasium."

While Hermann gushed, Ben studied his face. It was pale, almost cadaverous, and topped by an unruly mop of hair heavily flecked with dandruff. It was not the face of a man that beautiful women picked up off park benches.

"Gisèle and I were drawn to each other by a force greater than either one of us," Hermann giggled.

It was Gisèle who had suggested they go to the gymnasium for a swim. Afterwards, she had insisted on giving him a massage. One thing led to another and they ended up naked on a wrestling mat.

"Ben, I've never told anyone this, but I never, I mean I hadn't . . . I mean Gisèle is the first woman who . . . "

"Oh God," Ben moaned.

"What?"

"Is she Jewish?" Ben asked. Hermann looked startled.

"You know, I never thought to ask her, but I think she must be. She insisted I wear my yarmulke while we swam—and even when I . . . when we . . ."

"How many times have you seen her since you first met?" Ben interrupted.

"I haven't yet," Hermann said happily. "All this happened only yesterday but she . . . "

"Yesterday?" Ben sighed. "Hermann, why don't you show me where she lives?" Ben had a sinking feeling in the pit of his stomach.

It took them well over an hour to walk to Gisèle's neighborhood. As Ben suspected, it was located in one of Berlin's seamier areas, known for its cabarets and honky-tonk bars.

"That's the place!" Hermann pointed to a painted wooden building, covered with garish posters. "You don't see anything like that in Fulda."

"I'll bet," Ben remarked dryly as he started towards the front door. Hermann grabbed his arm.

"That's not the way in," he told Ben. "That entrance leads to a theater. We have to go down the alley and around the back."

"Let's see the show first," Ben suggested. "It's your first time in Berlin and you should take in a show."

"But I thought you . . . "

"Afterwards."

Hermann sputtered in confusion as he tried to keep up with Ben and hold onto his hat at the same time. Ben bought two tickets and they entered the theater.

It took a moment for their eyes to adjust to the dim half-light in the small room. A single row of chairs faced the end wall. Half were occupied by men with their eyes pressed to holes drilled in the plaster.

"This isn't a theater," Hermann whispered, bewildered by the bizarre interior. "There's no stage, no . . . "

"There's a stage, all right," Ben replied grimly. "Have a seat and take a look through one of the holes." Puzzled by Ben's attitude, Hermann did as he was told.

He recognized the "stage" immediately. "Ben! That's the place where . . . , " he faltered. An orthodox Jew, dressed in a swimsuit wandered into the room. He was followed by a woman with long blond hair. She led him over to a massage table, extolling his virility while she played with his yarmulke. Deftly, she slid out of her bathing suit and began to remove his.

Revolted by the degrading scene, Ben turned to find Hermann. His seat was empty. Ben stood up and nearly tripped over something in the narrow aisle.

Hermann had passed out.

Ben hauled him up and gently slapped the side of his face. Hermann's eyes fluttered open. "Ben?" he muttered.

"Yes, it's me. Can you walk now?" Ben was anxious to get out of the theater without causing a scene that might attract attention. Hermann clutched at his sleeve.

"The room, Ben . . . the place . . . it was the girl . . . Gisèle . . . ," he stammered.

"I'm sorry, Hermann," Ben sympathized. "It's called a peep-show."

"Then yesterday, I was the. . . ." His voice trailed off. He looked around at the men watching the peep holes and passed out again.

By the time Ben revived him, Hermann was trembling so badly that he was unable to speak. With the help of an attendant, Ben carried him out of the sleazy theater. After a few minutes in the open air, Hermann regained his equilibrium.

They walked homeward in silence until Hermann stopped and grabbed hold of Ben's arm.

"Why would she do that to me?" he blurted out. "She said she loved me and I loved her and I believed what she said—after what we said, after what we did . . . why? She even gave me chocolates and pastries when I left—the ones you had for breakfast. If she was a . . . a whore, wouldn't she have asked me for money? It doesn't make any sense."

"Not to you, Hermann, but trust me, it makes plenty of sense to the men who planned it."

"Men?" Hermann listened in a state of shock as Ben explained.

It was part of the training Ben had received at Nazi Headquarters. Though the Nazis did not yet possess the political power to dominate Germany, Adolf Hitler was keenly attuned to the value of propaganda and publicity, and manipulated both with consummate skill. The Nazis had already implemented a superbly organized strategy, designed to ridicule, degrade, and humiliate the Jews with accusations of betrayal, profiteering, and treason. The Nazis used demonstrations, leaflets, and the press to spread their message. No opportunity for harassment was lost, including the use of prostitutes to create public spectacles.

"It had nothing to do with you," Ben explained gently. "She saw your yarmulke and singled you out. She would have played you along, then created a final incident of some kind in public, maybe accused you of raping her."

Hermann began walking, immersed in thought. When he spoke again, it was to suggest they contact Ten Meineckestrasse.

"Your impulsiveness is what got you into trouble in the first place," Ben shook his head. "Why don't you just slow down? How's your family going to feel if they hear about it?"

Hermann thrust his jaw forward. "We must warn Ten Meineckestrasse. Forewarned is forearmed."

By dinner time, Hermann had fully recovered from the afternoon's disaster and held forth to the small group in Herschel's apartment. He was filled with a martyr's indignation. Ben had listened quietly to Hermann's recitation, turning an idea over in his mind.

"I think we should alert Agudath Israel," Ben interrupted. Agudath Israel was an organization of ultra-orthodox zealots. Like the congregation in Fulda, they believed that no Jew could return to Palestine until the Messiah appeared. Only He could end the millennia of exile and unite the Jewish people once again.

"But they're religious fanatics," Hermann blinked in surprise. "They spend all their time moaning and praying, not roaming around looking for excitement. They're not the type to get involved with strange women."

"Neither are you, Hermann. But when a beautiful woman throws herself at you, you have a tendency to forget you have a yarmulke on your head. The ultra-orthodox may be all the more vulnerable because they lead such an insulated existence." Everyone stared at Ben. The idea of using a peep show to humiliate orthodox Jews was almost too fantastic to believe. Ben stood up and started to pace.

"Did it ever strike any of you as odd that the Nazis seem to know everything there is to know about Jews? Their attacks are clever, well organized, and intended to accomplish specific purposes. Has it ever occurred to any of you that the most obvious target for the Nazis to attack is Ten Meineckestrasse? But, by and large, the Nazis don't bother them. Why? It's because Ten Meineckestrasse is devoted to getting Jews out of Germany. Right now, that fits in with Nazi strategey. On the other hand, the zealots and the rest of orthodox Jewry believe it blasphemous to return to Palestine. This peephole business has to be aimed at the ultra-orthodox,'' Ben continued. ''They make an ideal target because their dress and mannerisms make them stand out in a crowd. What the Nazis are doing is trying to prove that Jews are exactly what Henry Ford says they are: lying, deceitful, and hypocritical. Humiliating the ultra-orthodox is just the beginning. It terrifies me to imagine what they'll think of next.''

Herschel looked uneasy. It was becoming more difficult for him to shrug off what was happening outside the doors of Berlin University Hospital. He grinned lopsidedly and tried to minimize the incident.

''I think you're taking all this a little too seriously, Ben. There's no need to be paranoid. After all, Hermann wasn't harmed. Not only did he have a thrilling afternoon with a beautiful woman, completely free of charge, but he became the first Jew from Fulda to be martyred by the Nazis.''

''Herschel!'' Helen scolded.

''Remember, Herschel,'' Ben sighed. ''I've been in Nazi Head-quarters. I've seen first-hand how those people work. Their greatest allies are people like you who refuse to believe the evidence because it's so 'unbelievable.' You're underestimating these Nazis.''

''This just reinforced my own point. All the Jews must leave Germany,'' Hermann declared pompously. He gulped more tea and wiped his wispy mustache.

''The German Jews like my Uncle Kimmel in Fulda or Sarah's father are doomed. They're so in love with being German, they forget they will never be anything but Jews in the eyes of real Germans. They don't realize the lengths the Nazis will go to. We must all leave this place.'' Herschel wanted to know where Hermann intended to send all the Jews.

''I intend to go to America.''

''But what about Palestine?'' Ben cried. ''Last week you said. . . .''

''I found out the truth about Palestine since I came to Berlin. If anyone should go to Palestine, it's the *Ostjuden*, because they have no money and no future. I am a German Jew, so I'm eligible for a visa to go to the United States and don't have to end up in the middle of some scrubby desert scratching at flea bites.''

Suddenly, Ben's temper boiled over. ''Then *go!*'' he shouted. ''Do what you like—stay in Germany or go to America, it's nothing to me. But don't kid yourselves. Nothing will ever change, until *we* change it. Nothing will ever happen, unless *we* make it happen. Not until *we* fight back, not until *we* have a land of our own, will we be able to live in peace.''

He strode from the room. Silently, Bluma followed him. She

watched while he crammed clothes into a suitcase, then quietly walked over to the bed and refolded them neatly into the case. He smiled ruefully.

"I'm sorry, Bluma," he apologized. "I guess I lost my temper. Sometimes I get so frustrated. . . ."

"I know," she whispered, putting her arms around him. "I've been through all of it with you."

Ben caressed the back of her neck. "Do you think I'm right about leaving?"

"Ben, wherever you go and whatever you do, I'll be by your side as long as you want me there . . . 'whither thou goest . . .' " He looked into her eyes and felt his heart skip a beat.

"Bluma, wherever you are, is where I'll want to be." He kissed her deeply. Bluma's love was something he had always taken for granted, but now, holding her close to him, he realized that their love for each other formed the central core of his life. In the passion they felt for each other, everything else rang hollow and false.

• • •

The next morning, Ben and Bluma set out for Ten Meineckestrasse as though life had begun anew. All the old burdens and dark concerns sloughed away, leaving them carefree and lighthearted. Walking across the bridge spanning the Spree, they held hands and spoke of the future, of marriage, of children, and growing old. They tried to imagine what life would be like in Palestine, laughing as Bluma pantomimed herself plowing a field. Nothing stood between their hearts, and Ben sensed that his life finally had a meaning as well as a purpose.

As they approached Ten Meineckestrasse, Bluma pointed to a narrow side street. "Let's go that way," she said impulsively.

"That's the long way around."

"I know, but there's a little park I'd like to walk through." She snuggled up against him. "Please?"

"Who am I to say no?" he laughed. Bluma's eyes sparkled as they admired the displays in every shop window. They had all the time in the world. Crossing the street at the end of the block, they entered the park through an ornate archway.

"Isn't it lovely?" Bluma asked, squeezing Ben's arm. Delicately designed wrought-iron fencing traced the triangular perimeter, which was lined with rows of carefully tended evergreens. Bare-branched oaks and bright green benches dotted the walking paths.

As they strolled through the grounds, everything focused to crystal clarity for Ben. At last, there was a discernible pattern to the tapestry of his life, and contentment settled over him like a warm cloak. Unconsciously, he pulled Bluma closer to him.

Halfway through the park, they spotted a large crowd. The sound of strident voices pierced the silence. The crowd straddled the walking path, spilling over onto the green. Ben turned to take a different path.

Bluma pulled at his arm. "Let's see what it's all about."

"Who cares?" Ben was not about to allow anything to interfere with the magic of the day.

"Oh, come on," she coaxed, practically dragging him off in the direction of the crowd.

"All right, all right," he laughed. "But please, let me walk there myself."

From a wooden platform at the center of the park, a coatless speaker harangued the crowd. He wore a swastika armband, as did several other men positioned around the podium.

"When you go to the store," he yelled, raising his fist, "who takes your money?"

He paused theatrically and braced his fists against his hips.

"*Der Jude!*" he screamed. His face contorted with revulsion. A livid scar ran from the bridge of his nose to below his ear, pulsing red with his fury.

"Go to a Government office, and who orders you around?" he laughed hysterically. "Why, *der Jude*, of course!" He turned slowly, surveying his audience. His arm lashed out, pointing to the crowd.

"Who plays with our money so it becomes more worthless day by day?"

Suddenly, a few bystanders began to smile, captured by his oratory. "The Jews!" they shouted.

The crowd was not an ugly one, but Ben sensed it might turn that way in an instant. Most of the people responded as though they were singing the refrain of a beer house drinking song.

"I've seen enough," Bluma said in disgust. "I'm sorry I insisted. Let's get the hell out of here."

Ben didn't move.

"Ben? Let's go. Haven't you had enough of the Nazis?"

For Ben, the crowd had disappeared. There was only his own memory and the voice of the fascist standing on the small wooden platform. He remembered the mob outside the jail when Meilach had been arrested. He thought of Yitzakh and his inferiority complex within him, unable to find peace, and the slaughtered Jews of Fulda. He remembered the hatred in Dorpat and the young girl in Mina Cohen's story, slumped against a wall with blood running down her legs. Ben stood as though paralyzed.

"Ben, if one of the Nazis recognizes you, they'll try to kill you," Bluma kept casting nervous glances around them, certain Ben would be spotted.

"Who betrayed our valiant army during the war?" the speaker shrieked, the words like jagged glass.

"*Der Jude!*" The crowd roared back.

"That's a lie!"

Ben was hardly aware that the words came from his own mouth.

People craned to see who had spoken. Those standing closest to Ben and Bluma moved away quickly, afraid to be mistaken for hecklers.

"Ben, let's go! Please." Bluma began to tremble, but he ignored her.

"That's a lie and you are a liar!" Ben yelled. A feeling of exhilaration filled him. "The Jews fought for the Fatherland just as hard as any other Germans."

"You lie!" the Nazi screamed at Ben. Unprepared for any opposition, Ben's accusation had caught him off guard. The throng watched the two antagonists with eager anticipation, savoring the confrontation. They sensed blood.

Ben played a hunch. "You seem to know so much—tell us, what Wehrmacht unit did you serve in? Or did you sit out the war in a beerhall?" he shouted. The man just stared for a moment, open-mouthed. Then he recovered. There was a cunning look in his watery blue eyes.

"You're a dirty Jew!" He pointed at Ben, trying to shift attention from himself. "The man is a Jew—ask him to deny it."

"More Jews got Iron Crosses than any other group in the army," Ben roared, remembering Stiffler's story.

"You Jewish—" Derisive hoots and catcalls cut off the Nazi's attempt to speak. The crowd's sympathy began to shift.

"Are you defaming the German Army by saying that they sold those Crosses to the Jews?" Ben demanded.

Voices in the crowd murmured, "No! Impossible!" Momentum began to build.

"Are you saying that Hindenburg and Ludendorff sold all those Iron Crosses to the Jews?" Ben kept pounding. That was the spark that ignited the crowd. In spite of defeat, Hindenburg and Ludendorff were still cherished national heroes.

"You filthy piece of shit!" screamed an elderly man jabbing his umbrella at the Nazi. "This man speaks the truth, and you know it!" The Nazi's face was a frozen mask of hatred.

Other shouts broke from the throats of the mob as the Nazi became a lightning rod for their anger and frustration. Two of the Nazis standing at the base of the platform shoved their way through the crowd to Ben. The taller of the two men grabbed the front of Ben's coat.

"You stinking Jew," he sneered. "I'll teach you. . . ."

Ben reacted instantly, punching one Nazi in the face and dragging the other to the ground. He straddled the fallen man's body and pummeled his face.

The Nazi's companion rose unsteadily, watching for a moment as his friend absorbed Ben's blows. He saw the crowd enjoying the spectacle. Suddenly, his hand plunged into his coat and withdrew a revolver, which he cocked and aimed at Ben's back.

"Filthy Jew," he spat. Bluma screamed, throwing herself at the Nazi as the gun went off.

The crowd scattered in panic.

The Nazi had been standing less than ten feet from Ben and the stench of sulfur filled Ben's nostrils. He rolled to one side, certain he'd been hit.

Only then did he see Bluma lying face down in the snow. Scrambling to her side, he knelt down and carefully turned her towards him.

There was a large crimson blot on the snow. Panic rose in his throat, choking him. She moaned softly.

"Help is on the way," he whispered to keep his voice from cracking. "You'll be fine, I promise you." He spoke with a confidence he did not feel. Bluma's coat was open and Ben could see that her blouse was soaked with blood. "Somebody get an ambulance!" he screamed.

"I'm all right," she gasped weakly. "I'm all right. It's not too bad. I'm all right." Ben noticed a torn piece of cloth clutched in her left hand. Gently, he pried it from her fingers and slid it into his pocket without looking at it.

Slowly, the crowd reformed around Ben and Bluma, stilled by the sudden eruption of violence. Several people offered handkerchiefs to staunch the flow of blood.

Moments later an ambulance arrived. The attendants were brusque and efficient; violence in the streets of Berlin was not an uncommon occurrence. Quickly assessing the wound, they applied a large pressure bandage to Bluma's chest, and placed her on a stretcher. She was unconscious by the time they strapped her into the ambulance.

Ben crouched at the end of her stretcher, bracing Bluma's head against the violent motion of the vehicle. In the faint light of the open-backed ambulance, he could see that her face was pale and drawn. She was barely breathing.

For an instant, he caught the exotic scent of flowers from her body. Numbly, he prayed that she would live.

TWELVE

Berlin University Hospital
January 1925

Time spent in a hospital waiting room has a peculiar quality. The fading green walls sealed Ben into a separate universe, where the past and future merged into an eternal present. He sat like a dumb supplicant, caught in the nightmare grip of his own worst fears.

Herschel had been on duty when the ambulance arrived at the hospital. He had rushed Bluma directly to the emergency room, his face strained and tense. Since that time, there had been no activity in the corridor.

Ben slumped in a chair, staring at his clenched fists, not knowing what to think. Guilt, thick and bitter as bile, rose in his throat like a foul poison. He remembered the sensation of drunken exhilaration he experienced as he turned the crowd on the Nazis and shame washed over him. He should have been thinking about Bluma's safety, not his own gratification.

He waited a lifetime for news. Again and again, Ben turned the events of the day over in his mind, trying to assimilate the experience. They still had an unreal, dreamlike quality. Only hours ago, the future had seemed fixed and immutable, as though it was already happening, just as they'd planned it. Now, it had ceased to exist.

As he tried to reconstruct the sequence of events, he recalled the blue uniform of a policeman, standing on the edge of the crowd. The officer had witnessed the entire incident without interfering or making an arrest. The Nazis chose their friends well.

It was a harbinger of things to come.

This nightmare will end soon, Ben reassured himself. *Bluma and I will leave for Palestine as soon as she is well enough to travel.* He tried to organize their departure in his mind, as though planning the future would make it so.

"*Yihyeh tov*," Ben muttered aloud. "Everything will be all right." But nothing could purge the uncertainty from his subconscious. It lay there like a cold, unyielding knot. Why hadn't Herschel sent word?

The doors to the waiting area burst open as Zorach Hanovi strode into the room. Seeing him did not surprise Ben. Even if the shooting had not occurred practically across the street from Ten Meineckestrasse, Hanovi still would have been one of the first men in Berlin to hear about it. Hanovi sat down next to Ben, the bench creaking under his weight.

"Tell me about it," he said softly. "It is important that we know all the details." Ben recited the circumstances surrounding the shooting in a dispassionate monotone while Hanovi took notes.

Hanovi asked a number of questions. Could Ben identify the policeman? Did he recognize anyone in the crowd? How soon would Bluma be able to travel? Ben started to get annoyed.

"What's the purpose of all these questions?" he demanded petulantly. "More panic-mongering to get the Jews out of Berlin?"

"Berlin is no longer a safe place for Jews to remain," Hanovi replied evenly.

"*Ostjuden* or German Jews?" Hanovi ignored the jab and rose to leave.

"You're planning on using this, aren't you?" Ben asked resentfully. "Turning it into a first-class 'incident'?"

"It is a first-class incident. One of many more to come."

"You know what bothers me about you people from Ten Meineckestrasse? I don't really believe you give a damn. Not about flesh and blood people. They're just 'things' to be exploited, to be used as a means to an end. How you must love playing the game, being one of the manipulators, one of the planners. The woman I love is shot down in the street by an animal and you can't wait to tell the world about it. You don't care about her or anybody else. You know something, Hanovi, you make me sick."

"You're not thinking straight. You're all torn apart inside because you don't know whether Bluma Feldman is going to live or die."

"I can see why they call you 'the Prophet,' " Ben snapped sarcastically. He jumped to his feet. "You got what you came for, now why don't you get out of here and leave me alone. I'm tired of playing cloak and dagger games."

Hanovi stared at Ben, his eyes piercing through the cloud of the younger man's anger.

"You're right about one thing, Isaacson—we are playing games; war games. And they're not for children. There are no rules to this game, no guidelines, no referees. Our opponents have guns and clubs. The only weapon we have is the truth, and it's a weapon we must use with deadly accuracy.

"The Nazis are here to stay, but even if their party faded away tomorrow, their ideas would not. They'd be adopted by someone else on their way to the top. In five years those ideas will be a major force to be reckoned with. In ten years they'll rule the country.

"There are more than a million *Ostjuden* in Germany. That's twice the number of German Jews. The *Ostjuden* have no homes, no jobs, no future. They dress funny, and talk funny, and stand out like a sore thumb. They're a strain on the economy and they make an ideal scapegoat. Believe me, the pressure is going to keep building until it finally explodes."

"If you . . . ," Ben interrupted half-heartedly. He knew Hanovi was right; he had been acting like a fool.

"None of this is anything new to you. You're familiar with the story," Hanovi forged on. "The *Ostjuden* dream of America, where opportunities wait to be harvested like so many wild apples, free for the picking. They don't understand that the Americans don't want them. So they sit and rot, praying for a miracle. What happened to Bluma Feldman today presents us with a unique opportunity to display the truth for the entire world to see. A Nazi shoots down an innocent Jewish girl under the nose of a German policeman, then waltzes away, untouched, while she's left to bleed to death. That's the truth of what happened, Mr. Isaacson. I intend to see that people learn about it, and I will be needing your help."

Without waiting for Ben's reply, Hanovi walked towards the door. Grasping one of the handles, he hesitated a moment then turned. "Most people don't have much of a stomach for the truth, Mr. Isaacson. Do you?"

Ben stared at the exit long after Hanovi disappeared. He had never seen the man react passionately to anything. He was too cold, too calculating, never saying more than he had to say. Why the speech now? Hanovi's words echoed in his mind: "I intend to see that people learn about it, and I will be needing your help." Just what did that mean, Ben wondered.

As he sat back to speculate on Hanovi's outburst, Herschel appeared in the hallway. Ben's stomach turned over when he saw the blood on Herschel's hospital gown—Bluma's blood. His cousin's face was lined and dark. For a moment, Ben thought the worst, then Herschel broke into a tired smile.

"She's going to be all right, Ben."

Ben closed his eyes, holding back the tears. "Thank you, Herschel," he whispered.

"She's stable, but she'll be under the influence of the anaesthetic for a while. If you like, you can sit with her. Don't expect too much. She's lost a lot of blood and she's going to be pretty weak at first." Herschel promised him there would be no permanent damage. The bullet had entered her breast, then deflected off a rib.

He squeezed Ben's shoulder. "Helen and I will take good care of her. Go on now. She's in the third room on the right. I'll check in with you after my rounds."

Summoning his courage, Ben walked down the corridor and pushed open the door to her room. Bluma lay motionless on a small hospital bed with white iron side rails to keep her from rolling off. Her right arm was bound to her side.

Ben pulled a chair to the edge of the bed and reached for her left hand. She looked so pale and motionless, he feared she might have stopped breathing. Then he noticed the almost imperceptible rise and fall of her breasts. Tenderly, he kissed her hand.

"I love you, Bluma," he murmured.

He sat there as the hours passed, planning what he would say when she awoke. Herschel stopped in twice and Helen came by every half-hour. She suggested Ben go home and rest, but he was determined to be by Bluma's side when she awoke. He was unbearably anxious to reassure her that she was all right and nothing had changed; all their plans and hopes were still intact, just delayed for a few weeks. He had a mental image of the two of them, strolling on the boardwalk in Tel Aviv arm in arm, all pain and strife left behind. Just after midnight the duty nurse forced him to leave. Overriding his protests, she escorted him to the door, promising to send for him if Bluma awoke.

He walked back to Herschel's apartment through the deserted streets, trying to organize his thoughts. The apartment was dark and empty, underscoring his loneliness. He switched on the desk lamp and tried to write to his family and Bluma's mother. He was bone weary, but as he poured out his feelings on paper, his rage rekindled. He kept thinking of Bluma lying unconscious in the recovery room.

Restlessly, he began to pace the floor. He shoved his hands into his pockets and his right hand encountered the bunched cloth he had pried from Bluma's hand in the park. Slowly, he withdrew it. Seating himself at Herschel's desk, he smoothed the blood-red silk over the blotter and stared at the twisted swastika. Bluma must have ripped the armband from the Nazi as he shot her. Ben slammed his fist on the desktop in fury. They had shot her and there was nothing he could do to change that. But he could see they didn't get away with it. If the police would not give him justice, he would find it his own way. He jammed the armband in his back pocket and grabbed his coat, taking the stairs to the street three at a time.

North of Herschel's apartment, across the River Spree, was an area of Berlin known for its all night bars and taverns. At two o'clock in the morning, they were filled with the worst that Berlin had to offer. The shooting had set the rumor mills grinding, and Ben hoped the gunman would be stupid enough to boast about what he had done. Grimly, he entered the first bar. His questions netted plenty of rumors, but no one seemed to know who actually did the shooting. The same was true of the second place he tried. He became careless in the third bar, trying to leave too quickly after his casual inquiries failed to produce results. The bartender became suspicious and challenged him.

"Only a cop or a Jew would be so anxious to know who shot the Jew bitch." He pulled out a length of iron pipe from beneath the bar. "You don't look like a cop to me." Strangers asking too many questions in that section of Berlin were often found lying face down in a gutter.

Three men blocked the exit and the bar fell silent. The bartender stepped out from behind the bar and walked up to Ben.

"Me and my friends want to know who you really are." He smiled, revealing a mouthful of broken yellow teeth.

"I told you . . .," Ben began.

"Blond hair and blue eyes or not, he talks too perfect," growled a heavyset man with slablike features. "He must be a Jew."

"Strip off his pants and we'll have a look at him," one of them yelled. That was one test Ben could not bluff his way through. Furiously, his mind raced as they closed in on him.

"Wait!" he shouted at the top of his lungs. He snatched the armband from his pocket and waved it in front of the crowd. "Does this look like something that a stinking Jew would carry around?" They stared at the swastika.

He improvised quickly, telling them the Party had sent him out to look for the men who had done the shooting. The Party assumed they had gone underground to escape any repurcussions and wanted to help. It was Ben's job to locate the two men.

Ben met the bartender's scrutiny with an arrogant stare, knowing that the slightest sign of weakness or doubt on his part would mean disaster. After an eternity, the bartender slowly lowered his bludgeon.

"Sorry," he apologized gruffly. "But you never know these days. Have a drink on the house and tell your friends that Willy Imbach is as good a patriot as the next man."

Ben tried to decline the offer of a free beer but the other men forced him to drink with them. By the time Ben escaped their camaraderie, he was trembling with fear and exhilaration. He felt giddy and indestructible, but he was more careful in the next bar, a filthy, smoke-filled dive, smelling of stale beer, sweat, and urine. Ben sauntered over to the bar with a broad smile on his face.

"I need a beer!" he shouted, banging a fist on the table. "I want to raise my stein and toast the men who served the Fatherland so superbly this afternoon!"

The bartender filled a stein with foaming beer and slid it down the pitted wooden bartop with a wry smile. He was used to overenthusiastic drunks, especially late at night.

Ben caught the mug and lifted it high in the air, spilling some of the beer. "I don't know the names of those men but here's to their health. Let's hope they shoot another one tomorrow!"

"Hear, hear!" came the response from a dozen throats.

As Ben drained his stein, a brownshirted Nazi sporting a Sam Browne belt swaggered over. "*Grüss Gott*! May all the Jews rot in hell!" The Nazi emptied his glass. "Where're you from?"

"Lithuania," Ben replied casually. He gestured to the barkeeper to fill two more steins. "We've begun our own movement there called The Iron Fist. Good group of men. Fought for the Kaiser during the war. I would have too, if I'd been old enough. Now we have another war to fight. Against the Jews."

"Then we are brothers-in-arms! To our triumph!" Ben's drinking companion slapped him on the back.

"Listen," Ben whispered secretively. "You know what I'd really like to do?"

"No. What?" asked the Nazi, his eyes bleary from too much liquor.

"I would like to buy a drink for those men who had the guts to fight back against the Jews. If you ever see them, be sure to say that Walter Strauss wants to buy them a drink."

"Tell them yourself!" the Nazi burped. "They come in here almost every night. Tonight, I'm sure they decided to lay low because of the cops. If you come tomorrow night, you'll probably see them. Ask for Joachim and Hans.''

"Not Joachim Hetzer?'' Ben fished.

"No, no,'' the Nazi belched. "Wrong guy. Joachim Knaedl and Hans Festbach. Two good men. They might even turn up here later on. They live right nearby. They make the rounds of all the bars in the neighborhood.''

Ben pretended to slip off his stool. "Oops,'' he said drunkenly. "Looks like I've been celebrating too much. I better get home before I pass out.''

"Go safely, comrade-in-arms! We need all the help we can get to kill the Jew bastards!'' He raised his fist in a salute and Ben responded in kind, nearly keeling over. As he walked out, his former companion was still roaring with laughter.

Joachim Knaedl and Hans Festbach. Ben didn't need to repeat the names. He would remember them until the day he died. Now that he knew who they were, he would need help with the second part of his plan.

"Come,'' someone growled in response to Ben's tentative knock. Ben opened the door cautiously.

Stiffler was seated in a large chair diagonally opposite the door. He had a rifle leveled at Ben's chest.

"I thought you might be one of the Reds we've been skirmishing with. They know who I am,'' he explained, rising from his chair. He leaned the rifle in a corner. "What are you doing here at this hour? It must be close to four in the morning.''

Ben sat down at the small kitchen table. "You heard about the shooting this morning?''

"Who hasn't? It's all over town. A damned disgrace. Thugs gunning down women in broad daylight. The girl was a Jew, wasn't she?''

Ben nodded silently.

"Lousy Nazis,'' Stiffler spat. "They're an evil lot. They'll kill us all unless we wipe them out to a man. Did you know her?''

"It was Bluma.''

There was a moment of silence as Stiffler stared at Ben. "Bluma? They shot Bluma?''

"Yes. The bullet was meant for me.'' Ben felt his throat constrict. "She threw herself in the way.''

In the harsh light cast by the unshaded bulb that hung in the center of the room, Ben saw his friend's face pale.

"Do you know who they are, Ben?'' he asked quietly.

"Joachim Knaedl and Hans Festbach."

Stiffler's head snapped up. "I know those two."

"I was hoping to return this to them." Ben pulled the armband out of his pocket.

"Hand me my pants, Ben," Stiffler said grimly. "It's four o'clock and we still have a full night's work to do."

● ● ●

Ben was amazed at how quickly Stiffler assembled his "health and exercise" brigade; within fifteen minutes, ten men crammed the tiny apartment. Though some of the men had pistols, the working weapons were clubs and chains. All wore threadbare army uniforms and the standard-issue gray helmets. Ben was the only one wearing civilian clothes.

They left Stiffler's building and walked for ten minutes before stopping at the intersection of two small streets. Stiffler turned to one of his friends, a tall, muscular man named Kalman.

"Which buildings?" he asked.

Kalman pointed to a drab stone apartment house. "Festbach—there, second floor, first door on the right. Knaedl is in the one across the street—third floor, the only room."

"Gert!" Stiffler snapped. "Take Wilhelm, Eigner, Pfanzig, Olsendorf, and Dracht to grab Festbach. Everybody else, with me. I want them brought down here. Once you have them, don't worry about making noise. I want to make an example of these two."

Ben stayed with Stiffler's group and they strode into Knaedl's building like an avenging army. The front hall was dimly lit and reeked of mold and urine. Quietly, they climbed the stairs. One of the men in the lead warned the others not to trust the banister; most of the balusters were missing.

The third-floor landing was a cramped, narrow space that ended in front of Knaedl's door. Though Ben wanted the honor of breaking the door down, Stiffler insisted the job be left to professionals.

"If you don't break it in the first try, he'll have enough time to go for his gun. My plans for the evening don't include getting shot."

On Stiffler's signal, Kalman took the door down with a single lunge. The other men poured in behind him.

Knaedl's apartment was empty.

Stiffler started to set his men to knocking on doors, but Ben knew instinctively that Knaedl and Festbach were probably far from Berlin. Either someone in one of the bars tipped them off that Ben was looking for them, or the Nazis had spirited them out of Berlin to avoid trouble. Ben realized that his chances of finding them were practically nonexistent.

"Forget it, Kurt. They're long gone."

Stiffler kicked a rickety chair halfway across the room where it splintered against a bureau. "At least we tried," he sighed. He thanked his men for their support and sent them home.

"You should get Bluma out of Berlin as soon as you can," Stiffler warned Ben as they walked back through the deserted streets. "After tonight, the Nazis may try to finish her off. They're fond of symbols. And if they recognize you, the both of you have had it."

Stiffler dragged heavily on a cigarette. "It's getting worse, my friend," he muttered. "Every night, the dark things like those two animals become stronger. Every day, they get a little bolder. They'll try to dominate the streets, preying on the defenseless like the hyenas they are. The one thing I can't tolerate is an enemy that hides his face."

Half a block from Stiffler's apartment, they passed two drunks. One was sitting on the sidewalk drinking from a bottle, the other was urinating in a doorway.

"Look at that." Stiffler spat in disgust. "It's almost dawn and the drunks are still at it. You never saw that in the old days. People had respect. This used to be the greatest country in Europe. I remember my grandfather telling me when Bismarck. . . ." He stopped himself and frowned. "But that's old history."

They stopped in front of Stiffler's building and Ben thanked him for his help.

"Would that Knaedl and Festbach had been home. Then I could have been truly helpful." Stiffler grinned like a death's head. "Tell Bluma that I'll visit her in the hospital and bring her flowers to brighten her day."

"She'd like that."

"Think about what I said." Stiffler clasped Ben's hand. "Berlin is no place for the two of you."

"I'll think about it," Ben promised.

"Be well and do well," Stiffler grinned. He turned and disappeared into his building.

Ben walked back to the hospital, feeling drained and ragged. The doors were locked, and Ben had to bribe the night watchman with a mark to get in.

Bluma had been moved to one of the women's wards with eight or ten beds. Each bed was screened from the next by a rolling partition of metal tubing with curtains stretched over the frame. Taking care not to disturb any of the other patients, Ben found Bluma in the third bed.

He pulled a chair to her side and stared at the face of the woman he loved. She was still pale but no longer dead white, and she seemed to be breathing comfortably. He sat motionless until Herschel and Helen appeared just before seven o'clock. Herschel checked Bluma's vital signs and seemed pleased with the results. He told Ben not to worry.

After they left for morning rounds, the excitement of the preceding twenty-four hours wore off, and Ben had to fight to stay awake. His arms and legs felt leaden and his eyes were red and raw. He felt thick-witted and dull, hovering on the edge of collapse.

Bluma's hand twitched.

Ben jumped, instantly alert. It was the first time he had seen her move. He dared not speak for fear of waking her needlessly. She stirred uncomfortably and moaned. Her eyes fluttered open. She tried to speak, but her lips were too cracked and dry to form the words. Ben leaned forward and kissed her gently on the forehead.

"It's Ben, Bluma. Can you hear me?"

She nodded.

"You're in the hospital, and you're going to be all right. Don't try to move around, just relax." He poured a glass of water from the pitcher on the nightstand, bracing her head as she sipped the tepid liquid.

"My breast," she croaked. "Is it. . . ."

He saw the sudden terror in her eyes. "It's fine. You're going to be all right. Now don't try to talk any more. Herschel says you need lots of rest."

"Ben, I. . . ."

"Please. Don't talk, Bluma. Just listen." He kissed her hand and she squeezed his in return. Tenderly, he caressed her forehead.

"Whatever the future holds for us, I want you to know that I love you. Before you know it, all this will be a part of the past and when you've recovered, we'll do everything just as we planned. We'll go to Palestine, we'll get married, we'll. . . ."

The duty nurse suddenly appeared beside the bed and threatened him with dire consequences if he didn't leave immediately. Bluma was still too weak to see anyone for more than a couple of minutes.

Ben laughed, raising his hands in surrender. "I give up. I'll be back later, Bluma." But she didn't hear him; she had already fallen asleep.

•   •   •

The next three days passed slowly. Bluma remained in a great deal of discomfort, but her wound began to heal and Herschel's initial diagnosis proved correct; it looked as though there would be no permanent damage. She spent a great deal of time sleeping and Ben spent a great deal of time watching her. He fed her, massaged her, read to her, and held her hand. Gradually, the color returned to her cheeks.

The evening of the third day, Herschel asked Ben to follow him to the small examining room he used as an office. Zorach Hanovi literally filled one corner of it. Ben stared at him in silence, knowing what Hanovi had come for.

"The answer is yes," Ben said softly. "I do have the stomach for it."

Hanovi nodded. "Good."

"Stomach for what?" Herschel asked.

"Private joke," Hanovi smiled. "We should get started now."

Hanovi outlined the strategy Ten Meineckestrasse had planned. Berlin was no longer safe; for Ben and Bluma to remain any longer than absolutely necessary was to invite trouble. Once Bluma was well enough to travel, she and Ben would board a train bound for the Baltic States. Their base of operations would be the East Prussian city of Koenigsberg, a major staging area for refugees from the east. Hanovi explained that their mission would have a dual purpose.

First, they would describe the current situation in Berlin; nothing was as powerful as a first-hand account. People had to realize that no organized authority stood ready to accept responsibility for the Jews or guarantee their safety.

Secondly, Ben and Bluma were to organize mass demonstrations in front of all British Consulates in Estonia, Latvia, Lithuania, and east Prussia. If Jews were going to be shot down in the street, without cause or protection, the British would have to take some responsibility; it was their immigration restrictions that blocked the flow of refugees to Palestine.

When Ben voiced his concern about Bluma's health, Hanovi explained that Herschel and Helen would be going with them. It was typical of Hanovi's style; a personal physician would guarantee Bluma first-rate treatment and add a dramatic touch on the speaker's platform.

It was Herschel who surprised Ben. Almost overnight, he had done a complete about-face. Bluma's shooting had accomplished what all of Ben's rhetoric had not—it had turned Herschel into a committed Zionist.

"What if Bluma doesn't want to go?" Ben asked. He felt overwhelmed and a bit out of control. Everything was happening too fast.

Hanovi shrugged in response. "I'm not in a position to give anyone orders. I just offer suggestions from time to time. Will you talk to her?''

"I'll talk to her," Ben promised. But he already knew what her answer would be. So did Hanovi.

•   •   •

Two weeks later, Herschel, Helen, Zorach Hanovi, and Hermann Kishk gathered around Bluma's wheelchair on the eastbound platform of the Berlin Bahnhof.

Hanovi orchestrated their departure with meticulous attention to detail and issued his final instructions. Helen and Herschel were to wear their hospital whites at all times, and Bluma was to remain in a wheelchair whenever she appeared in public, even if she felt well enough to stand. Hanovi was anxious to display her condition to maximum effect.

Despite the promises he had made to Hanovi, Ben had felt uneasy about displaying Bluma like a side-show attraction; he had been having second thoughts. To everyone's surprise, it was Bluma who had erased all doubts about the project.

"What happened to me will happen to others, only they may not survive. We have an obligation to our people, Ben." She had spoken softly, but the iron resolve in her voice was crystal clear. Ben had listened with pride and affection. Few men could claim the love of a woman like Bluma Feldman.

Clustered on the platform, the small group surrounding Bluma achieved the precise effect Hanovi had hoped for. Bluma sat in the wheelchair swathed in blankets, her face pale and gaunt. Herschel stayed by her side, his black leather doctor's bag clutched in one hand. Tight-lipped and protective, Ben stood behind the wheelchair, talking with Helen and Hermann Kishk hovered over the luggage. After the incident, Hermann had flip-flopped again and reverted into an ardent Zionist. Though Ben had been reluctant to take him at first, Hanovi had correctly pointed out that an extra pair of hands might prove helpful.

Hanovi was pleased. Bluma's condition was bound to provide her with instant credibility; a pretty young girl strapped into a wheelchair would have no problem gaining a crowd's attention or sympathy. The people with her would only strengthen her presence; they were witnesses to the tragic event that had occurred and to the seriousness of her condition.

Hanovi wished them luck as he closed the compartment door. They watched him through the window as the train pulled away from the station. Hands in his pockets, shoulders hunched forward, Hanovi still towered a full head above the crowd. His eyes remained fixed on the train until it pulled away from the platform, but the neutral expression on his face never changed.

"Such a strange man," Bluma remarked. No one replied, but they all agreed.

•   •   •

Fifteen minutes out of Berlin, Bluma began to feel tired and depressed. Her wound ached ferociously and the sharp angle of the seat cut into her legs at the knee.

"Ben, I can't move my legs," she grimaced. Everyone rushed to make her more comfortable but nothing seemed to work.

"Put your head on my shoulder and lean against me," Ben instructed her. He put his arm around her and held her close.

Herschel eyed the two of them and suggested that he, Helen, and Hermann find temporary lodgings in another compartment, so Bluma could get some rest. After they left, she clutched Ben tightly.

"I feel so ashamed," she whispered.

"Ashamed of what?" Ben asked in surprise.

"I'm scared, Ben," she mumbled into his jacket.

"I know," he said, stroking her hair. It pleased him to have her lean on his strength. It made him feel needed. "I'll take care of you, and so will the others."

"I know that. But I can't help it. I feel like . . . like a part of me was taken away and I'll never be safe again."

"That will pass with time."

"I hope so, Ben. I never felt like this before."

"You've never been shot before. You have a right to feel the way you do."

She snuggled against him.

"You're strong, Bluma," he said gently. "It just takes time to get over things." Gradually, her breathing became measured and even. She slept soundly, and didn't awake when Herschel and the others returned.

Outside the snug compartment, winter lay cruelly on the land. Ice coated every exposed surface, hermetically sealing the land until spring broke its frozen grip. Rough-hewn farmhouses dotted the landscape and horse-drawn carts replaced automobiles. A biting Arctic wind sliced across the plains, rendering the landscape bleak and inhospitable. Jew or Gentile, its inhabitants led a hard, relentless existence, insulated from the strife of the outside world. Their lives were an endless round of sowing, planting, cultivating, and harvesting, and life was divided into good years and bad years. There were few good years.

They arrived in Koenigsberg around one in the morning. Ben and Helen wrapped Bluma in layers of wool blankets and carried her off the train in a wheelchair. She was exhausted after the long journey, but Herschel was reluctant to medicate her until they reached the hospital.

As the others unloaded the luggage, Bluma looked to the lights of the city beyond the open platform. A black wave of depression engulfed her. Even in the middle of the night, factory stacks spewed sulfurous clouds into the air, and the stench of rotting eggs wafted over the platform.

Her breast ached fiercely and a low moan escaped her lips. Herschel hurried off to send for an ambulance while Ben paced the platform impatiently until the medics arrived.

Half an hour later, Bluma was finally settled in a private room that was large enough to house a ward. Herschel gave her something for the pain, and she was asleep in minutes.

In the days that followed, Bluma addressed one group of local Jews after another. In graphic detail, she described the rising brutality and anti-Semitism spreading throughout Germany. Most of her listeners were young people, and as Hanovi had predicted, she quickly became a symbol to them.

The demonstrations Hanovi had wanted became a reality overnight; the frail young woman speaking Yiddish from her wheelchair was just the spark he had hoped for. British consulates all over northern Poland and the Baltics came to dread the news of her arrival. Her presence guaranteed that hundreds of angry demonstrators would be outside their offices the next morning, carrying signs and making demands they did not wish to hear.

Ben followed a different schedule. Hanovi had outlined a rigorous agenda for him before they left Berlin, leaving Ben barely enough time to eat between appointments. He and Bluma hardly saw each other.

He made the rounds in Koenigsberg and traveled to towns and villages in the surrounding countryside. Three times a day, and sometimes four, Ben faced a roomful of anxious faces eager to hear the truth from one who had witnessed it. Each time, he began his speech the same way: "Greetings from Berlin. I am here to tell you what is happening."

"In Berlin, a Jew can be spat upon be anyone."

"In Berlin, a Jew cannot walk the streets without fear of assault."

"In Berlin, Jews are banned from restaurants and public places."

"In Berlin, thousands of homeless Jews live in hopelessness, waiting for a visa that will never arrive."

Then he would pause dramatically, slowing his speech.

"In Berlin, no Jew dares speak his mind in a public place. I made that mistake, and my fiancée paid the price for it. With her blood."

His speaking abilities improved steadily, and he found himself enjoying the lectures. "*Lekh lekha!*" he urged over and over again. "Remember God's command to Abraham."

Ben used every weapon in his arsenal to convince his reluctant audiences that their future lay in Palestine. He told them about his experience on the Berlin Express, holding up his hands to show the scars; he described Nazi Headquarters and the evidence linking Henry Ford and Adolf Hitler; and too many times, he relived those agonizing moments in the park across from Ten Meineckestrasse.

While the young Jews tended to be responsive and enthusiastic, their elders were less receptive. But even though they countered Ben's logic and persuasive force with dogged resistance, gone was the attitude of casual indifference and bemused tolerance. People were brittle and argumentative, and he saw the raw fear in their eyes wherever he spoke.

At times, Ben felt a vague sense of guilt, as though he were unfairly manipulating people, just as he had accused Hanovi of doing. He had always despised demagogues who made a practice of waving bloody flags, people like Hanovi, who were obsessed by achieving a goal and not overly concerned with the means they used. Yet here he was, frightening people with apocalyptic visions of the future and exploiting the fear.

But the doubts only plagued him at the close of a long, frustrating day, or in the middle of a lonely night. They were counterbalanced by a sense of satisfaction and accomplishment that dispelled the negative moods; spreading the truth to his people carried its own rewards.

Just before leaving Berlin, Hanovi had given Ben one of the most powerful weapons of all—a thick packet of documents on American immigration. Most of the *Ostjuden* knew they had no future in Germany; that much they had learned the hard way. They were prepared to emigrate, but not to Palestine. Their destination was America. It was Ben's job to show them the simple truth—that America had made it impossible for any more than a minuscule handful of *Ostjuden* to enter the United States.

America's first immigration law had been passed in 1921 and based numerical immigration quotas for every European country on the census of 1910. The total number of immigrants was limited to 355,000. But the new law, the Johnson–Reed Act, passed in 1924, reduced the total number of immigrants to 155,000 and based the quotas on the census of

1890. Few eastern and southern Europeans had come to America at that time, so the quotas for those countries were meaningless. The intention and effect of the Johnson–Reed Act was to eliminate immigration from southern Europe and to bar the entry of hundreds of thousands of *Ostjuden* trapped in Germany. America did not want any more Greeks, Italians, or Jews. America did not want to "mongrelize" its Nordic racial stock.

There were no exceptions to the new law. It didn't matter whether or not you had relatives in America, or how much money you had, or whom you knew. And it didn't matter that the census of 1890 gave over 51,000 of the 155,000 openings to Germany. The architects of the Johnson–Reed Act specified that only *German-born* immigrants qualified for those slots. One qualified only for the quota assigned to the country of his birth.

As a result, the German quota was filled with Nazi sympathizers, welcomed by Henry Ford. The patriotic Germans had no desire to emigrate, least of all to a country that had just defeated them in a bloody war. Meanwhile, tens of thousands of eastern Jews struggled desperately to obtain entry to the United States.

Worst of all, there was no way to be certain whether or not a quota had been filled, so thousands simply "took their chances" and spent what money they had on a passage ticket, hoping for a miracle. It was a vain hope. The Johnson–Reed Act was strictly enforced; if the monthly quota had been filled, one was sent back to one's port of origin. In the course of a single month, dozens of ships crowded with homeless *Ostjuden* were returned to Europe because the tiny quotas had already been filled.

In every group Ben spoke to, there were *Ostjuden* who had been sent back at least once, past the Statue of Liberty, to a hopeless existence in Germany. It was heartbreaking and cruel, but the *Ostjuden* ignored the odds and kept on trying. They saw America as their only chance for a decent future.

Through one back-breaking round of meetings, lectures, and gatherings after another, Ben kept on pounding the message home: America would not take the *Ostjuden*, and until Jews possessed a homeland of their own and the strength to defend it, they would never be safe. Only Jews could guarantee the safety of the Jewish people.

The carousel continued for two weeks, until Bluma received an unsigned telegram from Berlin. Their mission in Koenigsberg was over.

While Herschel, Helen, and Hermann made plans to return to Berlin, Ben and Bluma discussed the future. Ben wanted to leave for Palestine as soon as possible, bypassing Berlin and booking passage directly from Hamburg. But Bluma had other plans; she wanted to visit her mother in Riga. It would probably be many years before she saw her family again, and Riga was less than two hundred miles from Koenigsberg.

At first, Ben tried to dissuade her. Bluma was feeling weak and discouraged after weeks on the road, and Ben feared her mother's influence. Bluma's mother was an overbearing, provincial woman given to carping and self-pity. She never failed to make Bluma feel guilty for having "deserted" her and she was bound to do everything in her power to prevent Bluma from going to Palestine; Ben didn't want to take the chance that she might suceed.

Bluma remained adamant.

Against his better judgment, Ben finally acceded to her wishes and tried to ignore his premonition of disaster. He was far from gracious in agreeing to go, but when he saw the expression of joy and relief flood across her pale features, he was glad that he had changed his mind.

• • •

Though the city of Koenigsberg was a major rail center and not quite 250 miles distant from Riga, it was impossible to travel directly from Poland to the Latvian capital by rail. Between the two countries sat Lithuania, engaged in a furious border dispute with neighboring Poland; the Lithuanians had closed the rail lines to Koenigsberg, just to spite the Poles.

The dispute forced Ben and Bluma to detrain at the border and travel a short distance by horsecart to the Lithuanian town of Etkunin, also known by its Slavic name, Verbalis. The two countries even refused to use one name for the same tiny village. It was typical of the insanity generated by postwar compromises in Europe; the end result was pleasing to none.

Verbalis Station was typical of small town rail stops throughout eastern Europe. Paint peeled from its weathered clapboards like huge scabs, its roof needed work, and there were deep grooves worn in the front steps from fifty years of use. Frost glazed the oversized windows, making them almost opaque. The horsecart pulled up to the main entrance.

A group of Jewish boys between the ages of fifteen and twenty practiced primitive military drills to one side of the station. They were unarmed and dressed in an odd assortment of clothes. A small group of their peers stood to one side, jeering them. Taking Bluma by the arm, Ben helped her out of the cart and up the front steps. The interior of the station was filled with young Jews passing the time of day. While Christian youths often congregated around their place of worship, Jewish youths tended to collect near the town railroad station. It was part of an unwritten social convention observed in small towns all over eastern Europe.

They entered the building to the sound of a half-dozen arguments that raged with adolescent intensity. As usual, Zionism provided the fuel for the debate. Ben suppressed a smile of amusement as they sat down on a bench. Most of the young people were followers of Vladimir Jabotinsky, who headed Betar, a protofascist group training young men to fight in Palestine. Jabotinsky did not believe the Balfour Declaration alone was sufficient guarantee of a Jewish homeland in Palestine; the Jews themselves would have to be prepared to fight for it. To do that, they would first have to learn how to fight.

Ben met Jabotinsky once, in Dorpat. He was a fiery, passionate orator, who envisioned a new nation of farmer-soldiers, armed and trained to fight. He spoke with unmatched intensity, sweating heavily and constantly shoving his steelwire-rim glasses back onto the bridge of his nose. He had no tolerance for the more conservative Zionists and ridiculed them as weaklings and appeasers. Jabotinsky was the father of self-defense Zionism and one of his most ardent followers was a young man by the name of Menachem Begin.

Jabotinsky's creed of action had tremendous appeal to the young, but he represented only one of the three main factions of the Zionist movement. The older, more conservative Jews sided with Weizmann and Sokolow and preferred to let the British honor their guarantees. Those who could not bring themselves to embrace Jabotinsky's violent nationalism, but still distrusted the British, followed Arlosoroff, whose Marxist–Labor orientation was compatible with their radical social beliefs.

Of the three, Ben felt the gratest kinship with Jabotinsky. Though Arlosoroff was a brilliant leader and a powerful speaker in his own right, Jabotinsky's belief in strength and action was an irresistible lure for Ben. Most of the young Jews who filled Verbalis Station seemed to agree.

Ben could not resist being drawn into the conversation, and asked a boy standing near them what had sparked all the excitement. He sensed that the present argument was somehow different from the day-to-day debate one expected to hear.

The boy pointed to a young couple sitting across the room.

"Yankele and Kreidal are leaving their parents so they can be married and go to Palestine. They're running away to join the labor movement in Palestine."

Yankele could not have been more than seventeen. He possessed a melancholy beauty, with pale skin, green eyes, and fine blond hair. He sat in the contemplative silence of a scholar. Next to him was a beautiful young girl with dark eyes and full, sensuous lips. She was fifteen or sixteen and she held her companion's hand with shy affection. Ben guessed their parents were not privy to their decision.

"It's a long way to Palestine," Ben called out. They nodded politely and smiled.

"What kind of preparations have you made?" Bluma wondered. They looked so inexperienced and vulnerable.

"Well," the girl answered hesitantly, "we've packed some food." She pointed to a small clothbound package.

A sad look came into Bluma's eyes and she asked Kreidal if they had papers, passports, money, or contacts. What kind of arrangements had they made? Yankele answered for her.

"All we have is our love for each other and the clothes you see us wearing."

Tears formed in the corners of Bluma's eyes. Yankele looked so earnest, so much in love. "Do your parents know?"

"No. Telling them would only make things more difficult. Our parents are out of touch with the world. They hide from the things that are happening. Instead of doing anything, they just pray and fast. Kreidal and I want to do something, to accomplish something."

"Don't you think it might be wise to wait until you're both a little better prepared?" Ben smiled.

"If we stay any longer, we'll be locked into their way of life forever," Kreidal replied intensely. "As long as we remain here, we'll never be free of the old traditions. We want to build a new life together, not live as our parents have."

That set off a new round of passionate arguments among the teenagers. As Ben listened, he marveled at the strength and vitality he saw. Trapped in a small isolated village, surrounded by hostility, the youngsters in Verbalis Station were busily debating the issues that the Jews in Leipzig refused even to discuss. Perhaps it was because they had so little, Ben thought. Only the poor welcome change.

A piercing whistle announced the approach of the train for Riga. Bluma stood up and gently kissed Kreidal on the cheek. "Cling to each other," she whispered. "Shalom."

●　　●　　●

For centuries, the Baltic port of Riga served as the connective tissue that bound Russian and European trade together. It was a city of great houses, universities, and cathedrals, with a history that stretched back a millennium. Strategically located on the River Dvina, less than six miles from the Gulf of Riga, the city had been a key objective of the German army during the First World War. Despite a devastating siege that lasted more than two years and ended in a German victory, the city had survived intact, its ancient Gothic landmarks and manicured parks untouched by shellfire.

Despite the Germanic culture and a virulent strain of anti-Semitism that erupted with periodic fury, the Jews of Riga were a prosperous lot. Like the Jews Ben knew in Dorpat, the Rigan Jews were generous in their financial support of Zionism. But money was the full extent of their commitment. They were deeply suspicious of the British and feared that the Balfour Declaration was just another trick; a clever ploy to lure them from lives of relative comfort to the uninhabitable wastes of Palestine. Insulated and conservative, they withheld the one possession most desperately needed by the Zionists—their children.

On a dozen occasions, Ben and Bluma had traveled to Riga, only to talk themselves hoarse explaining how the survival of the Jewish people depended on establishing a Jewish homeland and populating it. The Rigan Jews would always agree, always contribute, and always insist that someone else be the one to go. They saw no paradox in supporting a cause with their wallets, not their hearts. "I cannot go—I have responsibilities. . . . I cannot leave my house . . . my business. . . . My children haven't finished school yet. . . . Palestine is much too dangerous."

There were a thousand excuses. And every one of them was catalogued and endlessly parroted by Bluma's mother whenever Ben and Bluma came to visit. Riga was not a place Ben remembered with any great fondness.

As they neared Bluma's house, Ben began to feel nervous. Bluma looked fresh and excited, but Ben's doubts still continued to nag him. Zippe Feldman was one of the most domineering women he had ever met and he wondered if Bluma had the strength to resist her.

When they arrived at the house, Zippe promptly became hysterical. She cried and wailed, clutching Bluma in the doorway as though her daughter might disappear. After a while, Ben began to wonder if they would ever get in. Tactfully, he cleared his throat. Bluma's mother stared at him for a moment, then stood back, pressing her handkerchief against her face and motioned them into the tiny living room. Ben set the bags down in the foyer and they all sat down.

"I thought you were dead," Zippe began to cry again.

"I'm all right, Mama. . . ."

"All right? With a bullet in you?"

"They took it out."

"Don't lie to me! How do you take such a thing out without destroying a body? It can't be done. I know."

"Mama . . ."

"At least you're alive!" That set off another round of hysterical weeping which lasted until Bluma suggested that she and Ben settle in their separate rooms and wash up.

"Benjamin," Zippe said, blowing her nose. "You'll share a room with Bluma's brother." She always made the transition from hysterical to efficiency in the blink of an eye.

As the days passed, life settled into a numbing routine. Zippe nervously insisted on knowing where Bluma was at every minute, and Ben and Bluma were forced to sneak out at odd hours in order to have any time together.

Night after night, Ben watched Zippe earn a meager living by rolling cigarettes at the kitchen table. She specialized in Russian cigarettes with long hollow tips and chatted incessantly as she stacked the finished cigarettes into neat pyramids.

On several occasions, Bluma made the mistake of mentioning Palestine.

"You can't go to Palestine. I won't hear of it," Zippe said in shrill tone.

"Mother . . ."

"It's too dangerous, too dangerous." Furiously, she continued to roll cigarettes as her panic mounted. "What do you want to do? Kill me with worry? Is that what you want?"

"Mama, stop it!"

"Go ahead! Kill me with worry! Go off someplace and let them shoot you like an animal!"

Bluma covered her ears. "Mama, please!"

"You'll be dead in some foreign place, and even if I find out, I won't even know where your grave is, so I can. . . ."

Bluma ran to her room, pushing the other children out of the way. When Ben tried to rise and follow her, Zippe grabbed his arm.

"Benjamin, don't take her from me," she whined. "Bluma's all I have left. If you want to get married, get married, but stay here in Riga. I'm an old woman without long to live. Instead of being so selfish, you should consider my feelings."

Once again, Ben tried to explain his feelings about Palestine, but Zippe was not interested in listening.

"Nah!" she rasped with a derisive gesture. "You and my late husband." Zippe's husband had been a second-rate tailor who had thrived on the exciting pulse of Zionism. He had died of a stroke, listening to Sokolow speak during a Zionist rally. Characteristically, Zippe had turned her deceased husband into a martyr for the cause. "First my husband," she moaned. "Now they want my daughter."

"Mrs. Feldman," Ben said firmly. "I love Bluma, but. . . ."

"If you loved her, you wouldn't drag her off to the end of the world to die, leaving me with a broken heart." She had always been melodramatic; now she became impossible. Zippe never missed an opportunity to criticize their plans for the future or to bemoan her status as an impoverished widow in poor health. At first, Ben had simply ignored her, but as the days passed, her unrelenting tirades began to take their toll, especially on Bluma. Even Ben fet himself being sucked into a whirlpool. If he remained long enough, his own family, only a few hours away in Dorpat, would add their voices to Zippe's and he would be overwhelmed. The pressure became unbearable until one Tuesday night after supper, when Ben tried one last time to reason with Zippe. The result was a complete disaster. Afterwards, Ben took Bluma by the arm and guided her out the door. Silently they walked arm in arm to the edge of a canal.

"Bluma, my love, we can't put this off any longer." They sat down on a park bench, staring at the skim of black ice on the water. Ben felt her tense as he began to speak.

"Something has to change, Bluma," he said quietly.

There was a note of desperation in her reply. "Oh, Ben, I know it hasn't been easy for you. I want to go to Palestine with you, now, today, but I can't. I can't leave Mama like this."

"Bluma," he said dully, "your mother is choking us to death."

"Ben, she . . ."

"I don't think she's a bad woman, Bluma, but I do know she is so driven by fear she will never allow us a life of our own." He paused for a moment. "The time has come for us to go."

"I . . . I, oh, Ben, I don't know . . . ," Bluma stammered, her voice fraught with anxiety.

"Please!" Ben implored, holding her tightly. Her fingers dug into his flesh through the heavy fabric of his coat, as if to clutch him to her forever. "Bluma, I know you love me as I love you. Your mother doesn't need you. I do. Say you'll come."

"I want to, but I can't. Ben, we're young, we can spare a little time. We have our whole lives ahead of us. My mother is almost at the end of hers."

"Bluma, she'll live to be a hundred. Can't you see that she's playing on your sense of guilt? If we stay, we'll fall into the same trap Yankele and Kreidal were so afraid of. Don't you remember what you said to them? How they should cling to each other?"

"Ben, I know she's pathetic, but I just can't abandon her. Not now."

He had lost. She looked up at him, her eyes filled with tears and misery. Somehow, they would have to compromise.

"Bluma, I love you," he whispered. "We've shared more in the time we've been together than most couples do in a lifetime, but I can no longer remain here. There isn't anything for either one of us in Riga. I also have an obligation to my father and to myself that I have to fulfill."

"Then you must go," Bluma smiled through her tears. "And a part of me will go with you, until I can join you."

"If you think about it, you too have an obligation to your father. He never lived to see Palestine, so you must do it for him."

"I know. Ben, nothing between us has changed. We'll still do everything we planned to do, and we'll do it together. I want to go to Palestine, and believe me, I'll leave as soon as I can. Until then, know that my love is with you." The anguish on Bluma's face mirrored his own pain. They walked back to the house in silence.

"Where have you been?" Zippe demanded when they returned. "I've been worried sick."

She started to launch into a tirade, but Ben cut her off rudely and told her he was leaving in the morning. She made no attempt to conceal her satisfaction at the news.

Ben lay awake that night listening to Bluma's brother snoring and wondered what the future held for him and the woman he loved. Leaving her was the last thing he wanted to do, but something had to change. The way they were living was impossible. He had no other choice but to leave. He was still awake when the first light of dawn pierced the frost on the bedroom window.

At the railroad station, he and Bluma clung to each other wordlessly, then he broke away and boarded. He rolled down the compartment window and leaned out. Gently, she kissed him on the lips, then pulled back. As the train pulled away, they stared at each other like statues frozen in time.

THIRTEEN

Back in Berlin
January 1925

His first two weeks back in Berlin would always remain a blur in Ben's memory. He went through the motions of daily life with a mechanical precision, trying to ignore the void within him. Overcome by lethargy, he postponed his departure for Palestine; he seemed unable to make a decision. Helen and Herschel tried to help, but seeing their happiness as a couple only served as a reminder that he and Bluma were apart. After their wedding, he felt like an intruder, so he decided to find a room and move, despite their protests. He rented the first room he saw, a small cubicle with faded green wallpaper and a few pieces of ramshackle furniture. He had to share a bathroom with two other tenants, but he didn't really care as long as no one bothered him.

Somehow, the days passed.

The early morning hours were the worst. Alone in his room, it was impossible to escape from himself. During the day, he could convince himself that Bluma would probably rejoin him after she and Zippe had the opportunity to spend some time together. Once her mother unwound a bit, Bluma would regain her sense of proportion, and things would be as they had planned. Every evening when he returned to his colorless room, there would be a vague, flickering hope in his heart. Would she be there?

But in the cold, lonely hours that precede the dawn, his doubts would bubble to the surface, leaving him with the nagging suspicion that he and Bluma would never see each other again. He kept thinking of Bluma, living in the small flat with her neurotic mother and her brothers and sisters, suffocated by outdated traditions that proscribed a woman's role in life and perpetuated the mistakes of the past. Through it all, she would be alone, her heart encased in a brittle shell.

Then the recriminations would begin.

Guilt, black and heavy, would weigh him down with self-accusations. It became part of his nightly routine, a litany that he repeated to himself until he fell into an exhausted slumber, broken by nightmares he could not remember.

For the first time in his life, Ben truly drifted. He spent the days wandering aimlessly, trying to piece together the puzzle his life had become. Often, he returned to the park opposite Ten Meineckestrasse, staring at the spot where Bluma fell. Always, the same question arose: "Why?"

He understood a single act of violence—Knaedl and Festbach were a pair of psychotic bullies out on a spree. But they hardly represented an entire nation. Why was the venom they carried so potent, so addictive, so contagious? The German people as a whole were inordinately polite. They were an industrious people, serious by nature. How could such a people be suborned by a philosophy of destruction and hatred?

Part of the answer came to him from a most unlikely source. Trying to cheer him up, Herschel had insisted that Ben accompany him and Helen to see a cycle of operas by Richard Wagner. Ben refused at first, preferring the silence of his room, but in the end it was easier to go with Herschel than it was to argue with him.

Collectively entitled *Der Ring des Nibelungen*, the operas were based on an ancient German epic that chronicled a bloody saga of passion and violence. Watching the story unfold on stage, Ben realized that Wagner had caputred the essence of German romanticism. The cycle ended with *Gotterdammerung*, the "Twilight of the Gods," a final holocaust that left no victor, no vanquished—only the carnage of a terrible slaughter.

What stunned Ben was the way Wagner exalted destruction. Defeat could be glorious, if destruction was total and complete. He realized that deep within the German psyche lay a pagan death wish, waiting for the right catalyst to release it—a catalyst like Adolf Hitler. Eleven hundred years of Christian doctrine had not yet conquered the blood worship buried in the German soul. Ben studied the faces in the audience; they were glowing with a twisted pride. Listening to the audience's wild applause sealed his depression. Until that moment, in spite of everything he had said and done, Ben was not wholly convinced that Germany was beyond redemption. Now he knew better.

One night, he made himself a cup of tea and set it on the window sill to cool. Unbidden, an image of his grandmother filled his mind, and he remembered all the talks they'd had over countless cups of tea when he'd felt confused and angry. He wished she was there for him to talk to now. He had dealt with love, anger, fear, and loss, but never depression. It clung to him like a second skin, dulling his senses and leaving him helpless and despondent.

"What am I doing here?" he asked himself. "Why am I in this apartment, awake at this hour?"

He had left Bluma to fulfill a promise to his father and himself. He had made a choice to leave everything behind: home, family, friends. But now, he felt too hopelessly mired to summon the strength to carry out his plans. He tried to understand what he had received in exchange for the love and tenderness he had sacrificed, but there was nothing but emptiness. The feeling that he had foregone everything in return for doubt and uncertainty washed over him like a tidal wave of despair.

Giving up for the night, Ben finished his tea and placed the cup in the tiny kitchen sink. As he turned away, something caught his eye. Shoved halfway under his door was a picture postcard, unnoticed when he first came in. Stooping over to pick it up, he recognized Sarah's handwriting.

Dear Ben,

Katzele and I send you a big kiss hello, and want to know why you haven't written to us in so many weeks. Where have you been? You're our nearest family now, Benjamin, and we miss you.

I've written many letters to Mama and Papa, trying to explain to them that I'm doing what I want to do and that they shouldn't worry about me. I am learning more and more about Palestine every day, and it makes me unhappy to think that they might never understand. But I've got to keep trying.

Ben, it's been so long since I've seen you. Couldn't you come for a visit? Please come, or at least write. But, whatever you do, let me know how you are. I miss you very much.

Sarah

Suddenly, Ben realized that the answer to his questions lay between the lines of Sarah's letter. In a moment of insight, her words brought everything into focus for him.

She was emigrating to Palestine to make a new life for herself, predicating the rest of her life on a single decision. She had given up her home, her friends, and her family. The fact that she was not entirely happy living at home did not really bear on the emotional cost of exchanging the secure warmth and certainty of home for the unknown and the unfamiliar.

Like her, Ben had to tear himself free of the threads of affection and familiarity that weighed like chains. His own mother, his family, Bluma—all compelled him to remain, to live out his life as they envisioned it. In order to seek his own destiny, he would be forced to hurt them as well as himself. Without pain, growth was impossible. Somehow, he would have to find the strength to overcome that pain. With time, the hollow feeling would fade, returning only as the wistful memory of a path not taken. It was time he did something; anything. What he needed was a change.

He would pay Sarah a visit.

• • •

Bundled in a heavy coat, Ben braced himself against the uneven motion of the horsecart. Far removed from the clamor and meaningless activity of the city, he felt invigorated. The driver sang aloud, leading Ben's thoughts back to the last time he had journeyed from Fulda to the *hakhsharah* with Bluma and Sarah. He smiled at the memory, feeling an ache around his heart.

They pulled into the main yard, causing a small-scale riot. As always, people poured out of the buildings, flushed with excitement. When she recognized Ben, Sarah shouted with delight and threw herself into his arms.

"Whoa, whoa," he laughed, kissing her on the cheek. It felt good to hug her. "All right, everyone. I need help with the packages." Eagerly, a score of hands reached into the cart to help. They moved into the mess hall, where Ben directed them to place the packages on a table. Trudi Weiss and several other members of the staff leaned against the back wall, enjoying the excitement.

One by one the boxes were opened, yielding their surprises. Ben had gone on a spree, purchasing items he knew were in short supply at the *hakhsharah*: pens, pencils, pads of paper, scarves, woolen caps, and above all, books. The young people loved books with a passion. The isolated *hakhsharah* was far removed from theaters, concert halls, stores, libraries, and the stimulation of city living. The children longed for wider horizons, and books were the key that opened their imaginations to the outside world.

While the young people enjoyed their surprises, the staff brought out freshly baked bread and milk. Ben stood up and beckoned to Sarah, pulling a small package wrapped in pink and white paper out of his pocket. There was a large pink bow in the center, somewhat flattened by its journey in Ben's coat pocket.

She accepted the package with a shy grin, unwrapping it carefully so as not to damage the bow. Inside was a tin can of kosher sardines. Immediately there were cries for Sarah's cat and people scattered everywhere looking for her.

A lanky boy with tousled straw for hair finally found her under the stove in the kitchen. Triumphantly, he handed the cat to Sarah, who placed her on the floor next to the open tin.

The sardines were greedily devoured.

Ben glanced around the room. All around him, he sensed a warmth and tenderness, a mutual caring missing from his life since he and Bluma parted. Separated from their own families, the students at the *hakhsharah* had formed a family of their own. For the first time in weeks, Ben felt a sense of wholeness,

While the others enjoyed their presents, Ben took Sarah aside and handed her another small package. It was shaped like a long, thin rectangle and wrapped in plain brown butcher's paper. She opened it to find a black velvet jeweler's box. Inside was a gold Star of David on a thin gold chain. Sarah was speechless.

"Let me put it on you," he said.

"It's so beautiful," she whispered, touching it reverently.

"I'm glad you like it."

"You shouldn't have," she said shyly. Then she jumped up and hugged him. "But I'm glad you did!"

"Mazel tov."

"Come on. I'll show you the classrooms." Sarah looked as though she might burst from pride and excitement.

They spent most of the afternoon wandering around the *hakhsharah*, talking about everything and nothing. Sarah described her new life in glowing terms and listened in stunned silence while Ben told her about Bluma and explained why he hadn't written. When the mood became too serious, he lightened it by teasing her about having a boyfriend. She flushed beet red and denied it vigorously.

"Stop teasing me, Ben. You know I have enough trouble trying to convince Mama and Papa that we don't sleep with the boys."

He asked if she had heard from her parents. She laughed merrily, covering a grin with her hand.

"I've heard from them—and just what you'd expect. They've calmed down quite a bit, but Papa is still a long way from enthusiastic. He's embarrassed to have people know that I ran away to a *hakhsharah*, so he's told everyone that I'm visiting relatives. To tell the truth, I think they're both fine. Maybe they'll even come around to my point of view in a couple of years."

Ben studied the smile on her face, wondering why Bluma was unable to make the commitment that Sarah had. Maybe she will, he thought to himself. After she's had some time.

"It's nearly dark," Ben said. "Didn't you mention something about having chores to do?" Kitchen duties were part of Sarah's responsibilities at the *hakhsharah*. As they walked back through the building adjoining the dining hall, Ben noticed a girl sitting in a darkened classroom. He asked Sarah who she was.

"Her name is Sophie. She's an Austrian and she doesn't speak a word of Hebrew." Sarah explained that the girl had been at the *hakhsharah* for more than a week and wouldn't say more than two words to anyone but Katzele. Most of the students had pegged her as a snob.

"I think she's just lonely and afraid," Sarah whispered. "Would you talk to her? You're good at that. Maybe you can break through her reserve."

"I'll give it a try," Ben promised. Sarah kissed him and went running off towards the kitchen.

Ben lit a kerosene lamp near the door but Sophie just continued to stare, ignoring the intrusion. Ben scrutinized the room, searching for something that might serve as a common meeting ground. His eyes came to rest on the charcoal sketch of a young girl done by one of the *hakhsharah* students. It was simply framed with unpainted wood and hung over a corkboard. Ben placed a chair beneath the portrait, just a couple of feet from Sophie. Then he climbed up on it and busied himself looking for tacks.

"Would you please hold this for me?" he asked, holding out a ribbon without turning to look at the girl.

She didn't budge.

"I'm sorry, perhaps you didn't hear me. Please hold this ribbon for me," Ben repeated. He made an awkward pretense of having his hands full. "I'd like to pin it on this picture. I knew this girl before she left for a kibbutz in Israel. She always wore ribbons in her hair and I think she should have one now."

Ben waited for a few more seconds before feeling a gentle tug. With a great deal of effort, he used both hands to remove some tacks.

"She was certainly very pretty. You knew her, didn't you, Elizabeth?"

"My name is Sophie," came the timid response. It wasn't much, but it was a beginning.

Gradually, Ben drew her into conversation, asking her opinion on just where the ribbons should be placed and wondering what she thought of the portrait. When he finished, he stepped off the chair with a grin and asked if she liked the present he had brought for her.

"Present? Why would you bring a present for someone you don't even know?"

"I know I brought a gift for everyone. I'm positive I did. . . ."

Ben rummaged through his pockets. Suddenly he stopped and smiled broadly, holding up a bar of perfumed soap. It was still wrapped in soft green tissue.

Gracefully, she reached out and accepted the gift. She seemed so pale and fragile, almost doll-like, as though her aristocratic features were molded from fine porcelain. She carefully unwrapped the soap, closing her eyes to inhale the scent of lilacs.

"This is so lovely," she said. "I recognize the scent."

"From home?" Ben asked, sitting down in a chair opposite her.

"Yes. It smells like the soap my mother used to buy in Vienna when I was little. She was very beautiful and she always seemed bathed in flowers." At this her voice trailed off sadly. Ben saw the tears welling up.

"I'd be glad to send her a bar of soap for you."

"Oh, no," she whispered. "That would be very kind, but she cannot receive such tokens of esteem now. She passed away some time ago."

"I'm sorry, Sophie," Ben replied softly. "What about the rest of your family?"

The story she told was all too familiar. Sophie's father had been killed during the war and after her mother died of typhus in 1920, her grandmother had taken her to Prague. She was intensely unhappy there, having been raised in the privileged society of Viennese Jewry. The clannish attitudes and orthodox customs in Prague made her feel like a stranger among her own people. She stood it as long as she could, finally leaving her grandmother to seek out her father's relatives in Hamburg. She arrived only to discover that her cousins had left for America.

"I wanted to follow them, but I wasn't eligible for the German quota." She looked up at Ben. "That man said that I would never live long enough to get a visa for America."

"He spoke the truth, Sophie."

"My money ran out, so the Zionists sent me here," she explained listlessly. "I'm being sent to Palestine."

"You make it sound like a prison sentence," Ben joked. Sophie just looked away.

Ben was no longer surprised that Sophie had failed to find a niche at the *hakhsharah*. There were few Austrians in the camp, and no one with her education and cultural background. She was Jewish, but her Judaism was an ethnic factor, not a religious one.

When the social order of the Austro-Hungarian Empire collapsed at the end of the war, children like Sophie formed the cultured remnants of a vanished way of life. Ben studied her face. She had the classic features of court society. High, delicate cheekbones, ivory skin and clear green eyes. Her hair was a soft shade of red, thick and wavy.

She looked ready to burst into tears.

He understood how she felt. She was locked within the shell of the past, unable to envision the possibilities of the future. She needed to reach out, to be touched, to lose her fear and her sadness, to know that someone still cared.

"I must have looked rather foolish to you," Ben sighed.

She looked up in surprise. "Why?"

"Tacking hair ribbons onto a charcoal sketch."

She clasped her hands in her lap and looked down. "I know why you did it, and I thank you for caring. It's been a long time since anyone has been so kind to me."

"There are a lot of people here who would like to be your friend, Sophie."

"You are very nice," she smiled. "I am grateful for your efforts, but I do not think they need be continued. As you know, I am not here by my own choice. These people are strangers to me, and I'm not sure I understand what their intentions are. It's like Prague. Everything is so alien, so strange. I know that I cannot go on living in the past. Somehow I must make a new life for myself. But it takes time."

Ben nodded in admiration and pride. She was like many of the other girls in the *hakhsharah*: old before their time, adults in the bodies of children, prematurely aged by experience.

"You should know that the people here care about you," Ben said gently. "You must give them a chance."

"I know you're right. Just let me sit here a bit longer. I promise I'll join the others for dinner. I hope they won't hate me too much for being so unbearably cold."

"I think you might be surprised. Like you, most of them have had a very rough time."

"Thank you again for caring," she said with great dignity. She held out her right hand and he took it in his own, kissing the air above his thumb in accordance with Austrain court custom that never permitted lips to touch flesh. Then with a smile, Ben stood up and turned.

"I'll see you at dinner, Sophie."

As Ben opened the door and stepped out into the hallway, he nearly tripped over two girls who had been eavesdropping. When he snapped at them, they looked at each other and started to giggle.

"Please, grant me this favor," one of the girls parodied Sophie's courtly manners. "You see, I fear leaving my old life behind and dwelling here, amongst the peasants." With an exaggerated flourish, she held out her hand for her friend to kiss.

"That's enough," ben said coldly. "You two, of all people, should know better. Don't tell me that you've forgotten what it means to have your manners and your way of life mocked and ridiculed. You both know what it's like to be desperate and alone, to cry in your sleep over the people you'll never see again, to suffer hurt and loss, to fear that the place where you're going is worse than the one you're leaving. Have you forgotten what it feels like to wonder if you'll ever love or be loved again?" Then he saw the tears in their eyes and berated himself for being so harsh.

"I'm sorry," he sighed. "I know you didn't mean any harm. I'm just a little overtired, so why don't you go along to dinner, and I'll join you soon." The girls apologized and ran off to dinner. As he turned to leave, he caught sight of Sophie, peeking out through the classroom door.

"What have we here?" he smiled. "Another eavesdropper?"

"You want to cry for someone too, don't you?" she asked shyly.

"Someone I had to leave behind," Ben nodded, surprised at her perception.

"My father always said that there were two kinds of people in the world," she said gravely. "Those who give and those who take. I think you will always have people who will love you, because you are one of those who give, like my father was." She stretched and kissed him gently on the cheek.

Ben watched her as she walked off to join the other girls. She seemed so frail, so delicate, and yet Ben never doubted for a moment that she would survive. She carried within her the perseverance of her race.

Suddenly, Ben felt restored. He had touched someone and been touched in return. Somehow, he and Sophie had lightened each other's burdens.

At dinner that evening, the two eavesdroppers made a point of sitting with Sophie. By the time Ben and Sarah joined them, they were all laughing at Sophie's tales of life in Prague. Sarah was bright and bubbling and full of life. Again and again she unconsciously fingered the gold star that hung from her neck, stealing glances at Ben.

When the time arrived for Ben to depart, he did so with a pang of regret. For the first time since Riga, he felt like himself again. Though a part of his life would never be the same, and a score of unanswered questions still plagued him, Sarah's letter and his trip to the *hakhsharah* had begun the healing process.

From his compartment aboard the Berlin Express, he watched the countryside slip by and decided to pay Herschel and Helen a visit, regardless of what time the train arrived in Berlin. The thought of his room on Grenadierstrasse seemed claustrophobic and unbearably dreary; he needed to share his feelings with people who cared.

Three hours later, he was knocking on Herschel's door. No one answered. As Ben slipped his key in, he noticed a shiny *mezzuzah* nailed to the doorpost. Herschel had apparently lost his inhibition about displaying his Judaism. Reverently, Ben touched his fingers to the *mezzuzah*, then to his lips before entering the apartment. He stretched out on the couch and closed his eyes. It seemed like seconds later that the lights came on, startling him from a deep sleep.

"Ben!" Herschel exclaimed. "The prodigal son returns." He and Helen were loaded down with packages.

"Ben, where have you been?" Helen scolded. "You should have told us you wouldn't be home for the weekend."

"I went to Fulda to visit Sarah," he yawned. He noticed a large box from the bakery. "What's the cake for?"

"It's a present from Karl, to celebrate his turning anti-Nazi," Herschel announced gleefully. "He burned his uniform in front of the bakery."

"What brought that on?"

"He was severely beaten this weekend."

"Beaten?" Ben's eyebrows went up. "By whom? Communists?"

Twice Herschel tried to answer Ben, but he was laughing too hard to pronounce the words. Helen had to tell the story.

"He was beaten up by shoppers," Helen grinned. "They thought he was molesting my mother."

"Now you've really lost me," Ben shook his head.

Helen explained how her mother and father had gone to Wertheim's on a buying spree. Her father had just returned from a Nazi party meeting and hadn't bothered to change his uniform before going. They shopped for a while until Helen's mother picked out a dress she wanted to buy for Helen. That's when the trouble began.

Karl was in a cantankerous mood and announced that the dress was not suitable for his daughter. Helen's mother simply ignored him, which enraged Karl. He forbade her to buy it at the top of his lungs and when she turned her back, he ripped the dress off her arm. She screamed at him and a tug of war over the dress ensued.

The clerks and the other shoppers assumed that some Nazi was molesting a helpless woman, so they came to her rescue. Before she could stop them, they gave Karl a sound thrashing and ripped his uniform to shreds.

"You know what crowds are like once they get started," Herschel laughed. "They forgot all about Helen's mother—she got pushed into a counter and broke her little finger."

"Herschel, they're still my parents," Helen warned.

"I know, darling. I'm sorry."

"You don't sound very sincere," Helen said suspiciously.

"Anyway," Herschel continued, "they finally managed to escape. After what happened, Karl was practically naked and mortified to be seen wearing a Nazi uniform, so he tried to take a cab, but Helen's mother forced him to walk. She told him she was fed up with him, and she wanted everyone to see that Nazis were vulnerable, just like anyone else. Once they got home, Karl changed his clothes and built a small bonfire in front of the store. He burned what was left of his uniform, piece by tattered piece. Then he posted a big sign on the bakery that said: KEINE N—A—Z—I—S IN MEINE BACKEREI. "No Nazis in my bakery!"

"It sounds like I missed quite a weekend," Ben smiled.

"There's more to be celebrated," Helen said shyly.

"Oh?"

"Tell him, Herschel."

"Tell him what?" Herschel asked, opening a bottle of wine. She flashed him another warning glance. "Oh that—of course, my love. How stupid of me." He turned to Ben with a toothy grin. "Guess what."

"Helen is pregnant and you are planning to emigrate to Palestine after the baby is born."

"How right you are. Ben, you have convinced us."

"What about you, Ben?" Herschel asked. "What are your plans?"

"I'm not really sure. Maybe I'll just give myself some time to sort things out." Ben still clung to the hope that Bluma would meet him in Berlin.

Herschel knew what was going through his cousin's mind.

"I hate to say it, Ben, but you can't live your life waiting," he said gently.

Ben stared at him, knowing he was right. It was time he started living his life again.

An hour later, Ben sat in Zorach Hanovi's living room. They talked for a while until Hanovi sighed and smiled sadly. "Why don't you tell me the real reason why you've come tonight?"

"I think the time has come for me to fulfill my father's wishes," Ben explained, fingering the gold Star of David on his lapel. "I want to be standing on Mount Scopus for the opening of Hebrew University."

Hanovi rose from his chair and shook Ben's hand. "I envy you. And I'm glad you're getting out of Berlin for good. I'll make the necessary arrangements—it's the least we can do after what you've done for us. You can stop by the Messageries Maritimes office tomorrow. Your tickets will be waiting."

"Shalom," he said softly as Ben walked down the front steps. Then he hurried to his desk. He had a lot of planning to do before morning.

●　　●　　●

The next morning dawned icy and cold. Ben made himself a light breakfast, then donned his double-breasted blue coat and left to pick up his tickets. As he strode over the crusty snow, God's words to Abraham echoed in his heart. *Lekh lekha.* Go. Go, Jew, and find the land that I have made for thee. A rising sense of excitement coursed through Ben as though an enormous weight had been lifted from him, leaving him free to soar.

Although he could have taken a ship from Hamburg, Hanovi had recommended the more direct route preferred by Ten Meineckestrasse— by train to Marseilles, then on to Palestine by ship. Hanovi had felt it would make the journey more interesting; Ben had agreed.

There was another reason why Ten Meineckestrasse preferred the connection through Marseilles. The famed French shipping line, Messageries Maritimes handled so many bookings that it was impossible for the British to catch all of the Jews smuggled out of France.

Ben entered an unassuming store front bearing the company's name. The office was apparently empty. He called out several times, but no one replied. Idly, he examined the room, noticing a captain's hat lying on the counter.

It was navy blue with a laurel of gold braid on its peak. Impulsively,

Ben picked up the hat and placed it on his head. Admiring his reflection in a small wall mirror, he cocked the hat at a jaunty angle. With his stylish dark blue double-breasted coat, he looked the very image of a sea captain.

"You should have been a sailor, not a Zionist," he said to his reflection. He never heard the man come up behind him.

"Ah, Kapitan Landsdorf!"

Ben whirled around in embarrassment. Instinctively, he removed the hat, and tried to explain, but the man refused to listen.

"I beg you, Kapitan," he said firmly. "There is no time for the amenities. Please." He pointed to an Opel parked at the curb in front of the office. Its exhaust blew clouds of gray smoke into the clear morning air, swirling around two large men leaning up against the car.

In a moment, Ben was inside the car and being whisked away.

FOURTEEN

The Anhalter Bahnhof
Tuesday, February 3, 1925
10:00 AM

Ben sat in the back seat of the Opel, debating his next move. He was sandwiched between the two men who had been standing on the curb and they didn't look like the type to appreciate being taken in by an imposter. How had they mistaken him for a Messageries Maritimes captain? A chilling thought crossed his mind. What if it wasn't a case of mistaken identity? Were they Nazis? Had he been recognized by someone from Nazi Headquarters? He scanned the faces in the car, looking for a clue. The driver and the two men in the back had faces carved out of granite: cold, humorless, and sharp-edged; they would tell him nothing. The man sitting next to the driver, the one who had grabbed him in the office, seemed different. He was nervous and kept glancing in the rear-view mirror as if he expected to be followed. Of the four men, he would be most likely to let something slip.

Casually, Ben tried to start a conversation. "I assume we are going to the usual place?"

"*Jawohl*, Herr Kapitan." As Ben had guessed, the nervous one was first to speak. "The next shipment is due in less than thirty minutes."

Ben nodded indifferently, but inwardly, he was seething. What kind of shipment? The penalties for smuggling were severe. Getting caught by the police guaranteed an extended prison term; getting caught by one's competitors often meant a bullet in the back and a shallow unmarked grave. Ben cursed his stupidity. He should have put an end to the charade in the Messageries Maritimes office, but it was too late to stop it now. All he could do was wait for an opportunity to disengage himself.

The Opel veered around a corner, pressing Ben against the man on his left, and he suddenly realized how fast the car was moving. The driver swerved to avoid an elderly lady stepping off the curb, then accelerated and swerved again, narrowly missing a horse-drawn cart. Whatever the shipment contained, they were in a great hurry to receive it. The man next to the driver reached into the breast pocket of his overcoat and withdrew a smudged white envelope. Without turning around, he handed the envelope over his shoulder to Ben.

"Here is a copy of the manifest, Herr Kapitan," he said. "They may ask to see it."

Ben opened the flap. Inside were a half-dozen sheets of paper, each covered with orderly rows of names. He reclosed the flap and put the envelope in his pocket, more puzzled than ever. Was the list relevant? Or were they just trying to allay his suspicions?

The Opel bobbed through traffic, nearly causing several fatal mishaps, then turned at the entrance to the glass-domed Anhalter Bahnhof. Ben heaved a sigh of relief. If his companions were Nazis, they'd be headed out of town, to the deserted outskirts, not to a train depot in the middle of Berlin.

The main entrance of the station was mobbed with people. That in itself was unusual—one seldom saw large crowds at a station on weekday mornings. Ben also noticed the rows of empty buses double-parked along the sidewalk. He wondered if they had anything to do with the list of names in his breast pocket. The driver stopped in front of the station and turned to his nervous companion in the front seat.

"Good luck, Schimmel," he murmured. Like his face, his voice was hard and spare.

The man Ben now knew as Schimmel jumped out of the car and stood on the sidewalk, urging Ben to hurry. Ben smiled pleasantly and stepped out, then Schimmel slammed the doors shut. Perfect, Ben thought to himself. The three men in the Opel would not be going with them. Once he and Schimmel entered the station, Ben would have no problem disappearing into the crowd; Schimmel didn't look capable of stopping anyone from doing anything.

The concourse was choked with throngs of well-dressed Berliners. Though a few were obviously seeing someone off, the vast majority of people had no luggage. Instead, they carried large cardboard signs bearing the name of travelers they were to meet; names that were common to eastern Jewry. That could only mean incoming refugees. Schimmel confirmed Ben's guess.

"There are nearly six hundred *Ostjuden* on this train," he beamed proudly. "We're about as well prepared as we can be."

Why would a Messageries Maritimes captain be meeting a trainload of *Ostjuden*? Ben intended to find out. It was clear that he was in no danger and his curiosity was aroused. Schimmel and his friends probably worked for Ten Meineckestrasse—the entire setup smacked of Hanovi.

Ben started to walk towards the platform, but Schimmel grabbed his arm. "It would be best if you stayed out of the way, Herr Kapitan. These people have had a difficult trip; they'll be tired, hungry, and nervous. It's not uncommon for a lot of them to become hysterical with all the confusion. Children start crying, or get lost; people panic because they can't find friends or relatives. Sometimes we end up with a small riot on our hands. People who have spent their entire lives in a small village just aren't used to crowds or travel."

"I would think the sight of a uniform would have a calming effect," Ben pointed out.

"On the contrary," Schimmel replied. "It might cause panic. The only uniforms these people have ever seen were on Cossacks, soldiers, or policemen of one kind or another, and it's left them with a lifetime of harsh and bitter memories. Just the gold braid on your hat would be enough to make them break out in a cold sweat." He turned to Ben. "Please remember that your primary function is to appear in command and give the impression that everything is under control."

The last piece of the puzzle fell into place. Schimmel was using Captain Landsdorf to impress the German authorities, not the Jews. The *Ostjuden* were bound for a Messageries Maritimes ship to South Africa, South America, or even Palestine, and the Germans were probably worried that many might try to remain in Germany. The presence of a Messageries Maritimes captain would reassure the Germans that the company was committed to a smooth and orderly trans-shipment. Whether or not Ben could captain a ship was irrelevant; the gold laurles on his cap were all that nattered. A deafening whistle split the air, and an expectant hush fell over the crowd. Everywhere, people asked each other: "Is this the train from the east?"

It was.

Just then, an obese man in a blue serge suit appeared near the tracks. Even from a distance, Ben saw the sweat running down his face. The man moved purposefully, scanning the platform until his eyes met Ben's, then recognition spread across his face. He mopped his brow with a large handkerchief and waded through the milling crowd in Ben's direction. When they finally stood face to face, he clasped Ben's hand enthusiastically and introduced himself as Gregor Shultz. Panting heavily from his exertions, he told Ben that the situation was completely organized and well under control. Despite Shultz's confident patter, Ben could see he was tense and jumpy. He obviously had no idea that Ben was an imposter. Like everyone else, all that concerned Shultz was the gold braid on Ben's cap, not the face beneath it.

He shoved some papers into Ben's right hand, turned and raised his arm, then dropped it sharply, like an official starting a race. In response, dozens of men spread out along the platform, carrying placards that read:

WE ARE YOUR BROTHERS
PLEASE DO NOT ATTEMPT TO REMAIN HERE LONGER
THAN THE 72 HOURS GRANTED TO YOU

The train thundered into the station, belching sparks and steam. The brakes caught with a deafening screech of metal on metal and compartment doors flew open even before the engine came to a complete stop. Hundreds of passengers flooded out, colliding with the waiting crowd. Attendants placed at strategic points bellowed instructions in Yiddish while the exhaused *Ostjuden* inundated the platform, searching for friends, relatives, or contacts. The confusion was unbelievable.

Children clung tenaciously to their parents, terrified they would become separated and lost. Old people stumbled alongside the train, fearful of being crushed by the force of the mob. Nothing could be heard over the tremendous din that filled the station. Ben had never seen anything like it.

Volunteers began to organize the crowd with detached proficiency; they were accustomed to dealing with similar situations. Prior to the arrival, they had divided the platform into alphabetical areas, assigning each refugee's name to a sector. Now they circulated through the crowd, checking off names and directing people to their sectors.

Ben watched as their efforts settled the crowd and built order out of chaos. Awkwardly, he shifted from foot to foot, suddenly feeling self-conscious. Everyone seemed to have an assigned task but him.

It disappointed Ben that Kapitan Landsdorf did not have a more important role to play; no one had even bothered to talk to him. Ben had to laugh to himself. He should have been relieved that his role as an ersatz sea captain and the breakneck ride through the city were part of a harmless conspiracy. Instead, he was piqued by Landsdorf's meaningless role.

"Well, I've done my part," he thought and started towards an exit. Halfway there, Shultz appeared and practically dragged him behind a pillar. Shultz tried to speak in a conspiratorial whisper, but Ben couldn't hear him over the noise on the platform. Shultz ended up shouting that many of the passengers weren't carrying valid visas.

"But all of the appropriate agencies have been alerted," Shultz yelled, "and I assure you, they will act with all possible haste. I guarantee you, Herr Kapitan, that everything will be in order for the embarkation." He smiled, bowed obsequiously, and turned to leave.

Ben's hand shot out and closed around the man's forearm like a band of steel. Startled by the sudden gesture, Shultz nearly tripped and fell.

"Herr Kapitan," he mumbled in a shocked tone of voice, "there's no need to. . . ."

"I want some answers, and I want them now," Ben grinned crookedly, no longer caring about the subterfuge.

Shultz looked at him suspiciously and opened his mouth to protest, but when he saw the menacing expression on Ben's face, he changed his mind. Ben plied his captive with several questions, and the answers gave him all the information he needed. He released Shultz, who glared with indignation, and turned his attention back to the crowd.

The refugees milling around on the platform were all bound for Marseilles, where they were to board the *S.S. Asia* for Palestine—the same ship Hanovi had said Ben would be traveling on. Ben felt a sudden rush of excitement. Traveling to Palestine as a "tourist" was one thing, but traveling to Palestine in the company of hundreds of his own people was what he had always dreamed about. He felt like shouting out a welcome or embracing his shipmates.

As his eyes drifted across the platform, Ben glimpsed a disheveled woman holding a toddler in one arm and trying to drag a heavy trunk down the steps of her train compartment. A small boy stood on the other end of the trunk, pushing from inside the compartment. The woman was close to tears.

"Please," she called out, searching the platform for anyone with free hands. "Someone, please help us!" Her eyes met Ben's.

"Please help a poor widow," she shouted at him. In spite of her smudged face and bedraggled hair, she had an attractive aura. Ben smiled at her and started towards the train.

Before Ben reached them, the boy gave a final shove. The trunk teetered on the edge of the compartment, then tipped and thudded down the two steps, narrowly missing the woman and the girl. The boy fell head over heels, landing at Ben's feet. He sprang up and clutched at Ben's leg with such desperate force that it started to cut off the circulation. Ben laughed and offered the boy his hand, which was eagerly taken.

"I'll help you with the rest of your cases."

"Thank you," the boy's mother replied with a sigh of relief.

With surprising strength, the boy pulled Ben up the steps and led him into a third-class compartment where a large canvas suitcase sat on the floor. He pounced on it and insisted on helping Ben, calling him "*Tatte*" all the way back to the platform. It was the first time anyone had ever called Ben "daddy" in Yiddish. Ben set the case down in front of the woman and tipped his hat.

"I'm glad I was able to help," he shouted over the racket. "But for some reason, your son thinks I'm his "*Tatte*.""

"Oh, please," she begged. "Let Mendele think you're his father. It would mean so much to him and to me as well." Astonished, Ben asked if Mendele knew who his real father was.

"Yes, but it would give him a feeling of security in a strange land if you allow him to call you *Tatte*. It's such a small thing."

Ben thought it strange for any five-year-old boy to call a perfect stranger *Tatte*, but when he saw the expression on the woman's face, he let it pass. She was right, it was a small thing. The woman sank down on the trunk, holding the baby in her lap. She looked utterly exhausted.

"When did you last eat?"

"Last night," piped Mendele. It was impossible to mistake the hopeful note in his voice.

"I think we should remedy that situation right now," Ben grinned. "You stay right here and I'll be back with some food as quickly as I can find a vendor."

The woman just stared at him numbly, an unspoken fear clouding her dark eyes. She was terrified to be left alone with her children in the maelstrom on the platform. Ben signaled one of the men who had been organizing groups of *Ostjuden* and asked him to stay with the woman until he returned. The man's name was Jacob Berzig and he did not question Ben's instructions; he simply saluted and took up a post behind the suitcases. Ben set off to find something to eat.

Everywhere, people searched for other people, families struggled to find lost members, and strangers desperately sought aid, food, medicine, shelter, or papers. It took Ben the better part of twenty minutes to push through the crowd and find a food vendor. He bought sandwiches, fruit, and pastries, then fought his way back.

To his surprise, the woman had taken advantage of his brief absence to comb her hair, straighten her clothes, and somehow wash her face. She was extremely attractive. He dismissed Berzig with a brief salute; if he was going to play the role of an officer, he might as well play it to the hilt.

"What is your name?" Ben asked, handing the children sandwiches and fruit. They began to eat ravenously.

"Zelda Glovsky."

"You are Polish?"

"Yes. From Lemberg, in Galicia." She bit into her pastry.

"How old are you?"

"That I will not tell you, Herr Kapitan." In spite of her exhaustion, she managed a small smile. Ben guessed she was about twenty-four. They were barely beyond the introductions when Schimmel reappeared. He nodded to Ben, then gave Zelda Glovsky her bus assignment and asked her to hurry.

"Everyone must be aboard within twenty minutes. We need the buses to meet the other arrivals."

"Other arrivals?" Ben asked.

"There are groups arriving at nearly every station in Berlin. But this was the largest."

"Where are you going to put them all?"

"Most of them will be concentrated around Grenadierstrasse," Schimmel explained. "The young people have been assigned to special dormitories and the single adults to small hotels or boarding rooms. Families will be staying with local families or in shelters. They're only going to be here for forty-eight hours, so our main concern is food and shelter. Comfort we can't worry about."

"Where are we staying?" Zelda asked hesitantly.

"You and your children are assigned to Wiesenstrasse."

"Wiesenstrasse!" Ben exploded.

"The passenger manifest was matched to the list of available facilities. It was all arranged by the Jewish Hospitality Centers and the Ladies Auxiliary League. Besides, it's only for a couple of days."

Schimmel's casual attitude infuriated Ben. "The Ladies Auxiliary League must be insane to suggest that Wiesenstrasse is any place for a mother with two small children. You know what that place is like as well as I do." Ben's protective instincts bubbled to the surface. Impulsively, he turned to Zelda. "Come on, you're all going with me."

He drafted Schimmel to help with the luggage, then led Zelda and her children through the thinning crowd to a taxi. Just before getting in, he turned to Schimmel and grinned. "I assume you won't be needing me any more, Schimmel?"

"*Nein*, Herr Kapitan." Schimmel clicked his heels and bowed formally from the waist. Ben climbed into the cab and gave the driver his address.

Mendele was fascinated by the traffic as they crossed the River Spree and drove towards the Jewish section of Spandau. He was small, with dark curly hair like his mother's, and searching blue eyes. Diana, his two-year-old sister, was a trifle overwhelmed by the sights and the sounds of Berlin at midday. Solemnly, she tried to conceal her anxiety and listened to her brother, who was trying to teach her to call Ben *Tatte*. Ben could not resist the expression on her face. He leaned over and kissed her on the forehead, as though she were his own. She rewarded him with a happy smile.

When the taxi pulled to a stop in front of the apartment house, Ben instructed the driver to carry the bags to the second floor and shepherded his adopted family up the stairs. They were halfway up when Ben's landlady appeared on the landing, smiling and insatiably curious. When she heard Mendele call Ben *Tatte*, she made all the natural assumptions and rushed up the stairs to welcome Ben's family to Berlin.

"Most people leave their poor wives and children to suffer alone— leave them back in the east like so much unwanted baggage," she clucked to Zelda. There was a strident, self-righteous tone in her voice. "Not like your husband, who everyone knows is a fine, responsible man." She grinned widely, revealing two rows of poorly fitted false teeth.

Once everyone was in the apartment, the landlady beckoned Ben to the landing and told him that letters from Bluma, Sarah, and his family had arrived in the morning mail. He thanked her and was about to reenter the apartment when she clawed at his sleeve. To his surprise, she winked at him, crudely calculating that her discretion was of some value. Who knew how a man's wife would react to the news that he'd been receiving letters from other women? Ben kept a straight face and pressed a small coin into her hand.

"Please don't say anything," he whispered secretively. Her rheumy eyes blinked with excitement as she examined the coin.

"You can depend on me," she swore and pocketed the money. As Ben closed the door, he smiled to himself. For a pfennig more, he was certain she would sell him to the first buyer who made an offer. When he turned around, the two children stood staring at him. Zelda had collapsed on the couch.

"Why don't you and the children wash up while I go out for some groceries."

"That would be lovely," she smiled. "By the time you get back, the children will be hungry again."

Since returning to Berlin, Ben had discovered how lonely it was to sit at an empty table, and the thought of a family dinner warmed his heart. He ran to the kosher delicatessen around the corner and bought all the makings for a hot meal. On the way home, he even stopped to buy candy. The children were waiting for him and they shrieked with delight when Ben set his bundles down and swept them up in his arms. That was the difference between a room and a home—the sound of children's laughter.

As he hugged them tightly, he happened to notice Zelda's expression. Though she looked away quickly, he saw the tears in her eyes and realized how bitter and lonely she must be without her husband. He set the children down and let them carry the bags to the tiny kitchen.

Zelda prepared the food while Ben entertained the children, and when dinner was ready they sat down to eat as a family. Mendele let Ben cut up his food, then insisted on eating from Ben's plate. Ben leaned forward on his elbows, smiling at Mendele's effort to balance peas on the blade of his knife. "Use your fork, Mendele," he grinned, enjoying his role as surrogate father. Shyly, the boy obeyed.

Ben took advantage of Zelda's preoccupation with her daughter, Dianele, to study the delicate contours of her face. Her hair was pulled back into a severe bun, softened by a rebellious hank of curly black hair that fell over her left eye. Unconsciously, she kept brushing it back with a gesture that Ben found strangely intimate.

After dinner, the children curled up together against a bolster and promptly fell asleep on the floor. Zelda looked at them wistfully. "They seemed so content tonight," she whispered to Ben. "How I wish we could stay here in Berlin. I hate this traveling—never being settled, never knowing where we'll be sleeping tomorrow, running all the time."

"The running is almost over, Zelda. In a relatively short time, you and the children will be settled in Palestine, free to start a new life. You must be excited about that."

"I'm excited, and afraid, and exhausted, and God knows what else. I hardly know what I'm feeling anymore." She looked at him apologetically, brushing the wisp of hair back from her forehead. "I haven't even thanked you yet. How terrible. I'm ashamed of myself. I guess exhaustion makes one forget one's manners."

"Don't worry about it."

Zelda stood up and walked over to Ben. She sat next to him on the narrow sofa and folded her hands in her lap. He detected the scent of roses.

"Thank you for letting Mendele call you 'father'," she said quietly. "He just can't seem to accept his own father's death."

"It's nothing," Ben assured her. Filled with concern, he took her hand into his own. "I'm sorry for your misfortune." She leaned against him ever so slightly. Her body felt surprisingly soft.

"It was the will of God," she sighed with resignation.

She told Ben the story, her voice laced with sadness. Her husband had been a shopkeeper, a quiet man with a gentle sense of humor. He and Zelda were returning home from the shop late one afternoon when a team of horses went berserk. The driver fell off, leaving the helpless occupants of the carriage to careen down the street. Zelda's husband ran out and grabbed the check rein on the lead horse, but his coat caught in the harness and he was trampled to death. The carriage overturned, seriously injuring two of the occupants. One of the animals broke a leg and had to be destroyed. But her husband's death was only the beginning of Zelda Glovsky's problems.

The Poles blamed him for startling the horses in the first place, and people in the street would point to her as though she was responsible in some way for the accident and the dead horse. To most of her neighbors, a good horse was far more valuable than any Jew. At night, the doormat and windows would be smeared with chicken droppings or worse, and Mendele was beaten up regularly by the other children. When people threw rocks through the windows and threatened to burn the house, Zelda made the decision to leave. She sold the shop and everything she owned to raise five hundred dollars. Three hundred was used to purchase a valid travel pass, most of the balance went for bribes. It was a story Ben had heard before.

If you were a Jew, bribery was a way of life. No government official would speak to you until he had been paid; no policeman would guard your store until he had received his cut; no customs officer would pass your bags without a few marks for his trouble. Not even the street sweepers would touch a broom to your sidewalk unless you put a coin in their outstretched palms. Without money, a Jew did not exist. Even though Zelda had paid for the proper papers, she still had to pay someone to help her get away and bribe men on both sides of the border.

Ben nodded. "It's like Sholom Aleichem's story about the Jew who fought like a tiger to get a valid passport. When he finally succeeded, he was so terrified of the Czar's officials that he still paid to have himself smuggled across the border. But all that will be different in Palestine."

"Will it?" she sighed. "Maybe, maybe not. Perhaps we're just changing one set of oppressors for another. Who can say? All I know is that when you're caught in the fire, there's nothing to be lost by jumping out into the darkness. At least my children are happy and safe tonight."

She leaned towards Ben with a smile. Her face was close to his and he could see her eyes were a clear dark blue, very deep but very warm. Suddenly, she sat bolt upright as though something had startled her.

"I cannot believe how preoccupied I've become with my own problems! I should be making your bed for you. You must be tired," she said. Her voice was filled with concern. Though it was barely nine o'clock, the day had been long, difficult, and confusing.

"Don't bother," Ben replied. "I'll be staying at my cousin Herschel's tonight."

"But we can't put you out of your own home!"

"I spend more time at Herschel's than I spend here anyway."

Too exhausted to protest any further, she nodded gratefully. Together, they settled the children head to foot on the couch, then Zelda made up the bed. Ben watched her contentedly, enjoying the unaccustomed domesticity. His eyes felt leaden and he dozed off, drifting in a half-conscious state. He dreamed that a dark-haired woman was making the bed, smoothing the crisp white linen sheets. She covered them with a light blue and white woolen blanket, then a knitted afghan. Slipping into one side, she reached over and turned down the other for Ben. Her eyes met his and she whispered for him to join her. In the half light of dreams, he recognized Bluma's face a split second before he awoke with a start.

Zelda was already in her nightgown. The flimsy garment clung to her body sensuously, and something about the way she moved conveyed a clear invitation for him to spend the night with her. Though he felt a surge of desire, Ben was determined not to take advantage of her loneliness. He rose and walked quickly to the door.

"Sleep well," he said and left without waiting for a reply.

●　　●　　●

He rose early the next morning, planning to breakfast with his new family. When he arrived at the apartment, there was a note stuck on the door.

Ben—Please come to Ten Meineckestrasse immediately.
Urgent.   Z.H.

'Z.H.' would be Zorach Hanovi. Assuming that Hanovi's note was somehow connected with the charade of the previous day, he folded the message in half and slipped it into his pocket; Ten Meineckestrasse would have to wait. Ben had promised to breakfast with Zelda and the children and that was exactly what he intended to do. Zelda had been up early, eager to display her skills as a housewife: the children were scrubbed and dressed, the apartment was immaculate, and breakfast was ready to be served. The children greeted him joyfully.

"Good morning, Ben," she added shyly. "I hope you're hungry."

She wore a gray skirt and a frilled high-necked blouse; she looked radiant. Obviously, Zelda was out to impress him.

And she did.

They chatted through breakfast, which was superb, and if it were not for Hanovi's note, Ben would have been content to spend the rest of the day enjoying his new "family."

"Would you like more?" Zelda asked when she saw his empty plate.

"Thank you, no. I really must leave. I have some business to attend to, but I'll be back as soon as I finish."

●　　●　　●

Ben was intrigued to discover that it was really Kaplan who wanted to see him, not Hanovi. Kaplan greeted him brusquely and motioned to a chair opposite his own.

"No doubt, you've heard about the arrival of several hundred *Ostjuden* at the Anhalter Bahnhof yesterday?"

Ben was incredulous that Kaplan pretended not to know about his performance as Kapitan Landsdorf. "I was there," he said flatly. "You're not actually going to sit face to face with me and claim that you know nothing about my little charade as a sea captain."

"I haven't the vaguest idea of what you're talking about." Kaplan's gaze remained level and steady.

"Are you afraid of speaking freely?" Ben was irritated by Kaplan's game. "Are there British spies in the building?"

"Don't take that tone with me, Benjamin." Kaplan's eyes were a wintry gray.

"I have performed a number of functions for Ten Meineckestrasse," Ben retorted. "I understand the need for secrecy, and I respect it, but I won't be treated like an outsider any more. You people know everything that goes on out there," Ben pointed towards the street. "If you aren't aware of it, it didn't happen. So, Mr. Kaplan, please don't insult my intelligence or my good intentions."

"We need your assistance," Kaplan said smoothly, ignoring everything that Ben said. "You seem to have a unique talent for improvisation, which is exactly the skill we require to solve our problem."

"And exactly what is 'our problem'?" Ben asked.

"The *Ostjuden* bound for Marseilles create a delicate political situation. Once freed from the immediate perils of eastern Europe, they balk at leaving for Palestine. They either try to remain in Germany or want to emigrate to America. The net effect of either option is to swell the ranks of *Ostjuden* mired in Germany, adding to an already intolerable burden. That cannot be allowed to happen." Kaplan then revealed to Ben a secret agreement between the German Jewish community and Ten Meineckestrasse. In exchange for funding, Ten Meineckestrasse agreed to move the *Ostjuden* through Germany quickly, sparing everyone unnecessary "embarrassment."

"That's hardly a secret," Ben scoffed. "It's practically common knowledge."

Kaplan continued as though Ben hadn't spoken. "Our job is to see that no *Ostjude* remains behind. They have agreed to emigrate to Palestine, and it is up to us to see that they honor that agreement. If there is trouble, the German government will become involved, and they can make it very unpleasant for all of us. There always seem to be more arrivals than departures, but with a project involving hundreds of people, it is essential that no one be left behind. If there is, it could jeopardize future emigration."

"And what does this have to do with me?" Ben asked. Kaplan stared at him for a moment.

"We want you to see that every *Ostjude* who arrived in Berlin on Tuesday is aboard the Marseilles Express tomorrow and stays aboard until they reach the *S.S. Asia.*"

"Palestine?" Ben whispered, hardly able to believe it. "You want me to deliver those refugees to Palestine?" Kaplan nodded and let the news sink in.

"It's not a simple task," Kaplan warned him. "Most of these *Ostjuden* don't have visas or papers of any kind. They're going to have to be slipped into our country." Kaplan accented the "our country" ever so slightly.

"So I'll be smuggling them into Palestine."

Kaplan shrugged. "Call it what you will, but you've been waiting for this chance for months. You've done good work for us, and we have a great deal of faith in you. We've assigned several men to act as your aides, but you'll be in charge. It will be your job to get our people to Palestine, regardless of what happens. I won't accept any excuse for failure." Kaplan's expression was grim.

"We'll help you as much as we can along the way. We have eyes and ears all over Europe—they'll be watching out for you."

"How will I contact them?"

"You won't. If you don't know who they are, you can't betray them if you're arrested, but don't worry. They'll intervene if intervention is called for. You have a choice, which must be made now. You're free to go if you wish. What you do with your life is your own business. But we need you, and if you wish to help, this is your opportunity. What is your decision?"

It was Ben's turn to avoid Kaplan's question. He held up the captain's hat he'd brought along, originally intending to make a dramatic gesture by returning it to Kaplan.

"Do you think this gold braid will help me with the job?" he asked nonchalantly.

Kaplan smiled. "The Arabs despise all Europeans and fear military authority, but don't make the mistake of treating the British too lightly. They're not easily impressed or intimidated by gold braid or titles. They've got more than enough of their own."

Ben stood up. "Thank you for this opportunity, Mr. Kaplan. It's what I've always dreamed of. I won't disappoint you."

Kaplan came around from behind his desk and took Ben's hand in his own. For once, there was genuine warmth in Kaplan's voice when he spoke. "Ben, son of Anschel, remember that many lives are entrusted to your care."

•   •   •

Ben could hardly wait to break the news to Zelda. Part of him was relieved that she and the children would not have to make the trip alone. Another part of him wondered if they weren't becoming too close too fast. If he had had more experience with women, he would have realized that Zelda had already marked him as a husband. A widow with two children had a hard time attracting a good husband close to her own age and Ben had everything she dreamed of—confidence, money, looks. Most important of all, he was genuinely fond of the children. Time was what she needed, time to show him how good a wife she would be.

An hour after Ben left Kaplan's office, Zelda sat with him in a café off Grenadierstrasse, drinking coffee. She could hardly believe her good fortune when he told her they would be traveling together. Zelda naturally assumed his decision was motivated by her and she was ecstatic. She chattered happily about the future, allowing her excitement to get the best of her. She couldn't seem to stop herself. Ben finally interrupted her in the middle of her plans for Mendele.

"I've been meaning to ask you something about Mendele."

"Yes?" She looked at him brightly.

"I can understand how Mendele might not accept his father's death, but why does he think I'm his father? Do I look like him?"

"No, you don't. But Mendele believes that people come back looking . . . well . . . different. For some reason, when you came over to help with the luggage, he decided that you were his father, come back to him. It's a strange notion, but it seems to have helped him to adjust. I can't take that away from him. If he wants to think you're his father and you are kind enough to let him think so, then that is enough for me." She gazed at him fondly. "I'm very grateful to you, Ben."

Ben sipped his coffee silently. She sensed his disapproval, realizing she had perhaps presumed too much. It was time to back away. She chose her words carefully.

"We have a long, dangerous journey ahead of us, Ben. There's so much to learn. Please don't leave us, Ben, at least until we get to Palestine. You know I don't ask for much. Just peace of mind for myself and my children." She watched him closely for a sign of disapproval, or an indication she had driven him away, but he simply smiled.

"Everyone is entitled to a little peace of mind," he said. Zelda had a way of touching his emotions that he found irresistible. He leaned across the table and kissed her on the forehead. In response, she squeezed his hand.

"Now I'll take you back to the apartment," he boomed cheerfully. "I haven't seen my cousin or his wife for quite a while and it's time I explained what's been happening." He settled Zelda with the children, then he set off at a brisk pace for the Tiergarten.

Sitting with Herschel and Helen, Ben found it impossible to relax. He was fairly bursting with excitement at the assignment Kaplan had given him; it was the fulfillment of a lifetime dream. But Kaplan had insisted on absolute security; Ben had not even told Zelda that his real name was Isaacson. All he was permitted to say was that he was bound for Palestine.

Helen put her hand over Ben's. "You came into our lives like a storm and now you are leaving like one."

"Why leave so suddenly?" Herschel sounded puzzled. "Spend some time with us."

"It's the people at Messageries Maritimes," Ben lied. "They don't seem to be able to arrange their schedules very well." Helen rose from the couch and embraced him tightly.

"We'll miss you so much," she cried.

A wave of sadness washed over Ben and bittersweet memories tugged at his heart. He felt like an arrow about to be launched into endless space. Suddenly, he desperately wanted to take some fragment of home with him, so that he wouldn't be lost forever among strangers in a strange land.

As he held Helen, tears filled his eyes and his throat constricted with emotion. He wondered why leavetaking had to be so lonely. His family and friends—Bluma—it seemed as though everything he loved was being left behind. He had always dreamed of going to Palestine, but never reckoned with the heartache of saying the final good-bye.

Helen held him at arm's length and eyed him suspiciously. "Is there a special reason why you're going so soon? Is something wrong? Does it have anything to do with Zelda, the young woman you told me about?"

"Whoa," Ben laughed, hiding his sense of loss at leaving them. He explained that his decision had nothing to do with Zelda.

"I am going home at last," Ben whispered. Breaking away from them, he went to the bedroom to write his farewell letters.

The letter to Bluma was the most difficult. After a dozen false starts, he finally decided to simply say what he felt.

My Darling Bluma,
    By the time you receive this letter, I will have boarded the train for Marseilles, bound for the S.S. Asia and Palestine. I have but one true regret—that you are not with me.
    I won't speak of opportunities lost, or excuses, or reasons why. I just want you to remember that we are only given one life to live and I want to live mine with you. I am hoping you will feel the same way.
    From Riga, you can take the Wagonlit Express to Marseilles via Paris. You still have time to meet the Asia, but should you miss it, just take the next ship. I'll be waiting for you.
    I miss sharing my life with you.
    I love you.

                                                                    Ben

It was short and a trifle awkward but Ben knew she would read it with love and understand. He sealed it in an envelope and placed it on the growing stack of correspondence.

His final letter was addressed to Sarah and it was the easiest to write. "I wish that you and Katzele were sailing with me on the S.S. Asia," he wrote her. "We three travel well together." He shared with her his hopes for the future and ended by paraphrasing her own words to him: This year in Jerusalem!

His last night in Berlin was a sleepless one. He could barely wait for dawn, and left long before Herschel and Helen arrived home from the hospital. This would be his final day in the old world, and he felt as though he stood poised at the edge of a cliff, overlooking a new world. It was all too sad and too wonderful. Few men are able to fulfill their father's dream and their own dream at the same time.

It was not quite six in the morning when he arrived at his apartment in Grenadierstrasse. Zelda was a wreck, trying to pack and ready the two children, all at the same time. Mendele was crying, fearful that his *tatte* might miss the train, and Dianele needed to be changed. Zelda was vastly relieved to see Ben. He hugged everyone, then gave Zelda a pair of new suitcases inscribed with traditional Yiddish blessings for the traveler— *mazel und broche, fohrt gesunterhait*. Zelda read the words aloud to Mendele: Good luck and our blessings to you! Travel in health!

At last, the new luggage was packed and the children were ready. Zelda excused herself and disappeared into the bedroom. Fifteen minutes later, she emerged wearing an exquisite navy blue suit, a tailored white blouse, and matching high heel shoes.

"You look magnificent," he complimented her. She blushed like a schoolgirl.

There was a small station wagon parked by the curb, emblazoned with the Messageries Maritimes logo. The driver was dressed like a French sailor and as soon as Ben and Zelda appeared, he jumped out of the car and raced over to help with the luggage.

"I've been sent to drive you to the Potsdammer Bahnhof, sir," he saluted smartly. Ben returned the salute, inwardly admiring Kaplan's attention to detail.

"May I help you Madame Landsdorf?" the sailor asked. He was obviously impressed by Zelda's bearing and appearance. She smiled graciously and nodded, not bothering to correct his assumption.

The casual way Zelda allowed the sailor to address her as "Madame Landsdorf" rankled Ben. He liked Zelda, and he liked Mendele and Dianele, but he had been honest with her about his feelings for Bluma. At least he thought he had. He made a mental note to have a serious talk with her.

It never occurred to Ben that Zelda had sensed his own loneliness and saw herself as the ideal candidate to fill the void. She was, above all, a practical woman; he was lonely, she was lonely, and they liked each other. What more did a person need? Zelda was a woman who based her decisions on what happened in the present, not on what might happen in the future. Bluma was no more real to her than a fictional character in the novels she occasionally read. Reality was Zelda Glovsky and Benjamin Landsdorf.

• • •

The scene at the Potsdammer Bahnhof was a repetition of the arrival at Anhalter Bahnhof, only more organized. Children sang pioneering songs at the top of their lungs, marching in mock military formation, dozens of old men congregated together, swaying to and fro as they recited the *kaddish*, groaning in sadness, and each person on the platform struggled in his own way to relieve the fear and tension of a departure for the unknown. As Ben ushered Zelda and the children through the station, he heard someone bellow his name. Searching the sea of faces, he managed to spot Shultz plowing through the crowd. Berzig was with him.

"We need you for a moment, Herr Kapitan," Schultz panted. He always seemed to be short of breath. Ben assigned Berzig to stay with Zelda and the children, instructing him to see that they were safely boarded if he was delayed.

Shultz led Ben across the platforms to a deserted side corridor, indicating an unmarked door off the hall. It opened to a dingy room that reeked of mold and decay. A craggy-faced man with a dueling scar sat at a small table in the center of the room. An ill-fitting toupee jarred his otherwise serious appearance, and he did not smile or rise when Ben and Shultz entered. Except for the table and three chairs, the room was empty. Shultz dragged one of the chairs over for Ben, and another for himself. Nervously, he rubbed a handkerchief over his lips.

"Ben, we have a problem," Shultz began. "This is Herr Ludenkranz, who represents Messageries Maritimes. Apparently, the British are aware that many of our passengers are without papers, and they're pressuring the French into holding us up at the very least. Given enough time, they could stop us entirely."

Ludenkranz interrupted impatiently. "I am afraid it is no longer possible for you to continue as an associate of Ten Meineckestrasse. Your credentials must be beyond question. If we're going to get these people through, you have to be a bona fide employee of Messageries Maritimes. So, from now on, you are actually Kapitan Benjamin Landsdorf. Here are your papers. Please follow the orders we give you and everything will work out just fine. If you have any qualms or questions, call Kaplan. He'll confirm what I've just told you. I'm afraid we haven't any more time. Do you understand and agree?"

"It's nothing to me," Ben shrugged. Ten Meineckestrasse was up to its old tricks again. By disassociating itself from Ben, the Zionist organization would be free of any blame if something went wrong. Now, Messageries Maritimes would feel as though they had some control over Ben, while in reality, if he were arrested, they would bear the brunt of the responsibility. Ten Meineckestrasse was always careful to protect itself. Ben did not resent the apparently callous decision or its implications. If there was one thing he learned from Hanovi, it was "protect your flanks." No individual was more important than the organization or its goal of establishing a homeland in Palestine.

"If you have no further questions, our interview is at an end." Ludenkranz stood up, nodded curtly to Ben and strode from the room. After he left, Shultz handed Ben a well-cut Messageries Maritimes uniform.

"I don't know why you bothered," Ben remarked as he dressed. "It's not much different than my own suit."

"Your own suit was good enough for the *Ostjuden*, who don't know any better. I assure you that the French and the British are more discerning."

Outside, the Potsdammer Bahnhof continued to fill. By the time Ben and Shultz returned to the depot, there were more than a thousand passengers and well-wishers gathered on the platforms. Ben felt the pressure building.

It was now that the British agents would have an opportunity to mingle with the crowd, gathering information and evidence that would delay or halt the train on French soil. But the British underestimated Ten Meineckestrasse's intelligence capabilities. Hanovi's men had identified every British agent in Berlin; none made a move without Hanovi knowing about it. Though Hanovi was careful not to use his knowledge blatantly, there were times when risks had to be taken. This was one of them.

On Hanovi's orders, every British agent in the Potsdammer Bahnhof was tailed by a Zionist agent. On a prearranged signal, Hanovi's plants would feign outrage and accuse the Englishmen of being pickpockets. Even the most seasoned British intelligence officers were virtually speechless when someone else's walet turned up in their coat pockets. Once arrested by the German authorities, it usually took hours before the British agents were able to free themselves. Few spoke fluent German and none wished to reveal their true identity or purpose; foreign agents were hardly welcome on German soil. But the victory was only a small one.

Once the train cleared the station, nearly a thousand miles separated the emigrants from Marseilles and the temporary sanctuary of the *S.S. Asia*. Their planned route ran southwest through the medieval city of Magdeburg and across central Germany to Karlsruhe, on the French border. Traveling through Strasbourg, the train would turn south to Lyon, then on to Marseilles. Their itinerary included several necessary stops, each of which posed a potential crisis. Each one represented an opportunity for reluctant *Ostjuden* to disappear into the countryside or raised the possibility of interference by British agents. Disaster could strike anywhere.

Ben drifted through the crowd, doing what he could to resolve petty disputes and reassure frightened people. He was proud of the way the *Ostjuden* coped with an uncertain future and admired their courage and sense of humor. As he passed groups of people, he was fascinated by the snippets of conversation he heard.

"Why are you crying," shouted an older man with graying hair and three shiny gold teeth. He was berating a tearful woman. "You're here to pacify these people, not weep and wail like a. . . ."

"But they have such sad stories. . . ."

"What Jew doesn't?" he interrupted. "Just tell them jokes, make them laugh, and don't let them panic. Calm yourself, then calm them."

"How?" the woman sniffed.

"How should I know?" the man shook his fists in frustration. "Act Jewish!"

German Jews circulated through the crowd, listening to complaints, smoothing over difficulties, and easing frayed nerves. Ben listened to an earnest young man talking to a bedraggled woman and her daughter.

"Are we really getting away at last?" the woman asked.

"Of course, Sadie," the young man replied, his voice filled with sincerity. "Why should I lie to you?"

"I don't know," she whined. "You could have a reason."

"Are we definitely going to the ship?" he daughter asked.

"You have your tickets, don't you?"

"And what difference do tickets make?" the woman snorted derisively."

"They guarantee. . . ."

"They guarantee nothing," the woman sneered. "My ship was turned back from America, and I had tickets, visas, and an uncle in New York. Everything but a telegram from the President. So what good are your tickets?"

The young man hesitated for a moment, searching for an answer.

Then he smiled broadly. "You're going to love Palestine," he said. "I just know it."

Every Jewish agency in Berlin was represented on the platform. Groups of German Jews distributed kosher food, bottled water, and homemade wine; members of the school associations passed out books, and agents for Ten Meineckestrasse constantly worked on visa problems. Even Messageries Maritimes employees helped by distributing green and blue company flags to help identify the passengers. Everywhere, lists were checked and double checked to be certain that every *Ostjude* that arrived in Berlin on Tuesday would be bound for Marseilles that day.

Suddenly, a middle-aged woman wearing a black cloth coat stopped Ben and asked him to put out his hand. Startled, he did as she requested.

"Take this," she said, placing a small coin in his palm.

He stared at her. "What's this for?"

"So that God will know that you go to Palestine carrying money for the poor and not just for your own self-interest. Now it is God's responsibility to see that you arrive safely. You understand?" Ben nodded, and she turned to put another coin in the hand of another emigrant.

Everywhere were tearful good-byes and the repeated injunction: *Leshanah haba' ah b'Yerushalayim*, Next year in Jerusalem.

A whistle pierced the air; the train was ready to be boarded. The carriages attached to the engine looked like a patchwork quilt, made up of gray German coaches still bearing the faded stencil *Deutschland, Deutschland Uber Alles* and spanking new green and blue cars from France bearing the Wagonlit Express logo.

On a signal from the engineer, the station masters began to load the train with loud cries of "*Einsteigen! Einsteingen!*"—All aboard. Ben tried to cut across the crowd to join Zelda, but the forward motion of the crowd made any lateral movement impossible. He would have to board and move through the cars.

Ben worked his way through the coaches, reassuring the passengers with his presence. Already, families were settled into compartments, doing what people everywhere do when they're nervous and afraid and have time to pass: they eat. Ben savored the host of fragrant aromas permeating the air.

The Jewish organizations of Berlin had provided the *Ostjuden* with enormous quantities of food for the long journey that lay ahead. Families shared sticky pieces of *teigalach*, a honey-soaked pastry; bottles of kvas, a light root beer; and small satchels of chocolates and hard candies. Everyone carried stained paper bags or rolled cones of newspapers, laden with meat and fruit. Each compartment shared boxes of cheese and sandwiches made of chicken, occasionally layered with chewy slices of salt beef.

Some of the men rolled homemade cigarettes from the cheap Machorca tobacco favored in Russia, while the wealthier smoked Adas. Laps were laden with belongings too precious to place out of sight.

Again and again, Ben was called on to settle a petty dispute or calm a hysterical passenger. He moved through the train with quiet authority, and the sight of his gold-braided captain's hat quickly became a familiar and comforting sight. The boarding proceeded smoothly until one of the stationmasters cut through the crowd with a message for Ben.

"A German officer is demanding to speak with you, Herr Kapitan."

Visions of inspections and demands for credentials filled Ben's imagination. It would be like the German customs authorities to wait until the last possible minute, then keep everyone waiting until their questions were answered. Ben followed the stationmaster to the foot of the platform, prepared for a confrontation. A small knot surrounded the German officer, obscuring his face, but something about the set of the shoulders looked familiar.

It was Stiffler.

"What are you doing here?" Ben grinned. "I would think one sentimental good-bye was all you could stand." Ben had stopped by Stiffler's apartment to bid him farewell on his way back from Herschel's apartment and he hadn't expected to see his friend again.

"I couldn't let you leave without a memento," Stiffler explained. He surprised Ben with an awkward embrace, then stepped back and handed him a small package wrapped in plain brown paper. Inside was a picture portrait of Stiffler, complete with a uniform and monocle. The inscription reflected Stiffler's fondness for coining slogans. *Lekh lekha* he had written in a boyish scrawl. "Palestine for the Jews, Germany for the Germans." It was Stiffler's way of telling Ben that every people should have a country to call their own.

They stared at each other for a moment, not knowing what to say. Both realized they would probably never see one another again. Stiffler cleared his throat self-consciously.

"You look good in uniform, my friend, even if it is navy, not army."

Ben flushed in embarrassment. "I. . . ."

"Whatever you're doing, I wish you luck." Stiffler reached out and squeezed Ben's shoulder with affection. "*Auf wiedersehen, mein freund.*"

"Shalom," Ben replied solemnly. He watched Stiffler disappear into the crowd with a deep sense of loss. He suspected his friend would not fare well in Germany's new order.

"Kapitan Landsdorf?" a man tugged at Ben's sleeve. Turning away from his thoughts, Ben was quickly absorbed by the problems of loading the train.

Excitement began to mount as the train filled. Children played hide and seek among the piles of luggage. Officials did the best they could to calm wives whose husbands had not yet returned from running an errand. Individuals separated from their families frantically searched for the right compartments. Then the stationmasters turned their lamps around; there were just minutes left. Ben checked on Zelda and the children; they were fine.

It was nearly time to depart.

Ben was helping an elderly couple into Zelda's coach when he heard someone shouting "Benjamin! Ben!" Assuming another problem had arisen, Ben turned with a weary expression on his face. Again the voice called and Ben picked out Herschel's face from among the well-wishers mobbing the platform. Helen was with him. They ran towards each other and embraced.

Like Stiffler, Herschel and Helen had come to say their final farewells. Helen's eyes widened in shock when she saw Ben's uniform, and she started to ask what was going on. Herschel cut her off, knowing there wasn't time to explain.

"Helen, please, just give him the package!"

Like Stiffler, they had brought something for Ben: a small leather-bound family Bible with a paper thin silver book mark. The book was nearly two hundred years old, its cover worn smooth and shiny by generations of loving hands.

"You are the first of our family to return to the Land of Israel," Herschel explained. "This Bible represents all of us. Since you form the advance guard, we want you to carry it to Palestine for us. We hope to receive it back from you one day soon, standing on the soil God set aside for our people."

Compartment doors slammed shut all around them, and a conductor respectfully asked Ben to board. It was time to leave.

"Herschel. . . ."

"We marked a passage for you, Ben."

Without looking, Ben knew what passage was marked—Chapter Twelve of Genesis. He threw his arms around his cousin for one last time.

The train started to move and Mendele called out for him to hurry. Quickly, he embraced Helen, then hopped onto the coach riser.

"I love you both and I'll write as soon as I can!" Ben shouted.

As the train pulled out of the station, hundreds of people waved handkerchiefs and shouted final farewells drowned in the sounds of departure. Seeing tears on many of the faces in the crowd, Ben felt a stab of loneliness. He stepped into the compartment, facing Zelda and the children. In a way, they were his little "family." So he wouldn't really be leaving alone.

Then it occurred to him—the whole train was now his "family."

FIFTEEN

Aboard the Train Bound for Marseilles
Thursday, February 6th, 1925
10:00 AM

One of Ben's assistants, a young *Ostjude* named Zalmen, spotted two young women standing at the end of a corridor. One of them wore a rumpled brown coat and beret; the other was bareheaded. They looked nervous and out of place. The one wearing the beret clutched an oblong box, and her companion kept her hands in a large fur muff, despite the warmth in the corridor. Assuming they were frightened, Zalmen smoothed his white shirt over the *tallis-kotten* he wore underneath and walked over to the pair.

"May I help you with your package, Fraulein?" he asked the girl in the beret. Her coat was baggy and poorly cut, but it was still impossible to mistake her superb figure; the kind of figure Zalmen had often dreamed about.

"I don't need any help, thank you." The girl did not sound unfriendly, but she avoided his eyes.

Zalmen did not have a great deal of experience with women, but he was anxious to make a good impression. Suppressing his natural shyness, he made a determined effort to help the beautiful girl in front of him. Awkwardly, he reached out to help her with the package.

"Please," she snapped, pulling her package away. "You'll spill the contents."

Blushing at her tone, he stammered, "Wh . . . What's in it?" Zalmen always stuttered when he was nervous, and he was never more nervous than when standing in front of a pretty girl.

"Nothing that would interest you," she replied sharply. Her friend looked away.

Zalmen saw a trace of fear in her eyes. Why would she be afraid? He looked at the box suspiciously, then squared his shoulders, no longer the adolescent boy but now filled with the authority of his position as a "train warden." Stuttering heavily, he ordered her to show him what was in the package. Unfortunately for Zalmen's pride, the girl was not impressed by his display of authority.

"How dare you order me to do anything!" She glared ferociously. "I am an adult, unlike yourself, and have no problem taking care of myself. Besides, my friend and I have a Guardian Angel on the train. Now run off and play with your friends." She made a shooing motion with her free hand.

Though he was flustered and embarrassed, Zalmen refused to back off. His pride was at stake as well as his authority. She had left him no way to escape without looking like a complete fool, so he simply forged ahead, his stutter growing worse. "I'm a . . . a . . . afraid you're g . . . g . . . going to h . . . have to . . . ."

One of the passengers interrupted him with a tap on the shoulder and said, "Hey, go fly a kite, will you?"

Bewildered, Zalmen just stared at the man. With a sure instinct for the jugular, the girl with the beret smiled sweetly. "Make sure it's a blue and white kite with *tallis* fringes on all four sides." Unconsciously, his hands ran around his belt to see if his *tzitzes* were sticking out from under his shirt.

The crowd laughed at his discomfort and several people muttered "bravo" and "leave them alone."

Feeling miserable and humiliated, Zalmen turned to the small crowd standing behind him. "Listen, p . . . p . . . please. I h . . . have to examine th . . . that b . . . box for security r . . . reasons. D . . . Don't you underst . . . st . . . stand?"

"When you started to talk to the lady, young man, it wasn't the box you were interested in examining," one of the Russian men teased him. Mortified, Zalmen could not reply. It was, after all, the truth. He stood paralyzed until an old lady took pity on him.

"Give him a break," she cackled. "He's just trying to do his job and protect us all." Zalmen shot her a grateful glance.

"The old lady is right," laughed the Russian. "These girls could be a real threat to our security. They may attack us at any m . . . m . . . moment," he imitated Zalmen's stutter. Everyone roared with laughter. Ignoring him, the old woman walked over to the girl in the brown coat.

"I understand your reasons for refusing to allow a young man like Zalmen to examine your private belongings," she smiled. "So why don't you allow me to act on his behalf, with only women making a circle around me?"

"That won't be necessary."

"Why not?" asked the old woman. "Zalmen has a responsibility to fulfill and we are all anxious and worried. How can you refuse?"

"Thank you, but you needn't be concerned about us. We're just making our way to the next car." The girls started forward but no one moved to let them pass. The mood had changed; most people were no longer smiling.

"Well, what are you hiding in the package?" the Russian grinned.

"Nothing you'd be interested in, Grandpa."

The Russian clutched his chest as though mortally wounded.

The old woman was angry. "Just what do you have in that box that you're afraid to show us?" she said sharply. "Why are your belongings so different from ours? We allowed our bags to be examined when asked."

"These are just my own belongings—nothing that's any business of yours," the girl shot back. Suddenly, a sound came from the fur muff, low and grating, like a clock in need of oiling. The crowd recoiled.

"She's got a bomb!" someone cried out.

The stampede was on.

People scattered in all directions, jamming the exits to the compartments and filling the corridor with panic. Terrified, Zalmen backed from the compartment. "D . . . d . . . don't do anything rash," he pleaded. "I'll g . . . g . . . get Kapitan Landsdorf . . ." Without finishing the sentence, he bolted through the crush in the corridor.

Five minutes later, Ben was pushing his way towards the compartment. Zalmen breathlessly related the situation as they struggled through the throng.

"I tell you, she has a b . . . b . . . bomb in her m . . . muff. They m . . . must be B . . . B . . . British agents," he blurted out.

"British agents don't blow themsleves up," Ben retorted. He didn't want any wild rumors running through the train.

"They're c . . . c . . . crazy. The one with the b . . . beret said something ab . . . b . . . bout a 'G . . . G . . . Guardian An . . . g . . . gel' on b . . . b . . . board." Ben stopped dead and made Zalmen repeat himself.

"Guardian Angel?"

Zalmen's head bobbed vigorously.

"Oh, God," Ben muttered.

When he arrived at the scene of the commotion, his suspicions were confirmed. Standing alone in a deserted second-class compartment were Sophie and Sarah, looking like two innocent waifs.

"What in God's name are you doing here?" Ben burst out. Zalmen stared at him, watching in shock as the girls threw their arms around him, knocking his sides with their bundles and boxes. Ben heard a pitiful "meow" and looked just in time to see Katzele stick her head out of the muff.

"Oh, no," he groaned.

"We couldn't leave Katzele behind," Sarah explained blithely. "Not after all we've been through together."

"But we came prepared. See?" Sarah opened the box that started all the trouble. It was actually a narrow cabinet drawer filled with sand and crushed gravel for the cat. Shaking his head, Ben picked up the litter box and the cat and walked out into the corridor. The crowd shrank back at the sight of the box.

"This is the detonator," he said, holding up the purring cat. "Guess what's in the box."

The tension dissolved in an instant and everyone began to laugh. Slowly, they filed back to their seats. The crisis was over.

Ben closed the compartment door and turned back to Sarah and Sophie, his face clouded by disapproval. They stood side by side in wide-eyed innocence, as though their presence on the train should have been no surprise to anyone, least of all to Ben.

"Trudi Weiss would never have let you leave the *hakhsharah* alone," Ben frowned. "I assume you ran away."

Sophie's eyes were downcast. "We did leave her a note."

"With a postscript," Sarah added proudly. " 'We'll see you in Jerusalem.' "

"How did you know where to . . ."

"Your landlady," they replied in unison.

"I should have known." Ben studied their anxious faces. They're different, he thought to himself. The melancholy that had veiled Sophie's spirit was gone, and Sarah was poised and self-confident. She bore no resemblance to the frightened young girl he had taken to Fulda from her father's house. He was about to ask where they had raised the money to travel when he remembered that he had given her some pocket money in Fulda. She had to have saved every single penny in order to buy train tickets for Sophie and herself. He shook his head in admiration.

Despite the added burden of worry they posed, Ben was relieved to have them out of Germany. Papers would be a problem; having run away from the *hakhsharah*, they would have none of the benefits the camp provided to its graduates—birth certificates, sometimes genuine, sometimes forged, entry visas, tickets, and carefully planned travel arrangements. He would have to think of something. He tried to be stern but ended up spreading his arms to give them each a hug.

"Don't worry. I suppose we'll work something out," he sighed. "The British probably wouldn't notice two more imposters bound for Palestine."

"Speaking of imposters, since when are you Kapitan Landsdorf?" Sarah wondered. Ben explained the situation and warned them not to say anything.

"Your secret is safe with us," Sarah promised. "And don't worry about us being a bother. We intend to earn our way on this trip." She reached into a bulky canvas bag, producing a Hebrew book, pencils, paper, a map of Palestine, and a series of pamphlets on the Holy Land.

"You have all kinds of people running around here, totally confused, and just as many children underfoot," Sarah said with authority. "Now, if you'll give us half a chance, we'll take care of half your worries—the children. They need to learn elementary Hebrew. Most of them don't even know that Hebrew is written from right to left. We'll teach them."

"That's fantastic," Ben grinned. "You can start first thing tomorrow morning."

"We'll start today," Sophie grinned. The train lurched as it stopped to take on water.

Sophie noticed Mendele peering at them from the next compartment and asked Ben who he was. Turning around, Ben saw that Zelda had put him up to the glass. As he watched, Zelda pointed at him and the boy pressed his face against the glass, calling out "*Tatte, Tatte.*" Zelda was not one to miss an opportunity to keep herself in Ben's sight.

Resigned, he led Sarah and Sophie next door and introduced them to Zelda and the children. Sophie fell in love with little Dianele. Ben explained to Zelda that the girls were planning to run a simple school.

"Really? Why that's marvelous, Ben. It will give us more time to talk." Her voice was syrupy sweet but Ben caught the domineering undertone. He was beginning to resent Zelda's possessiveness.

Setting the baby down Sophie declared she was ready to go to work. "I think Sarah can set up one class here for the boys, and I'll take another class in the next car for the girls."

"Great," Sarah agreed. "We should also check the cars for other *hakhsharah* girls to help us. We could set up a regular staff.'' Sarah and Sophie were fairly bursting with excitement. They dashed out of the compartment to organize their school, dragging Mendele and Dianele with them. Ben straightened his cap and turned to leave.

"Where are you going?" Zelda cried in astonishment.

"I have to be certain that everyone is aboard and accounted for. We cannot afford to leave anyone behind."

"But you can't leave me now—when we're in such danger!"

"There's no danger, Zelda. If you need help, ask the girls. They're very capable." His tone was distinctly unsympathetic as he stepped out into the corridor. Bracing himself for a long evening, he began checking the compartments, one by one.

More than anything else, the train resembled a miniature city and each compartment formed a tiny community, with its own gossip, its own petty disputes, and its own particular character. The train was crowded, and as a result, individual compartments were hot and stuffy, full of noise and stale air. The seats were notoriously uncomfortable and everyone slept fitfully. The close quarters added to the tension.

As Ben walked through the train, he was able to distinguish some cars by their distinctive odors. Certain tobaccos and foods seemed to be favored by certain groups, filling a particular carriage with their unique aromas. Each group had its own slightly different set of priorities and problems, and Ben found it impossible to remember whether or not he had spoken with the occupants of a particular compartment. There were simply too many people and too many compartments.

There was one constant from car to car: the incessant talk. It never ended. Politics, literature, Palestine, America, the Germans, the Poles, the Russians, religion, business, and then back to politics again. What were the Nazis up to? Could they take power in Germany? Would the Jews be persecuted by the Arabs in Palestine? Why did the Jews have to leave Germany? If they couldn't stay in Berlin, why not the provincial capitals of smaller towns? How did one earn a living in Palestine?

Whenever Ben appeared, a tidal wave of questions washed over him. One of the most difficult parts of his job was learning to deflect questions without hurting anyone's feelings. He didn't have the time or the energy to answer them all.

A messenger ran up to him, something that happened a hundred times a day.

"Rosenbaum is planning to leave the train at Karlsruhe," he said importantly.

"Tell Berzig to take care of it. If there's a problem, have him speak to me and I'll talk to Rosenbaum myself." There was always someone planning to leave the train. So far, no one had succeeded and Ben intended to keep it that way.

He continued from compartment to compartment, checking visas, names, and lists. As he knocked on a door in one of the new French cars, the occupants stopped talking immediately. That usually spelled trouble.

There were only three people in the compartment; a middle-aged couple and a young girl of fifteen or sixteen. They were obviously a family, and by the sullen expression on the mother's face, Ben knew why the compartment was half empty: there was a family squabble in progress. Normally, Ben would have left them alone but the tension of the preceding twenty-four hours had left everyone's nerves on edge. It wouldn't take much to set people at each other's throats.

"All right," he said evenly. "What's going on here?"

"Nothing," replied the mother, her eyes downcast. Ben looked at the three of them. The man met his gaze but refused to say anything.

"I want to know what's happening here," Ben repeated.

"We're going to Palestine," the woman bit back.

"What a happy coincidence—so is everyone else on this train." Ben's tone was mild. He wasn't about to let her bait him into an argument. "Don't you think we have enough problems to face without adding more? Why don't you tell me about it?"

"You should be asking my daughter," she snapped. "For fifteen years, my husband and I worked to build up our business. We had good friends, good neighbors, and a good life. Then she falls in love with a Christian policeman. Did you ever try to forbid a Christian policeman from coming to your house? Thank God my mother wasn't alive to see it. All we could do was leave." She covered her mouth with her hand. "We had to leave like thieves in the night. We lost everything, all because our daughter's ego demanded a man she could never have. Young people today are all alike. They have no respect for the old traditions. All they think about is self-gratification."

Ben turned to the girl, who didn't appear at all upset over leaving the man she loved behind. She was neither sad nor resentful, and there was a hint of a supercilious grin at the corners of her mouth. She looked up at her mother.

"I think it's time I told you the truth, Mama," the girl said timidly.

"Oh my God! He didn't . . . you didn't . . ."

"Really Mama, you are impossible," the girl sighed. As her parents listened in shocked silence, she explained how she pretended to fall in love with a Christian because she knew that was the only way they would ever leave Poland and emigrate to Palestine. To have a child marry outside the faith was a sacrilege devout Jews would go to any extreme to prevent, and the girl knew her parents would choose the rigors of Palestine over the disgrace of intermarriage.

"You always laughed when I tried to talk to you about Palestine. I felt terrible lying to you, but I knew you would never listen to me. So I pretended to love a Christian; it was the only way. I hope you can forgive me."

Her parents were speechless.

Ben cleared his throat. "I don't think you'll be needing me here anymore." Quietly, he slid the door closed and shook his head with a smile. The stunned husband and wife in the compartment were the fourth set of parents he had come across whose children had intentionally forced them to emigrate. Some were not quite so subtle as the girl; they simply threatened to ignore the Jewish dietary laws, run away from home, or refuse to honor the customs and traditions that structured their parents' lives. Some parents would overcome their own fears and emigrate to keep the family together; others could not. Like Sarah's parents, they would never change. So their children often traded their life at home for an agricultural camp like Fulda, just as Sarah had done.

By dark, Ben was exhausted and weary. As he approached his own car, Sarah ran out of Zelda's compartment in tears. When she saw Ben, her expression changed from hurt to anger. She spun around and ran in the opposite direction. She was halfway through the second car before he caught her.

"Sarah, what happened?"

"Why didn't you tell me you were married?" Her voice trembled with rage. She was a Sarah he had never seen before; tough, angry, and hard.

"I'm not married," was all he could think to say.

"Don't make it worse by lying," she warned him. "Zelda told me herself."

It had all started in Ben's compartment. Sarah and Sophie had opened their makeshift school, and Mendele was one of their first pupils. When each of the children was asked to talk about their families, Mendele had told Sarah that Kapitan Landsdorf was his *tatte*. Sarah tried to correct him but he became hysterical. She took him back to his mother, expecting Zelda to clear up the misunderstanding. Instead, Zelda cradled the boy and told him not to listen to what other people said. Sarah hadn't waited to hear any more.

"I think we should have a talk with Zelda," Ben growled.

Sarah looked away. "I really don't care to—"

Ben grabbed her hand and dragooned her back towards Zelda's compartment, despite her furious protests.

He slid the compartment door open with a bang. Zelda sat in the far corner, clear-eyed and calm. She knew he would be angry and the best way to counter his anger was with composure. Zelda had intentionally allowed Sarah to draw the conclusion that she and Ben were married, hoping to discourage her. She had seen the way Sarah looked at Ben and intuitively knew the girl was in love with him. While Ben might be oblivious to Sarah's feelings, Zelda was not about to take any chances. She had marked him as her future husband, and she was not about to lose him to an adolescent with limpid eyes and the innocence of youth. Zelda intended to do everything in her power to reinforce Ben's perception of Sarah as a "little sister" who had overreacted to a simple misunderstanding. As she looked up, she did her best to appear surprised.

"Why Ben . . . Sarah . . . is there something wrong?"

"You are not my wife and your son is not my son."

"Ben, please, not in front of Mendele! Oh, I was afraid Sarah would misunderstand. She left in so much of a hurry." Mendele jumped off his seat and threw his arms around Ben with such force that Ben stumbled into Sarah. Gently he pried the boy away and knelt down, so they were face to face.

"Mendele, it's time for you to know the truth. You are a fine boy, and I care for you very much, but I am not your father. Someday, I hope to have a son like you, but for now, you must remember your real father and be proud of him. He was a very brave man who died trying to save other people. Do you understand?" Solemnly, Mendele nodded, tears streaming down his face.

"Will you still like me?"

"Of course I will," Ben laughed. He stood up and ruffled the boy's hair. "Now go and play."

After Mendele ran out, Zelda smiled at Sarah and apologized for the misunderstanding. "I didn't want to tell you about the little agreement Ben and I had while Mendele was still in the room. I know how you've confided in Ben, just like he was your own brother, and I understand how disappointed you must have felt to think he would not have told you about his own family. Had you stayed a bit longer, I would have explained. Few men have the capacity to care as much as Ben does."

Sarah had a vague feeling that she was somehow being manipulated, but she was too inexperienced to know just how. Ben, on the other hand, was just relieved to have the whole issue resolved. Careful not to overplay her hand, Zelda staged a perfect exit.

"I know how busy Ben is, and I have several things I must do, so you must excuse me." She shooed them out of the compartment. After she closed the door, Sarah turned to Ben and apologized for her outburst.

"Don't worry about it," he grinned. "It was time Mendele knew the truth. Now why don't you find Sophie and see what she's doing?"

"Oh, she's all right. She's found some Russian boy to talk to."

"Well, if you hurry, maybe you'll find one too," he laughed.

"Ben!" she scolded him. "Stop teasing me. I'm not a little girl anymore."

"Forgive me."

"Gladly," she smiled. "I have to go now. It's time to put the children to bed."

He gave her a peck on the cheek and she raced down the corridor, her short black hair bobbing up and down.

Later that evening, Ben shook off his fatigue and made one final round of the cars. He wanted to be sure that no one was missing. At the beginning of the trip, dozens of people had shifted their seats to be closer to relatives or friends, rendering the passenger manifest virtually useless. It was impossible to keep track of everyone, until Ben thought of appointing "car captains." Each coach had a captain responsible to Ben for headcounts and crowd control in his assigned car. The system seemed to be working.

Ben heard the whistle blow, announcing the stop outside Magdeburg. According to the itinerary, several freight cars were to be added and two removed. As the train lurched to a halt, people began to wake up. Confused, they started to pour out into the corridors, shouting questions in a half-dozen languages.

The panic began when the engines began the uncoupling and coupling procedures. Frightened that terrorists or anti-Semites were attacking the train, people milled about indecisively. It took the better part of an hour for the car captains to restore order, and Ben viewed it as a miracle that no one left the train.

The passengers abooard the Berlin–Marseilles Express were ready to degenerate into an undisciplined mob at the slightest provocation. They were raw and edgy from weeks of running. They were homesick, terrified, and unsophisticated—most had never been outside their own villages in Russia or Poland. Now they were traveling thousands of miles to a country that existed only in a book. To them, Palestine was the name of a place long vanished.

Every *Ostjude* on the train was a potential runaway, dangerous to the success of the present operation as well as future operations. Ben was just beginning to comprehend the complexity of the job he'd undertaken. He was actually more of a warden than a shepherd.

Ben settled in next to a window and propped his feet on the opposite seat, watching the shadowy landscape slip by his compartment window like a waking dream. It was close to midnight and starlight bathed the countryside, reflecting off the crusted snow and imparting an almost magical quality to the night.

Lulled by the rhythmic swaying of the car, Ben's thoughts drifted to the couple whose daughter had tricked them into emigrating. Why did so many Jews prefer Judaism as a collection of customs and traditions, rather than as a living faith, rooted in the land of their fathers? Even his own mother was no different. The only reason she had ever considered Palestine was Anschel's health.

His people represented a puzzling paradox—content to remain in exile, bearing indignity, insult, and even death, rather than leave the security of home for the land God set aside for them. But let the threat of a mixed marriage appear, and they were on the next train, sacrificing everything in order to prevent the sacrilege. He muttered a brief prayer of thanksgiving that he was not required to explain his people to anyone, not even himself, and gratefully he slipped into a dreamless sleep.

• • •

Ben awoke like an overwound spring when the train ground to a halt in Strasbourg to complete the formalities of crossing the French border. The first thing he saw was a sign in French, and it brought a smile to his lips. Germany was finally behind him, like a clearly remembered nightmare, powerless to hurt once it ended.

France was hardly a haven but it was far superior to Germany. The vicious anti-Semitism that had characterized French society at the turn of the century had finally dissipated, driven underground by the backlash from the Dreyfus Affair.

During the 1890s, Alfred Dreyfus, a Jew and an officer of the French General Staff, was falsely accused and convicted of treason. The specter of Jewish conspiracy and betrayal became a major issue, setting off a political firestorm in France that lasted more than a decade. In the end, the lies were exposed and Dreyfus was acquitted. Shamed and embarrassed, the French government awarded him the Legion of Honor. Anti-Semitism was no longer fashionable.

Although the French government sympathized with the plight of the *Ostjuden*, it spared no effort to ensure they did not settle in France. Immigration laws were highly restrictive, and shipping companies who allowed Jewish passengers from the east to remain in France longer than twenty-four hours were subject to heavy fines and penalties. Companies like Messageries Maritimes were forced to accept total responsibility for their passengers from the time they entered France to the time they left. Hanovi had warned Ben that if any number of *Ostjuden* escaped, it could lead to a situation where no shipping company would accept the risk of transporting *Ostjuden*. The southern route to Marseilles would be permanently closed. With that in mind, Ben's assistants were the first ones off the train and immediately set up an organized system to prevent any *Ostjude* from leaving the restricted areas of the station. The car captains were better organized than they had been at other stops and the *Ostjuden* were more exhausted. The only excitement occurred when a couple with four children and a half dozen suitcases cleverly tried to exit through Ben's command car. Sarah caught them and blocked the door, refusing to be intimidated by threats and waving fists. Ben and Berzig were paged, but by the time they arrived, Sarah had already returned the family back to their compartment by sheer force of will.

"You're an ingenious girl," Berzig complimented her.

"So she is," Ben said proudly. Sarah's pale features colored at Ben's praise. It always embarrassed her that her emotions played across her face so easily, especially in front of Ben. She longed to be subtle and sophisticated, not realizing how much her unconcealed honesty and openness appealed to him.

"I'll get us some coffee," Berzig volunteered.

After he left, Ben smiled at Sarah. "By the time we finish it, we should be in Lyon."

• • •

Lyon was the first high point of the journey. As the train pulled into the station, a small horde of Sephardic Jews laden with huge baskets and heavy platters of traditional delicacies descended on the train. The Sephardim actually gave the *Ostjuden* a standing ovation, overwhelming them with praise and admiration. The food was welcomed but the enthusiastic reception was what bouyed everyone's spirits.

The Sephardic Jews were heirs of the Jews of Africa, Moorish Spain, and the Middle East. Unlike the Ashkenazic Jews from northern and eastern Europe, the Sephardim ardently believed in a Jewish homeland in Palestine and many planned to emigrate as soon as they could.

For the first time, the *Ostjuden* on the train had contact with a group of fellow Jews who viewed Palestine as something other than a life sentence. Not a single passenger attempted to leave the train in Lyon, a fact Ben attributed to the Sephardic welcome they received. When it was time to leave, cries of "*Leshanah hazot b'Yerushalayim*" rang through the air. *This* year in Jerusalem! The train picked up speed, heading due south towards the coast.

Sunlight flooded the level plains of the Rhone Valley with Gallic warmth, and Ben began to feel that it was actually happening—they were going to Palestine and nothing could stop them. He made his usual rounds through the train with a cheerful smile and returned to his own compartment late in the afternoon to relax before Marseilles, the final stop.

Towards dusk, they entered the city. Nestled in a semicircle of bare hills, Marseilles was a gleaming white jewel set on the Gulf of Lyon. Beyond the harbor lights lay the Mediterranean, dark green in the fading light. To Ben, no sight could have been more welcome. The train slowed as it passed through the city.

Up close, Marseilles was something less than a jewel; it was dirty, grimy, and teeming with life. Its waterfront was the roughest in the world, bustling with legal and illegal trade; not even the police ventured down by the docks after nightfall. Sailors classed Marseilles with Hong Kong, Singapore, and the exotic ports of the Far East; the docks were ruled by their own laws. That was the main reason Ten Meineckestrasse routed their "shipments" via Marseilles; passenger manifests and bills of lading were just pieces of paper. Gold was the universal passport.

The train passed through a yard and was sidetracked to a small depot. Armed guards surrounded the area and a group of men in trenchcoats stood on the platform. Ben had seen enough bureaucrats to know they were not ordinary customs agents.

Berzig appeared in the doorway. "The men on the platform will want to see you, Kapitan Landsdorf."

"Somehow, I'm not surprised," Ben grimaced. It seemed like his entire life during the past few months had consisted of meeting men in trenchcoats or uniforms on station platforms. "If I never see another railroad station, it will be too soon, Berzig." Ben put on his hat and stepped off the train, almost colliding with a Frenchman in a steel gray coat.

The Frenchman introduced himself first. "I am Henri Villard. I assume you are Kapitan Landsdorf? Good. May I see your passport satchel? No one will be allowed to disembark until we have completed our examination.''

Ben's heart sank. They had come a thousand miles for nothing. Someone had tipped the authorities that nearly half of the *Ostjuden* had no papers.

While his agents began poring over the documents, Henri Villard turned to Ben. ''Cold, isn't it?'' he sniffed. ''So damp this time of year. It will probably rain tomorrow.''

''I'm sure you didn't come to discuss the weather,'' Ben replied. He made it a point to speak German, a gesture the Frenchman was bound to interpret as arrogant and insulting. Villard eyed him closely and abandoned any pretense.

''Shall we be frank, Herr Kapitan? We both know what my men will find. Half your passengers are most likely without papers of any kind, not even a birth certificate.''

Ben made no reply.

''Are you aware that handling illegal refugees is a serious offense under French law? This entire train could be returned to Germany.''

It was time to get aggressive, Ben decided. ''And are you aware that you are addressing a full captain of Messageries Maritimes?''

''You look a bit young to . . .''

''Check with my office,'' Ben snapped. ''I follow the orders I am given. I do not need to be insulted as well as inconvenienced.''

''My apologies, Monsieur,'' Villard replied, touching his fingers to the brim of his hat. ''No offense was intended.''

''What now?'' Ben demanded, ignoring the apology.

''Follow me, please.''

Villard stood six feet four and crossed the rail yard with a loping stride that forced Ben into an undignified dogtrot. Ben wondered if it was the Frenchman's way of repaying him for his remarks in German. Villard did not tell him where they were going, and Ben had no intention of giving him any satisfaction by asking. I'll stay above his games, Ben thought. The only weapon Ben had was his authority as a Messageries Maritimes captain; he had to hang onto that as long as he could.

Villard led him to an enclosed compound surrounded by a brick wall topped with jagged shards of glass. They entered a courtyard through double steel doors and came out facing a two-story building that looked like a prison. Ben steeled himself for the worst.

Villard identified himself to a uniformed guard at the door, then guided Ben through the interior of the building to an office. Within, a

French magistrate in full judicial robes sat writing at a plain wooden desk. The chair he occupied was the only one in the room but for a protrait of Rouget de Lisle, the walls were as bare as the room.

The magistrate finished placing a bundle of files into a jacket, then dismissed Villard with a flick of his fingers. He leaned back, studying Ben through his watery eyes.

"You are a Swedish citizen, Kapitan, are you not?"

"I am."

"I see you have a trainload of Jews bound for Palestine." The magistrate's expression was one of distaste.

"I do." Ben tried to keep the hostility out of his voice. There was nothing to be gained by antagonizing the man.

"Why do you involve yourself with these people?"

"They may seem peculiar but they're basically like people anywhere."

"Is that the only reason? I would have thought a full Kapitan with Messageries Maritimes could pick and choose his own post. Playing nursemaid to a flock of Jews must be rather distasteful to a man of your abilities."

"Perhaps it doesn't bother me because I'm one of them," Ben replied cooly. "Does that cause a problem for you?"

Idly the magistrate flicked a speck of invisible lint off his robes. Ben willed himself to remain calm. The man in front of him exercised a staggering degree of power over his life and the lives of his fellow Jews. Briefly, Ben wondered if his own papers would stand up to close scrutiny. Impersonating a French officer was a crime in France.

"Kapitan, Kapitan, what am I going to do with you? Half your passengers have no papers. This is a serious matter."

Ben felt desperate. The magistrate had been anyhting but sympathetic. If he was holding out for a bribe, he would be disappointed; Ben's resources were exhausted. Somehow Ben had to appeal to the magistrate's sense of justice. His eyes fell on the painting of Rouget de Lisle. He decided to gamble.

"I notice that you have a portrait of Rouget de Lisle."

"So? He's Marseilles' most honored citizen, the composer of the French national anthem. What does that have to do with your Jews?"

"It was this city that gave France her battle cry during the French Revolution. Before that revolution, the French people were no more than slaves. The French, of all people, should know what it means to yearn for freedom. My people are no different than yours. They too yearn for freedom. What you say is true. Half my people do not have proper papers, but neither did most of the people who stormed the Bastille. You have it within your power to free nearly a thousand men and women from a German yoke. All it would take is a stroke of your pen." If there was one thing a Frenchman despised, it was Germany. The magistrate thought for a moment.

"Have your passengers leave the train and prepare them for a sundown embarkation on your ship," the magistrate said abruptly. "They shall have their freedom."

Ben stared at the Frenchman in astonishment. The gamble had paid off, but it left one other problem. When Ben made no motion to leave, the magistrate looked up in annoyance.

"You're dismissed, Kapitan Landsdorf," he said curtly.

"As grateful as I am for your decision, I'm afraid there is another problem," Ben explained. "Our Holy Sabbath begins at sundown on Fridays, and we are forbidden to embark on journeys by sacred writ. Perhaps you could order us aboard immediately."

The magistrate shook his head ruefully and spat into a spittoon several feet away.

"Not possible," he muttered. "Everyone must be processed and that takes time. You realize, of course, that the entire train can be returned to Germany for such an inconvenience to the French people? Those with papers, as well as those without."

Ben kept his silence. The magistrate sighed and drummed his fingers on the desktop, idly humming the *Marseillaise.* he was hopelessly off-key but that wouldn't have bothered anyone in Marseilles but the composer.

Suddenly, Ben began to accompany him, imitating the sound of a trumpet and beating a staccato rhythm with his hands and feet. He continued to the end of the last refrain while the Frenchman sang.

"Bravo!" The magistrate gave him a standing ovation, and shook his hand as well. "You have a magnificent talent," he smiled for the first time.

"But the song is yours," Ben replied. The magistrate laughed.

"Tact as well as wit. I like that combination in a man. Take your damned Jews off the train and I will personally see to it that you are not troubled until your Sabbath is over and you can embark."

SIXTEEN

Marseilles
Friday, February 7th, 1925
4:00 PM.

As the first few *Ostjuden* shuffled through a makeshift customs station, Ben heaved a sigh of relief. It would take several hours before everyone was funneled into orderly lines and fully processed, but the biggest obstacles had been overcome. Ben's hundred-to-one gamble had paid off. He could hardly believe that he had been able to persuade the magistrate to ignore the lack of proper papers and allow the refugees to remain through the Sabbath; it left him with a heady feeling that nothing could stop him. Only one thing nagged at the back of his mind—the easy way Villard had accepted the magistrate's sudden reversal. Villard was a hard-liner, not the kind of man who believed in exceptions, and yet he had made no comment on the magistrate's decision; he had simply stubbed out his cigarette and suggested they return to the train. The Frenchman had not spoken during the walk back, but after he had instructed the gendarmes, he had turned to Ben and wished him good luck with a crooked grin. There had been no malice in his voice, only a flickering moment when his eyes seemed to betray some inner amusement, as though he were enjoying a joke at Ben's expense. It was odd, Ben thought. Then he became involved with the seething mass on the platform and forgot all about the mocking expression in the Frenchman's eyes.

As usual, the scene on the platform was like a three-ring circus.

Local vendors circulated through the crowd, selling sandwiches and French delicacies, fresh-baked brioches, iced fruit, and piping hot tea. After being cooped up on a train for days, refugees, no matter how poor, always had a few coins for something to eat or drink. A little something for the stomach always made the long wait for customs clearance pass quicker.

Dozens of local Jews helped organize the crowd and served as interpreters for the gendarmes. Once registered and cleared by the police, the *Ostjuden* were then guided through the gates to waiting buses. Provision for temporary shelter had been made well in advance with Ten Meineckestrasse's routine efficiency. If Kaplan and Hanovi had been handling logistics for the Allies during the war, Ben thought, Germany would have surrendered two years earlier. "The Prophet" and his planners never left anything to chance. Then something else occurred to Ben: why hadn't they foreseen the problem with the French authorities over papers or timed the arrival in Marseilles so it would not conflict with the Sabbath?

"Fire!"

Ben's head snapped up. The cry of alarm was picked up by a half-dozen voices and thrown across the crowd. Ben scanned the train for signs of smoke; he saw nothing. "Damn!" he muttered. Where there was fire, panic would not be far behind. Heart pounding, he pushed towards a knot of vendors and *Ostjuden* that seemed to be the source of the commotion.

A bearded Litvak Ben recognized from the train rocked back and forth on his knees, clutching at his stomach and shrieking in pain. A man wearing white coveralls marked with the red cross of the Marseilles Emergency Fire Squad knelt beside the Litvak, trying to calm him down. A second Frenchman rummaged through a first-aid kit attached to the front of a red wheelbarrow that was loaded with hand-pumped fire-fighting equipment. There was no sign of fire.

The *Ostjuden* surrounding the Litvak were obviously unnerved, by his screaming. They fidgeted like an anxious herd of deer, ready to bolt. Ben shouted for silence, then stepped forward to look at the Litvak for himself. He didn't appear to be burned, and Ben didn't see any blood, but to judge by the Litvak's contorted face and screams of agony, he had been mortally stricken. When he caught sight of Ben, the intensity of his shrieks increased.

"What's the matter with him?" Ben had to shout to be heard. One of the Frenchmen looked up in confusion.

"*Nous parlons Français seulement, monsieur. Nous . . .*"

"It's my husband, Boris Platzsky," a woman standing behind the Litvak broke in. "He thinks he's dying because he swallowed some oysters followed by plenty of *chazerei*."

"A few oysters and some junk food never killed anyone," Ben snapped. He crouched down next to Platzsky and shook his shoulder. "Stop acting like an idiot and tell me what happened."

Platzsky looked up, his chubby face twisted in agony.

"I was so hungry," he gasped. "The food smelled so good, I ate it without realizing it was *treif*, nonkosher. Now I am defiled." He bent over and cradled his stomach. "God will never forgive me and neither will my fellow Jew." Disgusted, Ben turned to the man's wife and asked why the firemen had been sent for.

"It's all a terrible misunderstanding," Mrs. Platzsky sobbed. "Once my husband realized what he had eaten, he started yelling, '*Mein hartz brent ve a fyer . . .*' "

"My heart burns me?"

"Yes. Some people misunderstood and thought he was on fire, so they sent for the firemen. Since they're here, do you think there's anything they can do for him?" Mrs. Platzsky wrung her hands in anguish.

Ben turned to the bewildered attendants and spoke rapidly in French. "The problem here is a combination of heartburn and guilt. Apparently, Mr. Platzsky has ingested several nonkosher oysters and is suffering terribly as a result. I would appreciate it if you would take him somewhere and end his suffering by cleansing his system." Ben grinned maliciously. "From both ends."

The Frenchmen laughed. "Rest assured, *Monsieur le Capitaine*, we will restore him to his sanctified condition." Together, they helped Platzsky to his feet and carried him towards the first-aid station with Mrs. Platzsky in tow.

Only when the crowd re-formed into orderly lines did Ben permit himself to relax. Rarely did a magistrate grant the "Immigrants in Transit" status allowing refugees to remain in France longer than twenty-four hours. That status could be revoked for the slightest infringement. If the French firemen had made a complaint to Villard about a false fire alarm, the entire train might have been returned to Germany, all because of a few lousy oysters. Ben did not think that an appeal to patriotism and his musical impersonations would persuade the magistrate a second time.

Normally, a mishap like Platzsky's would have occasioned a great deal of laughter and endless rounds of jokes. That no one so much as smiled was an indication of how tense and nervous the *Ostjuden* really were. Ben half expected disaster to rear its head at any moment, but there was no further trouble. The processing continued without interruption.

As the crowd on the platform dwindled, Ben realized that his role as Kapitan Landsdorf was over. The *Ostjuden* were now in the hands of the local Jewish organizations and Ben was now just another passenger on his way to Palestine. In less than forty-eight hours, they would all be aboard the *S.S. Asia* where a real Messageries Maritimes captain would assume command. No ship needed two captains.

He collected Berzig, who slouched against the side of the train, idly watching the vendors pack their carts, and together they returned to the command car. Sarah and Sophie were busy entertaining Zelda's children, while Zelda freshened herself up. They were already packed and ready to go. Everyone cheered with excitement when Ben and Berzig appeared.

Ben was delighted that everyone seemed to be getting along so well after the incident with Sarah. Zelda seemed relaxed and no longer tried to monopolize his time; she had made a real effort to become friendly with Sarah and Sophie. As for the children, they were in love with the girls.

He and Berzig had just started to ferry the luggage out to the platform when an attractive woman in her late forties called out to them.

"Is one of you gentlemen Mr. Isaacson?"

Startled by the sound of his real name, Ben looked up. She waved and walked towards him. There were two men with her.

"You must be he," she assumed extending her hand. "My name is Georgette LaForge. These gentlemen and I are from the local congregation." She introduced her two companions. "We waited for you by the exit gate, but we were delayed arriving, so we thought we might have missed you. I'm glad we managed to find you and your party."

Georgette LaForge looked like a hostess in search of a party. Her straw-colored hair, occasionally streaked by jets of white, was elegantly coiffed, and her makeup was flawless. She wore an apple green dress of watered silk that made a perfect showcase for the simple strand of large white pearls that draped from her neck. Ben wondered how she could have known his real name.

"What can I do for you, Madame LaForge?"

"Why, we're here to take you to your accommodations, of course. You're all to be staying with me. Oh, it's going to be wonderful! It's been years since I've had children and young people in the house! Come along now and we'll get you through this dreadful customs thing!"

Before Ben could respond to her invitation, she was already shepherding the children towards the exit and her two friends were helping Berzig with the luggage. Hanovi again, Ben thought. He had given

Georgette LaForge Ben's real name as a way of letting Ben know that she could be trusted. He picked a valise and followed the others.

As they waited for the French officials to stamp them through, a stunning woman with flame red hair joined them. She wore an expensive karakul coat with a matching fur hat and an embroidered scarf of Chinese silk. Ben had noticed her earlier on the crowded platform, drifting from person to person, chatting amiably and jotting notes in a small book. She had a brilliant smile used with telling effect. There was something familiar about her, but Ben couldn't pin it down.

Madame LaForge introduced her as Dora Hoffmann, another member of the Marseilles congregation. When she shook Ben's hand, her grasp was firm and dry, more like a man's handshake. It jarred his impression of her. Something about her eyes bothered him as well. They were sea green in color, but cold as ice, measuring him on an unknown scale.

"I hope we have the opportunity to know each other better," Dora Hoffmann smiled. Ben nodded politely.

After she left Ben turned to one of the men with Madame LaForge and asked him about Dora Hoffmann.

"She seemed nice enough, but something about her made me uncomfortable," Ben explained. "Who is she?"

The man laughed. "Your instincts must be good. She's a *shadchente*."

Now Ben understood the smooth, fast patter and the calculating eyes of green ice. "Just what I need," Ben thought, "a matchmaker." A good *shadchen* was like a force of nature; unstoppable when unleashed.

"Don't worry," the man grinned sympathetically. "You'll be safe at Madame LaForge's. It's built like a fortress."

And it was. Georgette LaForge lived in a stone-faced mansion that looked big enough to house the entire train. The travelers barely had enough time to absorb their new surroundings before their hostess ushered them to the dining room where a cold buffet had been set.

After dinner, everyone settled into their rooms. Ben tucked Mendele into bed, reassuring him that the house wasn't moving. The long hours of continuous motion aboard the Marseilles Express had left them all feeling a little shaky, but no one had any trouble falling asleep.

It was nearly nine o'clock in the morning when Madame LaForge roused Ben from sleep. He felt as though he had been drugged. She apologized for waking him.

"You have an urgent call," she told him. "You can take it in the study."

Ben dressed quickly and hurried downstairs. To his surprise, Berzig's voice echoed in the receiver.

"Why didn't you wake me when you got up?" Ben groused.

Berzig ignored him. "I'm at the synagogue right now, and I just got a message. We have a problem at the Coq d'Or. The hotel manager is nearly hysterical. He's prepared an enormous quantity of food, but our people won't get out of bed to eat it. In fact, they refuse to leave their rooms. I'll grab a cab and meet you there."

The first person Ben met at the Coq d'Or was the manager, a small, dark man with a nervous tic under his right eye. He looked on the verge of tears.

"*Mon Dieu*! Thank God someone in authority has arrived. I've tried coaxing, pleading, and shouting—nothing works. I warn you, Monsieur, if your people fail to eat, you will be billed for the food anyway, and if they don't vacate the rooms immediately, you'll be charged for an extra day's lodging. I run a good hotel, Monsieur, and I agreed to take on these people with the greatest reluctance, and now, my worst fears—"

Ben cut him off as Berzig strode into the lobby. "I would hazard a guess than any reluctance on your part was overcome with good French francs. Relax before you have a stroke."

The hotel manager was offended by the curt tone in Ben's voice but he held his tongue. Normally, he would have sent for the police and had the miserable Jews thrown out, but only half of what was owed had been paid. The manager wondered if the balance depended on the goodwill of the man in front of him. Perhaps it was best to humor the young blond stranger. After all, his entire hotel, all five floors, were occupied by *Ostjuden* and though he could break even on what he had already been paid, the second installment represented a huge profit. The thought of losing all that money filled him with dismay.

"A thousand apologies, Monsieur. I am distraught. Could you please talk to your people? The food is getting cold." The manager bowed obsequiously.

Ben took the stairs to the second floor two at a time, with Berzig and the manager close behind. He knocked on the first door he came to and a rangy Pole Ben knew by name answered the door. He was greatly relieved to see Ben.

"At last! Now we can get something to eat!"

"What do you mean by that?" Ben was thrown off guard; the hotel manager had claimed the food was ready and waiting.

"We can't get any breakfast! It was promised, but they won't deliver."

"But I have been told that breakfast is awaiting you downstairs."

"Let *him* eat downstairs," the man pointed to the hapless manager and slammed the door shut.

Ben knocked on another door and received a similar response from a woman, only she began to cry when he suggested she go downstairs for breakfast. She, too, slammed the door in his face.

Judging by the response Ben received, the manager decided that he might have overestimated Ben's authority. "Monsieur, I think the long trip has—how shall I say—unsettled your people. Evidently you are in no position to . . ."

"If I were you, I'd keep my mouth shut," Berzig snapped. He took a menacing step forward and the hotel manager retreated behind one of the stewards.

"What is the matter with these people?" Ben sputtered to Berzig. "Bang on all the doors. I want these people out in the hall so we can get to the bottom of this."

Five minutes later, the hallway was jammed with furious *Ostjuden*. When he saw the expression on their faces, the hotel manager suddenly wished they had stayed in their rooms; dealing with two or three people at a time was one thing—facing a small mob was another. Especially since the focus of their anger seemed to be him. He raised a handkerchief to his face to conceal the nervous tic under his right eye, which was jumping furiously, and he eyed the stairway, wishing he was closer to an exit.

"I want some answers," Ben yelled. "And I want them now."

"We're hungry and we want our food, as we were promised," someone shouted back. There were murmurs of indignant agreement.

"Then why don't you get dressed and go down and eat?"

"It's a matter of principle," retorted an ex-farmer with a weather-beaten face. "All our lives, people have done with us what they pleased because we were poor Jews. But we're not in Russia or Poland or Germany any more. We're on our way to the Holy Land, and we want to be treated just like anyone else."

"What am I missing?" Ben rolled his eyes in frustration. Berzig shrugged.

One of the Litvaks got irritated. "Didn't you see the sign downstairs, Herr Kapitan? Are you blind?"

"What sign?"

"The hotel sign reads: 'Breakfast in Bed—The Coq d'Or.' I, for one, intend to have my Sabbath breakfast where I'm entitled to have it—in bed. Now Herr Kapitan, whose side are you on?''

Litvaks were an argumentative, literal-minded people with a reputation for being *zeilem kopfs* or literally ''cross-heads.'' The term derived from an old folk saying that expressed life in terms of straight lines at right angles to each other, what the English called ''the straight and narrow.'' Arguing with a Litvak was like trying to move a mountain range, stone by stone.

Ben wracked his brain. Where would they have gotten the idea they were going to get breakfast in bed? There was nothing on the sign about . . . it suddenly dawned on Ben. The literal-minded *Ostjuden* had read the hotel sign from right to left, bottom to top, as though it had been written in Hebrew—Breakfast in Bed, The Coq d'Or. In fact it read, ''The Coq d'Or, Bed and Breakfast.''

He tried to explain what had happened but the Litvaks remained adamant. It was Saturday, the Holy Sabbath, and they had been promised breakfast in bed. They were not going to break the Sabbath injunction against unnecessary labor by going to the dining room to eat.

Ben finally gave up.

The hotel manager had followed the exchange anxiously, not understanding a word of Yiddish but knowing by the angry tones that things were not going well. When Ben turned to him, the manager was prepared for the worst.

Ben explained the misunderstanding. ''I'm afraid you're going to have to serve these people breakfast in bed.''

The manager envisioned the logistics of serving five floors of hungry guests and nearly fainted. ''Monsieur, for pity's sake, I beg you . . . I have no way of . . .''

Ben patted the manager on the back and flashed him an understanding smile. ''You don't know these people like I do. Believe me, if you don't serve them, they'll never leave their rooms. Take my advice. You have two dozen maids, standing around, waiting to clean the rooms. Put them to work with trays. Now, if you'll excuse me, Berzig and I will have breakfast in the dining room.''

Ben and Berzig enjoyed a leisurely breakfast, watching the maids, bellhops, and assistant cooks race back and forth from the kitchen with breakfast trays. By the time everyone had been served, the hotel staff looked ready to collapse.

''They earned their money today,'' Berzig grinned sardonically.

Ben laughed. ''See if you can get the powers that be to arrange for a decent tip. I doubt the hotel manager will show his appreciation to the staff for running up and down five flights of stairs.''

Berzig rose from the table. ''I'll do it now.''

After Berzig left, Ben watched the *Ostjuden* leaving the Coq d'Or for Sabbath services and decided to join them. It had been a long time since he entered a synagogue with no other thought than to pray.

As he listened to the rabbi praise the courage and fortitude of those bound for Palestine, Ben's thoughts drifted back to Dorpat and his father. He would never forget the sight of Anschel Isaacson, standing in front of the congregation in an austere black suit that emphasized his ascetic features. Anschel was an emotional speaker, exhorting his fellow Jews to obey God's injunction to return to the land He had given them. Of course, few people in the congregation had taken him seriously, but to Ben, his father was the very image of an Old Testament prophet. Now, as Ben stood on the eve of departure, ready to fulfill his father's wish, he felt humble and grateful.

The people around him were a confused and suspicious lot; narrow, provincial, and deeply mistrustful of the world outside their ken. They were a strange mass of contradictions. For centuries, they had suffered in stoic silence, but now, with freedom in sight, they became hysterical at the slightest excuse. They were fiercely loyal, but tormented each other with petty quarrels and meaningless arguments. One minute they were patient and understanding; the next, they were testy and unreasonable. Like their Old Testament ancestors, they were stubborn, stiff-necked, and reluctant to change. Ben was proud to be with them.

After the service, members of the French congregation mingled with the *Ostjuden*, listening to their complaints, offering moral support, and sharing the fears and hopes that lay ahead. Ben did not participate, content to remain in his seat and enjoy the tranquility that follows prayer.

His thoughts ranged back to Bluma, and he wished she was with him, so they could share the moment together. The thought of her no longer cut him with loneliness; instead there was a wistful ache, and understanding that she would always be with him, and he with her, no matter how long they were apart. His reverie was interrupted by Dora Hoffmann, who touched him on the shoulder.

''Mr. Isaacson—I thought we might find you here. I'd like you to meet Monsieur Lepatron, a dear friend of mine. I've just been telling him about your adventures on the Berlin Express.''

Lepatron was a distinguished-looking man in his mid-fifties. Clean shaven but for a razor thin mustache, Lepatron radiated an aura of unspoken authority. He gave Ben a brief, self-effacing smile as Ben stood to shake his hand.

"I understand you are a young man of considerable ingenuity."

"I had a lot of help," Ben replied.

"Isn't this wonderful?" Dora Hoffmann beamed at Ben. "Well, you will have to excuse me. I'm having lunch with the charming Mr. Berzig. Since you're dining with Monsieur Lepatron, you'll be safe from my wiles today." She was gone before Ben could get a word in edgewise. A frown crossed his face. He didn't like the feeling of being manipulated by Dora Hoffmann and the urbane Monsieur Lepatron.

"Madame Hoffmann is a formidable woman," Lepatron observed, sensing Ben's irritation. His tone was one of cultivated intimacy; two old friends sharing a private joke. "Shall we go to lunch?"

"Actually, I had made other plans." He hadn't but he was tired of having his life programmed by people he had never met.

"I understand," Lepatron nodded. "But perhaps you would indulge me. I am an elder in the congregation, and Madame Hoffmann felt we might all benefit if you would share the news from Berlin with me. We are most interested. I assure you, it won't take long. Then you'd be free to do . . . whatever you had planned."

Ben had the uncomfortable feeling that Lepatron could read his thoughts. "Why didn't Dora Hoffmann just say that?"

Lepatron gave a Gallic shrug. "Who knows? Matchmakers have their own ways of doing things." Adroitly, he slipped his arm through Ben's and guided him outside, chatting amiably about the rigors of the train ride.

Lepatron's car was a huge black limousine with a uniformed driver twice Ben's size. He looked more like a stevedore than a chauffeur. As Ben settled into the crushed velours upholstery, he noticed that the affable smile had disappeared from Lepatron's face. They were barely away from the curb when the Frenchman began asking questions, and they were not the casual inquiries one might expect from an elder of the synagogue; they were the knife-edged questions of an expert interrogator.

Lepatron made no pretense of conversation, but probed Ben's memory for details and information until he felt he had exhausted Ben's store of knowledge. Then he thanked Ben for his patience and once again reverted to Lepatron, the charming aristocrat. Though he had not bothered to take notes, Ben had no doubt that Lepatron remembered the precise details of everything Ben had told him.

To Ben's surprise, his host was not at all reluctant to answer Ben's questions about himself, and when he described himself as a businessman who owned "a few factories," Ben suspected that he was being overly modest. Lepatron had been to Palestine many times and Ben questioned him eagerly, absorbing the answers like a thirsty sponge.

Ben relished Lepatron's vivid descriptions of the Holy Land and found himself drawn to the man, but he wondered why Lepatron would bother to have lunch with him. They had already discussed the "news from Berlin," and Lepatron was not a man to waste time if he could possibly avoid it. Ben was about to ask when the limousine glided around a terraced curve, planted in mountain laurel, and onto a level plateau.

"Ah," Lepatron murmered, breaking into a congenial smile. "We have arrived."

The view took Ben's breath away. On one side lay the ocean, stretching towards the unseen coast of Africa. An enormous pool, surrounded by exotic plants and white wrought-iron furniture filled the foreground. The pool was contoured to the land and lined with cobalt blue tiles that matched the hue of the Mediterranean beyond. It was a setting designed with a single purpose in mind—to impress.

Lepatron's villa was of Spanish design, a dazzling white stucco topped by brick-red clay tiles. Broad stone steps led from the pool to a portico of Brindisi marble, and a frieze of Greek sculpture adorned the façade.

At the door, they were greeted by two Moroccan servants wearing spotless white jackets and the traditional black pants bound by a crimson sash. Without speaking, they helped Ben and Lepatron remove their coats, then led the way to an enormous vaulted drawing room. Extraordinary fauves by Derain and Vlaminck hung on the walls and a gigantic concert piano dominated the room.

Like the grounds, the interior of the house left Ben with a feeling of conspicuous opulence that jarred with Lepatron's conservative, old-world style. His speech, his clothing, and his habits were elegantly Spartan; nothing about him was frivolous or wasteful. He seemed out of place in such lush and decadent surroundings.

"Please, Benjamin, have a seat." Lepatron indicated an overstuffed leather club chair. As the servants brought out a magnificently prepared lunch, it was only natural for the conversation to turn to the *Ostjuden* bound for Palestine. Lepatron was concerned about the final stage of the journey from Marseilles to Jaffa.

"Surely the worst is behind us," Ben said.

Lepatron thought for a moment before he replied, filling the time by lighting a Cuban cigar. He didn't offer one to Ben; that seemed odd, given his impeccable manners. Ben wondered if Lepatron already knew he didn't use tobacco.

Lepatron exhaled a curly stream of thin blue smoke. "There are still many things that could go wrong. This year marks a turning point in the history of the Jewish people. Week after week, month after month, we have been shipping boatloads of refugees to Palestine and the United States without interference. All of a sudden, President Calvin Coolidge signed the Johnson–Reed Act, effectively barring immigration to America. The British simultaneously closed the doors to Palestine, bottling up tens of thousands of Jewish refugees in Germany. Adolf Hitler is free as a bird and *The Eternal Jew* is a best seller. A remarkable set of coincidences, don't you agree?"

Ben nodded. Despite the fact that Lepatron had said nothing that was not already common knowledge, he had a skillful way of making Ben feel as though he was sharing a confidence, trusting Ben with valuable information.

"You see, Benjamin, regardless of what we think of the Germans, to a fearful extent German history determines European history. It will take time, but before long the world will reap the bitter harvest sown in 1918. No one will suffer more than the Jews."

They were Anschel Isaacson's words, almost verbatim. Lepatron's voice was tinged with sadness; the sound of a powerful man resigned to an inevitable sequence of events beyond his control.

"Most people don't realize what is happening because the degeneration of a nation does not occur in a single day, or a week, or a month. It is a long, slow process of erosion. It begins innocently enough—an old man is taunted, a synagogue defaced, a threat of violence made. But gradually, it spreads like a cancer, feeding on healthy tissue. Germany is infected beyond cure. Now it's just a matter of time. We must all do what we can to get as many Jews out of Germany as possible."

"That's what I'm doing in Marseilles," Ben smiled.

"Listen to me!" Lepatron laughed and lightened the conversation. "I sound like an old man. Tell me about your family. One does not often meet Swedish Jews."

Ben and his host were still engrossed when a drab woman in a black evening gown interrupted them. Ben hadn't heard her walk in and the sound of her voice startled him. He rose to his feet.

"Dinner will be ready shortly, Maurice."

"Thank you, my dear," Lepatron smiled. "Benjamin, I'd like you to meet my charming wife, Nadine."

Ben held out his hand and she shook it limply. Madame Lepatron was nothing like her husband. *Dull* was the word that came to Ben's mind. Her hair was a mousey brown, tied back in a simple bun, and she had the kind of rounded, featureless face that people never looked at twice. Rather than enhance her appearance, the expensive jewelry she wore drew attention to her plainness. She was anything but charming.

"My dear, this is Kapitan Landsdorf. He'll be joining us for dinner." She nodded and left the room.

Lepatron's introduction struck a discordant note to Ben. The Frenchman knew his real name was Isaacson. So why say Kapitan Landsdorf? Ben was about to ask when Lepatron suggested they adjourn to the dining room, and the opportunity was lost. Ben's host had an uncanny knack of evading an uncomfortable question before it was asked.

"I hope you won't mind, Benjamin," he apologized. "My children will be joining us for dinner."

Lepatron's children, Jerome and Claudine, were two of the most unpleasant people Ben had ever met. Claudine was a beautiful young woman of twenty with wavy blond hair cut short in the latest fashion. Her smoky gray eyes sparked with impatience.

"This is an ungodly hour to dine, Papa," she complained.

"The Kapitan has responsibilities to return to, my dear. He can only stay with us a short time."

" 'Kapitan Landsdorf,' " Jerome mimicked. "He's no more a captain than I am and probably less." Jerome was a gangly, awkward teenager with narrow shoulders and a perpetual sneer in his light brown eyes. His complexion was dead white, broken by violent acne scars.

"Kapitan, what island lies at zero degrees of longitude and zero degrees of latitude? Can you tell me that?"

Ben stared at Jerome in shocked silence. He half expected Lepatron to rebuke the boy but Lepatron's attention seemed fixed on his soup. That a man like Lepatron would tolerate such unbelievable rudeness left Ben speechless.

"You see," the boy exclaimed triumphantly. "He doesn't know the most elementary fact of navigation. He's a liar."

"Jerome, please," his father said mildly.

"What's the matter? Can't we talk in front of him? I'd like to know what he's doing here."

"We never see you, Papa," Claudine pouted. "You're always away on business. I gave up an evening in town because you said we were having a family dinner. Now I find out you tricked me. He's not family." She pointed an accusing finger at Ben.

"Children, please," Nadine Lepatron murmured. It was an ineffectual request that her children didn't even bother to acknowledge.

Claudine examined her nails critically. "You're Polish, aren't you?" she asked Ben.

"Swedish."

"Really?" She looked away. The butler began serving the main course. To Ben's surprise, it was traditional Jewish cuisine, perfectly prepared.

"*Nom de Dieu!*" the boy cried in disgust. "I hope you don't expect us to eat this slop. You know how Claudine and I feel about eating Jewish food. What's wrong with French food?"

"You don't expect *him* to eat real food, do you?" the girl remarked snidely and gestured at Ben.

Ben was furious, but he reminded himself that he was a guest in Lepatron's house and made a conscious effort to ignore the Frenchman's bizarre family.

"The food is superb, Monsieur," Ben said.

"Thank you, Kapitan, I am gratified that you like it."

Claudine pushed her plate away violently. "I can't bear it! I'm sick and tired of having my feelings ignored. I won't eat this trash!"

"Then you'll eat nothing," her father replied. She glared at him sullenly.

"My father tells me you're going to Palestine," Jerome said between mouthfuls.

"That's correct," Ben replied coolly. He watched the boy devour his food. For someone who refused to eat slop, Jerome was managing more than his share.

"God knows why anyone would want to go there," Jerome smirked. "The place is full of vicious, dirty Arabs and bugs. You'll be lucky if you survive more than two days." Before Ben could reply, Claudine started to giggle.

"At least we'll have our revenge for being forced to eat this so-called 'food'. Our sailing captain will end up eating sand in Palestine just like the rest of those dreadful *Ostjuden*."

"I don't know," Jerome mused, helping himself to another serving of kugel. "The *Ostjuden* might do quite well in Palestine. After all, most of them look like camels to begin with—thick lips and bushy eyebrows." He began to snort and bounce, imitating a camel. Lepatron toyed with his pearl tie pin.

"Civilized people cannot survive in Palestine," Claudine announced blithely. "France is our promised land, *non*?"

"Not according to Papa," Jerome belched. Claudine threw her napkin down and pointed an accusing finger at Ben.

"How can you bring someone like that into our house?" she demanded. "He's responsible for taking hundreds of poor fools to an uninhabitable desert to die. Don't you realize that the British are only trying to prevent a slaughter? How can any intelligent person support Zionism? Anyone with any sensitivity can easily see that the British are right. Zionism is a form of suicide." Her eyes challenged Ben to respond.

Ben placed his fork on the table and thought for a moment. He had no desire to engage Lepatron's children in argument. He knew that any attempt at discussion was bound to degenerate into a shouting match, but it was impossible to say nothing.

"Mademoiselle, you are naturally free to believe what you will, and I am reluctant to argue with you at your father's table," Ben said quietly. "But I think that you should remember something."

"And what might that be?"

"You are a Jewish woman first, and a French mademoiselle second. Nothing can ever change that." He expected a sizzling protest but to his surprise the girl did not respond. Instead, she began eating.

'Jerome started in again by claiming he was a Frenchman first and a Jew second, and for the duration of the meal he and his sister continued to argue with Ben, trying to provoke him. Ben supposed that a man like Lepatron had little time for his family and that the children were using him to bait their father; there was no other explanation for their behavior. There were times Ben was tempted to lash out, but he held his temper in check and kept his voice reasonable.

Afterward, Lepatron walked Ben out to the car, never mentioning the unpleasantness at dinner. He shook Ben's hand warmly and apologized for not being able to ride back to Marseilles with him.

As Ben climbed into the car, Lepatron smiled. "I hope our paths will cross again, Benjamin."

All the way back to the city, Ben kept thinking about his afternoon with Lepatron. He liked the Frenchman and enjoyed his company, but he still couldn't fathom why Lepatron had spent the better part of a day with him. On the surface, his host was a charming businessman with a boring wife and two spoiled children, but the more Ben thought about it, the more uneasy he became. Nothing seemed to fit. Lepatron was a sleek predator, out of place in the sybaritic villa. And something about the wife was all wrong. When men like Lepatron married, it wasn't to a dowdy *hausfrau* like Nadine. And then there were Claudine and Jerome.

Lepatron had gone out of his way to be hospitable, yet allowed his children to insult him as well as Ben. Men like Lepatron did not tolerate insubordination in their associates, their business, or their families. Men like Lepatron were used to the prerogatives of wealth and command. They were accustomed to being obeyed. After all, they were the bosses, the men who . . . The words clicked in Ben's mind.

The bosses. That was it!

Lepatron was not a name at all. It was a title. The French words for "the boss"—le patron. Ben laughed out loud. Lepatron had to be head of the Zionist network in Marseilles. It was all another one of Ten Meineckestrasse's games; a setup, some kind of test.

Ben felt a rush of excitement. They wouldn't have bothered to test him unless they had something big in mind; something far more important than his role as Kapitan Benjamin Landsdorf. He knew he had handled himself well at Lepatron's dinner and whatever they had planned, Ben was to be a part of it. Impatience gnawed at him. Why did they always have to move in such convoluted circles?

He stared out the window at the approaching lights of Marseilles. Before he had come to Berlin, Zionism was a magnificent abstraction, a dream made of words. Now he was living the reality. In just six short weeks, he had experienced more than in the rest of his twenty-one years combined. Compared to the intensity of what he was doing now, the time he had spent making speeches and arguing with people who had already closed their minds seemed utterly meaningless, the words like so many dried leaves.

When his role as Kapitan Landsdorf had come to an end, his emotion was a feeling of relief; he was no longer responsible for the well-being of nearly a thousand people. But that initial feeling was soon replaced by a yearning to be back in the thick of the action. The tremendous stakes and the element of danger was like an addictive drug; once he had tasted it, the prospect of becoming a spectator again filled him with dismay. He knew in his gut that the afternoon with Lepatron was a prelude to something important, and the anticipation of a new assignment revived his spirits.

The car dropped him off at Georgette LaForge's house just after nine, but the smile faded from his face when he walked into the living room. Seated on the couch, holding one of Zelda's hands in her own, was Dora Hoffmann, the matchmaker. Ben sighed inwardly when he saw the doe-eyed expression on Zelda's face. The last thing he needed was a meddling shadchente trying to match him up with Zelda.

"Oh, Ben," Zelda breathed. "Dora and I were just talking about you."

No doubt, Ben thought sarcastically.

"I'm so glad to see you again, Benjamin," Dora Hoffmann gushed. "I simply must have a word with you. Would you mind getting my coat and seeing me to my car?"

It was impossible to refuse. Ben resigned himself to a lecture on Zelda's merits and the virtues of marriage.

Once outside, Dora Hoffmann's tone changed abruptly.

"Apparently, you did well tonight, Comrade Isaacson." The charm was gone from her voice, leaving a hard metallic edge to the words.

Ben stared in surprise. "Comrade Isaacson?"

"We haven't much time to talk . . ."

Ben cut her off. "How would you know 'how I did' tonight?"

Dora Hoffmann eyed him critically. "If you hadn't you wouldn't be here right now."

"Then you and Lepatron are . . ."

"I was told that you can be stubborn and argumentative and that you like to ask questions. I see that it's true. Now please simply shut up and listen to what I have to say."

Ben's ears burned at her rebuke, but he kept silent.

"Good. We have over 400 illegals that must board the *S.S. Asia* before she sails tomorrow. Once the boarding process begins, English agents here in Marseilles will be watching us like hawks on a henhouse. If they have enough evidence, they can force the French to stop us here or nail us off the coast of Palestine. Your job is to get on the *Asia* tonight and help us smuggle those illegals on board."

"Why me?" Ben asked.

"You've got a valid visa, so you won't arouse any suspicion. But even if you do, they can't touch you. You're completely legal. Just be sure you destroy Landsdorf's papers and use your own."

"Why all the intrigue with Lepatron?"

Dora Hoffmann lit a cigarette and drew on it heavily. "You've been attending too many lectures. When you're in the field, you forfeit the right to ask questions like that."

"I . . ."

"Another thing," Hoffmann interrupted. "The English always try to recruit spies from the passenger manifest; Gentiles willing to inform in exchange for money. There's a good chance you may be approached. You're the Nordic type and you hold a Swedish passport, so they won't take you for a Jew. If they try to recruit you, play along. That will make one less thing we need to worry about."

She turned and looked back at the house. Zelda was peering through the curtains watching them.

"What do you want me to do?" Ben asked. He felt like an overwound spring, about to be released.

"Put your clothes into a bundle or a battered case—nothing too fancy. You'll be playing the part of a moderately successful farm equipment dealer who's drunk, so bear that in mind when you dress. Don't tell anyone about this, not even Berzig. Just wait until they all go to bed, then be out on the street by eleven-fifteen. Someone will pick you up. Good luck and good-bye."

"You people are unbelievable," Ben shook his head as he closed the car door for her. "Are you really a *shadchente*?"

Dora Hoffmann rolled down the window and smiled tiredly. "I will tell you this much. That one has her hooks out for you." She nodded towards the front window, where Zelda still watched.

"I never would have guessed."

SEVENTEEN

The Docks of Marseilles
February 8th, 1925

Ben followed Dora Hoffmann's instructions to the letter. After packing his clothes in a travel-worn suitcase, he stood in front of the bathroom mirror and studied his reflection. More casual, he thought. He ruffled his hair and rethreaded his belt, intentionally missing a couple of loops. Carefully, he reknotted his tie and pulled it to one side. As a final touch, he buttoned his jacket on the wrong hole, giving him a slightly cockeyed look. Satisfied with his appearance, Ben picked up his suitcase and tiptoed down the hall to the head of the stairs. He was halfway to the foyer when Zelda's bedroom door opened.

When she saw the suitcase, her smile faded to a wounded expression.

"Ben," she whispered. "What are you doing?"

"Please, Zelda, just go back in your room."

"Ben, why are you leaving? Did I do something? Say something?"

"I have to go now," he replied grimly.

"You owe me an explanation!"

Ben looked at his watch. It was twelve minutes past eleven. There was no time to argue or explain, so he just turned and walked towards the front door. Zelda followed him, screaming at the top of her lungs. Bedroom doors began to open.

Ben stepped outside, hoping the cold would discourage Zelda, but she ignored it. Clad in her nightgown, she ran after him into the street. Anxiously, Ben scanned the block. There was no sign of a car. He turned to Zelda.

"For God's sake, Zelda, please. Go back to your room. This has nothing to do with you."

"How can you say that?" she wailed. "Why are you deserting me? Where are you going? Please tell me, please. You can't leave us now, we'll never get through without you—I'll do whatever you say. Just don't leave me." Lights came on in a neighbor's house. Two amused pedestrians stopped to watch.

There was still no sign of a car. Desperation constricted Ben's throat and his temples throbbed. No one was supposed to know what he was doing, and now half of Marseilles was watching the show.

"Zelda, get back in the house before I drag you back."

Zelda grabbed hold of his arm and began to sob hysterically. Just then, an old bakery truck rounded the corner and pulled up to the curb. The driver stuck his head out the window and shouted for Ben to get in the back. Ben tried to pry Zelda's fingers off his arm, but she held him in a death grip.

"You idiot," the driver yelled. "Dump her and get in or we leave without you."

Ben gave her a shove with his elbow and Zelda fell backwards into a low hedge.

"Sorry, Zelda," he muttered, running for the rear of the truck. In a single motion, he tossed his suitcase in the back and swung it over the tailgate. Zelda staggered to the curb, clutching her nightgown around her.

"If you leave me now, don't ever come back!" she screamed like a wounded animal. Mercifully, the driver accelerated and turned a corner. Zelda was still on the sidewalk, yelling and waving her fist. Ben slumped against the side wall of the truck and rubbed his forehead. How could things have gone so badly?

"Your wife is quite a woman," the driver shouted through the open panel separating the cab from the back of the truck. He laughed heartily. "I hope your mistress is more even-tempered."

It was not an auspicious beginning.

Fifteen minutes later the truck crossed a short bridge, turned, and skidded to a stop on the damp cobblestones. The smell of salt water and tidal decay filled Ben's nostrils.

"Get out!" the driver barked and stepped on the gas before Ben had both feet on the ground. He fell heavily, bruising his left side.

Three figures hurried towards him, silhouetted against a darkened warehouse. One of them was Dora Hoffmann. Ben stood up with a groan. His side throbbed painfully. A man took Ben's arm and practically dragged him into the building.

Dora Hoffmann put her face close to Ben's and whispered urgently. "You are going to be posing as a passenger. Being intoxicated, you mistook the departure time for twelve midnight instead of twelve noon. You're exhausted, drunk, and you don't have any place to stay. Keep your passport and ticket handy in case they want to check. Now listen carefully."

Dora Hoffmann handed Ben a magnum of champagne with a leather shoulder strap and explained that it had been doctored with a mild sedative that required ten or fifteen minutes to take effect. There were six guards aboard the *Asia*. Somehow, Ben had to get them to drink the champagne, then go below to pass out. By the time they came to, it would be too late to do anything about the people who had already boarded. The plan was crude, but it would have to work. The original plan, which called for a daylight boarding, had been aborted at the last minute. Dora Hoffmann had discovered that the British had managed to plant an informer among the guards but she didn't know who it was, and there wasn't time to find out.

"Forgive the question, but won't they be suspicious if I don't drink with them?" Ben asked.

"Of course. If they insist you drink, drink this." Dora Hoffmann handed him a silver flask of French brandy. She snapped her fingers and one of the men handed her a ladies hat box. "Use this like a drum and sing your way up the gangway."

"Piece of cake," Ben grinned.

"Just wipe the smug look off your face and take care of the guards. Once they're out, come and get us. We'll take care of the rest. *Mit mazel*."

Dora Hoffmann watched Ben walk towards the *Asia*. If he failed, they would have to chance the daylight boarding. Suddenly, she was aware of how fast her heart was beating. I'm getting too old for this, she thought.

The *S.S. Asia* dwarfed the dock. She was nearly six hundred feet long and had seen better days. Patches of rust and peeling paint marred the gray hull and parts of her superstructure were stained with soot. Two battered cranes bore mute witness to her service as a cargo ship. The overall effect was of a once grand old lady who had fallen on hard times. Only the smokestacks, which had been freshly painted in red, white, and blue to match the colors of the French flag, looked sharp and new.

Ben approached the gangway cautiously, avoiding the dim circles of light cast by the dock lamps. He wanted to be certain that no one spotted him before he was ready to begin his performance. The *Asia's* deck seemed to be deserted and the thin mist enshrouding the ship gave it a ghostly appearance. Ben drew a deep breath and set foot on the boarding ramp. He marched up the steep gangway, performing the Marseillaise like a one-man band. His boot heels clanged like cymbals on the metal ramp. The hatbox resounded with drumrolls, and instead of singing the words, Ben mimicked the sound of a trumpet. Three guards appeared at the railing, armed with truncheons. When they saw Ben lurching from side to side, they broke out laughing.

"Bravo!" one of them shouted and they all began to applaud.

Ben played his role to the hilt, stumbling at the head of the ramp so that one of the guards had to catch him. He bowed with a flourish and greeted the deckhands in atrocious French.

"*M'sierus, je viens partir le bateau,*" he announced, belching the last word. Then he saluted and began singing the words to the national anthem. The guards joined in, leading him back to their watch post.

It was bitterly cold on deck and the three remaining guards huddled over a small brazier, warming their hands. Ben noticed several empty wine bottles. Slurring his words, he explained his problem and was promptly invited to spend the night on board. In return, he offered them his bottle of champagne. Gleefully, they filled cracked beige coffee cups with the foaming liquor and toasted Ben's musical talents. They insisted that he imitate a trumpet while they sang the Marseillaise again. They finished the entire magnum in five minutes flat. Only the foreman, Jean, did not drink. Ben waited anxiously for the drug to take effect. Once the other five men were unconscious, he would have to figure out some way to get rid of Jean.

After what seemed like an eternity, one of the guards stood up and yawned. "I'm frozen to the bone and I can hardly keep my eyes open. How about it, Jean? Do you mind if I stretch out in the mess hall for a while? There's nothing happening up here anyway."

Jean looked at his men and grinned. "Why don't you all go below. You look too drunk to be any use to me anyway. If I need you, I'll call."

"Ah, Jean, one of the finest men who ever lived," one of the guards burped. They all stood to go below and tried to get Ben to join them. He feigned nausea, claiming he needed the fresh air.

When the other men disappeared, Jean bent over the brazier next to Ben. "Your French is lousy," he laughed.

"*Vraiment.*"

"Do you speak Spanish?"

"Not a word."

"Italian?"

"Nope."

"German?"

"Fluently, *mein freund*," Ben replied gleefully. "*Und sie?*"

"*Jawohl! Ich bin von Alzas.*"

The bosun's mate was from Alsace, on the French-German border. For hundreds of years, every time France and Germany fought, Alsace changed hands. The population was bilingual of necessity.

Ben pulled out the silver brandy flask and offered it to the bosun. Jean drank deeply then smacked his lips in satisfaction.

"Now that's what I call a drink!" he exclaimed. "Champagne is for children and old ladies." Ben noticed how thick Jean's wrists were. If it came to a physical confrontation, the beefy Frenchman would have a distinct advantage.

Jean pushed back his wool watchcap and rubbed his forehead. He was a simple kind-hearted man, and he had taken a liking to Ben. He took another swig from the flask and started to talk about Palestine and the Arabs, subjects on which he considered himself an authority.

"I fought the Arabs in Morocco. They're worse than animals. They love to castrate their captives, then slowly cut them into a hundred pieces. Believe me, I killed more than my share without a shred of regret."

Ben did not doubt it.

"Tell me something, blondie," Jean asked. "How come there are no poor Jews in France? All the ones I see are rich."

"They send the poor ones to Palestine to be eaten by the Arabs," Ben hiccupped.

Jean roared with laughter. He took another long sip of brandy, then offered Ben the flask. Ben declined.

The liquor had a melancholic effect on Jean, and he apologized for having to speak in German. That led to a maudlin account of the history of Alsace and how his people hated *les bosches*. Jean drank as he talked, apparently unaffected by the quantity of brandy he had consumed. Surreptitiously, Ben glanced at his watch. It was getting late. He had to do something about the bosun.

Suddenly, Jean squinted at Ben and asked to see his papers. Ben's mouth dropped open in surprise, and for a moment, the thought crossed his mind that Jean might be the British plant that Dora Hoffmann had warned him about. Silently, he pulled the papers out of his coat pocket. The bosun studied them in the dim light, then handed them back to Ben.

"*En ordre*," he nodded. He raised the flask to his lips and drained it. "So, you're a Swede, huh? Tell you what— you call me Alzas and I'll call you Swede." Some of his words were slurred. The liquor had begun to take effect. Ben prayed the bosun would pass out quickly, but Jean continued with his morose monologue.

"I tell you, Swede, the Germans are going to rise up and kill us all. Make the Great War look like a garden party. I say that from experience, you know. I fought in that war."

Once again, Jean went off on a tangent, castigating the German mentality and making dire predictions of another war. Ben liked the gruff bosun's mate, but he could feel the impatience rising in his gut. When was the man going to pass out?

To hold up his side of the conversation, Ben told Jean how his fiancée had been gunned down in Berlin. To Ben's surprise, tears streamed down Jean's cheeks and he gave Ben a bear hug.

"Where is this fiancée of yours? Why isn't she with you?" Jean sniffed.

"I'm going to make a home for us in Palestine first. Then she's going to join me." It was partly true, Ben thought.

"Poor girl. It's just terrible when you can be shot down in the street, just because you're a Jew."

"That's why I left," Ben explained.

"The Jews make Germany strong, you know," Jean rambled. "They own all the banks and industries. They run the hospitals and the government. It's funny that Hitler hates them so much—they're the ones that make Germany strong." Ben stared at the Frenchman. Unwittingly, his words gave Ben a lever to use if he was willing to chance it. Was the bosun what he appeared to be?

If Jean was a British informer, the entire exodus was in jeopardy. Trusting him could lead to disaster but time was running out. The risk had to be taken. If Ben guessed wrong, he would have to dispose of the affable Frenchman somehow. Ben eyed the wooden truncheon leaning against the base of the brazier. If necessary, he would overpower the bosun's mate and hide him ashore until the ship left. Jean's disappearance might raise suspicions, but there would be no proof. With luck, the bosun would be written off as a typical sailor off on a binge, and the *Asia* would be long gone before anyone was the wiser.

Ben searched the bosun's face for any sign of duplicity; all he saw was open curiosity. He decided to follow his instincts and take a chance that the Frenchman's hatred of the Germans was genuine.

"They're running away," he winked.

"Who's running away," the Frenchman asked drunkenly.

"Right here, on this ship." Ben deliberately confused the bosun.

"What?"

"Do you have any idea who's on the passenger list?" Ben dangled the bait.

"No." Jean took it.

"Scores of important German Jews and their families," Ben whispered as though they were conspirators.

"Like who?"

Ben thought quickly. Off the top of his head, he started naming important people that Jean might recognize, people like Gunther Wagner, head of Pelikan Tinte, the ink company, and Walter Schmiler, president of AEG, the German power company.

"That's incredible!"

"There are more." Ben went on listing prominent German companies like the Krupp Iron Works and Zeiss, certain military figures, and even Benjamin Tietz and Emilie Wertheim, the department store owners. Jean was impressed.

"You see, Alzas, the Germans would never let them leave. They're much too valuable, essential to the German economy. So we have to smuggle them out of Marseilles before the Germans find out." Ben was afraid the sound of his heart thudding against his ribs would give him away.

"They're disguised as refugees, Alzas, and they don't have any papers. You're going to have to look the other way for a while." Ben tried to keep the tension out of his voice. Everything depended on Jean's response.

Without a word, the Frenchman rose and disappeared through a bulkhead hatch before Ben could move. It was too late to stop him. Ben had visions of Jean and the other guards turning him over to the gendarmes.

In less than a minute, he reappeared. Alone.

"The others are asleep, and the rest of the ship is empty," he said with a wink. "Have your friends come up the gangway and hide in the hold, until the rest of the passengers board. They then can mix, and no one will notice the difference. *Vite, vite*." He smiled and went below.

Ben hurried down the gangway into the warehouse where he found Dora Hoffmann waiting for him. Quickly, he explained what had happened.

"We still have a problem," Hoffmann said grimly when Ben finished. She took him by the arm and led him to a narrow window. A man in a tan mackintosh paced slowly outside the warehouse gate; a British agent.

It was impossible to board the *Ostjuden* without his seeing them.

"Why don't we just get rid of him?" Ben fumed.

"Too risky. We've come up with an alternative plan."

The *Asia* was tied in a U-shaped berth with warehouses and broad docks lining both sides of the water. There was enough room for two ships, but the space next to the *Asia* was empty. Less than two hundred feet of open water separated her from the next dock.

The British agent was outside the fence surrounding the warehouse where Ben and Hoffmann were hiding, which meant that the *Asia* blocked his view of the opposite dock. With luck, the *Ostjuden* could be ferried across the water and boarded on the opposite side. Everyone was already assembled in an empty warehouse and the local Zionists had managed to scrounge some rowboats. All they needed was a way into the ship from the water side.

"There's got to be a cargo bay near the waterline," Ben guessed. "I'll find Alzas and we'll get it open. As soon as you see a light by the waterline, start bringing people over."

Ben raced back aboard the *Asia* and relayed the change in plans to Jean, who agreed to help. He led Ben through a maze of companionways down to a cargo bay off the passenger hold. Ben thanked his luck that Jean was not the informer. Alone, Ben would have had no chance of finding his way through the ship.

Jean cracked the hatch and the cargo door swung down to form a platform several feet above the water. He found a short rope ladder and attached it to the platform.

The faint light from the hold played out across the water, serving as a beacon to the Zionists waiting on the dock. As Ben peered into the darkness, a line of small rowboats appeared, filled with dark shapes. The first boat bumped against the hull with a hollow ring, and its occupants began climbing the rope ladder to the cargo platform.

There were only eight rowboats in all, and each boat held just six people plus two men to row. It was going to take hours before everyone was safely aboard. In order to save time, Dora Hoffmann had sent the young men first. They made the transfer faster and could help the women and children on the other end. Ben recruited the first few arrivals as "guides," and Jean showed them where to lead the *Ostjuden* once they entered the cargo bay.

The passenger hold was a series of interconnected rooms, illuminated by kerosene lamps. Each cabin contained six to eight bunks, stacked by twos, leaving an open space in the center for tables and chairs. Slowly, the cabins began to fill with people.

The first problem arose when a rotund Polish woman tried to climb the flimsy ladder, clutching a large satchel she refused to part with. Her foot slipped through one of the rungs and she plunged headlong into the icy water.

"*Jude im wasser!*" Jean said in a low voice and dove off the platform. Fortunately, the woman was paralyzed by the frigid water, so she neither screamed nor struggled when Jean swam her to the rowboat. Two men carried her aboard, shivering and gasping.

One other woman fell off the ladder, but she landed in the boat, twisting an ankle. She yelped in pain, but someone quickly clamped a hand across her mouth. Ben prayed the sounds had not carried to the agent on the dock.

Suddenly, two dark forms clustered around him—Sophie and Sarah. They hugged each other and Sarah began to cry softly.

"Ben," she sniffed, "how did you get here? We were terrified something had happened to you. Why didn't you tell us where you were going? Zelda went crazy."

"I'll tell you about it later," Ben promised. "You didn't forget Katzele, did you?"

Sophie giggled and opened her coat. The cat stuck its head out and meowed plaintively.

Ben laughed. "Take the beast below and please, do what you can to keep everyone calm and quiet, especially the children. We've got to keep our heads down until the rest of the passengers board at noon."

"You can count on us," Sarah whispered.

The last of the refugees boarded just before dawn. Ben helped Jean to close and bolt the cargo hatch. He clasped the Frenchman's shoulder.

"Alzas, I can't thank you enough."

The bosun's face split into a wide grin. "Anytime I can strike a blow at *les bosches*, I'm happy to do it, but next time, I'd just as soon skip the swim."

Ben walked Jean to the mess hall where he gathered his men. They were still groggy but none seemed to realize that the champagne had been drugged. Jean sent them up on deck to wait for the next shift.

"Some watchmen, heh?" Jean winked. I'll keep them on deck. If you can keep your people below until noon, no one will be the wiser."

He hugged Ben and kissed him on both cheeks, then disappeared up the companionway.

Ben walked back through the passenger hold to reassure everyone that things were going as planned. Having been awake all night, the exhausted *Ostjuden* were too tired to care about the future. Most of them were already asleep.

Sarah and Sophie were sharing an upper and lower bunk in the cabin adjacent to Zelda's. Ben stopped and joked with them for a few minutes. They were both giddy with excitement, too keyed up to sleep. He debated looking in on Zelda, but decided against it. He was in no mood for a scene.

It was just after nine when Ben went up on deck, and he spent the following two hours pacing restlessly, waiting for the legal passengers to embark at noon. Towards eleven, as the final time approached, he spotted Dora Hoffmann waving at him from the bottom of the gangway. He knew instantly, from the expression on her face, that something else had gone wrong. Ben jogged down the ramp.

"We have an unforeseen problem," she sighed. "Take a look around." The dock was swarming with British agents and their French counterparts. "As long as they're here, we're in trouble."

"How? All our illegals are already boarded. They've no way of knowing . . ."

"Do you know how many people boarded last night?"

"Four hundred or so," Ben guessed.

"Four hundred and forty-three, to be exact."

"So?"

"In two hours, it will be noon, and we'll be loading five hundred people onto the *S.S. Asia*, a ship with accommodations for more than a thousand passengers. If you were with British Intelligence, would you believe that Messageries Maritimes would sail with a ship half booked?"

Ben stared at her in astonishment. It was so obvious, no one had thought of it. "So we've outsmarted ourselves."

Hoffmann shot him an irritated glance. "You could put it that way. What we need now is a *tummel*, not an analysis." *Tummel* is a Yiddish word meaning chaos, pandemonium, and noise. Fortunately, eastern Jews did not need to be taught how to create a *tummel*. They did it naturally.

"We'll begin by boarding groups of twelve or fifteen. Out of every group, three or four will run back down the gangway immediately, yelling and carrying on about forgetting this or that. Thirty minutes later, they'll reboard as though they were new passengers."

"What about the lists? Won't they notice the same people getting on and off?"

"First, no one else here speaks Yiddish. You can imagine the kind of mileage that will give us. Once the back and forth begins, our British agents nursing Sunday morning hangovers will never be able to keep track. Besides, three quarters of our people have black or brown hair and wear dark clothing. Nearly all the men have heavy beards. To the British, they'll all look alike. They'll never be able to keep an accurate count, and the French officials won't bother. They couldn't care less.''

''What do you want me to do?''

She looked at him closely. ''You look terrible. Why don't you get yourself a cup of coffee somewhere. With luck, the British will try to recruit you and our final problem will be solved''

Taking her advice, Ben walked around the warehouse and across the street to a seedy-looking dive called the Café Mistral. The bar was already jammed with a rough-looking crowd downing one drink after another. Ben sat down at a table and beckoned to a waitress, who gave him a dirty look when all he ordered was coffee.

''Another big spender,'' she snarled. Her face was deeply pitted and her hands were filthy.

The coffee she brought him was bitter and topped by an oily film. Ben took a tentative sip, then put it down on the scarred table top. It was terrible, but it would keep him awake.

Suddenly, he had the uncomfortable feeling that someone was staring at him. He turned slightly and caught sight of a man he recognized from the docks. Like most of the Englishmen in Marseilles, he wore the obligatory ''uniform''—a tweed suit and light tan mackintosh. He had to be with British Intelligence.

Ben rummaged through his coat and pulled out his passport and visa. He made a great fuss of examining them for the agent's benefit. The man rose and walked over to Ben's table.

''*Pardon, monsieur. Allez-vous partir avec l'Asie?*'' His accent was terrible. Ben nodded, holding up his passport and ticket.

''You're Swedish!'' the Englishman exclaimed with delight.

''*Ja, ja,*'' Ben replied in a thick accent.

''Well, my name is Reginald Dobson and I'm with the British Consulate here in Marseilles.''

''Gud to mit you.''

''Indeed,'' the Englishman beamed. ''We're in charge here, you know. Got to see that the ships are properly loaded and everything is shipshape, you know.''

''Oh, *ja*, I can zee dat pretty gud.''

The waitress returned to the table. She looked at Dobson with a derisive expression.

"*Un cassis, s'il vous plait.*" His tone was polite, but the grimace on his face made it clear what he thought of the bar and his waitress.

"*Merveilleux,*" she snorted. "Between the two of you, I should be able to retire on the tip." She glared at the Englishman and stalked off.

"Strange people, these frogs," Dobson muttered.

Ben smiled inwardly, wondering if Dobson realized how strange he looked sitting in a waterfront bar dressed like an English country gentleman. The English never saw themselves as others did; to an Englishman, it was always the other person who was dressed wrong or spoke with an accent.

Dobson put on his best smile and brushed a curly lock of red hair off his forehead. Ben guessed he was about thirty-five, educated at Oxford, and a career civil servant. Dobson's eyes were already rheumy from too many late nights and too much whiskey.

Dobson made small talk for a while, nervously tracing the carvings on the table top with his forefinger. The Englishman was obviously uncomfortable and Ben enjoyed watching him squirm. Ben played along, smiling and nodding, waiting for Dobson to come to the point. It finally happened after the second *cassis.*

"Tell me, my friend," Dobson said expansively. "Why in God's name do you want to go to that godforsaken desert in Palestine? It's a terrible place, you know. You're not a Zionist, are you?" Ben finally identified the accent: Cambridge.

"No, no," Ben answered quickly, as if insulted to be taken for a Jew. "Due I hav to be a Zionist to goo to Palestine? I'm yung and I vant to zee de bisnezz opportoonities, *ja*? I gut de capitalist visa." Ben showed him the passport and visa. The Englishman checked the documents, then returned them. The waitress brought his third drink to the table.

"Have you seen any of the other passengers?" Dobson asked casually. He leaned forward. "You must be very careful. Ships like this one can be infested with reds and terrorists. Moscow smuggles them in to stir up the Arabs and the Jews. It can be very dangerous."

That's what I want to hear, Ben thought to himself. Just keep talking.

"We can tell these types in a flash you know," Dobson continued authoritatively. "They have to sneak on board like thieves. Honest people always have proper papers. The buggers without them are almost always bad actors of one sort or another." Ben studied the earnest expression on Dobson's face, realizing the Englishman believed what he was saying. Ben made a conscious effort to sympathize.

"Terrible, terrible," Ben clucked.

Dobson was pleased with Ben's reaction. "Do yourself a favor, old boy, and help us catch some of these buggers if you see them. I'll stand nearby, and if you see one, point. I'll do the rest. Incidentally, there's a reward as well.''

"*Ja?*" Ben feigned a sudden interest. He placed his coffee cup on the table and drew close to the Englishman. "How much?"

"Five pounds." Dobson withdrew a five-pound note from his pocket, flashing the printed side at Ben. He wrote Ben's name on the reverse side, which was blank. The English always joked that the five-pound notes were only printed on one side so a husband could write out a list of things to be bought on the reverse side, preventing his wife from buying frivolities. Agents like Dobson used the blank side to write the names of potential informers, as though the name on the back somehow guaranteed payment.

The Englishman rose, offering his hand. "I think we understand each other, old boy. Let's shake on it."

Ben took his hand and pumped it enthusiastically. He was home free.

Back at the wharf, the *tummel* had begun. Men, women, and children milled around in apparent confusion. People yelled, screamed, cried, moaned, and sang. The sound carried from one dock to another like breaking surf.

Ben lost himself in the crowd and, fifteen minutes later, he caught sight of Dobson near the foot of the gangway. The Englishman looked desperate. He was pinned against the edge of the dock by the *tummel* with a clipboard wedged under one arm, and he clung to the gangway railing with both hands like a drowning man clutching at a life preserver. The lack of sleep had made Ben a little punchy, and the sight of Reginald Dobson holding on for dear life sent him into a fit of laughter.

"What's so funny?" Dora Hoffmann startled him. He told her about Dobson, and she laughed as well. It was the first time Ben had heard her laugh when she wasn't playing the *shadchente*.

By four o'clock, it was over. Without anyone noticing, every one of the *Ostjuden* in the passenger hold had slipped on deck and mingled with the legal emigrants. The *tummel* had worked perfectly. Dobson and his men had no idea they had been hoodwinked, they were just grateful to be done with the job.

From a vantage point on the observation deck, Ben watched the refugees gather along the railing, proud of the role he had played in smuggling his fellow Jews aboard the *Asia*. He had been lucky with Jean, but he knew the real credit had to go to Lepatron and Dora Hoffmann and the nameless faces who made up the Zionist underground. In the middle of the night, they had gathered more than 400 frightened people, organized them, transported them to an empty warehouse, then rowed them to the *Asia*, right under the nose of British Intelligence. Once we have a land of our own, Ben thought, there's no limit to what we'll be able to accomplish.

Sarah and Sophie stood beside him at the rail, sharing the fear, the excitement, and the sense of anticipation that gripped every emigrant on board. The crew prepared to cast off. Suddenly, Ben caught sight of Zelda. He called out and waved.

She looked up with an angry glare. "I don't ever want to talk to you again," she screamed and shook her fist.

"You don't think she's mad at me?" Ben grinned. Sophie and Sarah broke into gales of laughter.

The ship was scheduled to sail at five, and as the sun began to set, the bosun growled the final order and the mooring lines were cast off. The ship's horn gave a deep, mournful blast, and a cheer rose from the crowd.

As the tugs edged the ship away from the dock, the emigrants took a last look at the shores of Europe. Centuries before, the legions of the Roman emperor Hadrian drove their ancestors from the Holy Land into exile in Europe. Now they were returning. Behind them lay the ghetto walls; the pogroms; and the bloody memories of shame and torture. As the ship left Marseilles in its wake, every Jew on board cast off the uniforms, the laws, and the hatreds that had bound them for a thousand years.

The time had come to leave a place of birth for a place of life.

It was time to go.

EIGHTEEN

Aboard the S. S. Asia
Sunday, February 9th, 1925
Evening

As the *Asia* cleared the harbor seawall, hundreds of people spontaneously linked arms, swaying together in song. There was a bittersweet melancholy to the singing, an unspoken admission that a final commitment had been made. A way of life that had sustained people for centuries was gone, vanished in the *Asia's* phosphorescent wake. There would be no going back.

The lights of Marseilles merged in the purple haze, becoming less distinct with every passing moment. As the lights grew smaller, then disappeared on the dark horizon, the singing stopped, and only the muffled throbbing of the Asia's engines broke the silence. People began to break off from the crowd on deck and return to their cabins.

Ben remained on the observation deck long after everyone else had gone below, reluctant to surrender the day to memory. He stood motionless at the railing, content to gaze out across the water and let the breeze riffle his hair. He wasn't wholly sure what he felt, but he knew that he would always look back on this moment as the real beginning of his life.

Sheer exhaustion finally drove him to his cabin, where he collapsed onto his narrow bunk fully clothed. Grateful that he'd been assigned a private cabin, even though there was barely enough room to take a single stride without hitting a bulkhead, Ben pulled a woolen blanket over himself and surrendered to sleep.

He was running across an endless courtyard; behind him, the sound of boot heels on cobblestones beat a staccato tattoo for the hoarse cries of angry men. He risked a glance over his shoulder, terror forming an icy knot in his gut. His pursuers were shrouded by the darkness; all he saw were the reaching hands, fish-white, the color of death. He tried to run faster, but his legs felt numb and leaden. They were gaining on him. Every step he took seemed to cover less ground, until he sensed the grasping hands reach out to pull him down and heard the snarls of triumph.

Ben awoke in a cold sweat, his throat dry, his heart thudding like a trip hammer. His cabin wall reverberated from the sound of shouting. Trembling from the realism of his nightmare, Ben stumbled from his bunk and collided with the opposite wall; he had forgotten how small the cabin was. Cursing in Swedish, he groped for the door, and yanked the handle open. The corridor was deserted; the echo of angry voices emanated from the mess hall around the corner. He ran towards the sound.

It took Ben's eyes a moment to adjust to the dim light in the dining room. At the far end, the ship's baker and two of his assistants were cornered by a dozen *Ostjuden*. The baker kept the furious *Ostjuden* at bay with a four-foot breadboard used to remove hot loaves from the oven. He was cursing at the top of his lungs and swinging the board in a vicious arc. Even from across the mess hall, Ben heard the whistle of the breadboard as it sliced through the air. The baker's two assistants cowered behind him.

The *Ostjuden* were yelling as well, only in Yiddish, threatening the baker with clenched fists. The language barrier aggravated the situation, and unless something was done immediately, it was certain that someone was bound to get hurt. Rather than elbow his way through the *Ostjuden*, Ben ran to the side entrance of the galley; by cutting across the kitchen, he would emerge between the antagonists. Before bursting in, he stopped to catch his breath, then pushed the door open and casually strolled into the melée.

"*Boker tov*," he boomed. "*Bonjour, bonjour*. Good morning."

Startled by his sudden entrance, everyone froze. Ben smiled. "Such a loud argument so early in the morning. You'll wake everyone on the ship." In French, he asked the baker for a moment's patience, then turned to the *Ostjuden* with a raised eyebrow. "Is there any special reason why you decided to attack the ship's baker and his assistants?"

"We weren't attacking him," one of the *Ostjuden* replied sullenly. "We were just trying to disarm them."

"Disarm them?"

The sullen *Ostjude* seemed to be the group's leader. "We're not going to be beaten any more. We came down here to get something to eat and when we saw them with the clubs, we decided to fight back.''

Ben looked at the baker. He was a big man and his stove-pipe chef's hat made him look even taller, but he was unarmed except for the breadboard. His assistants carried long loaves of French bread, cradled in their arms like firewood. Ben didn't see any weapons, just two terrified young men with flour-smudged faces. The *Ostjude* jabbed an accusing finger in their direction.

"Why don't you ask them where they were going with armloads of clubs at five o'clock in the morning?"

"Clubs?" Ben stared at the *Ostjude*. "Those aren't clubs, they're loaves of bread." Ben turned to the baker. "*Ils pensent que les baguettes sont des casse-têtes.*" Ben hoped that "head-breaker" was the right term. "*Vous connaissez? Peut-être un bâton.*"

The astonished baker turned and grabbed one of the loaves. "*Un bâton?*" he laughed. "*C'est du pain. Pain.*" The Frenchman shook the loaf at the dumbfounded *Ostjuden* in front of him. In the yellowish half-light of the mess hall, it looked exactly like a club.

"Bread doesn't look like that," the sullen *Ostjude* protested.

"It does in France," Ben grinned. "It's called a *baguette*. If you don't believe me, take a bite."

The suspicious *Ostjude* reached out and snatched the *baguette* away from the baker. Cautiously, he bit into one end; surprise spread across his face. "It is bread," he announced. The *Ostjuden* gathered around, touching the *baguette* for themselves.

Now that the situation had been defused, Ben was concerned about the three Frenchmen; bad blood between the crew and the passengers on the first day out would not bode well for the rest of the voyage. He tried to explain to the baker and his assistants how nervous and inexperienced the *Ostjuden* were, but it was difficult to rationalize how a dozen grown men had mistaken loaves of bread for clubs. To his relief, the Frenchmen found the entire misunderstanding quite humorous and reassured him they held no grudge. The baker then turned on the main lights and invited everyone to sit down to breakfast. When Ben left to wash up, the *Ostjuden* and bakers were laughing together and trying to communicate in sign language.

By the time Ben returned to the mess hall; the long benches were already jammed with people. Generous pots of creamery butter and homemade marmalade dotted the scarred wooden tabletops, and an endless supply of hard-boiled eggs and *baguettes* streamed from the galley. The hungry passengers devoured the food as quickly as the waiters brought it in and the ship's ovens ran continuously, turning out scores of fresh, hot loaves.

Ben savored his simple breakfast of bread, eggs, and strong black coffee, enjoying the spirited camaraderie that prevailed in the mess hall. The story of the "clubs" had already circulated through the ship, giving everyone on board the first decent laugh they'd had in days. The men who had been involved became minor celebrities, grinning sheepishly at the goodnatured ribbing and host of practical jokes that descended on them.

Children raced between the tables, whacking each other with the crusty *baguettes* until somebody's mother spoiled the fun by taking the bread away. Then they would run back to the kitchen where the sympathetic bakers would arm them again and the battle would begin anew.

As Ben sipped his second cup of coffee, he noticed two men standing alongside the table. He recognized the shorter of the two as Kopel Farkelstein, a bent-over Polish Jew who reminded him of Yitzakh. At first glance, Kopel and his friend appeared to be talking idly, but every so often, one would slip a *baguette* down one of his trouser legs. Ben watched them hide four or five loaves before he rose from his bench. When they saw him coming, they tried to hurry from the mess hall.

"Just a minute," Ben called out. The men stopped and turned to face him. They both flushed with embarrassment. Farkelstein started to stammer an explanation, waving one hand in the air and using the other to keep the *baguettes* from slipping down his trousers.

"Relax, Kopel. You haven't done anything wrong," Ben smiled. "I was just curious as to why you would steal your own bread."

Kopel Farkelstein nervously fumbled with the buttons on his coat, debating a range of excuses. He was a terrible liar; even small lies unnerved him. Everyone always knew when Kopel Farkelstein was telling less than the whole truth. Sweat would bead up and trickle down his forehead. He would become self-conscious and confused. And halfway through, he would forget what he had intended to say, trapping himself in his own story.

Kopel had always envied people who were able to save themselves from embarrassment with a harmless white lie, and tried desperately to think of a good reason why someone would hide *baguettes* in their trousers. Nothing came to him. The truth was that he had taken the bread out of fear, and the prospect of admitting that fear to Ben filled him with humiliation. Ben waited patiently for him to speak.

"Don't you think it's a good idea to keep a little something stowed away?'' Kopel finally mumbled. He looked up and saw the quizzical look on Ben's face. ''What if there's an emergency? What if they run out?''

Ben nodded with understanding. Since the war, most of the *Ostjuden* had lived hand to mouth, day by day. They never knew what tomorrow would bring; security was a matter of knowing that there would be food on the table for the next meal. Ben guessed that half the people in the dining room had squirreled away a loaf or two, just in case.

''There's enough food on board for twice our number,'' Ben smiled. ''Just ask, anytime, and they'll give you all you can eat. If you take it back to your cabin, the only ones who will end up enjoying it are the rats.'' He pointed to a sign in French, Yiddish, and German that warned passengers not to remove food from the mess hall.

''Besides, don't you remember what happened when the manna rained down from heaven and the people tried to hoard it? It just rotted. French bread is no different—it goes stale in a day. Now, why don't you and your friend brush the crumbs out of your underwear and go topside for some fresh air? Relax and enjoy the trip.''

Farkelstein hesitated, then pulled the *baguettes* out of their hiding place and set them back on the table. His friend followed suit.

''Old habits die hard,'' Kopel whispered softly.

After they left, Ben tossed the bread into a trash can and as he stepped away, he collided with a young man. They both stumbled.

''Oh my God, Ben, I'm sorry. I didn't think you were going to turn around.'' Yuri Grodberg's face was filled with concern.

''No harm done,'' Ben grinned. He had met Yuri Grodberg just once before, through Sophie, and had taken an immediate liking to the young Russian. Ben motioned to the bench in front of them. ''Why don't you sit down and have some breakfast?''

''I haven't time to talk,'' Yuri quickly replied. ''Do you know where Sophie is? I've looked everywhere and can't seem to find her. I wanted to . . .''

''Sit,'' Ben ordered. Yuri hesitated a moment, then sighed and sank down on the bench. He pulled a gold cigarette case out of his breast pocket and picked out a Gauloise. As he lit it, Ben noticed his hands were trembling. When Ben asked if there was something wrong, Yuri wouldn't meet his gaze.

''I was just looking for Sophie,'' he said defensively. ''I got nervous when I couldn't find her.'' Ben knew from Sophie that she and Yuri had been drawn to each other ever since they first met on the Marseilles Express.

Yuri Grodberg was no more than nineteen. He was slender but not frail, and had an almost feminine beauty. He had pale, sensitive features and eyes the color of gentian, set off by long blond lashes. High cheekbones and a finely chiseled nose gave his face an aristocratic cast, without the arrogance that usually implied. Yuri had a natural openness about him, a trusting innocence that appealed to the maternal instincts of every woman on board.

"Do you think Sophie is avoiding me?" Yuri blurted out. Although Ben had known him for less than a week, Yuri struck him as a well-educated, self-possessed young man—not the type inclined to adolescent insecurities.

"Sophie is very fond of you and you know it." Ben eyed him closely. Yuri looked strained and tense, and there were dark circles under his eyes. It was hard to believe he was so upset over not finding Sophie. When Ben told him that Sophie and Sarah were up on the promenade deck, organizing Hebrew lessons for the children, Yuri practically bolted from his seat. Ben grabbed his forearm and gently drew him back to the bench.

"Yuri, you're a bundle of nerves. And it isn't because you spent an hour looking for Sophie. I want you to tell me what's wrong."

Yuri hesitated, searching Ben's eyes as though debating whether or not to trust him. "I . . . I just feel strange. Out of place, maybe." Unconsciously, he straightened his tie.

Yuri's eyes darted around the messhall. The long tables were still occupied by dozens of *Ostjuden* enjoying a leisurely breakfast. There were two or three arguments raging over a Talmudic passage, and people were laughing, talking, and gossiping as usual—nothing out of the ordinary. Throughout the crowded room, people ate with gusto, smacking their lips and licking their fingers. Ben caught the expression of distaste that creased Yuri's handsome features.

Yuri Grodberg's family were wealthy Russians from St. Petersburg. Like Sophie, Yuri had enjoyed a sheltered and privileged existence until war and revolution had destroyed his world. Yuri's mother had died of influenza during the war; his father, though well connected and influential, had been arrested by the Communists in 1919 and simply vanished. Overnight, Yuri's way of life had disappeared, and he shuttled from one recently impoverished relative to another until he found himself an unwelcome burden wherever he went. It was then that he decided to go to Palestine.

Everything about Yuri was refined and elegant. Though his clothing was threadbare, he was fastidious about the way he dressed; Ben had often wondered how Yuri never seemed to be without a freshly starched shirt.

His tailored gray suit, his aristocratic accent, and his formal manners set him apart from the homespun gruffness that characterized the black-coated, heavily bearded *Ostjuden*. Although he was well liked, Yuri had nothing in common with most of his fellow travelers.

In the old days, Russian Jews in Yuri's class looked upon the Jews of the Pale—Jews like most of the *Ostjuden* on board the *Asia*—as no different from their Russian orthodox counterparts: uneducated, crude, superstitious, and coarse. It was a class prejudice, not a religious one, but Ben had noticed Yuri always referred to himself as a "Russian," never as a Jew.

The more fortunate of Yuri's peers had fled to France, where the right connections and enough money ensured a comfortable niche in Parisian society. Wealthy Russian Jews were considered emigrés, or political exiles, and were exempt from the usual prejudice and resentment reserved for Jewish refugees. Yuri would have been at home in Paris; aboard the *Asia*, he was an oddity.

It was a measure of Yuri's character that he evidenced no bitterness over the direction of his life. He had lost everything—family, friends, home, and he was desperately lonely. But there was no trace of self-pity in him, only a wistful longing to belong somewhere.

"I don't mean to sound like a snob," Yuri explained anxiously. "I guess I'm just different from the rest of the people here. I don't fit in. Palestine will probably be even worse."

"You're not as 'different' as you think," Ben laughed. "Everyone on this ship is just like you. None of them has a place they can truly call their own. That's what Palestine is all about. Palestine will forge us into a nation of Jews, as God intended, and 'Russian,' 'German,' or 'Estonian' will be words that describe where we came from, not who we are."

Ben gestured towards the crowded tables. "They might not talk like you, or look like you, but they're all Jews. That's the important thing to remember."

Yuri looked thoughtful. In his world, being a Jew was something one downplayed as much as possible. If you were a Jew in St. Petersburg, nothing killed a career faster than practicing your religion. His family had never even bothered to observe Hanukkah or Passover, and no one had ever instructed him in Judaism.

"I think I have a lot to learn," Yuri said quietly. "Sometimes, I get so confused . . ."

Ben reached out and ruffled Yuri's short blond hair. "I know one thing you're not confused about."

There was a question in Yuri's eyes.

"Sophie." Ben laughed. "I've got one stop to make, then we'll find her and Sarah."

Yuri grinned broadly. Ben was right, Sophie was the one thing in his life he had no doubts about.

Stopping to check on Zelda was certain to set off fireworks, but Ben wanted to be sure that the children were well and that Zelda was comfortable, if not happy.

He and Yuri found Zelda in her assigned cabin, lying on a lower bunk with a wet facecloth across her forehead. Mendele and Dianele were playing quietly until they spotted Ben. They jumped into his arms, shrieking with joy.

Zelda lifted the edge of the compress to glare at him. She threw the cloth to one side and sat up on the bunk.

"So, Mr. Bigshot, Mr. Ringleader, Herr Kapitan—I see you're finally able to spare a minute to see if we're still alive. All night I waited to see if you would ask after us! All night! If you brought poor Yuri with you for protection, you can forget it."

Yuri blushed with embarrassment.

"Zelda . . ." Ben sighed.

She jabbed a finger at him. "Do you see my eyes? How red they are? How exhausted I look? Not one wink did I sleep. Not a wink! If it weren't for Mottel Rubinstein, I don't know what we would have done. I thought you were different, more . . ."

While Zelda continued to harangue Ben for his lack of interest in her and the children, Yuri kept his eyes fixed on the deck.

Ben listened tolerantly to her list of complaints until she started to repeat herself. Gently, he interrupted her.

"I have to leave now, Zelda, but if you and the children need anything, let me know." He bent down and kissed the children, then led Yuri out the door.

Zelda crossed her arms defiantly. "We can do just fine on our own," she shouted down the corridor.

When Ben saw the horrified expression on Yuri's face, he started laughing. "Don't worry. Zelda's just exercising her prerogatives as a helpless widow. She'll be fine by tomorrow."

"Helpless?" The look on Yuri's face was a picture.

They found Sophie and Sarah just where Ben expected to find

them—up on the promenade deck, surrounded by children. Sarah saw them first and waved.

"Yuri!" Sophie shouted excitedly. She ran over breathlessly and they stood staring at each other in comfortable silence. She hardly noticed Ben, who suddenly felt like an intruder. Their love for each other was so plain for anyone to see that Ben wondered how long it would be before they told each other. Not long, he guessed. There was an almost visible electricity that jumped the gap between them; they both looked ready to burst. Yuri listened to Sophie chatter happily about the children and how much she enjoyed teaching them, then shyly made a request.

"You know, I speak German, Russian, English, and French, but the only words I know in Hebrew are *shalom* and *l'chayim*." Yuri hesitated. "Do you think you could teach me Hebrew?"

Sophie smiled and reached out for his hand, then led him towards the circle of children. He took a seat next to her and opened a Hebrew grammar book she handed him as though it was a sacred object. Ben doubted that he would see Yuri for the rest of the day.

Ben stood on the outskirts of the group until he grew restless, then idly strolled along the railing. The entire deck was dotted by makeshift Hebrew classes clustered around young *hakhsharah* graduates like Sophie and Sarah. Beyond reciting prayers and passages of Scripture, most *Ostjuden* had only a limited knowledge of Hebrew, and hoped to learn enough to survive their first few days in Tel Aviv.

People who hadn't seen the inside of a classroom for thirty years or more balanced notebooks on knees and chair arms, and struggled to conjugate irregular verbs. Ben felt as though he was walking through a gigantic, open-air yeshiva.

Listening to a young Russian boy arguing with an Austrian teenager in halting Hebrew, Ben remembered the emphasis his father had placed on learning the language. Biblical Hebrew had changed very little in two thousand years, but once Jewish pioneers in Palestine began to use it as a living language, thousands of new words and combinations came into being. Anschel had insisted that all of his children not only read and write fluent classical Hebrew, but learn the new words that were evolving every day. To keep abreast of the changes, Anschel had corresponded regularly with Eliezer Ben-Yehuda, a scholar originally from Vilna, Lithuania, who started the first Hebrew-language newspaper in Jerusalem and later founded the Hebrew Language Academy. When Ben-Yehuda published the first Hebrew dictionary in 1909, Ben's father was one of the first purchasers.

Like Anschel Isaacson, Ben-Yehuda was convinced that the creation of a Jewish homeland demanded the revival of the Hebrew language. Almost singlehandedly, Ben-Yehuda had struggled against bureaucrats, public opnion, and even the leaders of the Zionist movement to see that the mother tongue of the Old Testament became an official language of Eretz Yisrael. In 1922, just before he died, the British recognized Hebrew as one of the official languages of Palestine, in addition to English and Arabic.

Aside from their faith, new immigrants would now have a common language to bind them together, a common tongue that would help to forge a polyglot collection of refugees into a national entity. Ben shook his head at the thought of old Rabbi Shulmann back in Dorpat. Like many Jews, the Rabbi had believed the secular use of Hebrew in everyday speech was sacrilegious. Ben wished the old Rabbi could have been on the *Asia*, listening to the language come alive. The words Ben heard were fresh and vital, the voice of an ancient people speaking again for the first time in centuries. It was anything but blasphemous.

Ben had just decided to climb the companionway to the observation deck and find himself a comfortable chaise-lounge when one of the ship's stewards ran up to him. Ben's knowledge of French had earned him the unofficial role of "ship's translator," and whenever a language problem arose, Ben was called upon to mediate. The steward, a stocky Corsican with a handlebar mustache, was extremely agitated and had to repeat himself twice before Ben gathered there was a confrontation on C deck between an *Ostjude* and one of the waiters.

What Ben discovered on C deck was a Polish Jew in his late sixties launching a barrage of Yiddish invective at a French waiter. Ben couldn't remember the *Ostjude's* real name, but he recalled that people had nicknamed him "the Pessimist" for his gloomy predictions and his habit of wearing both belt and suspenders. A huge gray-white beard covered his chest, bristling like the quills on a porcupine as he shouted. Fleck of saliva flew from his lips; he looked exactly like an Old Testament prophet in full fury.

"Mendel!" the Pessimist growled. "Mendel Cohen is my name! What's wrong with everybody on this ship? Can't you even get a simple name right?"

"*Mais, M'sieur!*" The waiter cringed against the railing, desperately balancing his crowded serving tray. "*Je—*"

Enraged, Mendel cut him off. "You see! You did it again! How many times do I have to say it? Mendel! Mendel! Mendel!"

"*Naturellement, M'sieur . . . ,*" the beleaguered waiter pleaded.

"You want a fight, you misbegotten wretch? I'm just the man to give you one!" Mendel lunged unexpectedly and wrapped his fingers around the waiter's throat. The tray clattered to the deck and shards of china flew in all directions. The waiter struggled to free himself, gasping for breath, but Mendel was too strong.

Ben leaped forward and tried to pry the old man's fingers from the waiter's throat, but he couldn't get a decent grip. He gave up when he saw the Frenchman's eyes begin to bulge and simply grabbed Mendel's beard, yanking it backwards.

Mendel released the waiter with a yelp of pain and stumbled to his knees. He clambered to his feet, purple with rage, and started to come at Ben, who had interposed himself between the two men. Ben made no move to protect himself, but simply held up a warning finger.

"Have you forgotten the Commandments, Mendel? You almost killed that man."

Mendel hesitated, then stopped and spat at the waiter over Ben's shoulder. "Did you hear that? My name is Mendel!"

Horrified, the Frenchmen appealed to Ben. "*M'sieur*, you must help me. These people are crazy. Please, *M'sieur*."

"His name is Isaacson!" Mendel bellowed. He took a menacing step forward, but Ben held him at bay. The waiter curled into a ball against a bulkhead, trying to protect himself from Mendel's wrath.

Mendel stood eye to eye with Ben, waving his fist in self-righteous anger. "All I wanted was a cup of tea. When the wretch brought it, he started insulting me."

"How?"

"They call all of us by the same name. They think it's a great joke." Ben shook his head in disbeleif. "You don't believe me? Ask him what your name is."

"Okay," Ben sighed. He turned to the waiter. "Do you know my name?"

"*Non, M'sieur*," he replied respectfully. Mendel howled indignantly and smacked his palms together.

"You see! First he says he doesn't know your name, then he calls you Moishe! It's an insult! They call everyone Moishe! You ask for something they say 'Yes, Moishe!' You wonder what time it is, they say 'Nine, Moishe.' If one of them calls me 'Moishe' one more time, I'll . . . I'll . . ."

To judge by the faces around him, Ben saw that "the Pessimist" was not alone. The other *Ostjuden* standing behind him were equally furious.

Ben felt like laughing hysterically. "He's not calling you 'Moishe.' The French word for 'sir' is *'Monsieur.'* When properly pronounced, it's *M'sieur*. It only sounds like 'Moishe.' He was just being polite."

Mendel eyed Ben suspiciously, and it took another ten minutes of volatile conversation before he grudgingly conceded his mistake. He apologized to the waiter through Ben, then stooped to help the man clean up the mess. The waiter never took his eyes off the old man, as if he fully expected him to cut his throat with a broken plate or try to strangle him again. When the pieces had been stacked on the tray, the waiter backed away and ran down the companionway. He kept looking back over his shoulder.

Mendel watched him disappear, then turned to Ben. "I owe you an apology, Isaacson." He made it sound like a delinquent debt. Ben smiled and told him to forget it. He left Mendel lecturing a group of friends on the dangers of leaping to conclusions and found his way to one of the sun-washed upper decks. He promptly collapsed into a canvas deck chair, feeling like he had been drawn and quartered. His people were not doing very well out of their own element. First the *baguettes*, then "Moishe"; Ben wondered what would happen next.

He had thought the worst was over once the ship left Europe in its wake but he had been wrong. Things were getting worse, not better. The *Asia* should have been a temporary haven where people could relax and regain their bearings. Instead it was more like a pressure cooker, magnifying the tensions and frustrations of everyone on board.

It was like living on a powder keg.

Ben tried to relax, cleansing his mind of anxiety. His own nerves were getting frayed. He closed his eyes, enjoying the luxury of a few quiet moments. The sun felt marvelous on his face.

He spent the following half hour in a state of relaxation that bordered on sleep until the ship's bell roused him from his torpor. He pulled out his watch with a yawn. It was 11:00. He felt rested, more like himself. Since he had an hour or so to kill before lunch, he decided to look in on Dora Hoffmann.

He found her in one of the upper cabins near the bridge, seated behind a wide mahogany desk topped by a green leather blotter. A cigarette dangled from the corner of her mouth. She glanced up briefly, then continued jotting notes in Hebrew with a cheap steel-tipped pen.

She bore no resemblance to the Dora Hoffmann Ben had known in Marseilles. Her fine red hair was drawn back severely and pinned up with simple wooden combs; gone were the cosmetics and jewels. In place of a silk dress, she wore khaki shorts and a tan bush-shirt. A thin sheen of perspiration covered her forehead.

She flicked an ash into a horn tray overflowing with stale cigarette butts. "I've been expecting you. Sit down."

Ben eased his frame into a wooden armchair and grinned boyishly. "Well, Madame Hoffmann, you don't look much like a *shadchente* anymore."

"And you don't look like much of a sea captain, either," she replied tartly. She was not in the best of moods. "I understand that there was quite a bit of excitement this morning when the *baguettes* came out of the oven."

"That there was."

Dora pushed her chair back and kicked off her shoes with a groan. "I hope you realize that was only the beginning."

"I know." He told her about Mendel and shared his fears about the escalating tension. Dora agreed.

"People are frantic over papers. It has everyone living on a knife edge."

The ever-present threat of deportation to the port of origin hung over everyone's head like an axe suspended by thread, and at any given time, there were a dozen arguments raging over papers. People who were fortunate enough to possess legal visas and passports were jittery; the presence of illegal refugees aboard the *Asia* meant that the entire ship could be turned away once they got to Palestine. And despite everything the Zionists did to assuage their fears, people without valid documentation knew that discovery guaranteed deportation. No one was safe and the resulting uncertainty had created tremendous tension. So far, the incidents had been relatively minor; that could change at any moment.

"How are we going to deal with this?" Ben wondered.

Dora shrugged. "We'll do what we can to forestall their worst fears. We'll tell them that every contingency has been planned for; every obstacle foreseen; every problem anticipated. We'll ask them to believe that nothing has been left to chance."

"Is that the truth?"

"No."

Dora explained that the original plan had called for smuggling most of the illegals into Palestine right off the ship, but the British had doubled their patrols; smuggling was no longer a viable option.

Dora tapped her pen against the edge of the desk. "We actually have two separate problems. First, we have to keep a thousand people occupied and busy until we get to Palestine. That's more than a week. If we can keep their minds diverted, their imaginations will be less active. Second, we have to figure out a way to slip nearly five hundred illegals into Palestine. We have a way to solve both problems, but it's going to be tricky because of the numbers involved.'' Dora leaned forward, her eyes boring into Ben's. ''What we must do is stage three plays. During those plays, sixty or sevently illegals will be married off to legitimate visa holders. If one person—''

''That's impossible!'' Ben exclaimed. ''They'll never . . .''

''As I was about to say,'' Dora overrode him, ''if one person has a visa, everyone else in his family, including children and grandparents, is legally entitled to enter Palestine. By joining those sixty or seventy couples, nearly all of the illegals will become completely legal. It's the only way.''

''Playing the matchmaker has gone to your head,'' Ben snorted derisively. ''Most of these people are orthodox Jews. They'd never agree to holy vows that involved deception.''

''What if they don't know?''

Ben looked at Dora in sudden understanding. ''You mean forge the certificates?''

''My first choice,'' Dora sighed. ''But we'd need the captain's cooperation and he won't have anything to do with forging certificates. He's either a man of principle or I don't have enough money to bribe him. No, Ben, it's going to have to be real.''

''But how are you going to keep it a secret?'' Ben wondered. ''How are you going to marry them without their knowing it?''

Dora stubbed out a cigarette, automatically lighting another one. Her fingertips were stained a jaundiced yellow.

''There is a way,'' Dora smiled faintly. ''You know how Jews love the theater—there isn't a hamlet in eastern Europe that doesn't have a Yiddish theater or a group that stages a play at least once a year.''

''So?''

''So we're going to stage three plays. During the course of each play there will be a mass wedding with the captain presiding. Everyone will say ''I do'' without hesitation because they'll believe it's all part of the production. In reality, they'll be getting married.''

Ben looked dubious.

''It works, Ben. We've done it before, but never with so many people involved.''

Ben thought for a moment. ''Where are you going to get three plays like that in the middle of the Mediterranean?''

"We'll make them up. I have two 'playwrights' already, and I'm hoping that you'll be the third. It doesn't matter whether the play is good or bad, so long as it centers around weddings and involves the captain—at the appropriate moment, he'll have to marry everyone. Will you do it?"

Ben was still skeptical. "Do you really believe no one will catch on?"

"How? The captain speaks no Yiddish and only a few of the passengers speak French. Even those few who might understand the language would hardly be surprised—the play involves a wedding. They won't be expecting the real thing."

"Signatures on the marriage documents?"

"Same thing—the certificates will be written in French. All we have to do is tell people they're signing another immigration form. When we arrive in Palestine, we'll simply pretend that the plays gave us the idea of extending the charade in order to smuggle everyone into Palestine."

As they discussed the possibilities, Ben began to catch some of Dora's enthusiasm. Actually creating the plays posed no real problem— Yiddish dramas were always centered around the basic problems of everyday life and how ordinary people dealt with them. What was more basic than marriage? Besides providing a way to marry off the unsuspecting illegals to legitimate visa holders, Dora calculated that between rehearsals, staging, and the actual performances, more than half of the passengers could be kept fully occupied for the balance of the voyage. That alone made the plays worth staging.

Ben looked at Dora in admiration. "You know, it's just crazy enough to work. Let's set up some kind of schedule." Ben was to start a draft of his play immediately. At the same time, Dora would compile a list of legitimate visa holders who were single and match the names to unmarried passengers of the opposite sex.

"Just be sure you write a Rabbi into the plays." Startled, Ben turned quickly. A tall man with a ragged beard and thick glasses stood in the doorway. He had obviously been listening for some time.

"With all due respect, who invited you to this conference?" Ben snapped.

The intruder was a scholarly man with an emaciated appearance, commonly accepted as a bona fide, if somewhat eccentric, clergyman. He was known as "the Rabbi" for his habit of chanting prayers to himself in public, but no one really knew whether he was a real Rabbi or not.

"Just write me into the plays," the Rabbi instructed. "It will lend an aura of sanction to the proceedings from the captain's point of view."

"Doesn't it bother you, Rabbi, that these marriages are taking place under false pretenses?'' Ben was surprised by the Rabbi's attitude.

"Don't concern yourself with what bothers me—just do as I ask.''

Ben turned to Dora Hoffmann. "I don't know about—'' She cut him off in midsentence with a wave of her hand.

"You heard the decision,'' she said evenly.

Ben stared at the Rabbi. Through the heavy lenses, his eyes looked distorted and slightly comical, giving him an owlish appearance, but there was nothing comical about the expression on his face. Ben looked from one to the other, suddenly realizing that the Rabbi was the one with the power to make the final decisions. The frail cleric was no different than Kapitan Landsdorf, Madame Hoffmann the *Shadchente*, or Monsieur Lepatron the industrialist. He was just another actor playing out his part. As Ben stared at the innocuous man standing in front of him, the genius of the charade struck him. As a holy man, the Rabbi would be free to circulate, gather information, and dispense advice without incurring suspicion. He could control any situation by using people like Ben and Dora while preserving his own freedom through anonymity. It was simple, devious, and brilliant.

"Let me know when the first drafts are finished,'' the Rabbi murmured. "We have little time and much to do.'' He turned and left the cabin.

Ben looked at Dora, itching to ask a dozen questions.

"Don't bother to ask,'' she warned him. "You know I won't be able to answer. Just write your play and we'll go from there.''

• • •

Sarah poured another cup of strong black coffee and set it down in front of Ben; the coffee helped to keep him awake. He looked up from the script he was working on and gave her a smile.

"Aren't you having any?''

"No,'' she smiled back. Though it was well past midnight, Sarah wasn't the least bit tired. It was the first time she and Ben had been alone since leaving Germany, and she was enjoying every minute.

The officer's mess was deserted; everyone but the night watch had long since gone to bed. Only the low hum of the engines broke the quiet. Ben wrote steadily, filling reams of paper with terse notes and scrawled lines of dialogue. He was determined to come up with a draft of his play before morning. From time to time, he asked for Sarah's help or opinion, and she tried hard to conceal her feeling of pride and excitement when he wrote her suggestions into the play.

She sat across the table from him, content to watch him work. She longed to reach over and smooth the ruffled hair back from his forehead or touch her hand to his cheek. Just being with him was enough to make her heart beat faster and bring a flush to her face. Whenever they were together, Sarah felt like the rest of the world had ceased to exist. She kept hoping Ben would realize that she was a woman, not a child, but he never seemed to notice. Patience, she chided herself. If necessary, she was willing to wait forever. Meanwhile, being together was enough.

By the time they finished the rough draft, it was close to four in the morning. After they cleaned up the dirty cups, Ben saw Sarah back to her cabin.

"See you tomorrow," he smiled tiredly.

"Goodnight, Ben. Sleep well." She watched him disappear down the corridor, her heart aglow.

Ben stretched out on his bunk with a feeling of accomplishment. Writing a play had been easier than he thought, and Sarah's remarkable creative suggestions had made the job that much easier. He was well ahead of schedule.

Sleep did not come immediately, so Ben folded his hands beneath his head and thought about casting his play. Zelda was melodramatic and anxious to get married; now he would be able to oblige her. Smiling with satisfaction, he decided to cast Zelda as the main character. Opposite her, he would cast Mottel Rubinstein. Mottel was a widower with four children and a painful crush on Zelda Glovsky. They would be perfect for each other. Mendele and Dianele would finally have someone else to call *tatte*.

"I should have been a matchmaker," Ben laughed out loud.

Ben was up by six the next morning, shaved, dressed, and ready to begin. He was surprisingly refreshed and alert after just two hours of sleep. Over breakfast, he met with Dora and the two men who had written the other plays. They spent a half hour exchanging ideas, then broke to begin the work of recruiting participants.

At first, Ben had worried about generating enthusiasm for the plays, but his fears proved groundless. The news spred like wildfire and the three directors were surrounded by a host of would-be actors and actresses, clamoring to be considered for one role or another.

They started casting late that morning and the line of candidates stretched through the mess hall, out into the companionway, and onto the deck. Even though they were only interested in unmarried people with and without visas, the directors agreed to audition anyone who wished to try out. There was no point in raising any suspicions.

Auditions were an experience Ben would never forget.

His first aspirant was a stout grandmother in her late sixties. She wore a baggy dress with a faded floral pattern and black lace-up boots that were obviously too large for her. Awkwardly, she clomped across the improvised stage to Ben's chair and introduced herself as Ida Goldblum. Her dentures slipped when she spoke, but she crammed them back into place without missing a beat.

"I'm a dancer," she announced. When Ben asked her what kind of music she preferred, she chose the quadrille; Ida Goldblum was a woman of traditional tastes. Ben nodded to Abraham Schoenfeld, who sat at a battered piano bolted against the mess hall bulkhead, and Schoenfelt began to play the introductory bars.

"No, no, no," Ida admonished him. "Do I look like a cripple? Faster, faster."

Schoenfeld shrugged and increased the tempo slightly.

"Faster!" she yelled.

Schoenfeld looked at her, his dark eyes sparkling with amusement, then tripled his speed. Poor Ida was left behind during the second bar.

"All right, all right," she conceded. "So maybe a little slower would be better."

Ida began to dance, humming the music in a different key. She stumbled every third step, frequently lifting her dress to display a pair of spindly legs roped with varicose veins. Her boots were fitted with steel plates on the heels and toes that rattled against the iron deck like a radiator full of air. To judge by the rapt expression on her face, Ida Goldblum was seventeen years old, with a ripe figure that any man would be a fool to ignore. In reality, she was a one-woman disaster.

Ben ran his finger down the list of marriage candidates, praying that Ida Goldblum's name was not there. The thought of having to cast her in any part filled him with dread. Dora leaned over his shoulder.

"The Lord has been kind," she whispered. "Ida's husband is alive and well on B Deck. You'll be relieved to know that he is the holder of a bona fide capitalist visa."

Ben smiled in gratitude, then signaled the pianist to stop playing.

"Thank you, Ida. We'll let you know."

"But I wasn't finished," she protested. "You've missed the soul of my performance."

"Everyone gets just two minutes. I'm sorry, but there just isn't time for more. We'll let you know."

"Well, I want you to know that I was regarded as the finest dancer in all of Kaunas, Lithuania!" she huffed indignantly. "I danced with the best and if you think I'm going to—"

Gently, Berzig escorted her off the floor, sympathizing with her outrage.

By setting up three stations, and limiting everyone's audition to just two minutes, the three directors managed to finish just after ten that evening. By then, they had seen every imaginable kind of performance— jugglers, comedians, singers, and thundering recitations. One man had demonstrated his ability as a contortionist; another had fainted from stage fright the moment he stood up. To his astonishment, Ben auditioned two dancers who were actually worse than Ida Goldblum.

The one performance that commanded everyone's attention con- sisted of a husband and wife who played the roles of two angry people blaming each other for failing to get a part in the plays. Ben thought it was a brilliant and original idea for an audition, and was deeply impressed until one of the other directors, a man named Silverman, dryly pointed out that the couple had already tried out earlier in the day. Their dramatic perform- ance was a domestic quarrel, not an audition.

When the last audition was over, the exhausted directors moved from the mess hall to Dora Hoffmann's office.

"I haven't had a moment's peace since we started this morning," Silverman laughed. "Everyone I know is strong-arming to find out who's going to get the lead parts."

"Let's get to business," Dora said brusquely. Ben wondered why she was so reluctant to allow herself a laugh or a genuine smile. She did her job well, but without seeming to enjoy it.

"I'll begin by running down the list of couples, then you can match them to parts," Dora said. She began to read off the people she had matched together. "Geller and Kaminski; Greenblatt and Pearlman; Cheminsky and Hofner; Horshow and—"

"Wait a minute," Ben interrupted. "You can't possibly match Sophie Hofner to Morris Cheminsky. She's in love with Yuri Grodberg."

"I don't really care who she's in love with," Dora retorted. "Neither Sophie nor Yuri have any papers. They have to be married off to legiti- mate quota holders or they'll never get into Palestine."

"No way. I want them married to each other," Ben insisted stub- bornly. "I'll give her enough money to qualify for a special visa, then Yuri can enter on her papers."

Dora lit another cigarette, making no effort to conceal her irritation. "I thought I was supposed to be the matchmaker. I hope the rest of my list will meet with your approval.'' She shoved the list across the desk to him. He surprised her by scanning it. A frown creased his forehead.

"You've got Sarah marrying that obnoxious little Polish boy. You can't do that to her. She has to stay single.''

"Just what do you expect me to do?'' Hoffmann exploded. "Even with the weddings, I'll still have more than sixty people without papers. The Polish boy has papers, Sarah does not. They can get a divorce the day after we arrive in Palestine. None of these couples are going to stay together. It's a charade, remember?''

"I'll capitalize her,'' Ben retorted. He was determined to have Sarah remain single.

Dora threw up her hands in disgust. "Do what you like. Anything else?''

"I noticed that you left Zelda Glovsky unassigned. Why?''

A humorous expression came over Dora's face, and she looked at Silverman with a nod. Silverman cleared his throat.

"We assumed you would prefer to assign her yourself, Herr Kapitan Landsdorf.'' Silverman's eyes danced merrily. "We thought you might want to marry her so she could enter under your visa.''

Dora smiled with satisfaction at the look of horror that crossed Ben's face. Without speaking, Ben penciled in the name Mottel Rubinstein next to Zelda's.

When he looked up at Dora Hoffmann, the thought occurred to him that she might have a sense of humor after all.

NINETEEN

The Plays
February 10th, 1925

When the role assignments were posted outside the mess hall early Monday morning, shrieks of delights and triumphant cheers were counterbalanced by catcalls, derisive hoots, and groans of disappointment. Rehearsals and readings were scheduled to begin at nine sharp, and those who had been chosen for key parts basked in the envy of their friends.

Ben decided to tell Zelda in person that she had been selected for the leading role in his play. It was his way of making a peace offering, he told himself, but he did relish the vision of Zelda Glovsky exchanging valid marriage vows with Mottel Rubinstein.

As usual, Zelda was in her cabin. Mottel Rubinstein was with her. When Ben told her the news, she was ecstatic.

"Me? You want me to star in your play? Oh, Ben, I won't fail you—you won't be sorry, you'll be so proud of me. I used to see every production the Yiddish theater in our town put on. You and I will be perfect opposite each other." She was already posturing. "My mother always said I'd make a wonderful actress."

Your mother was right, Ben thought to himself. He smiled generously and explained that being the director precluded him from taking a part; Mottel had been chosen as her leading man. Zelda looked crestfallen; once again, she had misread Ben's motives.

Ben turned to Mottel. "What do you say? Would you play opposite Zelda?"

"I'd be honored," he answered shyly. "If Zelda doesn't object."

"Of course I don't mind, Mottel." Zelda recovered quickly; if she could not have Ben, Mottel would do just fine. But she didn't want to make it too easy for either of them. "You're a very nice man, but I wonder if you have the necessary experience . . ."

"With you coaching him, Zelda, I'm sure he'll have no problems at all." Ben handed them each a copy of the script and suggested they start practicing right away.

"Full rehearsals begin tomorrow," he warned them.

The first day was consumed with organizing the actors and blocking out the play. As Ben and Dora had hoped, the activity and excitement focused attention on opening night and diverted people from the issue of papers. Everyone seemed more relaxed, and with the exception of a few minor problems, the day passed without incident.

The following morning, Ben held his first full rehearsal with everyone walking through their parts and reading aloud from the script. Zelda had a great deal of trouble with her lines and kept losing her place. Mottel tried to help her, but she became increasingly agitated until she finally threw the script to the floor in a fit of pique.

"I can't possibly deliver these lines!" she complained. "I'm supposed to be a woman of the world! A woman of experience! These lines make me sound like a *kleinshtetldike chaye*— a small-town hick!"

Ben rubbed the bridge of his nose and forced himself to be patient. "The character you're playing is a pious widow who has spent her entire life in the same town. She's a modest, simple woman struggling to fend for herself and her family without a husband. She's supposed to be shy and unsophisticated. Trust me. Once you have your lines memorized, you'll see how the part comes together."

"You're trying to make me look like a fool!" Zelda pouted.

Mottel walked over and took her hand in his. "Zelda please. It's just a part."

"Well, I have to act it out. I should have some say."

"You're doing a wonderful job," he gushed. "Your character is so alive and vibrant. I feel so awkward by comparison."

"Oh, Mottel," she melted. "You've already memorized most of your lines, and I hardly know mine."

Mottel shrugged modestly. "Why don't you and I run over our lines together while Ben works with the rest of the cast?"

Relieved, Ben watched him lead Zelda to a corner of the mess hall. Unconsciously, Mottel Rubinstein provided Zelda with something she desperately needed: he worshipped the ground she walked on.

The balance of the day was hectic and exhausting, and when the three directors finished after-dinner rehearsals, the casts were only too grateful to go straight to their bunks. The plays absorbed everybody's nervous energy, leaving no time to worry about anything else.

After the mess hall emptied, Ben walked out on deck. It was a bright Mediterranean night, with the moon coloring the water a silver gray. A slight breeze barely rippled the surface, carrying with it a hint of Africa. He closed his eyes and took a deep breath, savoring the fragrance.

"How are rehearsals going?"

Ben opened his eyes to find Dora Hoffmann standing next to him at the rail. She readjusted the light gray sweater covering her shoulders and smiled at him. She looked different; softer, he thought. The hard lines of tension were gone from her face and Ben realized how attractive she was, even without makeup or jewelry.

"I'm not really sure that opening night will be able to top rehearsals," Ben laughed. He told her about some of the comical mishaps that had occurred, and she laughed with him. Everyone but Mottel had trouble with their parts, and Zelda had been so nervous that she delivered the same line incorrectly eight times in a row. Progress on the other plays was running about the same.

When he asked about the rest of the passengers, Dora told him that the only ongoing problem was Boris Platzsky. Having recovered from his bout with the French medics, Boris suddenly developed another series of complaints related to his liver. He had insisted on remaining in the infirmary and Dora had decided to leave him there, where his imagined "illnesses" would upset the least number of people.

"It sounds like you have everything under control," Ben smiled.

"Thanks to you and the other directors, Ben. I think you've done a superb job."

The compliment came as a surprise to him.

Dora Hoffmann was an enigma to Ben. At first, he had assumed she was exactly what she appeared to be: dedicated and serious, with a temperament forged from steel. On reflection, he hardly thought of her as a woman; she seemed to be almost sexless, a human machine driven by a single purpose. But just when he thought he understood her, she would surprise him by revealing yet another facet of herself and set him to speculating again.

In many ways, Dora's personality irritated Ben. She was authoritative, demanding, and not always appreciative. She had an uncanny knack of honing in on his weakest traits, and he frequently resented the way she manipulated people, particularly him. But at the same time, he admired her courage, her decisiveness, and her tireless energy. In those respects, she reminded him of Bluma before the shooting. Dora Hoffmann was one of a kind, he decided, and he liked her; he just wasn't sure where he stood in her estimation. He wondered if he subconsciously resented taking orders from a woman.

As they watched the foaming waves curl back from the *Asia's* prow and ripple away, Ben sensed the warmth beneath her facade of brusque competence, but he wasn't quite sure how to respond to it, so he said nothing. He was content to simply stand and watch the shifting pattern of the waves, waiting for Dora to speak.

"The world really does differ from place to place," she mused, breaking the silence. "When you travel, everything changes—even the air smells and feels different."

"Berzig told me that you've made this trip eight times. Don't you ever get tired of it?"

"Yes . . . and no. Every time Jaffa comes into sight over the prow, with the sun rising directly behind it, I vow that I'll never make this trip again. Then a few weeks go by, a telegram arrives, and before I know it, I'm on my way back to Europe."

"But why?" Ben was genuinely curious. "How did you get involved in all this?"

"The same way everyone on board did. I drifted into it. No one with a choice leaves the land of his birth gladly. No one voluntarily leaves the warmth of their home and family to travel thousands of miles to an unknown land. No happy person embarks on a dangerous journey willingly—only the rootless, the homeless, and the desperate."

"I haven't known you very long, Dora, but you don't strike me as rootless, homeless, or desperate."

Slowly, she turned away from him and clasped her arms around herself. "The sea is a frightening thing, Ben. It has an allure all its own. When it's too deep to see the bottom, it looks solid and firm. When you touch it, it seems too soft to be dangerous. But it can turn and swallow you without a trace."

She was no longer smiling. There was a melancholy sadness in her voice, as though she was about to take out an old family heirloom that had been locked in a closet for years and wipe the dust from it for him to see.

"I guess you could say I'm here because of my husband," she began. "Oscar was a thoroughly decent man, and that's a rarity anywhere. He was a first-rate trial lawyer with a highly successful practice in Poland. After we were married, we moved to a small town in Germany.

"It wasn't easy leaving a safe, comfortable life for the narrow-minded bigotry of rural Germany, but Oscar felt he was 'needed' more in a place where Jews were abused as a matter of course. No one wanted the kind of cases Oscar took; there was plenty of risk in representing destitute Jews, but no money. That didn't bother us.

"Oscar believed that Jews had to stand up for other Jews in need. I was very young then, Ben, and I shared his ideals. I was proud of him and what he was doing.

"One day, an *Ostjude* was accused of raping a young German girl. He was an intensely religious boy; quiet, studious, and devout. The charges were ludicrous, but by the time he came to trial, the town had been whipped into a fever. I don't have to tell you what that's like.

"I remember Oscar telling me the morning of the trial that despite all the hatred and prejudice, if we placed our trust in the law, we had nothing to fear. People respected the law and would obey it, if they understood it. All he had to do was show them. Oscar had great faith in the law.

"He defended the boy brilliantly and the judge had no choice but to acquit. Believe me, it was a genuine victory."

Dora paused to light a cigarette. As she inhaled, a cold foreboding encased Ben's heart. Somehow, he knew what she would say next.

"On his way back from the trial, they stopped my husband and put a bullet in the back of his head. They left a sign hung around his neck. It said: 'Here's real justice for the Jews.' They killed the boy that night."

"Oh, God," Ben whispered. He didn't know what else to say.

"It seems like a lifetime ago," Dora sighed. "Sometimes I even wonder if it really happened at all. It seems like some other woman had cried those tears."

She thought for a moment, then turned to him, her face illuminated by the faint glow of her cigarette. "I've watched you dealing with problems and crises, resolving petty disputes, taking care of a clinging widow and her children—you never seem to step out of the roles you play. Even when you're talking to Sarah or Sophie, you're still playing a part."

"That's not true," he said defensively. "Sarah and Sophie are very special to me and I . . ."

"And you play the part of a father to both of them, even though Sarah doesn't look at you that way. She's in love with you, you know."

Ben stared at her open-mouthed.

"But that's another matter. What I'm trying to say is that no one can play the game all the time. We're all vulnerable, and sooner or later, we either bend or break. Don't you have anyone you confide in? Anyone you share your fears with? Anyone who listens to your hopes?''

She was reaching out to him, and he suddenly felt very exposed and alone. He stood by the railing, looking out over the tranquil Mediterranean with an aching heart. He wanted to share his feelings with this knowing and sensitive woman, but something seemed to block the words.

"It's only for tonight, Ben," she said, resting a hand on his forearm. "People like us need to open up once in a while, to keep from going sour. We each have our own needs to be satisfied and our own fears to be buried. It's not a sign of weakness to admit it, Ben. It reminds us that we're human, just like everyone else."

Speaking slowly at first, then with increasing momentum as his emotions took hold, Ben poured out his loneliness to Dora Hoffmann. He told her about Dorpat and Berlin and the days shared with Bluma; about Sweden, his family, and the gold Star of David that he bore to Palestine in his father's name. Some of the feelings he expressed, he didn't even know he had, others had lain in darkness for years. And when he had finished, she hugged him for a while.

They talked like old lovers, comfortably, without pretense or fear. Theirs was a special intimacy, born of the struggles and pressures of extraordinary demands.

"Dora," he asked as they walked towards the *Asia's* stern. "Do you think you'll ever settle in Palestine?"

"I'm not sure I will," she replied. "It seems to be my fate to guide people to the Promised Land, not live there myself."

"Like Moses?" he teased.

She laughed heartily. It was a good sound. Then she pointed out that it was nearly three o'clock in the morning; time to turn in. Dora squeezed his forearm, turned, and disappeared below.

Ben stood at the railing a little longer, cherishing the fullness of the moment. He felt strengthened; Dora had been right. He hadn't realized how much he had needed to talk to someone.

●　　●　　●

The next day was the Sabbath, filled with prayer. All activities were suspended, including rehearsals, and the *S.S. Asia* became a floating temple. A small crisis arose when a delegation of orthodox men asked that the ship be stopped dead in the water because traveling on the Sabbath was expressly forbidden. An argument raged for twenty minutes until "the Rabbi" convinced everyone that it was the ship that moved, not they.

From eight in the morning until noon, the orthodox men chanted and prayed in their fringed prayer shawls, swaying and bowing from the waist. Though a group of younger men stood to the side, shunning the ancient rituals, a feeling of peace and harmony prevailed.

From noon until two, the devout ate and rested, returning to pray until nightfall. As the sun dipped below the horizon, Ben said *Kaddish* for his father, facing the ancient city of Jerusalem. Before long, he thought, I'll be there myself.

Many of the passengers returned to their cabins, fulfilled and emotionally drained by their first Sabbath away from Europe, but most of the younger *Ostjuden* remained on deck. Once freed of the Sabbath's restrictions, they began to sing and dance, their joyful voices traveling over the still water and echoing throughout the ship.

Flushed and excited by their exertions, they were no different than young people anywhere; able to forget the fears of tomorrow in a moment of pure delight at just being alive. As he watched them, it occurred to Ben that the refugees aboard the *S.S. Asia* were beginning to form a community of their own.

•　　•　　•

Early Sunday morning, rehearsals began again. Ben's play, which would unite the greatest number of couples, was scheduled for Monday night. The second play would be staged Tuesday afternoon, and the third Wednesday night.

When Dora broke the news to Captain Lefèvre that seventy or so couples were to be married, he responded with a Gallic shurg. He knew why the marriages had been arranged, but as long as the paperwork was in order, it was none of his concern.

The *Asia*'s crew pitched in enthusiastically, sharing in the growing excitement. With their help, the *Ostjuden* constructed a slightly elevated stage on the afterdeck. Volunteers began setting up chairs for the audience, lights were rigged, and the French deckhands cheerfully sewed together dozens of sheets to use as a curtain. Everything would be ready on time.

Monday morning, final rehearsals began for Ben's play and most of the participants suffered from the opening night jitters. Zelda was among the most anxious, fretting she would forget her lines or make a mistake in front of the entire ship. Mottel was her constant companion, catering to her every whim and reassuring her that she would be magnificent. Without realizing it, she came to depend on him more and more.

By early evening, everyone had the butterflies and few people were able to eat the early supper prepared by the ship's cook. Just before seven, Ben parted the curtain to check the noisy, impatient spectators that packed the afterdeck. Every seat was occupied and people crowded the railings. Members of the French crew filled one of the rear sections, and a special interpreter stood on a packing crate, ready to shout a French translation as the lines were spoken in Yiddish.

Ben felt a sudden presence behind him.

"It's time, don't you think?" the Rabbi asked. Ben nodded, then strode through the curtain to stage center. The crowd greeted him with enthusiastic applause. When the noise subsided, Ben drew a deep breath and began to speak.

"*Shalom*, brothers and sisters, and welcome. Before we begin, I would like to thank the captain of the S.S. *Asia* and his crew for their cooperation and invaluable aid." The audience applauded politely. "Tonight . . ."

"Louder! Louder!" someone bellowed.

"Tonight," Ben yelled, "we'll be seeing the title play of our trilogy, *A Wedding at Sea*. Later in the week, you'll be enjoying *The Necessary Marriage* and *A Marriage Mystery*.

"I can see we're playing to a full house," he continued. "Not many theaters in Europe can boast an audience of over 800 people."

The crowd roared its approval, and Ben was unable to speak until the racket subsided.

"The story you are about to see is as true as any. Zelda Levin and Mottel Rubinstein play a man . . ."

An *Ostjude* named Jacob Rubenstein jumped up with a grin. "Hey—that's my name!"

One of his friends grabbed him by the shoulder and pulled him back down. "You're an 'en' not an 'in,' " the man next to him shouted. Laughter rang through the crowd.

"We hope you'll all enjoy the play," Ben yelled, cutting his introduction short before any more interruptions occurred. He slipped behind the curtain and gave Berzig the signal to begin. To Ben's horror, Berzig shook his head and pointed towards a small group that had formed around Zelda. Ben ran across the stage thinking about the 800 spectators who expected the play to begin immediately.

"Oh, Ben, don't be angry with me," Zelda moaned when she saw him. "I just can't go on."

"Zelda, you'll be fine." He saw that she was genuinely terrified; she wasn't feigning.

"No, I won't be fine, I'll be awful. I'll forget my lines, and I know I look terrible," she wailed.

"Zelda, be quiet," he whispered fiercely. "The audience will hear you."

But it was too late. The first few rows had already overheard Zelda's wailing and roared with laughter while those farther back clamored to find out what was going on. Then, over the laughter of the crowd came the high-pitched voice of an old woman. "*Sei hoben noch nit chasene gehat un men cright sich shein arum*," she cackled in Yiddish. "They're not even married yet and already they're fighting like cats and dogs." That set off a new round of hysterical laughter. Ben was beside himself, but Zelda seemed oblivious to everything but herself.

"Zelda, please," Mottel begged her. "You look great. They'll love you, I know it."

"No, they won't. I've never done . . ."

"There are lots of things you've never done before, Zelda," Ben retorted. "For instance, you've never been happy unless you're at the center of attention, all the time. There's always some reason why you're special or different from everyone else, and frankly, I'm sick of it."

She stared at him in shock. He had never spoken to her that way before. Ben ordered the stage cleared, then turned back to her.

"Now, get out on the stage and just do what you do best: ACT!"

Ben turned on his heel and stalked off, hoping he had made her angry enough to forget her fears. The quality of her performance didn't concern him; he knew that the audience would be more than sympathetic. Nothing appealed more to the Yiddish heart than a lonely widower courting a widow with young children. If anything, Zelda's technical mistakes would endear her to the audience.

That was the intrinsic beauty of Yiddish theater. It was an emotional experience, not a critical performance. Accustomed to staging plays and readings in homes more often than theaters, Yiddish audiences were famous for their enthusiastic participation, which included everything from shouting advice and encouragement to the actors, to actually climbing up on stage to help out. As long as Zelda simply stayed on stage, she'd be all right.

Ben looked to stage center. Zelda was shaking, but her face was determined. Ben signaled for the play to begin.

A string quartet played softly as the curtain opened to reveal a park, with green benches and mock trees. Sarah sat to one side, singing softly with a group of children around a sand box. Couples strolled across the stage, arm in arm. Zelda sat on one of the benches, head down, hands clasped together. Mottel walked on stage and stopped in front of her, snatching his hat off; his knees trembled violently.

Mottel Rubinstein was not an actor by any stretch of the imagination, but his unspoken love for Zelda gave him the courage to walk on stage in front of hundreds of people, and that was half the battle. The audience would help him with the rest. Mottel's feelings for Zelda were a poorly kept secret and rumors began to circulate that the two of them might actually get married; it added a spicy element of suspense to the play.

Mottel kept twisting his felt hat, building his courage. The script called for Mottel to be nervous, and he had no trouble acting the part. When he spoke, the tremor in his voice was real.

MOTTEL. [Awkward and stiff]
Frau Levin, I am a patternmaker in the same factory where you are the bookkeeper.
ZELDA.
I'm afraid I don't really . . .
MOTTEL.
Please, Frau Levin, don't pretend that you don't know me. I know you do. Every day, I watch you through the window next to my work table. I've seen you walking up the street to the factory, dressed in black, with your head bent in sorrow. (He fidgets uncomfortably.) Frau Levin, may I be so bold . . . I mean, would you mind . . . could I . . .
ZELDA. [shyly]
You are Mottel Rubinstein.
MOTTEL.
You know my name?
ZELDA.
I'm the bookkeeper, remember? It's part of my job to know every-one's name.
MOTTEL. [slightly deflated]
Oh.
ZELDA.
Please call me Zelda.
MOTTEL.
And you must call me Mottel. We have a lot in common, you know. It must have been very painful for you when your husband died. I understand, because I lost my wife three months ago.
ZELDA.
I know.
MOTTEL.
You do?

ZELDA. [with compassion]

I have seen you at the cemetery, kneeling beside your wife's grave with your four children. The way you comforted them warmed my heart.

There was nothing special about the dialogue, no great truths concealed in the plot. Zelda and Mottel were two ordinary people, just playing themselves. The audience shared their loneliness and the problems they faced, knowing that their own lives were not much different from the play. People began to sniffle, then cry, and shouts of "Marry him!" broke out spontaneously. By the end of the first act, Mottel and Zelda had captured the hearts of the audience and the curtain closed to thunderous applause.

The stagehands hurried to remove the park props and replaced them with a perfectly reproduced kitchen set that would have been the envy of any European theater. Zelda collapsed into a chair, moaning how terrible her performance had been.

"You were magnificent!" Ben exclaimed without reservation. In truth, she was a fine actress, and her performance had been excellent.

"You're just saying that because you wrote the play."

"And you're just fishing for compliments," Ben teased her. Zelda's eyes sparkled with pleasure as Ida Goldblum touched up the makeup on her face. Ben urged her to hurry; it was nearly curtain time.

"Worry about yourself, Mr. Talent Scout, and leave the makeup to me," Ida glared in response. She still harbored a certain amount of resentment towards Ben over the auditions.

Ida Goldblum had failed to get a part, but she was not the type to sit on the sidelines. She had badgered Ben unmercifully, until he had given her the job of overseeing the makeup crew out of sheer desperation for a moment's peace. She discharged her responsibilities with a vengeance— Ben might be the director, but no one was going on stage until Ida approved their makeup. She put the finishing touches on Zelda, stepped back to admire her work, then pronounced Zelda ready for her public. The actors rushed to their places and the curtain made its lopsided journey upwards.

The second act opened in the kitchen with Zelda's mother scrubbing the floor on her hands and knees. She groaned melodramatically, rubbing her left hip and pretending to wipe the sweat off her forehead. The kitchen door opened and Zelda appeared in a nightgown, her hair disheveled.

ZELDA. [with a yawn]

Mama! Why are you scrubbing the floor at this hour of the morning? It's hardly six o'clock yet.

MOTHER.

So what else should a mother do when her own daughter won't confide in her any more?

ZELDA.

What?

MOTHER.

My own daughter is being courted by a descendant of the great Rabbi Stolzer, and I am the last to find out! Shut me out of your life, if you will, but don't think you can fool your old mother for long.

"Is that really true?" shouted an obese man with greasy black hair. Startled, the people on stage stopped in the middle of the scene. Hyman Cohen was a quarrelsome man with a pendulous belly that rolled from side to side like a tidal wave whenever he walked. Behind his back, the children called him *"Cohen der Grobber"*—Cohen the Fat.

Cohen struggled out of the two chairs he occupied. "Is Mottel Rubinstein really a descendant of Rabbi Stolzer? If he is, we're related!"

Cries of "sit down," "shut up," and "you're blocking our view," echoed across the deck.

"I must know if we're related," Cohen insisted. "I have a right." He was not the least bit fazed by the heckling, and refused to sit down.

Ben saw that Cohen wasn't going to give up and sent a pair of ushers to bring him backstage, where his obstinacy would not interfere with the play. Relishing his self-importance, Cohen puffed up like a pigeon and allowed himself to be led through the audience.

Ben knew that Cohen was using Mottel as an excuse to disrupt the play. *Der Grobber* held a grudge because no one had given him a part in the plays. There was a good reason why—no one liked Cohen *der Grobber*. He was abrasive, obnoxious, and dictatorial. Silverman wouldn't even let him work with the stage hands. Now Cohen was extracting his pound of flesh.

"If you don't send for Mottel Rubinstein this instant, I shall simply walk on stage and see him myself," Cohen said airily.

For one fleeting moment, Ben was tempted to let Cohen walk on stage and let the audience dispose of him, but reason prevailed.

"Tell you what. You can't talk to Mottel, but as long as you're here, we need some help. We've got to have another pole holder for the wedding ceremony. Will you do it?"

Cohen's face lit up. He pretended to be reluctant, but finally allowed

Ben to persuade him. When the stagehands led him away, he was giving orders for all the pole bearers to meet with him for final instructions.

"What next?" Berzig wondered with a broad grin. Ben grinned back, but he felt the sweat running down his sides.

On stage, the play progressed without a hitch. Zelda's mother cross-examined her like a prosecutor until she knew everything there was to know about Mottel and Zelda. Then she pointed out Zelda's perilous circumstances—a widow alone with two small children—and berated her "daughter" for allowing Mottel to dangle.

By this time, the people sitting in the front rows were an integral part of the production, dispensing advice like they were part of the family.

ZELDA. [Hesitating]
  I need some time to think, Mama.
MOTHER. [shouting in frustration]
  Think? Think? He needs a wife and you need a husband. So what's to think about? God give me strength.

Unable to decide, Zelda dissolved into sobs as her mother stormed offstage. Real tears coursed down her face, evoking cries of sympathy from the audience, and one of the old women in the front row actually climbed on stage to comfort her.

As the curtain fell, Zelda graciously led the old woman offstage, just as though it was all a planned part of the play. Watching from the side, Ben was filled with pride and admiration. Zelda played her role like a real professional.

Act III opened on a dining room scene. Six children sat around the long table: Mottel's four and Zelda's two. Zelda insisted that Mottel take his place at the head, while she and her mother sat at the foot. The dialogue began with the two eldest children giving the traditional blessing over the bread.

SHLOMO.
  Hold the bread tightly!
FEIVALE.
  But it's *hot*!

"Have pity on the child! He'll burn his tender fingers!" a woman three rows back cried out. Mendele, who was playing one of the children, started to giggle.

"It's not really hot," he shouted. "It's only pretend."

"The blessing, children. Now." Zelda ad-libbed between clenched teeth.

BOTH CHILDREN.
Baruch atah Adonai, eloheinu melech haolom hamotzi lekhem min haartez.

The entire audience responded as one with a deep "Amen." Then Sophie appeared, dressed in a long, gray maid's uniform, carrying a steaming tureen of stew. She made the rounds at the table, ladling the rich stew into everyone's plate. For the sake of realism, the ship's cooks had insisted on preparing it for the play and its delicious aroma permeated the air.

Before anyone could stop him, a man hauled himself on stage and brazenly picked up a plate. He held it out to Sophie, who filled it, not knowing what else to do. The man started to return to his seat, then stopped and walked back to the table for some bread as well.

"It's delicious," he announced, dipping his bread in the gravy. Ripples of laughter ran through the crowd and people began to stand.

Ben walked on stage and announced that a late supper would be served after the performance, praying the cooks would oblige him. He knew full well that it wouldn't take much encouragement to have half the audience up on stage for dinner.

Delighted at the promise of a feast after the play, the crowd settled down and the scene continued. Sophie left the stage and the courtship ritual began, meticulously orchestrated by Zelda's mother.

When Zelda gently resisted her mother's obvious attempts to bring up the subject of marriage, shouts rose from the audience, begging her to relent.

"You need a husband!" one old woman cried.

"And he needs a wife!" roared a Polish *Ostjude* with nine children. "Believe me, I know. And if he doesn't want that one, I'll take her and he can have my wife gratis!"

The Pole's wife, a short, stout woman sitting next to him, jumped up and seized her husband by the ear. He howled in pain and she yanked him back into his seat and abused him with a violent cascade of Yiddish.

The crowd laughed so hard that Zelda could hardly make herself heard over the noise. At that point, the script called for Zelda to leave the table and go to the parlor. Then Mottel was to follow her and end the scene by proposing, but as Zelda stood to excuse herself, Mottel rushed around the dining room table to her side, forgetting his lines.

"Zelda, let's get married—here and now!" he shouted spontaneously. Suspense gripped the audience. Zelda just stared at him, flabbergasted at his departure from the script.

"Zelda, I love you. I want to marry you tonight. Say you will," he pleaded, carried away by the moment.

Zelda found her voice and tried to stay with her lines. "I think I'll go into the living room and rest a bit."

"Stay!" the audience roared. "Say yes!"

"But who will marry us? We're on a boat." Zelda lost track of what was real and what was part of the play.

"The captain will marry us!" Mottel had forgotten there was a rabbi in the wings, waiting to come on stage during the final act.

"Mottel, it's only a play."

"Say you'll marry me!"

Zelda's response was drowned by the audience, shouting and yelling for her to agree. She collapsed into a chair, nodding her assent; there was no point in trying to stick with the script. Mottel ran offstage to get the captain and the curtain fell on the third act.

Zelda was furious with Mottel. Fortunately, her shrieking was drowned out by the audience's stomping and yelling for more action. Mottel hid behind Ben.

"Don't you dare protect that worm!" Zelda shouted. "He's ruined everything! I'm so humiliated! I'll never be able to show my face on this ship again!"

"Zelda, it's perfect," Ben shouted back. "They think it was all part of the script. All we have to do is improvise the fourth act and carry out the ceremony. They'll never know any different. That audience is hotter than hell, and they think you're a fantastic actress. You can't let them down now."

Zelda stubbornly refused to go back on stage.

While Ben argued with her, Berzig kept everyone backstage moving. The unwitting couples about to be married took their places around the perimeter of the stage, facing the audience like a Greek chorus. A raised podium was brought for the captain and the Rabbi, and the canopy was quickly set up for Zelda and Mottel to stand under. Hyman Cohen harangued his three fellow pole bearers continuously, jabbing his pudgy hand for emphasis, until one of them remarked that if Cohen didn't shut up, they'd set down their poles and drive him from the stage.

The captain appeared in his dress whites. looking more than a little overwhelmed.

"With all the brides and grooms we're going to have, I'll probably have to tell the cook to forget about breakfast," the captain laughed. "There isn't going to be anyone around to eat it." Everyone smiled politely, not understanding a word.

Fortunately, the captain knew only one word of Hebrew: "shalom"; and no one on stage understood French but Yuri, who was so busy looking at Sophie that he never heard anything the captain said.

Once the cast was assembled, Zelda relented and agreed to continue the performance. She turned on Mottel. He shrank under her withering gaze and meekly took his place.

As the final preparations were being made, Ben spotted Sarah trying to wriggle away from Morris Cheminsky's arm. He jogged over to them and grabbed Sarah and tried to lead her towards the wings, but she shook off his hand.

"Ben! What are you doing?"

"I'm sorry, Sarah, but you have to get offstage." He cursed the bullying tone in his voice, but there wasn't time to argue. Dora Hoffmann appeared behind him and tersely pointed out they were running late.

Ben whirled on her. "I thought we had discussed this earlier."

"Just an oversight. Take her offstage and let's get on with the play."

Sarah pleaded with him to let her stay, tears of frustration running down her cheeks. The hurt on her face struck him like a physical blow and his heart skipped a beat when she turned her back on him and ran offstage.

"Places!" Ben yelled. He hoped she would forgive him when she found out the truth.

The curtain opened to thunderous applause. When the noise subsided, the captain began speaking in French, explaining the significance of the ceremony. Only a handful of people understood him at all, and those who did naturally assumed it was part of the play.

On a cue from Berzig, all the couples forming a semicircle around Mottel and Zelda joined hands. Donning his reading glasses, Captain Lefèvre opened a small black book and read the service in Latin. Berzig cued everyone's responses from the wings, through an old-fashioned megaphone. Seven minutes later, the captain snapped the book shut to indicate that the civil ceremony was over and for the Rabbi to continue. The Rabbi gave his blessings in Biblical Hebrew sufficiently slow to simulate its effect. Pandemonium broke out in the cheering audience and the final curtain fell. The players received a standing ovation, and the makeshift curtain rose through two curtain calls, until it collapsed in a heap. The stage flooded with well-wishers and cries of "Mazel tov! Mazel tov!"

Ben leaned against one of the kitchen props and watched the crowds on the afterdeck thin to a handful of small groups.

Berzig had somehow arranged for the late supper Ben had promised and the celebration was gradually moving to the mess hall. Suddenly,

Dora Hoffmann appeared at Ben's side, holding out her cigarette for a light. She waited while he rummaged through his pockets for a box of matches.

"One down and two to go," he grinned, striking a match. She leaned over and drew on the cigarette. "Tell me, Dora. Does it bother you that all these people still think they're single?"

"No," Dora laughed. "My job is to get these people to Palestine safely; nothing else matters. Besides, these couples are all getting a honeymoon cruise, thrown in at no extra charge." Ben smiled at the thought as he took Dora's arm and led her below to join the late supper.

The rest of the week passed without incident, and the second play went smoothly, uniting fifteen couples. Silverman's play was the most professional of the three. His script included a ghost and a family curse which scared the daylights out of everyone. Twenty-two additional couples were wed during the Wednesday performance.

The next morning, Ben and Dora sat down and completed the paperwork on the marriages. Captain Lefèvre had married seventy-two holders of valid visas to seventy-two paperless spouses. Each couple was then assigned parents, grandparents, and children, creating an astonishing assortment. Many of the combinations were not only improbable, they were genetically impossible.

The three plays accomplished everything they were intended to accomplish. They solved the immediate problem of documentation for most of the passengers, they kept everyone's mind off the future, and they provided a perfect catalyst needed to dissolve the stress and tension accumulated during the previous weeks. All together, the plays united two hundred and fifty-three illegals with seventy-two holders of legitimate visas. As they made out the last of the documents, Ben felt exhilarated.

"You know what astounds me the most about this sham?" he said to Dora. "This is all completely legal—we've honored the letter of the law to the last dotted 'i' and crossed 't,' and all it took was a few words in Latin by a French sea captain to a Yiddish audience."

"Why do I feel like it took so much more?" Dora groaned, stretching her aching body. "It's times like this that I dream of a cottage in the Galilee."

"What you need is a husband," Ben observed solemnly.

She did not dignify his suggestion with a response.

●   ●   ●

For Ben, only one sour note remained—Sarah was still enraged. For two days, she refused to speak to him, despite Sophie's pleas on his behalf. When she relented at last, it was to chastise him for his heavy-handed lack of sensitivity. Ben did derive some consolation from watching Yuri and Sophie stroll the deck hand-in-hand like a pair of newlyweds. As far as they were concerned, it seemed, the ceremony had been real.

By Thursday evening, the humidity dropped to nil and the air became increasingly hot. Freed of responsibility, Ben ensconced himself at the *Asia's* prow, where there was at least a breath of wind generated by the forward motion of the ship.

To his surprise, the Rabbi joined him, making small talk for the better part of a half hour. The Zionist chief had never gone out of his way to spend any time with Ben, but all of a studden they were talking about each other's families and past like two old friends sitting around a café table.

Among other things, Ben learned that the Rabbi's real name was Spituna, and that his family were Sephardic Jews from Italy who had eventually settled in Holland. At fifteen, Spituna had run away from home to join an agricultural commune in Palestine. When he was twenty-two, the Zionists had recruited him as a bureau chief for their organization in Stettin. Ben wondered why a man as influential as Spituna would be tapped to shepherd *Ostjuden* to Palestine, and couldn't resist asking.

"This whole *aliyah* is in trouble, Ben," Spituna frowned.

Aliyah was the Hebrew word for emigration to the Land of Israel. Since the turn of the century, there had been four *aliyot*. The first two occurred in the bloody aftermath of the 1905 uprising and the Russian Revolution in 1917.

The third *aliyah* occurred at the end of the First World War and consisted mainly of idealistic young people committed to pioneering new settlements. They were desperately needed. Despite the previous *aliyot* the Jewish population of Palestine in 1919 was still only 58,000.

Ben's group was part of the fourth wave, called the Grabski *aliyah*, after the Polish minister who instigated repressive measures against the Jews throughout the east. It was by far the largest, drawing from the millions of Jews who had fled westward across the German border.

"We can't seem to stem the tide in the east," Spituna sighed. "Germany is bursting at the seams and we just can't relieve the pressure—too many people, too few visas, new regulations. It's getting harder all the time. This shipment has been the biggest yet and it's been hell to manage. A thousand Jews out of the millions waiting for something to happen. God have mercy on us." The Rabbi shook his head in despair. Gently, he placed a hand on Ben's shoulder and told him they were going to have to take some unusual steps to get everyone into Palestine.

"Like what?" Ben asked, his suspicions aroused.

"We may have to make some unscheduled stops. You'll be told when we've made the final decision. Just wanted you to know something was in the wind."

Despite Spituna's sudden interest in him, Ben was not flattered; Spituna never did anything without an ulterior motive. When Ben pressed him, Spituna straightened the *tallis* beneath his coarse cotton shirt and excused himself by claiming they were beginning to attract attention.

Ben speculated on what Spituna had said, but he didn't become alarmed until after dinner that night when Dora Hoffmann pulled him aside and warned him there might be trouble the next day. When he tried to pump her for more information, she cut him off.

"I can't tell you now. Just be prepared."

"Why can't you and Spituna let me in on this?" Ben exploded. "Is there some reason why I was trustworthy yesterday, but not today?"

"You know the rules. All I can say is that we've got to delay getting to Palestine until Sunday."

"The fewer who know, the better," Ben replied with disgust. He was furious. After all they had said and done, and been through together, he was still an outsider, still not trusted enough to become one of the "inner circle." How could he help if he didn't know what was happening? His anger got the better of him and he reminded her that without him, the train would have been returned to Germany.

When she wouldn't meet his eyes, he stopped, suddenly remembering the mocking expression in Villard's eyes after the magistrate granted the Immigrants in Transit status. What had Villard known that Ben didn't?

"Tell me about the magistrate," he said softly.

She looked at him long and hard. "The magistrate in Marseilles was a setup. He was paid off. So was Villard, the customs inspector you dealt with."

Ben recalled the pride he felt at persuading the magistrate to overlook the lack of papers. He remembered the way he had described the scene in the magistrate's office to Dora, and how impressed she had been. All along, Dora had known it meant nothing. It was all a lie.

"And that charade with Alzas?" Ben said bitterly. "Was that prearranged as well? Did you enjoy watching me make a fool of myself?"

"Stop acting like a child, Ben. If you're so insecure that you have to know, Alzas was for real. That's one you pulled off on your own." Abruptly, she turned and left him standing alone in the companionway.

●　　●　　●

He turned in early, feeling badly about his confrontation with Dora Hoffmann. Once again, she had been right. He had acted like a child, but that hardly mattered now. Something was desperately wrong. Apprehension knotted his stomach; why couldn't they just tell him? As he undressed he caught sight of himself in the tiny cabin mirror. His face was drawn and haggard. When sleep finally came, it was shallow and filled with nightmare images.

He awoke sluggishly, feeling as though his blood had thickened in his veins. As he climbed to consciousness, he realized that Sarah was shaking his shoulder, telling him that they had arrived in Palestine.

Fifteen minutes later, Ben stood at the rail with Sarah and dozens of other passengers, staring at the dark streak directly ahead. Everyone strained to catch sight of some detail that would transform the amorphous mass into a landscape with people and trees and buildings.

The sun was just beginning to peek over the horizon, illuminating the port side of the *Asia* with a faint glow. Ben felt a sudden sense of displacement; a nagging concern at the edge of his thoughts. He tried unsuccessfully to pinpoint the source, then gave up, ascribing his unease to exhaustion. He stifled a yawn and pulled Sarah closer to him.

The air had a sharp, spicy aroma, completely unlike the mossy earthiness of Europe. It carried a hot, clean scent that reminded Ben of ironing day in his grandmother's house.

He wondered about the trouble Dora feared. Would they be harassed by the British Navy? Forced to bribe officials? Quarantined? Inspected? At least they were in Palestine. What had she been so afraid of?

"I can see buildings!" Kopel Farkelstein shouted. Everyone at the rail struggled to see where he pointed. The sun climbed higher, revealing farms and palm trees lining the shore. Some one spied an Arab wearing the traditional *jebbalah* and flowing robes.

An enormous city spread out before them, gleaming brightly in the morning sun. Minarets dotted the landscape and from a distance, the whitewashed buildings looked like alabaster.

Eretz Yisrael. The Land of Israel. Silently, the words formed in a thousand hearts.

The centuries of slavery, oppression, and despair were over. All that separated the Jews aboard the *S.S. Asia* from the land of Jacob and Abraham were a few miles of clear blue water. The Diaspora was over. Two thousand years of exile were at an end.

Wishing that his father could have lived to witness such a moment, Ben surveyed the crowded deck with a full heart. As he watched Ida Goldblum waving a brown scarf at the curious Arabs on shore, Ben caught a glimpse of Dora Hoffmann and Spituna out of the corner of his eye. What he saw filled him with foreboding.

They stood on the flying bridge and stared straight over the bow. They did not smile or share in the elation sweeping the deck. Suddenly, Spituna looked down and his gaze met Ben's; his expression was grim. Ben left Sarah at the rail and climbed to the bridge.

Halfway there, he heard a piercing shriek. From his vantage point on the stairs, he saw people milling around in confusion, trying to discover the source of the scream. Someone howled ''Betrayal!'' The crowd took up the word, chanting it with rage and anguish. A young boy Ben recognized came rushing up the companionway.

''You lied to us,'' he yelled, aiming a vicious blow at Ben's face. Dodging to the side, Ben drove an elbow into the boy's gut, knocking the air out of him. The boy gasped for breath and would have rolled down the stairs if Ben hadn't caught him. Ben propped him against the wall and straightened. Numbly, he surveyed the panic on deck.

It was like a scene from Dante's *Inferno*.

There were people on their knees, keening in sorrow; others wandered aimlessly. Parents screamed for their children. A group of men struggled to free one of the lifeboats while members of the French crew tried to stop them. One woman fell against the metal railing at the foot of the companionway, splitting her forehead open. She staggered to her knees, shrieking incoherently, bright arterial blood spurting from between her fingers.

Hesitating for a moment, Ben ran down the steps to the woman's side. He was about to rip the tail of his shirt to make a pressure bandage, but Sarah was quicker. Expertly, she bound the wound with a strip of her slip. The woman moaned softly.

''What is it?'' Ben asked. ''What are you so afraid of?''

''They brought us back!'' she babbled. ''Back into slavery!''

''Stay with her, Sarah, I'm going up to the bridge.''

Setting foot on the stairway, he caught sight of a large warehouse, with white masonry walls and a black tile roof. Storage boxes obscured the writing on the walls, but not the giant white letters on the roof. They spelled disaster in English and Arabic. They spelled the bitterness of exile and slavery: ALEXANDRIA.

Alexandria! Egypt was the land of slavery. Once a year at Passover, every Jew on earth relived the exodus from Pharaoh's bondage. Bitter herbs reminded them of the bitterness of their captivity, and the unleavened Passover bread recalled the haste with which they left. Exodus was a triumph remembered in humility and thankfulness for God's mercy.

The sight of Alexandria before them conjured up centuries of anguish and exile. The *Ostjuden* were in despair.

Ben suddenly realized what nagged him about his first glimpse of the shoreline—it was Dora's remark about seeing the sun rise over Jaffa. The sun should have been dead ahead, not off to port! They had been traveling south, not east!

Boiling with anger, Ben bolted up the remainint stairs to confront Dora Hoffmann and Spituna. He burst onto the bridge, grabbed the Rabbi, and spun him around like a man possessed. Spituna's brown eyes were cold and hard as flint.

"Why? Why? Why?" Ben screamed. "Why have you brought us to Egypt?"

TWENTY

Alexandria
Saturday, February 15th, 1925
5:15 AM

Fear and dismay reigned on deck. Families searched frantically for lost children and relatives. Scores of people wept or moaned, collapsed against bulkheads and railings. There were dozens of cuts and bruises, but few serious injuries. It was just a matter of time before the undirected panic gave way to anger and the *Ostjuden* on deck took matters into their own hands.

For thousands of years, Jews had glorified their escape from Pharaoh's tyranny. Exodus was a living memory, preserved through the generations, an event just as real as though it had happened yesterday. Exodus was a promise of freedom to every Jew, living and unborn, a promise that God had delivered his people from Egypt's cruelty forever. They would not return to the land of Ramses without a fight; they would die first.

Face to face with Spituna, a blind fury clogged Ben's throat; no words would come. With both hands, he seized Spituna by his collar and shook him violently. The heavy glasses flew off. The Rabbi made no attempt to break free of Ben's grasp, but there was a cold-blooded look of contempt in his eyes that infuriated Ben even more.

''You traitor!'' Ben seethed, smashing the Rabbi against a bulkhead. ''Who are you really working for? How much did they pay you to bring us here?'' It wouldn't be the first time someone had sold out a boatload of refugees for money.

"Let him go, Ben,'' Dora said quietly. "There's been no betrayal.''

In response, Ben lifted Spituna off his feet and pinned him against the steel bridge wall.

"I'm not letting him go until—''

Dora suddenly stepped forward and slapped Ben's face. "You arrogant *chutzpenik*. Who the hell do you think you are? Moses? You're part of a team and you'll play the role you've been assigned. Now let him go.''

Ben allowed Spituna to slide to the deck, struggling to control his temper as he turned on Dora. He had trusted her, but whatever Spituna had done, Dora Hoffmann had to be a part of it. She had played him for a fool. Ben's jaws clenched together and his fists balled in anger.

"Don't ever do that again,'' he whispered. The side of his face bore the cherry red outline of Dora's palm.

Dora met his eyes unflinchingly, ignoring the threat in his voice. "Watch the deck, Mr. Isaacson.'' She pointed towards the main cargo hatch. Keeping one eye on Spituna, Ben leaned out over the bridge railing.

Four men dressed in white stood out like a beacon against the dark-suited mob of *Ostjuden*. They were trying unsuccessfully to move towards the rail with a stretcher; on the stretcher was Boris Platzsky. It was impossible to hear anything over the confusion, but Ben saw Platzsky's mouth working in howls of pain. His wife clutched the side of the stretcher, a handkerchief covering most of her face. Ben turned to Dora, his anger undiminished.

"So?''

"Mr. Platzsky developed a sudden case of appendicitis this morning,'' Dora explained. "We're stopping in Alexandria to get him to a hospital. Once people find out, they'll settle down.''

A diagnosis of appendicitis was practically a death warrant. All surgery was dangerous, but with appendicitis, the risk of infection was so high that few people could hope to survive. There was no defense against peritonitis.

As Ben watched, the *Ostjuden* nearest the stretcher stopped milling, and moved back to form a circle. Word spread quickly, focusing everyone's attention on Boris Platzsky, and just as Dora had predicted, the panic began to dissipate. Those farthest away stood on railings and craned their necks to see for themsleves. People closer in murmured their sympathy. On a few of the faces, Ben saw the harsh lines of judgment—there were some who viewed Platzsky's agony as God's punishment for violating the Jewish dietary laws. As silence took hold, Platzsky's screams of pain became audible, sending a tremor of fear through the crowd. Many on board had lost friends, relatives, and children to appendicitis. They all knew that without a miracle, Platzsky's wife would soon be a widow.

Taking advantage of the lull, Spituna stepped to the bridge rail with a megaphone and asked everyone to pray for Boris Platzsky. People were only too anxious to pray; it could just as easily have been one of them lying on the stretcher, waiting to die. As they prayed, the stretcher bearers carried Platzsky to the rail and set him down to wait for a launch. He lay on the stretcher in a fetal position, his screams fading to whimpers. Spituna concluded the prayer with a blessing, then dispersed the crowd without a problem.

"I trust this answers your questions, Mr. Isaacson," Dora said icily. Ben searched her face for the truth. He did not believe for a moment that Boris Platzsky had appendicitis; Platzsky was the excuse for their being in Alexandria, not the reason why.

"An admirable performance," Ben conceded. "But answer me two questions. First, if you knew Platzsky needed a hospital, why did you wait until the last possible minute to tell everyone? And second, why are we really here?"

When Dora started to reply, Spituna held up his hand. He trembled with suppressed rage and Ben recognized the look in his eyes. Spituna wanted to fight. The cold superiority was gone, replaced by undisguised hatred. Ben kept his hands at his sides, hoping Spituna would swing, but the Rabbi managed to control himself.

"You'll be told what you need to know and no more," Spituna spat. "Now get out of my way."

As Spituna strode past him to the companionway, Ben curbed an acid response, gripping the railing so hard that his knuckles turned white. The sound of Spituna's boots on the metal risers faded away, leaving Ben and Dora in an uncomfortable silence.

Dora stared at Ben's clenched knuckles, debating whether or not to disobey Spituna's orders. She knew the Rabbi was a good man and a brilliant tactician, but the continuous pressure had taken its toll. For the past three years, Spituna had driven himself like a man possessed, as though the success or failure of the *aliyah* depended on him alone. He had become obsessed by the threat of British Intelligence and fanatical about security.

When the telegram had arrived the previous evening, instructing them to lay over in Alexandria, it was Spituna who had thought of telling Platzsky he had appendicitis, creating a perfect reason to make the layover. But Spituna had insisted that no one be told of the diversion. Dora had warned him how the *Ostjuden* would react once they realized that it was Egypt that lay ahead, not Palestine. She had urged him, begged him, to circulate word through the ship they were stopping in Alexandria on a mercy mission, but Spituna had refused to listen. He was convinced that the less time the *Ostjuden* had to think about it, the better. He had been mistaken.

Spituna's paranoia was beginning to affect his judgment, Dora thought. It happens when people keep giving more than they have to give. Spituna was not the same man he had been six months before; that man would have avoided a confrontation, not created one.

Dora knew that Ben had every right to be furious, but that was no license to lose his temper. She did not regret slapping him, nor would she apologize for it; she did what the situation called for. But she did feel he was owed an explanation, and there was more involved than her own personal feelings.

It was part of Dora's standing orders to observe and recruit new ''talent'' whenever possible; there was a desperate shortage of agents like Dora and Spituna. It took time and testing to find someone with the right combination of skills and enough of the con man to overcome the kind of obstacles the Zionists faced. People who fit that description were few and far between.

Hers was a thankless, anonymous job, and in three and a half years, Dora Hoffmann had only found two people with the capabilities and inclination to do what she did. Instinctively, she had known from the beginning that Ben could be the third. With enough training and experience, Benjamin Isaacson had the potential to become a first-class operative. It was time to bring him in.

''Benjamin.''

He turned and met her gaze. She saw the maelstrom of conflicting emotions in his deep blue eyes.

''Why don't we go to my office. I think we have a lot to talk about.''

●　　●　　●

The way Dora and Spituna had smuggled nearly five hundred illegals onto the *Asia* was clever and daring, but it had been almost too easy. The British had to know there were illegals on board, yet they had been lax, even careless about gathering evidence. They had not bothered to lodge any formal complaint with the French government and the only effort made to plant anyone on board was Reginald Dobson's clumsy attempt to recruit Ben.

Ever since the ship cleared Marseilles, Dora Hoffmann had been asking herself why. The British were not stupid. Why had their surveillance been so half-hearted? Why hadn't they insisted on a shipboard check after the confusion of the *tummel*? The French were not in love with the British, but they seldom refused a reasonable request—all the British Consul had to do was ask.

Part of the answer had come at sea, a day out of Marseilles, when Spituna had received a coded telegram warning him that British patrols along the coast of Palestine had been doubled. That in itself was nothing unusual. British naval activity increased occasionally, usually as a political gesture to the Arabs; it demonstrated that the British were committed to their agreed policy of controlling illegal immigration. What was unusual was the timing—the day the *Asia* left Marseilles, the patrols had been doubled. It was enough of a coincidence for Zionist Headquarters to order a change in plans.

Routinely, when a refugee ship neared Palestine, *Ostjuden* without legal papers were taken off the ship in international waters, fifteen or twenty miles off the coast. Fishing boats then ferried them to a dozen different locations along the coast between Jaffa and Haifa. Once ashore, the refugees obtained proper visas through marriage or bribery.

Smuggling the entire complement of five hundred illegals had been ruled out by the British deployment. With the patrols doubled, the sheer number of people involved created a logistical problem that invited disaster. For that reason, Spituna had been instructed to arrange the marriages on board the *Asia*, which had left ninety-two men without papers.

Until Friday night, Dora and Spituna had assumed that those ninety-two men would be smuggled into Palestine aboard small fishing boats, as usual. Even though the patrols had been doubled, ferrying ninety-two illegals was still a viable strategy. The telegram that arrived shortly before midnight ruled out that option and confirmed Dora's worst fears.

The British had wanted the *Asia* and its cargo of illegal immigrants to clear Marseilles. They had no intention of interfering until the ship reached Palestine. The reason was simple.

They intended to make an example of the *Asia*.

Under the new rules, if just one illegal was found on board, or even linked to the *Asia*, it provided a legal pretext for returning the entire ship and everyone aboard to Marseilles. The law precluded exceptions or appeals. Any British naval commander who discovered illegal immigrants had the authority to either seize the ship or force it to return to its port of origin.

By making an example of the *Asia*, the British would achieve a number of objectives in a single masterstroke. Most important, it would prove to the Arabs that Great Britain intended to honor its agreements to curtail immigration to Palestine. That alone was political gold; it demonstrated that the British, who were supposed to remain neutral, were in fact choosing the Arabs over the Jews.

In addition, there was bound to be worldwide press coverage of the *Asia*'s return to Marseilles. That kind of publicity would deal a crippling blow to the Zionist refugee organizations. It would destroy their credibility and discourage *Ostjuden* from even considering Palestine as an alternative.

The British strategy was simple but effective. If it hadn't been for a sympathetic Egyptian secretary working in the High Commissioner's office in Jerusalem, the Zionists might well have blundered into the trap.

The Zionist chiefs never made the mistake of underestimating the opposition; if the British navy was looking for the *Asia*, they would find her. Once the *Asia* left Alexandria, the British would stick to her like glue, making any transfer impossible.

As he listened to Dora's explanation, Ben began to appreciate the magnitude of the stakes involved. If the *Asia* succeeded, she would become a symbol, proof that the stream of immigrants from Europe would continue to flow, regardless of what the British did. But if the *Asia* was returned in humiliation to Marseilles, it could take precious months or years to overcome the setback, time the Jews did not have. Many Jews, particularly the orthodox, would point to the Zionists' failure as a sign from God.

Everything hinged on the fate of the ninety-two illegal *Ostjuden*.

"What happens to those men now?" Ben asked. "Do we return them to Europe?" He could see no other alternative.

"That's not possible. We cannot afford to have a single Jew returned." Dora lit another cigarette. "We're going to put them overboard and let the Arabs handle them."

Ben stared at her, dumbfounded. "You must be out of your mind," he gasped. "You can't hand these men over to the Arabs. It's an invitation to a massacre. The Arabs are our sworn enemies!"

"Preconceptions can be fatal in this part of the world, Ben," Dora warned him. "The Middle East is a quagmire, full of contradictions and paradox. One of the first things you'll learn is that there is no such thing as an 'Arab.' "

Patiently, Dora explained to Ben that the Palestinians were the sworn enemies of the Jews, not the Egyptians. Though the overwhelming majority of people in the Middle East were Moslems, their common religion had no bearing on their political views. The Egyptians considered the rest of the Arab world as their social and cultural inferiors, just as most Jews ridiculed the Yemenite Jews as superstitious, ignorant, and backward. The Egyptians regarded their fellow "Arabs" with suspicion and contempt, and far from despising the Jews, the Egyptians viewed them as valued allies sharing a common enemy—the British.

"There is an ancient Greek adage," Dora smiled thinly. " 'The enemy of my enemies is my friend.' The Egyptians' greatest enemy is their colonial overlord, the British. They will be helping us to smuggle our ninety-two illegals overland, through the Sinai to Palestine, just as they have helped us in the past."

Within the hour, she told him, Egyptian customs and a group representing the *Sochnut*, the informal Jewish Government of Palestine, would board the *Asia*. Among the customs officials would be members of the Egyptian Freedom Fighters, who would make the necessary arrangements to handle the ninety-two illegal immigrants.

"Now you know the entire story." Dora coughed spasmodically and ground out a half-smoked Ada. As he watched her, Ben realized that their conversation marked a turning point in their relationship; he was no longer an outsider.

Dora looked up, her eyes filmy and bloodshot; exhaustion lined her face. Ben guessed she had not slept during the past twenty-four hours and felt a surge of guilt that his bout with Spituna had added to her burdens. He didn't like the Rabbi and probably never would, but now, he at least understood him.

"I think I owe you an apology, Dora. And Spituna as well. I have a lot to learn."

Dora nodded. "Now you'll have to excuse me. I have to prepare for customs and the *Sochnut*."

After he left, Dora allowed herself the luxury of closing her eyes for a few minutes. She felt like she had been awake for days, but she was glad she had taken Ben into her confidence. She made a mental note to introduce Ben to Ali Badawi when he came on board. There was a lot Ben could learn from the affable Egyptian.

●   ●   ●

Alexandria sprawled before Ben like an alabaster palace, covering every square foot of the narrow peninsula it was built on. Beyond, on the mainland, a thriving city stretched to the horizon. Tall, leafy palms and stucco buildings with tile roofs lined the wide boulevards. The streets teemed with life. It was close to the hour and the shrill cries of the muezzins drifted over the water, calling the faithful to morning prayer.

The city's outer harbor was relatively small and congested with activity. Single-masted dhows knifed through the bay, their graceful lateen sails casting triangular shadows on the pale blue water. Nut-brown Arabs, stripped to the waist, arranged their nets along the gunwales and regarded the *Asia* with studied indifference.

A small white cutter with official markings dodged through the maze of fishing boats and came alongside, offloading an Egyptian in a khaki uniform. The harbor pilot, Ben thought to himself. The Egyptian stopped by the stretcher, then pointed to the launch. Boris Platzsky was on his way to a hospital. Ben wondered if it would disappoint Platzsky to discover he did not have appendicitis.

The harbor pilot climbed the bridge companionway, smiling as he passed by Ben, and entered the wheelhouse. At his command, three squat red tugs nosed the *Asia* through a narrow channel to the spacious inner harbor. Ocean freighters occupied dozens of broad stone quays along the water's edge and trade goods from three continents filled the open-sided storage sheds. The sounds and smells of the great port filled the air.

They were still some distance from the dock when a motor launch rigged with a canvas canopy overtook the *Asia*. Ben watched the launch maneuver alongside and discharge a small contingent onto the ship's dock platform—all the formalities had to be completed before the *Asia* was allowed to anchor.

Dora Hoffmann and Spituna greeted the boarding party at the rail with smiles and embraces. It was plain to Ben that everyone knew each other well. Of the dozen or so people who came aboard, six were dark-complexioned and two wore fezzes; the rest looked European. Unable to contain his curiosity any longer, Ben descended to the main deck. To his surprise, one of the Egyptians walked over and introduced himself as Ali Badawi.

"Dora Hoffmann suggested I meet you," Badawi smiled beneath a razor-thin mustache. Ben guessed him to be in his late twenties or early thirties.

The Egyptian was attired in a spotless white linen suit, subtly tailored to emphasize his broad shoulders and athletic build. The dark complexion and curly black hair gave him a rakish look, enhanced by luminous brown eyes. His striking good looks hinted at a smoldering sensuality women would find irresistible.

Badawi chatted amiably about the weather and asked polite questions about the trip. As he spoke, he tapped a thin Egyptian cigarette on his thumbnail, then lit it with a gold lighter. Exhaling slowly, he brought up the reason for the *Asia*'s presence in Alexandria.

Ben feigned ignorance. ''I understand we had a case of acute appendicitis on board; that's why we stopped.''

''You are suspicious,'' Badawi laughed knowingly. ''That is good, but you have nothing to fear from me. Everything has been cleared through Spituna, your ersatz rabbi.'' Despite his casual charm and offhand manner, there was an underlying sense of coiled tension about Ali Badawi, a barely concealed violence waiting to be unleashed.

Badawi seemed sympathetic and knowledgeable, but Ben had no idea how he had discovered the real reason for their layover in Alexandria, but he was not about to trust the suave Egyptian. If Badawi was not one of the Egyptian Freedom Fighters, he had to be a British plant, probing for information. Anticipating Ben's suspicions, Badawi led him over to Dora, who vouched for the Egyptian's reliability.

Relieved, Ben apologized for his reservations. Badawi shrugged. ''It's how we all survive. Better not to gamble unless one has no other choice.''

Badawi was a ranking customs official assigned to handle special problems and unusual situations, such as the unexpected arrival of the *Asia* in Alexandria. It was a perfect cover for his illegal activities. No one would suspect that an Egyptian officer responsible for halting illegal immigration was the head of a smuggling ring.

Badawi was a fount of information on the intricate patchwork of allegiances and animosities that formed the basis of Middle Eastern politics. One by one, he answered Ben's questions with a mastery of the facts that revealed a cunning and perceptive mind concealed beneath the playboy exterior. Ben was not surprised to discover that Badawi had been schooled at Oxford. They spoke for the better part of an hour until the boarding party prepared to leave. One of the uniformed Egyptians called to Badawi and he acknowledged the summons with a casual wave. Then he turned back to Ben.

Ben smiled. ''I enjoyed talking with you. It's a shame we don't have more time.'' He liked Badawi, guessing that the Egyptian's animal magnetism and reckless nature would make him a formidable ally.

''Why don't you come ashore and let me give you a tour of the city?'' Ali suggested. Ben would have leaped at the opportunity but he thought of Sarah, Sophie, and Yuri. He explained to Badawi that he didn't really feel comfortable about leaving them.

''Bring them along!'' Ali cried expansively.

Ben rounded up his three friends and they followed Badawi onto the launch. By the time they reached the quay twenty minutes later, Sarah, Sophie, and Yuri were all under the spell of Badawi's considerable charm.

Once on the quay, the maelstrom that was Alexandria hit them with an almost physical force. The scent of fragrant woods imported from Europe mingled with the pungent odor of camel dung. Burly stevedores manhandled bales and crates of cargo while merchants shouted instructions and inventoried their stockpiled goods. Bales of dazzling white Nile cotton formed solid walls along the docks; without Ali to guide them through the maze, they would have been hopelessly lost.

The narrow aisle ways and streets were crowded by vendors selling bitter Egyptian tea from special carts or improvised backpacks designed to hold copper samovars. The aroma of savory Egyptian delicacies contrasted sharply with the odor of decay rising from the fetid water near the shore. But it was the oppressive heat that dominated the senses. It was all-pervasive and blanketed the newcomers like a thick outer skin.

Although the four Europeans began to sweat heavily from the moment they stepped ashore, Ben noticed that Badawi seemed cool and unaffected. The Egyptian grinned apologetically.

"It takes time to get used to the heat. Be sure you drink plenty of fluids—people who are new to the Middle East quite frequently suffer from sunstroke or dehydration. It will be a bit cooler once we're in the car." He wove through the crush with practiced ease.

It was strangely disconcerting to see bearded Moslems in blue striped *jebbalahs* arguing with businessmen in European three-piece suits. Every language in Africa, Europe, and the Middle East was spoken on the docks of Alexandria.

"Is this what Palestine is like?" Yuri gasped, overwhelmed by the variety.

"Yes, very similar, but don't worry," Badawi assured them. "You'll get used to the change very quickly." He put an arm around Sarah and Sophie.

"Despite what you might have heard, there is no more exciting place on earth than the Middle East, especially for young people. It's a tremendous challenge—a chance to build, to create a new way of life. It is not often that one has the opportunity to help shape the future of a nation. When you are old, you'll be able to sit back and admire the fruits of your labor, knowing that you had a part in it. Few people can claim such a tangible reward at the end of their lives."

As they reached the base of the pier, Badawi's driver pulled onto the sidewalk. Ben hesitated when he saw the car, a jet black Model T Ford. A grimace of distaste crossed his face.

Noticing Ben's expression, Badawi gestured to the car. "A Model T may not be the most comfortable automobile in the world, but I think you'll find it quite serviceable. My British counterpart has a Bentley, but I'm afraid we natives are paid rather poorly by comparison." He accented the word "natives" ever so slightly.

Ben saw the hooded look in Badawi's eyes; Badawi was deciding whether or not to be offended. The Egyptian came from a wealthy and prominent family. He could have had any car he wished, but he obviously drove the official car as a matter of principle. Ben had no wish to antagonize his new friend, but he could not bring himself to get into the Ford.

"We mean no offense," Sarah spoke up, realizing the reason for Ben's hesitation. "Today is our Sabbath and we are forbidden to ride in cars on our Holy Day." Ben acknowledged her quick thinking with a grateful squeeze.

Badawi studied her face, then relaxed. "Of course. Besides, the best way to know a city is to walk its streets."

Alexandria had been founded by Alexander the Great, three hundred years before the birth of Christ, and rapidly became a center of culture, learning, and trade without equal. Its Great Library was a wonder of the ancient world, containing over 700,000 scrolls, the sum total of written human knowledge. Caesar, Antony, and Cleopatra played out their drama in its palaces. Scientists, doctors, writers, and philosophers from all over the world journeyed to Alexandria to exchange ideas, to learn, and to teach. Claudius Ptolemaeus, one of the greatest astronomers, mathematicians, and geographers of all time, was one of its most prominent historical figures.

Badawi seemed to have an inexhaustible supply of historical anecdotes that brought Alexandria's past to life, and his tour of the old city was an experience none of them would forget. The thought crossed Sarah's mind that the handsome Egyptian would have made a superb teacher in another place and another time.

As they walked through an open park with a breathtaking view, Ali paused to point out a rock-strewn peninsula jutting out into the bay. "It is said that the Pharaos Lighthouse was built by Alexander the Great, right on those very rocks. For sixteen centuries, it earned Alexandria the nickname 'Jewel of the Mediterranean.' Some archeologists believe that the lighthouse was well over 500 feet high."

"What happened to it?" Yuri wondered.

"It was destroyed by an earthquake in the 1300s. Afterwards, trade languished and the city began to die. By the beginning of the eighteenth century, its population was less than 4,000. If our Ottoman rulers had not seen fit to revitalize the city during the late seventeen hundreds, Alexandria might still be an insignificant village, living on past glories."

They continued on towards the heart of the city, admiring the magnificent nineteenth-century structures erected during the Renaissance reign of Muhammed Ali, the Ottoman Pasha. Yuri, in particular, was fascinated by the domed architecture. Ruins of ancient temples dotted their route, their broken pillars a reminder of cultures long vanished.

"Are there many Jews in Alexandria?" Sarah asked. Since coming ashore, they had not seen a synagogue or anyone wearing a yarmulke.

"Well over 30,000 in Alexandria alone," Ali replied. "You won't notice them here as you would in Europe. Here, they dress as we do, speak as we do, and live as we do."

In Egypt, there were no prohibitions against Jewish ownership of property, and Jews played an important role in the city's cultural and economic life. The Egyptian Jews were Sephardim, forced to flee eastward during the terror of the Spanish Inquisition. Some settled along the Mediterranean's northern coast, in Italy, Greece, and Turkey; the rest migrated along the southern coast, settling in North Africa, Egypt, and the Middle East.

Ali explained that the Sephardic Jews of Alexandria considered themselves the aristocracy of world Jewry. They had no interest in Zionism and were not overly anxious to welcome hordes of Ashkenazim to Egypt. They considered intermarriage with their European brethren a disgrace and even association with Ashkenazim was regarded as distasteful. The Sephardic Jews of Alexandria were anxious to move the refugees on to Palestine as quickly as possible.

No different than the German Jews, like Sarah's father, Ben thought to himself.

"I'd like to take you somewhere," Badawi said in an offhand manner. He led them through a bewildering maze of side streets until they suddenly emerged on a main thoroughfare. Directly opposite was a magnificent park, carpeted with carefully tended beds of exotic flowers. The walkways were lined by palms. Centered in the park was an enormous white structure, flanked by slender columns of white marble. Its copper roof was green with age.

"How beautiful," Sarah breathed. "What is it? Who lives there?"

"No one lives there," Ali Badawi laughed. "It is the Eliyahu Hanavi, the central synagogue of the Alexandrian Jews."

Sarah was unable to tear her eyes off the building. "You must see the inside," Ali said kindly, but he needn't have spoken; nothing would have kept them from entering.

Wide marble steps led to a massive pair of bronze doors, covered with Arab friezework. The interior was cool and spacious, illuminated by enormous windows set in the upper tiers of the main building. Row after row of sculpted wooden pews faced an exquisitely carved tabernacle, raised above floor level. Lanterns of beaten copper filigreed with delicate patterns cast a soft glow over the magnificent altar, imparting a rich luster to the dark wood. The altar itself was a magnificent work of art, chiseled from a solid block of bleached white marble.

Badawi stood to one side while his four guests gaped at the synagogue. In Europe, such a temple would have been an invitation for a pogrom; it was too dangerous to invite comparison with the soaring cathedrals of Christian Europe. But the Eliyahu Hanavi had been built by Jews who were unfettered by shame or fear. The hands that designed and constructed such a monument had but one concern—the glorification of God.

Footfalls broke the magical silence as a man dressed in European clothing walked to the altar. He looked exactly as the four Europeans expected an Arab to look—nut-brown in color, with a close cropped beard and jet black hair. Instead of a yarmulke, he wore a heavy black beret embroidered with white silk. Ali explained he was one of the rabbis. Another man entered and began to speak in Ladino, the Sephardic equivalent of Yiddish. Ladino was derived from a combination of Hebrew and Spanish, instead of German and Hebrew.

"They seem so different from us," Yuri whispered.

"The Sephardim have a different heritage," Badawi reminded them. "While the Jews of Europe were being systematically persecuted, the Jews of Moorish Spain were honored citizens, teachers, and ministers. It was a different way of life." Ali admitted there had been times of conflict, but by and large, Arab and Jew had prospered together until the Christian reconquest of Spain forced the Sephardim to flee. Most had settled in the Islamic world.

Ali was delighted by Sarah's rapt attention; she seemed to hang on his every word. For a European Jew, it was inconceivable that Egyptian Jews enjoyed such freedom. Ali Badawi knew from experience how Jews were treated in Europe, and he went out of his way to show her just how much the Jews and Egyptians had in common. When he finally suggested they leave, her face registered intense disappointment.

"Perhaps you would like to remain for a while," Ali smiled. "We could pick you up on our way back to the ship."

"Oh, Ben, would you mind?" Her eyes shone.

"Of course not." Despite the changes in her life, Sarah Hessemann was still the devout young girl Ben had first met in Altona. Sophie and Yuri elected to stay with Sarah, exploring their new-found faith.

Since it was past noon, Badawi suggested they eat and led Ben to a nearby Egyptian restaurant wedged between a police substation and a public garden. Ben hesitated when he saw the uniformed British police-men walking in and out of the station; the thought of having lunch within earshot of the British police was not something that appealed to him.

"I know what you're thinking," Ali laughed. "But this café is a hotbed of sedition."

"Isn't that dangerous?"

"The British would never believe that anyone, even a wog, would be so stupid as to operate next to a police station. It's a perfect ruse."

A half-dozen people greeted Ali as they entered the restaurant; he seemed to know everyone. The maitre d' bowed deferentially and in-structed a young boy in a crimson skullcap and embroidered red vest to give them a table where they would enjoy a view and a slight breeze. The dining room was filled with Muslims in traditional and European garb, eating, arguing, and sipping cups of thick black coffee.

They had just taken their seats when a barrel-chested man with a broad mustache dashed up to the table. Rivulets of perspiration ran down his forehead and his greasy shirt was soaked with sweat. His shaven skull made a vivid contrast with the three days' growth of coarse black stubble on his rounded cheeks. With a shout of delight, he pulled Ali out of his chair and enfolded him in a bear hug.

"This is my cousin, Moustafa," Ali grinned, ignoring the sweat stains Moustafa's embrace left on his spotless linen jacket. He introduced Ben as a "comrade" in the struggle against the British.

"Splendid!" Moustafa exclaimed effusively. "For such a long fight, you will need to maintain your strength, and nothing satisfies the stomach and strengthens the body like a good Egyptian meal. My cousin has brought you to the right place."

"Moustafa serves the finest lamb in Alexandria," Ali interjected.

Moustafa was obviously pleased by the compliment, but frowned modestly. "The food is good, but not as impressive as I would like. Once the British dogs are gone, the Royal Family will be dead or on their way into exile, and I will have their head chef. Then my café will be the equal of any in Paris.'' Ali's cousin grinned evilly, revealing two uneven rows of broken yellow teeth. Something about the glint in Moustafa's eyes told Ben that the jolly cook was just as capable of slicing throats as he was cuts of meat. It was hard for him to believe that the suave customs official and the coarse restaurant owner were related. Moustafa rubbed his hands together gleefully.

"For my cousin and his friends—nothing but the best,'' he beamed. Moustafa insisted that Ben and Ali choose their own cuts of meat and propelled them through the crowded restaurant to a small room behind the kitchen. Dozens of freshly slaughtered lamb carcasses were suspended from ceiling hooks by their hind legs. The warm, sickly odor of blood made Ben slightly queasy. He tried to ignore the swarms of flies that settled on everything in sight.

"Why don't you choose for both of us, Ali,'' he suggested weakly.

Ali pointed out several cuts which Moustafa promptly severed from the carcass with a murderous-looking butcher knife. Promising them a magnificent meal, he swept the raw meat into a metal dish and disappeared into the kitchen's smoky interior.

They arrived back at the table just in time to be served hollow pitas stuffed with crisp vegetables and fresh humus, a paste of chickpeas seasoned with delicate herbs. Ben tried to forget about the bloody carcasses in the room behind the kitchen.

Ali suddenly stopped eating. "It suddenly occurs to me that anyone who would not ride in an automobile on his Sabbath would probably observe a kosher diet as well. How inconsiderate of me to . . .''

Ben shook his head. "Yes! Kosher food is my preference. To be honest, the Ford had nothing to do with religion.'' Feeling he owed Ali an explanation, Ben spelled out why he had been reluctant to set foot in a Model T.

Ali listened without interrupting, then nodded in understanding. "In my country, such an insult would be cause for a blood feud.''

As they enjoyed the appetizers, Ben asked about the ninety-two men who would have to be smuggled into Palestine illegally. All had Nansen Passports, a catch-all form of identity issued by the League of Nations to stateless people, but they were of little use without a visa.

Ali snapped his fingers and the waiter refilled their glasses of colored ice water. He drank deeply and set the glass down with a sigh of contentment.

"Without visas, we'd never get them in through regular channels, so we've developed an organization capable of moving groups of able-bodied men overland from Alexandria to Jaffa. The journey involves considerable physical hardships and a certain element of risk, but we've been very successful.''

'So it was hardly coincidence that every one of the ninety-two illegals were all strong, young men with sound bodies.

"The journey is long, hot, and tiring," Ali continued. "And much of it must be made on foot, but it's more a question of stamina than of danger."

The illegals would be broken into groups of eight or ten men, then guided to Palestine, avoiding the main roads and public transportation. Actually crossing the border was a simple matter; borders in the Middle East were just lines drawn on a map. The real threat was posed by British patrols conducting random spot checks for proper papers. By traveling the back roads in small groups, the risk of detection was greatly reduced, but there was always a chance they could be stopped in Alexandria, Jaffa, or any place in between.

"A certain amount of luck is required," Ali smiled.

Ben thought for a minute. "But how are you going to get them off the ship in broad daylight without the British finding out? They have agents on every dock."

"Simple. What happens when a ship rides at anchor in Alexandria?"

Whenever a ship put into port, the crew dropped rope ladders over the side every morning and allowed dozens of local vendors to swarm on board to peddle their wares. In port, the ships resembled floating bazaars.

Ali explained that the illegals would be assigned to groups while still on board the *Asia*, then dressed in native clothing and slipped over the side a few at a time. Those who could not pass for Arabs would be camouflaged with makeup. To ensure that no overzealous British agent would stop them, the *jebbalahs* they would wear had been left in a camel stable for several days. Few British officers familiar with the smell cared to come in close proximity.

"It's absolutely brilliant," Ben laughed. "No wonder the Arabs have such a reputation for scheming."

"You forget," Ali wagged a finger. "We are both Semites, descended from Abraham. That makes us brothers under the skin."

At that moment, the waiter brought out the roast lamb. It had been rubbed with garlic and rosemary, then glazed with honey. Sliced paper thin, it was served on a bed of fluffy rice. Ben felt his mouth water at the savory aroma. They ate hungrily, enjoying the conversation and each other's good company. Every time they emptied their plates, the waiter appeared out of nowhere to refill them. They finally had to beg Moustafa not to send any more food out.

When Ali tried to pay the bill, Moustafa flew out of the kitchen in a rage and indignantly refused to accept the money. He embraced his cousin, then turned to Ben.

"We share the fight. When next we meet, may every British throat be slit." Moustafa pumped Ben's hand vigorously and flashed him a conspiratorial smile. "*Inshallah.*"

"Shalom." Ben winced at Moustafa's grip and suppressed an involuntary shudder. He had no doubt that when the time came, Moustafa would be happy to slit more than his share of British throats.

As they strolled back towards the synagogue, Ben tried to sort out the paradoxes he had seen through Ali's eyes. He had no trouble understanding Moustafa's motives, or Ali's. What confused him was the divisiveness that split the Arab world. It only made sense to unite against the British, yet most Arabs spent more time battling each other and the Jews than the real enemy.

"Why is it that only the Egyptians see that there is strength in unity?" he wondered.

Ali laughed cynically. "Only the Egyptians form a true nation."

Ali tried to explain that Egypt differed greatly from the rest of the Arab world. While most Arabs still gloried in the days of the Caliphate, the Egyptians remembered beyond Alexander, Ptolemy, and Cleopatra. Hatshepsut and Amenhotep, Nefertiti and Thutmose had all ruled an empire while the rest of the world squatted around dung fires dressed in animal skins.

Four thousand years of history had bound the Egyptian people into a nation, but the other countries of the Middle East were European creations, born of the Great War. Their boundaries were arbitrary, drawn by planners without any regard for the cultural realities of the Middle East. For most of the Arab world, loyalty rested with family and tribe, not some abstract concept of nationhood. Most Arabs thought in biblical terms when it came to deciding who was an ally and who was an enemy. Issues of statehood and British rule were viewed as minor matters when compared to local blood feuds that had lasted for centuries.

"That's why it is essential for the Jews and Egyptians to work closely together," Ali said intensely. "We can expect help from no other quarter."

"My people will need time," Ben replied eagerly. "But when the right moment arrives, we'll be ready to fight."

Ali frowned in disapproval but said nothing. He guided Ben to a sidewalk café and ordered espresso and pastry over Ben's protests. Then he sat back and drew a cigarette from a silver case.

"You must understand that it is dangerous to think in terms of an armed clash with the British," Ali began. "There's no glory in assaulting English machine guns from the back of a camel."

Ben was about to argue that the only way to make an enemy respect you was to fight, but Ali held up his hand.

"No, Ben. We don't need violence to defeat the British, only time. Time is our greatest ally. We are here because God so willed. This is our home, our land, our birthright.

"The average Englishman sees no profit in the Middle East. They despise us and they're bored to death. They'd really prefer to be back in Great Britain, fishing for salmon in a Scottish stream. And that's how we'll defeat them. We'll use their boredom against them."

Ali was interrupted by the waiter, who set down two cups of thick, fragrant espresso with a lemon wedge on each saucer, and a plate of French pastries.

After the waiter left, Ali tried to explain that the British were driven by conflicting motives. Great Britain was a small, industrial nation. She needed raw materials, cheap labor, and new markets for her finished goods. Only an Empire could meet those needs, yet the reality of exploiting helpless nations was repugnant; conscience had to be satisfied.

To justify their Empire, the English created the myth of the "white man's burden," which gave conquest a veneer of selflessness. In the name of God and civilization, they sought to remake their conquered peoples into carbon copies of English gentlemen, and a whole new class of English-Arabs, English-Hindus, English-Chinese, and even English-Blacks was created.

"They all dance and bow and scrape with the best King's Row dandies," Ali said bitterly. "But let one of them try to enter an English club—and they're nothing more than wogs or niggers again." Ali spoke from personal experience.

Ali insisted that the British political strategy for the Middle East was bound to fail because it represented an attempt to cultivate British institutions on Middle Eastern soil. Churchill's plan called for a number of kingdoms to be established throughout the Middle East, governed by monarchs who would eventually share power with an elected parliament. These monarchs would naturally owe their allegiance to Great Britain and help to bring order out of political chaos. But there was one flaw in the plan.

The British did not understand the intertribal hatreds of the Middle East or the despotic streak in the Arab psyche. Once having acceded to power, no Arab would voluntarily relinquish it. They would use that power to establish their hegemony and eliminate their rivals. If the monarchies were established, the Middle East would remain fractured and vulnerable, torn by strife and rivalry. Even so, that situation would not adversely affect British interests; it was easier to deal with a despot dependent on their goodwill than a freely elected government.

Ali envisioned the Middle East as a collection of democracies, allied to protect their interests against the more powerful industrial nations. For years, the Europeans had used the policy of "divide and conquer" with enormous success; now the Arabs had the opportunity to do the same. By playing on the rivalry between the major powers, the Arab nations would have a fair chance of controlling their own destinies.

When the waiter appeared with the bill, Ali paid it and lapsed into silence. A brooding melancholy settled over his handsome features. Ben knew what he was thinking. In theory, his strategy was logical and sound; the British could be expelled without violence. In reality, it would probably come to a prolonged and bloody confrontation.

They left the café and walked for three or four blocks, sharing each other's silence. Suddenly, Ali stopped and his expression brightened considerably.

"Since we have been discussing all the marvelous things Jews and Egyptians can learn from one another, there's no reason why we can't begin right now." Ali's face split into a mischievous grin, and he dragged Ben down the street to a narrow two-story stone house with grimy windows and a battered wooden door.

Ali knocked on the weatherbeaten door and a small panel slid to one side. A narrow pair of eyes studied his face, then the panel slid closed and the door opened.

After having seen the plain, shabby exterior, Ben was completely unprepared for the opulence that greeted him beyond the paneled door. Thick Oriental carpets in deep reds and blues covered the stone floors, and the walls were hung with tapestries. Soft couches and elevated platforms littered with oversized pillows formed small circles around inlaid tables of brass and mahogany. Several dozen men sat or reclined around the tables.

As Ben and Ali walked through the main gallery, Ben realized how deceptive the front of the building had been. Though just fifteen feet wide at the street, the first floor flared out behind the shops on either side like a topheavy 'T,' creating a spacious interior. In the dim light, he noticed that the men were smoking from long rubber tubes attached to bottles filled with liquid. Pipe bowls sat atop the bottles, packed with different substances, and clouds of pungent, blue-gray smoke hung in the air. Ben found the odors sharp, but not unpleasing.

Ali led Ben through a curtain to a small, airless room off the main gallery, where they made themselves comfortable. A young man appeared with a pipe and a small vase containing a lumpy green substance. He placed it on the small table between them, then salaamed and left.

"We are about to embark on a great adventure," Ali grinned. "I know that you do not drink liquor or smoke tobacco. Neither does any devout Moslem. But this is different. It is called *hashish*." Ali broke off a chunk and placed it in the pipe bowl.

"Try to inhale deeply and retain as much smoke as you can." He touched a match to the hashish and drew deeply. Ben watched, fascinated, as the smoke bubbled through the liquid and gathered in the neck of the bottle. Holding his breath, Ali held out the rubber stem to Ben.

Against his better judgment, Ben accepted the rubber tube. He felt slightly foolish as he drew on the pipe. He inhaled the acrid smoke a little too heavily, and started to cough. His eyes began to tear.

"Don't feel embarrassed," Ali smiled. "It's a perfectly normal reaction. Don't draw so heavily next time."

At first, Ben was unable to detect any particular effect. But then, as he and Ali continued to talk, he noticed that Ali's voice seemed to be coming from a great distance and there was a grainy quality to his vision. He first ascribed it to the smoke-filled air and tried to clear his eyes by rubbing them. When he tried to focus on the striped cloth covering their table, its folds took on an intricate geometric beauty he had never seen before. He had the strange sensation of being able to feel the texture of the material with his eyes. Suddenly, he found himself laughing.

"No effect at all," he told Ali, wiping the tears of mirth from his eyes.

"Of course not." Ali's laugh was deep and throaty. "It's nearly three, Ben. We should be going." Ben could not believe they had been smoking for nearly an hour. When he rose to leave, he felt detached from his body. It was like watching himself go through the physical motions of leaving the building from somewhere above. Outside, the teeming activity of the city assailed his senses. Ben had never been so intensely aware of himself and his surroundings.

Sarah, Sophie, and Yuri were still at the synagogue, exhilarated by their meditations. They were all anxious to return to the *Asia*. For Ben, the trip back to the ship was a magical experience. The palms seemed to speak to him through the wind, and the docks vibrated with images of ancient explorers and warriors. Ben described his experience to the others while Ali grinned broadly.

By the time they arrived at the gangplank, everyone's sides ached from laughing. Sophie, Sarah, and Yuri thanked Ali, then dashed on board to tell their friends about Alexandria and the great Central Synagogue.

"They are our hope for the future," Ali said. He and Ben smiled at each other.

"Though I've only known you for a day, Ali Badawi, I feel as though we have been friends for a lifetime."

"I, too."

"Whatever the future brings, there will always be a special place in this Jew's heart for Egypt. May our two peoples always be friends."

"May Allah have it so," Ali extended his hand. "*Inshallah.*"

"Shalom, my friend." It was with a pang of regret that Ben watched Ali disappear into the crowd. Men like Ali Badawi were rare.

Back on the ship, the effects of the drug began to wear off, leaving Ben with a drowsy, pleasant feeling. He yawned and decided to check with Dora Hoffmann, to see if there had been any problems in smuggling the illegals ashore. The door to her office was ajar and he heard voices from within.

Dora was using her best "diplomatic" tone, trying to persuade two Egyptians to accept three hundred English pounds as a reward for their help in smuggling the illegals into Palestine. The Egyptians kept refusing the money.

"Many things we do for *baksheesh* or influence," one explained. *Baksheesh* was the organized system of tipping that governed life in the Arab world.

"What we do for your young men, we do for honor," the Egyptian continued. "Some day, Madame Hoffmann, the English will go and the Jews and Egyptians will have to live together. Only honor can govern such a relationship, not money." Ben heard the man push back his chair and stand. "*Salaam Aleikum.*"

"Shalom Aleichem," Dora replied. The door opened wide and two of the Egyptian officials that Ben met earlier walked out without noticing him. Dora was sitting alone, lighting another in an endless chain of cigarettes.

"Well, I see you finally decided to come back," she observed.

Ben slid into a chair opposite the desk and looked at her expectantly. Dora was in an expansive mood, relaxed and smiling. The ninety-two men had been safely offloaded without incident, and just as important, the *Asia*'s illegal refugees had been told how the lack of papers was to be circumvented.

"It worked like a charm," she smiled gleefully. "They accepted my explanation and thought it was a magnificent ruse. Everyone remarked what a marvelous coincidence it was that . . .'' Dora stopped in mid-sentence.

"Why are your eyes so bloodshot?'' she asked suspiciously.

He giggled in response.

She looked at him and her eyes narrowed.

"Hashish? I see that Ali Badawi has been teaching you the ways of the East. Next, I suppose you'll want your own hash pipe, then a camel, then a harem.''

She sent him off to his cabin with instructions to return to the bridge at eight that evening, when the *Asia* would weigh anchor. She laughed as Ben tried to negotiate the top of the companionway, remembering the first time Ali Badawi had taken her on a tour of Alexandria.

●   ●   ●

He woke at dusk, with the sound of Sarah's voice in his ear. "Ben, how can you sleep? We're sailing! We're pulling out! We're really on our way to Palestine.''

As Ben's head cleared, he heard the faint sound of singing—not elated, but solemn and gentle. He and Sarah hugged each other. Ben slipped on his shoes and together they went up on deck. Everywhere, groups of people had linked arms and were gently swaying to the words of *Hatikvah*, the Jewish pioneer's national anthem.

As the coast of Africa faded from sight, the singing ceased and a stillness fell over the ship. Old people stood along the rail, their faces radiating an eternal patience, a stoic willingness to wait, to suffer, to endure. They stood quietly, not daring to believe the ancient dream was about to become a reality.

The young people gathered in clusters and argued passionately about what the future would bring. They traded words and thoughts like white-hot blows, creating a minor disturbance, but no one rebuked them; they would need every bit of passion and vitality they could muster in order to hew a nation out of the desert within the course of a single lifetime. Only the unmistakable tension in their voices betrayed the hidden fears and uncertainties they all felt.

Suddenly, Ben realized that Sarah was crying softly. He put his arm around her, drawing her close.

"After tomorrow, will we be ordinary again?'' she blurted out. He looked at her, puzzled.

"Well, tomorrow we'll be in Palestine,'' she said, pausing to blow her nose. "The whole adventure will be over and we'll be just ordinary people, trying to live ordinary lives. You know—not special anymore."

Ben took her by the hand, and they strolled in silence for a moment.

"You know, Sarah," he began. "No one on this boat is ordinary. They were frightened, but somewhere, they found the courage to leave their homes and start a new life. They were poor, but they spent everything they had, gambling on the future. They lived in isolation and exile for centuries without losing their God or their faith. No one on this boat is ordinary. Tomorrow morning, we face the British on the soil of our forefathers. The adventure won't be over when we set foot in Palestine. That's where it will begin."

TWENTY-ONE

The Eastern Mediterranean
Sunday, February 16th, 1925

"They've had enough, Spituna!" Dora Hoffmann no longer tried to conceal the malice in her voice. Spituna stared at her, stoop-shouldered, his myopic eyes reduced to a pair of compressed black dots behind the gold-rimmed lenses. Lack of sleep and an inability to eat had made his face more angular since the *Asia* left Marseilles, and his skin had taken on an unhealthy yellowish cast, like old parchment. He looked stiff and artificial, like a papier-mâché caricature ready to crumble or blow away at the slightest breath of wind. Dora wondered if he had heard her.

Ever since Spituna had first mentioned staging a dry run through the immigration procedures they would face in Jaffa, Dora had been opposed to the idea. The *Ostjuden* were too tired, too nervous, and too numerous. Dora had argued that a good night's sleep would do more to prevent the possibility of an inadvertent mishap than a last-minute night drill, but Spituna became more unyielding with every argument Dora advanced. There was too much at stake, he insisted in a tired whisper, the thin, colorless lips barely moving. Even though everyone aboard was "legal," if someone should forget, or slip up, the British would initiate a series of individual interrogations that was bound to uncover the truth. Spituna was haunted by the "what-ifs."

"Just do it," he mumbled to Dora, shuffling back to the bridge. "I haven't the strength to argue with you."

For a moment, Dora debated ignoring his instructions. Only she and Ben knew who Spituna really was; his authority was based on their obedience. She considered sending everyone to bed, knowing there was nothing Spituna could do about it until they arrived in Jaffa the following day. As tempting as the thought was, she discarded it. It set a bad precedent, and somehow, she couldn't bring herslef to betray Spituna's trust. When we get to Jaffa, she promised herself. That's when I'll confront Spituna. Resigning herself to the Rabbi's will, Dora returned to her seat behind Ben to suprvise the practice runs. At the rate they were going, the process would continue until they were anchored off Jaffa.

"Next!" Ben snapped, his voice sharp and ragged; Spituna had told him to make the interrogations as realistic as posible. Dora watched as Jacob Zaminski stepped up to the table. He was a bearlike man in his early fifties, with grizzled features and a thick, squat neck set atop a massive pair of shoulders.

"Name!"

"Ja . . . Ja . . . Jacob Za . . . Zaminski."

"Passport!"

Self-consciously, Zaminski held out his passport, clutching his visa in the other hand. Ben snatched it away impatiently and demanded to know what kind of visa Zaminski had.

"Ca . . . Capitalist."

Ben examined it, then looked up sharply. "Where is the proof of your net worth?" Zaminski stared at him in a panic. Zaminski was not a man easily intimidated, yet he stood before Ben shaking like a leaf, even though it was only a rehearsal. Perhaps Spituna was right, Dora conceded to herself. Zaminski would have to do better or they might all be lost.

"Just relax, Mr. Zaminski," Ben smiled sympathetically. "It's important to relax. The British may try to trip you up, but don't worry. Don't be nervous. All you have to do is remember your papers are completely legal and in order."

Gratefully, Zaminski sat down and a man and woman followed by seven children stepped up to the desk. The man, Josef Rosenberg, had a capitalist visa for himself and his three children. Dora had married him off to a Ukrainian widow with four children of her own.

"Without turning around, Mr. Rosenberg, tell me, how many children do you have?" Ben asked politely.

"I . . . ah . . . I . . . I have seven children!" came the cautious reply. After having watched what happened to Zaminski, Rosenberg was not taking any chances.

"Their names, please."

The question was so obvious that it took Rosenberg completely by surprise. "Of course I know the names of—"

"Just repeat them, please. Without turning around."

There was a stricken look on Rosenberg's face. Nervously, he licked his lips and began. "Moishe, Sharon, Ida, Jacob, and . . ." He paused, mouthing the names silently.

"And?"

"And . . . David and Miriam!" he grinned triumphantly. There was a round of applause from his relieved "family."

"All right," Ben grinned. "But tomorrow, try to be a little more natural."

Four people stepped forward: a heavyset Latvian Jew, his "wife" and two old people. The Latvian spoke for the group. "I am Abraham Pinchas and this is my wife. I have a quota number that enables my wife and my grandparents to enter Palestine on my visa." Abraham Pinchas was smooth and well rehearsed. Ben examined the two "grandparents." The woman was from the Ukraine, the man was Polish. Because of the language difference, they could barely communicate with each other; they were the weak link.

Ben pointed to the "grandfather." "You, what is your name?"

"Isaac Pinchas."

Ben asked a few more simple questions, then suddenly turned on the woman.

"Name!"

"Sprinze Katz," she blurted out. A stillness fell over the room, hyphenated by Dora's sigh of despair.

Ben smiled maliciously. "Why is your last name different from your husband's?"

Sprinze Katz's eyes widened in fear, like those of a terrified animal, paralyzed by the harsh glare of a hunter's spotlight. "He . . . he's not my husband. My husband . . . my husband died three years ago . . ."

"Then you are attempting to enter the State of Palestine illegally!"

She burst into tears. Dora stepped out from behind Ben. "It's all right, mother," she comforted the old woman. "Just for today, your name is Pinchas, and just for today, this man is your husband. Do you understand?" Sprinze nodded slowly.

Abraham Pinchas wrung his hands nervously. "What if she forgets?"

Dora raised her voice so everyone in the crowded hall could hear. "She will not forget, because she must not forget. Each of you must play your parts. No one else can do it for you. Our safety and our futures rest with one another. We will not fail.''

Like Sprinze Pinchas, some people were reluctant to pose as someone else's wife or grandparent. Others simply forgot their new identities or faltered and told the truth when questioned sharply. Still, Spituna would not relent until everyone had been questioned at least once. It was two in the morning when they finished.

Hoarse and utterly exhausted, Ben propped himself against the bulkhead. He had no idea whether it was day or night. Within minutes, he was fast asleep.

● ● ●

As the *Asia* plowed through the blue-black Mediterranean night, her engines maintaining a steady ten knots, Dora Hoffmann stood alone on the bridge. She peered out into the blackness. Somewhere out there, though she could not see them, lay the British fleet. She knew they had been under constant surveillance from the time they left Alexandria.

Since the British had no way of knowing that the *Asia* had been alerted to their plan, they would take the utmost pains to remain out of sight until it became apparent that the *Asia* had been approached from shore. Then they would spring the trap. Suddenly, the blackness on the horizon was pierced by the naked flash of a semaphore. Dora wondered if it belonged to a British cruiser; who else would bother to use a semaphore? The Royal Navy wasn't communicating by wireless—Dora had bribed the *Asia*'s operator to monitor the traffic; there was nothing out of the ordinary. Perhaps they were using a submarine to trail the *Asia*, she speculated. Looking down, she checked her watch. It was almost time to send the messages.

Since Zionist Headquarters had no intention of tipping off the British that privileged information had been leaked, everything was to proceed as though the illegals were going to be smuggled off the *Asia*. Dora would despatch the simply coded signal used to inform Jaffa that the ship was approaching the rendezvous and the fishing boats would arrive on schedule, only this time, they would be fishing, not smuggling. Dora wondered if the British would stop the *Asia* and board her once they realized that no exchange had taken place.

As it happened, Dora Hoffmann wasn't the only one wondering how the night would end. Whitehall was waiting, so was the Foreign Office. Although the minister had retired, he had left strict instructions that he was to be awakened immediately when news of the *Asia* came through. A coup like that would strengthen his political position as Foreign Minister, boost his prestige with the Arabs, and give him a hefty salvo to fire at the liberals who were always cozying up to the Jews. He was already framing the speech in his mind.

Of all those involved on the British side, only the High Commissioner in Palestine had grave reservations about the snare set for the *Asia*. He understood the political necessities of the real world, but it disturbed him that Britain, so eager for Jewish support during the desperate days of 1917, suddenly seemed anxious to forget her pledges of a Jewish homeland in Palestine. The High Commissioner, Sir Herbert Samuel, had argued for continuing an official policy of strictly controlled immigration, which would satisfy the Arabs, while suggesting an unofficial policy that ignored illegal immigration. The commissioner had realized that it was a difficult diplomatic path to tread, nevertheless he urged the powers at 10 Downing Street that it was a better alternative than making an example out of a boatload of old people, helpless children, and homeless refugees. The last of his hopes were shattered when an answer arrived denying his request. The Jews would have to take care of of themselves.

● ● ●

When Ben openeed his eyes, Sarah placed a peeled Jaffa orange in front of him. He straightened up, groaning in discomfort as circulation returned to his limbs.

Sarah shook her head in disapproval. ''You must be practically crippled. Honestly, Ben, how could you fall asleep in a chair?''

''Would you like to see me do it again?'' he yawned.

''Eat your orange,'' she ordered. The sharp citrus aroma filled his nostrils. He bit into a section, spraying sweet juice.

''It's your first taste of Palestine,'' Sarah laughed.

''Let's hope the future is as sweet,'' he grinned. ''What time is it?''

''Nearly five. The sun will be coming up soon.''

''How come you're not asleep?''

''For the same reason that everyone on board is awake. A combination of fear and anticipation.'' She looked into Ben's eyes. ''I don't know exactly what you've done to smuggle us into Palestine, but I do know that nothing is foolproof. What will happen if something goes wrong?''

He started to tell her not to worry when something in her eyes stopped him. Suddenly, he realized that Sarah was no longer a child and she had a right to know the truth.

''If anything goes wrong, they'll ship us all back to Marseilles. We'd have to begin all over again.''

"Oh God," she whispered, keeping her eyes fixed on the tabletop. "Ben, I'm frightened."

"So am I," he replied, taking her hands in his. "So am I." They sat in silence, drawing strength from each other. The specter of exposure was almost too terrible to contemplate. Ben's stomach churned as he thought about the British Navy; what were they doing? Finally he stood, and took Sarah topside.

Dawn was just breaking over the Mediterranean. The sky was dark pearl gray, then the sun seemed to appear from nowhere, warming the air and changing the water's color from black to sea green. No clouds obscured the azure sky. It was going to be a magnificent day.

The *Asia*'s prow was crowded with people. Shielding their eyes against the sun's glare, they searched the horizon for a tell-tale line, each hoping to be the first to sight Palestine.

Ben and Sarah found a vantage point on the promenade deck and joined the watchers at the railing. Ben's thoughts ran to the past, to his father; how often had Anschel Isaacson dreamed of the moment his son was now living? Ben thought of his mother and the rest of his family, still clinging to the old ways, wagering their survival on the charity of their Christian neighbors. He thought of Meilach Gorsky and his family, bound by iron bonds to a disappearing way of life. Last of all, he thought of Bluma, who yearned to leave the past behind, but could not. How beautiful she would look, standing beside him at the rail, the wind keeping her long hair in disarray. He looked down, realizing his grasp on the rail was so tight that his knuckles had turned a dead white. He released his grip.

A shout arose, and one of the young boys standing near the prow began yelling with excitement that he could see the Holy Land. Ben squinted, but neither he nor Sarah could see anything but blue-green water.

Five minutes passed.

"Ben . . ." Sarah whispered. "Ben, look . . ." Directly ahead lay a very thin brown line, barely discernible from the haze that obscured the horizon.

Land.

Suddenly there were other shouts, and wild gestures. To the north, a British destroyer and a cruiser appeared, their course paralleling the *Asia*'s. To the south, another cruiser shadowed their wake. The *Asia* maintained her speed, closing on the coastline. As they approached, surface features began to appear. Swathes of green broke the tan shoreline, and areas of dazzling white marked the presence of a great city. A headland marking the mouth of a broad bay came into view, and the anxious passengers aboard the *Asia* were able to make out the outline of a dozen large cargo ships at anchor. Ben glanced towards the bridge, expecting Dora Hoffmann or Spituna to appear.

The bridge railing remained deserted. The British warships made no effort to close the gap.

Fifteen minutes later, they were able to see crewmen at work aboard the anchored ships. The royal blue of the Mediterranean depths changed as they neared the bay, which was large, but shallow. Its surface reflected a pale aqua, as though the bottom was lined with tile.

The bridge deck was still empty.

People began to fidget. Questions began to rise. Had something gone wrong? Were the British suddenly going to swoop down on them? Faces tense with anxiety and expectation kept turning towards the bridge. It was maddening.

The sound of a steel door slamming attracted his attention towards the bridge. Dora Hoffmann appeared at the railing with a megaphone in one hand, pausing for a moment to stare at the city beyond the harbor perimeter. Slowly, she raised the megaphone to her lips.

"Ladies and gentlemen, we are now arriving at the Port of Jaffa in Palestine, with the blessing of the Royal Navy."

No one moved.

Again and again, as a boy, an adolescent, and as an adult, Ben had tried to imagine how he would feel the moment he arrived in Palestine. What it would be like—the elation, the cries of joy, the feeling of exhilaration. But nothing happened; no one cheered or broke into song. No one wept. They stood transfixed by the sight of the Holy Land.

The ship's engines whined as they locked into reverse and the anchor chain rattled with a screeching protest, like nails dragged across a blackboard. There were no quays at Jaffa, no docks, no ramps—only ramshackle sheds on a sandy beach. The *Asia* shuddered briefly as her anchor caught, then the engines fell eerily silent. All along the rail, people stood staring at the city they had struggled to reach. Disappointment registered on many faces. It took no more than a glance to see that Jaffa was a far cry from Alexandria. Like the Egyptian city, nearly all the buildings in Jaffa were alabaster white, but there the similarity ended. Most of the construction was single story and relatively unimposing. Only an occasional minaret relieved the monotony.

Ben felt a hand on his shoulder. "It's plain, but it's home," Dora said proudly. "From here on in, we're just two more immigrants, waiting to enter the Holy Land. The rest is up to the French crew and the immigration authorities. Look!'' She pointed to the "taxis" headed for the *Asia*. Dozens of small boats, barely larger than canoes, pushed off the beach and bore down on the ship like an attacking fleet. Jaffa was not yet a real port with proper facilities, so scores of enterprising Arab boatmen made a living by ferrying people and their luggage to and from liners and freighters. Each boat was propelled by a single Arab in native garb.

The French crew flew into action, securing the *Asia* and preparing for debarkation. Their activity broke the solemn mood of the immigrants on deck and sent everyone scurrying below for luggage and personal belongings. According to plan, the immigrants would form lines on the main deck outside a large room where the authorities would set up a processing station. Once approved for entry to Palestine, the passengers would then be rowed ashore by the Arab "taxis," where their luggage would be fumigated. The fumigation procedure was a source of concern and embarrassment for every immigrant entering Palestine. The chemical process wrinkled spare clothing to the point where it had to be professionally cleaned and pressed. But there was also a minor stigma attached to badly wrinkled clothes—they labeled the wearer as a newcomer. Eager to avoid that label, everyone on board dressed in several layers of clothing—enough to take them through the first few days. Scrawny old men grew enormous paunches and thick legs absurdly disproportionate to their arms and shoulders. Most of the female passengers increased their bust by three sizes and all the girls appeared to have matured overnight. Those who were already plump became grossly obese.

They crowded the deck, waiting for the process to begin. Already, the early morning temperature promised a sweltering day.

"Look!" Ida Goldblum's piercing shriek set everyone's nerves jangling; she always managed to sound like someone falling overboard. The object of her concern was a long gray launch flying a British colonial flag. Two armed sailors stood in the prow. As it approached, officers of the French crew lined up along the gangway.

The launch tied alongside and offloaded her passengers. There were several British naval officers dressed in white shorts and a half-dozen English immigration officials in more formal uniform jackets and long pants. The Arab bureaucrats wore fezzes and white shirts buttoned to the neck. Last on board were the Jewish officials. Their open-necked short sleeve shirts gave them a casual appearance, belying their grave expressions.

The boarding party's chief was a lean, ruddy English colonel. As he clambered aboard, the French captain stepped forward and embraced him in Gallic fashion—a kiss on each cheek. Though the Englishman looked uncomfortable at the physical intimacy of the greeting, he laughed none-theless, responding like an old friend. The remaining officers on both sides shook hands and began to chat as though they were long lost friends.

Ben wasn't the only one surprised by the amicable relationship that seemed to exist between the French crew and the immigration authorities —people on deck began to mutter suspiciously about the possibility of a sellout. Their past experiences with authority had left them with an ingrained fear and instinctive distrust of uniforms. To compound the mood, the rising temperature and discomfort caused by layers of unneces-sary clothing had everyone sweating and edgy. On Spituna's instructions, aides began to circulate through the crowd, dealing with potential problems.

"Please, Mrs. Orlov, things will go smoother and quicker if we are calm and organized."

"There's nothing to worry about, Mr. Goralnik, just relax and remember your name."

"Answer the questions put to you with a simple yes or no whenever possible. Above all, don't volunteer any information."

"Everyone on board is legal. No one has anything to fear."

The crowds on deck responded to the gentle reassurance and formed orderly queues outside the closed doors of the processing area. The French crew set up a number of roped off areas according to the instructions of the immigration officials, and the delegation moved inside to begin the debarkation procedure.

At 8:00 A.M. sharp, the doors opened, revealing a long table. The Arabs sat at the near end, the British in the middle, and the Jews at the far end. The English colonel took his place in the center chair, looking bored and a little distracted as he signaled a sergeant-major directly across from him.

"First in line," the sergeant-major yelled. "To the fore!" An interpreter nudged the first group towards the table. Hesitantly, a couple "married" on board and their four "children" stepped in front of the Arab delegation. A dark-skinned Arab nodded slightly to the man and welcomed him to Palestine in a dry nasal tone that suggested he was anything but welcome. The Arab ignored the woman and children and asked for name and documentation.

"Chaim Wasserman," came the nervous reply as the precious sheaf of papers was handed over. He was never asked to identify his family, or answer a single question. Their papers were stamped, several new forms were filled out, then they were passed on to the British officials.

"First in line—to the fore!" shouted the sergeant-major again. Another couple stepped forward.

Meanwhile, the British finished with the Wassermans and passed them on to the Jewish authorities, who approved them with handshakes and broad smiles. Laden with reams of handwritten documents, the family shuffled before the Health Officer near the exit. He stacked the forms compulsively, asking several simple questions. Satisfied with the answers, he directed the Wassermans to a British orderly, who instructed them to gather their luggage and proceed ashore.

A spontaneous cheer arose from the line and the Wassermans walked hand-in-hand to the railing. As they disappeared over the *Asia*'s side, the tension dissipated and for the next hour and a half, everything went smoothly. Papers were closely scrutinized, but no attempt was made to browbeat anyone. The officials accepted legitimate papers at face value; the examinations seemed purely routine. Dora guessed the British did not want to arouse any suspicions; once they realized no transfer had occurred at sea, they had assumed that the illegals had somehow been offloaded in Alexandria and allowed the *Asia*'s deboarding to proceed through normal channels. If no illegals were found, they would wait for the next ship. The Royal Navy had plenty of time.

Trouble finally came in the person of Ira Malinski, a pale, nervous Latvian with a dandruff-flaked shock of coarse black hair. Ironically, Malinski and his wife and four children were all "legals," having obtained a legitimate capitalist visa in Berlin. The Arab immigration clerk was unable to find it in the thick wad of papers Malinski handed him and asked Malinski and his family to proceed to a roped off area opposite the desk.

Frantically, Malinski searched his pockets, his angular face twisted in fear. "But, I have one, I have a legitimate—"

"Please stand to the side," the Arab repeated firmly. "Now."

"Move it off now," the sergeant-major yelled, and took a menacing step forward. Terrified, Malinski's family left the line.

"Oh my God, Ben," Sarah whispered fearfully. "They're on to us."

"No, they're not," Ben reassured her. "It's just a foul-up. They'll find the papers. They're around someplace." A Zionist agent walked over to speak with Malinski's family. As the long line of immigrants slowly dwindled, twelve other families joined the Malinskis in temporary quarantine, but all were cleared in less than an hour. As each contingent of refugees passed through, the Arab boats, which held six or seven people, rowed them ashore, then returned for another group. Since it took a little over forty minutes to make a round trip, the French crew had arranged the queues so that large families and old people would be passed through first. Smaller groups and individuals would debark last, meaning that Sarah and Ben would be among the final few passed through. Sophie and Yuri stood just ahead of them, holding each other's hands. Periodically, Sarah would open her purse and check on Katzele, who was asleep in her handbag, thanks to the ship's doctor. Towards one o'clock in the afternoon, Sophie and Yuri stepped up to the Arab officials. The Arab passed them without even looking up. Then Ben and Sarah stood at the head of the line.

"First in line—to the fore!" the sergeant-major shouted hoarsely; the time had come. They stepped forward and the Arab asked for their names.

"Benjamin Isaacson and Sarah Isaacson, brother and sister."

Sarah squeezed his arm.

A gaunt little man with gold-rimmed glasses took their papers. "Welcome to Palestine," he smiled. Ben took him to be a Lebanese Christian, since he spoke in French. He scrutinized the papers, then passed them on. Sarah tightened her grip on Ben's arm.

The British approved them. For a moment, Ben thought Sarah might faint.

The Jewish officials welcomed them, and then the Health Officer sent them to the orderly.

It was over.

Sophie and Yuri waited in a ferry at the foot of the gangway, hardly able to contain their exuberance. They shouted gleefully as Ben and Sarah descended to the *Asia*'s sea dock, reaching out to help them board the unstable taxi. There was a tense moment when Sarah tried to step into the boat cradling her purse; it rocked wildly, and threatened to capsize, but the boatman was used to landlubbers and his hand shot out to steady her. He was a skinny Arab with blotchy skin, rickety legs, and thick yellow teeth constantly bared in an obsequious grin. "Shalom, Effendis, shalom," he kept repeating.

Once the boat was away from the ship, Sarah ripped open her bag, worried that Katzele might have smothered. Gently, she lifted the cat out of her bag and settled him on her lap for the twenty-minute ride. Though he appeared barely able to walk, their oarsman proved deceptively strong. With long, rhythmic strokes that sent the taxi skimming over the water's surface, he rowed them within a hundred feet from shore. Since the craft drew too much water to cross the shallow flats, Arab bearers splashed out to carry everyone ashore piggyback. Unwilling to wait, Ben tied his shoes around his neck and jumped into the warm water. It barely came up to his knees. While the others waited for the bearers, Ben waded to the beach alone.

Benjamin Isaacson stood on the soil of Eretz Yisrael.

The hot sand burned his bare feet and he turned, thrilled by the sight of dozens of boats ferrying the immigrants from the *Asia* to their new home. Behind him, the beach was roped off for a quarter of a mile and beyond the rope was an eight-foot barbed wire fence. Thousands of people crowded the far side, eager to greet the *Asia*'s passengers and guide them to their temporary quarters. Reverently, Ben reached up and touched the gold Star of David pinned to his shirt. A wave of elation swept over him and he leaped in the air with a shout.

"Ben!" Yuri called from the water's edge. Ben waved back and watched as they trudged up the beach to join him. No one could send them back now.

They walked towards the mobile wooden buildings near the exit gate where Arab porters were busy collecting everyone's luggage. Jabbering away, the porters placed bags and suitcases in a large round tank, then closed and latched a set of steel doors. Once the tank was secure, an attendant yanked a long lever, releasing a hot, gaseous cloud of poison with a sinister whoosh of air. The procedure left cardboard suitcases limp and floppy. Leather and canvas bags fared slightly better, but they were marred by large brown stains. One didn't have to guess what the contents looked like.

The last of the *Asia*'s passengers stood in line outside an adjacent building resembling a giant version of the luggage drum. As Ben and the others took their place at the end of the line, one of the Litvaks, a stubborn old man with hooded eyes and a flashpan temper, suddenly dragged his wife from the head of the line as though she were a piece of baggage. A young Jewish official in a white shirt hurried after them. The old man and his wife didn't get far before they were trapped against the perimeter fence and the sidewall of the fumigation building. He shielded his wife with his body and shook his fists at their pursuer. Not wanting to provoke his quarry, the young man stopped and hovered at a distance, repeatedly assuring the old Litvak that the fumigation process was completely safe and painless. In response, the old man's jaw set in defiance and he unloosed a string of Yiddish oaths bearing directly on the young man's family and ancestors. Then he jabbed a gnarled finger in the general direction of the fumigation chamber and spat.

"The others may have gone without a struggle, but they weren't Litvaks. You're not gassing my wife and me without a fight."

The young official covered his eyes in frustration. "*Adoni habibi!*" he muttered. "We're not going to *gas* you, just *cleanse* you. It's the law." The old man was not impressed.

"This process is designed to kill lice and other parasites that might—"

"Lice!" the old man bellowed. "You think I have lice!" That was almost worse than being gassed. By this time, the line had dissolved into a swirling mass of angry people; the Litvak had managed to stir everyone up against the fumigation crew. Though the advantage of the situation lay with the old man, recognition and relief flooded his face when he saw Ben pushing towards him.

"Mr. Isaacson, thank God you're here. That man believes we are unclean and wants us to step in there." Wrathfully, the old man pointed to the fumigation drum. His lips compressed with outrage. "They want to gas us."

"Look, Isaacson, or whatever your name is, I..." the young official began. Ben looked down and read his name tag: Meyer Fleischer. Gently he interrupted.

"Please, Meyer, let's hear what Mr. Krepski has to say." Fleischer wiped the sweat from his forehead and frowned impatiently. It was unbearably hot and Meyer Fleischer was tired and thirsty. His heavy blue-black beard always showed stubble by noontime, no matter how close he shaved, and now it itched ferociously. Although he was reluctant to surrender his authority to the blond stranger in front of him, Meyer was sick of the *Ostjuden* and their primitive superstitions. All he wanted was to be done with them as quickly as possible. Grudgingly, he nodded, which launched Krepski into a thundering monologue.

As Ben listened to Krepski's complaints and suspicions, all he could think about was the crowd at the Coq d'Or, demanding breakfast in bed, and the *Ostjuden* who had panicked over the *baguettes*. It was funny and sad at the same time. The Krepskis were like many of the refugees aboard the *Asia*—born and raised in small villages on the plains of the Ukraine, or in isolated hamlets along the Baltic. They were a simple people, without much use for change. Driven from their homes, they had been thrown into the mainstream of twentieth-century life and, when faced with the unfamiliar or the unknown, they floundered in confusion. They would accept change, but to be accepted, it first had to be understood.

Ben thought for a moment, then the official's words popped into his mind: "We're not going to gas you, just cleanse you!" It gave him an idea. He jumped on a chemical drum and cut Krepski off in mid-sentence, much to the old man's irritation.

"I really don't understand you people. You've come all this way, and you still never seem to learn," Ben shook his head in disappointment. Cries of "Learn what?" and "What is he talking about?" ran through the crowd.

"Are you all deaf?" Ben gestured to his ears. "Didn't you hear the man? He said that the purpose of this procedure is a cleansing." There was no reaction from the assembled immigrants. Ben feigned shock. "Cleansing! Cleansing! This is where you cleanse yourselves of the old life— Europe, the pogroms, the fear, the pain. Everyone of you now stands on the free soil of Eretz Yisrael. It's time to wash away the old bonds." They listened with rapt attention, fascinated by his performance.

"Go in and cleanse yourselves of the past! Wash away the shame! Wash away the degradation! Wash away the sadness!" As he spoke, some of the old women clapped their hands rhythmically and began to laugh.

"What are you waiting for?" he yelled joyously. "A new life awaits every one of us on the other side of this building! Can't you hear the people on the other side, calling to us? Let's go!" Laughing and singing, the crowd reformed into a line.

The immigrants entered the chamber looking like caricatures of themselves, blown out of proportion by excess clothing. People covered their faces and tried to hold their breath as the chemical mist descended on them. It evaporated quickly, leaving a faint odor of disinfectant behind. As they stepped outside the chamber, a British officer handed each person an identification paper and instructed them to claim their bags and proceed to the main gate. Once outside the restricted area, friends and relatives joyfully embraced the new immigrants, shouting words of greeting and jubilation. Even in the open air, the sound was deafening.

Every imaginable form of conveyance jammed the dirt road leading to the beach, from horse-drawn wagons, automobiles, donkey carts, trucks, and ramshackle buses to strange-looking hybrids, created in the workshops of Tel Aviv. People had parked anywhere, laughing and sweating as they tied pieces of luggage on roofs and running boards.

As Ben searched through the pile of soggy luggage, he heard someone call his name. He turned and scanned the faces peering through the barbed-wire barrier, finally spotting Dora and Berzig. He left Yuri to sort through the bags and trotted over to the fence with a broad smile.

"Shalom," they greeted him. "Welcome to the Holy Land." Dora looked cool and refreshed in a white cotton skirt, blouse, and tan leather sandals. Berzig's khaki shorts and short-sleeve bush shirt were crisp and freshly pressed.

"Shalom," he replied, suddenly aware of the sweat pouring down his forehead. "I see that rank has its privileges. You two look a lot more comfortable than I do."

'We'll remedy that quick enough," she promised and invited him to be the guest of the Jewish Agency of Palestine while he stayed in Tel Aviv.

"Great!" Ben replied. Sarah, Sophie, and Yuri were all bound for Bet Olim, a settlement house in Tel Aviv where newly arrived immigrants underwent a brief orientation period. Most would then be assigned to agricultural communes called kibbutzim. Those who decided against farming would await jobs and housing, or settle with relatives. Since Ben had funds of his own and had no plans to join a kibbutz, he had planned to stay in a boarding house until he found more permanent quarters.

Ben rejoined the others and picked up his battered suitcase. Together, they walked through the main gate to freedom.

Outside the gate, Dora and Berzig stood in front of a vehicle that could be described as a bus only by the kindest stretch of the imagination. The owner had welded a long, flat platform to a standard automobile chassis, creating a base that overhung the rear wheels by a good five feet. Upright steel pipes supported a roof of slatted boards, covered with tattered canvas. It was piled high with luggage and sagged in the middle. Two rows of short wooden benches lined either side of a narrow aisle, and passengers could avoid being pitched out the side only by clinging to a length of steel pipe that replaced the traditional sidewalls. It looked like a cross between a bus and military transport.

"Are we really going to ride in that?" Yuri asked incredulously. The rusty leaf springs no longer had an upward curve and the tires looked about to go flat. Berzig laughed and touted the unobstructed view. Filled with reservations, they climbed aboard and sat on three empty benches in the middle. The "bus" was so full that any motion set the entire vehicle rocking. Suddenly, it lurched to one side, the springs squealing in agony.

A huge woman had hoisted herself aboard, filling the tiny space next to the driver with her bulk. She was not more than five-five or five-six, but Ben guessed she weighed close to two hundred and fifty pounds. The driver asked her to wait for the next bus, but she spied the single remaining seat in the rear of the vehicle, and insisted on taking it. She squeezed down the aisle sideways, her broad girth overhanging the aisle seats. People tried to move away to give her space to maneuver, but there was not enough room. She knocked several passengers to one side or back into their seats. At the rear of the bus, she lowered herself onto the next to the last bench, bracing one huge buttock on her half of the seat and allowing the other to hang, suspended in midair.

The driver turned to the wheel with a look of despair and put the bus into first. As he released the ancient clutch, there was a spine-wrenching screech of gears and the bus jerked violently, then stalled. The front end reared in the air, sending the fat woman tumbling backwards with a scream. The force of her fall drove the tailpipe into the ground and her weight kept the front wheels a good two feet off the ground. Derisive hoots and laughter came from the front of the bus. Those in the rear were more preoccupied with the obese woman's attempts to right herself; a sudden lurch to one side or the other and someone might well be crushed. Only when it became evident that the woman was completely helpless did anyone come forward to aid her.

Bracing themselves against the tilted floor, passengers in adjoining seats struggled to pull the fat woman upright and help her towards the front, where her weight would balance the bus. As she moved forward, the front wheels banged down, knocking everyone from side to side. Flushed and angry, the woman buttressed herself in the aisle and yelled at the driver to start again. He begged her to wait for the next bus, but she was determined to remain aboard.

"Just move it out, *yeke*" she abused him in a shrill falsetto. All went well for a couple of hundred yards until the right front tire hit a deep pothole, throwing her off balance and causing the bus to upend again. Sarah clutched the railing with one hand and clamped the other over her mouth to keep from giggling. Sophie buried her face in Yuri's shoulder.

The second incident only deepened the fat woman's determination to make the trip. To avoid a possible disaster, several passengers swapped seats, allowing the fat woman to wedge herself in the front of the bus near the driver. Muttering a prayer, the driver started up again. The bus swayed, jerked, and hopped, but remained horizontal even though it continued to yaw from side to side. A cheer went up among the passengers when the bus finally entered the city limits of Tel Aviv.

Tel Aviv was actually a suburb of Jaffa, located just a few miles north of the debarkation area. Tel Aviv, which mean "Spring Mountain" in Hebrew, had been founded in 1910 by Jews seeking a modern alternative to the ancient, predominantly Moslem city of Jaffa. When the planners first began, Tel Aviv was an empty hill. Fifteen years later it was a bustling city boasting nearly 30,000 inhabitants. Nearly every structure in the city was built of white brick, fired from the region's clay, and new construction pockmarked the landscape. Like the immigrants crowding the ramshackle bus, Tel Aviv was new to Palestine, but there to stay.

Bet Olim turned out to be a large, unimposing building with the customary white brick façade and functional metal windows. On first glance, it struck Ben as having the same sterile, impersonal appearance as Wiesenstrasse. Once inside, however, the difference was plain to see. Wiesenstrasse reeked of loss and decay. Bet Olim was alive with hope and joy. Ben helped the others carry their cases in while Dora and Berzig waited on the bus.

The clerk checked his register, nodding in approval when he found Sarah ''Isaacson'' and Mr. and Mrs. Grodberg listed. He explained they would be staying for three nights before leaving for the kibbutz and apologized to Yuri; men and women were housed in different dormitories, which separated husbands and wives. Yuri and Sophie were pleased to be mistaken for husband and wife, but Yuri was about to correct the clerk when Ben broke in.

''I have some good news,'' he grinned. ''You and Sophie are man and wife.'' They looked at him in astonishment.

''Married? But you said the weddings were just part of the play . . .'' Sarah's voice trailed off.

''I said what had to be said at the time. They can stand under the canopy if they like, but since last Monday night, they've been legally married.'' The two young people embraced each other, too overcome to speak. When they finally broke apart, Sophie ran over and hugged Ben fiercely, tears running down her cheeks.

''Mazel tov,'' Ben whispered. Looking at Sarah over Sophie's shoulder, he started to laugh. ''Perhaps now you'll understand why I was so reluctant to allow you to become Mrs. Morris Cheminsky.'' Sarah paled visibly.

''Good God,'' she shuddered as the clerk handed her a bunk assignment.

After promising Sarah that they would all get together the following day, Ben rejoined Dora and Berzig on the bus. As they pulled away from Bet Olim, he asked about Zelda.

''Never satisfied until all the chicks are safely tucked in,'' Dora grinned, shaking her head. Mottel and Zelda and the children were sharing adjacent quarters on Rechov Bugrachoff, and Dora asked the driver to go slightly out of his way to drop them off. That was part of the magic of Tel Aviv in those days; everyone was family—friendly, caring, and willing to oblige a request whenever possible.

Rechov Bugrachoff was a broad residential street lined with attractive split-level homes. Like most of the roads in the city, only the center was paved. Tel Aviv's architects had insisted on wide, spacious avenues, but until the city's work force and financing caught up with its growth, the shoulders would remain bare white sand.

Zelda's host couple were warm, friendly people who provided just the right atmosphere of comfort and security after the escape from Europe. As they sat together in the living room, Ben was delighted to see that the children had adopted Mottel as their *tatte*. When Mottel left the room to brew some tea, Zelda confided that there was a very good chance she and Mottel might get married. He was older than she, Zelda conceded, and hadn't established himself yet, but on the whole, he might make a good husband.

"Just between us," Zelda said coyly, "I expect him to ask me any day."

Berzig and Dora looked away trying to maintain their composure, but Ben burst out laughing. When he told her that she and Mottel had been legally married for almost a week, her mouth dropped open in shock. For a minute, Ben actually thought she might be speechless, but as always, she recovered quickly.

"How dare you interfere with my life?" she sputtered indignantly. "What makes you think I wanted to get married? What gave you the right to play the matchmaker?"

"Didn't you just say . . ."

"What makes you think I would marry Mottel if he asked me?"

"After all, Zelda, you just—"

"Never mind what I just said!"

"You could always get a divorce," Berzig suggested.

"A divorce!" she gasped. "No one in my family has ever had a divorce! Think of the disgrace!"

"Better that than to be married to . . ."

"I'll just have to make do," she said firmly. "Who's going to tell poor Mottel? He'll probably faint with relief that he won't have to ask me officially." Berzig volunteered to convey the news out to the kitchen. As he rose, Zelda reached out and laid a hand on his forearm. "You can also tell him that he can forget any 'ideas' he might have until we stand in front of a real Rabbi. I have my self-respect to think of." Berzig smiled and disappeared into the kitchen.

Sixty seconds later, Mottel came rushing into the parlor, as flushed and incoherent as a teenager on his first date. He kept shaking everyone's hand until Dora finally suggested that it was time to go. Zelda walked Ben to the door. When he kissed her and wished her good luck, a melancholy look came into her eyes.

"Oh, Ben, I'm happy enough, but I would have liked something a little more romantic," she said wistfully. Zelda would always wish that her life could be different from what it was.

The accommodations that Dora arranged for Ben were in a small housing compound run by the Jewish Agency for visiting organizers and personnel. Since it was located just a few blocks from Rechov Bugrachoff, they decided to walk. Ten minutes later, Dora showed him to his room and introduced the Yemenite housekeeper, a plump woman named Deborah with iron-grey hair and a weathered face serrated by wrinkles and a ready smile. The house had been hastily built, and lacked the finish of most European homes, but to Ben, it looked fine. After his cabin on the *Asia*, anything seemed unbelievably spacious and luxurious.

Dora suggested they have lunch together, and thirty minutes later Ben sat down to a splendidly laid table; Deborah was a superb cook. After they had eaten, she cleared the dishes and left them to spend the balance of the afternoon talking on the back porch. Their conversation had a dream-like quality, as though everything around them might suddenly dissolve, leaving them to wake in a German relocation center or back aboard the *Asia* with a British escort, bound for Marseilles. As dusk approached, Dora and Berzig rose to leave. They were to be debriefed early the following morning and wanted to be well rested.

At the door, there was an awkward moment as the three friends stared at each other, reluctant to let the day end. The carefree afternoon they had spent laughing and retelling stories marked the end of a journey; by the next morning, it would all be a part of the past.

Ben leaned over and kissed Dora. She hugged him, then turned and stepped out into the street, leaving him alone with Berzig. They stood staring at each other, unable to find the words to express their feelings. Finally, Ben said. "Shalom, *u'lehitraot*. Farewell, comrade. Take good care of Dora."

"The lady takes care of herself," Berzig grinned, touching his forehead with a two-fingered salute. Then he, too, was gone.

Ben returned to his room and stretched out on the bed, intending to catch up on lost sleep. But sleep would not come. The mattress was too soft, the room too quiet, and his friends' departure had left too great a void within him. After the excitement and intensity of the past few months, tomorrow seemed like a yawning abyss. He tossed and turned restlessly until well after midnight, when sleep crept up on him like an unexpected but welcome visitor.

The next morning he awoke bleary-eyed, startled by a vision of Sarah standing in his doorway. Her hair was pinned up and she carried an armful of fresh flowers wrapped in newsprint. He rubbed his eyes. When he opened them again, she was still there.

"*Boker Tov*," she said brightly.

"And good morning to you," he replied, wondering how she managed to find him. She walked to the side of the bed and placed the bouquet in a handmande vase. Shyly, she detached a small white envelope from the flowers and gave it to him. He propped himself up on one elbow and withdrew a folded note which read, "Benjamin, I love you." He blushed in spite of himself and self-consciously pulled the sheet up to cover his bare chest.

"Sarah, I . . ."

"No, Ben, you don't have to say anything," she smiled happily. "I just wanted you to know how I feel." She had debated for hours over what to say in the note, finally deciding on the simple truth. If he didn't feel the same way about her, she could live with that, but she was tired of being the "little sister." It was time she told him how she felt.

Taken aback, Ben asked her to wait outside while he washed and dressed, buying a few minutes in which to think. Contrary to what Sarah thought, he realized she was no longer the insecure girl he had met in Hamburg. It was impossible to ignore her ripening figure and her poised self-confidence, or the way she looked at him when they were together. Ben was strongly attracted to Sarah and thoughts of their being together often came to him, unbidden. Yet he was still committed to Bluma, still hoping that she would come.

Once he became involved with Sarah, he knew himself well enough to know that Bluma would fade into memory, and he was not ready for that. He also suspected that Sarah was not quite ready to get involved in a relationship either. She had decided against joining a kibbutz, and Ben didn't want her making decisions just because she was at loose ends. They both had plenty of time, there was no need to rush.

When he stepped outside a half hour later, he found Sarah and Katzele out on the front porch, talking with the neighbor, whom Sarah introduced as Mrs. Blumenthal.

"Oh, Mr. Isaacson," the neighbor gushed, "Sarah has been telling me all about her escape from Germany. It must have been terrifying," she gasped, her lips forming a perfect red "o" of sympathy. "Then to be cooped up in a sterile, stuffy dormitory at Bet Olim . . . Well! It's just too much to ask of anyone! I know, because I was there when I first came from Germany with my husband. I'll tell you what, Sarah, why don't you come and live with me? You could help take care of the twins and the house—I can't pay much, but it would give you a place to stay until you decide what to do." How she managed to speak for so long without drawing a breath mystified Ben.

"Oh, Ben," Sarah exclaimed. "What do you think?"

"I think it's a fantastic idea."

Sarah and Katzele moved in that afternoon. As he helped her, Ben took advantage of their time alone to explain how he felt. To his relief, Sarah was neither surprised nor upset. She understood that he needed time to resolve his feelings about Bluma, and she needed time as well, to get herself settled. She reached out and squeezed his hand. "When you're ready, Ben, you know where I am." After he left, Sarah reflected on their conversation, thrilled with the outcome of her boldness. The words they exchanged hardly mattered—what did count was that for the first time, Ben had treated her as an equal, not as a child. That was more than enough, she thought, hugging Katzele. At least for now.

Ben found the freedom of the succeeding days pleasurable at first, then increasingly oppressive. Everyone seemed to have a direction but he. Yuri and Sophie had left for a kibbutz, Sarah was happy at Marta Blumenthal's, and even Zelda and Mottel were fully occupied planning for their wedding.

One afternoon when he was feeling particularly despondent, Dora Hoffmann came by with Berzig. After they talked for a while, Dora broached the real reason for their visit. They were bringing another boatload of *Ostjuden* through the blockade and they wanted Ben to join them. They tried to persuade him to return to Europe on the *Asia* the following week. At first, Ben was tempted to go with them. The work was important and exciting, and this time he would be a part of the team. But in the end, he decided against it. There were too many unsolved issues in his life.

"Maybe the next time," he promised.

Dora hesitated a moment, then smiled. "Ben, I know how you feel about Bluma and I pray it will happen for both of you. But don't delay too long. You have a life to lead, and I'd hate to see you waiting for something that will never happen."

After they left, he wrestled with his emotions until Deborah appeared with a mop and pail to clean the room, forcing him to pull on his shoes and leave the house. He walked aimlessly at first, exploring the neighborhood. Most of the houses were a couple of years old, but the land beyond was newly developed. Homes in various stages of completion dotted the white sand dunes; Tel Aviv was booming. Everywhere one turned, buildings were going up—apartments, duplexes, single family homes, office buildings, warehouses—the volume of new construction staggered the imagination.

Wandering down a dead-end street, Ben caught sight of a large sign in Hebrew and English, SILICAT BRICK WORKS, that overhung a rickety gate barring the main entrance. Off to one side was a small wooden gatehouse, occupied by an elderly man slouched over a newspaper. Having little else to do, Ben strolled over and greeted him.

The old man's name was Aaron, and he was obviously lonely and eager to talk. Aaron was not exactly a polished conversationalist, but he did prove to be a font of information on Tel Aviv and the brick industry, recalling the days when the city was an empty mound covered by olive trees and goats. As Aaron became more expansive, he volunteered a tour of the factory, but Ben refused, afraid the old man might get into trouble for deserting his post.

Aaron flashed him a toothless grin. "My brother-in-law owns the place. If he fires me, he'll have to live with my sister's wrath. Believe me, I wouldn't wish that on anyone." Aaron hauled the road barrier to an upright position so traffic wouldn't be blocked, then grabbed Ben's arm and led him towards one of the blast furnaces.

Silicat made plain white bricks, the mainstay of the building industry in Tel Aviv. The ovens ran around the clock and still couldn't meet the demand, because the constant influx of immigrants continued to outpace new construction. The result was a housing shortage that would last several years at least. Aaron detailed every step of the process and explained that orders were so brisk that the factory never had the opportunity to build up an inventory. The bricks were pulled out of the furnace, then directly loaded onto mule-drawn wagons for immediate delivery. They cooled on the way to the site.

"The bricks we make this morning could be part of a building by nightfall," Aaron boasted. Sweating heavily from the waves of heat, Ben watched the endless stream of bricks emerging from the kilns. What intrigued him the most was the line of wagons waiting to be loaded. There simply weren't enough bricks to go around. As they completed the tour and headed back towards the main gate, they were forced to walk around an enormous mountain of broken bricks that obscured the office building behind it.

"My brother-in-law's curse," the old man smirked, pointing to the brick pile. "He complains that his workers break more bricks than they make."

"What happens to all these bricks?" Ben wondered.

"Nothing. They're only good for fill. Usually, we wait until business is slow, then we load them on trucks and dump them somewhere."

"But business has been so good that you haven't had the time?"

Aaron shrugged his shoulders and nodded. As they walked back towards the gate, Ben kept thinking about the huge pile of bricks. It seemed like such a waste. "Do all the brickyards in Tel Aviv throw their broken bricks away?" An idea began to take form.

"We are the only factory of importance," Aaron replied proudly.

It didn't make sense. The brickyard could not manufacture bricks fast enough to meet the demand, yet they considered broken bricks worthless. His grandfather in Sweden would have found a dozen uses for those broken bricks—foundations, chimneys, slabs, driveways, walls, docks—the list was endless. Suddenly, Ben knew what he would be doing the next day.

When the *S.S. Asia* anchored in Jaffa, nearly a thousand *Ostjuden* became citizens of Eretz Yisrael. That was only half the battle. Many of those people would remain idle for months, searching for employment. Now, there was something Ben could do about that. He turned to Aaron, his heart pounding with excitement, and asked if anyone was still in the office.

"They're all there."

"Would you take me in and introduce me?"

The old man stared at him in mild surprise. "What for?"

"I want to take these broken bricks off their hands."

Aaron's brother-in-law was an unpleasant man in his mid-forties by the name of Mordecai Ravitz. Until the building boom began in Tel Aviv, Ravitz had scraped out a threadbare existence making bricks and tiles on an empty lot next to his home. The boom changed all that; now he was an important man with dozens of employees and a thriving business. Like many who attain sudden wealth that is largely undeserved and usually unexpected, Mordecai Ravitz was filled with small vanities and petty greed. At first, he was cagey, assuming that Ben wanted to be paid to haul the bricks away. Ravitz was open to such an arrangement and kept waiting to hear a price. When Ben explained that he was willing to haul the bricks away gratis, Ravitz was incredulous.

"What will you do with them?" he asked.

"Re-sell them for a profit." Ben saw no need for secrecy. Word would be out on the street within twenty-four hours anyway. Tel Aviv was still a small town.

Ravitz stared blankly at first, his tiny pig-eyes watering in disbelief, then he threw back his head and roared with laughter. He continued to laugh until Ben said he would sign a three-year contract and post a bond for 250 English pounds to be forfeited to Ravitz if Ben failed to uphold his part of the contract. A smarter man than Ravitz would have hesitated but Ravitz was too overwhelmed by his unexpected good fortune; all he could think of was the money he would save by not having to remove the bricks. Hurriedly, he sent for paper, pen, and ink, anxious to draw an agreement before the crazy European changed his mind. Poor Aaron earned himself a vicious rebuke for trying to warn Ben that the bricks were worthless. After Ben signed, Ravitz fawned on him all the way to the door. As Ben walked back up the road, his boots kicking up clouds of brick dust, Ravitz called out to him, "What's the name of your company?"

Ben thought for a moment, then yelled back, "The S.S. ASIA!"

"Never heard of it," Ravitz sneered.

"Before today, neither had I," Ben laughed in response.

That night, Ben hunched over the tiny desk in his room, jotting down lists of ideas, equipment he would need, and rough cost estimates. He had more than enough capital to fund the company, and he was convinced that a handsome profit lay buried in Mordecai Ravitz's brick pile. With the help of the *Ostjuden* off the *Asia*, Ben would turn those broken bricks into gold. He mapped out a careful strategy to cover the first thirty days of operation, trying to anticipate every contingency. He fell asleep propped up in bed, calculating the number of men he would be able to employ.

The following day, Ben bought two wagons and two pairs of mules. According to the mule trader, a wizened Arab from Tulkarem, the animals were a crossbreed between genuine Middle East donkeys and a renown purebred Arabian stallion. Ben did his best not to smile at the mule trader's sincerity attempts.

Ben's next step was to hire a crew of men off the ASIA, and he started with a roster of twenty men. He sold three wagon loads that first afternoon, to a contractor who saw the advantage of using broken bricks for foundation walls. That night, the men held a celebration in his honor, toasting each other with Rishon LeZion—'the wine of the first city in Zion.'

By the end of the week, Ben's efforts to find more buyers for his broken bricks paid off handsomely. He had to hire another dozen men and the mountainous brickpiles in Mordecai Ravitz's yard slowly began to dwindle. It came as no surprise to Ben when Ravitz suddenly tried to void their agreement; it had not taken the factory owner very long to realize the true value of his "useless" bricks.

Following common practice, Ben called on the labor union, the Histadrut, to mediate the dispute. Since nearly everyone in the work force was a member of the union, the Histadrut mediator's decision was usually binding; to reject his ruling was to invite a strike. Ben's disagreement was settled by none other than Chaim Arlosoroff, the charismatic union organizer. After listening to the facts, Arlosoroff quickly found in Ben's favor and Ravitz reluctantly agreed to abide by the decision.

As the business continued to flourish Ben came to rely more and more on Sarah. She had started by helping part-time with the bookkeeping, but within days, she was hard put to keep up with her work for the Blumenthals and with her responsibilities as company accountant for the S.S. ASIA.

During the second week, Ben moved out of the quarters provided by the Jewish Agency and into an unfinished house next to Shoshana, a friend of Bluma's from the University of Dorpat. When the house had become available, she had told Ben immediately and he had called the landlord, agreeing to rent the house without even seeing it. Even unfinished houses in Tel Aviv were impossibly difficult to find.

Three days later, Sarah quit her job at Mrs. Blumenthal's and became the SS ASIA's full time bookeeper. Ben set up a small office in his spare bedroom for Sarah to work in and at that point, it seemed only logical for her to accept Shoshana's invitation and move in next door to Ben's new house. But there was more than convenience involved; it was a way for Ben and Sarah to stay close to each other without raising any eyebrows among their orthodox neighbors. Outwardly, Shoshana and her husband made ideal "chaperones" for Sarah. In reality, Shoshana's husband was no more than a boarder; like so many of the illegals aboard the ASIA, he had entered Palestine thanks to Shoshana's good will and an ersatz marriage certificate.

During the ensuing month, Ben and Sarah saw Zelda and Motel united beneath the wedding canopy and helped to settle Sophie and Yuri on a kibbutz northeast of Tel Aviv. Zelda, Motel, and the children lived in a tiny cottage, but there was always room for two more people at the kitchen table; ben and Sarah were often guests for dinner. The Rubinsteins were a happy couple, even though Zelda never let Motel forget that she had married him because of Ben's intervention, not of her own free will. Motel had managed to secure a good job with a company that imported Singer sewing machines and with luck, by summertime they would be able to afford a larger house.

Shoshana was an engaging and entertaining young woman, and Ben and Sarah spent many pleasant evenings with her. To Ben's surprise,

Chaim Arlosoroff was a regular visitor. Apparently, he and Shoshana were good friends. Ben found his company stimulating and thought-provoking; Arlosoroff was that kind of man. Though the labor leader was only four years older than Ben, he was a man already marked for greatness.

Many times, Ben and Arlosoroff would argue passionately about the future until the small hours of the night. They shared a fascination for economics; like Ben, Arlosoroff had taken a degree in economics, but from the University of Berlin. Though they frequently found themselves in opposite camps, they both agreed that the survival of a Jewish Homeland in Palestine depended on its becoming self-sufficient.

One evening, Arlosoroff used Ben as a sounding board for a series of speeches he was planning to deliver in America. Taking his theme from the writings of the great Hebrew sage, Moses Maimonides, Arlosoroff wanted to convince American Jews that Palestine was not going to become a beggar's haven, forever dependent on the charity of others. Arlosoroff likened money given to the cause of a Jewish Homeland to Maimonides Eighth and highest degree of Charity; charity that was more than just alms. It was a way to help the needy to build factories, homes, and businesses, making it possible for them to become fully self-supporting. In turn, those Jews would help others in the same manner, creating a self-sufficient nation with its own resources. Ben felt the speeches would be a tremendous success.

Between the business, Sarah's presence, homespun dinners at the Rubinsteins, and the stimulating evenings spent with Arlosoroff, Ben hardly had a moment to himself. Life was full and exciting; every day seemed to be another adventure.

When Sarah closed the books on their first month of operation, the S.S. ASIA had netted a profit of just over 50 pounds sterling. Ben was delighted, but real reward was knowing that more than fifty families relied on the fledgling company to provide them with a fresh start in a new land. His experience with the S.S. ASIA convinced Ben that with ingenuity and enough hard work, there was no limit to what they could accomplish in Palestine.

Ben celebrated the company's success by paying everyone a bonus and rewarding Sarah and himself with a short vacation. It was nearly April and he wanted to take Sarah, Sophie, and Yuri to Jerusalem. There was something he wanted to witness, something he had planned on for a very long time—the opening of Hebrew University.

TWENTY-TWO

Jerusalem
March 30, 1925

Though Jerusalem was less than forty miles from Jaffa as the crow flies, traveling from one city to the other turned out to be an all-day affair. The Jerusalem Express creaked and rattled to a shuddering halt at every crossroad and watering stop along the way, taking on passengers, livestock, and trade goods. It was nearly dark when the ancient locomotive hissed to a final rest at Jerusalem Station. Outside the battered carriage door lay the Holy City, the City of David, the site of glorious victories and bitter defeats; the Wailing Wall, the Old City, and Mount Zion itself. Stepping off the train into Jerusalem was like entering another world.

Ben led the way through cobblestone avenues swarming with tourists and supplicants from all over the world: Christian, Moslem, and Jew. Buses, cars, and donkey carts shared the streets with pedestrians and long-robed Arabs leading camels. Jerusalem melded the centuries. They turned into a bazaar and were transported back to biblical times; emerging from the other side, they were nearly run over by a car. Festive electric globes illuminated the main thoroughfares, strung to celebrate the opening of the Hebrew University. Restaurants buzzed with activity. Countless shops and bazaars lined the streets. Vendors pushed carts laden with trade goods and momentos. Jerusalem radiated a sense of vitality that belied its age.

They made several wrong turns before coming to a halt in front of the

Amdursky Hotel. It was a two-story house with old-fashioned shutters and peeling paint; anything but imposing. The owner was an enterprising soul who had subdivided the original rooms into tiny cubicles, thereby quadrupling his capacity. The partitions separating the rooms were flimsy, creating just enough space for a bed, a chair, and a grubby white card that said: "Welcome to the Amdursky Hotel, ideally located in the Holiest of Cities."

They all laughed about the accommodations over dinner in a crowded restaurant, and afterwards, when Ben suggested they explore the city, Sarah was predictably eager to be off. Sophie and Yuri thanked Ben, but declined the invitation. The excursion to Jerusalem was their first time alone as man and wife since their arrival at the kibbutz. It was actually their honeymoon, and they were looking forward to spending some time alone.

Ben and Sarah left the restaurant and walked without purpose, purchasing sweets from an Arab vendor and a map of the city from a Christian peddler. Suddenly, Sarah grabbed Ben's arm and pointed to a woman leaning out a street-level window.

"Oh, Ben," she whispered. "Let's see if we can get ourselves invited into that woman's house."

"Whatever for?" he asked in astonishment.

"Can't you see the *mezzuzah* on the door? They're Jewish! What better way to learn about Jerusalem than from Jews who live here?" Reluctantly, he went along with her. They were promptly invited in, and Sarah was whisked off to the kitchen. Ben was given a yarmulke to wear, then ushered into a large room where a half dozen men sat around a table, pulling names out of a phone book, a Johannesburg phone book. Intrigued, Ben asked what they were doing.

"We earn a living by praying for the dead at the Wailing Wall," one of them explained brightly.

Working under the assumption that all American, British, Australian, and South African Jews were wealthy, the men drew Jewish surnames at random from urban phone books and wrote to them, offering to pray for loved ones at the Holy Wall. Since few Jews from abroad could perform the cherished task of praying at the Wall, local families prayed on their behalf in exchange for a small fee. The family increased its ability to handle a large volume of names by offering one kaddish for several subscribers.

Ben chatted with the men until Sarah emerged from the kitchen, flushed beet red. She smiled stiffly at her hostess and told Ben she was ready to go. Once outside, she gave vent to a howl of outrage.

"I can understand how these people believe that women are just chattels who belong in the kitchen or the nursery, but I never imagined that I would receive the kind of proposition that I did today." Sarah was livid. "That woman wanted me to ask my parents to pay for her son's education. He's thirteen and just about to enter the Yeshiva to obtain his higher education."

"And then?" Ben asked as they rounded a corner.

"And then, after he completed his education at my parents' expense, I would be allowed to marry the clod. In short, my parents would buy me a husband." Her expression was so outraged that Ben started laughing. Gradually a smile appeared on her lips and she laughed as well, her dark eyes sparkling with the joy of their being together.

•　　•　　•

The following morning they all congregated in the hotel lobby. Sophie and Yuri looked so radiant that Sarah wondered if they had something special planned for the day.

"Yes," Yuri's eyes glowed. "After you and Ben left us last night, we met several ultra-orthodox Jews who volunteered to guide us to the Kottel, the Wailing Wall. We hope you'll come with us."

"We wouldn't miss it," Ben smiled.

Their guides turned out to be pleasant and friendly, but very orthodox. Ben found out just how orthodox when he stopped to inhale the delicious aroma emanating from a native restaurant. The three men looked at him in horror; to them, even inhaling the odor of nonkosher food was sacrilegious. They hurried everyone away, following a serpentine route through the city that led down one twisting alley after another. Courtyards were a rare luxury in the Old City; most doors opened directly into the street. Ben started to believe that Jerusalem had no real streets, only narrow alleys where someone's front door might open in your face at any moment. Every so often, the alley would culminate in a series of broad, shallow steps.

Ben estimated they'd been walking for nearly an hour when their guides descended a particularly old and worn set of steps, coming to a stop at the bottom. They stood facing a massive stone wall, their view broken by the haphazard construction that opposed it. Great stone blocks rested atop one another, forming simple geometric patterns. No mortar filled the deep seams between the weathered blocks. The surface of the wall was rough and pitted, and from a distance, looked to be inscribed with ancient Hebrew lettering. Even up close it was hard to discern, and people commonly misread scratches and gouges as faded inscriptions. Men and boys in prayer shawls and phylacterics bowed and swayed before the Wall, intoning their devotions. Off to one side, a small group of women prayed quietly.

"Ben," Sarah whispered reverently. "Please put on your *tefillin*." She handed him a yarmulke bought from a vendor in front of the hotel. It was typical of her thoughtfulness.

Wordlessly, Ben set the yarmulke on the back of his head and drifted away from his companions. Overcome by emotion, he walked up to the wall and reached out to touch the rough surface. The cold stone spoke to him, as it had spoken to the heart and soul of Jewry since the time of Herod. Two thousand years of prayer and lamentation had imbued the unadorned blocks with the life pulse of a people.

Tears filled his eyes as he looked up. He felt unbearably sad, yet fulfilled at the same time. From far away, he heard his own voice. "Father," it whispered. "Father, I am here. I am here in Zion."

For a time, he stood motionless, aching with bittersweet memories. He fumbled for a handkerchief, then reached to his pocket and withdrew a folded piece of plain white paper, inscribed with a prayer for his father. Tenderly, he placed the note in an indentation between two blocks. Then he stepped back and covered his eyes to pray. When he finished, he found Sarah and the others were already waiting for him, drained and emotionally exhausted. As they retraced their steps through the noisy streets, no one spoke, each needing the time to assimilate the experience, each wanting to preserve their awareness of the moment a little longer. They shared a simple meal, then retired early.

Alone in his tiny room, Ben stretched out on his bed, hands folded behind his head, and tried to sort out his tangled emotions. He had come to Palestine as more of a Zionist than a Jew. Like his father, Ben's faith did not rest in religious nostrums or the observance of ritual, it rested in his people. But he began to understand how inseparable the two were, nation and faith wedded to each other through eternity. To be a Jew and to be alive was to be a living testament to God's covenant with the people of Eretz Yisrael. Now that the years of hostile exile were over, language, faith, and nation were united once more.

As the hours ticked by, he analyzed the past, reliving the formative experiences of his life. The carefree, joyful years in Sweden, his painful initiation to the rites of anti-Semitism, Madame Spitz trampling his sister's flowers, the roving gangs of bullies. He remembered the day his father arrived in Dorpat, half-dead from the winter snows; his grandmother's death, and his mother's sorrow when he left his home and family. He thought about the white-haired Nazi and that terrifying night on the Berlin Express; Hessemann's cold rejection, and Herschel's and Helen's warmth. There was Karl, kissing his Jewish wife, then leaving to beat up Jews in another part of town; Stiffler and his friendship; Maurice Kaplan weaving his sly webs; and Hanovi, gruff, efficient, and thorough. The pain of seeing Bluma shot came back to him, as fresh and sharp as though it had happened yesterday.

All things considered, he had conspired to smuggle hundreds of his people into a land he actually knew nothing about. Now that the task was over, he found himself examining his own motives, asking himself why, and what for. Was it because of a promise he'd made to his father? Only in the beginning. What he had done required an enormous amount of faith—no simple promise could have sustained him. But faith in what, he asked himself. He finally decided that it must be faith in the future.

"I'm here," he said aloud. "And this day, I paid my last debt to the past."

But what of the future? Was it just a great adventure, a challenge, a dare? In the past, whenever people asked him "why?" he always gave the same response: "To see the opening of the Hebrew University." But somehow, the meaning of that event had become lost in the floodtide of excitement. There was no time to consider something so distant while he faced the flaring despair of Wiesenstrasse or the panic in Alexandria. Given the backdrop of those events, the opening of a school seemed relatively unimportant. But as Ben tossed restlessly on his lumpy mattress, he knew that nothing could be further from the truth. The Hebrew University was much more than a school made of bricks and mortar. It symbolized the end of exile, the first wholly Jewish institution on Jewish soil since the Second Diaspora. It announced to the world: "We have come home, and we intend to stay." It marked the millennium, and he would be there to witness it.

The next morning, Ben rose early, intent on doing some exploring on his own. He wandered through the streets without a specific destination, trying to absorb the spirit of the city, and his initial impressions of Jerusalem changed radically as he observed its character beneath the surface color and activity. He could feel the anger and the tension seething beneath the casual façade of "business as usual." The impending dedication of the university had unleashed a maelstrom of passions.

The Arabs bitterly resented the university as a symbol of Jewish sovereignty and lost no opportunity to fight it. The orthodox Jews of the Agudat Yisrael viewed the opening of the university as a covert attempt to reestablish the Temple, an act forbidden until the advent of the Messiah, and they fought it with a vigor equal to that of the Arabs. Near the Mosque of Omar in the Arab section of the Old City, Ben saw Arabs and Jews arguing so fiercely that violence was only narrowly averted by a British colonial patrol that happened by. Jew fought with Jew just as passionately. In the Christian sectors, preachers, priests, and ministers lamented the cause of the troubles, advocating that the ceremonies be canceled. As the appointed day approached, the controversy built to a fever pitch.

Through it all, visitors continued to arrive from all over the world. Plainly earmarked as tourists by their expensive Western clothing, they strolled through the streets of Jerusalem as though they were on the Ringstrasse in Vienna or the Champs-Elysées in Paris; most were blissfully ignorant of the danger surrounding them on every side. The conspicuous presence of so many tourists made the British authorities feel nervous and impotent. Every street corner attracted a group of debaters, offering a potential opportunity for violence. The city was like a tinderbox. The mobs of tourists were too vulnerable, too visible—it was almost an invitation for some lunatic incited by the Grand Mufti or the ultrareligious to toss a bomb or run amok with a gun.

One particular group caught Ben's attention. A clean-shaven preacher with wiry black hair stood in the center of a small crowd with a Bible in one hand. "I was a Jew," he shouted fervently. "But I found grace in the love of Jesus Christ. You can find the same love. His blood was shed on this land . . ."

He was interrupted by another man who wanted to know how the preacher felt about the opening of the Hebrew University. Before he could reply, a third answered with his own rambling interpretation. Then the preacher spoke for a full five minutes, spouting inappropriate biblical references and grandiose sentiments. Bored, Ben was about to leave when an imposing man in threadbare Western clothes rose to speak. He was well over six feet tall, and needed no chair or soapbox to tower over the crowd. He spoke with a thick accent that Ben couldn't identify.

"I am not a student of theology, nor am I a preacher, or a religious fanatic. I am simply a follower of Jesus Christ, and I would like to share a bit of Scripture with you now." He reached into a dyed leather satchel and withdrew a worn Bible, trailing a length of red ribbon tied as a cross. Quoting the appropriate passages, he referred to Abraham, Isaac, and Jacob as the fathers of all three religions, giving every man in the audience, be he Christian, Moslem, or Jew, full authority to argue with one another to their heart's desire, but as brothers, not as enemies. In a deep, persuasive voice, he cited references from the Old and New Testaments, demonstrating that God had commanded Abraham and his people to occupy the land of Palestine. Then, he drew parallel quotations from Sura V of the Koran and Chapter 12 of Genesis, where God issued his command to Abraham, "*Lekh lekha!*"

He closed the book gently. "Can any of us thus deny that the Jews were commanded to return to Eretz Yisrael by the word of the Lord God?"—he challenged the crowd. "By what authority can we Christians and Moslems now contest His divine will and testament?"

Never had Ben heard the case for a Jewish homeland in Palestine stated so simply or so eloquently.

He spent the balance of the afternoon wandering through Jerusalem, past the Dome of the Rock, through the Gardens, and back into the Old City. Then, towards evening, he once again found himself facing the Wailing Wall. Bowing his head, he stood to one side and listened to the chanting.

A couple stood in front of him, unintentionally trapping him against the partially constructed building at his back. The man was in his mid-fifties, balding, and slightly paunchy, but handsome in a worn kind of way. The woman was blond, svelte, and at least ten years his junior. Ben knew without asking that they were married.

"I'm beat, Solomon. I've really had it," the blonde said tiredly. There was no whine to her voice; she sounded genuinely exhausted.

"I have to spend a few minutes here, Jenny," her husband replied. "Just a few minutes. Then we can go back to the hotel. Okay?" Reluctantly, she nodded.

He stepped forward, close to the wall, and drew a deep breath. A sheen of sweat covered his face. As he stood, Ben saw him tremble slightly, as though he had a fever. His wife noticed at the same time and ran to his side, her face furrowed with concern.

"Sol, you're too hot!" she scolded him. "We can look at rocks any day, but not if you end up with a stroke. Let's go back now! Please!"

"No!" he snapped. "Not yet."

The woman threw her hands up in disgust and Ben heard her mutter, "Now I know why it's called 'The Wailing Wall.' Some vacation."

The man walked past a group of elderly orthodox lost in prayer and found a small space for himself. Ben saw his expression tighten. By contrast, his wife looked bored and out of place; Ben suddenly realized that Solomon was a Jew and his wife was a Gentile.

Reverently, Solomon approached the wall. He hesitated a moment, then reached into his breast pocket and removed a folded piece of white paper. With an embarrassed glance at his wife, he slid the paper into an indentation in the wall, just as Ben and countless thousands of Jews had done before him. Then he closed his eyes and covered them with one of his hands, lips moving in silent prayer.

Solomon stood there for several minutes, while his wife frowned impatiently, arms across her chest. Then his lips stopped moving, but he still remained motionless at the wall. Ben watched her expression turn from impatience to worry when her husband's shoulders began shaking, as though he was crying. She hurried towards him.

"What's wrong Solly?" she asked gently, placing a hand on his shoulder.

"I'm all right, honey," he replied, wiping the tears from the corners of his eyes. "It's just . . . well, Jenny . . . it just feels like . . ." His face wrinkled in concentration as he searched for exactly the right word.

"What does it feel like?"

He suddenly relaxed and broke into a sad smile. "It feels just like coming home," he whispered. She gave him a hug, and they walked past Ben, hand in hand. As he looked after them, he caught sight of Mount Scopus, looming above the hills that surrounded Jerusalem. He knew exactly what the American meant. He, too, had come home, and when the doors to the Hebrew University finally opened, it would signal to the world: as a people, the Jews had come home.

At last.

TWENTY-THREE

The Summit of Mount Scopus
Jerusalem
Sunday, April 1st, 1925
2:30 PM

The sight was truly awesome.

Ben, Sarah, Sophie, and Yuri stood together on the pinnacle of Mount Scopus, watching thousands upon thousands of people crowd the road from Jerusalem, forming an unbroken line from the ancient city to the mountain's base. The exodus from Jerusalem had begun before dawn and had continued throughout the morning and early afternoon. Old people panting from exhaustion clung to relatives or sturdy walking staffs. Children scampered along the crowd's edge, singing and playing. Occasionally, an automobile loaded with dignitaries or wealthy tourists forced its way through the mob. But despite the long, tiring hike and steep incline to the summit, people were happy and smiling.

It was a day to remember.

Beyond the crowds lay the Judean Wilderness, the River Jordan, and the endless expanse of the Dead Sea. The brilliant white exterior of the university buildings stood out from the dusty mountaintop like a diamond lodged in a vein of clay. From its vantage point atop Mount Scopus, the university seemed poised like a watchtower over the ancient fortress-city of King David; a beacon to the descendants of his people. The only discordant note was struck by sullen groups of Arabs and ultra-orthodox Jews, gathered at the base of the mountain. Both groups were bitterly opposed to the opening and furious because they had failed to stop it. Members of Agudat Yisrael planned a retreat to their synagogues to pray that God would forgive the arrogance and blasphemy of their fellow Jews. The Arab *fellahin* were ordinarily peaceful enough, but capable of murderous rampages when aroused. There was good reason to fear such a possibility. When the Grand Mufti had failed to block the dedication of the university, his prestige had been tarnished; it would demand revenge.

Inevitably, the hatred would explode into violence, but on this particular day, the Arabs read their black-bordered newspapers, and waited. They screamed anti-Semitic insults, and waited. They listened to the litany of venom recited by the Grand Mufti, and waited, letting the pressue build, nurturing the tension to an unbearable pitch. One day soon, they would wreak havoc on the Jews of Palestine and once again, blood would stain the streets of the Old City.

But to the thousands participating in the celebrations, the reckoning would be paid another day, and the seeds of bitter discord were ignored. This day was a day for rejoicing.

The Jews of Palestine had fought, stolen, lied, smuggled, and begged to begin the great work, setting a cultural cornerstone of Jewish history. To the thousands present on top of Mount Scopus, the dedication of the university was the first step towards the revitalization of a Jewish national life. Thousands more, unable to be preent, gathered in cities, synagogues, and meeting halls all over the world, waiting to hear that the first Jewish institution to arise in two millennia was officially open.

The people streaming onto the university grounds represented a true cross section of Jewish society. The devout prayed aloud in Hebrew, and intellectuals, students, politicians, farmers, merchants, and tourists mingled with vendors, peddlers, and hucksters. It was a pitchman's dream and every spieler from Jerusalem and a fifty-mile radius around the city hawked one of two items—either food, or any salable piece of memorabilia bearing a portrait of Arthur James Balfour, author of the Balfour Declaration. Any article embellished by Lord Balfour's image was a guaranteed instant sale. Facsimilies of the Earl's face were printed, stamped, and embossed on every conceivable type of item—flags, posters, photographs, miniature paintings, postcards, luggage, handbags, scrolls, trays, plates, and mugs. The more enterprising combined the hero of the hour with edibles, insuring that sales would be brisk, and the Earl's elegant profile graced the sides of chocolate boxes, tins of soda crackers, pastry wrappers, and kosher delicacies.

In the future, men would accuse Balfour of insincerity and crass political opportunism, but to the celebrants on Mount Scopus and to Jews around the world, he was a genuine hero. Regardless of his motives, his personal efforts and the document that bore his name created a legal basis for a Jewish homeland.

The ceremonies were slated to be held in an open-air amphitheater, but despite its enormous capacity it was still not large enough to accommodate all who wished to attend. The vast majority of people had to be shunted off to makeshift benches constructed for the occasion or to open areas surrounding the perimeter of the amphitheater, where they could spread blankets on the ground. Scores of volunteers ushered people to their seats or led them to cordoned-off areas designed to accommodate the overflow.

Thanks to Dora Hoffmann, Ben and his friends had excellent seats close to the speaker's platform. The platform had been specially constructed and was draped with light blue and white bunting. Wreaths and fresh flowers decorated the rostrum. As they looked around, it appeared that the entire plateau atop Mount Scopus was covered with people. Only buildings and trees broke the sea of heads.

"My God," Sophie breathed with awe, "I would never have believed that there were this many Jews in the entire world. I've never seen a gathering of Jews larger than the congregation of a synagogue."

"In St. Petersburg, the secret police would have dispersed this meeting as subversive," Yuri remarked.

"It is," Ben laughed. They all looked at him in surprise. "It is a subversive gathering. From the time Julius Severus defeated Shimon Bar Kochba eighteen centuries ago, Jews have been suppressed and stripped of their freedom. Whenever an oppressed people yearn for freedom, they're classified as 'subversive' by those in power."

"When are they going to start?" Sarah asked impatiently. Groups of men wearing academic robes or formal clothing began filling three rows of straight-backed chairs at the rear of the stage. Yuri looked at his watch. It was close to three o'clock and the ceremonies still hadn't begun. The impatience and anticipation of the crowd around them was a palpable presence. Sarah pointed towards the speaker's platform, where ten or twelve chairs were arrayed in a privileged forward position. She asked if Ben recognized any of the men who occupied those seats.

Ben craned his neck. "The first man to your right is the Sephardic Chief Rabbi, Rabbi Meir. Next to him, in the dark hat, is Ashkenazic Chief Rabbi, Rabbi Kook."

"The man next to Rabbi Kook isn't Jewish, is he?" Sophie guessed.

"No, he's not," Ben answered. The man seated next to the Rabbi wore a cutaway morning suit and an elegant top hat. His name was already a part of history for the role he played during the war. "They call him the Conqueror of Palestine."

"Lord Allenby?"

"None other." Next to Allenby sat Sir Herbert Samuel, the British High Commissioner, then the man of the hour, Lord Balfour. Balfour wore his academic robes, marked with the colorful insignia of his degrees.

Yuri pointed to a man standing next to Balfour, wearing a fez. "I didn't expect to see any Arabs here today."

"You won't see any Arabs here," Ben explained, "even though the Arab leadership was invited. That fellow is Ahmed Seyydi Lutfi, the official Egyptian envoy. Ali Badawi promised me that his people would support us, and he spoke the truth." Once again, Egypt had chosen to stand by the Jews while her Arab cousins simmered in fury.

"The last man doesn't look Jewish or English," Sophie spoke up.

"Well, he's both," Ben laughed. "That's the Chief Rabbi of Great Britain, Rabbi Hertz."

Sophie stared at Ben, visibly impressed. "How do you know all those people?" Ben held up a special program showing photographs of all the major dignitaries attending the opening, and short biographies of each man.

Sophie's lips pressed together in mock rage. "Why didn't you tell us, you . . ."

Suddenly, an energetic man with a small goatee strode onto the platform and pulled up a seat next to Lord Balfour. No one atop the summit of Mount Scopus that day had any trouble recognizing the diminutive president of the World Zionist Organization—Chaim Weizmann. Weizmann chatted with Balfour for a moment, then rose and stepped to the raised dais on the main platform. He literally sprang to the lectern, his presence electrifying the audience.

Born in Russia, Weizmann was a brilliant chemist and the director of the British Admiralty Laboratories during the war. He knew every man on the dais socially as well as politically, and though the document creating a Jewish homeland in Palestine bore Balfour's name, in reality, Weizmann deserved equal credit.

He clasped the lectern on either side, and smiled at the crowd. Silence fell over the amphitheater and Weizmann stepped back from the microphones without speaking, signaling Rabbi Kook to come forward. The Rabbi walked to the speakers, then closed his eyes and raised his hands.

"Oh, Lord," he intoned. "We beseech you to give your blessing to this great endeavor, this center of learning in Your holiest of cities. From the far corners of the earth, we have gathered in Jerusalem to be a part of this event. Let this be, Lord, a place of wisdom and honor, that the Jewish people may ever merit Your continued blessing. Amen."

"Amen," responded the crowd in a single voice.

Weizmann stepped forward again, raising his arms as if to embrace the crowd. He looked calm, triumphant, and totally in control of the thousands watching him. "I now declare the Hebrew University officially open!"

It was done.

A roar of approval sprang from a thousand throats and echoed across the countryside. The restoration of a nation's pride had begun. Weizmann held up his hands for silence, but the crowd continued to cheer, oblivious to his repeated requests. They were not about to have the moment shortchanged.

Ben's seat afforded a magnificent view of Jerusalem, set beyond the cheering multitudes. A broad vista spread before him, forming a picture very much like one that hung in his parents' bedroom in Dorpat; during the long months of illness, Ben's father had stared at the picture, as though he could transport himself there by a force of will. "How you would have loved to be here," Ben murmured to himself.

The Mount of Olives, revered by Christians the world over, seemed close enough to touch in the clear afternoon light. At one end of the Jerusalem Basin, the Dead Sea shimmered in the sunlight. At the opposite end stood Rachel's tomb.

Ben suddenly realized that Jerusalem was more than just a city, it was the heart of his people's faith. Jerusalem's history, character, and destiny formed a living link to the God of Abraham, Isaac and Jacob, and its fate and future were unalterably intertwined with Jewish destiny. To abandon Jerusalem through some kind of partition would never be accepted; the Jews would never relinquish Jerusalem. Nor, Ben thought to himself, would God allow it.

Weizmann's high-pitched voice intruded on Ben's thoughts, reverberating over the loudspeakers. "Please, may I have silence!" Finally, the crowd quieted down and he was able to introduce Sir Herbert Samuel, who delivered the official greetings of His Majesty's Government. The audience approved his speech with enthusiastic applause. Again, it took nearly ten minutes to quiet the crowd.

Then Weizmann smiled broadly and without preamble, simply announced: "Lord Balfour!"

The audience went wild.

Ramrod straight, with a ruddy complexion and full shock of fine white hair, the author of the Balfour Declaration stood before the crowd, a patient smile on his lips. Most of the people in front of him were in Palestine as a result of the work he and Weizmann had done. They knew it, and they loved him for it. The cheering went on without a pause. When the passion finally abated, Balfour began to speak in slow, measured tones.

"What is that which has brought together this vast concourse from every quarter of the world, peoples often speaking their mother-tongue languages far separated in human speech, but all gathered here on this great, historic occasion in a land in which historic associations crowd upon the memory every step you take, from the north to the south, from the east to the west? It is the consciousness that this gathering marks a great epoch in the story of a people who made this little land of Palestine the centre of great religions, whose intellectual and moral destiny is, from a national point of view, reviving, and who will look back to this day we are celebrating as one of the great milestones in their future career.

"A few minutes ago I was reminded by friends that from where you are sitting you can see the very spot where the children of Israel first entered the Promised Land, and that it was from this very hill that the Roman destroyers of Jerusalem conducted their siege which brought to an end that great chapter in the life of the Jewish people.

"Could there be a more historic spot?

"From this hill you can see what then appeared to be an end of the Jewish community in the land they made illustrious.

"A new epoch has begun within the Palestine which came to end so many hundred years ago. Not that I would think for a moment that all Jewish culture in the interval between the destruction of Jerusalem and the expulsion of the Turks had ceased—far from it.

"It has been uninterrupted but it has been scattered. It has been the culture of Jewish people living within traditional limits of the country which they have rendered so famous; it was separate efforts of separate individuals, separate men of science, separate theologians, separate philosophers, scattered over the habitable globe. They have borne their share in the progress of civilization. I think it a profound mistake to suppose that men of Jewish birth have not borne their full share in the progress of knowledge and in the growth of civilization. The whole world over, they have done so, although scattered and unable to concentrate their peculiar national genius in a common task. I confidently expect in the future they will be able to give aid even more important.

"It is because of these peculiar past circumstances that we are now engaged in adapting Western methods and the Western form of the university to an Eastern site, and it is education which is to be in an Eastern language that is the new experiment. It has never been tried before under any circumstances parallel to those of which I speak.

"Unless I utterly misunderstand the signs of the times, unless I have profoundly mistaken the various Jewish people, the experiment is pre-destined to inevitable success, on which not only men of Jewish birth but others sharing the common civilization of the world will have reason to congratulate themselves.

"One problem which will naturally strike everybody is the one of language. It is true, Hebrew never has been a dead language, but it has not been a language, until recently, adapted to many phases of modern development. It is a great language. I say so with boldness, though I do not know any Hebrew, and I say so for the reason that all English-speaking people have been brought up on a translation into English of the Hebrew Scriptures, and that translation is one of the great literary treasures of all who speak the English tongue—it matters not what their creed may be or what their view of the historic value of the Hebrew Bible may be. Clearly, the Jewish people have a great instrument of literary instruction, capable of dealing with all the higher aspects of literary and imaginative literature: but does it follow that from that, Hebrew is fitted for modern uses? There is a great difference between Isaiah and microbiology. Is the language and poetical imagination of Isaiah fitted to deal with the laboratory work which is going to render this spot illustrious?

"I do not mean to suggest that all the great scientific work of the world has been done, or is going to be done, by men of Jewish birth; but it is worth noting by those looking with doubt upon the ideal of a Jewish university for Palestine, devoted to scientific research, what an important part in the problems interesting mankind the Jews are playing.

"I hope the Arabs will remember that in the darkest days of the dark ages, when Western civilization appeared almost extinct and smothered under barbaric influences, it was the Jews and Arabs together who gave the first sparks of light which illuminated that gloomy period.

"If, in the tenth century, for example, the Jews and Arabs could work together for the illumination of Europe, cannot Jews and Arabs work now in cooperation with Europe and make this not merely a Palestinian university but a Palestinian university from which all sections of the population of Palestine may draw intellectual and spiritual advantage?"

Despite Balfour's convoluted prose and halting delivery, the conclusion of his speech was greeted by thunderous applause that even Weizmann could not bring to an end. Again and again, Balfour stood, acknowledged the ovation with grace and dignity. Weizmann stood at the microphone, trying to shout, but the crowd's cheering drowned him out. Unable to speak, he shrugged and bowed deeply to the audience. As the speaker's platform began to empty, the crowd surged forward. Ben and the others were caught up in the confusion, involuntarily propelled towards the dais. Arms, legs, and elbows struck them from all sides, pushing them closer to the platform. Helpless to fight the momentum of the crowd, Ben kept checking to be sure that Sophie, Sarah, and Yuri were still near him—anyone who tripped or faltered risked serious injury. Carried along by the force of the crowd, Ben found himself at the foot of the speaker's platform, looking up at Chaim Weizmann.

"Dr. Weizmann!" he stuttered. Weizmann looked down with a smile, his dark eyes intense. For lack of anything better to say, Ben burst out, "Dr. Weizmann, it took me four months to get here."

Weizmann laughed. "You're fast, young man. It took the rest of us two thousand years." Instinctively, Ben reached up and shook Weizmann's hand. Weizmann barely had time to return the firm grasp before anxious aides pulled the leader of Zionism from the podium and hurried him offstage. They were afraid he might be injured or crushed by the overenthusiastic audience. Somehow, Ben felt as though he had truly been touched by history.

Ben braced himself against an inward angle of the platform and gathered the others around him. "We'll wait here until the confusion dies down," he yelled. From the relative safety of their niche, they watched the crowd twist and mill, forming a kaleidoscope of Judaism. Newly arrived Jews from eastern Europe in wrinkled clothes mingled with Yemenites in long, flowing robes. Sephardic Jews looked darkly Oriental in their Sabbath attire and remained clannishly aloof, even in the *tummel* surrounding them. With their clean-shaven faces and expensive Western suits, wealthy Jews from Europe and the United States made a studied contrast to their Palestinian counterparts.

Eventually, the crowd's inertia dwindled, and Ben and the others were finally able to push forward and grab a seat on the front row of benches. They drew a sigh of relief as the crowd slowly dispersed. Suddenly, a woman stumbled in the aisle, falling headlong into the seats. Had Yuri not reacted quickly enough, she would have struck her head on one of the risers. Gently, he helped her to her feet.

"Thank you," she gasped, brushing the tangled blond hair back from her face. "I could have broken my neck." To Ben's surprise, it was the Gentile woman, he'd seen at the Wailing Wall.

"Do I know you?" she asked, her clear blue eyes taking in the look of recognition on Ben's face.

"In a way," Ben smiled. "I saw you and your husband at the Wailing Wall yesterday. I'm Benjamin Isaacson."

"I'm Jenny Shair." She introduced herself with an outstretched hand. Her grip was firm and dry. "My husband, Sol, and I got separated in all the craziness."

After Jenny had met everyone, Ben suggested she wait with them until her husband appeared. Jenny Shair accepted the invitation without hesitation; she'd had enough jostling for one day. Fifteen minutes later, a worried Solomon Shair pushed through the thinning crowd and hurried to his wife's side. Worry and concern etched his sunburned face. His hair was disheveled, his suit rumpled.

"Thank God you're all right," he shook his head. "I thought you might have been trampled by the crowd." He thanked Ben and the others for their help, mopping his forehead with a limp white handkerchief. "The least I can do to show my appreciation is take everyone to lunch."

"Thank you," Sarah smiled, "but we brough a gigantic picnic feast that Yuri had to tote all the way from the hotel. If we don't eat it now, I can't guarantee what he might do."

"Why don't you join us?" Sophie broke in "We have plenty of food."

Within minutes, they were back at the top of the amphitheater, spreading a brightly colored blanket beneath an olive tree. Eager to serve a meal worthy of the occasion, Sarah and Sophie had outdone themselves, packing all kinds of kosher treats for the picnic.

Sarah handed Ben a beautifully twisted loaf of freshly baked challah and asked him to make the traditional blessing. Thoughtfully, Ben offered the loaf to Solomon, and asked him if he would like to make the blessing.

"I would be honored," Solomon replied. His Hebrew was rusty but passable. What he lacked in fluency, he made up for with enthusiasm.

They formed a typical Jewish gathering that day: A German, an Austrian, a Russian, a Swede, and two Americans, all from different backgrounds, united only by their common faith. Around them, people conversed in a dozen languages and it struck Ben as nothing short of a miracle that so many thousands of Jews could sit on a mountain in Palestine, free to talk, laugh, eat, dance, and sing to their heart's content.

By sundown, a full-blown festival was underway, and as Ben gazed out over the celebrants towards the city, his thoughts turned to Bluma. The letters she had sent were full of love, but each one ended the same way: she couldn't leave her family right now . . . perhaps in the future . . . could Ben come back to Riga? Ben knew they had reached a stalemate; she would never be able to break away from her family and he could never return to a life in eastern Europe. Though his love for Bluma would always remain with him, he sensed deep within himself that she was part of the past, a part of his life that might have been.

Ben watched Yuri and Sophi, lost in each other's eyes, and Sarah, busily entertaining a group of small children with Sol and Jenny. They had started their new lives, but Ben still felt attached to the past, as though some unseen tie continued to bind him. Sarah noticed the troubled expression on his face from where she played with the children and she knew instinctively that he was thinking about Bluma. Strangely, she was not jealous; she sensed that Bluma was no longer a part of Ben's future.

Below them, dusk settled over the valley and hundreds of exhausted people began the arduous trek to the foot of the mountain. Like their biblical ancestors, they used torches to light the way. The flames made bright points of light that merged at the road to form a flickering stream from the base of Mount Scopus all the way to Jerusalem.

As they watched, the city lights came on, turning Jerusalem into a jewel in the night. The young people who refused to end the day moved the festivities from Mount Scopus into the streets of the city. They crowded the alleys, singing, dancing, and blocking traffic. Here and there, groups of Arabs watched with open hostility, but most withdrew to their homes in silent protest.

Sol Shair and Ben sat slightly apart from the others, backs braced against the time-worn trunk of the old olive tree. Shair was a lawyer from Chicago, with a keen mind and razor-edged wit. Like Ben, he relished a good debate.

They talked freely, ranging from topic to topic until the conversation inevitably turned serious. As Ben described the way the Nazis were using anti-Semitism for political purposes, Shair shook his head in disgust, but nothing Ben said about the Nazis or Henry Ford seemed to surprise the American. Being deeply involved with B'nai B'rith, Shair was well acquainted with Henry Ford's activities. Only when Ben described the United States as a tottering democracy, ready to fall under Ford's domination, did Shair take exception. Sol readily conceded the strength of Ford's tremendous influence, but he insisted that Henry Ford did not speak for the majority of Americans.

"Just look at the treaty the United States signed with Great Britain," Sol argued. "If the American people were allied with Ford, the American government would never have formally acknowledged the British Mandate over Palestine and its promise of a Jewish homeland.''

"What about the immigration restrictions of the Johnson–Reed Act?'' Ben replied heatedly. "That was specifically directed against Eastern Jewry–''

"—and southern Europeans,'' Sol shot back. "It's more economic than–''

"Would you two please remember we're here to celebrate, not to argue!'' Sarah interrupted. She understood they were both enjoying the debate, but with Jenny's support, she insisted they change the subject to something less controversial. Sheepishly, Ben and Sol grinned at each other.

"I guess we got carried away,'' Ben apologized with a smile.

After the conversation around the picnic blanket resumed, Sol eyed Ben and cracked a smile. "Tell me, Ben, why did you really come to Palestine?'' Though the lawyer's question was posed half in jest, Ben decided to give his friend a serious answer.

"I came partly because of the past.'' Ben leaned back on one elbow, resting his head against the olive tree's smooth bark. "I had an obligation to fulfill my father's wishes. And my mother had given me a challenge, a challenge I wanted to meet. When I tried to emigrate instead of attending the university, she convinced me that Palestine needed more than farmers to become a nation. Without training or education, she told me, I'd just be another *batlen mit luftgescheften*, a bag of hot air. I'm glad I took her advice; I see now just how right she was.''

Ben thought for a moment, staring out over the valley, then he turned back to Sol. "Like you, I also came to see the opening of Hebrew University. You could even say that I came to escape a life I had no wish to lead. But to be honest, I came because I felt I had to. I can't really put it into words—I just know that the future of our people is here. That means my future is here.''

Yuri put his arm around Sophie in silent agreement.

"I think you've spoken for all of us, Ben,'' Sol said quietly. "The past is gone and the present is a maelstrom, changing too quickly for our senses to keep pace. All we're left with is the future. It is only the future that we can influence or change, and we must be prepared for it.'' Pensively, the lawyer stopped. Then a look of pride and determination suffused his face.

"I truly believe that Palestine is a land born of the past, but it has no definitive character, no form, no direction. We have an enormous opportunity here to mold a nation's character. One day, I may even come here to live. I never thought I would say that, but when I stood at the Wall, something happened inside. I felt like another person, locked inside me, was finally released.'' Shair looked over at Ben. ''I felt like a Jew.''

''But Sol, you never denied your Jewishness,'' Jenny spoke up. ''You're always forming some committee or leading some campaign. If you aren't out raising money for a Jewish Homeland in Palestine, you're organizing a charity ball or a fund drive to help homeless Jewish refugees marooned in Germany.'' There was more than just a trace of resentment in her voice, and Ben correctly guessed that she'd spent too many late evenings alone, waiting for Sol to come home.

''I know, honey,'' her husband interrupted gently, ''but I did those things as a member of an ethnic group, an association of people with something in common. But the other day at the Wall, I felt the presence of my faith for the first time since my childhood. Here I feel . . .''

''Is it so different in America?'' Sophie wondered.

''Everything is different there, Sophie. America is vital and exciting, filled with opportunity. But America does strange things to people. Those who didn't come over on the *Mayflower* try to act as though they did. They struggle to lose their accents, change their dress, and bury the old ways and traditions. Don't misunderstand me—there's nothing wrong with change, but people in America aren't interested in building on the past, they want to deny it, destroy it, pretend they were never poor.''

''But despite their best efforts,'' he continued, ''they are constantly reminded that a Jew is always a Jew. Neither God nor their neighbors will ever let them forget that. And the same is true if you're Black, Hispanic, Oriental—anything other than a white Anglo-Saxon Protestant. Every time I stand in front of a group of Jews to ask for their support I . . .''

''Oh, Sol!'' Jenny snapped. ''You're speechmaking again. All I ever hear is money, money, money—this isn't a charity dinner. Besides, have you noticed? Now when our friends see us coming, they look uncomfortable. They think you're going to ask them for a handout.''

''Money that supports a Homeland in Palestine is not a handout,'' Ben interrupted. He was dismayed at the way Sol and Jenny were sniping at each other, and the way they used the word 'charity' rankled him. He told them about Arlosoroff's planned trip to America and explained how the union chief intended to convey a clear message to his audience: Jews in Palestine did not want alms, they wanted financial independence.

''You must understand that there are two kinds of people in Palestine,'' Ben said. ''Those who have an independent livelihood and enjoy the freedom and dignity that implies, and those who are struggling to reach that goal.''

Sol grinned. "In America, we too are divided into two groups of people: capitalists and those who are striving to become capitalists."

"Then Americans should have no trouble understanding Arlosoroff when he explains that we need American capitalists to invest in the future of Palestine, not give us charity," Ben replied.

Suddenly, the sky exploded with showers of light. Starbursts of incandescent color blossomed like brilliant flowers against the ebony desert sky. Jets of alizarin crimson and emerald green corkscrewed across the night.

"Isn't it glorious!" Sarah cried exuberantly. "The sky itself is celebrating!"

Faint cheers welled up from the streets of Jerusalem and the sound of children laughing and clapping filled the night. For the next fifteen minutes, they watched the magnificent display in silence.

"Oh, Ben," Sarah whispered as the last fiery explosion faded away. "I wish tonight could last forever!"

"Always the romantic," Ben teased.

"You can't blame her," Sol laughed. "We Jews have always been romantics at heart—and how could we be any different? Just look at the stories of the Old Testament. Our Holy Books are filled with tales of faith, war, love, hate, and betrayal, all set in the land we now stand on. The Old Testament is peopled with enough heroes to inspire Christianity and Islam as well as Judaism; it's an epic unequalled by any other culture.

"As I think about it, I truly believe that we Jews have endured this long as a people because there is a place in the world we must fill, a role we must play, regardless of the efforts of others to stop us. In a way, you could say we must fulfill the will of God." The lawyer looked slighly embarrassed at his peroration.

Ben smiled. "All I know is that there are needs to be met and work to be done. I don't believe that God forces us into one mold or another, or predetermines our lives. We are free to choose. If we weren't, our love for Him would be meaningless. Life was meant to be a challenge that we can accept or deny."

"And who issues the challenge?" Sol asked.

"Every man, to himself," Ben answered.

"Or woman," Sarah interrupted archly. "Or did you two philosophers forget about us women?" Everyone laughed.

Sol clambered to his feet and stretched. "You're right, Sarah. We can argue and debate and speculate to the end of time, but down there," he pointed towards the city, "down there is reality."

Ben stood and looked out over the hills of Jerusalem. He stared at the lights of the city, the first great city of Jews, the cradle of his people's culture, civilization, and faith. For two thousand years, Jews had longed to return to Jerusalem. Now they once again danced joyfully in the streets, as they had centuries before. They celebrated because once again, they were building, not running, not hiding. The foundation had been inherited from the past, but the edifice would belong to the future. The hiatus created by the Exile was over. It was almost too good to be real. Suddenly, Ben felt the muscles of his throat constrict. He could hear the sound of conversation around him, but the words became an indistinguishable buzz. Inexplicably, Ben felt deeply shaken, as though something intensely private was about to emerge of its own volition and he didn't want Sarah or anyone else to witness even a part of it.

Sarah noticed how quiet he had become and saw the tension in his face. "Ben?" she whispered.

When he didn't answer, she laced her arm through his. "Are you all right?" Her voice was filled with concern.

Ben forced a smile. "Sure." As he broke away from her, he was unable to meet her eyes. "I think I'd like to be alone for a few minutes. Don't worry, I'll be back. I just need to walk to clear my head." Reluctantly, she let him go.

Ben hiked towards the crown of the summit, thinking about his friends. Sol had come with his wife to find himself and his heritage. Sophie and Yuri had come to rebuild the family they had lost. Sarah had escaped from a bleak and oppressive future. The simple act of reaching Palestine had meant success for all of them. Ben had thought it would be the same for him, but a sense of emptiness plagued him; a gnawing dissatisfaction. A piece of the circle was missing.

He stood just below the rounded cap of Mount Scopus, staring at the spidery web of lights that traced the streets of Jerusalem. The fireworks, the singing, the dancing, the warm sense of friendship he shared with the others—all conspired to leave him isolated and incomplete. Suddenly, a soft whimper intruded on his solitude. He turned to discover a small boy, crouched by a rock. The boy's eyes were swollen and red from crying, and when Ben looked at him, the boy hid his face in his striped *jebbalah*.

Ben coaxed him to speak and was rewarded with a few tentative words he recognized from his conversations with Deborah, the Yemenite housekeeper. Though Ben couldn't speak the language, it wasn't hard to guess that the boy was lost and crying for his mother. Ben knelt down next to the youngster and smiled, but the sudden movement frightened the boy and he began wailing at the top of his lungs. Ben reached out to comfort him, but the boy only began to wail even louder. Feeling utterly helpless,

Ben stood and turned in a circle, hoping to spot the boy's mother. To his relief, Ben saw Sarah coming up the path and he called to her. When she heard the boy's cries, she ran the last thirty yards.

"Ben!" she gasped, slightly out of breath. "What did you do?"

"All I did was smile."

"It must have been one of your intimidating smiles," Sarah frowned. She spoke to the boy in Hebrew. It was obvious he didn't understand, so she swept him up in her arms and stroked his hair, rocking him gently back and forth. When the boy's sobs finally subsided, Sarah held him at arm's length to get a closer look.

"Don't be afraid, little one," she reassured him. "You're safe with us." The boy never took his eyes off Sarah's face; he seemed to trust her. She cast a sidelong glance at Ben. "Do you think he's Jewish?"

"He's a Yemenite Jew," Ben explained. For centuries the Yemenites had been cut off from the rest of Jewry, surrounded by a sea of Islam. Their culture and language had become Arabic in character; so had their heart rending poverty.

Sarah drew the boy's head to her breast and crooned a Hebrew lullaby. When she finished, she and the boy regarded each other with great solemnity. Then she burst out laughing; so did the boy. Ben marveled at the way a smile and laugh jumped the barriers of language and culture.

"Yusef!" a shrill cry broke the magic of the moment. "Yusef!!" The boy pointed to the direction of the cry and shouted in a thin, high-pitched voice.

"It must be his mother," Ben guessed, hauling himself to his feet. He called out to the woman and waved his arms over his head to catch her attention. She stopped, staring suspiciously until she saw Sarah with her son. Then she uttered a cry of relief and rushed to embrace him, speaking rapidly in her own tongue. She held him for a moment, then released him with a sharp word and a gentle spank in his rear end. While Yusef clung to the hem of her *jebbalah*, his mother reached out and took Sarah's hand in her own.

"Thank you, thank you," she said in broken Hebrew. "I be frantic. I turn my back one minute and he is gone! I terrified he lost in crowd. God bless you both." She was darker than most Arabs, with broad cheekbones and a wide, flat forehead. Her eyes were the color of honey, her hair jet black and extremely fine.

"I'm afraid we didn't find your son," Ben explained. "He's the one who found us. Perhaps he was touring the grounds. Prospective students do that, you know."

The woman smiled wistfully. "To see Yusef study here is great dream for me. If God is kind . . . maybe my dream be true."

"You have every reason to expect that dream to come true," Ben said. He reached out and took Yusef's hand. The boy was still wary, but Ben smiled warmly and the youngster responded in kind.

"Look there, Yusef," Ben pointed to the faint white outline of the university buildings. "That is where your destiny lies. If you need help to get there, you'll find it. Here, everyone must help everyone else to achieve their heart's desire." The boy giggled at the strange words.

It seemed only natural to share the day with Yusef and his mother, so Sarah invited them to join the picnic. Shyly, Yusef's mother accepted the invitation and they all walked back down the darkened path to where the others waited.

While Sophie and Yuri busied themselves fixing plates for their two guests, Ben and Sarah settled in at the edge of the group, listening to the talk and laughter, content to be close to each other. Sarah leaned against him, resting her hand on his crossed knees, and he responded by wrapping his arm around her shoulders. When she looked up at him, her eyes were a luminous gold in the faint starlight. He smiled and she snuggled closer to him. Somehow the pressure of her body against his felt right and natural.

"Ben, I feel so full, so happy . . . like I might burst. But just now, when I feel the most content, sharing the moment with you, I think about my family and it makes me sad. They could be a part of this, but they never will be. Why? Why are they so afraid, so timid, so frightened? Why can't they understand that this is the life God meant us to live?"

"I know, Sarah." He too felt the same sadness. "Those are the same questions that I've asked myself over and over again. And since coming to Palestine, I think I've found the answer." He paused for a moment, studying the soft contours of her face.

"Maybe God never intended all Jews to live in Palestine," he said gently. "Perhaps He intends us to have the dignity of being a nation, to exist as a nation among nations, yet have that nation serve as the hub of a wheel that spans out across the earth. As Balfour said in his speech, we Jews have a contribution to make to mankind as a whole."

Sarah looked confused. "But what about Chapter Twelve of Genesis? Doesn't every Jew have an obligation to honor God's injunction to return?"

"Yes" Ben replied pensively, "but to return as a nation."

"Sarah, you remember the story of Moses and the twelve tribes who for forty years were wandering in the desert, waiting to hear from Moses that it was time to enter the Promised Land. When Moses finally gave the orders, two and a half tribes refused to go. ''Rather than tell them that they had to live in the Promised Land, Moses explained that all Jews were obligated by God to help found a nation.

''But once that duty was discharged it was their choice to live wherever they found comfort.''

Sarah looked thoughtful. ''So what you're saying is that '*lekh lekha*' really means that all Jews have an obligation to help build a Jewish homeland, but not all Jews are bound to live here.''

''Exactly. 'A Jew can pray to God anywhere,' my mother used to say, and she was right. Just as the two and a half tribes made their lives elsewhere, so are there Jews today who must find their destinies elsewhere.''

''But what about the hatred and persecution Jews suffer in other countries,'' Sarah wanted to know.

It is not the people we must fear. All people are God's people, and when we stand as a nation, Palestine will have citizens of all faiths from all over the world. Our real enemies are individuals, ambitious men who draw their power from hatred and ignorance. They're frustrated industrialists like Henry Ford or politicians like Hitler and Grabski who use anti-Semitism as a political weapon. These are the men we must fear.''

Ben paused, giving Sarah a moment to absorb what he had said. Then he asked her if she understood what he was trying to say.

Sarah squeezed his hand. ''Yes, Ben, I do. But my heart still aches.'' In response, Ben held her close.

When Ben looked up across the blanket, he happened to notice Yusef, crouched beside his mother. Though he couldn't understand a word that was being said, Yusef was obviously trying to follow the conversation. Something about the intensity of the boy's expression tugged at Ben's heart. Yusef's whole life lay before him; all the exciting possibilities of the future were within his young grasp. There were no limits to what Yusef and others like him could achieve. Suddenly, Ben realized why the circle remained unclosed.

His father.

More than anything, Anschel Isaacson had longed to walk the streets of Jerusalem, to pray at the Wall, to stand atop Mount Scopus and look out over the land of Goshen. Death denied him those dreams.

But Ben realized that was not entirely true. Everyone clustered around the blanket would make Anschel's dream a reality, each in his own way.

Smiling softly, Ben beckoned for Yusef to approach him. He reached to the lapel of his jacket for a part of his father he carried with him; a token of the past, his legacy to the future. As the boy watched in awe, Ben removed the gleaming Star of David from his coat and carefully pinned it to the collar of Yusef's *jebbalah*. Then he straightened and surveyed the small group around him. Sophie and Yuri, the Shairs, Sarah, Yusef, and his mother. Tenderly, he kissed Yusef on the forehead. "We are here to stay," he announced solemnly. He reached out for Sarah's hand, pulling her close to him. Like Yusef, she was the future.

He stood silently, feeling the tears run down his cheeks as he looked out over Jerusalem.

"Papa, we're home," he whispered.

The circle was closed.

Acknowledgments

My thanks to Messrs. Gil Alroy and Phil Gordon for their research assistance in coordinating dates, places and historical events.

I would like also to thank my editor Gregg Janson for bringing his skills and enthusiasm to this book.

I.C.